The Second Chronicles of Amber

OTHER BOOKS BY ROGER ZELAZNY

Novels

This Immortal
The Dream Master
Lord of Light
Isle of the Dead
Creatures of Light and Darkness
Damnation Alley
Jack of Shadows
Today We Choose Faces
To Die In Italbar
Deus Irae (with Philip K. Dick)
Bridge of Ashes
Doorways in the Sand
My Name is Legion
Roadmarks
Eye of Cat
Coils (with Fred Saberhagen)
A Dark Traveling
The Black Throne (with Fred
    Saberhagen)
The Mask of Loki (with Thomas T.
    Thomas)
Flare (with Thomas T. Thomas)
A Night in the Lonesome October
Wilderness (with Gerald Hausman)
Donnerjack (with Jane Lindskold)
Psychoshop (with Alfred Bester)
Lord Demon (with Jane Lindskold)

Collections

Four for Tomorrow
*The Doors of His Face, The Lamps of
    His Mouth and Other Stories*
The Last Defender of Camelot
Unicorn Variations
Frost and Fire
Manna From Heaven

The First Chronicles of Amber

Nine Princes in Amber
The Guns of Avalon
Sign of the Unicorn
The Hand of Oberon
The Courts of Chaos

The Changing Land

The Changing Land
Dilvish, The Damned

Wizard World

Changeling
Madwand

Azzie Elbub (with Robert Sheckley)

*Bring Me The Head of Prince
    Charming*
If At Faust You Don't Succeed
A Farce To Be Reckoned With

The Second Chronicles of Amber

TRUMPS OF DOOM
BLOOD OF AMBER
SIGN OF CHAOS
KNIGHT OF SHADOWS
PRINCE OF CHAOS

ROGER ZELAZNY

FANTASY

TRUMPS OF DOOM   Copyright © 1985 by the Amber Corporation

BLOOD OF AMBER   Copyright © 1986 by the Amber Corporation

SIGN OF CHAOS   Copyright © 1987 by the Amber Corporation

KNIGHT OF SHADOWS   Copyright © 1989 by the Amber Corporation

PRINCE OF CHAOS   Copyright © 1991 by the Amber Corporation

All rights reserved, including the right to reproduce this book or portions thereof in any form whatsoever.

First SFBC Science Fiction Printing: March 2005.

Published by arrangement with Eos,
a division of HarperCollins Publishers
10 East 53rd Street
New York, NY 10022

Visit The SFBC at *http://www.sfbc.com*

ISBN 0-7394-5184-7

Contents

TRUMPS
OF
DOOM

Again, Judy

1

It is a pain in the ass waiting around for someone to try to kill you. But it was April 30, and of course it would happen as it always did. It had taken me a while to catch on, but now I at least knew when it was coming. In the past, I'd been too busy to do anything about it. But my job was finished now. I'd only stayed around for this. I felt that I really ought to clear the matter up before I departed.

I got out of bed, visited the bathroom, showered, brushed my teeth, et cetera. I'd grown a beard again, so I didn't have to shave. I was not jangling with strange apprehensions, as I had been on that April 30 three years ago when I'd awakened with a headache and a premonition, thrown open the windows, and gone to the kitchen to discover all of the gas burners turned on and flameless. No. It wasn't even like the April 30 two years ago in the other apartment when I awoke before dawn to a faint smell of smoke to learn that the place was on fire. Still, I stayed out of direct line of the light fixtures in case the bulbs were filled with something flammable, and I flipped all of the switches rather than pushing them. Nothing untoward followed these actions.

Usually, I set up the coffee maker the night before with a timer. This morning, though, I didn't want coffee that had been produced out of my sight. I set a fresh pot going and checked my packing while I waited for it to brew. Everything I valued in this place resided in two medium-sized crates—clothing, books, paintings, some instruments, a few souvenirs, and so forth. I sealed the cases. A change of clothing, a sweatshirt, a good paperback, and a wad of traveler's checks went into the backpack. I'd drop my key off at the manager's on the way out, so he could let the movers in. The crates would go into storage.

No jogging for me this morning.

As I sipped my coffee, passing from window to window and pausing beside each for sidelong surveys of the streets below and the buildings across the way (last year's attempt had been by someone with a rifle), I thought back to the first time it had happened, seven years ago. I had simply been walking down the street on a bright spring afternoon when an oncoming truck had swerved, jumped the curb, and nearly combined me with portions of a brick wall. I was able to dive out of the way and roll. The driver never regained consciousness. It had seemed one of those freak occurrences that occasionally invade the lives of us all.

The following year to the day, however, I was walking home from my lady friend's place late in the evening when three men attacked me—one with a knife, the other two with lengths of pipe—without even the courtesy of first asking for my wallet.

I left the remains in the doorway of a nearby record store, and while I thought about it on the way home it did not strike me until the following day that it had been the anniversary of the truck crash. Even then, I dismissed it as an odd coincidence. The matter of the mail bomb that had destroyed half of another apartment the following year did cause me to begin wondering whether the statistical nature of reality might not be under a strain in my vicinity at that season. And the events of subsequent years served to turn this into a conviction.

Someone enjoyed trying to kill me once a year, it was as simple as that. The effort failing, there would be another year's pause before an attempt was made again. It seemed almost a game.

But this year I wanted to play, too. My main concern was that he, she, or it seemed never to be present when the event occurred, favoring stealth and gimmicks or agents. I will refer to this person as S (which sometimes stands for "sneak" and sometimes for "shithead" in my private cosmology), because X has been overworked and because I do not like to screw around with pronouns with disputable antecedents.

I rinsed my coffee cup and the pot and set them in the rack. Then I picked up my bag and departed. Mr. Mulligan wasn't in, or was sleeping, so I left my key in his mailbox before heading up the street to take my breakfast at a nearby diner.

Traffic was light, and all of the vehicles well behaved. I walked slowly, listening and looking. It was a pleasant morning, promising a beautiful day. I hoped to settle things quickly, so I could enjoy it at my leisure.

I reached the diner unmolested. I took a seat beside the window. Just as the waiter came to take my order I saw a familiar figure swinging along the street—a former classmate and later fellow employee—Lucas Raynard: six feet tall, red-haired, handsome in spite, or perhaps because, of an artistically broken nose, with the voice and manner of the salesman he was.

I knocked on the window and he saw me, waved, turned and entered.

"Merle, I was right," he said, coming up to the table, clasping my shoulder briefly, seating himself and taking the menu out of my hands. "Missed you at your place and guessed you might be here."

He lowered his eyes and began reading the menu.

"Why?" I asked.

"If you need more time to consider, I'll come back," the waiter said.

"No," Luke answered and read off an enormous order. I added my own. Then: "Because you're a creature of habit."

"Habit?" I replied. "I hardly eat here anymore."

"I know," he answered, "but you usually did when the pressure was on. Like, right before exams—or if something was bothering you."

"Hm," I said. There did seem to be something to that, though I had never before realized it. I spun the ashtray with its imprint of a unicorn's head, a smaller version of the stained-glass one that stood as part of a partition beside the doorway. "I can't say why," I finally stated. "Besides, what makes you think something's bothering me?"

"I remembered that paranoid thing you have about April 30, because of a couple of accidents."

"More than a couple. I never told you about all of them."

"So you still believe it?"

"Yes."

He shrugged. The waiter came by and filled our coffee cups. "Okay," he finally agreed. "Have you had it yet today?"

"No."

"Too bad. I hope it doesn't pall your thinking."

I took a sip of coffee.

"No problem," I told him.

"Good." He sighed and stretched. "Listen, I just got back to town yesterday . . ."

"Have a good trip?"

"Set a new sales record."

"Great."

"Anyhow . . . I just learned when I checked in that you'd left."

"Yeah. I quit about a month ago."

"Miller's been trying to reach you. But with your phone disconnected he couldn't call. He even stopped by a couple of times, but you were out."

"Too bad."

"He wants you back."

"I'm finished there."

"Wait'll you hear the proposition, huh? Brady gets kicked upstairs and you're the new head of Design—for a twenty percent pay hike. That's what he told me to tell you."

I chuckled softly.

"Actually, it doesn't sound bad at all. But, like I said, I'm finished."

"Oh." His eyes glistened as he gave me a sly smile. "You *do* have something lined up someplace else. He was wondering. Okay, if that's the case he told me to tell you to bring him whatever the other guys offered. He'll try like hell to top it."

I shook my head.

"I guess I'm not getting through," I said. "I'm finished. Period. I don't want to go back. I'm not going to work for anyone else either. I'm done with this sort of thing. I'm tired of computers."

"But you're really good. Say, you going to teach?"

"Nope."

"Well, hell! You've got to do something. Did you come into some money?"

"No. I believe I'll do some traveling. I've been in one place too long."

He raised his coffee cup and drained it. Then he leaned back, clasped his hands across his stomach, and lowered his eyelids slightly. He was silent for a time.

Finally: "You said you were finished. Did you just mean the job and your life here, or something else as well?"

"I don't follow you."

"You had a way of disappearing—back in college, too. You'd be gone for a while and then just as suddenly turn up again. You always were vague about it, too. Seemed like you were leading some sort of double life. That have anything to do with it?"

"I don't know what you mean."

He smiled.

"Sure you do," he said. When I did not reply, he added, "Well, good luck with it—whatever."

Always moving, seldom at rest, he fidgeted with a key ring while we had a second cup of coffee, bouncing and jangling keys and a blue stone pendant. Our breakfasts finally arrived and we ate in silence for a while.

Then he asked, "You still have the *Starburst?*"

"No. Sold her last fall," I told him. "I'd been so busy I just didn't have time to sail. Hated to see her idle."

He nodded.

"That's too bad," he said. "We had a lot of fun with her, back in school. Later, too. I'd have liked to take her out once more, for old times' sake."

"Yes."

"Say, you haven't seen Julia recently."

"No, not since we broke up. I think she's still going with some guy named Rick. Have you?"

"Yeah. I stopped by last night."

"Why?"

He shrugged.

"She was one of the gang—and we've all been drifting apart."

"How was she?"

"Still looking good. She asked about you. Gave me this to give to you, too."

He withdrew a sealed envelope from inside his jacket and passed it to me. It bore my name, in her handwriting. I tore it open and read:

Merle,
I was wrong. I know who you are and there is danger. I have to see you. I have something you will need. It is very important. Please call or come by as soon as you can.
Love,
                                                        Julia

"Thanks," I said, opening my pack and filing it.

It was puzzling as well as unsettling. In the extreme. I'd have to decide what to do about it later. I still liked her more than I cared to think about, but I wasn't sure I wanted to see her again. But what did she mean about knowing who I am?

I pushed her out of my mind, again.

I watched the traffic for a time and drank coffee and thought about how I'd first met Luke, in our freshman year, in the Fencing Club. He was unbelievably good.

"Still fence?" I asked him.

"Sometimes. How about you?"

"Occasionally."

"We never really did find out who was better."

"No time now," I said.

He chuckled and poked his knife at me a few times.

"I guess not. When are you leaving?"

"Probably tomorrow—I'm just cleaning up a few odds and ends. When that's done I'll go."

"Where are you heading?"

"Here and there. Haven't decided on everything yet."

"You're crazy."

"Um-hm. *Wanderjahr* is what they used to call it. I missed out on mine and I want it now."

"Actually it does sound pretty nice. Maybe I ought to try it myself sometime."

"Maybe so. I thought you took yours in installments, though."

"What do you mean?"

"I wasn't the only one who used to take off a lot."

"Oh, that." He dismissed it with the wave of a hand. "That was business, not pleasure. Had to do some deals to pay the bills. You going to see your folks?"

Strange question. Neither of us had ever spoken of our parents before, except in the most general terms.

"I don't think so," I said. "How're yours?"

He caught my gaze and held it, his chronic smile widening slightly.

"Hard to say," he replied. "We're kind of out of touch."

I smiled, too.

"I know the feeling."

We finished our food, had a final coffee.

"So you won't be talking to Miller?" he asked.

"No."

He shrugged again. The check came by and he picked it up.

"This one's on me," he said. "After all, I'm working."

"Thanks. Maybe I can get back at you for dinner. Where're you staying?"

"Wait." He reached into his shirt pocket, took out a match-book, tossed it to me. "There. New Line Motel," he said.

"Say I come by about six?"

"Okay."

He settled up and we parted on the street.

"See you," he said.

"Yeah."

Bye-bye, Luke Raynard. Strange man. We'd known each other for almost eight years. Had some good times. Competed in a number of sports. Used to jog together almost every day. We'd both been on the track team. Dated the same girls sometimes. I wondered about him again—strong, smart, and as private a person as myself. There was a bond between us, one that I didn't fully understand.

I walked back to my apartment's parking lot and checked under my car's hood and frame before I tossed my pack inside and started the engine. I drove slowly, looking at things that had been fresh and new eight years before, saying good-bye to them now. During the past week I had said it to all of the people who had mattered to me. Except for Julia.

It was one of those things I felt like putting off, but there was no time. It was either now or not at all, and my curiosity had been piqued. I pulled into a shopping mall's lot and located a pay phone, but there was no answer when I rang her number. I supposed she could be working full-time on a dayshift again, but she could also be taking a shower or be out shopping. I decided to drive on over to her place and see. It wasn't that far. And whatever it was that she had for me, picking it up would be a good excuse for seeing her this one last time.

I cruised the neighborhood for several minutes before I located a parking space. I locked the car, walked back to the corner, and turned right. The day had grown slightly warmer. Somewhere, dogs were barking.

I strolled on up the block to that huge Victorian house that had been converted into apartments. I couldn't see her windows from the front. She was on the top floor, to the rear. I tried to suppress memories as I passed on up the front walk, but it was no good. Thoughts of our times together came rushing back along with a gang of old feelings. I halted. It was silly coming here. Why bother, for something I hadn't even missed. Still . . .

Hell. I *wanted* to see her one more time. I wasn't going to back out now. I mounted the steps and crossed the porch. The door was open a crack so I walked in.

Same foyer. Same tired-looking potted violet, dust on its

leaves, on the chest before the gilt-framed mirror—the mirror that had reflected our embrace, slightly warped, many times. My face rippled as I went by.

I climbed the green-carpeted stairs. A dog began howling somewhere out back.

The first landing was unchanged. I walked the short hallway, past the drab etchings and the old end table, turned and mounted the second staircase. Halfway up I heard a scratching noise from overhead and a sound like a bottle or a vase rolling on a hardwood floor. Then silence again, save for a few gusts of wind about the eaves. A faint apprehension stirred within me and I quickened my pace. I halted at the head of the stairway and nothing looked to be out of order, but with my next inhalation a peculiar odor came to me. I couldn't place it—sweat, must, damp dirt perhaps— certainly something organic.

I moved then to Julia's door and waited for several moments. The odor seemed stronger there, but I heard no new sounds.

I rapped softly on the dark wood. For a moment it seemed that I heard someone stirring within, but only for a moment. I knocked again.

"Julia?" I called out. "It's me—Merle."

Nothing. I knocked louder.

Something fell with a crash. I tried the doorknob. Locked.

I twisted and jerked and tore the doorknob, the lock plate, and the entire locking mechanism free. I moved immediately to my left then, past the hinged edge of the door and the frame. I extended my left hand and applied gentle pressure to the upper panel with my fingertips.

I moved the door a few inches inward and paused. No new sounds ensued, and nothing but a slice of wall and floor came into view, with narrow glimpses of a watercolor, the red sofa, the green rug. I eased the door open a little farther. More of the same. And the odor was even stronger.

I took a half-step to my right and applied a steady pressure. Nothingnothingnothing . . .

I snatched my hand away when she came into view. Lying there. Across the room. Bloody . . .

There was blood on the floor, the rug, a bloody disarray near the corner off to my left. Upset furniture, torn cushions . . .

I suppressed an impulse to rush forward.

I took one slow step and then another, all of my senses alert. I crossed the threshold. There was nothing else/no one else in the room. Frakir tightened about my wrist. I should have said something then, but my mind was elsewhere.

I approached and knelt at her side. I felt sick. From the doorway I had not been able to see that half of her face and her right arm were missing. She was not breathing and her carotid was silent. She had on a torn and bloodied peach-colored robe; there was a blue pendant about her neck.

The blood that had spilled beyond the rug onto the hardwood floor was smeared and tracked. They were not human footprints, however, but large, elongated, three-toed things, well padded, clawed.

A draft of which I had been only half-consciously aware—coming from the opened bedroom door at my back—was suddenly diminished, as the odor intensified. There came another quick pulsing at my wrist. There was no sound, though. It was absolutely silent, but I knew that it was there.

I spun up out of my kneeling position into a crouch, turning—

I saw a large mouthful of big teeth, bloody lips curled back around them. They lined the muzzle belonging to several hundred pounds of doglike creature covered with coarse, moldy-looking yellow fur. Its ears were like clumps of fungi, its yellow-orange eyes wide and feral.

As I had no doubt whatever concerning its intentions I hurled the doorknob, which I had been clutching half-consciously for the past minute. It glanced off the bony ridge above its left eye without noticeable effect. Still soundless, the thing sprang at me.

Not even time for a word to Frakir . . .

People who work in slaughterhouses know that there is a spot on an animal's forehead to be found by drawing an imaginary line from the right ear to the left eye and another from the left ear to the right eye. They aim the killing blow an inch or two above the junction of this X. My uncle taught me that. He didn't work in a slaughterhouse, though. He just knew how to kill things.

So I spun forward and to the side as it sprang, and I struck a hammer blow at the death spot. It moved even faster than I'd anticipated, however, and when my fist struck it, it was already rushing by. Its neck muscles helped it to absorb the force of my blow.

This drew the first sound from it, though—a yelp. It shook its head and turned with great speed then, and it was at me again. Now a low, rumbling growl came up from its chest and its leap was high. I knew that I was not going to be able to sidestep this one.

My uncle had also taught me how to grab a dog by the flesh on the sides of its neck and under the jaws. You need a good grip if it's a big one, and you've got to get it just right. I had no real choice at the moment. If I tried a kick and missed it would probably take off my foot. My hands shot forward and snaked upward and I braced myself when we met. I was sure it outweighed me and I had to meet its momentum as well.

I'd had visions of losing fingers or a hand, but I got in under the jaw, caught hold and squeezed. I kept my arms extended and leaned into the impact. I was shaken by the force of its lunge, but I was able to maintain my grip and absorb it.

As I listened to the growls and regarded the slavering muzzle a foot or so away from my face I realized that I hadn't thought much beyond this point. With a dog, you might be able to bash its head against anything hard and handy; its carotids are too deeply buried to rely on direct pressure to take it out. But this thing was strong and my grip was already beginning to slip against its frantic twisting. As I held its jaws away from me and kept pushing it upward, I also realized that it was taller than I was when extended along the vertical. I could try for a kick at its soft underside, but I would probably go off balance as well as lose my grip, and then my groin would be exposed to its teeth.

But it twisted free of my left hand, and I had no choice but to use my right or lose it. So I pushed as hard as I could and retreated again. I had been looking for a weapon, any weapon, but there was nothing handy that would serve.

It lunged again, coming for my throat, coming too fast and high for me to manage a kick to its head. I couldn't get out of its way either.

Its forelegs were level with my midriff, and I hoped that my uncle had been right about this one too, as I seized them and twisted backward and inward with all of my strength, dropping to one knee to avoid those jaws, chin lowered to protect my throat, my head drawn back. Bones popped and crunched as I twisted and its head lowered almost immediately to attack my wrists. But by then I was already rising, thrusting forward, springing up.

It went over backward, twisted, and almost caught itself. When its paws struck the floor, however, it made a sound halfway between a whimper and a snarl and collapsed forward.

I was about to try for another blow to the skull when it recovered its footing, moving faster than I'd thought it could. It raised its right foreleg immediately upon standing and balanced itself on three legs, still growling, eyes fixed on my own, saliva dampening its lower jaw. I moved slightly to my left, certain that it was about to rush me yet again, angling my body, positioning myself in a way that no one had taught me, because I do occasionally have original thoughts.

It was a little slower when it came for me this time. Maybe I could have gone for the skull and gotten it. I don't know because I didn't try. I seized it once more by the neck, and this time it was familiar territory. It would not pull away as it had before in the few moments I needed. Without breaking its momentum I turned and dropped low and thrust and pulled, adding some guidance to its trajectory.

It turned in midair, its back striking the window. With a shattering, splintering sound it passed through, taking most of the frame, the curtain and the curtain rod along with it.

I heard it hit three stories below. When I rose and looked out I saw it twitch a few times and grow still, there on the concrete patio where Julia and I had often had a midnight beer.

I returned to Julia's side and held her hand. I began to realize my anger. Someone had to be behind this. Could it be S again? Was this my April 30 present for this year? I'd a feeling that it was and I wanted to do unto S as I had just done unto the creature that had performed the act. There had to be a reason. There ought to be a clue.

I rose, went to the bedroom, fetched a blanket, and covered Julia with it. Mechanically, I wiped my fingerprints from the fallen doorknob as I began my search of the apartment.

I found them on the mantelpiece between the clock and a stack of paperbacks dealing with the occult. The moment I touched them and felt their coldness I realized that this was even more serious than I had thought. They had to be the thing of mine she'd had that I would be needing—only they were not really mine, though as I riffled through I recognized them on one level and was puzzled by them on another. They were cards, Trumps, like yet unlike any I had ever seen before.

It was not a complete deck. Just a few cards, actually, and strange. I slipped them into my side pocket quickly when I heard the siren. Time for solitaire later.

I tore down the stairs and out the back door, encountering no one. Fido still lay where he had fallen and all the neighborhood dogs were discussing it. I vaulted fences and trampled flowerbeds, cutting through backyards on my way over to the side street where I was parked.

Minutes later I was miles away, trying to scrub the bloody pawprints from my memory.

2

I drove away from the bay until I came to a quiet, well-treed area. I stopped the car and got out and walked.

After a long while I located a small, deserted park. I seated myself on one of the benches, took out the Trumps and studied them. A few seemed half familiar and the rest were totally puzzling. I stared too long at one and seemed to hear a siren song. I put them down. I did not recognize the style. This was extremely awkward.

I was reminded of the story of a world-famous toxicologist who inadvertently ingested a poison for which there was no antidote. The question foremost in his mind was, Had he taken a lethal dose? He looked it up in a classic textbook that he himself had written years before. According to his own book he had had it. He checked another, written by an equally eminent professional. According to that one he had taken only about half the amount necessary to do in someone of his body mass. So he sat down and waited, hoping he'd been wrong.

I felt that way because I am an expert on these things. I thought that I knew the work of everyone who might be capable of producing such items. I picked up one of the cards, which held a peculiar, almost familiar fascination for me—depicting a small grassy point jutting out into a quiet lake, a sliver of something bright, glistening, unidentifiable, off to the right. I exhaled heavily upon it, fogging it for an instant, and struck it with my fingernail. It rang like a glass bell and flickered to life. Shadows swam and pulsed as the scene inched into evening. I passed my hand over it and it grew still once again—back to lake, grasses, daytime.

Very distant. Time's stream flowed faster there in relationship to my present situation. Interesting.

I groped for an old pipe with which I sometimes indulge myself, filled it, lit it, puffed it, and mused. The cards were functional all right, not some clever imitations, and though I did not understand their purpose, that was not my main concern at the moment.

Today was April 30, and I had faced death once again. I had yet to confront the person who had been playing with my life. S had again employed a proxy menace. And that was no ordinary dog I had destroyed. And the cards . . . where had Julia gotten them and why had she wanted me to have them? The cards and the dog indicated a power beyond that of an ordinary person. All along I had thought I'd been the subject of the unwelcome attention of some psycho, whom I could deal with at my leisure. But this morning's events put an entirely different complexion on the case. It meant that I had one hell of an enemy somewhere.

I shuddered. I wanted to talk to Luke again, get him to reconstruct their conversation of the previous evening, see whether Julia had said anything that might provide me with a clue. I'd like to go back and search her apartment more carefully, too. But that was out of the question. The cops had pulled up in front of the place as I was driving away. There'd be no getting back in for some time.

Rick. There was Rick Kinsky, the guy she'd begun seeing after we'd broken up. I knew him on sight—a thin, mustached, cerebral sort, thick glasses and all. He managed a bookstore I'd visited once or twice. I didn't know him beyond that, though. Perhaps he could tell me something about the cards and how Julia might have gotten into whatever situation it was that had cost her her life.

I brooded a little longer, then put the cards away. I wasn't about to fool with them any further. Not yet. First, I wanted as much information as I could get.

I headed back for the car. As I walked I reflected that this April 30 wasn't over. Suppose S didn't really consider this morning's encounter as aimed directly at me? In that case there was plenty of time for another attempt. I also had a feeling that if I began getting close S would forget about dates and go for my throat whenever there was an opening. I resolved not to let my guard down at all henceforth, to live as in a state of siege until this matter was settled. And all of my energies were now going to be directed toward settling it. My well-being seemed to require the destruction of my enemy, very soon.

Should I seek counsel? I wondered. And if so, from whom? There was an awful lot I still didn't know about my heritage . . .

No. Not yet, I decided. I had to make every effort to handle things myself. Beside the fact that I wanted to, I needed the practice. It's necessary to be able to deal with nasty matters where I come from.

I drove, looking for a pay phone and trying not to think of Julia as I had last seen her. A few clouds blew in from the west. My watch ticked on my wrist, next to unseen Frakir. The news on the radio was international and cheerless.

I stopped in a drugstore and used a phone there to try to reach Luke at his motel. He wasn't in. So I had a club sandwich and a milkshake in the dining area and tried again afterward. Still out.

Okay. Catch him later. I headed into town. The Browserie, as I recalled, was the name of the bookstore where Rick worked.

I drove by and saw that the place was open. I parked a couple of blocks up the street and walked back. I had been alert all of the way across town, but could not detect any sign that I was being followed.

A cool breeze touched me as I walked, hinting of rain. I saw Rick through the store's window, seated at his high counter reading a book. There was no one else in sight in the place.

A small bell jangled above the door as I entered, and he looked up. He straightened and his eyes widened as I approached.

"Hi," I said, pausing then for a moment. "Rick, I don't know whether you remember me."

"You're Merle Corey," he stated softly.

"Right." I leaned on the counter and he drew back. "I wondered whether you might be able to help me with a little information."

"What kind of information?"

"It's about Julia," I said.

"Look," he answered, "I never went near her until after you two had broken up."

"Huh? No, no, you don't understand. I don't care about that. It's more recent information that I need. She'd been trying to get in touch with me this past week and—"

He shook his head.

"I haven't heard from her for a couple of months."

"Oh?"

"Yeah, we stopped seeing each other. Different interests, you know?"

"Was she okay when you—stopped seeing each other?"

"I guess so."

I stared straight into his eyes and he winced. I didn't like that "I guess so." I could see that he was a little afraid of me so I decided to push it.

"What do you mean 'different interests'?" I asked.

"Well, she got a little weird, you know?" he said.

"I don't know. Tell me."

He licked his lips and looked away.

"I don't want any trouble," he stated.

"I'd rather not indulge either. What was the matter?"

"Well," he said, "she was scared."

"Scared? Of what?"

"Uh—of you."

"Me? That's ridiculous. I never did anything to frighten her. What did she say?"

"She never said it in so many words, but I could tell, whenever your name came up. Then she developed all these funny interests."

"You've lost me," I said. "Completely. She got weird? She got funny interests? What kind? What was going on? I really don't understand, and I'd like to."

He got to his feet and headed for the rear of the store, glancing at me as if I should follow him. I did.

He slowed when he reached a section full of books on natural healing and organic farming and martial arts and herbal remedies and having babies at home, but he went on past it into the hardcore occult section.

"Here," he said, halting. "She borrowed a few of these, brought them back, borrowed a few more."

I shrugged.

"That's all? That's hardly weird."

"But she really got into it."

"So do a lot of people."

"Let me finish," he went on. "She started with theosophy, even attended meetings of a local group. She got turned off on it fairly quick, but by then she'd met some people with different connections. Pretty soon she was hanging around with Sufis, Gurdjieffians, even a shaman."

"Interesting," I said. "No yoga?"

"No yoga. When I asked her that same thing she said that it was power she was after, not samadhi. Anyhow, she just kept finding stranger and stranger acquaintances. The atmosphere got too rarefied for me, so I said good-bye."

"I wonder why?" I mused.

"Here," he said, "take a look at this one."

He tossed me a black book and stepped back. I caught it. It was a copy of the Bible. I opened it to the publishing credits page.

"Something special about this edition?" I asked.

He sighed.

"No. I'm sorry."

He took it back and replaced it on the shelf.

"Just a minute," he said.

He returned to the counter and took a cardboard sign from a shelf beneath it. It read JUST STEPPED OUT. WE'LL REOPEN AT and there was a clock face beneath it with movable hands. He set them to indicate a time a half hour hence and went and hung the sign in the door's window. Then he shot the bolt and gestured for me to follow him to a room in the rear.

The back office contained a desk, a couple of chairs, cartons of books. He seated himself behind the desk and nodded toward the nearest chair. I took it. He switched on a telephone answering machine then, removed a stack of forms and correspondence from the blotter, opened a drawer and took out a bottle of Chianti.

"Care for a glass?" he asked.

"Sure, thanks."

He rose and stepped through the opened door of a small lavatory. He took a pair of glasses from a shelf and rinsed them. He brought them back, set them down, filled both, and pushed one in my direction. They were from the Sheraton.

"Sorry I tossed the Bible at you," he said, raising his glass and taking a sip.

"You looked as if you expected me to go up in a puff of smoke."

He nodded.

"I am really convinced that the reason she wants power has something to do with you. Are you into some form of occultism?"

"No."

"She talked sometimes as if you might even be a supernatural creature yourself."

I laughed. He did, too, after a moment.

"I don't know," he said then. "There're lots of strange things in the world. They can't all be right, but . . ."

I shrugged.

"Who knows? So you think she was looking for some system that would give her power to defend herself against me?"

"That was the impression I got."

I took a drink of the wine.

"That doesn't make sense," I told him.

But even as I said it I knew that it was probably true. And if I had driven her into the path of whatever had destroyed her, then I was partly responsible for her death. I suddenly felt the burden along with the pain.

"Finish the story," I said.

"That's pretty much it," he answered. "I got tired of people who wanted to discuss cosmic crap all the time and I split."

"And that's all? Did she find the right system, the right guru? What happened?"

He took a big drink and stared at me.

"I really liked her," he said.

"I'm sure."

"The Tarot, Caballa, Golden Dawn, Crowley, Fortune—that's where she went next."

"Did she stay?"

"I don't know for sure. But I think so. I only heard this after a while."

"Ritual magic, then?"

"Probably."

"Who does it?"

"Lots of people."

"I mean who did she find? Did you hear that?"

"I think it was Victor Melman."

He looked at me expectantly. I shook my head.

"I'm sorry. I don't know the name."

"Strange man," he mused, taking a sip and leaning back in his chair, clasping his hands behind his neck and bringing his elbows forward. He stared off into the lavatory. "I—I've heard it said—by a number of people, some of them fairly reliable—that he really has something going for him, that he has a hold on a piece of something, that he's known a kind of enlightenment, has been initiated, has a sort of power and is sometimes a great teacher. But he's got these ego problems, too, that seem to go along with that sort of thing. And there's a touch of the seamy side there. I've even heard it said that that's not his real name, that he's got a record, and there's more of Manson to him than Magus. I don't know. He's nominally a painter—actually a pretty good one. His stuff does sell."

"You've met him?"

A pause, then, "Yes."

"What were your own impressions?"

"I don't know. Well . . . I'm prejudiced. I can't really say."

I swirled the wine in my glass.

"How come?"

"Oh, I wanted to study with him once. He turned me down."

"So you were into this, too. I thought—"

"I'm not into anything," he snapped. "I tried everything at some time or other, I mean. Everybody goes through phases. I wanted to develop, expand, advance. Who doesn't? But I never found it." He unbent and took another gulp of wine. "Sometimes I felt that I was close, that there was some power, some vision that I could almost touch or see. Almost. Then it was gone. It's all a lot of crap. You just delude yourself. Sometimes I even thought I had it. Then a few days would go by and I realized that I was lying to myself again."

"All of this was before you met Julia?"

He nodded.

"Right. That might be what held us together for a while. I still like to talk about all this bullshit, even if I don't believe it anymore. Then she got too serious about it, and I didn't feel like going that route again."

"I see."

He drained his glass and refilled it.

"There's nothing to any of it," he said. "There are an infinite number of ways of lying to yourself, of rationalizing things into something they are not. I guess that I wanted magic, and there is no real magic in the world."

"That why you threw the Bible at me?"

He snorted.

"I could as easily have been the Koran or the Vedas, I suppose. It would have been neat to see you vanish in a flash of fire. But no go."

I smiled.

"How can I find Melman?"

"I've got it here somewhere," he said, lowering his eyes and opening a drawer. "Here."

He withdrew a small notebook and flipped through it. He copied out an address on an index card and handed it to me. He took another drink of wine.

"Thanks."

"It's his studio, but he lives there, too," he added.

I nodded and set down my glass.

"I appreciate everything you told me."

He raised the bottle.

"Have another drink?"

"No, thanks."

He shrugged and topped off his own. I rose.

"You know, it's really sad," he said.

"What?"

"That there's no magic, that there never was, there probably never will be."

"That's the breaks," I said.

"The world would be a lot more interesting place."

"Yeah."

I turned to go.

"Do me a favor," he said.

"What?"

"On the way out, set that sign for three o'clock and let the bolt in the door snap shut again."

"Sure."

I left him there and did those things. The sky had grown a lot darker, the wind a bit more chill. I tried again to reach Luke, from a phone on the corner, but he was still out.

We were happy. It had been a terrific day. The weather was perfect, and everything we did had worked out right. We went to a fun party that evening and afterward had a late dinner at a really good little place we'd stumbled upon by accident. We lingered over drinks, hating for the day to end. We decided then to prolong a winning streak, and we drove to an otherwise deserted beach where we sat around and splashed around and watched the moon and felt the breezes. For a long while. I did something then that I had sort of promised myself I would not. Hadn't Faust thought a beautiful moment worth a soul?

"Come on," I said, aiming my beer can at a trash bin and catching hold of her hand. "Let's take a walk."

"Where to?" she asked, as I drew her to her feet.

"Fairy land," I replied. "The fabled realms of yore. Eden. Come on."

Laughing, she let me lead her along the beach, toward a place where it narrowed, squeezing by high embankments. The moon was generous and yellow, the sea sang my favorite song.

We strolled hand in hand past the bluffs, where a quick turning of the way took us out of sight of our stretch of sand. I looked for the cave that should be occurring soon, high and narrow . . .

"A cave," I announced moments later. "Let's go in."

"It'll be dark."

"Good," I said, and we entered.

The moonlight followed us for about six paces. By then, though, I had spotted the turnoff to the left.

"This way," I stated.

"It *is* dark!"

"Sure. Just keep hold of me a little longer. It'll be okay."

Fifteen or twenty steps and there was a faint illumination to the right. I led her along that turning and the way brightened as we advanced.

"We may get lost," she said softly.

"I don't get lost," I answered her.

It continued to brighten. The way turned once more, and we proceeded along that last passage to emerge at the foot of a mountain in sight of a low forest, the sun standing at midmorning height above its trees.

She froze, blue eyes wide.

"It's daytime!" she said.

"Tempus fugit," I replied. "Come on."

We walked through the woods for a time, listening to the birds and the breezes, dark-haired Julia and I, and I led her after a while through a canyon of colored rocks and grasses, beside a stream that flowed into a river.

We followed the river until we came, abruptly, to a precipice from whence it plunged a mighty distance, casting rainbows and fogs. Standing there, staring out across the great valley that lay below, we beheld a city of spires and cupolas, gilt and crystal, through morning and mist.

"Where—are we?" she asked.

"Just around the corner," I said. "Come."

I led her to the left, then down a trail that took us back along the face of the cliff, passing finally behind the cataract. Shadows and diamond beads . . . a roaring to approach the power of silence . . .

We passed at last into a tunnel, damp at first but drying as it rose. We followed it to a gallery, open to our left and looking out upon night and stars, stars, stars. . . . It was an enormous prospect, blazing with new constellations, their light sufficient to cast our shadows onto the wall behind us. She leaned over the low parapet, her skin some rare polished marble, and she looked downward.

"They're down there, too," she said. "And to both sides! There is nothing below but more stars. And to the sides . . ."

"Yes. Pretty things, aren't they?"

We remained there for a long while, watching, before I could persuade her to come away and follow the tunnel farther. It bore us out again to behold a ruined classical amphitheater beneath a late afternoon sky. Ivy grew over broken benches and fractured pillars. Here and there lay a shattered statue, as if cast down by earthquake. Very picturesque. I'd thought she'd like it, and I was right. We took turns seating ourselves and speaking to each other. The acoustics were excellent.

We walked away then, hand in hand, down myriad ways beneath skies of many colors, coming at last in sight of a quiet lake with a sun entering evening upon its farther shore. There was a glittering mass of rock off to my right. We walked out upon a small point cushioned with mosses and ferns.

I put my arms around her and we stood there for a long time, and the wind in the trees was lute song counterpointed by invisible birds. Later still, I unbuttoned her blouse.

"Right here?" she said.

"I like it here. Don't you?"

"It's beautiful. Okay. Wait a minute."

So we lay down and loved till the shadows covered us. After a time she slept, as I desired.

I set a spell upon her to keep her asleep, for I was beginning to have second thoughts over the wisdom of making this journey. Then I dressed both of us and picked her up to carry her back. I took a shortcut.

On the beach from which we'd started I put her down and stretched out beside her. Soon I slept also.

We did not awaken till after the sun was up, when the sounds of bathers roused us.

She sat up and stared at me.

"Last night," she said, "could not have been a dream. But it couldn't have been real either. Could it?"

"I guess so," I said.

She furrowed her brow.

"What did you just agree to?" she asked.

"Breakfast," I said. "Let's go get some. Come on."

"Wait a minute." She put a hand on my arm. "Something unusual happened. What was it?"

"Why destroy the magic by talking about it? Let's go eat."

She questioned me a lot in the days that followed, but I was adamant in refusing to talk about it. Stupid, the whole thing was stupid. I should never have taken her on that walk. It contributed to that final argument that set us permanently apart.

And now, driving, as I thought about it, I realized something more than my stupidity. I realized that I had been in love with her, that I still loved her. Had I not taken her on that walk, or had I acknowledged her later accusation that I was a sorcerer, she would not have taken the route that she took, seeking power of her own—probably for self-protection. She would be alive.

I bit my lip and cried out. I cut around the braking car in front of me and crashed a light. If I had killed the thing I loved, I was certain that the opposite was not going to be true.

3

Grief and anger shrink my world, and I resent this. They seem to paralyze my memory of happier times, of friends, places, things, options. Squeezed by the grip of intense, unsettling emotion, I grow smaller in my single-mindedness. I suppose it is partly because I have discarded a range of choices, impairing in some measure my freedom of will. I don't like this, but after a point I have small control over it. It makes me feel that I have surrendered to a kind of determinism, which irritates me even more. Then, vicious cycle, this feeds back into the emotion that drives me and intensifies it. The simple way of ending this situation is the headlong rush to remove its object. The difficult way is more philosophical, a drawing back, the reestablishment of control. As usual, the difficult way is preferable. A headlong rush may also result in a broken neck.

I parked in the first place that I saw, opened the window, lit my pipe. I vowed not to depart until I had grown calm. All of my life I have had a tendency to overreact to things. It seems to run in my family. But I did not want to be like the others. They made a lot of trouble for themselves that way. The full-scale, all-or-nothing reaction may be all right if you always win, but that way also lies high tragedy or at least opera if you happen to be up against something extraordinary. And I did have indications that this was the case. Therefore, I was a fool. I told myself this till I believed it.

Then I listened to my calmer self as it agreed that I was indeed a fool—for not having seen my own feelings when I could have done something about them, for having displayed a power and denied its consequences, for not having at least guessed at the

strange nature of my enemy in all these years, for my present sim-
plification of the coming encounter. It would not do to seize Victor
Melman on sight and try to beat the truth out of him. I resolved to
proceed carefully, covering myself at all times. Life is never simple, I told myself. Sit still and gather, regroup.

Slowly, I felt the tension go out of me. Slowly, too, my world
grew again, and I saw within it the possibility that S really knew
me, knew me well, and may even have arranged events so that I
would dispense with thinking and surrender to the moment. No, I
would not be like the others . . .

I sat there and thought for a long while before I started the engine again and drove on slowly.

It was a grimy brick building situated on a corner. It was four
stories in height, with occasional spray-painted obscenities on the
alley side and on the wall facing the narrower street. I discovered
the graffiti, a few broken windows and the fire escape as I strolled
slowly about the place, looking it over. By then a light rain was
just beginning to fall. The lower two stories were occupied by the
Brutus Storage Company, according to a sign beside the stairs in a
small hallway I entered. The place smelled of urine, and there was
an empty Jack Daniels bottle lying on the dusty windowsill to my
right. Two mailboxes hung upon the flaking wall. One said "Brutus Storage", the other bore the legend "V.M." Both were empty.

I mounted the stair, expecting it to creak. It did not.

There were four knobless doors letting upon the second-floor
hallway, all of them closed. The outlines of what might be cartons
were visible through several of the frosted panes in their upper
sections. There were no sounds from within.

I surprised a black cat dozing on the next stairway. She arched
her back, showed me her teeth, made a hissing noise, then turned
and bounded up the stairs and out of sight.

The next landing also had four doors—three of them apparently nonfunctional, the fourth dark-stained and shellacked shiny.
It bore a small brass plate that read "Melman." I knocked.

There was no answer. I tried again several times, with the
same result. No sounds from within either. It seemed likely that
these were his living quarters and that the fourth floor, with the
possibility of a skylight, held his studio. So I turned away and
took the final flight.

I reached the top and saw that one of the four doors there was
slightly ajar. I halted and listened for a moment. From beyond it

came faint sounds of movement. I advanced and gave it a few knocks. I heard a sudden intake of breath from somewhere inside. I pushed on the door.

He stood about twenty feet away beneath a large skylight and he had turned to face me—a tall, broad-shouldered man with dark beard and eyes. He held a brush in his left hand and a palette in his right. He wore a paint-smeared apron over his Levi's and had on a plaid sport shirt. The easel at his back held the outlines of what could be a madonna and child. There were a great many other canvases about, all of them facing the walls or covered.

"Hello," I said. "You are Victor Melman?"

He nodded, neither smiling nor frowning, placed his palette on a nearby table, his brush into a jar of solvent. He picked up a damp-looking cloth then and wiped his hands with it.

"And yourself?" he asked, tossing the cloth aside and facing me again.

"Merle Corey. You knew Julia Barnes."

"I don't deny it," he said. "Your use of the past tense would seem to indicate—"

"She's dead all right. I want to talk to you about it."

"All right," he said, untying his apron. "Let's go downstairs then. No place to sit up here."

He hung the apron upon a nail near the door and stepped outside. I followed him. He turned back and locked the studio before proceeding down the stairs. His movements were smooth, almost graceful. I could hear the rain on the roof.

He used the same key to unlock the dark door on the third floor. He drew the door open and stood aside, gesturing for me to enter. I did, traversing a hallway that led past a kitchen, its counters covered with empty bottles, stacks of dishes, pizza cartons. Bursting bags of trash leaned against cupboards; the floor looked sticky here and there and the place smelled like a spice factory next door to a slaughterhouse.

The living room, which I came to next, was large, with a comfortable-looking pair of black sofas, facing each other across a battlefield of Oriental carpets and miscellaneous tables, each of which bore several overflowing ashtrays. There was a beautiful concert-sized piano in the far corner, before a wall covered with heavy red drapery. There were numerous low bookcases filled with occult materials, stacks of magazines beside them, atop them, and alongside a few easy chairs. What could be the corner of a pentacle protruded slightly from beneath the largest rug. The stale smells of incense and pot lingered in patches. To my right, there was an archway leading to another room, a closed door to my left. Paintings of a semireligious nature—which I took to be his work—were hung on several of the walls. There was a Chagall-like quality to them. Quite good.

"Have a seat."

He gestured toward an easy chair and I took it.

"Care for a beer?"

"Thank you, no."

He seated himself on the nearer sofa, clasped his hands, and stared at me.

"What happened?" he asked.

I stared back at him.

"Julia Barnes got interested in occult systems," I said. "She came to you to learn more about them. She died this morning under very unusual circumstances."

The left corner of his mouth twitched slightly. He made no other movement.

"Yes, she was interested in such matters," he said. "She came to me for instruction and I provided it."

"I want to know why she died."

He continued to stare.

"Her time was up," he said. "It happens to everybody, in the long run."

"She was killed by an animal that should not exist here. Do you know anything about it?"

"The universe is a stranger place than most of us can imagine."

"Do you know or don't you?"

"I know you," he said, smiling for the first time. "She spoke of you, of course."

"What does that mean?"

"It means," he answered, "that I know you are more than a little aware of such matters yourself."

"And so?"

"The Arts have a way of bringing the right people together at the proper moment when there is work in progress."

"And that's what you think this is all about?"

"I know it."

"How?"

"It was promised."

"So you were expecting me?"

"Yes."

"Interesting. Would you care to tell me more about it?"

"I'd rather show you."

"You say that something was promised. How? By whom?"

"All of that will become clear shortly."

"And Julia's death?"

"That, too, I'd say."

"How do you propose rendering me this enlightenment?"

He smiled. "I just want you to take a look at something," he said.

"All right. I'm willing. Show me."

He nodded and rose.

"It's in here," he explained, turning and heading toward the closed door.

I got to my feet and followed him across the room.

He reached into his shirtfront and drew up a chain. He lifted it over his head and I could see that it bore a key. He used it to unlock the door.

"Go in," he said, pushing it open and stepping aside.

I entered. It was not a large room, and it was dark. He flipped a switch and a blue light of small wattage came on within a plain fixture overhead. I saw then that there was one window, directly across from me, and that all of its panes had been painted black. There were no furnishings save for a few cushions scattered here and there across the floor. A portion of the wall to my right was covered with black drapery. The other walls were unadorned.

"I'm looking," I said.

He chuckled.

"A moment, a moment," he advised me. "Have you any idea of my major concern in the occult arts?"

"You're a cabalist," I stated.

"Yes," he admitted. "How could you tell?"

"People in Eastern disciplines tend to run a tight ship," I stated. "But cabalists always seem to be slobs."

He snorted.

"It is all a matter of what is really important to you," he said then.

"Exactly."

He kicked a cushion into the middle of the floor.

"Have a seat," he said.

"I'll stand."

He shrugged.

"Okay," he said, and he began muttering softly.

I waited. After a time, still speaking quietly, he moved to the black curtain. He opened it with a single quick movement and I stared.

A painting of the cabalistic Tree of Life was revealed, showing the ten sephira in some of their qlipphotic aspects. It was beautifully executed, and the sense of recognition that struck me as I regarded it was unsettling. It was no standard item from some head shop, but rather an original painting. It was not, however in the style of any of the works hanging in the other room. Still, it was familiar to me.

As I studied it I had no doubt whatsoever that it had been painted by the same person who had done the Trumps I had found in Julia's apartment.

Melman continued his incantation as I regarded the painting.

"Is this your work?" I asked him.

He did not answer me. Instead, he advanced and pointed, indicating the third sephiroth, the one called Binah. I studied it. It seemed to represent a wizard before a dark altar, and—

No! I couldn't believe it. It shouldn't—

I felt a contact with that figure. It was not just symbolic. He was real, and he was summoning me. He loomed larger, grew three-dimensional. The room began to fade about me. I was almost—

There.

It was a place of twilight, a small glade in a twisted wood. An almost bloody light illuminated the slab before me. The wizard, his face hidden by cowl and shadow, manipulated objects upon the stone, his hands moving too rapidly for me to follow. From somewhere, I still seemed to hear the chanting, faintly.

Finally, he raised a single object in his right hand and held it steady. It was a black, obsidian dagger. He laid his left arm upon the altar and brushed it across the surface, sweeping everything else to the ground.

He looked at me for the first time.

"Come here," he said then.

I began to smile at the stupid simplicity of the request. But then I felt my feet move without my willing them to do so, and I knew that a spell lay upon me in this dark shadow.

I thanked another uncle, who dwelled in the most distant place imaginable, as I began to speak in Thari, a spell of my own.

A piercing cry, as of some swooping night bird, rent the air.

The wizard was not distracted, nor my feet freed, but I was able to raise my arms before me. I kept them at the proper level, and when they reached the forward edge of the altar I cooperated with the summoning spell, increasing the force of each automatonlike step that I took. I let my elbows bend.

The wizard was already swinging the blade toward my fingers, but it didn't matter. I put all of my weight behind it and heaved at the stone.

The altar toppled backward. The wizard scurried to avoid it, but it struck one—perhaps both—of his legs. Immediately, as he fell to the ground, I felt the spell depart from me. I could move properly again and my mind was clear.

He drew his knees up to his chest and began to roll even as I leaped over the wrecked altar and reached toward him. I moved to follow as he somersaulted down a small slope and passed between two standing stones and into the darkened wood.

As soon as I reached the clearing's edge I saw eyes, hundreds of feral eyes blazing from the darkness at many levels. The incanting grew louder, seemed nearer, seemed to be coming from behind me.

I turned quickly.

The altar was still in wreckage. Another cowled figure stood behind it, much larger than the first. This one was doing the chanting, in a familiar masculine voice. Frakir pulsed upon my wrist. I felt a spell building about me, but this time I was not unprepared. The opposite of my walk, a summons, brought an icy wind that swept the spell away like so much smoke. My garments were lashed about me, changing shape and color. Purple, gray . . . light the trousers and dark the cloak, the shirtfront. Black my boots and wide belt, my gauntlets tucked behind, my silver Frakir woven into a bracelet about my left wrist, visible now and shining. I raised my left hand and shielded my eyes with my right, as I summoned a flash of light.

"Be silent," I said then. "You offend me."

The chanting ceased.

The cowl was blown back from his head and I regarded Melman's frightened face.

"All right. You wanted me," I stated, "and now you have me, heaven help you. You said that everything would become clear to me. It hasn't. Make it clear."

I took a step forward.

"Talk!" I said. "It can be easy or it can be hard. But you will talk. The choice is yours."

He threw back his head and bellowed: "Master!"

"Summon your master then, by any means," I said. "I will wait. For he, too, must answer."

He called out again, but there was no answer. He bolted then, but I was ready for this with a major summoning. The woods decayed and fell before he could reach them, and then they moved, were swept up in a mighty wind where there should be stillness. It circled the glade, gray and red, building an impenetrable wall to infinites above and below. We inhabited a circular island in the night, several hundred meters across, its edges slowly crumbling.

"He is not coming," I said, "and you are not going. He cannot help you. No one will help you. This is a place of high magic and you profane it with your presence. Do you know what lies beyond the advancing winds? Chaos. I will give you to it now, unless you tell me about Julia and your master and why you dared to bring me here."

He drew back from the Chaos and turned to face me.

"Take me back to my apartment and I will tell you everything," he said.

I shook my head.

"Kill me and you will never know."

I shrugged.

"In that case, you will tell me in order to stop the pain. Then I will give you to the Chaos."

I moved toward him.

"Wait!" He raised his hand. "Give me my life for what I am about to tell you."

"No bargain. Talk."

The winds swirled around us and our island shrank. Half-heard, half-intelligible voices babbled within the wind and fragments of forms swam there. Melman drew back from the crumbling edge of things.

"All right," he said, speaking loudly. "Yes, Julia came to me, as I had been told she would, and I taught her some things—not the things I would have taught her even a year ago, but pieces of some new things I had only learned myself more recently. I had been told to teach her in this manner, also."

"By whom? Name your master."

He grimaced.

"He was not so foolish as to give me his name," he said, "that I might seek some control over him. Like yourself, he is not human, but a being from some other plane."

"He gave you the painting of the Tree?"

Melman nodded.

"Yes, and it actually transported me to each sephiroth. Magic worked in those places. I gained powers."

"And the Trumps? He did those, too? He gave them to you to give to her?"

"I don't know anything about any Trumps," he answered.

"These!" I cried, drawing them from beneath my cloak, spreading them like a conjurer's fan and advancing toward him. I thrust them at him and let him stare for a few moments, withdrawing them before he got the idea that they might represent a means of escape.

"I never saw them before," he said.

The ground continued its steady erosion toward us. We withdrew to a point nearer the center.

"And you sent the creature that slew her?"

He shook his head vehemently.

"I did not. I knew that she was going to die, for he had told me that that was what would bring you to me. He told me, too, that it would be a beast from Netzach that would slay her—but I never saw it and I had no part in its summoning."

"And why did he want you to meet me, to bring me here?"

He laughed wildly.

"Why?" he repeated. "To kill you, of course. He told me that if I could sacrifice you in this place I would gain your powers. He said that you are Merlin, son of Hell and Chaos, and that I would become the greatest mage of all could I slay you here."

Our world was at best a hundred meters across now, and the rate of its shrinkage was accelerating.

"Was it true?" he asked. "Would I have gained had I succeeded?"

"Power is like money," I said. "You can usually get it if you're competent and it's the only thing you want in life. Would you have gained by it, though? I don't think so."

"I'm talking about the meaning of life. You know that."

I shook my head.

"Only a fool believes that life has but one meaning," I said. "Enough of this! Describe your master."

"I never saw him."

"What?"

"I mean, I saw him but I don't know what he looks like. He always wore a hood and a black trench coat. Gloves, too. I don't even know his race."

"How did you meet?"

"He appeared one day in my studio. I just turned around and he was standing there. He offered me power, said that he would teach me things in return for my service."

"How did you know he could deliver?"

"He took me on a journey through places not of this world."

"I see."

Our island of existence was now about the size of a large living room. The voices of the wind were mocking, then compassionate, frightened, sad and angry, too. Our wraparound vision shifted constantly. The ground trembled without letup. The light was still baleful. A part of me wanted to kill Melman right then, but if he had not really been the one who had hurt Julia . . .

"Did your master tell you why he wanted me dead?" I asked him.

He licked his lips and glanced back at the advancing Chaos.

"He said that you were his enemy," he explained, "but he never told me why. And he said that it was going to happen today, that he wanted it to happen today."

"Why today?"

He smiled briefly.

"I suppose because it's Walpurgisnacht," he replied, "though he never actually said that."

"That's all?" I said. "He never mentioned where he was from?"

"He once referred to something called the Keep of the Four Worlds as if it were important to him."

"And you never felt that he was simply using you?"

He smiled. "Of course he was using me," he replied. "We all use somebody. That is the way of the world. But he paid for this use with knowledge and power. And I think his promise may yet be fulfilled."

He seemed to be glancing at something behind me. It was the oldest trick in the world, but I turned. There was no one there. Immediately, I spun back to face him.

He held the black dagger. It must have been up his sleeve. He lunged at me, thrusting, mouthing fresh incantations.

I stepped back and swirled my cloak at him. He disengaged himself, sidestepping and slashing, turned and advanced again. This time he came in low, trying to circle me, his lips still moving. I kicked at the knifehand, but he snapped it back. I caught up the left edge of my cloak then, wrapping it about my arm. When he struck again, I blocked the thrust and seized his biceps. Dropping lower as I drew him forward, I caught hold of his left thigh with my right hand, then straightened, raising him high in the air, and threw him.

As I turned my body, completing the throw, I realized what I had done. Too late. With my attention focused on my adversary I had not kept track of the rapid, grinding advance of the destroying winds. The edge of Chaos was much nearer than I had thought, and Melman had time for only the most abbreviated of curses before death took him where he would incant no more.

I cursed, too, because I was certain there was still more information that I could have gotten from him; and I shook my head, there at the center of my diminishing world.

The day was not yet over and it was already my most memorable Walpurgisnacht ever.

4

It was a long walk back. I changed my clothes on the way.

My exit from the labyrinth took the form of a narrow alleyway between a pair of dirty brick buildings. It was still raining and the day had made its way into evening. I saw my parked car across the street at the edge of a pool of light cast by one of the unbroken streetlamps. I thought wistfully for a moment of my dry garments in the trunk, then I headed back toward the Brutus Storage sign.

A small light burned within the first-floor office, spilling a little illumination into the otherwise dark entranceway. I trudged on up the stairs, terminally moist and reasonably alert. The apartment door opened when I turned the knob and pushed. I switched on the light and entered, bolting the door behind me.

A quick prowl showed me that the place was deserted, and I changed out of my wet shirt into one from Melman's closet. His trousers were too big in the waist and a bit long for me, though. I transferred my Trumps to a breast pocket to keep them dry.

Step two. I began a systematic ransacking of the place. After a few minutes, I came across his occult diary in a locked drawer in his bedside table. It was as messy as the rest of the place, with misspellings, crossed-out words, and a few beer and coffee stains. It seemed to contain a lot of derivative stuff mixed with the usual subjective business—dreams and meditations. I flipped farther along in it, looking for the place where he'd met his master. I came to it and skimmed along. It was lengthy, and seemed mostly comprised of enthusiastic ejaculations over the workings of the Tree he had been given. I decided to save it for later and was about the stow it when a final riffling of the pages brought a brief poem into view. Swinburnian, overly allusive and full of rapture, the lines that first caught my eye were, "—the infinite shadows of Amber, touched with her treacherous taint." Too much alliteration, but it was the thought that counted. It revived my earlier feeling of vulnerability and caused me to ransack faster. I suddenly wanted only to get out, get far away and think.

The room held no further surprises. I departed it, gathered an armload of strewn newspapers, carried them to the john, tossed them into the bathtub, and set fire to them, opening the window on the way out. I visited the sanctum then, fetched out the Tree of Life painting, brought it back and added it to the blaze. I switched off the bathroom light and closed the door as I left. I'm one hell of an art critic.

I headed for the stacks of miscellaneous papers on the bookshelves then and began a disappointing search among them. I was halfway through my second heap when the telephone rang.

The world seemed to freeze as my thoughts sprinted. Of course. Today was the day when I was supposed to find my way here and be killed. Chances seemed decent that if it were going to happen it would have happened by now. So this could well be S, calling to learn whether my obituary had been posted. I turned and located the phone, back on the shadowy wall near the bedroom. I had known immediately that I was going to answer it. Moving toward it, I was allowing two to three rings—twelve to eighteen seconds—in which to decide whether my response was to consist of a wisecrack, an insult and a threat, or whether I was going to try to fake it and see what I might learn. As satisfying as the former could be, spoilsport prudence dictated the latter course and also suggested I confine myself to low monosyllables and pretend to be injured and out of breath. I raised the receiver, ready to hear S's voice at last and find out whether I knew him.

"Yes?" I said.

"Well? Is it done?" came the response.

Damn pronoun. It was a woman. Wrong gender but a right-sounding question. One out of two isn't bad, though.

I exhaled heavily, then: "Yeah."

"What's the matter?"

"I'm hurt," I croaked.

"Is it serious?"

"Think so. Got something—here—though. Better come—see."

"What is it? Something of his?"

"Yeah. Can't talk. Getting dizzy. Come."

I cradled the phone and smiled. I thought it very well played. I'd a feeling I'd taken her in completely.

I crossed the living room to the same chair I had occupied earlier, drew up one of the small tables bearing a large ashtray, seated myself, and reached for my pipe. Time to rest, cultivate patience, think a bit.

Moments later I felt a familiar, almost electrical tingling. I was on my feet in an instant, snatching up the ashtray, butts flying like bullets about me, cursing my stupidity yet again as I looked frantically about the room.

There! Before the red drapes, beside the piano. Taking form . . .

I waited for the full outline, then hurled the ashtray as hard as I could.

An instant later she was there—tall, russet-haired, dark-eyed, holding what looked like a .38 automatic.

The ashtray hit her in the stomach and she doubled forward with a gasp.

I was there before she could straighten.

I jerked the gun out of her hand and threw it across the room. Then I seized both her wrists, spun her around and seated her hard in the nearest chair. In her left hand she still held a Trump. I snatched it away. It was a representation of this apartment, and it was done in the same style as the Tree and the cards in my pocket.

"Who are you?" I snarled.

"Jasra," she spat back, "dead man!"

She opened her mouth wide and her head fell forward. I felt the moist touch of her lips upon the back of my left forearm, which still held her own right wrist against the chair's arm. Seconds later I felt an excruciating pain there. It was not a bite, but rather felt as if a fiery nail had been driven into my flesh.

I let go her wrist and jerked my arm away. The movement was strangely slow, weakened. A cold, tingling sensation moved down into the hand and up along the arm. My hand dropped to my side and seemed to go away. She extricated herself easily from my grip, smiled, placed her fingertips lightly upon my chest and pushed.

I fell backward. I was ridiculously weak and I couldn't control my movements. I felt no pain when I struck the floor, and it was a real effort to turn my head to regard her as she rose to her feet.

"Enjoy it," she stated. "After you awaken, the remainder of your brief existence will be painful."

She passed out of my line of sight, and moments later I heard her raise the telephone receiver.

I was certain she was phoning S, and I believed what she had just said. At least, I would get to meet the mysterious artist . . .

Artist! I twitched the fingers of my right hand. They still functioned, albeit slowly. Straining every bit of will and anatomy that remained under my control, I tried then to raise the hand to my chest. The movement that followed was a jerky, slow-motion thing. At least I had fallen upon my left side, and my back masked this feeble activity from the woman who had done me in.

My hand was trembling and seemed to be slowing even more when it came to the breast pocket. For ages after, I seemed to pick at the edges of pieces of pasteboard. Finally, one came free and I was able to twitch it high enough to view it. By then I was very dizzy and my vision was beginning to blur. I wasn't certain I could manage the transfer. From across a vast distance I could her Jasra's voice as she conversed with someone, but I was unable to distinguish the words.

I focused what remained of my attention upon the card. It was a sphinx, crouched upon a blue, rocky ledge. I reached for it. Nothing. My mind felt as if it were embedded in cotton. I possessed barely enough consciousness for one more attempt.

I felt a certain coldness and seemed to see the sphinx move slightly upon its stony shelf. I felt as if I were falling forward into a black wave that was rushing upward.

And that was all.

I was a long time coming around. My consciousness dribbled back, but my limbs were still leaden and my vision clouded. The lady's sting seemed to have delivered a neurotropic toxin. I tried flexing my fingers and toes and could not be certain whether I'd succeeded. I tried to speed up and deepen my breathing. That worked, anyway.

After a time, I heard what seemed a roaring sound. It stepped itself down a little later, and I realized it was my own rushing blood in my ears. A while after that I felt my heartbeat, and my vision began to clear. Light and dark and shapelessness resolved into sand and rocks. I felt little areas of chill, all over. Then I began to shiver, and this passed and I realized that I could move. But I felt very weak, so I didn't. Not for a while.

I heard noises—rustlings, stirrings—coming from somewhere above and before me. I also became aware of a peculiar odor.

"I say, are you awake?" This from the same direction as the sounds of movement.

I decided that I was not entirely ready to qualify for that state, so I did not answer. I waited for more life to flow back into my limbs.

"I really wish you'd let me know whether you can hear me," the voice came again. "I'd like to get on with it."

My curiosity finally overcame my judgment and I raised my head.

"There! I knew it!"

On the blue-gray ledge above me was crouched a sphinx, also blue—lion body, large feathered wings folded tight against it, a genderless face looking down upon me. It licked its lips and revealed a formidable set of teeth.

"Get on with what?" I asked, raising myself slowly into a sitting position and drawing several deep breaths.

"The riddling," it answered, "the thing I do best."

"I'll take a rain check," I said, waiting for the cramps in my arms and legs to pass.

"Sorry. I must insist."

I rubbed my punctured forearm and glared at the creature. Most of the stories I recalled about sphinxes involved their devouring people who couldn't answer riddles. I shook my head.

"I won't play your game," I said.

"In that case, you lose by forfeit," it replied, shoulder muscles beginning to tighten.

"Hold on," I said, raising my hand. "Give me a minute or two to recover and I'll probably feel differently."

It settled back and said, "Okay. That would make it more official. Take five. Let me know when you're ready."

I climbed to my feet and began swinging my arms and stretching. While I was about it, I surveyed the area quickly.

We occupied a sandy arroyo, punctuated here and there with orange, gray, and blue rocks. The stony wall whose ledge the sphinx occupied rose steeply before me to a height of perhaps twenty-five feet; another wall of the same height lay at about that distance to my rear. The wash rose steeply to my right, ran off in a more level fashion to my left. A few spiky green shrubs inhabited rifts and crevices. The hour seemed verging upon dusk. The sky was a weak yellow with no sun in sight. I heard a distant wind but did not feel it. The place was cool but not chill.

I spotted a rock the size of a small dumbbell on the ground

nearby. Two ambling paces—as I continued swinging my arms and stretching—and it lay beside my right foot.

The sphinx cleared its throat.

"Are you ready?" it asked.

"No," I said. "But I'm sure that won't stop you."

"You're right."

I felt an uncontrollable desire to yawn and did so.

"You seem to lack something of the proper spirit," it observed. "But here it is: I rise in flame from the earth. The wind assails me and waters lash me. Soon I will oversee all things."

I waited. Perhaps a minute passed.

"Well?" the sphinx finally said.

"Well what?"

"Have you the answer?"

"To what?"

"The riddle, of course!"

"I was waiting. There was no question, only a series of statements. I can't answer a question if I don't know what it is."

"It's a time-honored format. The interrogative is implied by the context. Obviously, the question is, 'What am I?' "

"I could just as easily be, 'Who is buried in Grant's tomb?' But okay. What is it? The phoenix, of course—nested upon the earth, rising in flames above it, passing through the air, the clouds, to a great height—"

"Wrong."

It smiled and began to stir.

"Hold on," I said. "It is not wrong. It fits. It may not be the answer you want, but it is an answer that meets the requirements."

It shook its head.

"I am the final authority on these answers. I do the defining."

"Then you cheat."

"I do not!"

"I drink off half the contents of a flask. Does that make it half full or half empty?"

"Either. Both."

"Exactly. Same thing. If more than one answer fits, you have to buy them all. It's like waves and particles."

"I don't like that approach," it stated. "It would open all sorts of doors to ambiguity. It could spoil the riddling business."

"Not my fault," I said, clenching and unclenching my hands.

"But you do raise an interesting point."

I nodded vigorously.

"But there *should* only be one correct answer."

I shrugged.

"We inhabit a less than ideal world," I suggested.

"Hm."

"We could just call it a tie," I offered. "Nobody wins, nobody loses."

"I find that esthetically displeasing."

"It works okay in lots of other games."

"Also, I've grown a bit hungry."

"The truth surfaces."

"But I am not unfair. I serve the truth, in my fashion. Your mention of a tie raises the possibility of a solution."

"Good. I'm glad you see things—"

"That being a tie breaker. Ask me your riddle."

"This is silly," I said. "I don't have any riddles."

"Then you'd better come up with one fast. Because it's the only way out of our deadlock—that, or I judge you the loser."

I swung my arms and did a few deep kneebends. My body felt as if it were afire. It also felt stronger.

"Okay," I said. "Okay. Just a second."

What the hell . . .

"What's green and red and goes round and round and round?"

The sphinx blinked twice, then furrowed its brow. I used the time that followed for some more deep breathing and some running in place. The fires subsided, my head grew clearer, my pulse steadied . . .

"Well?" I said some minutes later.

"I'm thinking."

"Take your time."

I did a little shadowboxing. Did some isometrics, too. The sky had darkened a bit more and a few stars were now visible off to my right.

"Uh, I hate to rush you," I said, "but—"

The sphinx snorted. "I'm still thinking."

"Maybe we should set a time limit."

"It shouldn't be much longer."

"Mind if I rest?"

"Go ahead."

I stretched out on the sand and closed my eyes, muttering a guard word to Frakir before I slept.

*   *   *

I woke with a shiver, light in my eyes and a breeze upon my face. It took me several moments to realize that it was morning. The sky was brightening to my left, stars were fading to my right. I was thirsty. Hungry, too.

I rubbed my eyes. I got to my feet. I located my comb and ran it through my hair. I regarded the sphinx.

". . . and goes round and round and round," it muttered.

I cleared my throat. No reaction. The beast was staring past me. I wondered whether I might simply be able to slip off . . .

No. The gaze shifted to me.

"Good morning," I said cheerfully.

There was a brief gnashing of teeth.

"All right," I said, "you've taken a lot longer than I did. If you haven't got it by now I don't care to play any longer."

"I don't like your riddle," it said at last.

"Sorry."

"What is the answer?"

"You're giving up?"

"I must. What is the answer?"

I raised a hand.

"Hold on," I said. "These things should be done in proper order. I should have the preferred answer to yours before I tell you mine."

It nodded.

"There is some justice in that. All right—the Keep of the Four Worlds."

"What?"

"That is the answer. The Keep of the Four Worlds."

I thought of Melman's words. "Why?" I asked.

"It lies at the crossroads of the worlds of the four elements, where it rises from the earth in flames, assailed by the winds and waters."

"What about the business of overseeing all things?"

"It could refer to the view, or to its master's imperialistic designs. Or both."

"Who is its master?"

"I don't know. That information is not essential to the answer."

"Where'd you pick up this riddle, anyhow?"

"From a traveler, a few months back."

"Why'd you choose this one, of all the riddles you must know, to ask me?"

"It stopped me, so it had to be good."

"What became of the traveler?"

"He went on his way, uneaten. He'd answered my riddle."

"He had a name?"

"He wouldn't say."

"Describe him, please."

"I can't. He was well muffled."

"And he said nothing more about the Keep of the Four Worlds?"

"No."

"Well," I said. "I believe I'll follow his example and take a walk myself."

I turned and faced the slope to my right.

"Wait!"

"What?" I asked.

"Your riddle," it stated. "I've given you the answer to mine. You must now tell me what it is that is green and red and goes round and round and round."

I glanced downward, scanned the ground. Oh, yes, there it was—my dumbbell-shaped stone. I took several steps and stood beside it.

"A frog in a Cuisinart," I said.

"What?"

Its shoulder muscles bunched, its eyes narrowed and its many teeth became very apparent. I spoke a few words to Frakir and felt her stir as I squatted and caught hold of the stone with my right hand.

"That's it," I said, rising. "It's one of those visual things—"

"That's a rotten riddle!" the sphinx announced.

With my left index finger I made two quick movements in the air before me.

"What are you doing?" it asked.

"Drawing lines from your ears to your eyes," I said.

Frakir became visible at about that moment, sliding from my left wrist to my hand, twining among my fingers. The sphinx's eyes darted in that direction. I raised the stone level with my right shoulder. One end of Frakir fell free and hung writhing from my extended hand. She began to brighten, then glowed like a hot silver wire.

"I believe the contest is a draw," I stated. "What do you think?"

The sphinx licked its lips.

"Yes," it finally said, sighing. "I suppose you are right."

"Then I will bid you good day," I said.

"Yes. Pity. Very well. Good day. But before you go may I have you name—for the record?"

"Why not?" I said. "I am Merlin, of Chaos."

"Ah," it said, "then someone would have come to avenge you."

"It's possible."

"Then a draw is indeed best. Go."

I backed farther off before turning and proceeding up the slope to my right. I remained on guard until I was out of that place, but there was no pursuit.

I began jogging. I was thirsty and hungry, but I wasn't likely to turn up breakfast in this desolate, rocky place under a lemon sky. Frakir recoiled and faded. I began drawing deep breaths as I headed away from the risen sun.

Wind in my hair, dust in my eyes . . . I bore toward a cluster of boulders, passed among them. Seen from amid their shadows the sky grew greenish above me. Emerging, I came upon a softer plain, glitters in the distance, a few clouds rising to my left.

I maintained a steady pace, reaching a small rise, mounting it, descending its farther side where sparse grasses waved. A grove of mop-topped trees in the distance . . . I headed for them, startling a small orange-furred creature that sprang across my path and tore away to the left. Moments later, a dark bird flashed by, uttering a wailing note, headed in the same direction. I ran on, and the sky continued to darken.

Green the sky and thicker the grasses, green the grasses, too . . . Heavy gusts of wind at irregular intervals . . . Nearer the trees . . . A singing sound emerges from their branches . . . The clouds sweep onward . . .

A tightness goes out of my muscles and a familiar fluidity enters . . . I pass the first tree, treading upon long, fallen leaves . . . I pass among hairy-barked boles . . . The way I follow is hard-packed, becomes a trail, strange foot marks cast within it . . . It drops, curves, widens, narrows again . . . The ground rises at either hand . . . the trees sound bass viol notes . . . Patches of sky amid the leaves are the color of Morinci turquoise . . . Streamers of cloud snake forward like silver rivers . . . Small clusters of blue flowers appear on the trail walls . . . The walls rise higher, passing above my head . . . The way grows rocky . . . I run on . . .

My path widens, widens, descending steadily . . . Even before I see or hear it, I smell the water . . . Carefully now, among the stones . . . A bit slower here . . . I turn and see the stream, high, rocky banks at either hand, a meter or two of shoreline before the rise . . .

Slower still, beside the gurgling, sparkling flow . . . To follow its meandering . . . Bends, curves, trees high overhead, exposed roots in the wall to my right, gray and yellow talus-fall along the flaky base . . .

My shelf widens, the walls lower . . . More sand and fewer rocks beneath my feet . . . Lowering, lowering . . . Head-height, shoulder-height . . . Another bending of the way, slope descending . . . Waist high . . . Green-leafed trees all about me, blue sky overhead, off to the right a hard-packed trail . . . I mount the slope, I follow it . . .

Trees and shrubs, bird notes and cool breeze . . . I suck the air, I lengthen my stride . . . I cross a wooden bridge, footfalls echoing, creek flowing to the now-masked stream, moss-grown boulders beside its cool . . . Low stone wall to my right now . . . Wagon ruts ahead . . .

Wildflowers at either hand . . . A sound of distant laughter, echoing . . . The neigh of a horse . . . Creak of a cart . . . Turn left . . . Widening of the way . . . Shadow and sunlight, shadow and sunlight . . . Dapple, dapple . . . River to the left, wider now, sparkling . . . Haze of smoke above the next hill . . .

I slow as I near the summit. I reach it walking, dusting my garments, brushing my hair into place, limbs tingling, lungs pumping, bands of perspiration cooling me. I spit grit. Below me and to the right lies a country inn, some tables on its wide, rough-hewn porch, facing the river, a few in a garden nearby. Bye-bye, present tense. I am arrived.

I walked on down and located a pump at the far side of the building, where I washed my face, hands and arms, my left forearm still sore and slightly inflamed where Jasra had attacked me. I made my way to the porch then and took a small table, after waving to a serving woman I saw within. After a time, she brought me porridge and sausages and eggs and bread and butter and strawberry preserves and tea. I finished it all quickly and ordered another round of the same. The second time through a feeling of returning normalcy occurred, and I slowed and enjoyed it and watched the river go by.

It was a strange way to wind up the job. I had been looking forward to some leisurely travel, to a long lazy vacation, now my work had been done. The small matter of S had been all that stood in my way—a thing I had been certain I could settle quickly. Now I was in the middle of something I did not understand, something dangerous and bizarre. Sipping my tea and feeling the day warm about me, I could be lulled into a momentary sense of peace. But I knew it for a fleeting thing. There could be no true rest, no safety for me, until this matter was settled. Looking back over events, I saw that I could no longer trust my reactions alone for my deliverance, for a resolution of this affair. It was time to formulate a plan.

The identity of S and S's removal were high on my list of things that needed knowing and doing. Higher still was the determination of S's motive. My notion that I was dealing with a simple-minded psycho had dissolved. S was too well organized and possessed some very unusual abilities. I began searching my past for possible candidates. But though I could think of quite a few capable of managing what had occurred thus far, none of these were particularly ill-disposed toward me. However, Amber *had* been mentioned in that strange diary of Melman's. Theoretically, this made the whole thing a family matter and I suppose put me under some obligation to call it to the attention of the others. But to do so would be like asking for help, giving up, saying that I couldn't manage my own affairs. And threats on my life were my own affair. Julia was my affair. The vengeance on this one was to be mine. I had to think about it some more . . .

Ghostwheel?

I mulled it over, dismissed it, thought about it again. Ghostwheel . . . No. Untried. Still developing. The only reason it had occurred to me at all was because it was my pet, my major accomplishment in life, my surprise for the others. I was just looking for an easy way out. I would need a lot more data to submit, which meant I had to go after it, of course.

Ghostwheel . . .

Right now I needed more information. I had the cards and the diary. I didn't want to fool with the Trumps any more at this point, since the first one had seemed something of a trap. I would go through the diary soon, though my initial impression had been that it was too subjective to be of much help. I ought to go back to Melman's for a final look around, though, in case there was anything I had missed. Then I ought to look up Luke and see whether he could tell me anything more—even some small remark—that might be of value. Yes . . .

I sighed and stretched. I watched the river a little longer and finished my tea. I ran Frakir over a fistful of money and selected sufficient transformed coinage to pay for my meal. Then I returned to the road. Time to run on back.

5

I came jogging up the street in the light of late afternoon and halted when I was abreast of my car. I'd almost failed to recognize it. It was covered with dust, ashes, and water stains. How long had I been away, anyhow? I hadn't tried to reckon the time differential between here and where I'd been, but my car looked as if it had been standing exposed for over a month. It seemed intact, though. It had not been vandalized and—

My gaze had drifted past the hood and on ahead. The building that had housed the Brutus Storage Company and the late Victor Melman no longer stood. A burnt-out, collapsed skeleton of the place occupied the corner, parts of two walls standing. I headed toward it.

Walking about it, I studied what was left. The charred remains of the place were cold and settled. Gray streaks and sooty fairy circles indicated that water had been pumped into it, had since evaporated. The ashy smell was not particularly strong.

Had I started it, with that fire in the bathtub? I wondered. I didn't think so. Mine had been a small enough blaze, and well confined, with no indication of its spreading while I was waiting.

A boy on a green bicycle pedaled past while I was studying the ruin. Several minutes later he returned and halted about ten feet from me. He looked to be about ten years old.

"I saw it," he announced. "I saw it burn."

"When was that?" I asked him.

"Three days ago."

"They know how it started?"

"Something in the storage place, something flam—"

"Flammable?"

"Yeah," he said through a gap-toothed smile. "Maybe on purpose. Something about insurance."

"Really?"

"Uh-huh. My dad said maybe business was bad."

"It's been known to happen," I said. "Was anybody hurt in the fire?"

"They thought maybe the artist who lived upstairs got burned up because nobody could find him. But they didn't see any bones or anything like that. It was a good fire. Burned a long time."

"Was it nighttime or daytime?"

"Nighttime. I watched from over there." He pointed to a place across the street and back in the direction from which I had come. "They put a lot of water on it."

"Did you see anyone come out of the building?"

"No," he said. "I got here after it was burning pretty good."

I nodded and turned back toward my car.

"You'd think bullets would explode in all that fire, wouldn't you?" he said.

"Yes," I answered.

"But they didn't."

I turned back.

"What do you mean?" I asked.

He was already digging in a pocket.

"Me and some of my friends were playing around in there yesterday," he explained, "and we found a mess of bullets."

He opened his hand to display several metallic objects.

As I moved toward him, he squatted and placed one of the cylinders on the sidewalk. He reached out suddenly, picked up a nearby rock and swung it toward it.

"Don't!" I cried.

The rock struck the shell and nothing happened.

"You could get hurt that way—" I began, but he interrupted.

"Naw. No way these suckers will explode. You can't even set that pink stuff on fire. Got a match?"

"Pink stuff?" I said as he moved the rock to reveal a mashed shell casing and a small trailing of pink powder.

"That," he said, pointing. "Funny, huh? I thought gunpowder was gray."

I knelt and touched the substance. I rubbed it between my fingers. I sniffed it. I even tasted it. I couldn't tell what the hell it was.

"Beats me," I told him. "Won't even burn, you say?"

"Nope. We put some on a newspaper and set the paper on fire. It'll melt and run, that's all."

"You got a couple of extras?"

"Well . . . yeah."

"I'll give you a buck for them," I said.

He showed me his teeth and spaces again as his hand vanished into the side of his jeans. I ran Frakir over some odd Shadow cash and withdrew a dollar from the pile. He handed me two soot-streaked double 30's as he accepted it.

"Thanks," he said.

"My pleasure. Anything else interesting in there?"

"Nope. All the rest is ashes."

I got into my car and drove. I ran it through the first car wash I came to, since the wipers had only smeared the crap on the wind-shield. As the rubbery tentacles slapped at me through a sea of foam, I checked to see whether I still had the matchbook Luke had given me. I did. Good. I'd seen a pay phone outside.

"Hello. New Line Motel," a young, male voice answered.

"You had a Lucas Raynard registered there a couple of days ago," I said. "I want to know whether he left a message for me. My name's Merle Corey."

"Just a minute."

Pause. Shuffle.

Then: "Yes, he did."

"What does it say?"

"It's in a sealed envelope. I'd rather not—"

"Okay. I'll come by."

I drove over. I located the man matching the voice at the desk in the lobby. I identified myself and claimed the envelope. The clerk—a slight, blond fellow with a bristly mustache—stared for a moment, then: "Are you going to see Mr. Raynard?"

"Yes."

He opened a drawer and withdrew a small brown envelope, its sides distended. Luke's name and room number were written on it.

"He didn't leave a forwarding address," he explained, opening the envelope, "and the maid found this ring on the bathroom counter after he'd checked out. Would you give it to him?"

"Sure," I said, and he passed it to me.

I seated myself in a lounge area off to the left. The ring was of pink gold and sported a blue stone. I couldn't recall ever having seen him wear it. I slipped it on the ring finger of my left hand and it fit perfectly. I decided to wear it until I could give it to him.

I opened the letter, written on motel stationery, and read:

Merle,
Too bad about dinner. I did wait around. Hope everything's okay. I'm leaving in the morning for Albuquerque. I'll be there three days. Then up to Santa Fe for three more. Staying at the Hilton in both towns. I did have some more things I wanted to talk about. Please get in touch.

                                                                    Luke

Hm.

I phoned my travel agent and discovered that I could be on an afternoon flight to Albuquerque if I hustled. In that I wanted a face-to-face rather than a phone talk, I did that thing. I stopped by the office, picked up my ticket, paid cash for it, drove to the airport and said good-bye to my car as I parked it. I doubted I would ever see it again. I hefted my backpack and walked to the terminal.

The rest was smooth and easy. As I watched the ground drop away beneath me, I knew that a phase of my existence had indeed ended. Like so many things, it was not at all the way I had wanted it to be. I'd thought to wind up the matter of S pretty quickly or else decide to forget about it, and then visit people I'd been meaning to see for some time and stop at a few places I'd long been curious about. Then I would take off through Shadow for a final check on Ghostwheel, heading back to the brighter pole of my existence after that. Now, my priorities had been shuffled—all because S and Julia's death were somehow connected, and because it involved a power from elsewhere in Shadow that I did not understand.

It was the latter consideration that troubled me most. Was I digging my grave as well as jeopardizing friends and relatives because of my pride? I wanted to handle this myself, friendly skies, but the more I thought about it the more impressed I became with the adversary powers I had encountered and the paucity of my knowledge concerning S. It wasn't fair not to let the others know—not if they might be in danger, too. I'd love to wrap the whole thing up by myself and give it to them for a present. Maybe I would, too, but—

Damn it. I *had* to tell them. If S got me and turned on them, they needed to know. If it were a part of something larger, they needed to know. As much as I disliked the idea, I would have to tell them.

I leaned forward and my hand hovered above my backpack beneath the seat in front of me. It wouldn't hurt, I decided, to wait until after I'd spoken with Luke. I was out of town and probably safe now. There was the possibility of picking up a clue or two from Luke. I'd rather have more to give them when I told my story. I'd wait a little longer.

I sighed. I got a drink from the stewardess and sipped it. Driving to Albuquerque in a normal fashion would have taken too long. Short-cutting through Shadow would not work, because I'd never been there before and didn't know how to find the place. Too bad. I'd like to have my car there. Luke was probably in Santa Fe by now.

I sipped and I looked for shapes in the clouds. The things I found matched my mood, so I got out my paperback and read until we began our descent. When I looked again ranks of mountains filled my prospect for a time. A crackly voice assured me that the weather was pleasant. I wondered about my father.

I hiked in from my gate, passed a gift shop full of Indian jewelry, Mexican pots, and gaudy souvenirs, located a telephone, and called the local Hilton. Luke had already checked out, I learned. I phoned the Hilton in Santa Fe then. He had checked in there but was not in his room when they rang it for me. I made a reservation for myself and hung up. A woman at an information counter told me that I could catch a Shuttlejack to Santa Fe in about half an hour and sent me in the proper direction to buy a ticket. Santa Fe is one of the few state capitals without a major airport, I'd read somewhere.

While we were heading north on I-25, somewhere among lengthening shadows in the vicinity of Sandia Peak, Frakir tightened slightly upon my wrist and released the pressure a moment later. Again. Then once again. I glanced quickly about the small bus, seeking the danger against which I had just been warned.

I was seated in the rear of the vehicle. Up near the front was a middle-aged couple, speaking with Texas accents, wearing an ostentatious quantity of turquoise and silver jewelry; near the middle were three older women, talking about things back in New York; across the aisle from them was a young couple, very absorbed in each other; two young men with tennis racquets sat diagonally to the rear of them, talking about college; behind them was a nun, reading. I looked out the window again and saw nothing particularly threatening on the highway or near it. I did not want to draw to myself the attention that any location practices would involve either.

So I spoke a single word in Thari as I rubbed my wrist, and the warnings ceased. Even though the rest of the ride was uneventful, it bothered me, though an occasional false warning was possible just because of the nature of nervous systems. As I watched red shale and red and yellow earth streak by, bridged arroyos, viewed distant mountains and nearer slopes dotted with piñon, I wondered. S? Is S back there somewhere, somehow, watching, waiting? And if so, why? Couldn't we just sit down and talk about it over a couple of beers? Maybe it was based on some sort of misunderstanding.

I'd a feeling it was not a misunderstanding. But I'd settle for just knowing what was going on, even if nothing were resolved. I'd even pay for the beers.

The light of the setting sun touched flashes of brightness from streaks of snow in the Sangre de Cristos as we pulled into town; shadows slid across gray-green slopes; most of the buildings in sight were stuccoed. It felt about ten degrees cooler when I stepped down from the bus in front of the Hilton than it had when I'd boarded in Albuquerque. But then, I'd gained about two thousand feet in altitude and it was an hour and a quarter further along in the direction of evening.

I registered and found my room. I tried phoning Luke, but there was no answer. I showered then and changed into my spare outfit. Rang his room once more then, but still no answer. I was getting hungry and I'd hoped to have dinner with him.

I decided to find the bar and nurse a beer for a while, then try again. I hoped he didn't have a heavy date.

A Mr. Brazda, whom I approached in the lobby and asked for directions, turned out to be the manager. He asked about my room, we exchanged a few pleasantries and he showed me the corridor leading off to the lounge. I started in that direction, but didn't quite make it.

"Merle! What the hell are you doing here?" came a familiar voice.

I turned and regarded Luke, who had just entered the lobby. Sweaty and smiling, he was wearing dusty fatigues and boots, a fatigue cap, and a few streaks of grime. We shook hands and I said, "I wanted to talk to you." Then: "What'd you do, enlist in something?"

"No, I've been off hiking in the Pecos all day," he answered. "I always do that when I'm out this way. It's great."

"I'll have to try it sometime," I said. "Now it seems it's my turn to buy dinner."

"You're right," he answered. "Let me catch a shower and change clothes. I'll meet you in the bar in fifteen, twenty minutes. Okay?"

"Right. See you."

I headed up the corridor and located the place. It was medium-sized, dim, cool and relatively crowded, divided into two widely connected rooms, with low, comfortable-looking chairs and small tables.

A young couple was just abandoning a corner table off to my left, drinks in hand, to follow a waitress into the adjacent dining room. I took the table. A little later a cocktail waitress came by, and I ordered a beer.

Sitting there, several minutes later, sipping, and letting my mind drift over the perversely plotted events of the past several days, I realized that one of the place's passing figures had failed to pass. It had come to a halt at my side—just far enough to the rear to register only as a dark peripheral presence.

It spoke softly: "Excuse me. May I ask you a question?"

I turned my head, to behold a short, thin man of Spanish appearance, his hair and mustache flecked with gray. He was sufficiently well dressed and groomed to seem a local business type. I noted a chipped front tooth when he smiled so briefly—just a twitch—as to indicate nervousness.

"My name's Dan Martinez," he said, not offering to shake hands. He glanced at the chair across from me. "Could I sit down a minute?"

"What's this about? If you're selling something, I'm not interested. I'm waiting for somebody and—"

He shook his head.

"No, nothing like that. I know you're waiting for someone—a Mr. Lucas Raynard. It involves him, actually."

I gestured at the chair.

"Okay. Sit down and ask your question."

He did so, clasping his hands and placing them on the table between us. He leaned forward.

"I overheard you talking in the lobby," he began, "and I got the impression you knew him fairly well. Would you mind telling me for about how long you've known him?"

"If that's all you want to know," I answered, "for about eight years. We went to college together, and we worked for the same company for several years after that."

"Grand Design," he stated, "the San Francisco computer firm. Didn't know him before college, huh?"

"It seems you already know quite a bit," I said. "What do you want, anyway? Are you some kind of cop?"

"No," he said, "nothing like that. I assure you I'm not trying to get your friend into trouble. I am simply trying to save myself some. Let me just ask you—"

I shook my head.

"No more freebies," I told him. "I don't care to talk to strangers about my friends without some pretty good reasons."

He unclasped his hands and spread them wide.

"I'm not being underhanded," he said, "when I know you'll tell him about it. In fact, I want you to. He knows me. I want him to know I'm asking around about him, okay? It'll actually be to his benefit. Hell, I'm even asking a friend, aren't I? Someone who might be willing to lie to help him out. And I just need a couple simple facts—"

"And I just need one simple reason: why do you want this information?"

He sighed. "Okay," he said. "He offered me—tentatively, mind you—a very interesting investment opportunity. It would involve a large sum of money. There is an element of risk, as in most ventures involving new companies in a highly competitive area, but the possible returns do make it tempting."

I nodded.

"And you want to know whether he's honest."

He chuckled. "I don't really care whether he's honest," he said. "My only concern is whether he can deliver a product with no strings on it."

Something about the way this man talked reminded me of someone. I tried, but couldn't recall who it was.

"Ah," I said, taking a sip of beer. "I'm slow today. Sorry. Of course this deal involves computers."

"Of course."

"You want to know whether his present employer can nail him if he goes into business out here with whatever he's bringing with him."

"In a word, yes."

"I give up," I said. "It would take a better man than me to answer that. Intellectual properties represent a tricky area of the law. I don't know what he's selling and I don't know where it comes from—he gets around a lot. But even if I did know, I have no idea what your legal position would be."

"I didn't expect anything beyond that," he said, smiling.

I smiled back.

"So you've sent your message," I said.

He nodded and began to rise.

"Oh, just one thing more," he began.

"Yes?"

"Did he ever mention places," he said, staring full into my eyes, "called Amber or the Courts of Chaos?"

He could not have failed to note my startled reaction, which had to have given him a completely false impression. I was sure that he was sure I was lying when I answered him truthfully.

"No, I never heard him refer to them. Why do you ask?"

He shook his head as he pushed his chair back and stepped away from the table. He was smiling again.

"It's not important. Thank you, Mr. Corey. *Nus a dhabzhun dhuilsha.*"

He practically fled around the corner.

"Wait!" I called out, so loudly that there was a moment of silence and heads turned in my direction.

I got to my feet and started after him, when I heard my name called.

"Hey, Merle! Don't run off! I'm here already!"

I turned. Luke had just come in through the entrance behind me, hair still shower-damp. He advanced, clapped me on the shoulder, and lowered himself into the seat Martinez had just vacated. He nodded at my half-finished beer as I sat down again.

"I need one of those," he said. "Lord, am I thirsty!" Then, "Where were you off to when I came in?"

I found myself reluctant to describe my recent encounter, not least because of its strange conclusion. Apparently, he had just missed seeing Martinez.

So: "I was heading for the john."

"It's back that way," he told me, nodding in the direction from which he had entered. "I passed it on the way in."

His eyes shifted downward.

"Say, that ring you have on—"

"Oh, yeah," I said. "You left it at the New Line Motel. I picked it up for you when I collected your message. Here, let me . . ."

I tugged at it, but it wouldn't come off.

"Seems to be stuck," I noted. "Funny. It went on easy enough."

"Maybe your finger's swollen," he remarked. "It could have something to do with the altitude. We're up pretty high."

He caught the waitress's attention and ordered a beer, while I kept twisting at the ring.

"Guess I'll just have to sell it to you," he said. "Give you a good deal."

"We'll see," I told him. "Back in a minute."

He raised one hand limply and let it fall as I headed toward the rest room.

There was no one else in the facility, and so I spoke the words that released Frakir from the suppression spell I had uttered back aboard the Shuttlejack. There followed immediate movement. Before I could issue another command, Frakir became shimmeringly visible in the act of uncoiling, crept across the back of my hand and wound about my ring finger. I watched, fascinated, as the finger darkened and began to ache beneath a steady tightening.

A loosening followed quickly, leaving my finger looking as if it had been threaded. I got the idea. I unscrewed the ring along the track that had been pressed into my flesh. Frakir moved again as if to snag it and I stroked her.

"Okay," I said. "Thanks. Return."

There seemed a moment of hesitation, but my will proved sufficient without a more formal command. She retreated back across my hand, rewound herself about my wrist, and faded.

I finished up in there and returned to the bar. I passed Luke his ring as I seated myself, and took a sip of beer.

"How'd you get if off?" he asked.

"A bit of soap," I answered.

He wrapped it in his handkerchief and put it in his pocket.

"Guess I can't take your money for it, then."

"Guess not. Aren't you going to wear it?"

"No, it's a present. You know, I hardly expected you to make the scene here," he commented, scooping a handful of peanuts from a bowl that had appeared in my absence. "I thought maybe you'd just call when you got my message, and we could set something up for later. Glad you did, though. Who knows when later might have been. See, I had some plans that started moving faster than I'd thought they would—and that's what I wanted to talk to you about."

I nodded.

"I had a few things I wanted to talk to you about, too."

He returned my nod.

I had decided back in the lavatory definitely to refrain from mentioning Martinez yet, and the first things he had said and implied. Although the entire setup did not sound as if it involved anything in which I had any interest any longer, I always feel more secure in talking with anyone—even friends—when I have at least a little special information they don't know I have. So I decided to keep it that way for now.

"So let's be civilized and hold everything important till after dinner," he said, slowly shredding his napkin and wadding the pieces, "and go somewhere we can talk in private then."

"Good idea," I agreed. "Want to eat here?"

He shook his head.

"I've been eating here. It's good, but I want a change. I had my heart set on eating at a place around the corner. Let me go and see if they've got a table."

"Okay."

He gulped the rest of his drink and departed.

. . . And then the mention of Amber. Who the hell was Martinez? It was more than a little necessary that I learn this, because it was obvious to me that he was something other than he appeared to be. His final words had been in Thari, my native tongue. How this could be and why it should be, I had no idea. I cursed my own inertia, at having let the S situation slide for so long. It was purely a result of my arrogance. I'd never anticipated the convoluted mess the affair would become. Served me right, though I didn't appreciate the service.

"Okay," Luke said, rounding the corner, digging into his pocket, and tossing some money on the table. "We've got a reservation. Drink up, and let's take a walk."

I finished, stood and followed him. He led me through the corridors and back to the lobby, then out and along a hallway to the rear. We emerged into a balmy evening and crossed the parking lot to the sidewalk that ran along Guadaloupe Street. From there it was only a short distance to the place where it intersected with Alameda. We crossed twice there and strolled on past a big church, then turned right at the next corner. Luke pointed out a restaurant called La Tertulia across the street a short distance ahead.

"There," he said.

We crossed over and found our way to the entrance. It was a low adobe building, Spanish, venerable, and somewhat elegant inside. We went through a pitcher of sangria, orders of pollo adova, bread puddings, and many cups of coffee, keeping our agreement not to speak of anything serious during dinner.

During the course of the meal Luke was greeted twice, by different guys passing through the room, both of whom paused at the table to pass a few pleasantries.

"You know everybody in this town?" I asked him a bit later.

He chuckled. "I do a lot of business here."

"Really? It seems a pretty small town."

"Yes, but that's deceptive. It *is* the state capital. There're a lot of people here buying what we're selling."

"So you're out this way a lot?"

He nodded. "It's one of the hottest spots on my circuit."

"How do you manage all this business when you're out hiking in the woods?"

He looked up from the small battle formation he was creating from the things on the table. He smiled.

"I've got to have a little recreation," he said. "I get tired of cities and offices. I have to get away and hike around, or canoe or kayak or something like that—or I'd go out of my gourd. In fact, that's one of the reasons I built up the business in this town— quick access to a lot of good places for that stuff."

He took a drink of coffee.

"You know," he continued, "it's such a nice night we ought to take a drive, let you get a feeling of what I mean."

"Sounds good," I said, stretching my shoulders and looking for our waiter. "But isn't it too dark to see much?"

"No. The moon'll be up, the stars are out, the air's real clear. You'll see."

I got the tab, paid up, and we strolled out. Sure enough, the moon had risen.

"Car's in the hotel lot," he said as we hit the street. "This side."

He indicated a station wagon once we were back in the parking lot, unlocked it, and waved me aboard. He drove us out, turned at the nearest corner, and followed the Alameda to the Paseo, took a right leading uphill on a street called Otero and another onto Hyde Park Road. From then on traffic was very light. We passed a sign indicating that we were heading toward a ski basin.

As we worked our way through many curves, heading generally upward, I felt a certain tension going out of me. Soon we had left all signs of habitation behind us, and the night and the quiet settled fully. No streetlights here. Through the opened window I smelled pine trees. The air was cool. I rested, away from S and everything else.

I glanced at Luke. He stared straight ahead, brow furrowed. He felt my gaze, though, because he seemed to relax suddenly and he shot me a grin.

"Who goes first?" he asked.

"Go ahead," I answered.

"Okay. When we were talking the other morning about your leaving Grand D, you said you weren't going to work anywhere else and you weren't planning on teaching."

"That's right."

"You said you were just going to travel around."

"Yep."

"Something else did suggest itself to me a little later on."

I remained silent as he glanced my way.

"I was wondering," he said after a time, "whether you might not be shopping around—either for backing in getting your own company going, or for a buyer for something you have to sell. You know what I mean?"

"You think I came up with something—innovative—and didn't want Grand Design to have it."

He slapped the seat beside him.

"Always knew you were no fool," he said. "So you're screwing around now, to allow decent time for its development. Then you hunt up the buyer with the most bread."

"Makes sense," I said, "if that were the case. But it isn't."

He chuckled.

"It's okay," he said. "Just because I work for Grand D doesn't make me their fink. You ought to know that."

"I do know it."

"And I wasn't asking just to pry. In fact, I had other intentions completely. I'd like to see you make out with it, make out big."

"Thanks."

"I might even be of some assistance—valuable assistance—in the matter."

"I begin to get the drift, Luke, but—"

"Just hear me out, huh? But answer one thing first, though, if you would: You haven't signed anything with anybody in the area, have you?"

"No."

"Didn't think so. It would seem a little premature."

The roadside trees were larger now, the night breeze a bit more chill. The moon seemed bigger, more brilliant up here than it had in the town below. We rounded several more curves, eventually commencing a long series of switchbacks that bore us higher and higher. I caught occasional glimpses of sharp drops to the left. There was no guard rail.

"Look," he said, "I'm not trying to cut myself in for nothing. I'm not asking you for a piece of the action for old times' sake or anything like that. That's one thing and business is another— though it never hurts to do a deal with someone you know you can trust. Let me tell you some of the facts of life. If you've got some really fantastic design, sure, you can go sell it for a bundle to lots of people in the business—if you're careful, damn careful. But that's it. Your golden opportunity's flown then. If you really want to clean up, you start your own outfit. Look at Apple. If it really catches on you can always sell out then, for a lot more than you'd get from just peddling the idea. You may be a whiz at design, but I know the marketplace. And I know people—all over the country—people who'd trust me enough to bankroll us to see it off the ground and out on the street. Shit! I'm not going to stay with Grand D all my life. Let me in and I'll get us the financing. You run the shop and I'll run the business. That's the only way to go with something big."

"Oh, my," I sighed. "Man, it actually sounds nice. But you're following a bum scent. I don't have anything to sell."

"Come on!" he said. "You know you can level with me. Even if you absolutely refuse to go that way, I'm not going to talk about it. I don't screw my buddies. I just think you're making a mistake if you don't develop it yourself."

"Luke, I meant what I said."

He was silent for a little while. Then I felt his gaze upon me again. When I glanced his way I saw that he was smiling.

"What," I asked him, "is the next question?"

"What is Ghostwheel?" he said.

"What?"

"Top secret, hush-hush, Merle Corey project. Ghostwheel," he answered. "Computer design incorporating shit nobody's ever seen before. Liquid semiconductors, cryogenic tanks, plasma—"

I started laughing.

"My God!" I said. "It's a joke, that's what it is. Just a crazy hobby thing. It was a design game—a machine that could never be built on Earth. Well, maybe most of it could. But it wouldn't function. It's like an Escher drawing—looks great on paper, but it can't be done in real life." Then after a moment's reflection, I asked, "How is it you even know about it? I've never mentioned it to anyone."

He cleared his throat as he took another turn. The moon was raked by treetops. A few beads of moisture appeared upon the windshield.

"Well, you weren't all that secret about it," he answered. "There were designs and graphs and notes all over your work table and drawing board any number of times I was at your place. I could hardly help but notice. Most of them were even labeled 'Ghostwheel.' And nothing anything like it ever showed up at Grand D, so I simply assumed it was your pet project and your ticket to security. You never impressed me as the impractical dreamer type. Are you sure you're giving this to me straight?"

"If we were to sit down and build as much as could be constructed of that thing right here," I replied honestly, "it would just sit there and look weird and wouldn't do a damned thing."

He shook his head.

"That sounds perverse," he said. "It's not like you, Merle. Why the hell would you waste your time designing a machine that doesn't function?"

"It was an exercise in design theory—" I began.

"Excuse me, but that sounds like bullshit," he said. "You mean to say there's no place in the universe that damn machine of yours would kick over?"

"I didn't say that. I was trying to explain that I designed it to operate under bizarre hypothetical conditions."

"Oh. In other words, if I find a place like that on another world we can clean up?"

"Uh, yeah."

"You're weird, Merle. You know that?"

"Uh-huh."

"Another dream shot to shit. Oh, well . . . Say, is there anything unusual about it that could be adapted to the here and now?"

"Nope. It couldn't perform its functions here."

"What's so special about its functions, anyhow?"

"A lot of theoretical crap involving space and time and some notions of some guys named Everett and Wheeler. It's only amenable to a mathematical explanation."

"You sure?"

"What difference does it make, anyhow? I've got no product, we've got no company. Sorry. Tell Martinez and associates it was a blind alley."

"Huh? Who's Martinez?"

"One of your potential investors in Corey and Raynard, Inc.," I said. "Dan Martinez—middle-aged, a bit short, kind of distinguished-looking, chipped front tooth . . ."

His brow furrowed. "Merle, I don't know who the hell you're talking about."

"He came up to me while I was waiting for you in the bar. Seemed to know an awful lot about you. Started asking questions on what I can now see as the potential situation you just described. Acted as if you'd approached him to invest in the thing."

"Uh-uh," he said. "I don't know him. How come you didn't tell me sooner?"

"He beat it, and you said no business till after dinner. Didn't seem all that important, anyway. He even as much as asked me to let you know he'd been inquiring about you."

"What, specifically, did he want to know?"

"Whether you could deliver an unencumbered computer property and keep the investors out of court, was what I gathered."

He slapped the wheel. "This makes no sense at all," he said. "It really doesn't."

"It occurs to me that he might have been hired to investigate a bit—or even just to shake you up some and keep you honest—by the people you've been sounding out to invest in this thing."

"Merle, do you think I'm so damn stupid I'd waste a lot of time digging up investors before I was even sure there was something to put the money into? I haven't talked to anybody about this except you, and I guess I won't be now either. Who do you think he could have been? What did he want?"

I shook my head, but I was remembering those words in Thari. Why not?

"He also asked me whether I'd ever heard you refer to a place called Amber."

He was looking in the rearview mirror when I said it, and he jerked the wheel to catch a sudden curve.

"Amber? You're kidding."

"No."

"Strange. It has to be a coincidence—"

"What?"

"I did hear a reference to a kind of dreamland place called Amber, last week. But I never mentioned it to anybody. It was just drunken babbling."

"Who? Who said it?"

"A painter I know. A real nut, but a very talented guy. Name's Melman. I like his work a lot, and I've bought several of his paintings. I'd stopped by to see whether he had anything new this last time I was in town. He didn't, but I stayed pretty late at his place anyway, talking and drinking and smoking some stuff he had. He got pretty high after a while and he started talking about magic. Not card tricks, I mean. Ritual stuff, you know?"

"Yes."

"Well, after a time he started doing some of it. If it weren't that I was kind of stoned myself I'd swear that it worked—that he levitated, summoned sheets of fire, conjured and banished a number of monsters. There had to've been acid in something he gave me. But damn! It sure seemed real."

"Uh-huh."

"Anyway," he went on, "he mentioned a sort of archetypal city. I couldn't tell whether it sounded more like Sodom and Gomorrah or Camelot—all the adjectives he used. He called the place Amber, and said that it was run by a half-mad family, with the city itself peopled by their bastards and folks whose ancestors they'd brought in from other places ages ago. Shadows of the family and the city supposedly figure in most major legends and such—whatever that means. I could never be sure whether he was talking in metaphor, which he did a lot, or just what the hell he meant. But that's where I heard the place mentioned."

"Interesting," I said. "Melman is dead. His place burned down a few days ago."

"No, I didn't know." He glanced into the mirror again. "Did you know him?"

"I met him—after you left this last time. Kinsky told me Julia'd been seeing him, and I looked the guy up to see what he could tell me about her. You see—well, Julia's dead."

"How'd it happen? I just saw her last week."

"In a very bizarre fashion. She was killed by a strange animal."

"Lord!"

He braked suddenly and pulled off the road onto a wide shoulder to the left. It looked upon a steep, tree-filled drop. Above the trees I could see the tiny lights of the city across a great distance.

He killed the engine and the headlights. He took a Durham's bag from his pocket and began rolling a cigarette. I caught him glancing upward and ahead.

"You've been checking that mirror a lot."

"Yes," he replied. "I was just about sure a car had been following us all the way from the parking lot down at the Hilton. It was a few turns behind us for the longest damned while. Now it seems to have disappeared."

He lit his cigarette and opened the door.

"Let's get some air."

I followed him and we stood for a few moments staring out across the big spaces, the moonlight strong enough to cast the shadows of some trees near to us. He threw down the cigarette and stamped on it.

"Shit!" he said. "This is getting too involved! I knew Julia was seeing Melman, okay? I went to see her the night after I'd seen him, okay? I even delivered a small parcel he'd asked me to take her, okay?"

"Cards," I said.

He nodded.

I withdrew them from my pocket and held them toward him. He barely glanced at them there in the dim light, but he nodded again.

"Those cards," he said. Then: "You still liked her, didn't you?"

"Yes, I guess I did."

"Oh, hell," he sighed. "All right. There are some things I'm going to have to tell you, old buddy. Not all of them nice. Give me just a minute to sort it all out. You've just given me one big problem—or I've given it to myself, because I've just decided something."

He kicked a patch of gravel and the stones rattled down the hillside.

"Okay," he said. "First, give me those cards."

"Why?"

"I'm going to tear them into confetti."

"The hell you are. Why?"

"They're dangerous."

"I already know that. I'll hang onto them."

"You don't understand."

"So explain."

"It's not that easy. I have to decide what to tell you and what not to."

"Why not just tell me everything?"

"I can't. Believe me—"

I hit the ground as soon as I heard the first shot, which ricocheted off a boulder to our right. Luke didn't. He began running in a zigzag pattern toward a cluster of trees off to our left, from which two more shots were fired. He had something in his hand and he raised it.

Luke fired three times. Our assailant got off one more round. After Luke's second shot I heard someone gasp. I was on my feet by then and running toward him, a rock in my hand. After his third shot I heard a body fall.

I reached him just as he was turning the body over, in time to see what seemed a faint cloud of blue or gray mist emerge from the man's mouth past his chipped tooth and drift away.

"What the hell was that?" Luke asked as it blew away.

"You saw it, too? I don't know."

He looked down at the limp form with the dark spot growing larger on its shirtfront, a .38 revolver still clutched in the right hand.

"I didn't know you carried a gun," I said.

"When you're on the road as much as I am, you go heeled," he answered. "I pick up a new one in each city I hit and sell it when I leave. Airline security. Guess I won't be selling this one. I never saw this guy, Merle. You?"

I nodded.

"That's Dan Martinez, the man I was telling you about."

"Oh, boy," he said. "Another damn complication. Maybe I should just join a Zen monastery someplace and persuade myself it doesn't matter. I—"

Suddenly, he raised his left fingertips to his forehead. "Oh-oh," he said then. "Merle, the keys are in the ignition. Get in the car and drive back to the hotel right away. Leave me here. Hurry!"

"What's going on? What—"

He raised his weapon, a snub-nosed automatic, and pointed it at me.

"Now! Shut up and go!"

"But—"

He lowered the muzzle and put a bullet into the ground between my feet. Then he aimed it squarely at my abdomen.

"Merlin, son of Corwin," he said through clenched teeth, "if you don't start running right now you're a dead man!"

I followed his advice, raising a shower of gravel and laying some streaks of rubber coming out of the U-turn I spun the wagon through. I roared down the hill and skidded around the curve to my right. I braked for the next one to my left. Then I slowed.

I pulled off to the left, at the foot of a bluff, near some shrubbery. I killed the engine and the lights and put on the parking brake. I opened the door quietly and did not close it fully after I'd slipped out. Sounds carry too well in places like this.

I started back, keeping to the darker, righthand side of the road. It was very quiet. I rounded the first turn and headed for the next one. Something flew from one tree to another. An owl, I think. I moved more slowly than I wanted to, for the sake of silence, as I neared the second turning.

I made my way around that final corner on all fours, taking advantage of the cover provided by rocks and foliage. I halted then and studied the area we had occupied. Nothing in sight. I advanced slowly, cautiously, ready to freeze, drop, dive, or spring up into a run as the situation required.

Nothing stirred, save branches in the wind. No one in sight.

I rose into a crouch and continued, still more slowly, still hugging the cover.

Not there. He had taken off for somewhere. I moved nearer, halted again and listened for at least a minute. No sounds betrayed any moving presences.

I crossed to the place where Martinez had fallen. The body was gone. I paced about the area but could locate nothing to give me any sort of clue as to what might have occurred follow-

ing my departure. I could think of no reason for calling out, so I
didn't.

I walked back to the car without misadventure, got in and
headed for town. I couldn't even speculate as to what the hell was
going on.

I left the wagon in the hotel lot, near to the spot where it had
been parked earlier. Then I went inside, walked to Luke's room,
and knocked on the door. I didn't really expect a response, but it
seemed the proper thing to do preparatory to breaking and entering.

I was careful to snap only the lock, leaving the door and the
fame intact, because Mr. Brazda had seemed a nice guy. It took a
little longer, but there was no one in sight. I reached in and turned
on the light, did a quick survey, then slipped inside quickly. I
stood listening for a few minutes but heard no sounds of activity
from the hall.

Tight ship. Suitcase on luggage rack, empty. Clothing hung in
closet—nothing in the pockets except for two matchbooks, and a
pen and pencil. A few other garments and some undergarments in
a drawer, nothing with them. Toiletries in shaving kit or neatly ar-
rayed on countertop. Nothing peculiar there. A copy of B. H. Lid-
dell Hart's *Strategy* lay upon the bedside table, a bookmark about
three-quarters of the way into it.

His fatigues had been thrown onto a chair, his dusty boots
stood next to it, socks beside them. Nothing inside the boots but
a pair of blousing bands. I checked the shirt pockets, which at
first seemed empty, but my fingertips then discovered a number
of small white paper pellets in one of them. Puzzled, I unfolded
a few. Bizarre secret messages? No . . . No sense getting completely paranoid, when a few brown flecks on a paper answered
the question. Tobacco. They were pieces of cigarette paper. Obviously he stripped his butts when he was hiking in the wilderness. I recalled a few past hikes with him. He hadn't always
been that neat.

I went through the trousers. There was a damp bandana in one
hip pocket and a comb in the other. Nothing in the right front
pocket, a single round of ammo in the left. On an impulse, I pocketed the shell, then went on to look beneath the mattress and behind the drawers. I even looked in the toilet's flush box. Nothing.
Nothing to explain his strange behavior.

Leaving the car keys on the bedside table I departed and returned to my own room. I did not care that he'd know I'd broken in. In fact, I rather liked the idea. It irritated me that he'd poked around in my Ghostwheel papers. Besides, he owed me a damned good explanation for his behavior on the mountain.

I undressed, showered, got into bed, and doused my light. I'd have left him a note, too, except that I don't like to create evidence and I had a strong feeling that he wouldn't be coming back.

6

He was a short, heavy-set man with a somewhat florid complexion, his dark hair streaked with white and perhaps a bit thin on top. I sat in the study of his semirural home in upstate New York, sipping a beer and telling him my troubles. It was a breezy, star-dotted night beyond the window and he was a good listener.

"You say that Luke didn't show up the following day," he said. "Did he send a message?"

"No."

"What exactly did you do that day?"

"I checked his room in the morning. It was just as I'd left it. I went by the desk. Nothing, like I said. Then I had breakfast and I checked again. Nothing again. So I took a long walk around the town. Got back a little after noon, had lunch, and tried the room again. It was the same. I borrowed the car keys then and drove back up to the place we'd been the night before. No sign of anything unusual there, looking at it in the light of day. I even climbed down the slope and hunted around. No body, no clues. I drove back, replaced the keys, hung around the hotel till dinnertime, ate, then called you. After you told me to come on up, I made a reservation and went to bed early. Caught the Shuttlejack this morning and flew here from Albuquerque."

"And you checked again this morning?"

"Yeah. Nothing new."

He shook his head and relit his pipe.

His name was Bill Roth, and he had been my father's friend as well as his attorney, back when he'd lived in this area. He was possibly the only man on Earth Dad had trusted, and I trusted him, too. I'd visited him a number of times during my eight years—most recently, unhappily, a year and a half earlier, at the time of his wife, Alice's, funeral. I had told him my father's story, as I had heard it from his own lips, outside the Courts of Chaos, because I'd gotten the impression that he had wanted Bill to know what had been going on, felt he'd owed him some sort of explanation for all the help he'd given him. And Bill actually seemed to understand and believe it. But then, he'd known Dad a lot better than I did.

"I've remarked before on the resemblance you bear your father."

I nodded.

"It goes beyond the physical," he continued. "For a while there he had a habit of showing up like a downed fighter pilot behind enemy lines. I'll never forget the night he arrived on horseback with a sword at his side and had me trace a missing compost heap for him." He chuckled. "Now you come along with a story that makes me believe Pandora's box has been opened again. Why couldn't you just want a divorce like any sensible young man? Or a will written or a trust set up? A partnership agreement? Something like that? No, this sounds more like one of Carl's problems. Even the other stuff I've done for Amber seems pretty sedate by comparison."

"Other stuff? You mean the Concord—the time Random sent Fiona with a copy of the Patternfall Treaty with Swayvil, King of Chaos, for her to translate and you to look at for loopholes?"

"That, yes," he said, "though I wound up studying your language myself before I was done. Then Flora wanted her library recovered—no easy job—and then an old flame traced—whether for reunion or revenge I never learned. Paid me in gold, though. Bought the place in Palm Beach with it. Then—Oh, hell. For a while there, I thought of adding 'Counsel to the Court of Amber' to my business card. But that sort of work was understandable. I do similar things on a mundane level all the time. Yours, though, has that black magic and sudden-death quality to it that seemed to follow your father about. It scares the hell out of me, and I wouldn't even know how to go about advising you on it."

"Well, the black magic and sudden-death parts are my area, I guess," I observed. "In fact, they may color my thinking too much. You're bound to look at things a lot differently than I do. A blind spot by definition is something you're not aware of. What might I be missing?"

He took a sip of his beer, lit his pipe again.

"Okay," he said. "Your friend Luke—where's he from?"

"Somewhere in the Midwest, I believe he said: Nebraska, Iowa, Ohio—one of those places."

"Mm-hm. What line of work is his old man in?"

"He never mentioned it."

"Does he have any brothers or sisters?"

"I don't know. He never said."

"Doesn't that strike you as somewhat odd—that he never mentioned his family or talked about his home town in the whole eight years you've known him?"

"No. After all, I never talked about mine either."

"It's not natural, Merle. You grew up in a strange place that you *couldn't* talk about. You had every reason to change the subject, avoid the issues. He obviously did, too. And then, back when you came you weren't even certain how most people here behaved. But didn't you ever wonder about Luke?"

"Of course. But he respected my reticence. I could do no less for him. You might say that we had a sort of tacit agreement that such things were off limits."

"How'd you meet him?"

"We were freshmen together, had a lot of the same classes."

"And you were both strangers in town, no other friends. You hit it off from the beginning . . ."

"No. We barely talked to each other. I thought he was an arrogant bastard who felt he was ten times better than anybody he'd ever met. I didn't like him, and he didn't like me much either."

"Why not?"

"He felt the same way about me."

"So it was only gradually that you came to realize you were both wrong?"

"No. We were both right. We got to know each other by trying to show each other up. If I'd do something kind of—outstanding—he'd try to top it. And vice versa. We got so we'd go out for the same sport, try to date the same girls, try to beat each other's grades."

"And . . . ?"

"Somewhere along the line I guess we started to respect each other. When we both made the Olympic finals something broke. We started slapping each other on the back and laughing, and we went out and had dinner and sat up all night talking and he said he didn't give a shit about the Olympics and I said I didn't either. He said he'd just wanted to show me he was a better man and now he didn't care anymore. He'd decided we were both good enough, and he'd just as soon let the matter stand at that. I felt exactly the same way and told him so. That was when we got to be friends."

"I can understand that," Bill said. "It's a specialized sort of friendship. You're friends in certain places."

I laughed and took a drink.

"Isn't everyone?"

"At first, yes. Sometimes always. Nothing wrong with that. It's just that yours seems a much more highly specialized friendship than most."

I nodded slowly. "Maybe so."

"So it still doesn't make sense. Two guys as close as you got to be—with no pasts to show to each other."

"I guess you're right. What does it mean?"

"You're not a normal human being."

"No, I'm not."

"I'm not so sure Luke is either."

"What, then?"

"That's your department."

I nodded.

"Apart from that issue," Bill continued, "something else has been bothering me."

"What?"

"This Martinez fellow. He followed you out to the boondocks, stopped when you did, stalked you, then opened fire. Who was he after? Both of you? Just Luke? Or just you?"

"I don't know. I'm not sure which of us that first shot was aimed for. After that, he was firing at Luke—because by then Luke was attacking and he was defending himself."

"Exactly. If he were S—or S's agent—why would he even have bothered with that conversation with you in the bar?"

"I now have the impression that the whole thing was an elaborate buildup to that final question of his, as to whether Luke knew anything about Amber."

"And your reaction, rather than your answer, led him to believe that he did."

"Well, apparently Luke does—from the way he addressed me right there at the end. You think he was really gunning for someone from Amber?"

"Maybe. Luke is no Amberite, though?"

"I never heard of anyone like him in the time I spent there after the war. And I got plenty of lectures on genealogy. My relatives are like a sewing circle when it comes to keeping track of such matters—a lot less orderly about it than they are in Chaos—can't even decide exactly who's oldest, because some of them were born in different time streams—but they're pretty thorough—"

"Chaos! That's right! You're also lousy with relatives on that side! Could—?"

I shook my head. "No way. I have an even more extensive knowledge of the families there. I believe I'm acquainted with just about all of the ones who can manipulate Shadow, traverse it. Luke's not one of them and—"

"Wait a minute! There are people in the Courts who can walk in Shadow, also?"

"Yes. Or stay in one place and bring things from Shadow to them. It's a kind of reverse—"

"I thought you had to walk the Pattern to gain that power?"

"They have a sort of equivalent called the Logrus. It's a kind of chaotic maze. Keeps shifting about. Very dangerous. Unbalances you mentally, too, for a time. No fun."

"So you've done it?"

"Yes."

"And you walked the Pattern as well?"

I licked my lips, remembering.

"Yes. Damn near killed me. Suhuy'd thought it would, but Fiona thought I could make it if she helped. I was—"

"Who's Suhuy?"

"He's Master of the Logrus. He's an uncle of mine, too. He felt that the Pattern of Amber and the Logrus of Chaos were incompatible, that I could not bear the images of both within me. Random, Fiona, and Gérard had taken me down to show me the Pattern. I got in touch with Suhuy then and gave him a look at it. He said that they seemed antithetical, and that I would either be destroyed by the attempt or the Pattern would drive the image of the Logrus from me—probably the former. But Fiona said that the Pattern should be able to encompass anything, even the Logrus, and from what she understood of the Logrus it should be able to work its way around anything, even the Pattern. So they left it up to me, and I knew that I had to walk it. So I did. I made it, and I still bear the Logrus as well as the Pattern. Suhuy acknowledged that Fi had been right, and he speculated that it had to do with my mixed parentage. She disagreed, though—"

Bill raised his hand. "Wait a minute. I don't understand how you got your uncle Suhuy down into the basement of Amber Castle on a moment's notice."

"Oh, I have a set of Chaos Trumps as well as a set of Amber Trumps, for my relatives back in the Courts."

He shook his head. "All of this is fascinating, but we're straying from the point. Is there anyone else who can walk in Shadow? Or are there other ways of doing it?"

"Yes, there are different ways it could be done. There are a number of magical beings, like the Unicorn, who can just wander wherever they want. And you can follow a Shadow walker or a magical being through Shadow for so long as you can keep track of it, no matter who you are. Kind of like Thomas Rhymer in the ballad. And one Shadow walker could lead an army through. And then there are the inhabitants of the various Shadow kingdoms nearest to Amber and to Chaos. Those at both ends breed mighty sorcerers, just because of their proximity to the two power centers. Some of the good ones can become fairly adept at it—but their images of the Pattern or the Logrus are imperfect, so they're never quite as good as the real thing. But on either end they don't even need an initiation to wander on in. The Shadow interfaces are thinnest there. We even have commerce with them, actually. And established routes become easier and easier to follow with time. Going outward is harder, though. But large attacking forces have been known to come through. That's why we maintain patrols. Julian in Arden, Gérard at sea, and so forth."

"Any other ways?"

"A Shadow-storm perhaps."

"What's that?"

"It's a natural but not too well-understood phenomenon. The best comparison I can think of is a tropical storm. One theory as to their origin has to do with the beat frequencies of waves that pulse outward from Amber and from the Courts, shaping the nature of shadows. Whatever, when such a storm rises it can flow through a large number of shadows before it plays itself out. Sometimes they do a lot of damage, sometimes very little. But they often transport things in their progress."

"Does that include people?"

"It's been known to happen."

He finished his beer. I did the same with mine.

"What about the Trumps?" he asked. "Could anybody learn to use them?"

"Yes."

"How many sets are there kicking around?"

"I don't know."

"Who makes them?"

"There are a number of experts in the Courts. That's where I learned. And there are Fiona and Bleys back in Amber—and I believe they were teaching Random—"

"Those sorcerers you spoke of—from the adjacent kingdoms . . . Could any of them do up a set of Trumps?"

"Yes, but theirs would be less than perfect. It is my understanding that you have to be an initiate of either the Pattern or the Logrus to do them properly. Some of them could do a sort of half-assed set, though, one you'd be taking your chances on using—maybe winding up dead or in some limbo, sometimes getting where you were headed."

"And the set you found at Julia's place . . . ?"

"They're the real thing."

"How do you account for them?"

"Someone who knew how to do it taught someone else who was able to learn it, and I never heard about it. That's all."

"I see."

"I'm afraid none of this is too productive."

"But I need it all to think with," he replied. "How else can I come up with lines of inquiry? You ready for another beer?"

"Wait."

I closed my eyes and visualized an image of the Logrus—shifting, ever shifting. I framed my desire and two of the swimming lines within the eidolon increased in brightness and thickness. I moved my arms slowly, imitating their undulations, their jerkings. Finally, the lines and my arms seemed to be one, and I opened my hands and extended the lines outward, outward through Shadow.

Bill cleared his throat.

"Uh—what are you doing, Merle?"

"Looking for something," I replied. "Just a minute."

The lines would keep extending through an infinitude of Shadow till they encountered the objects of my desire—or until I ran out of patience or concentration. Finally, I felt the jerks, like bites on a pair of fishing lines.

"There they are," I said, and I reeled them in quickly.

An icy bottle of beer appeared in each of my hands. I grasped them as they did and passed one to Bill.

"That's what I meant by the reverse of a Shadow walk," I said, breathing deeply a few times. "I sent out to Shadow for a couple of beers. Saved you a trip to the kitchen."

He regarded the orange label with the peculiar green script on it.

"I don't recognize the brand," he said, "let alone the language. You sure it's safe?"

"Yes, I ordered real beer."

"Uh—you didn't happen to pick up an opener, too, did you?"

"Oops!" I said. "Sorry. I'll—"

"That's all right."

He got up, walked out to the kitchen, and came back a little later with an opener. When he opened the first one it foamed a bit and he had to hold it over the wastebasket till it settled. The same with the other.

"Things can get a bit agitated when you pull them in fast the way I did," I explained. "I don't usually get my beer that way and I forgot—"

"That's okay," Bill said, wiping his hands on his handkerchief . . .

He tasted his beer then.

"At least it's good beer," he observed. "I wonder . . . Naw."

"What?"

"Could you send out for a pizza?"

"What do you want on it?" I asked.

The next morning we took a long walk beside a wandering creek, which we met at the back of some farmland owned by a neighbor and client of his. We strolled slowly, Bill with a stick in his hand and a pipe in his mouth, and he continued the previous evening's questioning.

"Something you said didn't really register properly at the time," he stated, "because I was more interested in other aspects of the situation. You say that you and Luke actually made it up to the finals for the Olympics and then dropped out?"

"Yes."

"What area?"

"Several different track and field events. We were both runners and—"

"And his time was close to yours?"

"Damn close. And sometimes it was mine that was close to his."

"Strange."

"What?"

The bank grew steeper, and we crossed on some stepping-stones to the other side where the way was several feet wider and relatively flat, with a well-trod path along it.

"It stikes me as more than a little coincidental," he said, "that this guy should be about as good as you are in sports. From all I've heard, you Amberites are several times stronger than a normal human being, with a fancy metabolism giving you unusual stamina and recuperative and regenerative powers. How come Luke should be able to match you in high-level performances?"

"He's a fine athlete and he keeps himself in good shape," I answered. "There are other people like that here—very strong and fast."

He shook his head as we started out along the path.

"I'm not arguing that," he said. "It's just that it seems like one coincidence too many. This guy hides his past the same way you do, and then it turns out that he really knows who you are anyhow. Tell me, is he really a big art buff?"

"Huh?"

"Art. He really cared enough about art to collect it?"

"Oh. Yes. We used to hit gallery openings and museum exhibits fairly regularly."

He snorted and swung his stick at a pebble, which splashed into the stream.

"Well," he observed, "that weakens one point, but hardly destroys the pattern."

"I don't follow . . ."

"It seemed odd that he also knew that crazy occultist painter. Less odd, though, when you say that the guy was good and that Luke really did collect art."

"He didn't have to tell me that he knew Melman."

"True. But all of this plus his physical abilities . . . I'm just building a circumstantial case, of course, but I feel that guy is very unusual."

I nodded.

"I've been over it in my mind quite a few times since last night," I said. "If he's not really from here, I don't know where the hell he's from."

"Then we may have exhausted this line of inquiry," Bill said, leading me around a bend and pausing to watch some birds take flight from a marshy area across the water. He glanced back in the direction from which we had come, then, "Tell me—completely off the subject—what's your—uh, rank?" he asked.

"What do you mean?"

"You're the son of a Prince of Amber. What does that make you?"

"You mean titles? I'm Duke of the Western Marches and Earl of Kolvir."

"What does that mean?"

"It means I'm not a Prince of Amber. Nobody has to worry about me scheming, no vendettas involving the succession—"

"Hm."

"What do you mean, 'Hm'?"

He shrugged. "I've read too much history. Nobody's safe."

I shrugged myself. "Last I heard, everything was peaceful on the home front."

"Well, that's good news, anyway."

A few more turnings brought us to a wide area of pebbles and sand, rising gently for perhaps thirty feet to the place where it met an abrupt embankment seven or eight feet in height. I could see the high water line and a number of exposed roots from trees that grew along the top. Bill seated himself on a boulder back in their shade and relit his pipe. I rested on one nearby, to his left. The water splashed and rippled in a comfortable key, and we watched it sparkle for a time.

"Nice," I said, a bit later. "Pretty place."

"Uh-huh."

I glanced at him. Bill was looking back the way we'd come.

I lowered my voice. "Something there?"

"I caught a glimpse a little earlier," he whispered, "of someone else taking a walk this way—some distance behind us. Lost sight of him in all the turnings we took."

"Maybe I should take a stroll back."

"Probably nothing. It's a beautiful day. A lot of people do like to hike around here. Just thought that if we waited a few minutes he'd either show up or we'd know he'd gone somewhere else."

"Can you describe him?"

"Nope. Caught only the barest glimpse. I don't think it's anything to get excited about. It's just that thinking about your story made me a little wary—or paranoid. I'm not sure which."

I found my own pipe and packed it and lit it and we waited. For fifteen minutes or so we waited. But no one showed.

Finally, Bill rose and stretched. "False alarm," he said.

"I guess."

He started walking again and I fell in step beside him.

"Then that Jasra lady bothers me," he said. "You say she seemed to trump in—and then she had that sting in her mouth that knocked you for a loop?"

"Right."

"Ever encounter anyone like her before?"

"No."

"Any guesses?"

I shook my head.

"And why the Walpurgisnacht business? I can see a certain date having significance for a psycho, and I can see people in various primitive religions placing great importance on the turning of the seasons. But S seems almost too well organized to be a mental case. And as for the other—"

"Melman thought it was important."

"Yes, but he was into that stuff. I'd be surprised if he didn't come up with such a correspondence, whether it was intended or not. He admitted that his master had never told him that that was the case. It was his own idea. But you're the one with the background in the area. Is there any special significance or any real power that you know of to be gained by slaying someone of your blood at this particular time of year?"

"None that I ever heard of. But of course there are a lot of things I don't know about. I'm very young compared to most of the adepts. But which way are you trying to go on this? You say you don't think it's a nut, but you don't buy the Walpurgis notion either."

"I don't know. I'm just thinking out loud. They both sound shaky to me, that's all. For that matter, the French Foreign Legion gave everyone leave on April 30 to get drunk, and a couple of days after that to sober up. It's the anniversary of the battle of Camerone, one of their big triumphs. But I doubt that figures in this either.

"And why the sphinx?" he said suddenly. "Why a Trump that takes you someplace to trade dumb riddles or get your head bitten off?"

"I'd a feeling it was more the latter that was intended."

"I sort of think so, too. But it's certainly bizarre. You know what? I'll bet they're all that way—traps of some kind."

"Could be."

I put my hand in my pocket, reaching for them.

"Leave them," he said. "Let's not look for trouble. Maybe you should ditch them, at least for a while. I could put them in my safe, down at the office."

I laughed.

"Safes aren't all that safe. No thanks. I want them with me. There may be a way of checking them out without any risk."

"You're the expert. But tell me, could something sneak through from the scene on the card without you—"

"No. They don't work that way. They require your attention to operate. More than a little of it."

"That's something, anyway. I—"

He looked back again. Someone was coming. I flexed my fingers, involuntarily.

Then I heard him let go a big breath.

"It's okay," he said. "I know him. It's George Hansen. He's the son of the guy who owns the farm we're behind. Hi, George!"

The approaching figure waved. He was of medium height and stocky build. Had sandy hair. He wore Levi's and a Grateful Dead T-shirt, a pack of cigarettes twisted into its left sleeve. He looked to be in his twenties.

"Hi," he answered, drawing near. "Swell day, huh?"

"Sure is," Bill answered. "That's why we're out walking in it, instead of sitting at home."

George's gaze shifted to me.

"Me, too," he said, raking his teeth over his lower lip. "Real good day."

"This is Merle Corey. He's visiting me."

"Merle Corey," George repeated, and he stuck out his hand. "Hi, Merle."

I took it and shook it. It was a little clammy.

"Recognize the name?"

"Uh—Merle Corey," he said again.

"You knew his dad."

"Yeah? Oh, sure!"

"Sam Corey," Bill finished, and he shot me a glance over George's shoulder.

"Sam Corey," George repeated. "Son of a gun! Good to know you. You going to be here long?"

"A few days, I guess," I replied. "I didn't realize you'd known my father."

"Fine man," he said. "Where you from?"

"California, but it's time for a change."

"Where you headed?"

"Out of the country, actually."

"Europe?"

"Farther."

"Sounds great. I'd like to travel sometime."

"Maybe you will."

"Maybe. Well, I'll be moving on. Let you guys enjoy your walk. Nice meeting you, Merle."

"My pleasure."

He backed away, waved, turned, and walked off.

I glanced at Bill then and noticed that he was shaking.

"What's the matter?" I whispered.

"I've known that boy all his life," he said. "Do you think he's on drugs?"

"Not the kind you have to make holes in your arms for. I didn't see any tracks. And he didn't seem particularly spacey."

"Yeah, but you don't know him the way I do. He seemed very—different. It was just on impulse that I used the name Sam for your dad, because something didn't seem right. His speech patterns have changed, his posture, his gait . . . Intangibles. I was waiting for him to correct me, and then I could have made a joke about premature senility. But he didn't. He picked up on it instead. Merle, this is scary! He knew your father real well—as Carl Corey. Your dad liked to keep his place nice, but he was never much for weeding and mowing or raking leaves. George did his yard work for him for years while he was in school. He knew his name wasn't Sam."

"I don't understand."

"Neither do I," he said, "and I don't like it."

"So he's acting weird—and you think he was following us?"

"Now I do. This is too much of a coincidence, timed with your arrival."

I turned.

"I'm going after him," I said. "I'll find out."

"No. Don't."

"I won't hurt him. There are other ways."

"It might be better to let him think he's got us fooled. It might encourage him to do something or say something later that could prove useful. On the other hand, anything you do—even something subtle or magical—might let him, or something, know that we're on to him. Let it ride, be grateful you're warned and be wary."

"You've got a point there," I agreed. "Okay."

"Let's head on back and drive into town for lunch. I want to stop by the office and pick up some papers and make some phone calls. Then I have to see a client at two o'clock. You can take the car and knock around while I'm doing that."

"Fine."

As we strolled back I did some wondering. There were a number of things I had not told Bill. For instance, there had been no reason to tell him that I wore an invisible strangling cord possessed of some rather unusual virtues, woven about my left wrist. One of these virtues is that it generally warns me of nasty intentions aimed in my direction, as it had done in Luke's presence for almost two years until we became friends. Whatever the reason for George Hansen's unusual behavior, Frakir had not given me any indication that he meant me harm.

Funny, though . . . there was something about the way he talked, the way he said his words . . .

I went for a drive after lunch while Bill took care of his business. I headed out to the place where my father had lived years ago. I'd been by it a number of times in the past, but I'd never been inside. No real reason to, I guess, anyway. I parked up the road on a rise, off on the shoulder, and regarded it. A young couple lived there now, Bill had told me, with some kids—a thing I could see for myself from some scattered toys off to the side of the yard. I wondered what it would have been like, growing up in a place like that. I supposed that I could have. The house looked well kept, sprightly even. I imagined that the people were happy there.

I wondered where he was—if he were even among the living. No one could reach him via his Trump, though that didn't necessarily prove anything. There are a variety of ways in which a Trump sending can be blocked. In fact one of these situations was even said to apply in his case, though I didn't like to think about it.

One rumor had it that Dad had been driven mad in the Courts of Chaos by a curse placed upon him by my mother, and that he now wandered aimlessly through Shadow. She refused even to comment on this story. Another was that he had entered the universe of his own creation and never returned, which it seemed possible could remove him from the reach of the Trumps. Another was simply that he had perished at some point after his departure from the Courts—and a number of my relatives there assured me that they had seen him leave after his sojourn. So, if the rumor of his death were correct, it did not occur in the Courts of Chaos. And there were others who claimed to have seen him at widely separated sites afterward, encounters invariably involving bizarre behavior on his part. I had been told by one that he was traveling in the company of a mute dancer—a tiny, lovely lady with whom he communicated by means of sign language—and that he wasn't talking much himself either. Another reported him as roaring drunk in a raucous cantina, from which he eventually expelled all the other patrons in order to enjoy the music of the band without distraction. I could not vouch for the authenticity of any of these accounts. It had taken me a lot of searching just to come up with this handful of rumors. I could not locate him with a Logrus summoning either, though I had tried many times. But of course if he were far enough afield my powers of concentration may simply have been inadequate.

In other words, I didn't know where the hell my father, Corwin of Amber, was, and nobody else seemed to know either. I regretted this sorely, because my only long encounter with him had been on the occasion of hearing his lengthy story outside the Courts of Chaos on the day of the Patternfall battle. This had changed my life. It had given me the resolve to depart the Court, with the determination to seek experience and education in the shadow world where he had dwelled for so long. I'd felt a need to understand it if I were to understand him better. I believed that I had now achieved something of this, and more. But he was no longer available to continue our conversation.

I believed that I was about ready to attempt a new means of locating him—now that the Ghostwheel project was almost off the ground—when the most recent fecal missile met the rotating blades. Following my cross-country trip, scheduled to wind up at Bill's place a month or two from now, I was going to head off to my personal anomaly of a place and begin the work.

Now . . . other things had crowded in. The matters at hand would have to be dealt with before I could get on with the search.

I drove past the house slowly. I could hear the sounds of stereo music through open windows. Better not to know exactly what it was like inside. Sometimes a little mystery is best.

That evening after dinner I sat on the porch with Bill, trying to think of anything else I should run through his mind. As I kept drawing blanks, he was the first to renew our serial conversation:

"Something else," he began.

"Yes?"

"Dan Martinez struck up his conversation with you by alluding to Luke's attempts to locate investors for some sort of computer company. You later felt that the whole thing could simply have been a ploy, to get you off guard and then hit you with that question about Amber and Chaos."

"Right."

"But then Luke really did raise the matter of doing something along those lines. He insisted, though, that he had not been in touch with potential investors and that he had never heard of Dan Martinez. When he saw the man dead later he still maintained that he'd never met him."

I nodded.

"Then either Luke was lying, or Martinez had somehow learned his plans."

"I don't think Luke was lying," I said. "In fact, I've been thinking about that whole business some more. Just knowing him as I do, I don't believe Luke *would* have gone around looking for investors until he was sure there was something to put the money into. I think he was telling the truth on that, too. It seems more likely to me that this might have been the only real coincidence in everything that's happened so far. I have the feeling that Martinez knew a lot about Luke and just wanted that one final piece of information—about his knowledge of Amber and the Courts. I think he was very shrewd, and on the basis of what he knew already he was able to concoct something that seemed plausible to me, knowing I'd worked for the same company as Luke."

"I suppose it's possible," he said. "But then when Luke really did—"

"I'm beginning to believe," I interrupted, "that Luke's story was phoney, too."

"I don't follow you."

"I think he put it together the same way Martinez did, and for similar reasons—to sound plausible to me so that he could get some information he wanted."

"You've lost me. What information?"

"My Ghostwheel. He wanted to know what it was."

"And he was disappointed to learn that it was just an exercise in exotic design, for other reasons than building a company?"

Bill caught my smile as I nodded.

"There's more?" he said. Then: "Wait. Don't tell me. You were lying, too. It's something real."

"Yes."

"I probably shouldn't even ask—unless you think it's material and want to tell me. If it's something big and very important it could be gotten out of me, you know. I have a low tolerance for pain. Think about it."

I did. I sat there for some time, musing.

"I suppose it could be," I said finally, "in a sort of peripheral way I'm sure you're not referring to. But I don't see how it could be—as you say—material. Not to Luke or to anyone else—because nobody even knows what it is but me. No. I can't see how it enters the equation beyond Luke's curiosity about it. So I think I'll follow your suggestion and just keep it off the record."

"Fine with me," he said. "Then there is the matter of Luke's disappearance—"

Within the house, a telephone rang.

"Excuse me," Bill said.

He rose and went into the kitchen.

After a few moments, I heard him call, "Merle, it's for you!"

I got up and went inside. I gave him a questioning look as soon as I entered and he shrugged and shook his head. I thought fast and recalled the locations of two other phones in the house. I pointed at him, pointed in the direction of his study and pantomimed the motion of picking up a receiver and holding it one's ear. He smiled slightly and nodded.

I took the receiver and waited a while, till I heard the click, only beginning to speak then, hoping the caller would think I'd picked up an extension to answer.

"Hello," I said.

"Merle Corey?"

"That's me."

"I need some information I think you might have."

It was a masculine voice, sort of familiar but not quite.

"Who am I talking to?" I asked.

"I'm sorry. I can't tell you that."

"Then that will probably be my answer to your question, too."

"Will you at least let me ask?"

"Go ahead," I said.

"Okay. You and Luke Raynard are friends."

He paused.

"You could say that," I said, to fill the space.

"You have heard him speak of places called Amber and the Courts of Chaos."

Again, a statement rather than a question.

"Maybe," I said.

"Do you know anything of these places yourself?"

Finally, a question.

"Maybe," I said again.

"Please. This is serious. I need something more than a 'maybe.'"

"Sorry. 'Maybe' is all you're going to get, unless you tell me who you are and why you want to know."

"I can be of great service to you if you will be honest with me."

I bit back a reply just in time and felt my pulse begin to race. That last statement had been spoken in Thari. I maintained my silence.

Then: "Well, that didn't work, and I still don't really know."

"What? What don't you know?" I said.

"Whether he's from one of those places or whether it's you."

"To be as blunt as possible, what's it to you?" I asked him.

"Because one of you may be in great danger."

"The one who is from such a place or the one who is not?" I asked.

"I can't tell you that. I can't afford another mistake."

"What do you mean? What was your last one about?"

"You won't tell me—either for purposes of self-preservation, or to help a friend?"

"I might," I said, "if I knew that that were really the case. But for all I know, it might be you that's the danger."

"I assure you I am only trying to help the right person."

"Words, words, words," I said. "Supposing we were both from such places?"

"Oh, my!" he said. "No. That couldn't be."

"Why not?"

"Never mind. What do I have to do to persuade you?"

"Mm. Wait a minute. Let me think," I answered. "All right. How about this? I'll meet you someplace. You name the place. I get a good look at you and we trade information, one piece at a time, till all the cards are on the table."

There was a pause.

Then: "That's the only way you'll do it?"

"Yes."

"Let me think about it. I'll be back in touch soon."

"One thing—"

"What?"

"If it is me, am I in danger right now?"

"I think so. Yes, you probably are. Good-bye."

He hung up.

I managed to sigh and swear at the same time as I recradled the phone. People who knew about us seemed to be coming out of the woodwork.

Bill came into the kitchen, a very puzzled expression on his face.

"How'd whoever-the-hell-he-is even know you're here?" were his first words.

"That was my question," I said. "Think up another."

"I will. If he wants to set something up, are you really going?"

"You bet. I suggested it because I want to meet the guy."

"As you pointed out, he may be the danger."

"That's okay by me. He's going to be in a lot of danger, too."

"I don't like it."

"I'm not so happy with it myself. But it's the best offer I've had so far."

"Well, it's your decision. It's too bad there isn't some way of locating him beforehand."

"That passed through my mind, too."

"Listen, why not push him a little?"

"How?"

"He sounded a little nervous, and I don't think he liked your suggestion any more than I do. Let's not be here when he calls back. Don't let him think you're just sitting around waiting for the phone to ring. Make him wait a little. Go conjure up some fresh clothes and we'll drive over to the country club for a couple of hours. It'll beat raiding the icebox."

"Good idea," I said. "This was supposed to be a vacation, one time. That's probably the closest I'll get. Sounds fine."

I renewed my wardrobe out of Shadow, trimmed my beard, showered, and dressed. We drove to the club then and had a leisurely meal on the terrace. It was a good evening for it, balmy and star-filled, running with moonlight like milk. By mutual consent we refrained from discussing my problems any further. Bill seemed to know almost everyone there, so it seemed a friendly place to me. It was the most relaxed evening I'd spent in a long while. Afterward we stopped for drinks in the club bar, which I gathered had been one of my dad's favorite watering spots, strains of dance music drifting through from the room next door.

"Yeah, it was a good idea," I said. "Thanks."

"De nada," he said. "I had a lot of good times here with your old man. You haven't, by any chance—?"

"No, no news of him."

"Sorry."

"I'll let you know when he turns up."

"Sure. Sorry."

The drive back was uneventful, and no one followed us. We got in a little after midnight, said good night, and I went straight to my room. I shrugged out of my new jacket and hung it in the closet, kicked off my new shoes and left them there, too. As I walked back into the room, I noticed the white rectangle on the pillow of my bed.

I crossed to it in two big steps and snatched it up.

SORRY YOU WERE NOT IN WHEN I CALLED BACK, it said, in block capitals. BUT I SAW YOU AT THE CLUB AND CAN CERTAINLY UNDERSTAND YOUR WANTING A NIGHT OUT. IT GAVE ME AN IDEA. LET'S MEET IN THE BAR THERE, TOMORROW NIGHT, AT TEN. I'D FEEL BETTER WITH LOTS OF PEOPLE AROUND BUT NONE OF THEM LISTENING.

Damn. My first impulse was to go and tell Bill. My first thought following the impulse, though, was that there was nothing he could do except lose some sleep over it, a thing he probably needed a lot more than I did. So I folded the note and stuck it in my shirt pocket, then hung up the shirt.

Not even a nightmare to liven my slumber. I slept deeply and well, knowing Frakir would rouse me in the event of danger. In fact, I overslept, and it felt good. The morning was sunny and birds were singing.

I made my way downstairs to the kitchen after splashing and combing myself into shape and raiding Shadow for fresh slacks and a shirt. There was a note on the kitchen table. I was tired of finding notes, but this one was from Bill, saying he'd had to run into town to his office for a while and I should go ahead and help myself to anything that looked good for breakfast. He'd be back a little later.

I checked out the refrigerator and came up with some English muffins, a piece of cantaloupe and a glass of orange juice. Some coffee I'd started first thing was ready shortly after I finished, and I took a cup with me out onto the porch.

As I sat there, I began to think that maybe I ought to leave a

note of my own and move on. My mysterious correspondent—
conceivably S—had phoned here once and broken in once. How S
had known I was here was immaterial. It was a friend's house, and
though I did not mind sharing some of my problems with friends,
I did not like the idea of exposing them to danger. But then, it was
daylight now and the meeting was set for this evening. Not that
much longer till some sort of resolution was achieved. Almost
silly to depart at this point. In fact, it was probably better that I
hang around till then. I could keep an eye on things, protect Bill if
anything came up today—

Suddenly, I had a vision of someone forcing Bill to write that
note at gunpoint, then whisking him away as a hostage to pressure
me into answering questions.

I hurried back to the kitchen and phoned his office. Horace
Crayper, his secretary, answered on the second ring.

"Hi, this is Merle Corey," I said. "Is Mr. Roth in?"

"Yes," he replied, "but he's with a client right now. Could I
have him call you back?"

"No, it's not that important," I said, "and I'll be seeing him
later. Don't bother him. Thanks."

I poured myself another cup of coffee and returned to the
porch. This sort of thing was bad for the nerves. I decided that if
everything wasn't squared away this evening I would leave.

A figure rounded the corner of the house.

"Hi, Merle."

It was George Hansen. Frakir gave me the tiniest of pulses, as
if beginning a warning and then reconsidering it. Ambiguous.
Unusual.

"Hi, George. How's it going?"

"Pretty well. Is Mr. Roth in?"

"Afraid not. He had to go into town for a while. I imagine he'll
be back around lunchtime or a little after."

"Oh. A few days ago he'd asked me to stop by when I was
free, about some work he wanted done."

He came nearer, put his foot on the step.

I shook my head.

"Can't help you. He didn't mention it to me. You'll have to
catch him later."

He nodded, unwound his pack of cigarettes, shook one out and
lit it, then rewound the pack in his shirt sleeves. This T-shirt was a
Pink Floyd.

"How are you enjoying your stay?" he asked.

"Real well. You care for a cup of coffee?"

"Don't mind if I do."

I rose and went inside.

"With a little cream and sugar," he called after me.

I fixed him one and when I returned with it he was seated in the other chair on the porch.

"Thanks."

After he'd tasted it, he said, "I know your dad's name's Carl even though Mr. Roth said Sam. His memory must've slipped."

"Or his tongue," I said.

He smiled.

What was it about the way he talked? His voice could almost be the one I'd heard on the phone last night, though that one had been very controlled and slowed just enough to neutralize any number of speech clues. It wasn't that comparison that was bothering me.

"He was a retired military officer, wasn't he? And some sort of government consultant?"

"Yes."

"Where is he now?"

"Doing a lot of traveling—overseas."

"You going to see him on your own trip?"

"I hope so."

"That'll be nice," he said, taking a drag on his cigarette and another sip of coffee. "Ah! that's good!"

"I don't remember seeing you around," he said suddenly then. "You never lived with your dad, huh?"

"No, I grew up with my mother and other relatives."

"Pretty far from here, huh?"

I nodded. "Overseas."

"What was her name?"

I almost told him. I'm not certain why. But I changed it to "Dorothy" before it came out.

I glanced at him in time to see him purse his lips. He had been studying my face as I spoke.

"Why do you ask?" I said.

"No special reason. Or genetic nosiness, you might say. *My* mother was the town gossip."

He laughed and gulped coffee.

"Will you be staying long?" he asked then.

"Hard to say. Probably not real long, though."

"Well, I hope you have a good time of it." He finished his coffee and set the cup on the railing. He rose then, stretched and added, "Nice talking to you."

Partway down the stairs he paused and turned.

"I've a feeling you'll go far," he told me. "Good luck."

"You may, too," I said. "You've a way with words."

"Thanks for the coffee. See you around."

"Yes."

He turned the corner and was gone. I simply didn't know what to make of him, and after several attempts I gave up. When inspiration is silent reason tires quickly.

I was making myself a sandwich when Bill returned, so I made two. He went and changed clothes while I was doing this.

"I'm supposedly taking it easy this month," he said while we were eating, "but that was an old client with some pressing business, so I had to go in. What say we follow the creek in the other direction this afternoon?"

"Sure."

As we hiked across the field I told him of George's visit.

"No," he said, "I didn't tell him I had any jobs for him."

"In other words—"

"I guess he came by to see you. It would have been easy enough to see me leave, from their place."

"I wish I knew what he wanted."

"If it's important enough he'll probably wind up asking you, in time."

"But time is running," I said. "I've decided to leave tomorrow morning, maybe even tonight."

"Why?"

As we made our way down the creek, I told him of last night's note and this evening's rendezvous. I also told him my feelings about exposing him to stray shots, or intended ones.

"It may not be that serious," he began.

"My mind's made up, Bill. I hate to cut things short when I haven't seen you for so long, but I hadn't counted on all this trouble. And if I go away you know that it will, too."

"Probably so, but . . ."

We continued in this vein for a while as we followed the watercourse. Then we finally dropped the matter as settled and returned to a fruitless rehashing of my puzzles. As we walked I looked back occasionally but did not see anyone behind us. I did hear a few sounds within the brush on the opposite bank at infrequent intervals, but it could easily have been an animal disturbed by our voices.

We had hiked for over an hour when I had the premonitory feeling that someone was picking up my Trump. I froze.

Bill halted and turned toward me.

"What—"

I raised my hand.

"Long distance call," I said.

A moment later I felt the first movement of contact. I also heard the noise in the bushes again, across the water.

"Merlin."

It was Random's voice, calling to me. A few seconds later I saw him, seated at a desk in the library of Amber.

"Yes?" I answered.

The image came into solidity, assumed full reality, as if I were looking through an archway into an adjacent room. At the same time, I still possessed my vision of the rest of my surroundings, though it was growing more and more peripheral by the moment. For example, I saw George Hansen start up from among the bushes across the creek, staring at me.

"I want you back in Amber right away," Random stated.

George began to move forward, splashing down into the water.

Random raised his hand, extended it.

"Come on through," he said.

By now my outline must have begun shimmering, and I heard George cry out, "Stop! Wait! I have to come with—!"

I reached out and grasped Bill's shoulder.

"I can't leave you with this nut," I said. "Come on!"

With my other hand I clasped Random's.

"Okay," I said, moving forward.

"Stop!" George cried.

"The hell you say," I replied, and we left him to clasp a rainbow.

7

Random looked startled as the two of us came through into the library. He rose to his feet, which still left him shorter than either of us, and he shifted his attention to Bill.

"Merlin, who's this?" he asked.

"Your attorney, Bill Roth," I said. "You've always dealt with him through agents in the past. I thought you might like to—"

Bill began dropping to one knee, "Your Majesty," on his lips, but Random caught him by the shoulders.

"Cut the crap," he said. "We're not in Court." He clasped his hand, then said, "Call me Random. I've always intended to thank you personally for the work you did on that treaty. Never got around to it, though. Good to meet you."

I'd never seen Bill at a loss for words before, but he just stared, at Random, at the room, out of the window at a distant tower.

Finally, "It's real . . ." I heard him whisper moments later.

"Did I not see someone springing toward you?" Random said to me, running a hand through his unruly brown hair. "And surely your last words back there were not addressed to me?"

"We were having a little problem," I answered. "That's the real reason I brought Bill along. You see, someone's been trying to kill me, and—"

Random raised his hand. "Spare me the details for the moment. I'll need them all later, but—but let it be later. There is more nastiness than usual afoot at the moment, and yours may well be a part of it. But I've got to breathe a bit."

It was only then that some deepened lines in his naturally

youthful face registered and I began to realize that he was under a strain.

"What's the matter?" I asked.

"Caine is dead. Murdered," he replied. "This morning."

"How did it happen?"

"He was off in Shadow Deiga—a distant port with which we have commerce. He was with Gérard, to renegotiate an old trade agreement. He was shot, through the heart. Died instantly."

"Did they catch the bowman?"

"Bowman, hell! It was a rifleman, on a rooftop. And he got away."

"I thought gunpowder didn't work around here."

He made a quick palms-up gesture.

"Deiga may be far enough off in Shadow for it to work. Nobody here can remember ever testing any there. For that matter, though, your father once came up with a compound that worked here."

"True. I'd almost forgotten."

"Anyway, the funeral is tomorrow—"

"Bill! Merlin!"

My aunt Flora—who had turned down Rossetti's offers, one of them being to model for him—had entered the room. Tall, slim and burnished, she hurried forward and kissed Bill on the cheek. I had never seen him blush before. She repeated the act for me, too, but I was less moved, recalling that she had once been my father's warden.

"When did you get in?" Her voice was lovely, too.

"Just now," I said.

She immediately linked arms with both of us and attempted to lead us off.

"We have so much to talk about," she began.

"Flora!" This from Random.

"Yes, brother?"

"You may give Mr. Roth the full tour, but I require Merlin's presence for a time."

She pouted slightly for a moment, then released my arm.

"Now you know what an absolute monarchy is," she explained to Bill. "You can see how power corrupts."

"I was corrupt before I had power," Random said, "and rich is better. You have my leave to depart, sister."

She sniffed and led Bill away.

"It's always quieter around here when she finds a boyfriend off somewhere in Shadow," Random observed. "Unfortunately, she's been home for the better part of a year this time."

I made a tsking sound.

He gestured toward a chair and I took it. He crossed to a cabinet then.

"Wine?" he asked.

"Don't mind if I do."

He poured two glasses, brought me one, and seated himself in a chair to my left, a small table between us.

"Someone also took a shot at Bleys," he said, "this afternoon, in another shadow. Hit him, too, but not bad. Gunman got away. Bleys was just on a diplomatic mission to a friendly kingdom."

"Same person, you think?"

"Sure. We've never had rifle sniping in the neighborhood before. Then two, all of a sudden? It must be the same person. Or the same conspiracy."

"Any clues?"

He shook his head and tasted the wine.

"I wanted to talk to you alone," he said then, "before any of the others got to you. There are two things I'd like you to know."

I sipped the wine and waited.

"The first is that this really scares me. With the attempt on Bleys it no longer appears to have been simply a personal thing directed at Caine. Somebody seems to have it in for us—or at least some of us. Now you say there's someone after you, too."

"I don't know whether there's any connection—"

"Well, neither do I. But I don't like the possible pattern I see developing. My worst fear is that it may be one or more of us behind it."

"Why?"

He glowered into his goblet.

"For centuries the personal vendetta has been our way of settling disagreements, not necessarily proceeding inevitably to death—though that was always a possibility—but certainly characterized by intrigues, to the end of embarrassing, disadvantaging, maiming, or exiling the other and enhancing one's own position. This reached its latest peak in the scramble for the succession. I thought everything was pretty much settled, though, when I wound up with the job, which I certainly wasn't looking for. I had no real axes to grind, and I've tried to be fair. I know how touchy everyone here is. I don't think it's me, though, and I don't think it's the succession. I haven't had any bad vibes from any of the others. I'd gotten the impression they had decided I was the lesser of all possible evils and were actually cooperating to make it work. No, I don't believe any of the others is rash enough to want my crown. There was actually amity, goodwill, after the succession was settled. But what I'm wondering now is whether the old pattern might be recurring—that some of the others might have taken up the old game again to settle personal grievances. I really don't want to see that happen—all the suspicion, precautions, innuendoes, mistrust, double dealings. It weakens us, and there's always some possible threat or other against which we should be strong. Now, I've spoken with everyone privately, and of course they all deny any knowledge of current cabals, intrigues, and vendettas, but I could see that they're getting suspicious of each other. It's become a habit of thought. And it wasn't at all difficult for them to dig up some old grudge each of the others might still have had against Caine, despite the fact that he saved all our asses by taking out Brand. And the same with Bleys—everyone could find motives for everyone else."

"So you want the killer fast, because of what he's done to morale?"

"Certainly. I don't need all this backbiting and grudgehunting. It's all still so close to the surface that we're likely to have real cabals, intrigues, and vendettas before long, if we don't already, and some little misunderstanding could lead to violence again."

"*Do* you think it's one of the others?"

"Shit! I'm the same as they are. I get suspicious by reflex. It well may be, but I haven't really seen a bit of evidence."

"Who else could it be?"

He uncrossed and recrossed his legs. He took another drink of wine.

"Hell! Our enemies are legion. But most of them wouldn't have the guts. They all know the kind of reprisal they could expect once we found them out."

He clasped his hands behind his head and stared at the rows of books.

"I don't know how to say this," he began after a time, "but I have to."

I waited again. Then he said quickly, "There's talk it's Corwin, but I don't believe it."

"No," I said softly.

"I told you I don't believe it. Your father means a lot to me."

"Why would anybody believe it?"

"There's a rumor he's gone crazy. You've heard it. What if he's reverted to some past state of mind, from the days when his relations with Caine and Bleys were a lot less than cordial—or with any of us, for that matter? That's what they're saying."

"I don't believe it."

"I just wanted you to be aware that it's being kicked around."

"Nobody'd better kick it in my direction."

He sighed. "Don't *you* start. Please. They're upset. Don't look for trouble."

I took a drink of wine.

"Yes, you're right," I said.

"Now I have to listen to your story. Go ahead, complicate my life some more."

"Okay. At least I'm fresh on it," I told him.

So I ran through it again. It took a long while, and it was getting dark by the time I finished. He had interrupted me only for occasional clarifications and had not indulged in the exploration of contingencies the way Bill had when he'd heard it.

When I had finished, he rose and lit a few oil lamps. I could almost hear him thinking.

Finally he said, "No, you've got me on Luke. He doesn't ring any bells at all. The lady with the sting bothers me a bit, though. It seems I might have heard something about people like that, but I can't recall the circumstances. It'll come to me. I want to know more about this Ghostwheel project of yours, though. Something about it troubles me."

"Sure," I said. "But there is something else I am reminded to tell you first."

"What's that?"

"I covered everything for you pretty much the way I did when I was talking to Bill. In fact, my just having been through it recently made me almost use it like a rehearsal. But there was something I didn't mention to Bill because it didn't seem important at the time. I might even have forgotten it entirely in the light of everything else, till this business about the sniper came up—and then you reminded me that Corwin once developed a substitute for gunpowder that will work here."

"Everybody remembered it, believe me."

"I forgot about two rounds of ammunition I have in my pocket that came from the ruins of that warehouse where Melman had his studio."

"So?"

"They don't contain gunpowder. There's some kind of pink stuff in them instead—and it won't even burn. At least back on that shadow Earth . . ."

I dug one out.

"Looks like a 30–30," he said.

"I guess so."

Random rose and drew upon a braided cord that hung beside one of the bookshelves.

By the time he'd returned to his seat there was a knock on the door.

"Come in," he called.

A liveried servant entered, a young blond fellow.

"That was quick," Random said.

The man looked puzzled.

"Your Majesty, I do not understand . . ."

"What's to understand? I rang. You came."

"Sire, I was not on duty in the quarters. I was sent to tell you that dinner is ready to be served, awaiting your pleasure."

"Oh. Tell them I'll be along shortly. As soon as I've spoken with the person I've called."

"Very good, Sire."

The man departed backward with a quick bow.

"I thought that was too good to be true," Random muttered.

A little later another guy appeared, older and less elegantly garbed.

"Rolf, would you run down to the armory and talk to whoever's on duty?" Random said. "Ask him to go through that collection of rifles we have from the time Corwin came to Kolvir with them, the day Eric died. See if he can dig up a 30–30 for me, in good shape. Have him clean it and send it up. We're going down to dinner now. You can just leave the weapon in the corner over there."

"30–30, Sire?"

"Right."

Rolf departed, Random rose and stretched. He pocketed the round I'd given him and gestured toward the door.

"Let's go eat."

"Good idea."

There were eight of us at dinner: Random, Gérard, Flora, Bill, Martin—who had been called back a little earlier in the day,

Julian—who had just arrived from Arden, Fiona—who had also just come in, from some distant locale, and myself. Benedict was due in the morning, and Llewella later this evening.

I sat to Random's left, Martin to his right. I hadn't seen Martin in a long while and was curious what he'd been about. But the atmosphere was not conducive to conversation. As soon as anyone spoke everyone else evinced unusually acute attention—far beyond the dictates of simple politeness. I found it rather unnerving, and I guess Random did, too, because he sent for Droppa Ma-Pantz, the court jester, to fill the heavy silences.

Droppa had a rough time at first. He began by juggling some food, eating it as it moved by until it was gone, wiped his mouth on a borrowed napkin, then insulted each of us in turn. After that, he commenced a stand-up routine I found very funny.

Bill, who was at my left, commented softly, "I know enough Thari to catch most of it, and that's a George Carlin shtick! How——"

"Oh, whenever Droppa's stuff starts sounding stale, Random sends him off to various clubs in Shadow," I explained, "to pick up new material. I understand he's a regular at Vegas. Random even accompanies him sometimes, to play cards."

He did start getting laughs after a while which loosened things up a bit. When he knocked off for a drink it became possible to talk without being the center of attention, as separate conversations had sprung up. As soon as this happened, a massive arm passed behind Bill and fell upon my shoulder. Gérard was leaning back in his chair and sideward toward me.

"Merlin," he said, "good to see you again. Listen, when you get a chance I'd like to have a little talk with you in private."

"Sure," I said, "but Random and I have to take care of something after dinner."

"When you get a chance," he repeated.

I nodded.

A few moments later I had the feeling that someone was trying to reach me via my Trump.

"Merlin!"

It was Fiona. But she was just sitting at the other end of the table . . .

Her image came clear, however, and I answered her, "Yes?" and then I glanced down the table and saw that she was staring into her handkerchief. She looked up at me then, smiled, and nodded.

I still retained the mental image of her, simultaneously, and I heard it say, *"I dislike raising my voice, for a number of reasons. I'm certain that you will be rushed off after dinner, and I just wanted to let you know that we ought to take a walk, or row out on one of the ponds, or Trump out to Cabra or go look at the Pattern together sometime soon. You understand?"*

"I understand," I said. "I'll be in touch."

"Excellent."

The contact was broken then, and when I glanced her way she was folding her handkerchief and studying her plate.

Random did not linger, but rose quickly after he had finished his dessert, bidding the others a good night and gesturing for Martin and me to accompany him as he departed.

Julian brushed by me on the way out, trying to look somewhat less than sinister and almost succeeding.

"We must go riding together in Arden," he said, "soon."

"Good idea," I told him. "I'll be in touch."

We departed the dining room. Flora caught me in the hall. She still had Bill in tow.

"Stop by my room for a nightcap," she said, "before you turn in. Or come by for tea tomorrow."

"Thank you," I said. "We'll get together. It all depends on how things run, as to just when."

She nodded and hit me with the smile that had caused numerous duels and Balkan crises in the past. Then she moved on and we did, too.

As we mounted the stair on the way to the library, Random asked, "Is that everyone?"

"What do you mean?" I said.

"Have they all set up assignations with you by now?"

"Well, they're all tentative things, but yes."

He laughed. "Didn't think they'd waste any time. You'll get everybody's pet suspicions that way. Might as well collect them. Some might come in handy later. They're probably all looking for allies, too—and you should seem a pretty safe choice."

"I do want to visit with all of them. It's just a shame it has to be this way."

He gestured as we came to the top of the stairs. We turned up the hallway and headed toward the library.

"Where are we going?" Martin asked.

Although he resembled Random, Martin looked a little less sneaky, and he was taller. Still, he was not a really big guy.

"To pick up a rifle," Random said.

"Oh? Why?"

"I want to test some ammo Merlin brought back. If it actually fires, our lives have just acquired an additional complication."

We entered the library. The oil lamps were still burning. The rifle was standing in a corner. Random went to it, dug the shell out of his pocket, and loaded it.

"Okay. What should we try it on?" he mused.

He stepped back out into the hall and looked around.

"Ah! Just the thing!"

He shouldered it, aimed at a suit of armor up the hall, and squeezed the trigger. There followed a sharp report and the ringing of metal. The armor shook.

"Holy shit!" Random said. "It worked! Why me, Unicorn? I was looking for a peaceful reign."

"May I try it, father," Martin asked. "I've always wanted to."

"Why not?" Random said. "You still got that other round, Merlin?"

"Yes," I said, and I rummaged about in my pocket and brought out two. I passed them to Random. "One of these shouldn't work, anyway," I said. "It just got mixed in with the other two."

"All right."

Random accepted both, loaded one. He passed the weapon to Martin then and began explaining its operation. In the distance I heard the sounds of alarm.

"We're about to have the entire palace guard descend upon us," I observed.

"Good," Random answered, as Martin raised the piece to his shoulder. "A little realistic drill every now and then never hurts."

The rifle roared and the armor rang a second time. Martin looked startled and quickly passed the weapon back to Random. Random glanced at the shell in his hand, said, "What the hell!", loaded the final round and fired without sighting.

There was a third report, followed by sounds of a ricochet, just as the guard reached the top of the stair.

"I guess I just don't live right," Random remarked.

After Random had thanked the guard for their prompt response to a training exercise and I overheard a mutter about the king being in his cups, we returned to the library and he asked me the question.

"I found the third one in the pocket of Luke's field jacket," I answered, and I proceeded to explain the circumstances.

"I can no longer afford *not* to know about Luke Raynard," he finally said. "Tell me how you read what just happened."

"The building that burned down," I began. "Upstairs was Melman who wanted to sacrifice me. Downstairs was the Brutus Storage Company. Brutus apparently was storing ammo of this sort. Luke admitted that he knew Melman. I had no idea that there might be some connection with Brutus and the ammunition, also. The fact that they were located in the same building is too much, though."

"If they're turning it out in such quantities that it requires warehousing, then we're in big trouble," Random said. "I want to know who owned that building—and who owned the company, if it's a different person."

"It shouldn't be too difficult to check."

"Who should I send to do it?" he mused. Then he snapped his fingers and smiled. "Flora is about to undertake an important mission for the Crown."

"Inspired," I said.

Martin smiled at that and then shook his head. "I'm afriad I don't understand what's going on," he told us, "and I want to."

"Tell you what," Random said. "You fill him in while I go give Flora her assignment. She can leave right after the funeral."

"Yes," I said as he departed, and I began telling my tale once again, editing for brevity.

Martin had no fresh insights and no new information, not that I had expected any of him. He had spent the past few years off in a more pastoral setting, I learned. I got the impression that he was more fond of the countryside than of cities.

"Merlin," he said. "You should have brought this whole mess home to Amber sooner. We're all affected."

And what of the Courts of Chaos? I wondered. Would that rifle have fired there? Still, it had been Caine and Bleys who had been targets. No one had summoned me back to the Courts to brief me on any incidents. Still . . . perhaps I ought to bring my other relatives aboard at some point.

"But up until a few days ago matters were a lot simpler," I told Martin, "and then when things began developing fast I was too caught up in them."

"But all those years . . . those attempts on your life . . ."

I said, "I don't call home whenever I stub my toe. Nobody else does either. I couldn't see any connection, all that time."

But I knew that he was right and I was wrong. Fortunately, Random returned about then.

"I couldn't quite get her to believe it was an honor," he said, "but she'll do it."

We talked for a while then about more general matters, mostly what we had been doing for the past several years. I recalled Random's curiosity about Ghostwheel and mentioned the project to him. He changed the subject immediately, giving the impression he wanted to save it for a fully private conversation. After a time, Martin began to yawn and it was contagious. Random decided to bid us good night and rang for a servant to show me to my room.

I asked Dik, who had led me to my quarters, to find me some drawing materials. It took him about ten minutes to turn up everything that I needed.

It would have been a long, difficult walk back and I was tired. So I seated myself beside a table and commenced the construction of a Trump for the bar at the country club Bill had taken me to the previous evening. I worked for perhaps twenty minutes before I was satisfied.

Now it was just a matter of time differential, a thing that was subject to variation, the 2.5-to-1 ratio being only a rule of thumb between Amber and the shadow I had recently inhabited. It was quite possible that I had missed my rendezvous with the nameless housebreaker.

I set everything aside except for the Trump. I rose to my feet.

There came a knock on my door. I was tempted not to answer it, but my curiosity won out. I crossed the room, unbolted the door, and opened it.

Fiona stood there, her hair down for a change. She had on an attractive green evening dress and a small jeweled pin that matched her hair perfectly.

"Hello, Fi," I said. "What brings you around?"

"I felt you working with certain forces," she answered, "and I didn't want anything happening to you before we had our talk. May I come in?"

"Of course," I said, stepping aside. "But I am in a hurry."

"I know, but perhaps I can be of help."

"How?" I asked, closing the door.

She looked about the room and spotted the Trump I'd just finished. She shot the bolt on the door and crossed to the table.

"Very nice," she observed, studying my handiwork. "So that's where you're headed? Where is it?"

"The bar at a country club in the place I just came from," I replied. "I'm supposed to meet an unknown party there at ten, local time. Hopefully, I will obtain information as to who has been trying to kill me, and why, and possibly even learn something of other matters that have been troubling me."

"Go," she said, "and leave the Trump behind. That way, I can use it to spy, and if you should suddenly need help I will be in a position to provide it."

I reached out and squeezed her hand. Then I took up a position beside the table and focused my attention.

After several moments, the scene took on depth and color. I sank into the emerging textures, and everything advanced toward me, growing larger, crowding out my immediate surroundings. My gaze sought the wall clock I remembered, to the right of the bar . . .

9:48. I couldn't have cut things much closer.

I could see the patrons now, hear the sounds of their voices. I looked for the best point of arrival. Actually, there was no one at the right end of the bar, near that clock. Okay . . .

I was there. Trying to look as if I had been, all along. Three of the patrons snapped glances in my direction. I smiled and nodded. Bill had introduced me to one of the men the previous evening. The other I had seen, but not spoken with at that time. Both of them returned my nod, which seemed to satisfy the third that I was real, as he immediately turned his attention back to the woman he was with.

Shortly, the bartender came up to me. He recalled me from last night, also, because he asked whether Bill was around.

I had a beer from him and retired with it to the most secluded table, where I sat and nursed it, my back to the wall, glancing occasionally at the clock, watching the room's two entrances between times. If I tried I could feel Fiona's presence.

Ten o'clock came and went. So did a few patrons, new and old. None of them seemed particularly interested in me, though my own attention was drawn to an unescorted young lady with pale hair and a cameolike profile, which ends the resemblance because cameos don't smile much and she did the second time she glanced at me, right before she looked away. Damn, I thought, why did I have to be wrapped up in a life-and-death situation? Under almost any other circumstances I would have finished the beer, walked over for another, passed a few pleasantries, then asked her whether she'd care to join me. In fact . . .

I glanced at the clock.

10:20.

How much longer should I give the mystery voice? Should I just assume it had been George Hansen, and that he'd given up on tonight when he'd seen me fade? How much longer might the lady hang around?

I growled softly. Stick to business. I studied the narrowness of her waist, the swell of her hips, the tension of her shoulders . . .

10:25.

I noticed that my mug was empty. I took it over for a refill. Dutifully, I watched the progress of the mug.

"I saw you sitting there," I heard her say. "Waiting for someone?"

She smelled strongly of a strange perfume.

"Yes," I said. "But I'm beginning to think it's too late."

"I've a similar problem," she said, and I turned toward her. She was smiling again. "We could wait together," she concluded.

"Please join me," I said. "I'd much rather pass the time with you."

She picked up her drink and followed me back to the table.

"My name's Merle Corey," I told her, as soon as we were seated.

"I'm Meg Devlin. I haven't seen you around before."

"I'm just visiting. You, I take it, are not?"

She shook her head slightly.

"Afraid not. I live in that new apartment complex a couple of miles up the road."

I nodded as if I knew where it was located.

"Where are you from?" she wanted to know.

"The center of the universe," I said, then hastily added, "San Francisco."

"Oh, I've spent a lot of time there. What do you do?"

I resisted a sudden impulse to tell her that I was a sorcerer, and instead described my recent employment at Grand Design. She, I learned in turn, had been a model, a buyer for a large store, and later manager of a boutique.

I glanced at the clock. It was 10:45. She caught the look.

"I think we've both been stood up," she said.

"Probably," I agreed, "but we ought to give them till eleven to be decent about it."

"I suppose."

"Have you eaten?"

"Earlier."

"Hungry?"

"Some. Yes. Are you?"

"Uh-huh, and I noticed some people had food in here earlier. I'll check."

I learned we could get sandwiches, so we got two, with some salad on the side.

"I hope your date didn't include a late supper," I said suddenly.

"It wasn't mentioned, and I don't care," she replied, taking a bite.

Eleven o'clock came and went. I'd finished my drink with the food, and I didn't really want another.

"At least the evening wasn't a total loss," she said, crumpling her napkin and setting it aside.

I watched her eyelashes because it was a pleasant thing to do. She wore very little or very pale makeup. It didn't matter at all. I was about to reach out and cover her hand with my own, but she beat me.

"What were you going to do tonight?" I asked her.

"Oh, dance a bit, have a few drinks, maybe take a walk in the moonlight. Silly things like that."

"I hear music in the next room. We could stroll on over."

"Yes, we could," she said. "Why don't we?"

As we were leaving the bar, I heard Fiona, like a whisper: *"Merlin! If you leave the scene on the Trump you will be out of range to me."*

"Hold on a minute," I answered.

"What?" Meg asked me.

"Uh—I want to visit the rest room first," I said.

"Good idea. I'll do the same. Meet you in the hall here in a couple of minutes."

The place was vacant, but I took a stall in case anyone wandered in. I located Fiona's Trump in the packet I carried. Moments later, I reached Fiona.

"Listen, Fi," I said. "Obviously, no one's going to show. But the rest of the evening promises to shape up nicely, and I might as well have a little fun while I'm here. So thanks for your help. I'll just wander on back later."

"I don't know," she said. *"I don't like you going off with a stranger, under the circumstances. There may still be danger around there for you, somewhere."*

"There isn't," I replied. "I have a way of knowing, and it doesn't register for her. Besides, I'm sure it was a fellow I'd met here and that he gave up when I trumped out. I'll be all right."

"I don't like it," she said.

"I'm a big boy. I can take care of myself."

"I suppose so. Call me immediately if there are any problems."

"There won't be. You might as well turn in."

"And call me when you're ready to come back. Don't worry about waking me. I want to bring you home personally."

"Okay, I'll do that. Good night."

"Stay wary."

"I always am."

"Good night, then."

She broke the contact.

A few minutes later we were on the dance floor, turning and listening and touching. Meg had a strong tendency to lead. But what the hell, I can be led. I even tried being wary occasionally but there was nothing more threatening than loud music and sudden laughter.

At eleven-thirty we checked the bar. There were several couples there, but her date wasn't. And no one even gave me a nod. We returned to the music.

We looked again a little after midnight with similar results. We seated ourselves then and ordered a final drink.

"Well, it was fun," she said, resting her hand where I could cover it with my own. So I did.

"Yes," I replied. "I wish we could do it more often. But I'm going to be leaving tomorrow."

"Where are you headed?"

"Back to the center of the universe."

"A pity," she said. "Do you need a ride anywhere?"

I nodded "Anywhere you're going."

She smiled and squeezed my hand.

"All right," she agreed. "Come on over and I'll make you a cup of coffee."

We finished our drinks and headed out to the parking lot, pausing a few times to embrace along the way. I even tried being wary again, but we seemed to be the only people in the lot. Her car was a neat little red Porsche convertible with the top down.

"Here we are. You care to drive?" she asked.

"No, you do it and I'll watch for headless horsemen."

"What?"

"It's a lovely night, and I've always wanted a chauffeur who looked exactly like you."

We got in and she drove. Fast, of course. It just seemed to follow. The roads were deserted and a feeling of exhilaration swept over me. I raised one hand and summoned a lighted cigar from Shadow. I took a few puffs and tossed it away as we roared over a bridge. I regarded the constellations, which had grown familiar to me these past eight years. I drew a deep breath and let it out slowly. I tried to analyze my feelings and realized that I was happy. I hadn't felt that way in a long while.

A mess of light occurred beyond a fringe of trees up ahead. A minute later we rounded a curve and I saw that it came from a small apartment complex off to the right. She slowed and turned there when we reached it.

She parked in a numbered slot, from whence we made our way along a shrub-lined walk to the building's entrance. She let us in and we crossed the lobby to the elevators. The ride up was over too soon, and once we reached her apartment she really did make coffee.

Which was fine with me. It was good coffee, and we sat together and sipped it. Plenty of time . . .

One thing finally did lead to another. We found ourselves in the bedroom a bit later, our clothes on a nearby chair, and I was congratulating myself that the meeting for which I had returned had not come off. She was smooth and soft and warm, and there was just enough of her in all the right places. A vise in velvet, with honey . . . the scent of her perfume . . .

We lay there, much later, in that peaceful state of temporary fatigue on which I will not waste metaphors. I was stroking her hair when she stretched, turned her head slightly, and regarded me through half-lidded eyes.

"Tell me something," she said.

"Sure."

"What was your mother's name?"

I felt as if something prickly had just been rolled along my spine. But I wanted to see where this was leading. "Dara," I told her.

"And your father?"

"Corwin."

She smiled.

"I thought so," she said, "but I had to be sure."

"Do I get some questions now? Or can only one play?"

"I'll save you the trouble. You want to know why I asked."

"You're on the ball."

"Sorry," she said, moving her leg.

"I take it their names mean something to you?"

"You are Merlin," she stated, "Duke of Kolvir and Prince of Chaos."

"Damn!" I observed. "It seems everybody in this shadow knows who I am! Do you all belong to a club or something?"

"Who else knows?" she asked quickly, her eyes suddenly wide.

"A fellow named Luke Raynard, a dead man named Dan Martinez, and a local man named George Hansen, probably—and another dead man named Victor Melman . . . Why? These name ring any bells?"

"Yes, the dangerous one is Luke Raynard. I brought you here to warn you about him, if you were the right one."

"What do you mean 'the right one'?"

"If you were who you are—the son of Dara."

"So warn me."

"I just did. Don't trust him."

I sat up and propped a pillow behind me.

"What's he after? My stamp collection? My traveler's checks? Could you be a little more specific?"

"He tried several times to kill you, years ago—"

"What? How?"

"The first time it involved a truck that almost ran you down. Then the next year—"

"Gods! You really do know! Give me the dates, the dates he tried it."

"April 30, always April 30."

"Why? Do you know why?"

"No."

"Shit. How do you know all of this?"

"I was around. I was watching."

"Why didn't you do something about it?"

"I couldn't. I didn't know which of you was which."

"Lady, you've lost me completely. Who the hell are you, and what's your part in this?"

"Like Luke, I am not what I seem," she began.

There came a sharp buzzing sound from the next room.

"Oh my!" she said and sprang out of bed.

I followed her, arriving in the foyer as she pushed a button beside a small grating and said, "Hello?"

"Honey, it's me," came the reply. "I got home a day early. Buzz me in, will you? I'm carrying a bunch of packages."

Oh-oh.

She released the one button and pushed another, turning toward me as she did so.

"The husband," she said, suddenly breathless. "You've got to leave now. Please! Take the steps!"

"But you haven't told me anything yet!"

"I've told you enough. Please don't make trouble!"

"Okay," I said, hurrying back to the bedroom, pulling on my pants and slipping my feet into my loafers.

I stuffed my socks and underwear into my hip pockets and drew on my shirt.

"I'm not satisfied," I said. "You know more and I want it."

"Is that all you want?"

I kissed her cheek quickly.

"Not really. I'll be back," I said.

"Don't," she told me. "It won't be the same. We shall meet again, when the time is right."

I headed for the door.

"That's not good enough," I said as I opened it.

"It will have to be."

"We'll see."

I tore off up the hall and pushed open the door beneath the EXIT sign. I buttoned my shirt and tucked it in on my way down the steps. I paused at the bottom to draw on my socks. I ran a hand through my hair then and opened the door to the lobby.

No one in sight. Good.

As I left the building and headed down the walk a black sedan pulled up in front of me and I heard the hum of a power window and saw a flash of red.

"Get in, Merlin," came a familiar voice.

"Fiona!"

I opened the door and slid inside. We began moving immediately.

"Well, was she?" she asked me.

"Was she what?" I said.

"The one you went to the club to meet."

I hadn't thought of it that way until she said it.

"You know," I said a little later. "I think maybe she was."

She turned onto the road and drove back in the direction from which we had come earlier.

"What kind of game was she playing?" Fiona asked.

"I'd give a lot to know," I answered.

"Tell me about it," she said, "and feel free to edit certain portions."

"Well, all right," I said, and I let her have it.

We were back in the country club parking lot before I was finished.

"Why are we here again?" I asked.

"This is where I got the car. It might belong to a friend of Bill's. I thought I'd be nice and bring it back."

"You used the Trump I'd made to go through to the bar in there?" I asked, gesturing.

"Yes, right after you went in to dance. I watched you for about an hour, mostly from the terrace. And I'd told you to be wary."

"Sorry, I was smitten."

"I'd forgotten they don't serve absinthe here. I had to make do with a frozen marguerita."

"Sorry about that, too. Then you hot-wired a car and followed us when we left?"

"Yes. I waited in her parking lot and maintained the most peripheral of touches with you via your Trump. If I'd felt danger I would have come in after you."

"Thanks. How peripheral?"

"I am not a voyeur, if that's what you mean. Very well, we're up to date."

"There's a lot more to the story than this last part."

"Keep it," she said, "for now. There is only one thing I am curious about at the moment. Would you happen to have a picture of this Luke Raynard?"

"I might," I told her, reaching for my wallet. "Yes, I think I do."

I withdrew my shorts from my hip pocket and explored further.

"At least you don't wear jockeys," she remarked.

I withdrew my wallet and turned on the overhead light. As I flipped the wallet open she leaned toward me, resting her hand on my arm. Finally, I found a clear colored photo of Luke and me at the beach, with Julia and a girl named Gail whom Luke used to date.

I felt her grip tighten as she drew in a short, sharp breath.

"What is it?" I asked. "You know him?"

She shook her head too quickly.

"No. No," she said. "Never saw him before in my life."

"You're a lousy liar, Auntie. Who is it?"

"I don't know," she said.

"Come on! You nearly broke my arm when you saw him."

"Don't push me," she said.

"It involves my life."

"It involves more than your life, I think."

"So?"

"Let it be, for now."

"I'm afraid I can't do that. I must insist."

She turned more fully and both of her hands came up between us. Smoke began to rise from her well-manicured fingertips. Frakir throbbed upon my wrist, which meant she was sufficiently pissed off to lean on me if it came to that.

I made a warding gesture and decided to back off.

"Okay, let's call it a day and head home."

She flexed her fingers and the smoke fled. Frakir became still. She withdrew a packet of Trumps from her purse and shuffled out the one for Amber.

"But sooner or later I'm going to have to know," I added.

"Later," she said, as the vision of Amber grew before us.

One thing I always liked about Fiona: she didn't believe in hiding her feelings.

I reached up and switched off the dome light as Amber came on all around us.

8

I guess that my thoughts at funerals are typical. Like Bloom in *Ulysses,* I usually think the most mundane things about the deceased and the current goings-on. The rest of the time my mind wanders.

On the wide strand of shoreline at the southern foot of Kolvir there is a small chapel dedicated to the Unicorn, one of several such throughout the realm at places where she had been sighted. This one seemed most appropriate for Caine's service in that—like Gérard—he had once expressed a desire to be laid to rest in one of the sea caves at the mountain's foot, facing the waters he had sailed so long, so often. One such had been prepared for him, and there would be a procession after the service to inter him there. It was a windy, misty, sea-cool morning with only a few sails in sight, moving to or from the port over half a league westward of us.

Technically, I suppose Random should have officiated, since his kingship automatically made him high priest, but aside from reading an opening and closing passage on the Passing of Princes from the Book of the Unicorn, he turned the service over to Gérard to perform in his stead, as Caine had gotten along with Gérard better than with anyone else in the family. So Gérard's booming voice filled the small stone building, reading long sections involving the sea and mutability. It was said that Dworkin himself had penned the Book in his saner days, and that long passages had come direct from the Unicorn. I don't know. I wasn't there. It is also said that we are descended of Dworkin and the Unicorn, which gives rise to some unusual mental images. Origins of anything tend to fade off into myth, though. Who knows? I wasn't around then.

". . . And all things return to the sea," Gérard was saying. I looked about me. Besides the family, there were perhaps forty or fifty people present, mostly nobility from the town, a few merchants with whom Caine had been friendly, representatives of realms in several adjacent shadows where Caine had spent time on both official and personal business, and of course Vinta Bayle. Bill had expressed a desire to be present, and he stood to my left. Martin was at my right. Neither Fiona nor Bleys was present. Bleys had pleaded his injury and excused himself from the service. Fiona had simply vanished. Random had been unable to locate her this morning. Julian departed partway through the service, to check on the guard he had posted along the strand, someone having pointed out that a would-be assassin could rack up a high score with that many of us together in one small space. Consequently, Julian's foresters, with short sword, dagger, and longbow or lance, were spotted strategically all over the place— and every now and then we'd hear the baying of one of his hellhounds, to be answered almost immediately by several others, a mournful, unnerving thing, counter-pointing waves, wind, and reflections upon mortality. Where had she gotten off to? I wondered. Fiona? Fear of a trap? Or something to do with last night? And Benedict . . . he had sent regrets and regards, mentioning sudden business that precluded his making it back in time. Llewella simply hadn't shown, and could not be reached by Trump. Flora stood ahead and to the left of me, knowing she looked lovely in dark colors, too. Perhaps I do her an injustice. I don't know. But she seemed more fidgety than contemplative.

At the conclusion of the service we filed out, four seamen bearing Caine's casket, and we formed up into a procession that would lead to the cave and his sarcophagus. A number of Julian's troops came up to pace us as an armed escort.

As we walked along, Bill nudged me and gestured upward with his head, toward Kolvir. I looked in that direction and beheld a black-cloaked and cowled figure standing upon a ledge in the shadow of a rocky projection. Bill leaned close so that I could hear him above the sound of the pipes and strings that were now playing.

"Is that one some part of the ceremony?" he asked.

"Not that I know of," I answered.

I broke out of line and moved forward. In another minute or so we would pass directly beneath the figure.

I caught up with Random and put my hand on his shoulder. When he looked back I pointed upward. He halted and stared, squinting.

His right hand rose to his breast, where he wore the Jewel of Judgment, as on most state occasions. Instantly, the winds rose.

"Halt!" Random called out. "Stop the procession! Everyone stay where you are!"

The figure moved then, slightly, head turning as if to stare at Random. In the sky, as if by trick photography, a cloud blew itself together, growing, above Kolvir. A red, pulsing glow emerged from beneath Random's hand.

Suddenly, the figure looked upward and a hand flashed beneath the cloak, emerging moments later to perform a quick casting movement. A tiny black object hung in the air, then began its descent.

"Everybody down!" Gérard called out.

Random did not move as the others of us dropped. He remained standing, watching, as lightning emerged from the cloud and played across the face of the cliff.

The thunder that followed coincided almost exactly with the explosion that occurred high overhead. The distance had been too great. The bomb had gone off before it reached us—though it would probably have scored had we continued as we were, to pass beneath the ledge and have it dropped directly upon us. When the spots stopped dancing before my eyes, I regarded the cliff again. The dark figure was gone.

"Did you get him?" I asked Random.

He shrugged as he lowered his hand. The jewel had ceased its pulsing.

"Everybody on your feet!" he called out. "Let's get on with this funeral!"

And we did. There were no more incidents, and the business was concluded as planned.

My thoughts, and probably everyone else's, were already playing family games as the box was being fitted into the vault. Might the attacker have been one of our absent kin? And if so, which one? What motives might each of them possess for the act? Where were they now? And what were their alibis? Could there have been a coalition involved? Or could it have been an outsider? If so, how was access obtained to the local supply of explosives? Or was this imported stuff? Or had someone local come up with the proper formula? If it were an outsider, what was the motive and where was the person from? Had one of us imported an assassin? Why?

As we filed past the vault I did think fleetingly of Caine, but more as part of the puzzle picture than as an individual. I had not known him all that well. But then, several of the others had told me early on that he was not the easiest person to get to know. He was tough and cynical and had a streak of cruelty in his nature. He had made quite a few enemies over the years and seemed even to be proud of this fact. He had always been decent enough with me, but then we'd never been at cross-purposes over anything. So my feelings did not run as deep for him as they did for most of the others. Julian was another of this cut, but more polished on the surface. And no one could be certain what lay beneath that surface on any given day. Caine . . . I wish I'd gotten to know you better. I am certain that I am diminished by your passing in ways that I do not even understand.

Departing, afterward, heading back to the palace for food and drink, I wondered, not for the first time, how my problems and everyone else's were connected. For I felt they were. I don't mind small coincidences, but I don't trust big ones.

And Meg Devlin? Did she know something of this business, too? It seemed possible that she might. Husband or no husband, I decided, we had a date. Soon.

Later, in the big dining hall, amid the buzz of conversation and the rattle of cutlery and crockery, one vague possibility occurred to me and I resolved to pursue it immediately. Excusing myself from the cold but attractive company of Vinta Bayle, third daughter of some minor nobility and apparently Caine's last mistress, I made my way to the far end of the hall and the small knot of people surrounding Random. I was standing there for several minutes, wondering how to break in, when he spotted me. He excused himself from the others immediately, advanced upon me, and caught hold of my sleeve.

"Merlin," he said, "I don't have time now, but I just wanted to let you know that I don't consider our conversation concluded. I want to get together with you again later this afternoon or this evening—as soon as I'm free. So don't go running off anywhere till we've talked, okay?"

I nodded.

"One quick question," I said, as he began turning back toward the others.

"Shoot," he said.

"Are there any Amberites currently in residence on the shadow Earth I just departed—agents of any sort?"

He shook his head.

"I don't have any, and I don't believe any of the others do just now. I have a number of contacts there in different places, but they're all natives—like Bill."

His eyes narrowed. "Something new come up?" he asked then.

I nodded again.

"Serious?"

"Possibly."

"I wish I had the time to hear it, but it'll just have to keep till we talk later."

"I understand."

"I'll send for you," he said, and he returned to his companions.

That shot down the only explanation I could think of for Meg Devlin. It also foreclosed the possibility of my taking off to see her as soon as I could leave the gathering.

I consoled myself with another plate of food. After a time, Flora entered the hall, studied all the knots of humanity, then made her way among them to settle beside me on the window seat.

"No way of talking to Random right now without an audience," she said.

"You're right," I replied. "May I get you something to eat or drink?"

"Not now. Maybe you can help. You're a sorcerer."

I didn't like that opening, but I asked, "What's the problem?"

"I went to Bleys' rooms, to see whether he wanted to come down and join us. He's gone."

"Wasn't his door locked? Most people do that around here."

"Yes, from the inside. So he must have trumped out. I broke in when he didn't answer, since there'd been one attempt on his life already."

"And what would you want of a sorcerer?"

"Can you trace him?"

"Trumps don't leave tracks," I said. "But even if I could, I'm not so sure that I would. He knows what he's doing, and he obviously wants to be left alone."

"But what if he's involved? He and Caine had been on opposite sides in the past."

"If he's mixed up in something dangerous to the rest of us you should be happy to see him go."

"So you can't help—or won't?"

I nodded. "Both, I guess. Any decision to seek him out should really come from Random, don't you think?"

"Maybe."

"I'd suggest keeping it to yourself till you can talk to Random. No use stirring up fruitless speculations among the others. Or I'll tell him, if you'd like. I'm going to be talking with him a bit later."

"What about?"

Ouch.

"Not sure," I said. "It's something he wants to tell me, or ask me."

She studied me carefully.

"We haven't really had our own little talk yet," she said then.

"Looks like we're having it now."

"Okay. May I hear about your problems in one of my favorite shadows?"

"Why not?" I said, and I launched into a synopsis of the damned thing again. I felt that this would be the final time, though. Once Flora knew it I was confident it would make the rounds.

She had no information bearing upon my case that she cared to share. We chatted for a while then—local gossip—and she finally decided to get something to eat. She departed in the direction of the food and did not return.

I talked with a few of the others, too—about Caine, about my father. I did not hear anything that I did not already know. I was introduced to a number of people I had not met before. I memorized a mess of names and relationships since I had nothing better to do.

When things finally broke up, I kept an eye on Random and contrived to depart at about the same time he did.

"Later," he said as we passed, and he went off with a couple of guys he'd been talking with.

So I went back to my rooms and stretched out on the bed. When things are brewing you take your rest whenever you can.

After a time I slept, and I dreamed . . .

I was walking in the formal garden behind the palace. Someone else was with me, but I did not know who it was. This did not seem to matter. I heard a familiar howling. Suddenly, there were growling noises near at hand. The first time I looked about I saw nothing. But then, abruptly, they were there—three huge, doglike creatures similar to the one I had slain in Julia's apartment. They were racing toward me across the garden. The howling continued, but they were not its authors. They restricted themselves to growl-

ing and slavering as they came on. Just as suddenly, I realized that
this was a dream and that I had dreamt it several times before only
to lose track of it upon awakening. The knowledge that it was a
dream, however, in no way detracted from the feeling of menace
as they rushed toward me. All three of them were surrounded by a
kind of light—pale, distorting. Looking past them, through their
haloes, I did not see the garden but caught glimpses of a forest.
When they drew near and sprang to attack it was as if they had encountered a glass wall. They fell back, rose and dashed toward me
once more only to be blocked again. They leaped and growled and
whined and tried again. It was as if I stood beneath a bell jar or
within a magic circle, though. They could not get at me. Then the
howling came louder, came nearer and they turned their attention
away from me.

"Wow!" Random said. "I should charge you something for
pulling you out of a nightmare."

. . . And I was awake and lying on my bed and there was darkness beyond my window—and I realized that Random had called
me via my Trump and tuned in on my dream when he'd made
contact.

I yawned and thought him my answer, *Thanks*.

"Finish waking up and let's have our talk," he said.

"Yes. Where are you?"

"Downstairs. The little sitting room off the main hall to the
south. Drinking coffee. We've got it to ourselves."

"See you in five."

"Check."

Random faded. I sat up, swung my feet over the side of the
bed, and rose. I crossed the room to the window and flung it wide.
I inhaled the crisp evening air of autumn. Spring on the shadow
Earth, fall here in Amber—my two favorite seasons. I should be
heartened, uplifted. Instead—a trick of the night, the tag-end of
the dream—it seemed for a moment that I heard the final note of
the howling. I shuddered and closed the window. Our dreams are
too much with us.

I hiked down to the designated room and took a seat on one of
its sofas. Random let me get through half a cup of coffee before he
said, "Tell me about the Ghostwheel."

"It's a kind of—paraphysical surveillance device and library."

Random put down his cup and cocked his head to one side.

"Could you be more specific?" he said.

"Well, my work with computers led me to speculate that basic data-processing principles could be employed with interesting results in a place where computer mechanics themselves would not operate," I began. "In other words, I had to locate a shadow environment where the operations would remain pretty much invariant but where the physical construct, all of the peripherals, the programming techniques and the energy inputs would be of a different nature."

"Uh, Merlin," Random said. "You've lost me already."

"I designed and built a piece of data-processing equipment in a shadow where no ordinary computer could function," I replied, "because I used different materials, a radically different design, a different power source. I also chose a place where different physical laws apply, so that it could operate along different lines. I was then able to write programs for it which would not have operated on the shadow Earth where I'd been living. In doing so, I believe that I created an unique artifact. I called it the Ghostwheel because of certain aspects of its appearance."

"And it's a surveillance device and a library? What do you mean by that?"

"It riffles through Shadow like the pages of a book—or a deck of cards," I said. "Program it for whatever you want checked out and it will keep an eye on it for you. I was planning it as a surprise. You could, say, use it to determine whether any of our potential enemies are mobilizing, or to follow the progress of Shadowstorms, or—"

"Wait a minute," he said, raising a hand. "How? How does it flip through shadows that way? What makes it work?"

"In effect," I explained, "it creates the equivalent of multitudes of Trumps in an instant, then—"

"Stop. Back up. How can you write a program for the creation of Trumps? I thought they could only be done by a person who had an initiate of either the Pattern or the Logrus."

"But in this case," I said, "the machine itself is of that same class of magical objects as Dad's blade, Grayswandir. I incorporated elements of the Pattern itself into its design."

"And you were going to surprise us with this?"

"Yes, once it's ready."

"When will that be?"

"I'm not sure. It had to gather certain critical amounts of data before its programs could become fully operational. I set it to do that a while back, and I haven't had a chance to check on it recently."

Random poured some more coffee, took a drink.

"I don't see where it would save that much in the way of time and effort," he said a little later. "Say I'm curious about something in Shadow. I go and investigate, or I send someone. Now, say that instead I want to use this thing to check it out. I still have to spend the time going to the place where you keep it."

"No," I told him. "You summon a remote terminal."

"Summon? A terminal?"

"Right."

I unearthed my Amber Trumps and dealt myself the one off the bottom. It showed a silver wheel against a dark background. I passed it to Random and he studied it.

"How do you use it?" he asked.

"Same as the others. You want to call it to you?"

"You do it," he said. "I want to watch."

"Very well," I answered. "But while I've set it to gathering data across the shadows it still won't know a whole lot that's useful at this point."

"I don't want to question it so much as I want to see it."

I raised the card and stared, seeing through it with my mind's eye. After a few moments, there was contact. I called it to me.

There followed a small crackling sound and a feeling of ionization in the air as a glowing wheel about eight feet in diameter materialized before me.

"Diminish terminal size," I ordered.

It shrank down to about a third of what it had been and I ordered it to halt at that point. It looked like a pale picture frame, occasional sparks dancing within it, the view across the room constantly rippling as seen through its center.

Random began to extend a hand.

"Don't," I said. "You might get a shock. I still don't have all the bugs out."

"It can transmit energy?"

"Well, it could. No big deal."

"If you ordered it to transmit energy . . . ?"

"Oh, sure. It has to be able to transmit energy here to sustain the terminal, and through Shadow to operate its scanners."

"I mean, could it discharge it at this end?"

"If I told it to it could build up a charge and let it go. Yes."

"What are its limits in this?"

"Whatever it has available."

"And what does it have available?"

"Well, in theory an entire planet. But—"

"Supposing you ordered it to appear beside someone here, build up a large charge and discharge it into that person. Could it do an electrocution?"

"I guess so," I said. "I don't see why not. But that's not its purpose—"

"Merlin, your surprise is certainly a surprise. But I'm not sure I like it."

"It's safe," I explained. "No one knows where it's located. No one goes there. This Trump I have is the only one. Nobody else can reach it. I was going to make one more card, just for you, and then show you how to operate the thing when it was ready."

"I'm going to have to think about this . . ."

"Ghost, within five thousand Shadow veils, this location— how many Shadow-storms are currently in existence?"

The words came as if spoken within the hoop: "Seventeen."

"Sounds like—"

"I gave it my voice," I told him. "Ghost, give us some pictures of the biggest one."

A scene of chaotic fury filled the hoop.

"Another thought just occurred to me," Random stated. "Can it transport things?"

"Sure, just like a regular Trump."

"Was the original size of that circle its maximum size?"

"No, we could make it a lot larger if you wanted. Or smaller."

"I don't. But supposing you made it larger—and then told it to transmit that storm, or as much of it as it could manage?"

"Wow! I don't know. It would try. It would probably be like opening a giant window onto it."

"Merlin, shut it down. It's dangerous."

"Like I said, nobody knows where it is but me, and the only other way to reach it is—"

"I know, I know. Tell me, could anybody access it with the proper Trump, or just by finding it?"

"Well, yes. I didn't bother with any security codes because of its inaccessibility."

"That thing could be an awesome weapon, kid. Shut it down. Now."

"I can't."

"What do you mean?"

"You can't dump its memory or kill its power from a remote terminal. I would actually have to travel to the site itself to do that."

"Then I suggest you get going. I want it turned off until there are a lot more safeguards built into it. Even then—well, we'll see. I don't trust a power like that. Not when I don't have any defenses against it. It could strike almost without warning. What were you thinking of when you built that thing?"

"Data-processing. Look, we're the only ones—"

"There's always a possibility someone will get wise to it and find a way to get at it. I know, I know—you're in love with your handiwork—and I appreciate what you had in mind. But it's got to go."

"I have done nothing to offend you." It was my voice, but it came from the wheel.

Random stared at it, looked at me, looked back at it.

"Uh—that's not the point," he addressed it. "It's your potential that I'm concerned about."

"Merlin, turn off the terminal!"

"End transmission," I said. "Withdraw terminal."

It wavered a moment, then was gone.

"Had you anticipated that comment from the thing?" Random asked me.

"No. I was surprised."

"I'm beginning to dislike surprises. Maybe that shadow environment is actually altering the thing in subtle ways. You know my wishes. Give it a rest."

I bowed my head. "Whatever you say, sir."

"Cut it out. Don't be a martyr. Just do it."

"I still think it's just a matter of installing a few safeguards. No reason to crash the whole project."

"If things were quieter," he said, "maybe I'd go along with it. But there's too much shit coming down right now, with snipers and bombers and all the things you've been telling me about. I don't need another worry."

I got to my feet. "Okay. Thanks for the coffee," I said. "I'll let you know when it's done."

He nodded. "Good night, Merlin."

"Good night."

As I was stalking out through the big entrance hall I saw Julian, in a green dressing gown, talking with two of his men. On the floor between them lay a large dead animal. I halted and stared. It was one of those same damned dog things I had just dreamed about, like at Julia's.

I approached. "Hi, Julian. What is it?" I asked gesturing.

He shook his head. "Don't know. But the hellhounds just killed three of them in Arden. I trumped these guys up with one of the carcasses, to show Random. You wouldn't know where he is, would you?"

I stabbed with my thumb back over my shoulder. "In the sitting room."

He walked off in that direction. I went nearer and prodded the animal with my toe. Should I go back and tell Random I'd met one before?

The hell with it, I decided. I couldn't see how the information would be of any vital use.

I returned to my rooms and washed up and changed my clothes. Then I stopped by the kitchen and filled my backpack with food. I didn't feel like saying good-bye to anyone, so I just headed for the back and took the big rear staircase down into the gardens.

Dark. Starry. Cool. Walking, I felt a sudden chill as I neared the spot where, in my dream, the dogs had appeared.

No howls, no growls. Nothing. I passed through that area and continued on my way to the rear of that well-kept site, to the place where a number of trails led off through a more natural landscape. I took the second one from the left. It was a slightly longer route than another I might have chosen—with which it intersected later, anyway—but was easier going, a thing I felt I needed in the night. I was still not all that familiar with the irregularities of the other way.

I hiked the crest of Kolvir for the better part of an hour before I located the downward trail I was seeking. I halted then, took a drink of water and rested for a few minutes before I began the descent.

It is very difficult to walk in Shadow on Kolvir. One has to put some distance between oneself and Amber in order to do it properly. So all I could do at this point was hike—which was fine with me, because it was a good night for walking.

I was well on my way down before a glow occurred overhead and the moon crested a shoulder of Kolvir and poured its light upon my twisting trail. I increased my pace somewhat after that. I did want to make it off the mountain by morning.

I was angry with Random for not giving me a chance to justify my work. I hadn't really been ready to tell him about it. If it hadn't been for Caine's funeral I would not have returned to Amber until I'd had the thing perfected. And I wasn't even going to mention Ghostwheel this time around, except that it had figured in a small way in the mystery that had engulfed me and Random had wanted to know about it in order to have the whole story. Okay. He didn't like what he'd seen, but the preview had been premature. Now, if I shut it down as I'd been ordered I would ruin a lot of work that had been in progress for some time now. Ghostwheel was still in a Shadow-scanning, self-education phase. I would have been checking on it about now, anyway, to see how it was coming along and to correct any obvious flaws that had crept into the system.

I thought about it as the trail grew steeper and curved on Kolvir's western face. Random had not exactly ordered me to dump everything it had accumulated thus far. He'd simply told me to shut it down. Viewed the way I chose to view it, that meant I could exercise my own judgment as to means. I decided that gave me lee-way to check everything out first, reviewing systems functions and revising programs until I was satisfied that everything was in order. Then I could transfer everything to a more permanent status be fore shutting it down. Then nothing would be lost; its memory would be intact when the time came to restore its functions again.

Maybe . . .

What if I did everything to make it shipshape, including throwing in a few—as I saw it—unnecessary safeguards to make Random happy? Then, I mused, supposing I got in touch with Random, showed him what I'd done, and asked him whether he was happy with it that way? If he weren't, I could always shut it down then. But perhaps he'd reconsider. Worth thinking about . . .

I played over imaginary conversations with Random until the moon had drifted off to my left. I was more than halfway down Kolvir by then and the going was becoming progressively easier. I could already feel the force of the Pattern as somewhat diminished.

I halted a couple of more times on the way down, for water and once for a sandwich. The more I thought about it, the more I felt that Random would just get angry if I proceeded along the lines I had been thinking and probably wouldn't even give me a full hearing. On the other hand, I was angry myself.

But it was a long journey with few shortcuts. I'd have plenty of time to mull it over.

The sky was growing lighter when I crossed the last rocky slope to reach the wide trail at the foot of Kolvir to the northwest. I regarded a stand of trees across the way, one large one a familiar landmark—

With a dazzling flash that seemed to sizzle and a bomblike

report of thunder the tree was split, not a hundred meters away. I'd flung up both hands at the lightning stroke, but I could still hear cracking wood and the echo of the blast for several seconds afterward.

Then a voice cried out, "Go back!"

I assumed I was the subject of this conversational gambit. "May we talk this over?" I responded.

There was no reply.

I stretched out in a shallow declivity beside the trail, then crawled along it for several body lengths to a place where the cover was better. I was listening and watching the while, hoping that whoever had pulled that stunt would betray his position in some fashion.

Nothing happened, but for the next half minute I surveyed the grove and a portion of the slope down which I had come. From that angle their proximity gave me a small inspiration.

I summoned the image of the Logrus, and two of its lines became my arms. I reached then, not through Shadow but up the slope to where a fairly good-sized rock was poised above a mass of others.

Seizing hold, I drew upon it. It was too heavy to topple easily, so I began rocking it. Slowly, at first. Finally, I got it to the tipping point and it tumbled. It fell among the others and a small cascade began. I withdrew further as they struck and sent new ones bouncing. Several big ones began to roll. A fracture line gave way when they fell upon its edge at a steeper place. An entire sheet of stone groaned and cracked, began to slide.

I could feel the vibration as I continued my withdrawal. I had not anticipated setting off anything this spectacular. The rocks bounced, slid and flew into the grove. I watched the trees sway, saw some of them go down. I heard the crunching, the pinging, the breaking.

I gave it an extra half minute after what seemed its end. There was much dust in the air and half of the grove was down. Then I rose to my feet, Frakir dangling from my left hand, and I advanced upon the grove.

I searched carefully, but there was no one there. I climbed upon the trunk of a fallen tree.

"I repeat, do you care to talk about it?" I called out.

No answer.

"Okay, be that way," I said, and I headed north into Arden.

* * *

I heard the sound of horses occasionally as I hiked through that ancient forest. If I was being followed, though, the horsemen showed no interest in closing with me. Most likely, I was passing in the vicinity of one of Julian's patrols.

Not that it mattered. I soon located a trail and began the small adjustments that bore me farther and farther from them.

A lighter shade, from brown to yellow, and slightly shorter trees . . . Fewer breaks in the leafy canopy . . . Odd bird note, strange mushroom . . .

Little by little, the character of the wood was altered. And the shifting grew easier and easier the farther this took me from Amber.

I began to pass sunny clearings. The sky grew a paler blue . . . The trees were all green now, but most of them saplings . . .

I broke into a jog.

Masses of clouds came into view, the spongy earth grew firmer, drier . . .

I stepped up my pace, heading downhill. Grasses were more abundant. The trees were divided into clusters now, islands in a waving sea of those pale grasses. My view took in a greater distance. A flapping, beaded curtain off to my right: rain.

Rumbles of thunder came to me, though sunlight continued to light my way. I breathed deeply of the clean damp air and ran on.

The grasses fell away, ground fissured, sky blackened . . . Waters rushed through canyons and arroyos all about me . . . Torrents poured from overhead onto the rocking terrain . . .

I began slipping. I cursed each time I picked myself up, for my overeagerness in the shifting.

The clouds parted like a theater curtain, to where a lemon sun poured warmth and light from a salmon-colored sky. The thunder halted in mid-rumble and a wind rose . . .

I made my way up a hillside, looked down upon a ruined village. Long-abandoned, partly overgrown, strange mounds lined its broken main street.

I passed through it beneath a slate-colored sky, picked my way slowly across an icy pond, faces of those frozen beneath me staring sightlessly in all directions . . .

The sky was soot-streaked, the snow hard-packed, my breath feathery as I entered the skeletal wood where frozen birds perched: an etching.

Slipping downhill, rolling, sliding into melting and spring . . .

Movement again, about me . . . Mucky ground and clumps of green . . . Strange cars on distant highway . . .

A junkyard, smelling, oozing, rusting, smoldering . . . Threading my way amid acres of heaps . . . Rats scurrying . . .

Away . . . Shifting faster, breathing harder . . . Skyline beneath smog cap . . . Delta bottom . . . Seashore . . . Golden pylons along the road . . . Countryside with lakes . . . Brown grasses beneath green sky . . .

Slowing . . . Rolling grassland, river and lake . . . Slowing . . . Breeze and grass, sealike . . . Mopping my brow on my sleeve . . . Sucking air . . . Walking now . . .

I moved through the field at a normal pace, preferring to do my resting in a congenial spot such as this, where I could see for a good distance. The wind made soft noises as it passed among the grasses. The nearest lake was a deep lime color. Something in the air smelled sweet.

I thought I saw a brief flash of light off to my right, but when I looked that way there was nothing unusual to be seen. A little later, I was certain that I heard a distant sound of hoofbeats. But again, I saw nothing. That's the trouble with shadows—you don't always know what's natural there; you're never certain what to look for.

Several minutes passed, and then I smelled it before I saw anything.

Smoke.

The next instant there was a rush of fire. A long line of flame cut across my path.

And again the voice: "I told you to go back!"

The wind was behind the fire, pushing it toward me. I turned to head away and saw that it was already flanking me. It takes a while to build up the proper mental set for shadow-shifting, and I had let mine go. I doubted I could set it up again in time.

I began running.

The line of flame was curving about me, as if to describe a huge circle. I did not pause to admire the precision of the thing, however, as I could feel the heat by then and the smoke was getting thicker.

Above the fire's crackling it seemed that I could still hear the drumming of hoofs. My eyes were beginning to water, though, and streams of smoke further diminished my vision. And again, I detected no sign of the person who had sprung the trap.

Yet—definitely—the ground was shaking with the rapid progress of a hooved creature headed in my direction. The flames flashed higher, drew nearer as the circle rushed toward closure.

I was wondering what new menace was approaching, when a horse and rider burst into view through the gap in the fiery wall. The rider drew back the reins, but the horse—a chestnut—was not too happy at the nearness of the flames. It bared its teeth, biting at the bit, and tried several times to rear.

"Hurry! Behind me!" the rider cried, and I rushed to mount.

The rider was a dark-haired woman. I caught only a glimpse of her features. She managed to turn the horse back in the direction from which she had come, and she shook the reins. The chestnut started forward, and suddenly it reared. I managed to hang on.

When its front hooves struck the ground, the beast wheeled and tore off toward the light. It was almost into the flames when it wheeled again.

"Damn!" I heard the rider say, as she worked almost frantically with the reins.

The horse turned again, neighing loudly. Bloody spittle dripped from its mouth. And by then the circle was closed, the smoke was heavy and the flames very near. I was in no position to help, beyond giving it a pair of sharp kicks in the flanks when it began moving in a straight line again.

It plunged into the flames to our left, almost screaming as it went. I had no idea how wide the band of fire was at that point. I could feel a searing along my legs, though, and I smelled burning hair.

Then the beast was rearing again, the rider was screaming back at it, and I found that I could no longer hold on. I felt myself sliding backward just as we broke through the ring of fire and into a charred, smoldering area where the flames had already passed. I fell amid hot black clumps; ashes rose about me. I rolled frantically to my left, and I coughed and squeezed my eyes shut against the cloud of ashes that assailed my face.

I heard the woman scream and I scrambled to my feet, rubbing my eyes. My vision came clear in time for me to see the chestnut rising from where he had apparently fallen atop his rider. The horse immediately tore off, to be lost among clouds of smoke. The woman lay very still and I rushed to her side. Kneeling, I brushed sparks from her clothing and checked for breathing and a pulse. Her eyes opened while I was doing this.

"Back's—broken—I think," she said, coughing. "Don't feel—much. . . . Escape—if you can. . . . Leave me. I'll die—anyway."

"No way," I said. "But I've got to move you. There's a lake nearby, if I remember right."

I removed my cloak from where it was tied about my waist and I spread it out beside her. I inched her onto it as carefully as I could, folded it over her to protect her against the flames and began dragging her in what I hoped was the proper direction.

We made it through a shifting patchwork of fire and smoke. My throat was raw, my eyes watering steadily and my trousers on fire when I took a big step backward and felt my heel squish downward into mud. I kept going.

Finally, I was waist deep in the water and supporting her there. I leaned forward, pushed a flap of the cloak back from her face. Her eyes were still open, but they looked unfocused and there was no movement. Before I could feel for a carotid pulse, however, she made a hissing noise, then she spoke my name.

"Merlin," she said hoarsely, "I'm—sorry—"

"You helped me and I couldn't help you," I said. "*I'm* sorry."

"Sorry—I didn't last—longer," she continued. "No good—with horses. They're—following you."

"Who?" I asked.

"Called off—the dogs, though. But the—fire—is—someone—else's. Don't know—whose."

"I don't know what you're talking about."

I splashed a little water onto her cheeks to cool them. Between the soot and her singed, disheveled hair it was difficult to judge her appearance.

"Someone—behind—you," she said, her voice growing fainter. "Someone—ahead—too. Didn't know—about—that one. Sorry."

"Who?" I asked again. "And who are you? How do you know me? Why—"

She smiled faintly. ". . . Sleep with you. Can't now. Going . . ."

Her eyes closed.

"No!" I cried.

Her face contorted and she sucked in a final breath. She expelled it then, using it to form the whispered words, "Just—let me—sink here. G'bye . . ."

A cloud of smoke blew across her face. I held my breath and shut my eyes as a larger billow followed, engulfing us.

When the air finally cleared again, I studied her. Her breathing had ceased and there was no pulse, no heartbeat. There was no nonburning, nonmarshy area available for even an attempt at CPR. She was gone. She'd known she was going.

I wrapped my cloak about her carefully, turning it into a shroud. Last of all, I folded a flap over her face. I fixed everything into place with the clasp I'd used to close it at my neck when I'd worn it. Then I waded out into deeper water. "Just let me sink here." Sometimes the dead sink quickly, sometimes they float . . .

"Good-bye, lady," I said. "Wish I knew your name. Thanks again."

I released my hold upon her. The waters swirled. She was gone. After a time, I looked away then moved away. Too many questions and no answers.

Somewhere, a maddened horse was screaming . . .

9

Several hours and many shadows later I rested again, in a place with a clear sky and not much tinder about. I bathed in a shallow stream and afterward summoned fresh clothing out of Shadow. Clean and dry then, I rested on the bank and made myself a meal.

It seemed as if every day were now an April 30. It seemed as if everyone I met knew me, and as if everyone were playing an elaborate double-game. People were dying all about me and disasters were becoming a common occurrence. I was beginning to feel like a figure in a video game. What would be next? I wondered. A meteor shower?

There had to be a key. The nameless lady who had given her life to pull me out of the fire had said that someone was following me and that there was someone ahead of me, also. What did that mean? Should I wait for my pursuer to catch up and simply ask him, her, or it what the hell was going on? Or should I push on fast, hopefully catch the other party and make inquiry there? Would either give me the same answer? Or were there two different answers involved? Would a duel satisfy someone's honor? I'd fight it, then. Or a bribe. I'd pay it. All I wanted was an answer followed by a little peace and quiet. I chuckled. That sounded like a description of death—though I wasn't that sure about the answer part.

"Shit!" I commented, to no one in particular, and I tossed a stone into the stream.

I got to my feet and crossed the water. Written in the sand on its opposite shore were the words GO BACK. I stepped on them and broke into a run.

The world spun about me as I touched the shadows. Vegetation fell away. The rocks grew into boulders, lightening, taking on a sparkle . . .

I ran through a valley of prisms beneath an awesome purple sky . . . Wind among rainbow stones, singing, Aeolian music . . .

Garments lashed by gales . . . Purple to lavender above . . . Sharp cries within the strains of sound . . . Earth cracking . . .

Faster.

I am giant. Same landscape, infinitesimal now . . . Cyclopean, I grind the glowing stones beneath my feet . . . Dust of rainbows upon my boots, puffs of cloud about my shoulders . . .

Atmosphere thickening, thickening, almost to liquid, and green . . . Swirling . . . Slow motion, my best efforts . . .

Swimming in it . . . Castles fit for aquaria drift by . . . Bright missiles like fireflies assail me . . . I feel nothing . . .

Green to blue . . . Thinning, thinning . . . Blue smoke and air like incense . . . The reverberation of a million invisible gongs, incessant . . . I clench my teeth.

Faster.

Blue to pink, spark-shot . . . A catlick of fire . . . Another . . . Heatless flames dance like sea plants . . . Higher, rising higher . . . Walls of fire buckle and crackle . . .

Footfalls at my back.

Don't look. Shift.

Sky split down the middle, by sun a comet streaking . . . Here and gone . . . Again. Again. Three days in as many heartbeats . . . I breathe the air spicy . . . Swirl the fires, descend to purple earth . . . Prism in the sky . . . I race the course of a glowing river across a field of fungus color of blood, spongy . . . Spores that turn to jewels, fall like bullets . . .

Night on a plain of brass, footfalls echoing to eternity . . . Knobbed machinelike plants clanking, metal flowers retracting back to metal stalks, stalks to consoles . . . Clank, clank, sigh . . . Echoes only, at my back?

I spin once.

Was that a dark figure ducking behind a windmill tree? Or only the dance of shadows in my shadow-shifting eyes?

Forward. Through glass and sandpaper, orange ice, landscape of pale flesh . . .

There is no sun, only pale light . . . There is no earth . . . Only thin bridges and islands in the air . . . The world is crystal matrix . . .

Up, down, around . . . Through a hole in the air and down a chute . . .

Sliding . . . To a cobalt beach beside a still copper sea . . . Twilight without stars . . . Faint glow everywhere . . . Dead, dead this place . . . Blue rocks . . . Broken statues of inhuman beings . . . Nothing stirring . . .

Stop.

I drew a magic circle about me in the sand and invested it with the forces of Chaos. I spread my new cloak then at its center, stretched out and went to sleep. I dreamed that the waters rose up to wash away a portion of the circle, and that a green, scaly being with purple hair and sharp teeth crept out of the sea and came to me to drink my blood.

When I awoke, I saw that the circle was broken and a green, scaly being with purple hair and sharp teeth lay dead upon the beach a half-dozen yards from me, Frakir knotted tightly about its throat and the sand disturbed all around. I must have slept very deeply.

I retrieved my strangling cord and crossed another bridge over infinity.

On the next leg of my journey I was nearly caught up in a flash flood the first time I paused to rest. I was no longer unwary, however, and I kept ahead of it long enough to shift away. I received another warning—in burning letters on the face of an obsidian mountain—suggesting I withdraw, retire, go home. My shouted invitation to a conference was ignored.

I traveled till it was time to sleep again, and I camped then in the Blackened Lands—still, gray, musty, and foggy. I found myself an easily defended cleft, warded it against magic and slept.

Later—how much later, I am uncertain—I was awakened from a dreamless slumber by the pulsing of Frakir upon my wrist.

I was instantly awake, and then I wondered why. I heard nothing and I saw nothing untoward within my limited field of vision. But Frakir—who is not 100 percent perfect—always has a reason when she does give an alarm. I waited, and I recalled my image of the Logrus while I did so. When it was fully before me I fitted my hand within it as if it were a glove and I reached . . .

I seldom carry a blade above the length of a middle-sized dagger. It's too damned cumbersome having several feet of steel hanging at my side, bumping into me, catching onto bushes, and occasionally even tripping me up. My father, and most of the others in Amber and the Courts, swear by the heavy, awkward things, but they are probably made of sterner stuff than myself. I've nothing against them in principle. I love fencing, and I've had a lot of training in their use. I just find carrying one all the time to be a nuisance. The belt even rubs a raw place on my hip after a while. Normally, I prefer Frakir and improvisation. However . . .

This, I was willing to admit, might be a good time to be holding one. For now I heard bellowslike hissing sounds and scrambling noises from somewhere outside and to my left.

I extended through Shadow, seeking a blade. I extended, I extended . . .

Damn. I had come far from any metalworking culture of the appropriate anatomy and at the proper phase in its historical development.

I continued to reach, sweat suddenly beading my brow. Far, very far. And the sounds came nearer, louder, faster.

There came rattling, stamping, and spitting noises. A roar.

Contact!

I felt the haft of the weapon in my hand. Seize and summon! I called it to me, and I was thrown against the wall by the force of its delivery. I hung there a moment before I could draw it from the sheath in which it was still encased. In that moment, things grew silent outside.

I waited ten seconds. Fifteen. Half a minute . . .

Nothing now.

I wiped my palms on my trousers. I continued to listen. Finally, I advanced.

There was nothing immediately before the opening save a light fog, and as the peripheral lines of sight opened there was still nothing to behold.

Another step . . .

No.

Another.

I was right at the threshold now. I leaned forward and darted a quick glance in either direction.

Yes. There was something off to the left—dark, low, unmoving, half masked by the fog. Crouched? Ready to spring at me?

Whatever it was, it did not stir and it kept total silence. I did the same. After a time, I noticed another dark form of the same general outline beyond it—and possibly a third even farther away. None of them showed any inclination to raise the sort of hell I had been listening to but minutes before.

I continued my vigil.

Several minutes must have passed before I stepped outside. Nothing was roused by my movement. I took another step and waited. Then another.

Finally, moving slowly, I approached the first form. An ugly brute, covered with scales the color of dried blood. A couple of hundred pounds' worth of creature, long and sinuous . . . Nasty teeth, too, I noted, when I opened its mouth with the point of my weapon. I knew it was safe to do this, because its head was almost completely severed from the rest of it. A very clean cut. A yellow-orange liquid still flowed from the wound.

And I could see from where I stood that the other two forms were creatures of the same sort. In all ways. They were dead, too. The second one I examined had been run through several times and was missing one leg. The third had been hacked to pieces. All of them oozed, and they smelled faintly of cloves.

I inspected the well-trampled area. Mixed in with that strange blood and the dew were what seemed to be the partial impressions of a boot, human-scale. I sought farther and I came across one intact footprint. It was pointed back in the direction from which I had come.

My pursuer? S, perhaps? The one who had called off the dogs? Coming to my aid?

I shook my head. I was tired of looking for sense where there wasn't any. I continued to search, but there were no more full tracks. I returned to the cleft then and picked up my blade's sheathe. I fitted the weapon into it and hung it from my belt. I fastened it over my shoulders so that it hung down my back. The hilt would protrude just above my backpack once I'd shouldered that item. I couldn't see how I could jog with it at my side.

I ate some bread and the rest of the meat. Drank some water, too, and a mouthful of wine. I resumed my journey.

I ran much of the next day—though "day" is something of a misnomer beneath unchanging stippled skies, checkered skies, skies lit by perpetual pinwheels and fountains of light. I ran until I was tired, and I rested and ate and ran some more. I rationed my food, for I'd a feeling I'd have to send far for more and such an act places its own energy demands upon the body. I eschewed short-cuts, for flashy shadows-spanning hellruns also have their price and I did not want to be all whacked out when I arrived. I checked behind me often. Usually, I saw nothing suspicious. Occasionally, though, I thought that I glimpsed distant pursuit. Other explanations were possible, however, considering some of the tricks the shadows can play.

I ran until I knew that I was finally nearing my destination. There came no new disaster followed by an order to turn back. I wondered fleetingly whether this was a good sign, or if the worst were yet to come. Either way, I knew that one more sleep and a little more journeying would put me where I wanted to be. Add a little caution and a few precautions and there might even be reason for optimism.

I ran through a vast, forestlike stand of crystalline shapes. Whether they were truly living things or represented some geological phenomenon, I did not know. They distorted perspectives and made shifting difficult. However, I saw no signs of living things in that glossy, glassy place, which led me to consider making my final campsite there.

I broke off a number of the limbs and drove them into the pink ground, which had the consistency of partly set putty. I constructed a circular palisade standing to about shoulder-height, myself at its center. I unwound Frakir from my wrist then voiced the necessary instructions as I placed her atop my rough and shining wall.

Frakir elongated, stretching herself as thin as a thread and twining among the shardlike branches. I felt safe. I did not believe anything could cross that barrier without Frakir's springing loose and twining herself to deathly tightness about it.

I spread my cloak, lay down, and slept. For how long, I am not certain. And I recall no dreams. There were no disturbances either.

When I woke I moved my head to reorient it, but the view was the same. In every direction but down the view was filled with interwoven crystal branches. I climbed slowly to my feet and pressed against them. Solid. They had become a glass cage.

Although I was able to break off some lesser branches, these were mainly from overhead, and it did nothing to work my release. Those which I had planted initially had thickened considerably, having apparently rooted themselves solidly. They would not yield to my strongest kicks.

The damned thing infuriated me. I swung my blade and glassy chips flew all about. I muffled my face with my cloak then and swung several times more. Then I noticed that my hand felt wet. When I looked at it, I saw that it was running with blood. Some of those splinters were very sharp. I desisted with the blade and returned to kicking at my enclosure. The walls creaked occasionally and made chiming noises, but they held.

I am not normally claustrophobic and my life was not in imminent peril, but something about this shining prison annoyed me out of all proportion to the situation itself. I raged for perhaps ten minutes before I forced myself to sufficient calmness that I might think clearly.

I studied the tangle until I discerned the uniform color and texture of Frakir running through it. I placed my fingertips upon her and spoke an order. Her brightness increased and she ran through the spectrum and settled into a red glow. The first creaking sound occurred a few seconds later.

I quickly withdrew to the center of the enclosure and wrapped myself fully in my cloak. If I crouched, I decided, some of the overhead pieces would fall a greater distance, striking me with more force. So I stood upright, protecting my head and neck with my arms and hands as well as with the cloak.

The creaking sounds became cracking sounds, followed by rattling, snapping, breaking. I was suddenly struck across the shoulder, but I maintained my footing.

Ringing and crunching, the edifice began to fall about me. I held my ground, though I was struck several times more.

When the sounds ceased and I looked again I saw that the roof had been removed, and I stood calf-deep amid fallen branches of the hard, corallike material. Several of the side members had splintered off at near to ground level. Others now stood at unnatural angles, and this time a few well-placed kicks brought them down.

My cloak was torn in a number of places, and Frakir coiled now about my left ankle and began to migrate to my wrist. The stuff crunched underfoot as I departed.

I shook out my cloak and brushed myself off. I traveled for perhaps half an hour then, leaving the place far behind me, before I halted and took my breakfast in a hot, bleak valley smelling faintly of sulfur.

As I was finishing, I heard a crashing noise. A horned and tusked purple thing went racing along the ridge to my right pursued by a hairless orange-skinned creature with long claws and a forked tail. Both were wailing in different keys.

I nodded. It was just one damned thing after another.

* * *

I made my way through frozen lands and burning lands, under skies both wild and placid. Then at last, hours later, I saw the low range of dark hills, an aurora streaming upward from behind them. That was it. I needed but approach and pass through and I would see my goal beyond the last and most difficult barrier of all.

I moved ahead. It would be good to finish this job and get on with more important matters. I would trump back to Amber when I was finished there, rather than retracing my steps. I could not have trumped in to my destination, though, because the place could not be represented on a card.

In that I was jogging, I first thought that the vibrations were my own. I was disabused of this notion when small pebbles began to roll aimlessly about the ground before me.

Why not?

I'd been hit with just about everything else. It was as if my strange nemesis were working down through a checklist and had just now come to "Earthquake." All right. At least there was nothing high near at hand to fall on me.

"Enjoy yourself, you son of a bitch!" I called out. "One day real soon it won't be so funny!"

As if in response the shaking grew more violent, and I had to halt or be thrown from my feet. As I watched, the ground began to subside in places, tilt in still others. I looked about quickly, trying to decide whether to advance, retreat, or stay put. Small fissures had begun to open, and now I could hear a growling, grinding sound.

The earth dropped abruptly beneath me—perhaps six inches—and the nearest crevices widened. I turned and began sprinting back the way I had come. The ground seemed less disturbed there.

A mistake perhaps. A particularly violent tremor followed, knocking me from my feet. Before I could rise a large crack appeared within reaching distance. It continued to widen even as I watched. I sprang to my feet, leapt across it, stumbled, rose again, and beheld another opening rift—widening more rapidly than the one I had been fleeing.

I sprang once more, onto a tilting tabletop of land. The ground seemed torn everywhere now with the dark lightning strokes of rifts, heaving themselves open widely to the accompaniment of awful groans and screechings. Big sections of ground slipped from sight into abysses. My small island was already going.

I leaped again, and again, trying to make it over to what appeared to be a more stable area.

I didn't quite manage it. I missed my footing and fell. But I managed to catch hold of the edge. I dangled a moment then and began to draw myself upward. The edge began to crumble. I clawed at it and caught a fresh hold. Then I dangled again, coughing and cursing.

I sought for footholds in the clayey wall against which I hung. It yielded somewhat beneath the thrusting of my boots and I dug in, blinking dirt from my eyes, trying for a firmer hold overhead. I could feel Frakir loosening, tightening into a small loop, one end free and flowing over my knuckles, hopefully to locate something sufficiently firm-set to serve as an anchor.

But no. My lefthand hold gave way again. I clung with my right and groped for another. Loose earth fell about me as I failed, and my right hand was beginning to slip.

Dark shadow above me, through dust and swimming eyes.

My right hand fell loose. I thrust with my legs for another try.

My right wrist was clasped as it sped upward and forward once again. A big hand with a powerful grip held me. Moments later, it was joined by another and I was drawn upward, quickly, smoothly. I was over the edge and seeking my footing in an instant. My wrist was released. I wiped my eyes.

"Luke!"

He was dressed in green, and blades must not have bothered him the way they do me, for a good-sized one hung at his right side. He seemed to be using a rolled cloak for a backpack, and he wore its clasp like a decoration upon his left breast—an elaborate thing, a golden bird of some sort.

"This way," he said, turning, and I followed him.

He led me a course back and to the left, tangent to the route I had taken on entering the valley. The footing grew steadier as we hurried that way, mounting at last a low hill that seemed completely out of range in the disturbance. Here we paused to look back.

"Come no farther!" a great voice boomed from that direction.

"Thanks, Luke," I panted. "I don't know how you're here or why but—"

He raised a hand. "Right now I just want to know one thing," he said, rubbing at a short beard he seemed to have grown in an amazingly brief time, and causing me to note that he was wearing the ring with the blue stone.

"Name it," I told him.

"How come whatever it was that just spoke has your voice?" he asked.

"Uh-oh. I knew it sounded familiar."

"Come on!" he said. "You must know. Every time you're threatened and it warns you back it's your voice that I hear doing it—echolike."

"How long have you been following me, anyhow?"

"Quite a distance."

"Those dead creatures outside the cleft where I'd camped—"

"I took them out for you. Where are you going, and what is that thing?"

"Right now I have only suspicions as to exactly what's going on, and it's a long story. But the answer should lie beyond that next range of hills."

I gestured toward the aurora.

He stared off in that direction, then nodded.

"Let's get going," he said.

"There is an earthquake in progress," I observed.

"It seems pretty much confined to this valley," he stated. "We can cut around it and proceed."

"And quite possibly encounter its continuance."

He shook his head. "It seems to me," he said, "that whatever it is that's trying to bar your way exhausts itself after each effort and takes quite a while to recover sufficiently to make another attempt."

"But the attempts are getting closer together," I noted, "and more spectacular each time."

"Is it because we're getting closer to their source?" he asked.

"Possibly."

"Then let's hurry."

We descended the far side of the hill, then went up and down another. The tremors, by that time, had already subsided to an occasional shuddering of the ground and shortly these too, ceased.

We made our way into and along another valley, which for a while headed us far to the right of our goal, then curved gently back in the proper direction, toward that final range of barren hills, lights flickering beyond them against the low, unmoving base of a cloudlike line of white under a mauve to violet sky. No freah perils were presented.

"Luke," I asked after a time, "what happened on the mountain, that night in New Mexico?"

"I had to go away—fast," he answered.

"What about Dan Martinez's body?"

"Took it with me."

"Why?"

"I don't like leaving evidence lying about."

"That doesn't really explain much."

"I know," he said, and he broke into a jog.

I paced him.

"And you know who I am," I continued.

"Yes."

"How?"

"Not now," he said. "Not now."

He increased his pace. I matched it.

"And why were you following me?"

"I saved your ass, didn't I?"

"Yeah, and I'm grateful. But it still doesn't answer the question."

"Race you to that leaning stone," he said, and he put on a burst of speed.

I did, too, and I caught him. Try as I could I couldn't pass him, though. And we were breathing too hard by then to ask or answer questions.

I pushed myself, ran faster. He did, too, keeping up. The leaning stone was still a good distance off. We stayed side by side and I saved my reserve for the final sprint. It was crazy, but I'd run against him too many times. It was almost a matter of habit by now. That, and the old curiosity. Had he gotten a little faster? Had I? Or a little slower?

My arms pumped, my feet thudded. I got control of my breathing, maintained it in an appropriate rhythm. I edged a little ahead of him and he did nothing about it. The stone was suddenly a lot nearer.

We held our distance for perhaps half a minute, and then he cut loose. He was abreast of me, he was past me. Time to dig in.

I drove my legs faster. The blood thudded in my ears. I sucked air and pushed with everything I had. The distance between us began to narrow again. The leaning rock was looking bigger and bigger . . .

I caught him before we reached it, but try as I might I could not pull ahead. We raced past it side by side and collapsed together.

"Photo finish," I gasped.

"Got to call it a tie," he panted. "You always surprise me—right at the end."

I groped out my water bottle and passed it to him. He took a swig and handed it back. We emptied it that way, a little at a time.

"Damn," he said then, getting slowly to his feet. "Let's see what's over those hills."

I got up and went along.

When I finally recovered my breath the first thing I said was, "You seem to know a hell of a lot more about me than I do about you."

"I think so," he said after a long pause, "and I wish I didn't."

"What does that mean?"

"Not now," he replied. "Later. You don't read *War and Peace* on your coffee break."

"I don't understand."

"Time," he said. "There's always either too much time or not enough. Right now there's not enough."

"You've lost me."

"Wish I could."

The hills were nearer and the ground remained firm beneath our feet. We trudged steadily onward.

I thought of Bill's guesswork, Random's suspicions, and Meg Devlin's warning. I also thought of that round of strange ammunition I'd found in Luke's jacket.

"That thing we're heading toward," he said, before I could frame a fresh question of my own. "That's your Ghostwheel, isn't it?"

"Yes."

He laughed. Then: "So you were telling the truth back in Santa Fe when you told me it required a peculiar environment. What you didn't say was that you'd found that environment and built the thing there."

I nodded. "What about your plans for a company?" I asked him.

"That was just to get you to talk about it."

"And what about Dan Martinez—the things he said?"

"I don't know. I really didn't know him. I still don't know what he wanted, or why he came at us shooting."

"Luke, what is it that you want, anyhow?"

"Right now I just want to see that damned thing," he said. "Did building it out here in the boonies endow it with some sort of special properties?"

"Yes."

"Like what?"

"Like a few I didn't even think of—unfortunately," I answered.

"Name one."

"Sorry," I said. "Question and answer is a two-way game."

"Hey, I'm the guy who just pulled you out of a hole in the ground."

"I gather you're also the guy who tried to kill me on a bunch of April thirtieths."

"Not recently," he said. "Honest."

"You mean you really did?"

"Well . . . yeah. But I had reasons. It's a long story and—"

"Jesus, Luke! Why? What did I ever do to you?"

"It's not that simple," he answered.

We reached the base of the nearest hill and he started climbing it.

"Don't," I called to him. "You can't go over."

He halted. "Why not?"

"The atmosphere ends thirty or forty feet up."

"You're kidding."

I shook my head.

"And it's worse on the other side," I added. "We have to find a passage through. There's one farther to the left."

I turned and headed in that direction. Shortly, I heard his footfalls.

"So you gave it your voice," he said.

"So?"

"So I see what you're up to and what's been going on. It's become sentient in that crazy place you built it. It went wild, and you're heading to shut it down. It knows it and it's got the power to do something about it. It's your Ghostwheel that's been trying to get you to turn back, isn't it?"

"Probably."

"Why didn't you just trump in?"

"You can't construct a Trump for a place that keeps changing. What do you know about Trumps, anyway?"

"Enough," he said.

I saw the passage I was seeking up ahead.

I approached the place and I halted before I entered it.

"Luke," I said, "I don't know what you want or why or how you got here, and you don't seem to care to tell me. I will tell you something for free, though. This could be very dangerous. Maybe you ought to go back to wherever you came from and let me handle it. There's no reason to place you in jeopardy."

"I think there is," he said. "Besides, I might be useful."

"How?"

He shrugged. "Let's get on with it, Merlin. I want to see that thing."

"Okay. Come on."

I led the way into the narrow place where the stone had been riven.

10

The passage was long and dark and occasionally tight, growing progressively colder as we advanced, but at length we emerged onto the wide, rocky shelf that faced the steaming pit. There was an ammonialike odor in the air, and my feet were cold and my face flushed, as usual. I blinked hard several times, studying the latest outlines of the maze through the shifting mist. A pearl-gray pall hung over the entire area. Intermittent orange flashes penetrated the gloom.

"Uh—where is it?" Luke inquired.

I gestured straight ahead, toward the site of the latest flicker. "Out there," I told him.

Just then, the mists were swept away, revealing file upon file of dark, smooth ridges separated by black declivities. The ridges zigged and zagged their way out toward a fortresslike island, a low wall running about it, several metallic structures visible beyond.

"It's a—maze," he remarked. "Do we travel it down in the passages or up on top of the walls?"

I smiled as he studied it.

"It varies," I said. "Sometimes up and sometimes down."

"Well, which way do we go?"

"I don't know yet. I have to study it each time. You see, it keeps changing, and there's a trick to it."

"A trick?"

"More than one, actually. The whole damn thing is floating on a lake of liquid hydrogen and helium. The maze moves around. It's different each time. And then there's a matter of the atmosphere. If you were to walk upright along the ridges you would be above it in most places. You wouldn't last long. And the temperature ranges from horribly cold to roasting hot over a range of a few feet in elevation. You have to know when to crawl and when to climb and when to do other things—as well as which way to go."

"How do you tell?"

"Un-uh," I said. "I'll take you in, but I'm not giving you the secret."

The mists began to rise again from the depths and to collect into small clouds.

"I see now why you can't make a Trump for it," he began.

I continued to study the layout.

"All right," I said then. "This way."

"What if it attacks us while we're in the maze?" he asked.

"You can stay behind if you want."

"No. Are you really going to shut it down?"

"I'm not sure. Come on."

I took several steps ahead and to the right. A faint circle of light appeared in the air before me, grew brighter. I felt Luke's hand upon my shoulder.

"What—?" he began.

"No farther!" the voice I now recognized as my own said to me.

"I think we can work something out," I responded. "I have several ideas and—"

"No!" it answered. "I heard what Random said."

"I am prepared to disregard his order," I said, "if there is a better alternative."

"You're trying to trick me. You want to shut me down."

"You're making things worse with all these power displays," I said. "I'm coming in now and—"

"No!"

A heavy gust of wind blew out of the circle and struck against me. I was staggered by it. I saw my sleeve turn brown, then orange. It began to fray even as I watched.

"What are you doing? I have to talk to you, explain—"

"Not here! Not now! Never!"

I was hurled back against Luke, who caught me, dropping to one knee as he did so. An arctic blast assailed us and icy crystals danced before my eyes. Bright colors began to flash then, half blinding me.

"Stop!" I cried, but nothing did.

The ground seemed to tilt beneath us and suddenly there was no ground. It did not feel as if we were falling, however. It seemed rather as if we hung suspended in the midst of a blizzard of light.

"Stop!" I called out once again, but the words were swept away.

The circle of light vanished, as if retreating down a long tunnel. I realized, however, through the sensory overload, that it was Luke and I who were receding from the light, that we had already been blasted a great enough distance to drive us halfway through the hill. But there was nothing solid in any direction about us.

A faint buzzing sound began. It grew into a humming, then a dull roar. In the distance, I seemed to see a tiny steam locomotive negotiating a mountainside at an impossible angle, then an upside-down waterfall, a skyline beneath green waters. A park bench passed us quickly, a blue-skinned woman seated upon it, clutching at it, a horrified expression on her face.

I dug frantically within my pocket, knowing we might be destroyed at any moment.

"What," Luke screamed into my ear, his grip now almost dislocating my arm, "is it?"

"Shadow-storm!" I cried back. "Hang on!" I added unnecessarily.

A batlike creature was blown into my face, was gone an instant later, leaving a wet slash upon my right cheek. Something struck against my left foot.

An inverted mountain range flowed past us, buckling and rippling. The roaring increased in volume. The light seemed to pulse by us now, in wide bands of color, touching us with a near-physical force. Heat lamps and wind chimes . . .

I heard Luke cry out as if he had been struck, but I was unable to turn to his aid. We traversed a region of lightninglike flashes where my hair stood on end and my skin tingled.

I gripped the packet of cards within my pocket and withdrew it. At this point we were beginning to spin and I was afraid they would be torn from my hand. I held them tightly, fearing to sort through them, keeping them close to my body. I drew them upward slowly, carefully. Whichever one lay on top would have to be our exit.

Dark bubbles formed and broke about us, discharging noxious fumes.

I saw, as I raised my hand, that my skin was gray in appearance, sparkling with fluorescent swirls. Luke's hand upon my arm looked cadaverous, and when I glanced back at him a grinning death's head met my gaze.

I looked away, turned my attention back to the cards. It was hard to focus my vision, through the grayness, through a peculiar distancing effect. But it finally came clear. It was the grassy spit of land I had regarded—how long ago?—quiet waters about it, the edge of something crystalline and bright jutting into view off toward the right.

I held it within my attention. Sounds from beyond my shoulder indicated that Luke was trying to address me, but I could not distinguish his words. I continued to regard the Trump and it grew clearer. But slowly, slowly. Something struck me hard, below the right side of my rib cage. I forced myself to ignore it and continued to concentrate.

At last the scene on the card seemed to move toward me, to grow larger. There was a familiar sense of coldness to it now as the scene engulfed me and I it. An almost elegiac feeling of stillness hung over that little lake.

I fell forward into the grass, my heart pounding, my side throbbing. I was gasping, and the subjective sense of worlds rushing by me was still present, like the afterimages of highways upon closing one's eyes at the end of a long day's drive.

Smelling sweet water, I passed out.

I was vaguely aware of being dragged, carried, then helped, stumbling along. There followed a spell of full unconsciousness, shading over into sleep and dreaming.

. . . I walked the streets of a ruined Amber beneath a lowering sky. A crippled angel with a fiery sword stalked the heights above me, slashing. Wherever its blade fell, smoke, dust, and flame rose up. Its halo was my Ghostwheel, pouring forth mighty winds ridden by abominations that streamed past the angel's face like a dark, living veil, working disorder and ruin wherever they fell. The palace was half collapsed, and there were gibbets nearby where my relatives hung, twisting in the gusts. I'd a blade in one hand and Frakir dangled from the other. I was climbing now, going up to meet and do battle with the bright-dark nemesis. An awful feeling lay upon me as I mounted my rocky way, as if my imminent failure was a thing foregone. Even so, I decided, the creature was going to leave here with wounds to lick.

It took note of me as I drew near, turning in my direction. Its face was still hidden as it raised its weapon. I rushed forward, regretting only that I had not had time to envenom my blade. I spun twice as I went in, feinting, to strike somewhere in the vicinity of its left knee.

There followed a flash of light and I was falling, falling, bits of flame descending about me, like a burning blizzard.

I fell so for what seemed an age and a half, coming to rest at last upon my back atop a large stone table marked out like a sundial, its stylus barely missing impaling me—which seemed crazy even in a dream. There were no sundials in the Courts of Chaos, for there is no sun there. I was located at the edge of a courtyard beside a high, dark tower, and I found myself unable to move, let alone rise. Above me, my mother, Dara, stood upon a low balcony in her natural form, looking down at me in her awful power and beauty.

"Mother!" I cried. "Free me!"

"I have sent one to help you," she answered.

"And what of Amber?"

"I do not know."

"And my father?"

"Speak not to me of the dead."

The stylus turned slowly, positioned itself above my throat, began a gradual but steady descent.

"Help me!" I cried. "Hurry!"

"Where are you?" she called out, head turning, eyes darting. "Where have you gone?"

"I'm still here!" I yelled.

"Where are you?"

I felt the stylus touch the side of my neck—

The vision broke and fell apart.

My shoulders were propped against something unyielding, my legs were stretched out before me. Someone had just squeezed my shoulder, the hand brushing against my neck.

"Merle, you okay? Want a drink?" a familiar voice was asking.

I took a deep breath and sighed it out. I blinked several times. The light was blue, the world a field of lines and angles. A dipper of water appeared before my mouth.

"Here." It was Luke's voice.

I drank it all.

"Want another?"

"Yes."

"Just a minute."

I felt his weight shift, heard his footsteps recede. I regarded the diffusely illuminated wall six or seven feet before me. I ran my hand along the floor. It seemed to be of the same material.

Shortly, Luke returned, smiling, and passed me the dipper. I drained it and handed it back.

"Want more?" he asked.

"No. Where are we?"

"In a cave—a big, pretty place."

"Where'd you get the water?"

"In a side cavern, up that way." He gestured. "Several barrels of it in there. Also lots of food. Want something to eat?"

"Not yet. Are you okay?"

"Kind of beat," he replied, "but intact. You don't seem to have any broken bones, and that cut on your face has stopped bleeding."

"That's something, anyway," I said.

I climbed slowly to my feet, the final strands of dreams withdrawing slowly as I rose. I saw then that Luke had turned and was walking away. I followed him for several paces before I thought to inquire, "Where are you going?"

"In there," he answered, pointing with the dipper.

I followed him through an opening in the wall and into a cold cavern about the size of my old apartment's living room. Four large wooden barrels stood along the wall to my left, and Luke proceeded to hang the dipper upon the upper edge of the nearest. Against the far wall were great stacks of cartons and piles of sacks.

"Canned goods," he announced. "Fruit, vegetables, ham, salmon, biscuits, sweets. Several cases of wine. A Coleman stove. Plenty of Sterno. Even a bottle or two of cognac."

He turned and brushed quickly past me, headed on up the hall again.

"Now where?" I asked.

But he was moving fast and did not reply. I had to hurry to catch up. We passed several branches and openings before he halted at another, nodding.

"Latrine in there. Just a hole with some boards over it. Good idea to keep it covered, I'd say."

"What the hell is this?" I asked.

He raised his hand. "It will all become clear in a minute. This way."

He swung around a sapphire corner and vanished. Almost completely disoriented, I moved in that direction. After several turns and one cutback, I felt totally lost. Luke was nowhere in sight.

I halted and listened. Not a sound except for my own breathing.

"Luke? Where are you?" I called.

"Up here," he answered.

The voice seemed to be coming from overhead and some-where off to my right. I ducked beneath a low arch and came into a bright blue chamber of the same crystalline substance as the rest of the place. I saw a sleeping bag and a pillow in one corner. Light streamed in from a small opening about eight feet overhead.

"Luke?" I asked again.

"Here," came his reply.

I moved to position myself beneath the hole, squinting against the brightness as I stared upward. Finally, I shaded my eyes. Luke's head and shoulders were limned above me, his hair a crown of coppery flame in what could be the light of early morning or of evening. He was smiling again.

"That, I take it, is the way out," I said.

"For me," he answered.

"What do you mean?"

There followed a grating noise and the view was partly occluded by the edge of a large boulder.

"What are you doing?"

"Moving this stone into a position where I can block the opening quickly," he replied, "and stick in a few wedges afterward."

"Why?"

"There are sufficient tiny openings for air so that you shan't suffocate," he went on.

"Great. Why am I here, anyway?"

"Let's not get existential just now," he said. "This isn't a philosophy seminar."

"Luke! Damn it! What's going on?"

"It should be obvious that I'm making you a prisoner," he said. "The blue crystal, by the way, will block any Trump sendings and negate your magical abilities that rely on things beyond the walls. I need you alive and fangless for now, in a place where I can get to you in a hurry."

I studied the opening and the nearby walls.

"Don't try it," he said. "I have the advantage of position."

"Don't you think you owe me an explanation?"

He stared at me for a moment, then nodded.

"I have to go back," he said finally, "and try to get control of the Ghostwheel. Any suggestions?"

I laughed. "It's not on the best of terms with me at the moment. I'm afraid I can't help you."

He nodded again. "I'll just have to see what I can do. God, what a weapon! If I can't swing it myself I'll have to come back and pick your brains for some ideas. You be thinking about it, okay?"

"I'll be thinking about a lot of things, Luke. You're not going to like some of them."

"You're not in a position to do much."

"Not yet," I said.

He caught hold of the boulder, began to move it.

"Luke!" I cried.

He paused, studied me, his expression changing to one I had never seen before.

"That's not really my name," he stated, after a moment.

"What, then?"

"I am your cousin Rinaldo," he said slowly. "I killed Caine, and I came close with Bleys. I missed with the bomb at the funeral, though. Someone spotted me. I will destroy the House of Amber with or without your Ghostwheel—but it would make things a lot easier if I had that kind of power."

"What's your bitch, Luke? . . . Rinaldo? Why the vendetta?"

"I went after Caine first," he continued, "because he's the one who actually killed my father."

"I—didn't know." I stared at the flash of the Phoenix clasp upon his breast. "I didn't know that Brand had a son," I finally said.

"You do now, old buddy. That's another reason why I can't let you go, and why I have to keep you in a place like this. Don't want you warning the others."

"You're not going to be able to pull this off."

He was silent for several seconds, then he shrugged.

"Win or lose, I have to try."

"Why April 30?" I said suddenly. "Tell me that."

"It was the day I got the news of my dad's death."

He drew upon the boulder and it slid into the hole, blocking it fully. There followed some brief hammerings.

"Luke!"

He did not answer. I could see his shadow through the translucent stone. After a while it straightened, then dropped from sight. I heard his boots strike the ground outside.

"Rinaldo!"

He did not answer and I heard his retreating footsteps.

I count the days by the lightening and darkening of the blue crystal walls. It has been over a month since my imprisonment, though I do not know how slowly or rapidly time flows here in relation to other shadows. I have paced every hall and chamber of this great cave, but I have found no way out. My Trumps do not work here, not even the Trumps of Doom. My magic is useless to me, limited as it is by walls the color of Luke's ring. I begin to feel that I might enjoy even the escape of temporary insanity, but my reason refuses to surrender to it, there being too many puzzles to trouble me: Dan Martinez, Meg Devlin, my Lady of the Lake . . . Why? And why did he spend all of that time in my company, Luke, Rinaldo, my enemy? I have to find a way to warn the others. If he succeeds in turning Ghostwheel upon them then Brand's dream—my nightmare of vengeance—will be realized. I see now that I have made many mistakes . . . Forgive me, Julia . . . I will pace the measure of my confinement yet again. Somewhere there must be a gap in the icy blue logic that surrounds me, against which I hurl my mind, my cries, my bitter laughter. Up this hall, down that tunnel. The blue is everywhere. The shadows will not bear me away, for there are no shadows here. I am Merlin the pent, son of Corwin the lost, and my dream of light has been turned against me. I stalk my prison like my own ghost. I cannot let it end this way. Perhaps the next tunnel, or the next . . .

BLOOD
OF
AMBER

For Kirby McCauley

Reflections in a Crystal Cave

My life had been relatively peaceful for eight years—not counting April thirtieths, when someone invariably tried to kill me. Outside of that, my academic career with its concentration on computer science went well enough and my four years' employment at Grand Design proved a rewarding experience, letting me use what I'd learned in a situation I liked while I labored on a project of my own on the side. I had a good friend in Luke Raynard, who worked for the same company, in sales. I sailed my little boat, I jogged regularly—

It all fell apart this past April 30, just when I thought things were about to come together. My pet project, Ghostwheel, was built; I'd quit my job, packed my gear and was ready to move on to greener shadows. I'd stayed in town this long only because that morbidly fascinating day was near, and this time I intended to discover who was behind the attempts on my life and why.

At breakfast that morning Luke appeared with a message from my former girlfriend, Julia. Her note said that she wanted to see me again. So I stopped by her place, where I found her dead, apparently killed by the same doglike beast which then attacked me. I succeeded in destroying the creature. A quick search of the apartment before I fled the scene turned up a slim packet of strange playing cards, which I took along with me. They were too much like the magical Tarots of Amber and Chaos for a sorcerer such as myself not to be interested in them.

Yes. I am a sorcerer. I am Merlin, son of Corwin of Amber and Dara of the Courts of Chaos, known to local friends and acquaintances as Merle Corey: bright, charming, witty, athletic. . . . Go read Castiglione and Lord Byron for particulars, as I'm modest, aloof and reticent, as well.

The cards proved to be genuine magical objects, which seemed appropriate once I learned that Julia had been keeping company with an occultist named Victor Melman after we had broken up. A visit to this gentleman's studio resulted in his attempting to kill me in a ritual fashion. I was able to free myself from the constraints of the ceremony and question him somewhat, before local conditions and my enthusiasm resulted in his death. So much for rituals.

I'd learned enough from him to realize that he'd been but a cat's-paw. Someone else had apparently put him up to the sacrifice bit—and it seemed quite possible that the other person was the one responsible for Julia's death and my collection of memorable April thirtieths.

I had small time to reflect upon these matters, though, because I was bitten (yes, bitten) shortly thereafter by an attractive redhaired woman who materialized in Melman's apartment, following my brief telephone conversation with her in which I'd tried to pose as Melman. Her bite paralyzed me, but I was able to depart before it took full effect by employing one of the magical cards I'd found at Julia's place. It bore me into the presence of a sphinx, which permitted me to recover so that it could play that silly riddle game sphinxes love so well because they get to eat you when you lose. All I can say about it is that this particular sphinx was a bad sport.

Anyhow, I returned to the shadow Earth where I'd been making my home to discover that Melman's place had burned down during my absence. I tried phoning Luke, because I wanted to have dinner with him, and learned that he had checked out of his motel, leaving me a message indicating that he had gone to New Mexico on business and telling me where he'd be staying. The desk clerk also gave me a blue-stone ring Luke had left behind, and I took it with me to return when I saw him.

I flew to New Mexico, finally catching up with Luke in Santa Fe. While I waited in the bar for him to get ready for dinner, a man named Dan Martinez questioned me, giving the impression that Luke had proposed some business deal and that he wanted to be assured Luke was reliable and could deliver. After dinner, Luke and I went for a drive in the mountains. Martinez followed us and started shooting as we stood admiring the night. Perhaps he'd decided Luke was not reliable or couldn't deliver. Luke surprised me by drawing a weapon of his own and shooting Martinez. Then an even stranger thing happened. Luke called me by name—my real name, which I'd never told him—and cited my parentage and told me to get into the car and get the hell out. He emphasized his point by placing a shot in the ground near my feet. The matter did not seem open to discussion so I departed. He also told me to destroy those strange Trumps that had saved my life once already. And I'd learned on the way up that he'd known Victor Melman. . . .

I didn't go far. I parked downhill and returned on foot. Luke was gone. So was Martinez's body. Luke did not return to the hotel, that night or the next day, so I checked out and departed. The only person I was sure I could trust, and who actually might have some good advice for me, was Bill Roth. Bill was an attorney who lived in upstate New York, and he had been my father's best friend. I went to visit him, and I told him my story.

Bill got me to wondering even more about Luke. Luke, by the way, is a big, smart, red-haired natural athlete of uncanny prowess—and though we'd been friends for many years I knew next to nothing (as Bill pointed out) concerning his background.

A neighboring lad named George Hansen began hanging out near Bill's place, asking strange questions. I received an odd phone call, asking similar questions. Both interrogators seemed curious as to my mother's name. Naturally, I lied. The fact that my mother is a member of the dark aristocracy of the Courts of Chaos was none of their business. But the caller spoke my language, Thari, which made me curious enough to propose a meeting and a trade-off of information that evening in the bar of the local country club.

But my Uncle Random, King of Amber, called me home before that, while Bill and I were out hiking. George Hansen, it turned out, was following us and wanted to come along as we shifted away across the shadows of reality. Tough; he wasn't invited. I took Bill along because I didn't want to leave him with anyone acting that peculiar.

I learned from Random that my Uncle Caine was dead, of an assassin's bullet, and that someone had also tried to kill my Uncle Bleys but only succeeded in wounding him. The funeral service for Caine would be the following day.

I kept my date at the country club that evening, but my mysterious interrogator was nowhere in sight. All was not lost, however, as I made the acquaintance of a pretty lady named Meg Devlin—and, one thing leading to another, I saw her home and we got to know each other a lot better. Then, at a moment when I would have judged her thoughts to be anywhere but there, she asked me my mother's name. So, what the hell, I told her. It did not come to me until later that she might really have been the person I'd gone to the bar to meet.

Our liaison was terminated prematurely by a call from the lobby—from a man purportedly Meg's husband. I did what any gentleman would do. I got the hell out fast.

My Aunt Fiona, who is a sorceress (of a different style from my own), had not approved of my date. And apparently she approved even less of Luke, because she asked me whether I had a picture of him after I'd told her somewhat concerning him. I showed her a photo I had in my wallet, which included Luke in the group. I'd have sworn she recognized him from somewhere, though she wouldn't admit it. But the fact that she and her brother Bleys both disappeared from Amber that night would seem more than coincidental.

The pace of events was accelerated even more after that. A crude attempt at knocking off most of the family with a thrown bomb was made the next day, following Caine's funeral. The would-be assassin escaped. Later, Random was upset at a brief demonstration on my part of the power of the Ghostwheel, my pet project, my hobby, my avocation during those years at Grand Design. Ghostwheel is a—well, it started out as a computer that required a different set of physical laws to operate than those I'd learned in school. It involved what might be called magic. But I found a place where it could be built and operated, and I'd constructed it there. It was still programming itself when I'd left it. It seemed to have gone sentient, and I think it scared Random. He ordered me to go and turn it off. I didn't much like the idea, but I departed.

I was followed in my passage through Shadow; I was harassed, threatened and even attacked. I was rescued from a fire by a strange lady who later died in a lake. I was protected from vicious beasts by a mysterious individual and saved from a bizarre earthquake by the same person—who turned out to be Luke. He accompanied me to the final barrier, for a confrontation with Ghostwheel. My creation was a bit irritated with me and banished us by means of a shadow-storm—a thing it is not fun to be caught in, with or without an umbrella. I delivered us from the vicissitudes by means of one of the Trumps of Doom, as I'd dubbed the odd pasteboards from Julia's apartment.

We wound up outside a blue crystal cave, and Luke took me in. Good old Luke. After seeing to my needs he proceeded to imprison me. When he told me who he was, I realized that it was a resemblance to his father which had upset Fiona when she'd seen his photo. For Luke was the son of Brand, assassin and arch traitor, who had damn near destroyed the kingdom and the rest of the universe along with it some years back. Fortunately, Caine had killed him before he'd accomplished his designs. Luke, I learned then, was the one who'd killed Caine, to avenge his father. (And it turned out he'd gotten the news of his father's death on an April thirtieth and had had a peculiar way of observing its anniversary over the years.) Like Random, he too had been impressed by my Ghostwheel, and he told me that I was to remain his prisoner, as I might become necessary in his efforts to gain control of the machine, which he felt would be the perfect weapon for destroying the rest of the family.

He departed to pursue the matter, and I quickly discovered that my powers were canceled by some peculiar property of the cave, leaving me with no one to talk to but you, Frakir, and no one here for you to strangle. . . .

Would you care to hear a few bars of "Over the Rainbow"?

1

I threw the hilt away after the blade had shattered. The weapon had done me no good against that blue sea of a wall in what I had taken to be its thinnest section. A few small chips of stone lay at my feet. I picked them up and rubbed them together. This was not the way out for me. The only way out seemed to be the way I had come in, and it wasn't working.

I walked back to my quarters, meaning that section of the caves where I had cast my sleeping bag. I sat down on the bag, a heavy brown one, uncorked a wine bottle and took a drink. I had worked up a sweat hacking away at the wall.

Frakir stirred upon my wrist then, unwound herself partway and slithered into the palm of my left hand, to coil around the two blue chips I still held. She knotted herself about them, then dropped to hang and swing pendulum-like. I put the bottle aside and watched. The arc of her swing paralleled the lengthwise direction of the tunnel I now called home. The swinging continued for perhaps a full minute. Then she withdrew upward, halting when she came to the back of my hand. She released the chips at the base of my third finger and returned to her normal hidden position about my wrist.

I stared. I raised the flickering oil lamp and studied the stones. Their color. . . .

Yes.

Seen against skin, they were similar in appearance to the stone in that ring of Luke's I had picked up at the New Line Motel some time ago. Coincidence? Or was there a connection? What had my strangling cord been trying to tell me? And where had I seen another such stone?

Luke's key ring. He'd a blue stone on it, mounted on a piece of metal. . . . And where might I have seen another?

The caverns in which I was imprisoned had the power to block the Trumps and my Logrus magic. If Luke carried stones from these walls about with him, there was probably a special reason. What other properties might they possess?

I tried for perhaps an hour to learn something concerning their nature, but they resisted my Logrus probes. Finally, disgusted, I pocketed them, ate some bread and cheese and took another swallow of wine.

Then I rose and made the rounds once more, inspecting my traps. I'd been a prisoner in this place for what seemed at least a month now. I had paced all these tunnels, corridors, grottoes, seeking an exit. None of them proved a way out. There were times when I had run manic through them and bloodied my knuckles upon their cold sides. There were times when I had moved slowly, seeking after cracks and fault lines. I had tried on several occasions to dislodge the boulder that barred the entranceway—to no avail. It was wedged in place, and I couldn't budge it. It seemed that I was in for the duration.

My traps. . . .

They were all as they had been the last time I had checked—deadfalls, boulders nature had left lying about in typical careless fashion, propped high and ready now to be released from their wedging when someone tripped any of the shadow-masked lengths of packing cord I'd removed from crates in the storeroom.

Someone?

Luke, of course. Who else? He was the one who'd imprisoned me. And if he returned—no, *when* he returned—the booby traps would be waiting. He was armed. He would have me at a disadvantage from the overhead position of the entrance if I merely waited for him below. No way. I would not be there. I would make him come in after me—and then—

Vaguely troubled, I returned to my quarters.

Hands behind my head, I lay there and reviewed my plans. The deadfalls could kill a man, and I did not want Luke dead. This had nothing to do with sentiment, though I had thought of Luke as a good friend until fairly recently—up until the time I learned that he had killed my Uncle Caine and seemed intent upon destroying the rest of my relatives in Amber as well. This was because Caine had killed Luke's father—my Uncle Brand—a man whom any of the others would gladly have done in also. Yes, Luke—or Rinaldo, as I now knew him—was my cousin, and he had a reason for engaging in one of our in-family vendettas. Still, going after everybody struck me as a bit intemperate.

But neither consanguinity nor sentiment bade me dismantle my traps. I wanted him alive because there were too many things about the entire situation that I did not understand and might never understand were he to perish without telling me.

Jasra . . . the Trumps of Doom . . . the means by which I had been tracked so easily through Shadow . . . the entire story of Luke's relationship with the painter and mad occultist Victor Melman . . . anything he knew about Julia and her death. . . .

I began again. I dismantled the deadfalls. The new plan was a simple one, and it drew upon something of which I believed Luke had no knowledge.

I moved my sleeping bag to a new position, in the tunnel just outside the chamber whose roof held the blocked entranceway. I shifted some of the food stores there, also. I was determined to remain in its vicinity for as much of the time as possible.

The new trap was a very basic thing: direct and just about unavoidable. Once I'd set it there was nothing to do but wait. Wait, and remember. And plan. I had to warn the others. I had to do something about my Ghostwheel. I needed to find out what Meg Devlin knew. I needed to . . . lots of things.

I waited. I thought of Shadow storms, dreams, strange Trumps and the Lady in the Lake. After a long spell of drifting, my life had become very crowded in a matter of days. Then this long spell of doing nothing. My only consolation was that this time line probably outpaced most of the others that were important to me right now. My month here might only be a day back in Amber, or even less. If I could deliver myself from this place soon, the trails I wished to follow might still be relatively fresh.

Later, I put out the lamp and went to sleep. Sufficient light filtered through the crystal lenses of my prison, brightening and waning, for me to distinguish day from night in the outside world, and I kept my small series of routines in accord with its rhythms.

During the next three days I read through Melman's diary again—a thing heavy in allusion and low in useful information—and just about succeeded in convincing myself that the Hooded One, as he referred to his visitor and teacher, had probably been

Luke. Except for a few references to androgyny, which puzzled me. References to the sacrifice of the Son of Chaos near the end of the volume were something I could take personally, in light of my present knowledge of Melman's having been set up to destroy me. But if Luke had done it, how to explain his ambiguous behavior on the mountain in New Mexico, when he had advised me to destroy the Trumps of Doom and had driven me away almost as if to protect me from something? And then he had admitted to several of the earlier attempts on my life, but denied the later ones. No reason to do that if he were indeed responsible for all of them. What else might be involved? Who else? And how? There were obviously missing pieces to the puzzle, but I felt as if they were minor, as if the smallest bit of new information and the slightest jiggling of the pattern would suddenly cause everything to fall into place, with the emerging picture to be something I should have seen all along.

I might have guessed that the visitation would be by night. I might have, but I didn't. Had it occurred to me, I would have changed my sleep cycle and been awake and alert. Even though I felt fairly confident of my trap's efficiency, every little edge is important in truly crucial matters.

I was deeply asleep, and the grating of rock upon rock was a distant thing. I stirred but slowly as the sounds continued, and it was several seconds more before the proper circuits closed and I realized what was occurring. Then I sat up, my mind still dusty, and moved into a crouch beside the wall of the chamber nearest the entranceway, knuckling my eyes, brushing back my hair, seeking lost alertness on sleep's receding shore.

The first sounds I heard must have accompanied the removal of the wedges, which apparently had entailed some rocking or tipping of the boulder. The continuing sounds were muffled, echoless—external.

So I ventured a quick glance into the chamber. There was no opened adit, showing stars. The overhead vibrations continued. The rocking sounds were now succeeded by a steady crunching, grating noise. A ball of light with a diffuse halo shone through the translucent stone of the chamber's roof. A lantern, I guessed. Too steady to be a torch. And a torch would be impractical under the circumstances.

A crescent of sky appeared, holding two stars near its nether horn. It widened, and I heard the heavy breathing and grunts of what I took to be two men.

My extremities tingled as I felt additional adrenaline doing its biological trick within me. I hadn't counted on Luke's bringing anyone with him. My foolproof plan might not be proof against this—meaning I was the fool.

The boulder rolled more quickly now, and there was not even time for profanity as my mind raced, focused upon a course of action and assumed its appropriate stance.

I summoned the image of the Logrus and it took shape before me. I rose to my feet, still leaning against the wall, and began moving my arms to correspond with the random-seeming movements of two of the eidolon's limbs. By the time I achieved a satisfactory conjunction, the sounds from overhead had ceased.

The opening was now clear. Moments later the light was raised and moved toward it.

I stepped into the chamber and extended my hands. As the men, short and dark, came into view above me my original plan was canceled completely. They both carried unsheathed poignards in their right hands. Neither of them was Luke.

I reached out with my Logrus gauntlets and took hold of each of them by the throat. I squeezed until they collapsed within my grip. I squeezed a little longer, then released them.

As they dropped from sight I hooked the high lip of the entrance with my glowing lines of force and drew myself upward with them. As I reached the opening I paused to recover Frakir, who was coiled about its underside. That had been my trap. Luke, or anyone else, would have been passing through a noose to enter, a noose ready to tighten instantly upon anything moving through.

Now, though. . . .

A trail of fire ran down the slope to my right. The fallen lantern had shattered, its spilled fuel become a burning rivulet. The men I had choked lay sprawled at either hand. The boulder that had blocked this opening rested to the left and somewhat to the rear of me. I remained where I was—head and shoulders above the opening, resting on my elbows—with the image of the Logrus dancing between my eyes, the warm tingling of its power lines yet a part of my arms, Frakir moving from my left shoulder down to my biceps.

It had been almost too easy. I couldn't see Luke trusting a couple of lackeys to question, kill or transport me—whichever of these had been their mission. That is why I had not emerged fully, but scanned the nighted environs from my vantage of relative security.

Prudent, for a change. For someone else shared the night with me. It was sufficiently dark, even with the dwindling fire trail, that my ordinary vision did not serve to furnish me this intelligence. But when I summon the Logrus, the mental set that grants me vision of its image permits me to view other nonphysical manifestations as well.

So it was that I detected such a construct beneath a tree to my left, amid shadows where I would not have seen the human figure before which it hovered. And a strange pattern at that, reminiscent of Amber's own; it turned like a slow pinwheel, extending tendrils of smoke-shot yellow light. These drifted toward me across the night and I watched, fascinated, knowing already what I would do when the moment came.

There were four big ones, and they came on slowly, probing. When they were within several yards of me they halted, gained slack, then struck like cobras. My hands were together and slightly crossed, Logrus limbs extended. I separated them with a single sweeping motion, tilting them slightly forward as I did so. They struck the yellow tendrils, casting them away to be thrown back upon their pattern. I felt a tingling sensation in my forearms as this occurred. Then, using my right-hand extension as if it were a blade, I struck at the now-wavering pattern as if it were a shield. I heard a short sharp cry as that image grew dim, and I struck again quickly, hauled myself out of my hole and started down the slope, my arm aching.

The image—whatever it had been—faded and was gone. By then, however, I could make out more clearly the figure leaning against the tree trunk. It appeared to be that of a woman, though I could not distinguish her features because of some small object she had raised and now held before her near to eye level. Fearing that it was a weapon, I struck at it with a Logrus extension, hoping to knock it from her hand.

I stumbled then, for there was a recoil which jolted my arm with considerable force. It would seem to have been a potent sorcerous object which I had struck. At least I had the pleasure of seeing the lady sway also. She uttered a short cry, too, but she hung on to the object.

A moment later a faint polychrome shimmering began about her form and I realized what the thing was. I had just directed the force of the Logrus against a Trump. I had to reach her now, if only to find out who she was.

But as I rushed ahead I realized that I could not get to her in time. Unless . . .

I plucked Frakir from my shoulder and cast her along the line of the Logrus force, manipulating her in the proper direction and issuing my commands as she flew.

From my new angle of view and by the faint rainbow halo that now surrounded her I finally saw the lady's face. It was Jasra, who had damn near killed me with a bite back in Melman's apartment. In a moment she would be gone, taking with her my chance of obtaining some answers on which my life might depend.

"Jasra!" I cried, trying to break her concentration.

It didn't work, but Frakir did. My strangling cord, glowing silver now, caught her about the throat, whipping out with a free end to lash tightly about the branch that hung near, to Jasra's left.

The lady began to fade, apparently not realizing that it was too late. She couldn't trump out without decapitating herself.

She learned it quickly. I heard her gurgling cry as she stepped back, grew solid, lost her halo, dropped her Trump and clawed at the cord encircling her throat.

I came up beside her, to lay my hand upon Frakir, who uncoiled one end from the tree limb and rewound it about my wrist.

"Good evening, Jasra," I said, jerking her head back. "Try the poison bite again and you'll need a neck brace. You understand?"

She tried to talk but couldn't. She nodded.

"I'm going to loosen my cord a bit," I said, "so you can answer my questions."

I eased Frakir's grip upon her throat. She began coughing, then, and gave me a look that would have turned sand to glass. Her magical construct had faded completely, so I let the Logrus slip away also.

"Why are you after me?" I asked. "What am I to you?"

"Son of perdition!" she said, and she tried to spit at me but her mouth must have been too dry.

I jerked lightly on Frakir and she coughed again.

"Wrong answer," I said. "Try again."

But she smiled then, her gaze shifting to a point beyond me. I kept the slack out of Frakir and chanced a glance. The air was beginning to shimmer, behind me and to the right, in obvious preparation to someone's trumping in.

I did not feel ready to take on an additional threat at this time, and so I dipped my free hand into my pocket and withdrew a handful of my own Trumps. Flora's was on top. Fine. She'd do.

I pushed my mind toward her, through the feeble light, beyond the face of the card. I felt her distracted attention, followed by a sudden alertness.

Then, *Yes . . . ?*

"Bring me through! Hurry!" I said.

Is it an emergency? she asked.

"You'd better believe it," I told her.

Uh—okay. Come on.

I had an image of her in bed. It grew clearer, clearer. She extended her hand.

I reached out and took it. I moved forward just as I heard Luke's voice ring out, crying, "Stop!"

I continued on through, dragging Jasra after me. She tried to draw back and succeeded in halting me as I stumbled against the side of the bed. It was then I noted the dark-haired, bearded man regarding me with wide eyes from the bed's farther side.

"Who—? What—?" he began as I smiled bleakly and regained my balance.

Luke's shadowy form came into view beyond my prisoner. He reached forward and seized Jasra's arm, drawing her back away from me. She made a gurgling noise as the movement drew Frakir more tightly about her throat.

Damn! What now?

Flora rose suddenly, her face contorted, the scented lavender sheet falling away as she drove a fist forward with surprising speed.

"You bitch!" she cried. "Remember me?"

The blow fell upon Jasra's jaw, and I barely managed to free Frakir in time to keep from being dragged backward with her into Luke's waiting arms.

Both of them faded, and the shimmer was gone.

The dark-haired guy in the meantime had scrambled out of the bed and was snatching up articles of clothing. Once he had them all in his grasp he did not bother to don any, but simply held them in front of him and backed quickly toward the door.

"Ron! Where are you going?" Flora asked.

"Away!" he answered, and he opened the door and passed through it.

"Hey! Wait!"

"No way!" came the reply from the next room.

"Damn!" she said, glaring at me. "You have a way of messing up a person's life." Then, "Ron! What about dinner?" she called.

"I have to see my analyst," came his voice, followed shortly by the slamming of another door.

"I hope you realize what a beautiful thing you just destroyed," Flora told me.

I sighed. "When did you meet him?" I asked.

She frowned. "Well, yesterday," she replied. "Go ahead and smirk. These things are not always a mere function of time. I could tell right away that it was going to be something special. Trust someone crass like you or your father to cheapen a beautiful—"

"I'm sorry," I said. "Thanks for pulling me through. Of course he'll be back. We just scared the hell out of him. But how could he fail to return once he's known you?"

She smiled. "Yes, you *are* like Corwin," she said. "Crass, but perceptive."

She rose and crossed to the closet, took out a lavender robe and donned it.

"What," she said, belting it about her, "was that all about?"

"It's a long story—"

"Then I'd better hear it over lunch. Are you hungry?" she asked.

I grinned.

"It figures. Come on."

She led me out through a French Provincial living room and into a large country kitchen full of tiles and copper. I offered to help her, but she pointed at a chair beside the table and told me to sit.

As she was removing numerous goodies from the refrigerator, I said, "First—"

"Yes?"

"Where are we?"

"San Francisco," she replied.

"Why have you set up housekeeping here?"

"After I finished that business of Random's I decided to stay on. The town looked good to me again."

I snapped my fingers. I'd forgotten she'd been sent to determine the ownership of the warehouse where Victor Melman had had his apartment and studio, and where Brutus Storage had a supply of ammo that would fire in Amber.

"So who owned the warehouse?" I asked.

"Brutus Storage," she replied. "Melman rented from them."

"And who owns Brutus Storage?"

"J. B. Rand, Inc."

"Address?"

"An office in Sausalito. It was vacated a couple of months ago."

"Did the people who owned the place have a home address for the renter?"

"Just a post office box. It's been abandoned too."

I nodded. "I'd a feeling it would be something like that," I said. "Now tell me about Jasra. Obviously you know the lady."

She sniffed. "No lady," she said. "A royal whore is what she was when I knew her."

"Where?"

"In Kashfa."

"Where's that?"

"An interesting little shadow kingdom, a bit over the edge of the Golden Circle of those with which Amber has commerce. Shabby barbaric splendor and all that. It's kind of a cultural backwater."

"How is it you know it at all, then?"

She paused a moment in stirring something in a bowl.

"Oh, I used to keep company with a Kashfan nobleman I'd met in a wood one day. He was out hawking and I happened to have twisted my ankle—"

"Uh," I interjected, lest we be diverted by details. "And Jasra?"

"She was consort to the old king Menillan. Had him wrapped around her finger."

"What have you got against her?"

"She stole Jasrick while I was out of town."

"Jasrick?"

"My nobleman. Earl of Kronklef."

"What did His Highness Menillan think of these goings-on?"

"He never knew. He was on his deathbed at the time. Succumbed shortly thereafter. In fact, that's why she really wanted Jasrick. He was chief of the palace guard and his brother was a general. She used them to pull off a coup when Menillan expired. Last I heard, she was queen in Kashfa and she'd ditched Jasrick. Served him proper, I'd say. I think he had his eye on the throne, but she didn't care to share it. She had him and his brother executed for treason of one sort or another. He was really a handsome fellow. . . . Not too bright, though."

"Do the people of Kashfa have any—uh—unusual physical endowments?" I asked.

She smiled. "Well, Jasrick was one hell of a fellow. But I wouldn't use the word 'unusual' to—"

"No, no," I interrupted. "What I meant was some sort of anomaly of the mouth—retractable fangs or a sting or something of that sort."

"Un-uh," she said, and I could not tell whether her heightened coloring came from the heat of the stove. "Nothing like that. They're built along standard lines. Why do you ask?"

"When I told you my story back in Amber I omitted the part where Jasra bit me, and I was barely able to trump out because of some sort of poison she seemed to have injected. It left me numb, paralyzed and very weak for a long while."

She shook her head. "Kashfans can't do anything like that. But then, of course, Jasra is not a Kashfan."

"Oh? Where's she from?"

"I don't know. But she's a foreigner. Some say a slaver brought her in from a distant land. Others say she just wandered in herself one day and caught Menillan's eye. It was rumored she was a sorceress. I don't know."

"I do. That rumor's right."

"Really? Perhaps that's how she got Jasrick."

I shrugged. "How long ago was your—experience—with her?"

"Thirty or forty years, I'd guess."

"And she is still queen in Kashfa?"

"I don't know. It's been a long time since I've been back that way."

"Is Amber on bad terms with Kashfa?"

She shook her head. "No special terms at all, really. As I said, they're a bit out of the way. Not as accessible as a lot of other places, with nothing greatly desirable for trade."

"No real reason then for her to hate us?"

"No more than for hating anyone else."

Some delightful cooking odors began to fill the room. As I sat there sniffing them and thinking of the long, hot shower I would head for after lunch, Flora said what I had somehow known she would say.

"That man who dragged Jasra back. . . . He looked familiar. Who was he?"

"He was the one I told you about back in Amber," I replied. "Luke. I'm curious whether he reminds you of anyone."

"He seems to," she said, after a pause. "But I can't say just who."

As her back was to me I said, "If you're holding anything that might break or spill if you drop it, please put it down."

I heard something set to rest on the countertop. Then she turned, a puzzled expression on her face.

"Yes?"

"His real name is Rinaldo, and he's Brand's son," I told her. "I was his prisoner for over a month in another shadow. I just now escaped."

"Oh, my," she whispered. Then, "What does he want?"

"Revenge," I answered.

"Against anyone in particular?"

"No. All of us. But Caine, of course, was first."

"I see."

"Please don't burn anything," I said. "I've been looking forward to a good meal for a long time."

She nodded and turned away. After a while she said, "You knew him for a pretty long time. What's he like?"

"He always seemed to be a fairly nice guy. If he's crazy, like his dad, he hid it well."

She uncorked a wine bottle, poured two glasses and brought them over. Then she began serving the meal.

After a few bites she paused with her fork half raised and stared at nothing in particular.

"Who'd have thought the son of a bitch would reproduce?" she remarked.

"Fiona, I think," I told her. "The night before Caine's funeral she asked me whether I had a photo of Luke. When I showed her one I could tell that something was bothering her, but she wouldn't say what."

"And the next day she and Bleys were gone," Flora said. "Yes. Now I think of it, he does look somewhat the way Brand did when he was very young—so long ago. Luke seems bigger and heavier, but there is a resemblance."

She resumed eating.

"By the way, this is very good," I said.

"Oh, thanks." She sighed then. "That means I have to wait till you're finished eating to hear the whole story."

I nodded, because my mouth was full. Let the empire totter. I was starved.

2

Showered, trimmed, manicured and garbed in fresh-conjured finery, I got a number out of Information and placed a call to the only Devlin listed in Bill Roth's area. The voice of the woman who answered did not possess the proper timbre, though I still recognized it.

"Meg? Meg Devlin?" I said.

"Yes," came the reply. "Who is this?"

"Merle Corey."

"Who?"

"Merle Corey. We spent an interesting night together some time back—"

"I'm sorry," she said. "There must be some mistake."

"If you can't talk freely now I can call whenever you say. Or you can call me."

"I don't know you," she said, and she hung up.

I stared at the receiver. If her husband were present I'd assumed she'd play it a bit cagey but would at least give some indication that she knew me and would talk another time. I had held off on getting in touch with Random because I'd a feeling he'd summon me back to Amber immediately, and I'd wanted to talk to Meg first. I certainly couldn't spare the time to go and visit her. I could not understand her response, but for now at least I was stuck with it. So I tried the only other thing that occurred to me. I got hold of Information again and obtained the number for Bill's next-door neighbors, the Hansens.

It was answered on the third ring—a woman's voice I recognized as Mrs. Hansen's. I had met her in the past, though I had not seen her on my most recent trip to the area.

"Mrs. Hansen," I began. "It's Merle Corey."

"Oh, Merle. . . . You were just up here a while ago, weren't you?"

"Yes. Couldn't stay long, though. But I did finally get to meet George. Had several long talks with him. In fact, I'd like to speak with him right now if he's handy."

The silence ran several beats too long before she responded.

"George. . . . Well, George is over at the hospital just now, Merle. Is it something you could tell me?"

"Oh, it's not urgent," I said. "What happened to George?"

"It—it's nothing real bad. He's just an outpatient now, and to-day's his day to get checked over and pick up some medication. He had a—sort of—breakdown last month. Had a couple days' worth of amnesia, and they can't seem to figure what caused it."

"I'm sorry to hear that."

"Well, the X-rays didn't show any damage—like he'd hit his head or anything. And he seems okay now. They say he'll proba-bly be fine. But they want to keep an eye on him a little longer. That's all." Suddenly, as if struck by inspiration, she asked, "How'd he seem when you were talking with him, anyway?"

I'd seen it coming, so I didn't hesitate.

"He seemed fine when I talked with him," I answered. "But of course I hadn't known him before, so I couldn't tell whether he was acting any different."

"I see what you mean," she said. "Do you want him to call you back when he gets in?"

"No. I'm going to be going out," I said, "and I'm not sure when I'll be getting back. It was nothing really important. I'll get in touch again one of these days."

"Okay, then. I'll tell him you called."

"Thanks. G'bye."

That one I'd almost expected. After Meg. George's behavior had been overtly weird, at the end there. What had bothered me was that he'd seemed to know who I really was and to know about Amber—and he even wanted to follow me through a Trump. It was as if he and Meg had both been subjected to some strange manipulation.

Jasra came to mind immediately in this regard. But then she was Luke's ally, it seemed, and Meg had warned me against Luke.

Why would she do that if Jasra were controlling her in some fashion? It didn't make sense. Who else did I know who might be capable of causing such phenomena?

Fiona, for one. But then she'd been party to my later return to this shadow from Amber and had even picked me up after my evening with Meg. And she'd seemed just as puzzled about the course of events as I was.

Shit. Life is full of doors that don't open when you knock, equally spaced amid those that open when you don't want them to.

I went back and knocked on the bedroom door, and Flora told me to come in. She was seated before a mirror, applying makeup.

"How'd it go?" she asked.

"Not too well. Totally unsatisfactory, actually." I summarized the results of my calls.

"So what are you going to do now?" she inquired.

"Get in touch with Random," I said, "and bring him up to date. I've got a feeling he'll call me back to hear it all. So I wanted to say good-bye, and thanks for helping me. Sorry if I broke up your romance."

She shrugged, her back still to me, as she studied herself in the mirror.

"Don't worry—"

I did not hear the remainder of her sentence, though she continued talking. My attention was snatched away by what seemed the beginning of a Trump contact. I made myself receptive and waited. The feeling grew stronger but the caller's presence did not become manifest. I turned away from Flora.

"Merle, what is it?" I heard her say then.

I raised one hand to her as the feeling intensified. I seemed to be staring down a long black tunnel with nothing at its farther end.

"I don't know," I said, summoning the Logrus and taking control of one of its limbs. "Ghost? Is that you? Are you ready to talk?" I asked.

There was no reply. I felt a chill as I remained receptive, waiting. I had never experienced anything quite like this before. I'd a strong feeling that if I but moved forward I would be transported somewhere. Was this a challenge? A trap? Whatever, I felt that only a fool would accept such an invitation from the unknown. For all I knew, it might deliver me back to the crystal cave.

"If there is something you want," I said, "you are going to have to make yourself known and ask. I've given up on blind dates."

A sense of presence trickled through, then, but no intimations of identity.

"All right," I said. "I'm not coming and you have no message. The only other thing I can think of is that you're asking to come to me. If that's the case, come ahead."

I extended both of my apparently empty hands, my invisible strangling cord writhing into position in my left, an unseen Logrus death bolt riding my right. It was one of those times when courtesy demanded professional standards.

A soft laughter seemed to echo within the dark tunnel. It was purely a mental projection, however, cold and genderless.

Your offer is, of course, a trick, came to me then. *For you are not a fool. Still, I grant your courage, to address the unknown as you do. You do not know what you face, yet you await it. You even invite it.*

"The offer is still good," I said.

I never thought of you as dangerous.

"What do you want?"

To regard you.

"Why?"

There may come a time when I will face you on different terms.

"What terms?"

I feel that our purposes will be crossed.

"Who are you?"

Again, the laughter.

No. Not now. Not yet. I would merely look upon you, and observe your reactions.

"Well? Have you seen enough?"

Almost.

"If our purposes are crossed, let the conflict be now," I said. "I'd like to get it out of the way so I can get on with some important business."

I appreciate arrogance. But when the time comes the choice will not be yours.

"I'm willing to wait," I said, as I cautiously extended a Logrus limb out along the dark way.

Nothing. My probe encountered nothing. . . .

I admire your performance. Here!

Something came rushing toward me. My magical extension informed me that it was soft—too soft and loose to do me any real harm—a large, cool mass showing bright colors. . . .

I stood my ground and extended through it—beyond, far,

farther—reaching for the source. I encountered something tangible but yielding: a body perhaps, perhaps not; too—too big to snap back in an instant.

Several small items, hard and of sufficiently low mass, recommended themselves to my lightning search. I seized upon one, tore it free of whatever held it and called it to me.

A wordless impulse of startlement reached me at the same time as the rushing mass and the return of my Logrus summoning.

It burst about me like fireworks: flowers, flowers, flowers. Violets, anemones, daffodils, roses. . . . I heard Flora gasp as hundreds of them rained into the room. The contact was broken immediately. I was aware that I held something small and hard in my right hand, and the heady odors of the floral display filled my nostrils.

"What the hell," said Flora, "happened?"

"I'm not sure," I answered, brushing petals from my shirtfront. "You like flowers? You can have these."

"Thanks, but I prefer a less haphazard arrangement," she said, regarding the bright mound that lay at my feet. "Who sent them?"

"A nameless person at the end of a dark tunnel."

"Why?"

"Down payment on a funeral display, maybe. I'm not sure. The tenor of the whole conversation was somewhat threatening."

"I'd appreciate it if you'd help me pick them up before you go."

"Sure," I said.

"There are vases in the kitchen and the bathroom. Come on."

I followed her and collected several. On the way, I studied the object I had brought back from the other end of the sending. It was a blue button mounted in a gold setting, a few navy blue threads still attached. The cut stone bore a curved, four-limbed design. I showed it to Flora and she shook her head.

"It tells me nothing," she said.

I dug into my pocket and produced the chips of stone from the crystal cave. They seemed to match. Frakir stirred slightly when I passed the button near her, then lapsed again into quiescence, as if having given up on warning me about blue stones when I obviously never did anything about them.

"Strange," I said.

"I'd like some roses on the night table," Flora told me, "and a couple of mixed displays on the dresser. You know, no one's ever sent *me* flowers this way. It's a rather intriguing introduction. Are you sure they were for you?"

I growled something anatomical or theological and gathered rosebuds.

Later, as we sat in the kitchen drinking coffee and musing, Flora remarked, "This thing's kind of spooky."

"Yes."

"Maybe you ought to discuss it with Fi after you've talked with Random."

"Maybe."

"Speaking of whom, shouldn't you be calling Random?"

"Maybe."

"What do you mean, 'maybe'? He's got to be warned."

"True. But I've a feeling that being safe won't get any questions answered for me."

"What do you have in mind, Merle?"

"Do you have a car?"

"Yes, I just got it a few days back. Why?"

I withdrew the button and the stones from my pocket, spread them on the table and regarded them again. "It just occurred to me while we were picking up flowers where I might have seen another of these."

"Yes?"

"There is a memory I must have been blocking, because it was very distressing: Julia's appearance when I found her. I seem to recall now that she had on a pendant with a blue stone. Maybe it's just coincidence, but—"

She nodded. "Could be. But even so, the police probably have it now."

"Oh, I don't want the thing. But it reminds me that I didn't really get to look over her apartment as well as I might have if I hadn't had to leave in a hurry. I want to see it again before I go back to Amber. I'm still puzzled as to how that—creature—got in."

"What if the place has been cleaned out? Or rented again?"

I shrugged. "Only one way to find out."

"Okay, I'll drive you there."

A few minutes later we were in her car and I was giving her directions. It was perhaps a twenty-minute drive beneath a sunny late-afternoon sky, stray clouds passing. I spent much of the time making certain preparations with Logrus forces, and I was ready by the time we reached the proper area.

"Turn here and go around the block," I said, gesturing. "I'll show you where to park if there's a place."

There was, close to the spot where I'd parked on that day.

When we were stopped beside the curb she glanced at me. "Now what? Do we just go up to the place and knock?"

"I'm going to make us invisible," I told her, "and I'm going to keep us that way till we're inside. You'll have to stay close to me in order for us to see each other, though."

She nodded.

"Dworkin did it for me once," she said, "when I was a child. Spied on a lot of people then." She chuckled. "I'd forgotten."

I put the finishing touches to the elaborate spell and laid it upon us, the world growing dimmer beyond the windshield as I did. It was as if I regarded our surroundings through gray sunglasses as we slipped out the passenger side of the car. We walked slowly up to the corner and turned right.

"Is this a hard spell to learn?" she asked me. "It seems a very handy one to know."

"Unfortunately, yes," I said. "Its biggest drawback is that you can't just do it at a moment's notice if you don't have it hanging ready—and I didn't. So, starting from scratch, it takes about twenty minutes to build."

We turned up the walk to the big old house.

"Which floor?" she asked me.

"Top."

We climbed to the front door and found it locked. No doubt they were more particular about such matters these days.

"Break it?" Flora whispered.

"Too noisy," I answered.

I placed my left hand upon the doorknob and gave Frakir a silent command. She unwound two turnings of her coil from about my wrist, coming into view as she moved across the lock plate and slithered into the keyhole. There followed a tightening, a stiffening and several rigid movements.

A soft click meant the bolt was drawn, and I turned the knob and pulled gently. The door opened. Frakir returned to bracelethood and invisibility.

We entered, closing the door quietly behind us. We were not present in the wavery mirror. I led Flora up the stairs.

There were soft voices from one of the rooms on the second floor. That was all. No wind. No excited dogs. And the voices grew still before we reached the third floor.

I saw that the entire door to Julia's apartment had been replaced. It was slightly darker than the other and it sported a bright new lock. I tapped upon it gently and we waited. There was no response, but I knocked again after perhaps half a minute and we waited again.

No one came. So I tried it. It was locked, but Frakir repeated her trick and I hesitated. My hand shook as I recalled my last visit. I knew her mutilated corpse was no longer lying there. I knew no killer beast was waiting to attack me. Yet the memory held me for several seconds.

"What's the matter?" Flora whispered.

"Nothing," I said, and I pushed the door open.

The place had been partly furnished, as I recalled. The part that had come with it remained—the sofa and end tables, several chairs, a larger table—but all Julia's own stuff was gone. There was a new rug on the floor, and the floor itself had been buffed recently. It did not appear that the place had been re-let, as there were no personal items of any sort about.

We entered and I closed the door, dropping the spell that had cloaked us as I began my circuit through the rooms. The place brightened perceptibly as our magic veils faded.

"I don't think you're going to find anything," Flora said. "I can smell wax and disinfectant and paint. . . ."

I nodded.

"The more mundane possibilities seem to be excluded," I said. "But there is something else I want to try."

I calmed my mind and called up the Logrus-seeing. If there were any remaining traces of a magical working, I hoped I could spot them in this fashion. I wandered slowly then, through the living room, regarding everything from every possible angle. Flora moved off, conducting her own investigation, which consisted mainly in looking under everything. The room flickered slightly for me as I scanned at those wavelengths where such a manifestation was most likely to be apparent—at least, that was the best way to describe the process in this shadow.

Nothing, large or small, escaped my scrutiny. But nothing was revealed to it. After long minutes I moved into the bedroom.

Flora must have heard my sudden intake of breath, because she was into the room and at my side in seconds, and staring at the chest of drawers before which I stood.

"Something in it?" she inquired, reaching forward, then withdrawing her hand.

"No. Behind it," I said.

The chest of drawers had been moved in the course of purging the apartment. It used to occupy a space several feet farther to the right. That which I now saw was visible to its left and above it, with more of it obviously blocked to my sight. I took hold of the thing and pushed it back to the right, to the position it had formerly occupied.

"I still don't see anything," Flora said.

I reached out and caught hold of her hand, extending the Logrus force so that she, too, saw what I saw.

"Why"—she raised her other hand and traced the faint rectangular outline on the wall—"it looks like a . . . doorway," she said.

I studied it—a dim line of faded fire. The thing was obviously sealed and had been for some time. Eventually it would fade completely and be gone.

"It *is* a doorway," I answered.

She pulled me back into the other room to regard the opposite side of the wall.

"Nothing here," she observed. "It doesn't go through."

"Now you've got the idea," I said. "It goes somewhere else."

"Where?"

"Wherever the thing that killed Julia came from."

"Can you open it?"

"I am prepared to stand in front of it for as long as I have to," I told her, "and try."

I returned to the other room and studied it once again.

"Merlin," she said, as I released her hand and raised mine before me, "don't you think this is the point where you should get in touch with Random, tell him exactly what has been happening and perhaps have Gérard standing next to you if you succeed in opening that door?"

"I probably should," I agreed, "but I'm not going to."

"Why not?"

"Because he might tell me not to."

"He might be right, too."

I lowered my hands and turned toward her. "I have to admit you have a point," I said. "Random has to be told everything, and I've probably put it off too long already. So here is what I would like you to do: Go back to the car and wait. Give me an hour. If I'm not out by then, get in touch with Random, tell him everything I told you and tell him about this, too."

"I don't know," she said. "If you don't show, Random's going to be mad at me."

"Just tell him I insisted and there was nothing you could do. Which is actually the case, if you stop to think about it."

She pursed her lips. "I don't like leaving you—though I'm not anxious to stay either. Care to take along a hand grenade?"

She raised her purse and began to open it.

"No. Thanks. Why do you have it, anyway?"

She smiled. "I always carry them in this shadow. They sometimes come in handy. But okay, I'll go wait."

She kissed me lightly on the cheek and turned away.

"And try to get hold of Fiona," I said, "if I don't show. Tell her the whole story, too. She might have a different angle on this."

She nodded and departed. I waited until I heard the door close, then focused my attention fully upon the bright rectangle. Its outline seemed fairly uniform, with only a few slightly thicker, brighter areas and a few finer, dimmer ones. I traced the lines slowly with the palm of my right hand at a height of about an inch above the wall's surface. I felt a small prickling, a heatlike sensation as I did this. Predictably, it was greater above the brighter areas. I took this as an indication that the seal was slightly less perfect in these spots. Very well. I would soon discover whether the thing could be forced, and these would be my points of attack.

I twisted my hands deeper into the Logrus until I wore the limbs I desired as fine-fingered gauntlets, stronger than metals, more sensitive than tongues in the places of their power. I moved my right hand to the point nearest it, on a level with my hip. I felt the pulse of an old spell when I touched that spot of greater brightness. I narrowed my extension as I pushed, making it finer and finer until it slipped through. The pulsing then became a steady thing. I repeated the exercise on a higher area to my left.

I stood there, feeling the force that had sealed it, my fine filament extensions throbbing within its matrix. I tried moving them, first upward, then down. The right one slid a little farther than the left, in both directions, before a tightness and resistance halted it. I summoned more force from the body of the Logrus, which swam specterlike within and before me, and I poured this energy into the gauntlets, the pattern of the Logrus changing form again as I did so. When I tried once more to move it, the right one slid downward for perhaps a foot before the throbbing trapped it; when I pushed it upward it rose nearly to the top. I tried again on the left. It moved all the way to the top, but it only passed perhaps six inches below the starting point when I drew it downward.

I breathed deeply and felt myself beginning to perspire. I pumped more power into the gauntlets and forced their extensions farther downward. The resistance was even greater there, and the throbbing passed up my arms and into the very center of my being. I paused and rested, then raised the force to an even higher level of intensity. The Logrus writhed again and I pushed both hands all the way to the floor, then knelt there panting before I began working my way along the bottom. The portal was obviously meant never to be opened again. There was no artistry for this, only brute force.

When my forces met in the middle, I withdrew and regarded the work. To the right, to the left and along the bottom, the fine red lines had now become broad fiery ribbons. I could feel their pulsation across the distance that separated us.

I stood and raised my arms. I began to work along the top, starting at the corners, moving inward. It was easier than it had been earlier. The forces from the opened areas seemed to add a certain pressure, and my hands just flowed to the middle. When they met I seemed to hear something like a soft sighing sound. I dropped them and considered my work. The entire outline flared now. But more than that. It seemed almost as if the bright line were flowing, around and around. . . .

I stood there for several minutes, regrouping, relaxing, settling. Working up my nerve. All I knew was that the door would lead to a different shadow. That could mean anything. When I opened it something could, I suppose, leap out and attack me. But then, it had been sealed for some time. More probably any trap would be of a different sort. Most likely, I would open it and nothing would happen. I would then have a choice of merely looking around from where I stood or entering. And there probably wouldn't be very much to see, just standing there, looking. . . .

So I extended my Logrus members once again, taking hold of the door at either side, and I pushed. A yielding occurred on the side to my right, so I released my hold on the left. I continued my pressure on the right and the whole thing suddenly swung inward and away. . . .

I was looking down a pearly tunnel, which appeared to widen after a few paces. Beyond that was a ripple effect, as of distant heat patterns above the road on a hot summer day. Patches of redness and indeterminate dark shapes swam within it. I waited for perhaps half a minute, but nothing approached.

I prepared Frakir for trouble. I maintained my Logrus connection. I advanced, extending probes before me. I passed within.

A sudden change in the pressure gradient at my back caused me to cast a quick glance in that direction. The doorway had closed and dwindled, now appearing to me in the distance as a tiny red cube. My several steps could, of course, have borne me a great distance also, should the rules of this space so operate.

I continued, and a hot wind flowed toward me, engulfed me, stayed with me. The sides of my passageway receded, the prospect before me continued to shimmer and dance, and my pace became more labored, as if I were suddenly walking uphill. I heard something like a grunt from beyond the place where my vision misbehaved, and my left Logrus probe encountered something that it jolted slightly. Frakir began to throb simultaneous with my sensing an aura of menace through the probe. I sighed. I hadn't expected this was going to be easy. If I'd been running the show I wouldn't have let things go with just sealing the door.

"All right, asshole! Hold it right there!" a voice boomed from ahead.

I continued to trudge forward.

It came again. "I said halt!"

Things began to swim into place as I advanced, and suddenly there were rough walls to my right and left and a roof overhead, narrowing, converging—

A huge rotund figure barred my way, looking like a purple Buddha with bat ears. Details resolved themselves as I drew nearer: protruding fangs, yellow eyes that seemed to be lidless, long red claws on its great hands and feet. It was seated in the middle of the tunnel and made no effort to rise. It wore no clothing, but its great swollen belly rested upon its knees, concealing its sex. Its voice had been gruffly masculine, however, and its odor generically foul.

"Hi," I said. "Nice day, wasn't it?"

It growled and the temperature seemed to rise slightly. Frakir had grown frantic and I calmed her mentally.

The creature leaned forward and with one bright nail inscribed a smoking line in the stone of the floor. I halted before it.

"Cross that line, sorcerer, and you've had it," it said.

"Why?" I asked.

"Because I said so."

"If you're collecting tolls," I suggested, "name the price."

It shook its head. "You can't buy your way past me."

"Uh—what makes you think I'm a sorcerer?"

It opened the dingy cavern of its face, displaying even more lurking teeth than I'd suspected, and it did something like the rattling of a tin sheet way down deep in back.

"I felt that little probe of yours," it said. "It's a sorcerer's trick. Besides, nobody but a sorcerer could have gotten to the place where you're standing."

"You do not seem to possess a great deal of respect for the profession."

"I eat sorcerers," it told me.

I made a face, thinking back over some of the old farts I've known in the business.

"To each, his, her or its own, I guess," I told it. "So what's the deal? A passage is no good unless you can get through it. How do I get by here?"

"You don't."

"Not even if I answer a riddle?"

"That won't do it for me," it said. But a small gleam came into its eye. "Just for the hell of it, though, what's green and red and goes round and round and round?" it asked.

"You know the sphinx!"

"Shit!" it said. "You've heard it."

I shrugged. "I get around."

"Not here you don't."

I studied it. It had to have some special defense against magical attacks if it were set to stop sorcerers. As for physical defense it was fairly imposing. I wondered how fast it was. Could I just dive past and start running? I decided that I did not wish to experiment along that line.

"I really do have to get through," I tried. "It's an emergency."

"Tough."

"Look, what do you get out of this, anyway? It seems like a pretty crummy job, sitting here in the middle of a tunnel."

"I love my work. I was created for it."

"How come you let the sphinx come and go?"

"Magical beings don't count."

"Hm."

"And don't try to tell me you're really a magical being, and then pull some sorcerous illusion. I can see right through that stuff."

"I believe you. What's your name, anyhow?"

It snorted. "You can call me Scrof, for conversational purposes. Yourself?"

"Call me Corey."

"Okay, Corey. I don't mind sitting here bullshitting with you, because that's covered by the rules. It's allowed. You've got three choices and one of them would be real stupid. You can turn around and go back the way you came and be none the worse for wear. You can also camp right where you are for as long as you like and I won't lift a finger so long as you behave. The dumb thing to do would be to cross this line I've drawn. Then I'd terminate you. This is the Threshold and I am the Dweller on it. I don't let anybody get by."

"I appreciate your making it clear."

"It's part of the job. So what'll it be?"

I raised my hands and the lines of force twisted like knives at each fingertip. Frakir dangled from my wrist and began to swing in an elaborate pattern.

Scrof smiled. "I not only eat sorcerers, I eat their magic, too. Only a being torn from the primal Chaos can make that claim. So come ahead, if you think you can face that."

"Chaos, eh? Torn from the primal Chaos?"

"Yep. There's not much can stand against it."

"Except maybe a Lord of Chaos," I replied, as I shifted my awareness to various points within my body. Rough work. The faster you do it the more painful it is.

Again, the rattling of the tin sheet.

"You know what the odds are against a Chaos Lord coming this far to go two out of three with a Dweller?" Scrof said.

My arms began to lengthen and I felt my shirt tear across my back as I leaned forward. The bones in my face shifted about and my chest expanded and expanded. . . .

"One out of one should be enough," I replied, when the transformation was complete.

"Shit," Scrof said as I crossed the line.

3

I stood just within the mouth of the cave for some time, my left shoulder hurting and my right leg sore also. If I could get the pain under control before I retransformed myself there was a chance that much of it would fade during the anatomical reshuffling. The process itself would probably leave me pretty tired, however. It takes a lot of energy, and switching twice this close together could be somewhat prostrating, following my bout with the Dweller. So I rested within the cave into which the pearly tunnel had eventually debouched, and I regarded the prospect before me.

Far down and to my left was a bright blue and very troubled body of water. White-crested waves expired in kamikaze attacks on the gray rocks of the shore; a strong wind scattered their spray and a piece of rainbow hung within the mist.

Before me and below me was a pocked, cracked and steaming land which trembled periodically, as it swept for well over a mile toward the high dark walls of an amazingly huge and complex structure, which I immediately christened Gormenghast. It was a hodgepodge of architectural styles, bigger even than the palace at Amber and somber as all hell. Also, it was under attack.

There were quite a few troops in the field before the walls, most of them in a distant nonscorched area of more normal terrain and some vegetation, though the grasses were well trampled and many trees shattered. The besiegers were equipped with scaling ladders and a battering ram, but the ram was idle at the moment and the ladders were on the ground. What appeared to have been an entire village of outbuildings smoldered darkly at the wall's base. Numerous sprawled figures were, I assumed, casualties.

Moving my gaze even farther to the right, I encountered an area of brilliant whiteness beyond that great citadel. It looked to be the projecting edge of a massive glacier, and gusts of snow or ice crystals were whipped about it in a fashion similar to the sea mists far to my left.

The wind seemed a constant traveler through these parts. I heard it cry out high above me. When I finally stepped outside to look upward, I found that I was only about halfway up a massive stony hillside—or low mountainside, depending on how one regards such matters—and the whining note of the wind came down even more loudly from those broken heights. There was also a *thump* at my back, and when I turned I could no longer locate the cave mouth. My journey along the route from the fiery door had been completed once I exited the cave, and its spell had apparently clamped down and closed the way immediately. I supposed that I could locate the outline upon the steep wall if I wanted to, but at the moment I had no such desire. I made a little pile of stones before it, and then I looked about again, studying details.

A narrow trail curved off to my right and back among some standing stones. I headed in that direction. I smelled smoke. Whether it was from the battle site or the area of vulcanism below I could not tell. The sky was a patchwork of cloud and light above me. When I halted between two of the stones and turned to regard the scene below once again, I saw that the attackers had formed themselves into new groups and that the ladders were being borne toward the walls. I also saw what looked like a tornado rise on the far side of the citadel and begin a slow counterclockwise movement about the walls. If it continued on its route it would eventually reach the attackers. Neat trick. Fortunately it was their problem and not mine.

I worked my way back into a stony declivity and settled myself upon a low ledge. I began the troublesome shapeshifting work, which I paced to take me half an hour or so. Changing from something nominally human to something rare and strange—perhaps monstrous to some, perhaps frightening—and then back again is a concept some may find repugnant. They shouldn't. We all of us do it every day in many different ways, don't we?

When the transformation was completed I lay back, breathing deeply, and listened to the wind. I was sheltered from its force by the stones and only its song came down to me. I felt vibrations from distant tremors of the earth and chose to take them as a gentle massage, soothing. . . . My clothes were in tatters, and for the moment I was too tired to summon a fresh outfit. My shoulder seemed to have lost its pain, and there was only the slightest twinge in my leg, fading, fading. . . . I closed my eyes for a few moments.

Okay, I'd made it through, and I'd a strong feeling that the answer to the matter of Julia's killer lay in the besieged citadel below. Offhand, I didn't see any easy way into the place at the moment, to make inquiry. But that was not the only way I might proceed. I decided to wait where I was, resting, until it grew dark—that is, if things here proceeded in a normal dark-light fashion. Then I'd slip downstairs, kidnap one of the besiegers and question him. Yes. And if it didn't get dark? Then I'd think of something else. Right now, though, just drifting felt best. . . .

For how long I dozed, I was uncertain. What roused me was the clicking of pebbles, from somewhere off to the right. I was instantly alert, though I didn't stir. There was no effort at stealth, and the pattern of approaching sounds—mainly slapping footfalls, as of someone wearing loose sandals—convinced me that only a single individual was moving in this direction. I tensed and relaxed my muscles and drew a few deep breaths.

A very hairy man emerged from between two of the stones to my right. He was about five and a half feet in height, very dirty, and he wore a dark animal skin about his loins; also, he had on a pair of sandals. He stared at me for several seconds before displaying the yellow irregularities of his smile.

"Hello. Are you injured?" he asked, in a debased form of Thari that I did not recall ever having heard before.

I stretched to make sure and then stood. "No," I replied. "Why do you ask that?"

The smile persisted. "I thought maybe you'd had enough of the fighting below and decided to call it quits."

"Oh, I see. No, it's not exactly like that. . . ."

He nodded and stepped forward. "Dave's my name. What's yours?"

"Merle," I said, clasping his grimy hand.

"Not to worry, Merle," he told me. "I wouldn't turn in anybody who decided to take a walk from a war, unless maybe there was a reward—and there ain't on this one. Did it myself years ago and never regretted it. Mine was goin' the same way this one seems to be goin', and I had sense enough to get out. No army's ever taken that place down there, and I don't think one ever will."

"What place is it?"

He cocked his head and squinted, then shrugged. "Keep of the Four Worlds," he said. "Didn't the recruiter tell you anything?"

I sighed. "Nope," I said.

"Wouldn't have any smokin' stuff on you, would you?"

"No," I answered, having used all my pipe tobacco back in the crystal cave. "Sorry."

I moved past him to a point where I could look downward from between the stones. I wanted another look at the Keep of the Four Worlds. After all, it was the answer to a riddle as well as the subject of numerous cryptic references in Melman's diary. Fresh bodies were scattered all over before its walls, as if cast about by the whirlwind, which was now circling back toward the point whence it had risen. But a small party of besiegers had apparently made it to the top of the wall despite this. And a fresh party had formed below and was headed for the ladders. One of its members bore a banner I could not place, but which seemed vaguely familiar—black and green, with what might be a couple of heraldic beasts having a go at each other. Two ladders were still in place, and I could see some fierce fighting going on behind the battlements.

"Some of the attackers seem to have gotten in," I said.

Dave hurried up beside me and stared. I immediately moved upwind.

"You're right," he acknowledged. "Now, that's a first. If they can get that damn gate open and let the others in they might even have a chance. Never thought I'd live to see it."

"How long ago was it," I asked, "when the army you were with attacked the place?"

"Must be eight, nine—maybe ten years," he muttered. "Those guys must be pretty good."

"What's it all about?" I asked.

He turned and studied me. "You really don't know?"

"Just got here," I said.

"Hungry? Thirsty?"

"As a matter of fact, yes."

"Come on, then." He took hold of my arm and steered me back between the stones, then led me along a narrow trail.

"Where are we headed?" I asked.

"I live nearby. I make it a point to feed deserters, for old times' sake. I'll make an exception for you."

"Thanks."

The trail split after a short while, and he took the right-hand branch, which involved some climbing. Eventually this led us to a series of rocky shelves, the last of which receded for a considerable distance. There were a number of clefts at its rear, into one of which he ducked. I followed him a short distance along it, and he halted before a low cave mouth. A horrible odor of putrefaction drifted forth, and I could hear the buzzing of flies within.

"This is my place," he announced. "I'd invite you in, but it's a little—uh—"

"That's okay," I said. "I'll wait."

He ducked inside, and I realized that my appetite was rapidly vanishing, especially when it came to anything he might have stored in that place.

Moments later he emerged, a duffel bag slung over his shoulder. "Got some good stuff in here," he announced.

I started walking back along the cleft. "Hey! Where you headed?"

"Air," I said. "I'm going back out on the shelf. It's a bit close back there."

"Oh. Okay," he said, and he fell into step behind me.

He had two unopened bottles of wine, several canteens of water, a fresh-looking loaf of bread, some tinned meat, a few firm apples and an uncut head of cheese in the bag, I discovered, after we'd seated ourselves on a ledge out in the open and he'd gestured for me to open the thing and serve myself. Having prudently remained upwind, I took some water and an apple for openers.

"Place has a stormy history," he stated, withdrawing a small knife from his girdle and cutting himself a piece of cheese. "I'm not sure who built it or how long it's been there."

When I saw that he was about to dig the cork out of a wine bottle with the knife I halted him and essayed a small and surreptitious Logrus sending. The response was quick, and I passed him the corkscrew immediately. He handed me the entire bottle after he'd uncorked it and opened the other for himself. For reasons involving public health I was grateful, though I wasn't in the mood for that much wine.

"That's what I call being prepared," he said, studying the corkscrew. "I've needed one of these for some time. . . ."

"Keep it," I told him. "Tell me more about that place. Who lives there? How did you come to be part of an invading army? Who's attacking it now?"

He nodded and took a swig of wine.

"The earliest boss of the place that I know of was a wizard

named Sharu Garrul. The queen of my country departed suddenly and came here." He paused and stared off into the distance for a time, then snorted. "Politics! I don't even know what the given reason for the visit was at the time. I'd never heard of the damned place in those days. Anyhow, she stayed a long while and people began to wonder: Was she a prisoner? Was she working out an alliance? Was she having an affair? I gather she sent back messages periodically, but they were the usual bland crap that didn't say anything—unless of course there were also secret communications folks like me wouldn't have heard about. She had a pretty good-sized retinue with her, too, with an honor guard that was not just for show. These guys were very tough veterans, even though they dressed pretty. So it was kind of debatable what was going on at that point."

"A question, if I may," I said. "What was your king's part in all this? You didn't mention him, and it would seem he ought to know—"

"Dead," he announced. "She made a lovely widow, and there was a lot of pressure on her to remarry. But she just took a succession of lovers and played the different factions off against each other. Usually her men were military leaders or powerful nobles, or both. She'd left her son in charge when she made this trip, though."

"Oh, so there was a prince old enough to sit in control?"

"Yes. In fact, he started the damned war. He raised troops and wasn't happy with the muster, so he got in touch with a childhood friend, a man generally considered an outlaw, but who commanded a large band of mercenaries. Name of Dalt—"

"Stop!" I said.

My mind raced as I recalled a story Gérard had once told me, about a strange man named Dalt who had led a private army against Amber, unusually effectively. Benedict himself had had to be recalled to oppose him. The man's forces had been defeated at the foot of Kolvir, and Dalt himself severely wounded. Though no one ever saw his body, it was assumed he would have died of such injuries. But there was more.

"Your home," I said. "You never named it. Where are you from, Dave?"

"A place called Kashfa," he replied.

"And Jasra was your queen?"

"You've heard of us. Where're you from?"

"San Francisco," I said.

He shook his head. "Don't know the place."

"Who does? Listen, how good are your eyes?"

"What do you mean?"

"A little while ago, when we looked down on the fighting, could you make out the flag the attackers were carrying?"

"Eyes ain't what they used to be," he said.

"It was green and black with some sort of animals on it."

He whistled. "A lion rending a unicorn, I'll bet. Sounds like Dalt's."

"What is the significance of that device?"

"He hates them Amberites, is what it means. Even went up against them once."

I tasted the wine. Not bad.

The same man, then. . . .

"You know why he hates them?" I asked.

"I understand they killed his mother," he said. "Had something to do with border wars. They get real complicated. I don't know the details."

I pried open a tin of meat, broke off some bread and made myself a sandwich.

"Please go ahead with your story," I said.

"Where was I?"

"The prince got hold of Dalt because he was concerned about his mother, and he needed more troops in a hurry."

"That's right, and I was picked up for Kashfan service about that time—foot soldier. The prince and Dalt led us through dark ways till we came to that place below. Then we did just what them guys downstairs were doing."

"And what happened?"

He laughed. "Went bad for us at first," he said. "I think it's somehow easy for whoever's in charge down there to control the elements—like that twister you saw a while ago. We got an earthquake and a blizzard and lightning. But we pressed on to the walls anyhow. Saw my brother scalded to death with boiling oil. That's when I decided I'd had enough. I started running and climbed on up here. Nobody chased me, so I waited around and watched. Probably shouldn't have, but I didn't know how things would go. More of the same, I'd figgered. But I was wrong, and it was too late to go back. They'd have whacked off my head or some other valuable parts if I did."

"What happened?"

"I got the impression that the attack forced Jasra's hand. She'd apparently been planning to do away with Sharu Garrul all along and take over the place herself. I think she'd been setting him up, gaining his confidence before she struck. I believe she was a little afraid of the old man. But when her army appeared on the doorstep she had to move, even though she wasn't ready. She took him on in a sorcerous duel while her guard held his men at bay. She won, though I gather she was somewhat injured. Mad as hell, too, at her son—for bringing in an army without her ordering it. Anyway, her guard opened the gates to them, and she took over the Keep. That's what I meant about no army taking the place. That one was an inside job."

"How did you learn all this?"

"Like I said, when deserters head this way I feed 'em and get the news."

"You gave me the impression that there have been other attempts to take the place. These would have had to be after she'd taken over."

He nodded and took another drink of wine.

"Yup. There was apparently a coup back in Kashfa, with both her and her kid away—a noble named Kasman, brother of one of her dead lovers, a fellow named Jasrick. This Kasman took over, and he wanted her and the prince out of the way. Must've attacked this place half a dozen times. Never could get in. Finally resigned himself to a standoff, I think. She sent her son off somewhere later, maybe to raise another army and try to win back her throne. I don't know. That was long ago."

"What about Dalt?"

"They paid him off with some loot from the Keep—there was apparently a lot of good stuff in there—and he took his troops and went back to wherever he hangs out."

I took another sip of wine myself and cut off a piece of the cheese. "How come you've stayed around all these years? It seems like a hard life."

He nodded. "Truth of it is, I don't know the way home. Those were strange trails they brought us in on. I thought I knew where they were, but when I went lookin' I couldn't never find 'em. I suppose I could have just taken off, but then I'd probably get lost more than ever. Besides, I know I can make out here. A few weeks and those outbuildings will be rebuilt and the peasants will move back in, no matter who wins. And they think I'm a holy man,

prayin' up here and meditatin'. Any time I wander down that way
they come out for a blessin' and give me enough food and drink to
hold me for a long while."

"Are you a holy man?" I asked.

"I just pretend," he said. "Makes them happy and keeps me
fed. Don't go tellin' that, though."

"Of course not. They wouldn't believe me, anyway."

He laughed again. "You're right."

I got to my feet and walked back along the trail a little way, so
that I could see the Keep once again. The ladders were on the
ground, and I beheld even more scattered dead. I saw no signs of
the struggle within.

"Is the gate open yet?" Dave called.

"No. I don't think the ones who got in were sufficient to the
task."

"Is that green and black banner anywhere in sight?"

"I can't see it anywhere."

He rose and came over, carrying both bottles. He passed me
mine and we both took a drink. The ground troops began to fall
back from the area before the wall.

"Think they're giving up or re-forming for another rush?" he
asked me.

"Can't say yet," I told him.

"Whichever it is, there should be a lot of good loot down there
tonight. Stick around and you'll have all you can carry."

"I'm curious," I said, "why Dalt would be attacking again, if
he's on good terms with the queen and her son."

"I think it's just the son," he said, "and he's gone. The old
lady's supposed to be a real bitch. And after all, the guy *is* a mercenary. Maybe Kasman hired him to go after her."

"Maybe she's not even in there," I said, having no idea how
this time stream ran, but thinking of my recent encounter with the
lady. The image of it, though, caused a strange train of thought.
"What's the prince's name, anyway?" I asked.

"Rinaldo," he answered. "He's a big red-haired guy."

"She's his mother!" I said involuntarily.

He laughed. "That's how you get to be a prince," he said.
"Have the queen be your mother."

But then, that would mean. . . .

"Brand!" I said. Then, "Brand of Amber."

He nodded. "You've heard the story."

"Not really. Just that much," I replied. "Tell it to me."

"Well, she snared herself an Amberite—the prince called Brand," he said. "Rumor had it they met over some magical operation and it was love at first blood. She wanted to keep him, and I've heard it said they actually were married in a secret ceremony. But he wasn't interested in the throne of Kashfa, though he was the only one she might have been willing to see on it. He traveled a lot, was away for long stretches of time. I've heard it said that he was responsible for the Days of Darkness years ago, and that he died in a great battle between Chaos and Amber at that time, at the hands of his kinsmen."

"Yes," I said, and Dave gave me a strange look, half puzzlement, half scrutiny. "Tell me more about Rinaldo," I said quickly.

"Not much to say," he replied. "She bore him, and I've heard she taught him something of her Arts. He didn't know his father all that well, Brand being away so much. Kind of a wild kid. Ran away any number of times and hung out with a band of outlaws—"

"Dalt's people?" I asked.

He nodded. "Rode with them, they say—even though his mother'd placed bounties on many of their heads at that time."

"Wait a minute. You say that she really hated these outlaws and mercenaries—"

" 'Hate' may be the wrong word. She'd never bothered about them before, but when her son got friendly with them I think she just got mad."

"She thought they were a bad influence?"

"No, I think she didn't like it that he'd run to them and they'd take him in whenever he had a falling out with her."

"Yet you say that she saw Dalt paid off out of the Keep's treasure and allowed him to ride away, after they'd forced her hand against Sharu Garrul."

"Yup. Big argument at the time, too, between Rinaldo and his mom, over just that point. And she finally gave in. That's the way I heard it from a couple of guys who were there. One of the few times the boy actually stood up to her and won, they say. In fact, that's why the guys deserted. She ordered all witnesses to their argument executed, they told me. They were the only ones managed to get away."

"Tough lady."

"Yup."

We walked on back to the area where we'd been seated and ate some more food. The song of the wind rose in pitch and a storm began out at sea. I asked Dave about big doglike creatures, and he told me that packs of them would probably be feasting on the battle's victims tonight. They were native to the area.

"We divide the spoils," he said. "I want the rations, the wine and any valuables. They just want the dead."

"What good are the valuables to you?" I said.

He looked suddenly apprehensive, as if I were considering the possibility of robbing him.

"Oh, it don't really amount to much. It's just that I've always been a thrifty person," he said, "and I make it sound more important than it is.

"You never can tell," he added.

"That's true," I agreed.

"How'd you get here anyway, Merle?" he asked quickly, as if to get my mind off the subject of his loot.

"Walked," I said.

"That don't sound right. Nobody comes here willingly."

"I didn't know I was coming here. Don't think I'll be staying long either," I said, as I saw him take up the small knife and begin toying with it. "No sense going below and begging after hospitality at a time like this."

"That's true," he remarked.

Was the old coot actually thinking of attacking me, to protect his cache? He could be more than a little mad by now, living up here alone in his stinking cave, pretending to be a saint.

"Would you be interested in returning to Kashfa," I said, "if I could set you on the right trail?"

He gave me a crafty look. "You don't know that much about Kashfa," he said, "or you wouldn't have been asking me all those questions. Now you say you can send me home?"

"I take it you're not interested?"

He sighed. "Not really, not any more. It's too late now. This is my home. I enjoy being a hermit."

I shrugged. "Well, thanks for feeding me, and thanks for all the news." I got to my feet.

"Where you going now?" he asked.

"I think I'll look around some, then head for home." I backed away from that small lunatic glow in his eyes.

He raised the knife, his grip tightened on it. Then he lowered it and cut another piece of cheese.

"Here, you can take some of the cheese with you if you want," he said.

"No, that's okay. Thanks."

"Just trying to save you some money. Have a good trip."

"Right. Take it easy."

I heard his chuckling all the way back to the trail. Then the wind drowned it.

I spent the next several hours reconnoitering. I moved around in the hills. I descended into the steaming, quaking lands. I walked along the seashore. I passed through the rear of the normal-seeming area and crossed the neck of the ice field. In all of this, I stayed as far from the Keep itself as possible. I wanted to fix the place as firmly in mind as I could, so that I could find my way back through Shadow rather than crossing a threshold the hard way. I saw several packs of wild dogs on my journey, but they were more intent upon the battle's corpses than anything that moved.

There were oddly inscribed boundary stones at each topo-graphical border, and I found myself wondering whether they were mapmakers' aids or something more. Finally, I wrestled one from the burning land over about fifteen feet into a region of ice and snow. I was knocked down almost immediately by a heavy tremor; I was able to scramble away in time, however, from the opening of a crevice and the spewing of geysers. The hot area claimed that small slice of the cold land in less than half an hour. Fortunately, I moved quickly to get out of the way of any further turmoil, and I observed the balance of these phenomena from a distance. But there was more to come.

I crouched back among the rocks, having reached the foothills of the range from which I had started by crossing through a sec-tion of the volcanic area. There, I rested and watched for a time while that small segment of terrain rearranged itself and the wind smeared smoke and steam across the land. Rocks bounced and rolled; dark carrion birds went out of their way to avoid what had to be some interesting thermals.

Then I beheld a movement which I first assumed to be seismic in origin. The boundary stone I had shifted rose slightly and jogged to the side. A moment later, however, and it was elevated even farther, appearing almost as if it had been levitated slightly above the ground. Then it drifted across the blasted area, moving in a straight line at a uniform speed, until—as nearly as I could judge—it had recovered its earlier position. And there it settled. Moments later the turmoil recommenced, and this time it was a jolting shrug of the ice sheet, jerking back, reclaiming the invaded area.

I called up my Logrus sight, and I was able to make out a dark glow surrounding the stone. This was connected by a long, straight, steady stream of light of the same general hue, extending from a high rear tower of the Keep. Fascinating. I would have given a lot for a view of the interior of that place.

Then, born with a sigh, maturing to a whistle, a whirlwind rose from the disputed area, growing, graying, swaying, to advance suddenly toward me like the swung proboscis of some cloudy, sky-high elephant. I turned and climbed higher, weaving my way amid rocks and around the shoulders of hillsides. The thing pursued, as if there were an intelligence guiding its movements. And the way it hung together while traversing that irregular terrain indicated an artificial nature, which in this place most likely meant magic.

It takes some time to determine an appropriate magical defense, and even more time to bring it into being. Unfortunately, I was only about a minute ahead of the posse, and that margin was probably dwindling.

When I spotted the long narrow crevice beyond the next turning, jagged as a limb of lightning, I paused only an instant to peer into its depth, and then I was descending, my tattered garments lashed about me, the windy tower a rumbling presence at my back. . . .

The way ran deep and so did I, following its jogs, its twistings. The rumble rose to a roar, and I coughed at the cloud of dust that engulfed me. A hailstorm of gravel assailed me. I threw myself flat then, about eight feet below the surface of the land, and covered my head with my arms, for I believed that the thing was about to pass directly above me.

I muttered warding spells as I lay there, despite their minuscule parrying effect at this distance against such an energy-intensive manifestation.

I did not jump up when the silence came. It could be that the tornado's driver had withdrawn support and collapsed the funnel on seeing that I might be out of reach. It could also be the eye of the storm, with more to come, by and by.

While I did not jump up, I did look up, because I hate to miss educational opportunities.

And there was the face—or, rather, the mask—at the center of the storm, regarding me. It was a projection, of course, larger than life and not fully substantial. The head was cowled; the mask was full and cobalt bright and strongly reminiscent of the sort worn by goalies in ice hockey; there were two vertical breathing slits from which pale smoke emerged—a touch too theatrical for my taste; a lower series of random punctures was designed to give the impression of a sardonically lopsided mouth. A distorted sound of laughter came down to me from it.

"Aren't you overdoing it a bit?" I said, coming up into a crouch and raising the Logrus between us. "For a kid on Halloween, yes. But we're all adults here, aren't we? A simple domino would probably serve—"

"You moved my stone!" it said.

"I've a certain academic interest in such matters," I offered, easing myself into the extensions. "Nothing to get upset about. Is that you, Jasra? I—"

The rumbling began again, softly at first, then building once more.

"I'll make a deal," I said. "You call off the storm, and I'll promise not to move any more markers."

Again, the laughter as the storm sounds rose. "Too late," came the reply. "Too late for you. Unless you're a lot tougher than you look."

What the hell! The battle is not always to the strong, and nice guys tend to win because they're the ones who get to write their memoirs. I'd been fiddling with the Logrus projections against the insubstantiality of the mask until I found the link, the opening leading back to its source. I stabbed through it—a thing on the order of an electrical discharge—at whatever lay behind.

There came a scream. The mask collapsed, the storm collapsed, and I was on my feet and running again. When whatever I'd hit recovered I did not want to be in the same place I had been because that place might be subject to sudden disintegration.

I had a choice of cutting off into Shadow or seeking an even faster path of retreat. If a sorcerer were to tag me as I started shadow-slipping I could be followed. So I dug out my Trumps and shuffled forth Random's. I rounded the next turning of the way then, and I would have had to halt there anyway, I saw, because it narrowed to a width impossible for me to pass. I raised the card and reached with my mind.

There followed contact, almost immediately. But even as the images solidified I felt a probe. I was certain that it was my blue-masked nemesis seeking me once more.

But Random came clear, seated before a drum set, sticks in hand. He set aside the drumsticks and rose.

"It's about time," he said, and he extended his hand.

Even as I reached I felt something rushing toward me. As our fingers touched and I stepped forward, they burst about me like a giant wave.

I passed through into the music room in Amber. Random had opened his mouth to speak again when the cascade of flowers fell upon us.

Brushing violets from his shirtfront, he regarded me. "I'd rather you said it with words," he remarked.

4

Portrait of the artists, purposes crossed, temperature falling. . . .

Sunny afternoon, and walking through small park following light lunch, us, prolonged silences and monosyllabic responses to conversational sallies indicating all's not well at other end of communication's taut line. Upon bench, seated then, facing flower beds, souls catch up with bodies, words with thoughts. . . .

"Okay, Merle. What's the score?" she asks.

"I don't know what game you're talking about, Julia."

"Don't get cute. All I want's a straight answer."

"What's the question?"

"That place you took me, from the beach, that night. . . . Where was it?"

"It was—sort of a dream."

"Bullshit!" She turns sideways to face me fully, and I must meet those flashing eyes without my face giving anything away. "I've been back there, several times, looking for the way we took. There is no cave. There's nothing! What happened to it? What's going on?"

"Maybe the tide came in and—"

"Merle! What kind of an idiot do you take me for? That walk we took isn't on the maps. Nobody around here's ever heard of anything like those places. It was geographically impossible. The times of day and the seasons kept shifting. The only explanation is supernatural or paranormal—whatever you want to call it. What happened? You owe me an answer and you know it. What happened? Where were you?"

I look away, past my feet, past the flowers.

"I—can't say."

"Why not?"

"I—" What could I say? It was not only that telling her of Shadow would disturb, perhaps destroy, her view of reality. At the heart of my problem lay the realization that it would also require telling her how I knew this, which would mean telling her who I am, where I am from, what I am—and I was afraid to give her this knowledge. I told myself that it would end our relationship as surely as telling her nothing would; and if it must end either way, I would rather we parted without her possessing this knowledge. Later, much later, I was to see this for the rationalization it was; my real reason for denying her the answers she desired was that I was not ready to trust her, or anyone, so close to me as I really am. Had I known her longer, better—another year, say—I might have answered her. I don't know. We never used the word "love," though it must have run through her mind on occasion, as it did through mine. It was, I suppose, that I didn't love her enough to trust her, and then it was too late. So, "I can't tell you," were my words.

"You have some power that you will not share."

"Call it that, then."

"I would do whatever you say, promise whatever you want promised."

"There is a reason, Julia."

She is on her feet, arms akimbo. "And you won't even share that."

I shake my head.

"It must be a lonely world you inhabit, magician, if even those who love you are barred from it."

At that moment it seems she is simply trying her last trick for getting an answer from me. I screw my resolve yet tighter. "I didn't say that."

"You didn't have to. It is your silence that tells me. If you know the road to Hell too, why not head that way? Good-bye!"

"Julia. Don't. . . ."

She chooses not to hear me.

Still life with flowers. . . .

Awakening. Night. Autumn wind beyond my window. Dreams. Blood of life without the body . . . swirling. . . .

I swung my feet out of bed and sat rubbing my eyes, my temples. It had been sunny and afternoon when I'd finished telling

Random my story, and he'd sent me to get some shuteye afterward. I was suffering from shadow lag and felt completely turned around at the moment, though I was not certain exactly what the hour might be.

I stretched, got up, repaired myself and donned fresh clothing. I knew that I would not be able to get back to sleep; also, I was feeling hungry. I took a warm cloak with me as I departed my quarters. I felt like going out rather than raiding the larder. I was in the mood for some walking, and I hadn't been outside the palace and into town in—years, I guessed.

I made my way downstairs, then cut through a few chambers and a big hall, connecting up at the rear with a corridor I could have followed all the way from the stair if I'd cared to, but then I'd have missed a couple of tapestries I'd wanted to say hello to: an idyllic sylvan scene, with a couple making out following a picnic lunch; and a hunting scene of dogs and men pursuing a magnificent stag, which looks as if it might yet have a chance of getting away, if it will dare a stupendous leap that lies ahead. . . .

I passed through and made my way up the corridor to a postern, where a bored-looking guard named Jordy suddenly strove to seem attentive when he heard me coming. I stopped to pass the time with him and learned that he didn't get off duty till midnight, which was almost two hours away.

"I'm heading down into town," I said. "Where's a good place to eat this time of night?"

"What've you got a taste for?"

"Seafood," I decided.

"Well, Fiddler's Green—about two thirds of the way down the Main Concourse—is very good for seafood. It's a fancy place. . . ."

I shook my head. "I don't want a fancy place," I said.

"The Net's still supposed to be good—down near the corner of the Smiths and Ironmongers Street. It's not real fancy."

"But you wouldn't go there yourself?"

"Used to," he replied. "But a number of the nobles and big merchants discovered it recently. I'd feel kind of uncomfortable there these days. It's gotten sort of clubby."

"Hell! I don't want conversation or atmosphere. I just want some nice fresh fish. Where would you go for the best?"

"Well, it's a long walk. But if you go all the way down to the docks, at the back of the cove, it's a little to the west. . . . But maybe you shouldn't. It's kind of late, and that isn't the best neighborhood after dark."

"Is that by any chance Death Alley?"

"They do sometimes call it that, sir, as bodies are occasionally found there of a morning. Maybe you'd better go to the Net, seeing as you're alone."

"Gérard took me through that area once, during the day. I think I could find my way around it, all right. What's the name of the place?"

"Uh, Bloody Bill's."

"Thanks. I'll say hi to Bill for you."

He shook his head. "Can't. It was renamed after the manner of his demise. His cousin Andy runs it now."

"Oh. What was it called before?"

"Bloody Sam's," he said.

Well, what the hell. I bade him a good night and set out walking. I took the path to the short stairway down the slope, which led to the walkway through a garden and over to a side gate, where another guard let me out. It was a cool night with the breezed smells of autumn burning down the world about me. I drew it into my lungs and sighed it out again as I headed for the Main Concourse, the distant, almost-forgotten, slow clopping sounds of hoofs on cobbles coming to me like something out of dream or memory. The night was moonless but filled with stars, and the concourse below flanked by globes of phosphorescent liquid set atop high poles, long-tailed mountain moths darting about them.

When I reached the avenue I strolled. A few closed carriages rolled by as I passed along the way. An old man walking a tiny green dragon on a chain leash touched his hat to me as I passed and said, "Good evening." He had seen the direction from which I had come, though I was sure he did not recognize me. My face is not that well-known about town. My spirits loosened a bit after a time, and I felt a spring come into my step.

Random had not been as angry as I'd thought he might. Since Ghostwheel had not been stirring up any trouble, he had not charged me to go after it immediately and try again for a shutdown. He had merely told me to think about it and come up with the best course of action we might pursue. And Flora had been in touch earlier and told him who Luke was—a thing that seemed to have eased his mind somehow, knowing the identity of the enemy. Though I'd asked, he would not tell me what plans he might have formulated for dealing with him. He did allude to the recent dispatch of an agent to Kashfa, though, to obtain certain unspecified information. The thing that seemed to trouble him the most, actually, was the possibility that the outlaw Dalt was still to be numbered among the living.

"Something about that man . . ." Random began.

"What?" I'd asked.

"For one thing, I saw Benedict run him through. That generally tends to terminate a person's career."

"Tough son of a bitch," I said. "Or damn lucky. Or both."

"If he is the same man, he's the son of the Desacratrix. You've heard of her?"

"Deela," I said. "Wasn't that her name? Some sort of religious fanatic? Militant?"

Random nodded. "She caused a lot of trouble out around the periphery of the Golden Circle—mostly near Begma. You ever been there?"

"No."

"Well, Begma's the nearest point on the circle to Kashfa, which is what makes your story particularly interesting. She'd raided a lot in Begma and they couldn't handle her by themselves. They finally reminded us of the protection alliance we have with almost all the Circle kingdoms—and Dad decided to go in personally and teach her a lesson. She'd burned one Unicorn shrine too many. He took a small force, defeated her troops, took her prisoner and hanged a bunch of her men. She escaped, though, and a couple of years later when she was all but forgotten she came back with a fresh force and started the same crap all over. Begma screamed again, but Dad was busy. He sent Bleys in with a larger force. There were several inconclusive engagements—they were raiders, not a regular army—but Bleys finally cornered them and wiped them out. She died that day, leading her troops."

"And Dalt's her son?"

"That's the story, and it makes some sense, because he did everything he could to harass us for a long time. He was after revenge, pure and simple, for his mother's death. Finally, he put together a fairly impressive fighting force and tried to raid Amber. Got a lot farther than you'd think, right up to Kolvir. But Benedict was waiting, his pet regiment at his back. Benedict cut them to pieces, and it sure looked as if he'd wounded Dalt mortally. A few of his men were able to carry him off the field, so we never saw the body. But hell! Who cared?"

"And you think he could be the same guy who was Luke's friend when he was a kid—and later?"

"Well, the age is about right and he seems to hail from that same general area. I suppose it's possible."

I mused as I strolled. Jasra hadn't really liked the guy, according to the hermit. So what was his part in things now? Too many unknowns, I decided. It would take knowledge rather than reasoning to answer that one. So let it ride and go enjoy dinner. . . .

I continued on down the concourse. Near to its farther end I heard laughter and saw where some hardy drinkers still occupied a few tables at a sidewalk cafe. One of them was Droppa, but he didn't spot me and I passed on. I did not feel like being amused. I turned onto Weavers Street, which would take me over to where West Vine wound its way up from the harbor district. A tall masked lady in a silver cloak hurried by and into a waiting carriage. She glanced back once and smiled beneath her domino. I was certain that I didn't know her, and I found myself wishing I did. It was a pretty smile. Then a gust of wind brought me the smokesmell of someone's fireplace and rattled a few dead leaves as it went by. I wondered where my father was.

Down along the street then and left on West Vine. . . . Narrower here than the concourse, but still wide; a greater distance between lights, but still sufficiently illuminated for night travelers. A pair of horsemen clopped slowly by, singing a song I did not recognize. Something large and dark passed overhead a bit later, to settle upon a roof across the street. A few scratching noises came from that direction, then silence. I followed a curve to the right, then another to the left, entering what I knew to be a long series of switchbacks. My way grew gradually steeper. A harbor breeze came up at some point a little later, bearing me my first salt sea smells of the evening. A short while afterward—two turns, I believe—and I had a view of the sea itself, far below: bobbing lights on a sparkling, swelling slickness over black, pent by the curving line of bright dots, Harbor Road. To the east the sky was powdered slightly. A hint of horizon appeared at the edge of the world. I thought I caught a glimpse of the distant light of Cabra minutes later, then lost it again with another turning of the way.

A puddle of light like spilled milk pulsed on the street to my right, outlining a ghostly gridwork of cobbles at its farthest downhill reach; the stippled pole above it might advertise some spectral barbershop; the cracked globe at its top still showed a faint phosphorescence, skull-on-a-stick style, reminding me of a game we used to play as kids back in the Courts. A few lighted footprints proceeded downhill away from it, faint, fainter, gone. I passed on, and across the distance I heard the cries of sea birds. Autumn's smells were submerged in ocean's. The powdered light beyond my left shoulder rose higher above the water, drifted forward across the wrinkled face of the deep. Soon. . . .

My appetite grew as I walked. Ahead, I beheld another dark-cloaked stroller on the other side of the street, a slight glowing at the edges of the boots. I thought of the fish I would soon be eating and hurried, breasting the figure and passing. A cat in a doorway paused at licking her asshole to watch me go by, hind leg held vertical the while. Another horseman passed, this one headed up the hill. I heard the fringes of an argument between a man and a woman from upstairs in one of the darkened buildings. Another turning and the shoulder of the moon came into sight like some magnificent beast surfacing, shrugging droplets from bright bathic grottoes. . . .

Ten minutes later I had reached the port district and found my way over to Harbor Road, its lack of all but occasional globes supplemented by window spillage, a number of buckets of burning pitch and the glow of the now-risen moon. The smells of salt and sea-wrack were more intense here, the road more cluttered with trash, the passersby more colorfully garbed and noisier than any on the concourse, unless you counted Droppa. I made my way to the rear of the cove, where the sounds of the sea came to me more strongly: the rushing, building advances of waves, then their crashing and splashing out beyond the breakwater; the gentler falls and slopping withdrawals nearer at hand; the creaking of ships, the rattling of chains, the bumping of some smaller vessel at pier or moor post. I wondered where the Starburst, my old sailboat, might be now.

I followed the curve of the road over to the western shore of the harbor. A pair of rats chased a black cat across my path as I wandered briefly, checking several sidestreets for the one I sought. The smells of barf as well as solid and liquid human waste mingled with other odors here, and I heard the cries, crashes and thuds of a struggle from somewhere nearby, leading me to believe that I was in the proper neighborhood. From somewhere distant a buoy bell rattled; from somewhere nearby I heard an almost bored-sounding string of curses preceding a pair of sailors who rounded the nearest corner to my right, reeling, staggered on past me, grinning, and broke into song moments later, receding. I advanced and checked the sign on that corner. SEABREEZE LANE, it read.

That was it, the stretch commonly called Death Alley. I turned there. It was just a street like any other. I didn't see any corpses or even collapsed drunks for the first fifty paces, though a man in a doorway tried to sell me a dagger and a mustachioed stock character offered to fix me up with something young and tight. I declined both, and learned from the latter that I wasn't all that far from Bloody Bill's. I walked on. My occasional glances showed me three dark-cloaked figures far to the rear which, I supposed, could be following me; I had seen them back on Harbor Road too. Also, they might not. In that I was not feeling particularly paranoid, I reflected that they could be anybody going anywhere and decided to ignore them. Nothing happened. They kept to themselves, and when I finally located Bloody Bill's and entered they passed on by, crossing the street and going into a small bistro a little farther down along the way.

I turned and regarded Bill's. The bar was to my right, tables to my left, suspicious-looking stains on the floor. A board on the wall suggested I give my order at the bar and say where I was sitting. The day's catch was chalked beneath this.

So I went over and waited, collecting glances, until a heavy-set man with gray and amazingly shaggy brows came over and asked what I wanted. I told him the blue sea scut and pointed at an empty table to the rear. He nodded and shouted my order back through a hole in the wall, then asked me whether I wanted a bottle of Bayle's Piss to go with it. I did, he got it for me, and a glass, uncorked it and passed it over. I paid up there, headed back to the table I had chosen and seated myself with my back to the wall.

Oil flames flickered through dirty chimneys in brackets all about the place. Three men—two young, one middle-aged—played cards at the corner table in the front and passed a bottle. An older man sat alone at the table to my left, eating. He had a nasty-looking scar running both above and below his left eye, and there was a long wicked blade about six inches out of its scabbard resting on the chair to his right. He, too, had his back to the wall. Men with musical instruments rested at another table: between numbers, I guessed. I poured some of the yellow wine into my glass and took a sip: a distinctive taste I remembered from across the years. It was okay for quaffing. Baron Bayle owned a number of vineyards about thirty miles to the east. He was the official vintner to the Court, and his red wines were generally excellent. He was less successful with the whites, though, and often wound up dumping a lot of second-rate stuff onto the local market. It bore his emblem and a picture of a dog—he liked dogs—so it was sometimes called Dog Piss and sometimes Bayle's Piss, depending on who you talked to. Dog lovers sometimes take offense at the former appellation.

About the time my food arrived I noticed that two young men near the front of the bar were glancing in my direction more than occasionally, exchanging a few indistinguishable words and laughing and smiling a lot. I ignored them and turned my attention to my meal. A little later the scarred man at the next table said softly, without leaning or looking toward me, his lips barely moving, "Free advice. I think those two guys at the bar noticed you're not wearing a blade, and they've marked you for trouble."

"Thanks," I said.

Well. . . . I was not overly concerned about my ability to deal with them, but given a choice I'd rather avoid the occasion entirely. If all that it required was a visible blade, that was easily remedied.

A moment's meditation and the Logrus danced before me. Shortly thereafter, I was reaching through it in search of the proper weapon—neither too long nor too heavy, properly balanced, with a comfortable grip—with a wide dark belt and scabbard. It took me close to three minutes, partly because I was so fussy about it, I suppose—but hell, if prudence required one, I wanted comfort—and partly because it is harder reaching through Shadow in the vicinity of Amber than it is almost anywhere else.

When it came into my hands I sighed and mopped my brow. Then I brought it up slowly from beneath the table, belt and all, drew it about half a foot from its scabbard, to follow a good example, and placed it on the seat to my right. The two guys at the bar caught the performance and I grinned back at them. They had a quick consultation, and this time they weren't laughing. I poured myself a fresh glass of wine and drank it off at a single draught. Then I returned to my fish, about which Jordy had been right. The food here was very good.

"Neat trick, that," the man at the next table said. "I don't suppose it's an easy one to learn?"

"Nope."

"It figures. Most good things aren't, or everybody'd do 'em. They may still go after you, though, seeing as you're alone. Depends on how much they drink and how reckless they get. You worried?"

"Nope."

"Didn't think so. But they'll hit someone tonight."

"How can you tell?"

He looked at me for the first time and grinned a nasty grin. "They're generic, like wind-up toys. See you around."

He tossed a coin onto the table, stood, buckled on his sword belt, picked up a dark, feathered hat and headed for the door.

"Take care."

I nodded.

" 'Night."

As he passed out of the place the two guys began whispering again, this time glancing after him rather than at me. Some decision reached, they rose and departed quickly. For a moment I was tempted to follow, but something restrained me. A little later, I heard the sounds of a scuffle from up the street. Not too long after that, a figure appeared in the doorway, hovered a moment, then fell forward. It was one of the two drinkers. His throat had been cut.

Andy shook his head and dispatched his waiter to inform the local constabulary. Then he took hold of the body by the heels and dragged it outside, so as not to impede the flow of customers.

Later, when I was ordering another fish, I asked Andy about the occurrence. He smiled grimly.

"It is not good to mess with an emissary of the Crown," he said. "They tend to pick them tough."

"That guy who was sitting next to me works for Random?"

He studied my face, then nodded. "Old John worked for Oberon, too. Whenever he passes through he eats here."

"I wonder what sort of mission he was on?"

He shrugged. "Who knows? But he paid me in Kashfan currency, and I know he ain't from Kashfa."

As I worked on my second platter I pondered that one. Whatever it was that Random had wanted from Kashfa was probably on its way to the castle right now, unless of course it was unavailable. It would almost have to concern Luke and Jasra. I wondered what it was, and of what benefit it might be.

I sat there for a long while after that, thinking, and the place was a lot less noisy than it had been for most of an hour, even when the musicians began a fresh set. Had it been John the guys had been watching all along, with both of us misinterpreting their gazes as directed toward me? Or had they simply decided to go after the first person who left alone? I realized from these reflections that I was beginning to think like an Amberite again—seeking plots everywhere—and I hadn't been back all that long. Something in the atmosphere, I guessed. Probably it was a good thing that my mind was moving along these lines once more, since I was involved in so much already and it seemed an investment in self-preservation.

I finished my glass of wine and left the bottle on the table with a few drinks still in it. It occurred to me that I shouldn't be fogging my senses any further, all things considered. I rose and buckled on my sword belt.

As I passed the bar Andy nodded. "If you run into anyone from the palace," he said softly, "you might mention that I didn't know that was going to happen."

"You knew them?"

"Yeah. Sailors. Their ship came in a couple of days ago. They've been in trouble here before. Blow their pay fast, then look for some more the quick way."

"Do you think they might be professionals at—removing people?"

"Because of John's being what he is, you mean? No. They got caught once too often, mainly for being stupid. Sooner or later they were bound to run into someone who knew what he was doing and end up this way. I don't know anyone who'd hire them for something serious."

"Oh, he got the other one too?"

"Yep. Up the street a way. So you might mention that they just happened to be in the wrong place at the wrong time."

I stared at him and he winked.

"I saw you down here with Gérard, several years ago. I make it a point never to forget a face that might be worth remembering."

I nodded. "Thanks. You serve a good meal."

Outside, it was cooler than it had been earlier. The moon hung higher and the sea was noisier. The street was deserted in my immediate vicinity. Loud music poured from one of the places back toward Harbor Street, with accompanying sounds of laughter. I glanced within as I passed it and saw where a tired-looking woman on a small stage appeared to be giving herself a gynecological examination. From somewhere nearby I heard a sound of breaking glass. A drunk reeled toward me from between two buildings, one hand outstretched. I walked on. The wind sighed amid masts in the harbor, and I found myself wishing Luke were at my side—like in the old days, before things got complicated—someone of my own age and cast of mind to talk to. All my relatives here had too many centuries of cynicism or wisdom for us to see things and feel them in much the same way.

Ten paces later, Frakir pulsed wildly upon my wrist. In that there was no one anywhere near me at that moment, I did not even draw my new blade. I threw myself flat, then rolled toward the shadows to my right. Simultaneous with this, I heard a *thunk* from the side of the building across the street. The first glance I could spare in that direction showed me an arrow protruding from a wall, its height and position such that had I not taken the dive it might well have hit me. Its angle also indicated that I had just cast myself in the direction from which it had been discharged.

I raised myself enough to draw my blade and looked to my right. There were no opened windows or doors in the immediately adjacent building, a darkened place, its front wall only about six feet away now. But there was a gap between it and the buildings on either side, and geometry told me that the arrow had come from the open area ahead of me.

I rolled again, bringing myself up beside the low, roofed porch which ran the full width of the place. I scrambled up onto it before I rose fully. Staying near the wall I advanced, cursing the slowness silence demanded. I was almost near enough to the opening to be able to rush any archer who might step out, before he could release another arrow. The possibility of his circling and catching me from behind did pass through my mind, though, and I flattened myself against the wall, blade extended forward, and cast quick glances behind as I moved. Frakir writhed into my left hand and hung ready.

If I reached the corner and no one emerged I was uncertain what I would do next. The situation seemed to demand a magical offensive. But unless the spells were already hung—and I'd been remiss in this—one can seldom spare the attention it requires in life-and-death situations. I halted. I controlled my breathing. I listened. . . .

He was being careful, but I heard faint sounds of movement from the roof, coming forward. But this did not preclude another, or even several, being around the corner. I had no idea how many persons might be involved in this ambush, though it was beginning to strike me as a little too sophisticated for a simple robbery. In such a case, I doubted there would be only one. And their forces might be split several ways. I held my position, my mind racing. When the attack came, it would be concerted, I was certain of that. I imagined an archer around the corner, arrow nocked, waiting for a signal. The one on the roof would most likely have a blade. I guessed at blades for any others, too. . . .

I pushed aside any questions as to who might be after me and how they had located me here—if it were indeed me, personally, whom they were after. Such considerations made no difference at this point. I would be just as dead were they random thugs seeking my purse as I would be if they were assassins, should they succeed in the present enterprise.

Again. A sound from above. Someone was directly overhead. Any moment now. . . .

With a shuffling noise and a great cry a man leaped from the roof to the street before me. His shout was apparently the signal to the archer, also, for there was immediate movement at the corner of the building, accompanied by the sounds of rapid footfalls from the building's other corner, to my rear.

Before his feet even struck the ground I had cast Frakir at the man from the roof with a command to kill. And I was rushing the archer before he had even rounded the corner completely, my blade already swinging. My cut passed through his bow, his arm and his lower abdomen. On the minus side, there was a man with a drawn blade right behind him and someone was running toward me along the porch.

I placed my left foot upon the folding archer's chest and propelled him backward into the man behind him. I used the recoiling momentum from the push to spin, my blade sweeping through a wide, wild parry which I had to adjust immediately to stop a head cut from the man who had crossed the porch. As I riposted to his chest and had my own cut parried I became peripherally aware of the one from the roof kneeling now in the street and tearing at his throat, in evidence that Frakir was doing her job.

The man somewhere to my rear made my back feel very exposed. I had to do something fast or his blade would be in me within seconds. So. . . .

Rather than riposting, I pretended to stumble, actually gathering my weight, positioning myself.

He lunged, cutting downward. I sprang to the side and thrust with a twisting movement of my body. If he were able to adjust the angle of that cut as I moved I would feel it in seconds. Dangerous, but I couldn't see any other choice.

Even as my blade entered his chest I did not know whether he had connected with me. Not that it mattered now. Either he had or he hadn't. I had to keep moving until I stopped or was stopped.

I used my blade like a lever, turning him as I continued my counterclockwise movement, him at its center, hoping to position him between that fourth man and myself. The maneuver was partly successful. It was too late to interpose my skewered and sagging adversary fully, but in time at least to cause a small collision between him and the other. Time enough, I hoped, as the other stumbled to the side, stepping down from the porch. All I needed do now was wrench my blade free, and it would be one-on-one.

I yanked at it. . . .

Damn, damn, damn. The thing was wedged into bone and wouldn't come free. And the other man had regained his footing. I kept turning the body to keep it between us while with my left hand I tried to free my most recent adversary's own blade from his still-clenched right fist.

Ditto the damns. It was locked in a death grip, his fingers like metal cables about the haft.

The man in the street gave me a nasty smile while moving his blade about, looking for an opening. It was then that I caught the flash of the blue-stone ring he wore, answering my question as to whether it was me in particular who had been sought, here, tonight.

I bent my knees as I moved and positioned my hands low upon the dead man's body.

Situations such as this are, for me, sometimes videotaped into memory—a total absence of conscious thought and a great mass of instant perceptions—timeless, yet only subject to serial review when the mind indulges in later replay.

There were cries from various places along the street, from within and without. I could hear people rushing in my direction. There was blood on the boards all around me, and I recall cautioning myself not to slip on it. I could see the archer and his bow, both of them broken, on the ground past the far edge of the porch. The garroted swordsman was sprawled in the street, off to the right of the man who menaced me now. The body I steered and positioned had become dead weight. To my small relief I saw that no more attackers had emerged from anywhere to join the final man I faced. And that man was sidestepping and feinting, getting ready to make his rush.

Okay. Time.

I propelled the corpse toward my attacker with all my strength and did not wait to observe the result of my action. The risk I was about to take granted me no time for such indulgence.

I dove into the street and did a shoulder roll past the supine figure, who had dropped his blade in trying to use his hands against Frakir. As I moved I heard the sound of some impact followed by a grunt from above and somewhere to the rear, indicating that I had been at least partly on target when I'd pushed the dead man toward the other. How effectively this would serve me still remained to be seen.

My right hand snaked out as I went by, catching the hilt of the fallen man's blade. I rolled to my feet, facing back in the direction from which I had come, extending the blade, crossing my legs and springing backward. . . .

Barely in time. He was upon me with a strong series of attacks, and I backed away fast, parrying wildly. He was still smiling, but my first riposte slowed his advance and my second one stopped it.

I settled and stood my ground. He was strong, but I could see that I was faster. There were people near at hand now, watching us. A few shouts of useless advice reached me. To which of us it was directed, I could not say. It didn't matter, though. He stood for a few moments as I began to press my attack, and then he began to give ground, slowly, and I was sure that I could take him.

I wanted him alive, though, which would make things a little more difficult. That blue-stoned ring flashing and retreating before me held a mystery to which he had the answer, and I needed that answer. Therefore, I had to keep pressing him, to wear him down. . . .

I tried turning him, a little at a time, as subtly as I could. I was hoping to press him into stumbling over the dead man to his rear. It almost worked, too.

When his rear foot fell upon the arm of the sprawled man, he shifted his weight forward to maintain his balance. In one of those instants of inspiration on which one must act immediately without thinking, he turned this movement into a rush, seeing that my blade was out of line in preparation for the heavy rush I was about to give him as he stumbled. Wrong of me to have anticipated that much, I guess.

He beat my blade cross-body with a heavy swing, throwing his own weapon way out of line also and bringing us *corps à corps,* with him turning in the same direction I was facing and unfortunately providing him with the opportunity to drive his left fist into my right kidney with the full force of his momentum.

Immediately, his left foot shot out to trip me, and the impact of the blow as we came together showed me that he was going to succeed. The best thing I could manage was to catch hold of my cloak with my left hand, spinning it out and dragging it back, entangling both our blades as we fell, while I tried hard to turn on the way down, so as to land on top of him. I did not succeed in falling upon him. We came down side by side, still facing each other, and the guard of someone's blade—my own, I think—hit me hard in the ribs on my left side.

My right hand was caught beneath me and my left was still tangled in my cloak. His left was free, though, and high. He clawed at my face with it, and I bit his hand but couldn't hold it. In the meantime, I finally managed to drag my own left hand free and I thrust it into his face. He turned his head away, tried to knee me and hit my hip, then thrust stiff fingers toward my eyes. I caught his wrist and held it. Both of our right hands were still pinned and our weights seemed about equal. So all that I had to do was squeeze.

The bones of his wrist crunched within my grip, and for the first time he cried out. Then I simply pushed him away, rolled into a kneeling position and started to rise, dragging him up along with me. End of the game. I had won.

He slumped suddenly against me. For a moment, I thought it a final trick, and then I saw the blade protruding from his back, the hand of the grim-faced man who had put it there already tightening to pull it out again.

"You son of a bitch!" I cried in English—though I'm sure the meaning came through—and I dropped my burden and drove my fist into the stranger's face, knocking him over backward, his blade remaining in place. "I needed him!"

I caught hold of my former adversary and raised him into the most comfortable position I could manage.

"Who sent you?" I asked him. "How did you find me?"

He grinned weakly and dribbled blood. "No freebies here," he said. "Ask somebody else," and he slumped forward and got blood on my shirtfront.

I drew the ring from his finger and added it to my collection of goddamned blue stones. Then I rose and glared at the man who had stabbed him. Two other figures were helping him to his feet.

"Just what the hell did you do that for?" I asked, advancing upon them.

"I saved your damn life," the man growled.

"The hell you did! You might have just cost me it! I needed that man alive!"

Then the figure to his left spoke, and I recognized the voice. She placed her hand lightly upon the arm I did not even realize I had raised to strike the man again.

"He did it on my orders," she said. "I feared for your life, and I did not understand that you wanted him prisoner."

I stared at her pale proud features within the dark cloak's raised cowl. It was Vinta Bayle, Caine's lady, whom I had last seen at the funeral. She was also the third daughter of the Baron Bayle, to whom Amber owed many a bibulous night.

I realized that I was shaking slightly. I drew a deep breath and caught control of myself.

"I see," I said at last. "Thank you."

"I am sorry," she told me.

I shook my head. "You didn't know. What's done is done. I'm grateful to anybody who tries to help me."

"I can still help you," she said. "I might have misread this one, but I believe you may still be in danger. Let's get away from here."

I nodded. "A moment, please."

I went and retrieved Frakir from about the neck of the other dead man. She disappeared quickly into my left sleeve. The blade I had been using fit my scabbard after a fashion, so I pushed it home and adjusted the belt, which had pulled around toward the rear.

"Let's go," I said to her.

The four of us strode back toward Harbor Street. Interested bystanders got out of our way quickly. Someone was probably already robbing the dead behind us. Things fall apart; the center cannot hold. But what the hell, it's home.

5

Walking, with the Lady Vinta and two servingmen of the House of Bayle, my side still hurting from its encounter with a sword hilt, beneath a moonbright, starbright sky, through a sea mist, away from Death Alley. Lucky, actually, that a bump on the side was all I acquired in my engagement with those who would do me harm. How they had located me so quickly upon my return, I could not say. But it seemed as if Vinta might have some idea about this, and I was inclined to trust her, both because I knew her somewhat and because she had lost her man, my Uncle Caine, to my former friend Luke, from whose party anything involving a blue stone seemed to have its origin.

When we turned onto a seaward side way off Harbor Street, I asked her what she had in mind.

"I thought we were heading for Vine," I said.

"You know you are in danger," she stated.

"I guess that's sort of obvious."

"I could take you to my father's place up in town," she said, "or we could escort you back to the palace, but someone knows you are here and it didn't take long to reach you."

"True."

"We have a boat moored down this way. We can sail along the coast and reach my father's country place by morning. You will have disappeared. Anyone seeking you in Amber will be foiled."

"You don't think I'd be safe back in the palace?"

"Perhaps," she said. "But your whereabouts may be known locally. Come with me and this won't be the case."

"I'll be gone and Random will learn from one of the guards

that I was heading for Death Alley. This will cause considerable consternation and a huge brouhaha."

"You can reach him by Trump tomorrow and tell him that you're in the country—if you have your cards with you."

"True. How did you know where to find me this evening? You can't persuade me that we met by coincidence."

"No, we followed you. We were in the place across the way from Bill's."

"You anticipated tonight's happenings?"

"I saw the possibility. If I'd known everything, of course I'd have prevented it."

"What's going on? What do you know about all of this, and what's your part in it?"

She laughed, and I realized it was the first time I had ever heard her do it. It was not the cold, mocking thing I would have guessed at from Caine's lady.

"I want to sail while the tide is high," she said, "and you want a story that will take all night. Which will it be, Merlin? Security or satisfaction?"

"I'd like both, but I'll take them in order."

"Okay," she said, then turned to the smaller of the two men, the one I had hit. "Jarl, go home. In the morning, tell my father that I decided to go back to Arbor House. Tell him it was a nice night and I wanted to sail, so I took the boat. Don't mention Merlin."

The man touched his cap to her. "Very good, m'lady."

He turned and headed back along the way we had come.

"Come on," she said to me then, and she and the big fellow— whose name I later learned was Drew—led me down among the piers to where a long sleek sailboat was tied up. "Do much sailing?" she asked me.

"Used to," I said.

"Good enough. You can give us a hand."

Which I did. We didn't talk much except for business while we were getting unbuttoned and rigged and casting off. Drew steered and we worked the sails. Later, we were able to take turns for long spells. The wind wasn't tricky. In fact, it was just about perfect. We slid away, rounded the breakwater and made it out without any problems. Having stowed our cloaks, I saw that she wore dark trousers and a heavy shirt. Very practical, as if she'd planned for something like this ahead of time. The belt she stowed bore a real, full-length blade, not some jeweled dagger. And just from watching the way she moved, I'd a feeling she might be able to use the thing pretty well. Also, she reminded me of someone I couldn't quite place. It was more a matter of mannerisms of gesture and voice than it was of appearance. Not that it mattered. I had more important things to think about as soon as we settled into routine and I had a few moments to stare across the dark waters and do some quick reviewing.

I was familiar with the general facts of her life, and I had encountered her a number of times at social gatherings. I knew she knew that I was Corwin's son and that I had been born and raised in the Courts of Chaos, being half of that bloodline which was linked anciently with Amber's own. In our conversation the last time we met, it became apparent that she was aware that I had been off in Shadow for some years, going native and trying to pick up something of an education. Presumably, Uncle Caine had not wanted her ignorant of family matters—which led me to wonder how deeply their relationship might have run. I'd heard that they had been together for several years. So I wondered exactly how much she knew about me. I felt relatively safe with her, but I had to decide how much I was willing to tell her in exchange for the information she obviously possessed concerning those who were after me locally. This, because I had a feeling it would probably be a trade-off. Other than doing a favor for a member of the family, which generally comes in handy, there was no special reason for her having an interest in me personally. Her motivation in the whole matter pretty much had to be a desire for revenge, so far as I could see, for Caine's killing. With this in mind, I was willing to deal. It is always good to have an ally. But I had to decide how much I was willing to give her of the big picture. Did I want her messing around in the entire complex of events that surrounded me? I doubted it, even as I wondered how much she would be asking. Most likely she just wanted to be in on the kill, whatever that might be. When I glanced over to where moonlight accentuated the planes of her angular face, it was not difficult to superimpose a mask of Nemesis upon those features.

Out from shore, riding the sea breeze east, passing the great rock of Kolvir, the lights of Amber like jewels in her hair, I was taken again by an earlier feeling of affection. Though I had grown up in darkness and exotic lighting amid the non-Euclidean paradoxes of the Courts, where beauty was formed of more surreal elements, I felt more and more drawn to Amber every time I visited her, until at last I realized she was a part of me, until I began to think of her, too, as home. I did not want Luke storming her slopes with riflemen, or Dalt performing commando raids in her vicinity. I knew that I would be willing to fight them to protect her.

Back on the beach, near the place where Caine had been laid to rest, I thought I saw a flash of prancing whiteness, moving slowly, then quickly, then vanishing within some cleft of the slope. I would have said it was a Unicorn, but with the distance and the darkness and the quickness of it all, I could never be certain.

We picked up a perfect wind a little later, for which I was grateful. I was tired, despite my day-long slumber. My escape from the crystal cave, my encounter with the Dweller, and the pursuit by the whirlwind and its masked master all flowed together in my mind as the nearly continuous action that they were. And now the postadrenal reaction from my latest activity was settling in. I wanted nothing more than to listen to the lapping of the waves while I watched the black and craggy shoreline slide by to port or turned to regard the flickering sea to starboard. I did not want to think, I did not want to move. . . .

A pale hand upon my arm.

"You're tired," I heard her say.

"I guess so," I heard myself say.

"Here's your cloak. Why don't you put it on and rest? We're holding steady. The two of us can manage easily now. We don't need you."

I nodded as I drew it about me. "I'll take you up on that. Thanks."

"Are you hungry or thirsty?"

"No. I had a big meal back in town."

Her hand remained on my arm. I looked up at her. She was smiling. It was the first time I had seen her smile. With the fingertips of her other hand she touched the bloodstain on my shirtfront.

"Don't worry. I'll take care of you," she said.

I smiled back at her because it seemed she wanted me to. She squeezed my shoulder and left me then, and I stared after her and wondered whether there were some element I had omitted from my earlier equation concerning her. But I was too tired now to solve for a new unknown. My thinking machinery was slowing, slowing. . . .

Back braced against the port gunwale, rocked gently by the swells, I let my head nod. Through half-closed eyes I saw the dark blot she had indicated upon my white shirtfront. Blood. Yes, blood. . . .

"First blood!" Despil had cried. "Which is sufficient! Have you satisfaction?"

"No!" Jurt had shouted. "I barely scratched him!" and he spun on his stone and waved the triple claws of his *trisp* in my direction as he prepared to have at me again.

The blood oozed from the incision in my left forearm and formed itself into beads which rose into the air and drifted away from me like a handful of scattered rubies. I raised my *fandon* into a high guard position and lowered my *trisp,* which I held far out to the right and angled forward. I bent my left knee and rotated my stone 90 degrees on our mutual axis. Jurt corrected his own position immediately and dropped a half-dozen feet. I turned another 90 degrees, so that each of us seemed to be hanging upside down in relation to the other.

"Bastard son of Amber!" he cried, and the triple lances of light raked toward me from his weapon, to be shattered into bright, mothlike fragments by the sweep of my *fandon,* to fall, swirling, downward into the Abyss of Chaos above which we rode.

"Up yours," I replied, and squeezed the haft of my *trisp,* triggering the pulsed beams from its three hair-fine blades. I extended my arm above my head as I did so, slashing at his shins.

He swept the beams away with his *fandon,* at almost the full extent of their eight-foot effective range. There is about a three-second recharge pause on a *trisliver,* but I feinted a dead cut toward his face, before which he raised *fand* reflexively, and I triggered the *trisp* for a swirl cut at his knees. He broke the one-second pulse in low *fand,* triggered a thrust at my face and spun over backward through a full 360, counting on the recharge time to save his back and coming up, *fandon* high, to cut at my shoulder.

But I was gone, circling him, dropping and rotating erect. I cut at his own exposed shoulder but was out of range. Despil, on his beachball-sized stone, was circling also, far to my right, while my own second—Mandor—high above, was dropping quickly. We clung to our small stones with shapeshifted feet, there on an outer current of Chaos, drifting, as at the whirlpool's rim. Jurt rotated to follow me, keeping his left forearm—to which the *fandon* is attached, elbow and wrist—horizontal, and executing a slow circular movement with it. Its three-foot length of filmy mesh, *mord*-weighted at the bottom, glittered in the balefire glow, which occurred at random intervals from many directions. He held his *trisp* in middle attack position, and he showed his teeth but was not smiling as I moved and he moved at opposite ends of the diameter of a ten-foot circle which we described over and over, looking for an opening.

I tilted the plane of my orbit and he adjusted his own immediately to keep me company. I did it again, and so did he. Then I did the dive—90 degrees forward, *fandon* raised and extended—and I turned my wrist and dropped my elbow, angling my raking cut upward beneath his guard.

He cursed and cut, but I scattered his light, and three dark lines appeared upon his left thigh. The *trisliver* only cuts to a depth of about three quarters of an inch through flesh, which is why the throat, eyes, temples, inner wrists and femoral arteries are particularly favored targets in a serious encounter. Still, enough cuts anywhere and you eventually wave goodbye to your opponent as he spins downward in a swarm of red bubbles into that place from whence no traveler returns.

"Blood!" Mandor cried, as the beads formed upon Jurt's leg and drifted. "Is there satisfaction, gentlemen?"

"I'm satisfied," I answered.

"I'm not!" Jurt replied, turning to face me as I drifted to his left and rotated to my right. "Ask me again after I've cut his throat!"

Jurt had hated me from sometime before he had learned to walk, for reasons entirely his own. While I did not hate Jurt, liking him was totally beyond my ability. I had always gotten along reasonably well with Despil, though he tended to take Jurt's side more often than my own. But that was understandable. They were full brothers, and Jurt was the baby.

Jurt's *trisp* flashed and I broke the light and riposted. He scattered my beams and spun off to the side. I followed. Our *trisps* flared simultaneously, and the air between us was filled with flakes of brilliance as both attacks were shattered. I struck again, this time low, as soon as I had recharge. His came in high, and again both attacks died in *fand*. We drifted nearer.

"Jurt," I said, "if either of us kills the other, the survivor will be outcast. Call it off."

"It will be worth it," he said. "Don't you think I've thought about it?"

Then he slashed an attack at my face. I raised both arms reflexively, *fandon* and *trisp*, and triggered an attack as shattered light showered before me. I heard him scream.

When I lowered my *fandon* to eye level I saw that he was bent forward, and his *trisp* was drifting away. So was his left ear, trailing a red filament that quickly beaded itself and broke apart. A flap of scalp had also come loose, and he was trying to press it back into place.

Mandor and Despil were already spiraling in.

"We declare the duel ended!" they were shouting, and I twisted the head of my *trisp* into a safety-lock position.

"How bad is it?" Despil asked me.

"I don't know."

Jurt let him close enough to check, and a little later Despil said, "He'll be all right. But Mother is going to be mad."

I nodded. "It was his idea," I said.

"I know. Come on. Let's get out of here."

He helped Jurt steer toward an outcropping of the Rim, *fandon* trailing like a broken wing. I lingered behind. Sawall's son Mandor, my stepbrother, put his hand on my shoulder.

"You didn't even mean him that much," he said. "I know."

I nodded and bit my lip. Despil had been right about the Lady Dara, our mother, though. She favored Jurt, and somehow he'd have her believing this whole thing was my fault. I sometimes felt she liked both of her sons by Sawall, the old Rim Duke she'd finally married after giving up on Dad, better than me. I'd once overheard it said that I reminded her of my father, whom I'd been told I resembled more than a little. I wondered again about Amber and about other places, out in Shadow, and felt my customary twinge of fear as this recalled to me the writhing Logrus, which I knew to be my ticket to other lands. I knew that I was going to try it sooner than I had originally intended.

"Let's go see Suhuy," I said to Mandor, as we rose up out of the Abyss together. "There are more things I want to ask him."

When I finally went off to college I did not spend a lot of time writing home.

". . . home," Vinta was saying, "pretty soon now. Have a drink of water," and she passed me a flask.

I took several long swallows and handed it back. "Thanks."

I stretched my cramped muscles and breathed the cold sea air. I looked for the moon and it was way back behind my shoulder.

"You were really out," she said.

"Do I talk in my sleep?"

"No."

"Good."

"Bad dreams?"

I shrugged. "Could be worse."

"Maybe you made a little noise, right before I woke you."

"Oh."

Far ahead I saw a small light at the end of a dark promontory. She gestured toward it.

"When we've passed the point," she said, "we will come into sight of the harbor at Baylesport. We'll find breakfast there, and horses."

"How far is it from Arbor House?"

"About a league," she replied. "An easy ride."

She stayed by me in silence for a while, watching the coastline and the sea. It was the first time we had simply sat together, my hands unoccupied and my mind free. And my sorcerer's sense was stirred in that interval. I felt as if I were in the presence of magic. Not some simple spell or the aura of some charmed object she might be bearing, but something very subtle. I summoned my vision and turned it upon her. There was nothing immediately obvious, but prudence suggested I check further. I extended my inquiry through the Logrus. . . .

"Please don't do that," she said.

I had just committed a faux pas. It is generally considered somewhat gauche to probe a fellow practitioner in such a fashion.

"I'm sorry," I said. "I didn't realize you were a student of the Art."

"I am not," she answered, "but I am sensitive to its operations."

"In that case, you would probably make a good one."

"My interests lie elsewhere," she said.

"I thought perhaps someone had laid a spell upon you," I stated. "I was only trying to—"

"Whatever you saw," she said, "belongs. Let it be."

"As you would. Sorry."

She must have known I couldn't let it rest at that, though, when unknown magic represents possible danger. So she went on, "It is nothing that can do you harm, I assure you. Quite the contrary."

I waited, but she did not have anything further to say on the matter. So I had to let it drop, for the moment. I shifted my gaze back to the lighthouse. What was I getting into with her, anyhow? How had she even known that I was back in town, let alone that I would visit Death Alley when I did? She must have known that the question would occur to me, and if there was to be good faith on both our parts she should be willing to explain it.

I turned back toward her, and she was smiling again.

"The wind changes in the lee of the light," she said, and she rose. "Excuse me. I've work to do."

"May I give you a hand?"

"In a bit. I'll call you when I need you."

I watched her move away, and as I did I had the eerie feeling that she was watching me also, no matter where she was looking. I realized, too, that this feeling had been with me for some time, like the sea.

By the time we had docked and put everything in order and headed up a hill along a wide cobbled way toward an inn with smoke snaking from its chimney, the sky was growing pale in the east. After a hearty breakfast, morning's light lay full upon the world. We walked then to a livery stable where three quiet mounts were obtained for the ride to her father's estate.

It was one of those clear crisp autumn days which become rarer and dearer as the year winds down. I finally felt somewhat rested, and the inn had had coffee—which is not that common in Amber, outside the palace—and I enjoy my morning cup. It was good to move through the countryside at a leisurely pace and to smell the land, to watch the moisture fade from sparkling fields and turning leaves, to feel the wind, to hear and watch a flock of birds southbound for the Isles of the Sun. We rode in silence, and nothing happened to break my mood. Memories of sorrow, betrayal, suffering and violence are strong but they do fade, whereas interludes such as this, when I close my eyes and regard the calendar of my days, somehow outlast them, as I see myself riding with Vinta Bayle under morning skies where the houses and fences are stone and stray seabirds call, there in the wine country to the east of Amber, and the scythe of Time has no power in this corner of the heart.

When we arrived at Arbor House we gave the horses into the care of Bayle's grooms, who would see to their eventual return to town. Drew departed for his own quarters then, and I walked with Vinta to the huge hilltop manor house. It commanded far views of rocky valleys and hillsides where the grapes were grown. A great number of dogs approached and tried to be friendly as we made our way to the house, and once we had entered their voices still reached us on occasion. Wood and wrought iron, gray flagged floors, high beamed ceilings, clerestory windows, family portraits, a couple of small tapestries of salmon, brown, ivory and blue, a collection of old weapons showing a few touches of oxidation, soot smudges on the gray stone about the hearth. . . . We passed through the big front hall and up a stair.

"Take this room," she said, opening a darkwood door, and I nodded as I entered and looked about. It was spacious, with big windows looking out over the valley to the south. Most of the servants were at the Baron's place in town for the season. "There is a bath in the next room," she told me, indicating a door to my left.

"Great. Thanks. Just what I need."

"So repair yourself as you would." She crossed to the window and looked downward. "I'll meet you on that terrace in about an hour, if that is agreeable."

I went over and looked down upon a large flagged area, well shaded by ancient trees—their leaves now yellow, red and brown, many of them dotting the patio—the place bordered by flower beds, vacant now, a number of tables and chairs arranged upon it, a collection of potted shrubs well disposed among them.

"Fine."

She turned toward me. "Is there anything special you would like?"

"If there is any coffee about, I wouldn't mind another cup or two when I meet you out there."

"I'll see what I can do."

She smiled and seemed to sway slightly toward me for a moment. It almost seemed in that instant as if she wanted me to embrace her. But if she did not, it could be slightly awkward. And under the circumstances I wanted no familiarity with her anyway, having no idea as to the sort of game she was playing. So I returned her smile, reached out and squeezed her arm, said, "Thank you," and stepped away. "I guess I'll see about that bath now."

I saw her to the door and let her out.

It was good to get my boots off. It was far better to soak, for a long, warm time.

Later, in fresh-conjured attire, I made my way downstairs and located a side door that let off the kitchen onto the patio. Vinta, also scrubbed and refitted, in brown riding pants and a loose tan blouse, sat beside a table at the east end of the patio. Two places were set upon it, and I saw a coffeepot and a tray of fruit and cheeses. I crossed over, leaves crunching beneath my feet, and sat down.

"Did you find everything to your satisfaction?" she asked me.

"Entirely," I replied.

"And you've notified Amber of your whereabouts?"

I nodded. Random had been a bit irritated at my taking off without letting him know, but then he had never told me not to. He was less irritated, however, when he learned that I hadn't gone all that far, and he even acknowledged finally that perhaps I had done a prudent thing in disappearing following such a peculiar attack. "Keep your eyes open and keep me posted," were his final words.

"Good. Coffee?"

"Please."

She poured and gestured toward the tray. I took an apple and took a bite.

"Things have begun happening," she said ambiguously, as she filled her own cup.

"I can't deny it," I acknowledged.

"And your troubles have been manifold."

"True."

She took a sip of coffee. "Would you care to tell me about them?" she finally said.

"They're a little too manifold," I replied. "You said something last night about your story being a long one, too."

She smiled faintly. "You must feel you have no reason to trust me more than necessary at this point," she said. "I can see that. Why trust anyone you don't have to when something dangerous is afoot, something you do not completely understand? Right?"

"It does strike me as a sound policy."

"Yet I assure you that your welfare is of the highest concern to me."

"Do you think I may represent a means of getting at Caine's killer?"

"Yes," she said, "and insofar as they may become your killers I would like to get at them."

"Are you trying to tell me that revenge is not your main objective?"

"That's right. I would rather protect the living than avenge the dead."

"But that part becomes academic if it's the same individual in both cases. Do you think it is?"

"I am not certain," she said, "that it was Luke who sent those men after you last night."

I placed my apple beside my cup and took a long drink of coffee. "Luke?" I said. "Luke who? What do you know of any Luke?"

"Lucas Raynard," she said steadily, "who trained a band of

mercenaries in the Pecos Wilderness in northern New Mexico, issued them supplies of a special ammunition that will detonate in Amber, and sent them all home with it to await his orders to muster and be transported here—to attempt something your father once tried years ago."

"Holy shit!" I said.

That *would* explain a lot—like Luke's showing up in fatigues back at the Hilton in Santa Fe, with his story about liking to hike around in the Pecos, with that round of peculiar ammunition I'd found in his pocket; and all the other trips he'd been making there—more, actually, than seemed absolutely necessary on his sales route. . . . That angle had never occurred to me, but it made a lot of sense in light of everything I'd since learned.

"Okay," I acknowledged, "I guess you know Luke Raynard. Mind telling me how you came by this?"

"Yes."

"Yes?"

"Yes, I mind. I'm afraid I'm going to have to play this game your way and trade you information a piece at a time. Now that I think of it, it will probably make me feel more comfortable too. How does that sound to you?"

"Either one of us can call it quits at any time?"

"Which stops the trading, unless we can negotiate it."

"All right."

"So you owe me one. You just returned to Amber the other day. Where had you been?"

I sighed and took another bite of the apple. "You're fishing," I said finally. "That's a big question. I've been to a lot of places. It all depends on how far back you want to go."

"Let's take it from Meg Devlin's apartment to yesterday," she said.

I choked on a piece of apple. "Okay, you've made the point— you have some damn good sources of information," I observed. "But it has to be Fiona for that one. You're in league with her some way, aren't you?"

"It's not your turn for a question," she said. "You haven't answered mine yet."

"Okay, Fi and I came back to Amber after I left Meg's place. The next day Random sent me on a mission, to turn off a machine I'd built called Ghostwheel. I failed in this but I ran into Luke along the way. He actually helped me out of a tight spot. Then, following a misunderstanding with my creation, I used a strange

Trump to take both Luke and myself to safety. Luke subsequently imprisoned me in a crystal cave—"

"Aha!" she said.

"I should stop there?"

"No, go on."

"I was a prisoner for a month or so, though it amounted to only a few days, Amber time. I was released by a couple of fellows working for a lady named Jasra, had an altercation with them and with the lady herself and trumped out to San Francisco, to Flora's place. There, I revisited an apartment where a murder had occurred—"

"Julia's place?"

"Yes. In it, I discovered a magical gateway which I was able to force open. I passed through it to a place called the Keep of the Four Worlds. A battle was in progress there, the attackers probably being led by a fellow named Dalt, of some small notoriety hereabouts at one time. Later, I was pursued by a magical whirlwind and called names by a masked wizard. I trumped out and came home—yesterday."

"And that's everything?"

"In capsule form, yes."

"Are you leaving out anything?"

"Sure. For instance, there was a Dweller on the threshold of the gateway, but I was able to get by."

"No, that's part of the package. Anything else?"

"Mm. Yes, there were two peculiar communications, ending in flowers."

"Tell me about them."

So I did.

She shook her head when I'd finished. "You've got me there," she said.

I finished my coffee and the apple. She refilled my cup.

"Now it's my turn," I said. "What did you mean by that 'Aha!' when I mentioned the crystal cave?"

"It was blue crystal, wasn't it? And it blocked your powers."

"How'd you know?"

"It was the color of the stone in the ring you took from that man last night."

"Yes."

She got to her feet and moved around the table, stood a moment, then pointed to the vicinity of my left hip.

"Would you empty that pocket onto the table, please?"

I smiled. "Sure. How'd you know?"

She didn't answer that one, but then it was a different question. I removed the assortment of blue stones from my pocket—the chips from the cave, the carved button I'd snatched, the ring—and placed them upon the table.

She picked up the button, studied it, then nodded.

"Yes, that's one also," she stated.

"One what?"

She ignored the query and dipped her right forefinger into a bit of spilled coffee within her saucer. She then used it to trace three circles around the massed stones, widdershins. Then she nodded again and returned to her seat. I'd summoned the vision in time to see her build a cage of force about them. Now, as I continued to watch, it seemed as if they were exhaling faint wisps of blue smoke that remained within the circle.

"I thought you said you weren't a sorcerer."

"I'm not," she replied.

"I'll save the question. But continue answering the last one. What is the significance of the blue stones?"

"They have an affinity for the cave, and for each other," she told me. "A person with very little training could hold one of them and simply begin walking, following the slight psychic tugging. It would eventually lead him to the cave."

"Through Shadow, you mean?"

"Yes."

"Intriguing, but I fail to see any great value to it."

"But that is not all. Ignore the pull of the cave, and you will become aware of secondary tuggings. Learn to distinguish the signature of the proper stone, and you can follow its bearer anywhere."

"That does sound a little more useful. Do you think that's how those guys found me last night, because I had a pocket full of the things?"

"Probably, from a practical standpoint, they helped. Actually, though, in your case, they should not even have been necessary at this point."

"Why not?"

"They have an additional effect. Anyone who has one in his possession for a time becomes attuned to the thing. Throw it away and the attunement remains. You can still be tracked then, just as if you had retained the stone. You would possess a signature of your own."

"You mean that even now, without them, I'm marked?"

"Yes."

"How long does it take to wear off?"

"I am not certain that it ever does."

"There must be some means of deattunement."

"I do not know for certain, but I can think of a couple of things that would probably do it."

"Name them."

"Walking the Pattern of Amber or negotiating the Logrus of Chaos. They seem almost to break a person apart and do a re-assemblement into a purer form. They have been known to purge many strange conditions. As I recall, it was the Pattern that restored your father's memory."

"Yes—and I won't even ask you how you know about the Logrus—you may well be right. As with so much else in life, it seems enough of a pain in the ass to be good for me. So, you think they could be zeroing in on me right now, with or without the stones?"

"Yes."

"How do you know all this?" I asked.

"I can sense it—and that's an extra question. But I'll give you a free one in the interests of expedition."

"Thanks. I guess it's your turn now."

"Julia was seeing an occultist named Victor Melman before she died. Do you know why?"

"She was studying with him, looking for some sort of development—at least, that's what I was told by a guy who knew her at the time. This was after we broke up."

"That is not exactly what I meant," she said. "Do you know why she desired this development?"

"Sounds like an extra question to me, but maybe I owe you one. The fellow I'd spoken with told me that I had scared her, that I'd given her to believe that I possessed unusual abilities, and that she was looking for some of her own in self-defense."

"Finish it," she said.

"What do you mean?"

"That's not a complete answer. *Did* you actually give her cause to believe that and to be afraid of you?"

"Well, I guess I did. Now my question: How could you possibly know anything about Julia in the first place?"

"I was there," she answered. "I knew her."

"Go ahead."

"That's it. Now it's my turn."

"That's hardly complete."

"But it's all you're getting on that one. Take it or leave it."

"According to our agreement I can call it quits over that."

"True. Will you?"

"What do you want to know next?"

"Did Julia develop the abilities she sought?"

"I told you that we'd stopped seeing each other before she got involved in that sort of thing. So I have no way of knowing."

"You located the portal in her apartment from which the beast that slew her had presumably emerged. Two questions now—not for you to answer for me, just for you to think over: Why would anyone want her dead in the first place? And does it not seem a very peculiar way to have gone about it? I can think of a lot simpler ways of disposing of a person."

"You're right," I agreed. "A weapon is a hell of a lot easier to manage than magic any day. As for why, I can only speculate. I had assumed it was a trap for me, and that she had been sacrificed as part of the package—my annual April thirtieth present. Do you know about them, too?"

"Let's save that business for later. You are obviously aware that sorcerers have styles, the same as painters, writers, musicians. When you succeeded in locating that gateway in Julia's apartment, was there anything about it which we might refer to as the author's signature?"

"Nothing special that I can recall. Of course, I was in a hurry to force it. I wasn't there to admire the aesthetics of the thing. But no, I can't associate it with anyone with whose work I am familiar. What are you getting at?"

"I just wondered whether it were possible that she might have developed some abilities of her own along these lines, and in the course of things opened that gateway herself and suffered those consequences."

"Preposterous!"

"All right. I am just trying to turn up some reasons. I take it then that you never saw any indication that she might possess latent abilities for sorcery?"

"No, I can't recall any instances."

I finished my coffee, poured a refill.

"If you don't think Luke is after me now, why not?" I asked her then.

"He set up some apparent accidents for you, years ago."

"Yes. He admitted that recently. He also told me that he quit doing it after the first few times."

"That is correct."

"You know, it's maddening—not knowing what you know and what you do not."

"That is why we're talking, isn't it? It was your idea to go about it this way."

"It was not! You suggested this trade-off!"

"This morning, yes. But the idea was originally yours, some time ago. I am thinking of a certain telephone conversation, at Mr. Roth's place—"

"You? That disguised voice on the phone? How could that be?"

"Would you rather hear about that or about Luke?"

"That! No, Luke! Both, damn it!"

"So it would seem there is a certain wisdom in keeping to the format we've agreed upon. There is much to be said for orderliness."

"Okay, you've made another point. Go on about Luke."

"It seemed to me, as an observer, that he quit that business as soon as he got to know you better."

"You mean back about the time we became friendly—that wasn't just an act?"

"I couldn't tell for sure then—and he certainly countenanced the years of attacks on you—but I believe that he actually sabotaged some of them."

"Who was behind them after he quit?"

"A red-haired lady with whom he seemed to be associated."

"Jasra?"

"Yes, that was her name—and I still don't know as much about her as I'd like to. Do you have anything there?"

"I think I'll save that for a big one," I said.

For the first time, she directed a narrow-eyed, teeth-clenched expression toward me.

"Can't you see that I'm trying to help you, Merlin?"

"Really, what I see is that you want information I have," I said, "and that's okay. I'm willing to deal because you seem to know things I want, too. But I've got to admit that your reasons are murky to me. How the hell did you get to Berkeley? What were you doing calling me at Bill's place? What is this power of yours you say isn't sorcery? How—"

"That's three questions," she said, "and the beginning of a fourth. Would you prefer to write them all out, and have me do the same for you? Then we can both go off to our rooms and decide which ones we want to answer?"

"No," I replied. "I'm willing to play the game. But you are aware of my reason for wanting to know these things. It's a matter of self-preservation to me. I thought at first that you wanted information that would help you to nail the man who killed Caine. But you said no, and you didn't give me anything to put in its place."

"I did, too! I want to protect you!"

"I appreciate the sentiment. But why? When it comes down to it, you hardly know me."

"Nevertheless, that is my reason and I don't feel like going behind it. Take it or leave it."

I got to my feet and began pacing the patio. I didn't like the thought of giving away information that could be vital to my security, and ultimately that of Amber—though I had to admit I was getting a pretty good return for what I'd given. Her stuff did sound right. For that matter, the Bayles had a long history of loyalty to the Crown, for whatever that was worth. The thing that bothered me the most, I decided, was her insistence that it was not actually revenge that she was after. Apart from this being a very un-Amberlike attitude, if she were any judge at all as to what would go over with me she need but have agreed that blood was what she wanted, in order to make her concern intelligible. I would have bought it without looking any further. And what did she offer in its place? Airy nothings and classified motives. . . .

Which could well mean she was telling the truth. Disdaining the use of a workable lie and offering something more cumbersome in its place would seem the mark of genuine honesty. And she did, apparently, have more answers that I wanted—

I heard a small rattling sound from the table. I thought at first that she might be drumming on it with her fingertips as a sign of her irritation with me. But when I glanced back I saw that she was sitting perfectly still, not even looking at me.

I drew nearer, seeking the source. The ring, the pieces of blue stone and even the button were jiggling about on the tabletop, as of their own accord.

"Something you're doing?" I asked.

"No," she replied.

The stone in the ring cracked and fell out of its setting.

"What, then?"

"I broke a link," she said. "I believe something may be trying to reestablish it and failing."

"Even so, if I'm still attuned they don't need them in order to locate me, do they?"

"There may be more than one party involved," she observed. "I think I should have a servant ride back to town and throw the things into the ocean. If someone wishes to follow them there, fine."

"The chips should just lead back to the cave, and the ring to the dead man," I said. "But I'm not ready to throw the button away."

"Why not? It represents a big unknown."

"Exactly. But these things would have to work both ways, wouldn't they? That would mean that I could learn to use the button to find my way to the flower thrower."

"That could be dangerous."

"And not doing it could prove more dangerous in the long run. No, you can throw the rest of them into the sea, but not the button."

"All right. I'll keep it pent for you."

"Thanks. Jasra is Luke's mother."

"You're joking!"

"Nope."

"That explains why he didn't lean on her directly about the later April thirtieths. Fascinating! It opens up a whole new lane of speculation."

"Care to share them?"

"Later, later. In the meantime, I'll take care of these stones right now."

She scooped them all out of the circle and they seemed, for a moment, to dance in her hand. She stood.

"Uh—the button?" I said.

"Yes."

She put the button into her pocket and kept the others in her hand.

"You're going to get attuned yourself if you keep the button that way, aren't you?"

"No," she said, "I won't."

"Why not?"

"There's a reason. Excuse me while I find a container for the others, and someone to transport them."

"Won't that person get attuned?"

"It takes a while."

"Oh."

"Have some more coffee—or something."

She turned and left. I ate a piece of cheese. I tried to figure out whether I'd gotten more answers or more new questions during the course of our conversation. I tried to fit some of the new pieces into the old puzzle.

"Father?"

I turned, to see who had spoken. There was no one in sight.

"Down here."

A coin-sized disk of light lay within a nearby flower bed, otherwise empty save for a few dry stalks and leaves. The light caught my attention when it moved slightly.

"Ghost?" I asked.

"Uh-huh," came the reply from among the leaves. "I was waiting to catch you when you were alone. I'm not sure I trust that woman."

"Why not?"

"She doesn't scan right, like other people. I don't know what it is. But that's not what I wanted to talk to you about."

"What, then?"

"Uh—well, did you mean what you said about not really intending to turn me off?"

"Jeez! After all the sacrifices I made for you! Your education and everything. . . . And lugging all your damn components out to a place like that where you'd be safe! How can you ask me that?"

"Well, I heard Random tell you to do it—"

"You don't do everything you're told either, do you? Especially when it comes to assaulting me when I just wanted to check out a few programs? I deserve a little more respect than that!"

"Uh—yeah. Look, I'm sorry."

"You ought to be. I went through a lot of crap because of you."

"I looked for you for several days, and I couldn't find you."

"Crystal caves are no fun."

"I don't have much time now. . . ." The light flickered, faded almost to the point of vanishing, returned to full brilliance. "Will you tell me something fast?"

"Shoot."

"That fellow who was with you when you came out this way—and when you left—the big red-haired man?"

"Luke. Yes?"

The light grew dimmer again.

"Is it okay to trust him?" Ghost's voice came faintly, weakly.

"No!" I shouted. "That would be damn stupid!"

Ghost was gone, and I couldn't tell whether he'd heard my answer.

"What's the matter?" Vinta's voice, from above me.

"Argument with my imaginary playmate," I called out.

Even from that distance I could see the expression of puzzlement on her face. She sought in all directions about the patio and then, apparently persuading herself that I was indeed alone, she nodded.

"Oh," she said. Then, "I'll be along in a little while."

"No hurry," I answered.

Where shall wisdom be found, and where is the place of understanding? If I knew, I'd walk over and stand there. As it was, I felt as if I stood in the midst of a large map, surrounded by vague areas wherein were penned the visages of particularly nasty-looking random variables. A perfect place for a soliloquy, if one had anything to say.

I went back inside to use the john. All that coffee.

6

Well, maybe.

With Julia, I mean.

I sat alone in my room, thinking by candlelight.

Vinta had stirred a few sunken memories to the surface. It was later on, when we weren't seeing much of each other. . . .

I'd met Julia first in a Computer Science course I was taking. We'd started seeing each other occasionally, just coffee after class and like that, at first. Then more and more frequently, and pretty soon it was serious.

Now it was ending as it had started, a little more each time. . . .

I felt her hand on my shoulder as I was leaving the supermarket with a bag of groceries. I knew it was her and I turned and there was no one there. Seconds later, she hailed me from across the parking lot. I went over and said hello, asked her if she were still working at the software place where she'd been. She said that she wasn't. I recalled that she was wearing a small silver pentagram on a chain about her neck. It could easily—and more likely should—have been hanging down inside her blouse. But of course I wouldn't have seen it then, and her body language indicated that she wanted me to see it. So I ignored it while we exchanged a few generalities, and she turned me down on dinner and a movie, though I asked after several nights.

"What are you doing now?" I inquired.

"I'm studying a lot."

"What?"

"Oh, just—different things. I'll surprise you one of these days."

Again, I didn't bite, though an over-friendly Irish setter approached us about then. She placed her hand on its head and said, "Sit!" and it did. It became still as a statue at her side, and remained when we left later. For all I know, there's a dog skeleton still crouched there, near the cart return area, like a piece of modern sculpture.

It didn't really seem that important at the time. But in retrospect, I wondered. . . .

We had ridden that day, Vinta and I. Seeing my growing exasperation of the morning, she must have felt a break was in order. She was right. Following a light lunch, when she made the suggestion that we take a ride about the estate, I agreed readily. I had wanted a little more time in which to think before continuing our cross-examination and discourse game. And the weather was good, the countryside attractive.

We made our way along a curling trail through arbors, which led at length into the northern hills from where we were afforded long views across the rugged and cross-hatched land down to the sun-filled sea. The sky was full of winds and wisps of cloud, passing birds. . . . Vinta seemed to have no special destination in mind, which was all right with me. As we rode, I recalled a visit to a Napa Valley winery, and the next time we drew rein to rest the horses I asked her, "Do you bottle the wine here at the estate? Or is that done in town? Or in Amber?"

"I don't know," she said.

"I thought you grew up here."

"I never paid attention."

I bit back a remark about patrician attitudes. Unless she were joking, I couldn't see how she'd fail to know something like that.

She caught my expression, though, and added immediately, "We've done it various ways at various times. I've been living in town for several years now. I'm not sure where the principal bottling has been done recently."

Nice save, because I couldn't fault it. I hadn't intended my question as any sort of trap, but I felt as if I had just touched on something. Possibly from the fact that she didn't let it go at that. She went on to say that they shipped large casks all over the place and often sold them in that fashion. On the other hand, there were smaller customers who wanted the product bottled. . . . I stopped listening after a time. On the one hand, I could see it, coming from a vintner's daughter. On the other, it was all stuff I could have made up myself on the spot. There was no way for me to check on any of it. I got the feeling that she was trying to snow me, to cover something. But I couldn't figure what.

"Thanks," I said when she paused for breath, and she gave me a strange look but took the hint and did not continue.

"You have to speak English," I said in that language, "if the things you told me earlier are true."

"Everything I told you is true," she replied, in unaccented English.

"Where'd you learn it?"

"On the shadow Earth where you went to school."

"Would you care to tell me what you were doing there?"

"I was on a special mission."

"For your father? For the Crown?"

"I'd rather not answer you at all than lie to you."

"I appreciate that. Of course, I must speculate."

She shrugged.

"You said you were in Berkeley?" I asked.

A hesitation, then, "Yes."

"I don't remember ever seeing you around."

Another shrug. I wanted to grab her and shake her. Instead, I said, "You knew about Meg Devlin. You said you were in New York—"

"I believe you're getting ahead of me on questions."

"I didn't know we were playing the game again. I thought we were just talking."

"All right, then: Yes."

"Tell me one more thing and perhaps I can help you."

She smiled. "I don't need any help. You're the one with problems."

"May I, anyway?"

"Go ahead and ask. Every time you question me you tell me things I wish to know."

"You knew about Luke's mercenaries. Did you visit New Mexico, too?"

"Yes, I've been there."

"Thanks," I said.

"That's all?"

"That's all."

"You've come to some conclusion?"

"Perhaps."

"Care to tell me what it is?"

I smiled and shook my head.

I left it at that. A few oblique queries on her part as we rode on led me to believe that I had her wondering what I might have guessed or suddenly seen. Good. I was determined to let it smolder. I needed something to balance her reticence on those points about which I was most curious, to lead hopefully to a full trade of information. Besides, I *had* reached a peculiar conclusion concerning her. It was not complete, but if it were correct I would require the rest of the answer sooner or later. So it was not exactly as if I were setting up a bluff.

The afternoon was golden, orange, yellow, red about us, with an autumn-damp smell behind the cool nips of the breezes. The sky was very blue, like certain stones. . . .

Perhaps ten minutes later I asked her a more neutral question. "Could you show me the road to Amber?"

"You don't know it?"

I shook my head. "I've never been this way before. All I know is that there are overland routes coming through here that lead to the Eastern Gate."

"Yes," she said. "A bit farther to the north, I believe. Let's go find it."

She headed back to a road we had followed for a time earlier and we turned right on it, which seemed logical. I did not remark on her vagueness, though I expected a comment from her before too long in that I had not elaborated on my plans and I'd a feeling she was hoping that I would.

Perhaps three quarters of a mile later we came to a crossroads. There was a low stone marker at the far left corner giving the distance to Amber, the distance back to Baylesport, the distance to Baylecrest in the east and to a place called Murn, straight ahead.

"What's Murn?" I asked.

"A little dairy village."

No way I could check that, without traveling six leagues.

"You plan on riding back to Amber?" she asked.

"Yes."

"Why not just use a Trump?"

"I want to get to know the area better. It's my home. I like it here."

"But I explained to you—about the danger. The stones have marked you. You can be tracked."

"That doesn't mean I *will* be tracked. I doubt that whoever sent the ones I met last night would even be aware this soon that they'd found me and failed. They'd still be lurking about if I hadn't decided to go out for dinner. I'm sure I have a few days' grace in which to remove the markings you spoke of."

She dismounted and let her horse nibble a few blades of grass. I did the same. Dismounted, that is.

"You're probably right. I just don't like to see you taking *any* chances," she said. "When are you planning on heading back?"

"I don't know. I suppose that the longer I wait the more likely it is that the person behind last night's business will get restless and maybe send more muscle."

She took hold of my arm and turned, so that she was suddenly pressed against me. I was somewhat surprised by the act, but my free arm automatically moved to hold the lady as it tends to on such occasions.

"You weren't planning on leaving now, were you? Because if you are, I'm going with you."

"No," I answered truthfully. Actually, I'd been thinking of departing the following morning, following a good night's sleep.

"When, then? We still have a lot of things to talk about."

"I think we've pushed the question-and-answer business about as far as you're willing to let it go."

"There are some things—"

"I know."

Awkward, this. Yes, she was desirable. And no, I didn't care to have anything to do with her that way. Partly because I felt she wanted something else as well—what, I wasn't sure—and partly because I was certain she possessed a peculiar power to which I did not wish to expose myself at intimate range. As my Uncle Suhuy used to say, speaking technically as a sorcerer, "If you don't understand it, don't screw around with it." And I had a feeling that anything beyond a friendly acquaintanceship with Vinta could well turn into a duel of energies.

So I kissed her quickly to stay friendly and disengaged myself.

"Maybe I'll head back tomorrow," I told her.

"Good. I was hoping you'd spend the night. Perhaps several. I will protect you."

"Yes, I'm still very tired," I said.

"We'll have to feed you a good meal and build up your strength."

She brushed my cheek with her fingertips then, and I suddenly realized that I did know her from somewhere. Where? I couldn't say. And that, too, frightened me. More than a little. As we mounted and headed back toward Arbor House I began making my plans for getting out of there that night.

So, sitting in my room, sipping a glass of my absent host's wine (the red) and watching the candles flicker in the breeze from an opened window, I waited—first for the house to grow quiet (which it had), then for a goodly time to pass. My door was latched. I had mentioned how tired I felt several times during dinner, and then I had retired early. I am not so egotistically male that I feel myself constantly lusted after, but Vinta had given indication that she might stop by and I wanted the excuse of heavy sleeping. Least of all did I wish to offend her. I had problems enough without turning my strange ally against me.

I wished I still had a good book about, but I'd left my last one at Bill's place, and if I were to summon it now I did not know but that Vinta might sense the sending, just as Fiona had once known I was creating a Trump, and come pounding on the door to see what the hell was going on.

But no one came pounding, and I listened to the creakings of a quiet house and the night sounds without. The candles shortened themselves and the shadows on the wall behind the bed ebbed and flowed like a dark tide beyond their swaying light. I thought my thoughts and sipped my wine. Pretty soon. . . .

An imagining? Or had I just heard my name whispered from some undetectable place?

"Merle. . . ."

Again.

Real, but—

My vision seemed to swim for a moment, and then I realized it for what it was: a very weak Trump contact.

"Yes," I said, opening and extending. "Who is it?"

"Merle, baby. . . . Give me a hand or I've had it. . . ."

Luke!

"Right here," I said, reaching, reaching, as the image grew clear, solidified.

He was leaning, his back against a wall, shoulders slumped, head hanging.

"If this is a trick, Luke, I'm ready for it," I told him. I rose quickly and, crossing to the table where I had laid my blade, I drew it and held it ready.

"No trick. Hurry! Get me out of here!"

He raised his left hand. I extended my left hand and caught

hold of it. Immediately he slumped against me, and I staggered. For an instant I thought it was an attack, but he was dead weight and I saw that there was blood all over him. He still clutched a bloody blade in his right hand.

"Over here. Come on."

I steered him and supported him for several paces, then deposited him on the bed. I pried the blade from his grip, then placed it along with mine on a nearby chair.

"What the hell happened to you?"

He coughed and shook his head weakly. He drew several deep breaths, then, "Did I see a glass of wine," he asked, "as we passed a table?"

"Yeah. Hold on."

I fetched it, brought it back, propped him and held it to his lips. It was still over half full. He sipped it slowly, pausing for deep breaths.

"Thanks," he said when he'd finished, then his head turned to the side.

He was out. I took his pulse. It was fast but kind of weak.

"Damn you, Luke!" I said. "You've got the worst timing. . . ."

But he didn't hear a word. He just lay there and bled all over the place.

Several curses later I had him undressed and was going over him with a wet towel to find out where, under all that blood, the injuries lay. There was a nasty chest wound on the right, which might have hit the lung. His breathing was very shallow, though, and I couldn't tell. If so, I was hoping he'd inherited the regenerative abilities of Amber in full measure. I put a compress on it and laid his arm on top to hold it in place while I checked elsewhere. I suspected he had a couple of fractured ribs, also. His left arm was broken above the elbow and I set it and splinted it, using loose slats from a chair I'd noticed in the back of the closet earlier, and I strapped it to him. There were over a dozen lacerations and incisions of various degrees of severity on his thighs, right hip, right arm and shoulder, his back. None of them, fortunately, involved arterial bleeding. I cleaned all of these and bound them, which left him looking like an illustration in a firstaid handbook. Then I checked his chest wound again and covered him up.

I wondered about some of the Logrus healing techniques I knew in theory but had never had a chance to practice. He was looking pretty pale, so I decided I had better try them. When I'd finished, some time later, it seemed as if his color had returned to his face. I added my cloak to the blanket which covered him. I took his pulse again and it felt stronger. I cursed again, just to stay in practice, removed our blades from the chair and sat down on it.

A little later my conversation with Ghostwheel returned to trouble me. Had Luke been trying to do a deal with my creation? He'd told me he wanted Ghost's power, to prosecute his designs against Amber. Then Ghost had asked me earlier today whether Luke was to be trusted, and my answer had been emphatically negative.

Had Ghost terminated negotiations with Luke in the fashion I saw before me?

I fetched forth my Trumps and shuffled out the bright circle of the Ghostwheel. I focused on it, setting my mind for contact, reaching out, calling, summoning.

Twice I felt near to something—agitated—during the several minutes I devoted to the effort. But it was as if we were separated by a sheet of glass. Was Ghost occupied? Or just not inclined to talk with me?

I put my cards away. But they had served to push my thoughts into another channel.

I gathered Luke's gory clothing and did a quick search. I turned up a set of Trumps in a side pocket, along with several blank cards and a pencil—and yes, they seemed to be rendered in the same style as the ones I had come to call the Trumps of Doom. I added to the packet the one depicting myself, which Luke had been holding in his hand when he had trumped in.

His were a fascinating lot. There was one of Jasra, and one of Victor Melman. There was also one of Julia, and a partly completed one of Bleys. There was one for the crystal cave, another for Luke's old apartment. There were several duplicated from the Trumps of Doom themselves, one for a palace I did not recognize, one for one of my old pads, one for a rugged-looking blond guy in green and black, another of a slim, russet-haired man in brown and black, and one of a woman who resembled this man so closely it would seem they must be related. These last two, strangely, were done in a different style; even by a different hand, I'd say. The only unknown one I felt relatively certain about was the blond fellow, who, from his colors, I would assume to be Luke's old friend Dalt, the mercenary. There were also three separate attempts at something resembling Ghostwheel—none of them, I would guess, completely successful.

I heard Luke growl something, and I saw that his eyes were open and darting.

"Take it easy," I said. "You're safe."

He nodded and closed his eyes. A few moments later, he opened them again.

"Hey! My cards," he said weakly.

I smiled. "Nice work," I remarked. "Who did them?"

"Me," he answered. "Who else?"

"Where'd you learn?"

"My dad. He was real good at it."

"If you can do them, you must have walked the Pattern."

He nodded.

"Where?"

He studied me a moment, then performed a weak shrug and winced. "Tir-na Nog'th."

"Your father took you, saw you through it?"

Again, a nod.

Why not push it, since I seemed to be on a roll? I picked up a card.

"And here's Dalt," I said. "You used to be Cub Scouts together, didn't you?"

He did not reply. When I looked up I saw narrowed eyes and a furrowed brow.

"I've never met him," I added. "But I recognize the colors, and I know he's from out your way—around Kashfa."

Luke smiled. "You always did your homework back in school, too," he said.

"And usually on time," I agreed. "But with you I've been running late. Luke, I can't find a Trump for the Keep of the Four Worlds. And here's someone I don't know."

I picked up the slim lady's card and waved it at him.

He smiled. "Gettin' weak and losin' my breath again," he said. "You been to the Keep?"

"Yep."

"Recently?"

I nodded.

"Tell you what," he said at last. "Tell me what you saw at the Keep and how you learned some of that stuff about me and I'll tell you who she is."

I thought quickly. I could say things so that I probably wouldn't be telling him anything he didn't already know.

So, "The other way around," I said.

"Okay. The lady," he stated, "is Sand."

I stared so hard that I felt the beginnings of a contact. I smothered it.

"The long-lost," he added.

I raised the card depicting the man who resembled her. "Then this must be Delwin," I said.

"Right."

"You didn't do these two cards. They're not your style, and you probably wouldn't have known what they looked like to begin with."

"Perceptive. My father drew them, back in the time of the troubles—for all the good it did him. They wouldn't help him either."

"Either?"

"They weren't interested in helping me, despite their disaffection with this place. Count them as out of the game."

"This place?" I said. "Where do you think you are, Luke?"

His eyes widened. He cast his gaze about the room. "The camp of the enemy," he answered. "I had no choice. These are your quarters in Amber, right?"

"Wrong," I replied.

"Don't bait me, Merle. You've got me. I'm your prisoner. Where am I?"

"Do you know who Vinta Bayle is?"

"No."

"She was Caine's mistress. This is her family's place, way out in the country. She's just up the hall somewhere. Might even stop by. I think she's got a crush on me."

"Uh-oh. She a tough lady?"

"Very."

"What you doing making out with her this soon after the funeral? That's hardly decent."

"Huh! If it weren't for you there wouldn't have been any funeral."

"Don't give me that indignation crap, Merle. If it had been *your* dad, Corwin, he'd killed, wouldn't you have gone after him?"

"That's not fair. My father wouldn't have done all those things Brand did."

"Maybe, maybe not. But supposing he had? Even then. Wouldn't you have gone after Caine?"

I turned away. "I don't know," I said finally. "It's too damned hypothetical."

"You'd have done it. I know you, Merle. I'm sure you would have."

I sighed. "Maybe," I said. "Well, okay. Maybe I might have. But I would have stopped there. I wouldn't have gone after the others too. I don't want to make you feel any worse than you do about it, but your old man was psycho; you must know that. And you're not. I know you as well as you know me. I've been thinking about this for some time. You know, Amber recognizes the personal vendetta. You've got an arguable case there for one. And the death didn't even occur within Amber, if Random were really looking for an out for you."

"Why should he be?"

"Because I'd be vouching for your integrity in other matters."

"Come on, Merle—"

"You've got a classic vendetta defense—a son avenging his father's death."

"I don't know. . . . Hey, you trying to get out of telling me the stuff you promised to?"

"No, but—"

"So you made it to the Keep of the Four Worlds. What did you learn there and how did you learn it?"

"Okay. You think about what I said, though," I replied.

His expression remained unchanged.

Then, "There was an old hermit named Dave," I began.

Luke fell asleep before I finished. I just let my voice trail off and sat there. After a time, I rose and located the wine bottle and poured a little into the glass, since Luke had drunk most of mine. I took it with me to the window and stared down and out across the patio, where the wind was rattling leaves. I wondered about what I'd said to Luke. It wasn't a full picture I'd given him, partly because I hadn't had time to go into it thoroughly, mainly because he hadn't seemed interested. But even if Random did let him off the hook officially in the matter of Caine's death, Julian or Gérard would probably be looking to kill him under the same vendetta code I'd been talking about. I didn't really know what to do. I was obliged to tell Random about him, but I'd be damned if I'd do it yet. There were still too many things I had to learn from him, and getting at him might be a lot harder if he were a prisoner back in Amber. Why had he ever gotten himself born as Brand's son, anyway?

I returned to the bedside seat, near which I had left our weapons and Luke's Trumps. I moved these items across the room, to where I seated myself in the more comfortable chair I had occupied earlier. I studied his cards again. Amazing. A whole bunch of history in my hand. . . .

When Oberon's wife Rilga had shown less hardihood than many by aging rapidly and retiring to a reclusive life at a country shrine, he had gone off and remarried, somewhat to the chagrin of their children—Caine, Julian and Gérard. But to confuse genealogists and sticklers for family legality, he had done it in a place where time flowed far more rapidly than in Amber. Interesting arguments both for and against the bigamous nature of his marriage to Harla may be made. I'm in no position to judge. I had the story from Flora years ago, and in that she'd never gotten along too well with Delwin and Sand, the offspring of that union, she was inclined to the pro-bigamy interpretation. I'd never seen pictures of Delwin or Sand until now. There weren't any hanging around the palace, and they were seldom mentioned. But they had lived in Amber for the relatively short time Harla was queen there. Following her death, they grew unhappy with Oberon's policies toward her homeland—which they visited often—and after a time they departed, vowing not to have anything to do with Amber again. At least that's the way I'd heard it. There could easily have been all sorts of sibling politicking involved, too. I don't know.

But here were two missing members of the royal family, and obviously Luke had learned of them and approached them, hoping to revive old resentments and gain allies. He admitted that it hadn't worked. Two centuries is a long time to hold a grudge at high pitch. That's about how long it had been since their departure, as I understood it. I wondered fleetingly whether I should get in touch with them, just to say hello. If they weren't interested in helping Luke I didn't suppose they'd be interested in helping the other side either, now they were aware there was another side. It did seem proper that I should introduce myself and pay my respects, as a family member they'd never met. I decided that I would do it sometime, though the present moment was hardly appropriate. I added their Trumps to my own collection, along with good intentions.

And then there was Dalt—a sworn enemy of Amber, I gathered. I studied his card again, and I wondered. If he were indeed such a good friend of Luke's, perhaps I should let him know what had happened. He might even know of the circumstances involved and mention something I could use. In fact, the more I thought about it—recalling his recent presence at the Keep of the Four Worlds—the more tempting it became to try to reach him. It seemed possible I could even pick up something about what was now going on in that place.

I gnawed a knuckle. Should I or shouldn't I? I couldn't see any harm that could come of it. I wasn't planning on giving anything away. Still, there were a few misgivings.

What the hell, I decided finally. Nothing ventured. . . .

Hello, hello. Reaching out through the suddenly cold card. . . .

A startled moment somewhere, and the sense of an *Aha!*

Like a portrait come to life, my vision stirred.

"Who are you?" the man asked, hand on hilt, blade half drawn.

"My name is Merlin," I said, "and we've a mutual acquaintance named Rinaldo. I wanted to tell you that he'd been badly injured."

By now, we both hovered between our two realities, solid and perfectly clear to each other. He was bigger than I'd thought from his representation, and he stood at the center of a stone-walled room, a window to his left showing a blue sky and a limb of cloud. His green eyes, at first wide, were now narrowed and the set of his jaw seemed a bit truculent.

"Where is he?" he inquired.

"Here. With me," I answered.

"How fortunate," he replied, and the blade was in his hand and he moved forward.

I flipped the Trump away, which did not sever the contact. I had to summon the Logrus to do that—and it fell between us like the blade of a guillotine and jerked me back as if I had just touched a live wire. My only consolation was that Dalt had doubtless felt the same thing.

"Merle, what's going on?" Luke's voice came hoarsely. "I saw—Dalt. . . ."

"Uh, yeah. I just called him."

He raised his head slightly. "Why?"

"To tell him about you. He's your friend, isn't he?"

"You asshole!" he said. "He's the one that did this to me!"

Then he began coughing and I rushed to his side.

"Get me some water, huh?" he said.

"Coming up."

I went off to the bathroom and fetched him a glass. I propped him and he sipped it for a time.

"Maybe I should have told you," he said finally. "Didn't think—you'd play games—that way, though—when you don't know—what's going on. . . ."

He coughed again, drank more water.

"Hard to know what to tell you—and what not to," he continued, a while later.

"Why not tell me everything?" I suggested.

He shook his head slightly. "Can't. Probably get you killed. More likely both of us."

"The way things have been going, it seems as if it could happen whether you tell me or not."

He smiled faintly and took another drink.

"Parts of this thing are personal," he said then, "and I don't want anyone else involved."

"I gather that your trying to kill me every spring for a while there was kind of personal, too," I observed, "yet somehow I felt involved."

"Okay, okay," he said, slumping back and raising his right hand. "I told you I cut that out a long time ago."

"But the attempts went on."

"They weren't my doing."

Okay, I decided. Try it. "It was Jasra, wasn't it?"

"What do you know about her?"

"I know she's your mother, and I gather this is her war too."

He nodded. "So you know. . . . All right. That makes it easier." He paused to catch his breath. "She started me doing the April thirtieth stuff for practice. When I got to know you better and quit, she was mad."

"So she continued it herself?"

He nodded.

"She wanted you to go after Caine," I said.

"So did I."

"But the others? She's leaning on you about them, I'll bet. And you're not so sure they have it coming."

Silence.

"Are you?" I said.

He shifted his gaze away from my own and I heard his teeth grind together.

"You're off the hook," he said at last. "I've no intention of hurting you. I won't let her do it either."

"And what about Bleys and Random and Fiona and Flora and Gérard and—"

He laughed, which cost him a wince and a quick clutch at his chest.

"They've nothing to worry about from us," he said, "right now."

"What do you mean?"

"Think," he told me. "I could have trumped back to my old apartment, scared hell out of the new tenants and called an ambulance. I could be in an emergency room right now."

"Why aren't you?"

"I've been hurt worse than this, and I've made it. I'm here because I need your help."

"Oh? For what?"

He looked at me, then looked away again. "She's in bad trouble, and we've got to rescue her."

"Who?" I asked, already knowing the answer.

"My mother," he replied.

I wanted to laugh, but I couldn't when I saw the expression on his face. It took real balls to ask me to help rescue the woman who'd tried to kill me—not once, but many times—and whose big aim in life seemed to be the destruction of my relatives. Balls, or—

"I've no one else left to turn to," he said.

"If you talk me into this one, Luke, you'll deserve the Salesman of the Year Award," I said. "But I'm willing to listen."

"Throat's dry again," he said.

I went and refilled the glass. As I returned with it, it seemed there was a small noise in the hall. I continued listening while I helped Luke to a few more sips.

He nodded when he was finished, but I had heard another sound by then. I raised my finger to my lips and glanced at the door. I put down the glass, rose and crossed the room, retrieving my blade as I did so.

Before I reached the door, however, there was a gentle knock.

"Yes?" I said, advancing to it.

"It's me," came Vinta's voice. "I know that Luke is in there, and I want to see him."

"So you can finish him off?" I asked.

"I told you before that that is not my intention."

"Then you're not human," I said.

"I never claimed I was."

"Then you're not Vinta Bayle," I said.

There followed a long silence, then, "Supposing I'm not?"

"Then tell me who you are."

"I can't."

"Then meet me halfway," I said, drawing upon all of my accumulated guesswork concerning her, "and tell me who you were."

"I don't know what you mean."

"Yes, you do. Pick one—any one. I don't care."

There was another silence, then, "I dragged you from the fire," she said, "but I couldn't control the horse. I died in the lake. You wrapped me in your cloak. . . ."

That was not an answer I had anticipated. But it was good enough.

With the point of my weapon I raised the latch. She pushed the door open and glanced at the blade in my hand.

"Dramatic," she remarked.

"You've impressed me," I said, "by the perils with which I am beset."

"Not sufficiently, it would seem." She entered, smiling.

"What do you mean?" I asked.

"I didn't hear you ask him anything about the blue stones and what he might have homing in on you as a consequence of your attunement."

"You've been eavesdropping."

"A lifetime habit," she agreed.

I turned toward Luke and introduced her. "Luke, this is Vinta Bayle—sort of."

Luke raised his right hand, his eyes never leaving her face. "I just want to know one thing," he began.

"I'll bet you do," she replied. "Am I going to kill you or aren't I? Keep wondering. I haven't decided yet. Do you remember the time you were low on gas north of San Luis Obispo and you discovered your wallet was missing? You had to borrow money from your date to get back home. She had to ask you twice, too, before you paid her back."

"How could you know that?" he whispered.

"You got in a fight with three bikers one day," she went on. "You almost lost an eye when one of them wrapped a chain around your head. Seems to have healed up nicely. Can't see the scar—"

"And I won," he added.

"Yes. Not too many people can pick up a Harley and throw it like you did."

"I have to know," he said, "how you learned these things."

"Maybe I'll tell you that too, sometime," she said. "I just mentioned them to keep you honest. Now I'm going to ask you some questions, and your life is going to depend on giving me honest answers. Understand—"

"Vinta," I interrupted, "you told me that you weren't interested in killing Luke."

"It's not at the top of my list," she replied, "but if he's in the way of what is, he goes."

Luke yawned. "I'll tell you about the blue stones," he muttered. "I don't have anybody on a blue-stone detail after Merle now."

"Might Jasra have someone tracking him that way?"

"Possible. I just don't know."

"What about the ones who attacked him in Amber last night?"

"First I've heard of it," he said, and he closed his eyes.

"Look at this," she ordered, removing the blue button from her pocket.

He opened his eyes and squinted at it.

"Recognize it?"

"Nope," he said, and closed his eyes again.

"And you don't mean Merle any harm now?"

"That's right," he answered, his voice drifting off.

She opened her mouth again and I said, "Let him sleep. He's not going anywhere."

She gave me an almost angry look, then nodded. "You're right," she said.

"So what are you going to do now—kill him while he's out?"

"No," she replied. "He was telling the truth."

"And does it make a difference?"

"Yes," she told me, "for now."

7

I actually did get a fairly decent night's sleep despite everything, including a distant dogfight and a lot of howling. Vinta had been disinclined to continue at questions and answers, and I hadn't wanted her bothering Luke any more. I persuaded her to leave and let us rest. I sacked out on the comfortable chair, with my feet propped on the other one. I was hoping to continue my conversation with Luke in private. I remember chuckling right before I fell asleep as I tried to decide which of them I distrusted less.

I was awakened by the first brightening of the sky and a few arguments of birds. I stretched several times then and made my way to the bathroom. Half an ablution later I heard Luke cough and then whisper my name.

"Unless you're hemorrhaging, wait a minute," I replied, and I dried myself off. "Need some water?" I asked while I was doing it.

"Yeah. Bring some."

I threw the towel over my shoulder and took him a drink.

"Is she still around?" he asked me.

"No."

"Give me the glass and go check the hall, will you? I'll manage."

I nodded and passed it to him. I kept it quiet as I eased the door open. I stepped out into the hall, walked up to the corner. There was no one in sight.

"All clear," I whispered as I came back into the room.

Luke was gone. A moment later I heard him in the bathroom.

"Damn! I'd have helped you!" I said.

"I can still take a leak by myself," he replied, staggering back into the room, his good hand on the wall. "Had to see whether I could negotiate," he added, lowering himself to the edge of the bed. He put his hand against his rib cage and panted. "Shit! that smarts!"

"Let me help you lie back."

"Okay. Listen, don't let her know I can do even that much."

"Okay," I said. "Take it easy now. Rest."

He shook his head. "I want to tell you as much as I can before she comes busting back in here," he said, "and she will, too—believe me."

"You know that for a fact?"

"Yes. She's not human, and she's more attuned to both of us than any blue stone ever was. I don't understand your style of magic, but I've got my own and I know what it tells me. It was your question about who she was that got me to working on the problem, though. Have you figured her out yet?"

"Not completely, no."

"Well, I know she can switch bodies like changing clothes—and she can travel through Shadow."

"Do the names Meg Devlin or George Hansen mean anything to you?" I asked.

"No. Should they?"

"Didn't think so. But she was both of them, I'm sure."

I'd left out Dan Martinez, not because he'd shot it out with Luke and telling Luke would raise his distrust of her even further, but because I didn't want him to know that I was aware of the New Mexico guerrilla operation—and I could see that it might lead in that direction.

"She was also Gail Lampron."

"Your old girlfriend, back in school?" I said.

"Yes. I thought there was something familiar about her immediately. But it didn't hit me till later. She has all of Gail's little mannerisms—the way she turns her head, the way she uses her hands and eyes when she's talking. Then she mentioned two events to which there had only been a single common witness—Gail."

"It sounds as if she wanted you to know."

"I believe she did," he agreed.

"Why didn't she just come out and say it then, I wonder?"

"I don't think she can. There's something could be a spell on her, only it's hard to judge, her not being human and all." He glanced furtively at the door as he said this. Then, "Check again," he added.

"Still clear," I said. "Now what about—"

"Another time," he said. "I've got to get out of here."

"I can see your wanting to get away from her—" I began.

He shook his head. "That's not it," he said. "I've got to hit the Keep of the Four Worlds—soon."

"The shape you're in—"

"That's it. That's what I mean. I've got to get out of here so I can be in shape soon. I think old Sharu Garrul's gotten loose. That's the only way I can figure what happened."

"What *did* happen?"

"I got a distress call from my mother. She'd gone back to the Keep after I'd gotten her away from you."

"Why?"

"Why, what?"

"Why'd she head for the Keep?"

"Well, the place is a power center. The way the four worlds come together there releases an awful lot of free power, which an adept can tap into—"

"Four worlds actually do come together there? You mean you're in a different shadow depending on the direction you might take off in?"

He studied me for a moment. "Yes," he finally said, "but I'll never get this thing told if you want all the little details."

"And I won't understand it if too much gets left out. So she went to the Keep to raise some power and got in trouble instead. She called you to come help her. What did she want that power for, anyway?"

"Mm. Well, I'd been having trouble with Ghostwheel. I thought I almost had him talked into coming over to our side, but she probably thought I wasn't making progress fast enough and apparently decided to try binding him with a massive spell after—"

"Wait a minute. You were talking to Ghost? How did you get in touch? Those Trumps you drew are no good."

"I know. I went in."

"How'd you manage it?"

"In scuba gear. I wore a wet suit and oxygen tanks."

"Son of a gun. That's an interesting approach."

"I wasn't Grand D's top salesman for nothing. I almost had him convinced, too. But she'd learned where I'd stashed you, and she decided to try expediting matters by putting you under control, then using you to clinch the deal—as if you'd come over to our side. Anyhow, when that plan fell through and I had to go and get her away from you, we split up again. I thought she was headed for Kashfa, but she went to the Keep instead. Like I said, I think it was to try a massive working against Ghostwheel. I believe something that she did there inadvertently freed Sharu, and he took the place over again and captured her. Anyhow, I got this frantic sending from her, so—"

"Uh, this old wizard," I said, "had been locked up there for—how long?"

Luke began to shrug, thought better of it. "Hell, I don't know. Who cares? He's been a cloak rack since I was a boy."

"A cloak rack?"

"Yeah. He lost a sorcerous duel. I don't really know whether she beat him or whether it was Dad. Whoever it was, though, caught him in midinvocation, arms outspread and all. Froze him like that, stiff as a board. He got moved to a place near an entranceway later. People would hang cloaks and hats on him. The servants would dust him occasionally. I even carved my name on his leg when I was little, like on a tree. I'd always thought of him as furniture. But I learned later that he'd been considered pretty good in his day."

"Did this guy ever wear a blue mask when he worked?"

"You've got me. I don't know anything about his style. Say, let's not get academic or she'll be here before I finish. In fact, maybe we ought to go now, and I can tell you the rest later."

"Uh-uh," I said. "You are, as you noted last night, my prisoner. I'd be nuts to let you go anywhere without knowing a hell of a lot more than I do. You're a threat to Amber. That bomb you tossed at the funeral was pretty damn real. You think I want to give you another shot at us?"

He smiled, then lost it. "Why'd you have to be born Corwin's son, anyway?" he said. Then, "Can I give you my parole on this?" he asked.

"I don't know. I'm going to be in a lot of trouble if they find out I had you and didn't bring you in. What terms are you talking? Will you swear off your war against Amber?"

He gnawed his lower lip. "There's no way I can do that, Merle."

"There are things you're not telling me, aren't there?"

He nodded. Then he grinned suddenly. "But I'll make you a deal you can't refuse."

"Luke, don't give me that hard-sell crap."

"Just give me a minute, okay? And you'll see why you can't afford to pass this one up."

"Luke, I'm not biting."

"Only one minute. Sixty seconds. You're free to say no when I'm done."

"All right," I said. "Tell me."

"Okay. I've got a piece of information vital to the security of Amber, and I'm certain nobody there has an inkling of it. I'll give it to you, after you've helped me."

"Why should you want to give us something like that? It sounds kind of self-defeating."

"I don't, and it is. But it's all I've got to offer. Help me get out of here to a place I have in mind where the time flow is so much faster that I'll be healed up in a day or so in terms of local time at the Keep."

"Or here, for that matter, I'd guess."

"True. Then—uh-oh!"

He sprawled on the bed, clutched at his chest with his good hand and began to moan.

"Luke!"

He raised his head, winked at me, glanced at the door and commenced moaning again.

Shortly, there came a knocking.

"Come in," I said.

Vinta entered and studied us both. For a moment, there seemed to be a look of genuine concern on her face as she regarded Luke. Then she advanced to the bed and placed her hands upon his shoulders. She stood there for about half a minute, then announced, "You're going to live."

"At the moment," Luke replied, "I don't know whether that's a blessing or a curse." Then he slipped his good arm around her, drew her to him suddenly and kissed her. "Hi, Gail," he said. "It's been a long time."

She drew away with less haste than she might have. "You seem improved already," she observed, "and I can see that Merle's worked something to help you along." She smiled faintly for an instant, then said, "Yes, it has been, you dumb jock. You still like your eggs sunny-side up?"

"Right," he acknowledged. "But not half a dozen. Maybe just two today. I'm out of sorts."

"All right," she said. "Come on, Merle. I'll need you to supervise."

Luke gave me a funny look, doubtless certain she wanted to talk with me about him. And for that matter, I wasn't certain I wanted to leave him alone even though I had all of his Trumps in my pocket. I was still uncertain as to the extent of his abilities, and I knew a lot less concerning his intentions. So I hung back.

"Maybe someone should stay with the invalid," I told her.

"He'll be all right," she said, "and I might need your help if I can't scare up a servant."

On the other hand, maybe she had something interesting to tell me. . . .

I found my shirt and drew it on. I ran a hand through my hair.

"Okay," I said. "See you in a bit, Luke."

"Hey," he responded, "see if you can turn up a walking stick for me, or cut me a staff or something."

"Isn't that rushing things a bit?" Vinta asked.

"Never can tell," Luke replied.

So I fetched my blade and took it along. As I followed Vinta out and down the stairs, it occurred to me that when any two of us got together we would probably have something to say about the third.

As soon as we were out of earshot, Vinta remarked, "He took a chance, coming to you."

"Yes, he did."

"So things must be going badly for him, if he felt you were the only one he could turn to."

"I'd say that's true."

"Also, I'm sure he wants something besides a place to recover."

"Probably so."

" 'Probably,' hell! He must have asked by now."

"Perhaps."

"Either he did or he didn't."

"Vinta, obviously you've told me everything you intend to tell me," I said. "Well, vice versa. We're even. I don't owe you explanations. If I feel like trusting Luke, I will. Anyhow, I haven't decided yet."

"So he *has* made you a pitch. I might be able to help you decide if you'll let me know what it is."

"No, thanks. You're as bad as he is."

"It's your welfare I'm concerned with. Don't be so quick to spurn an ally."

"I'm not," I said. "But if you stop to think about it, I know a lot more about Luke than I do about you. I think I know the things on which I shouldn't trust him as well as I do the safe ones."

"I hope you're not betting your life on it."

I smiled. "That's a matter on which I tend to be conservative."

We entered the kitchen, where she spoke with a woman I hadn't met yet who seemed in charge there. She left our breakfast orders with her and led me out the side door and onto the patio. From there, she indicated a stand of trees off to the east.

"You ought to be able to find a good sapling in there," she said, "for Luke's staff."

"Probably so," I replied, and we began walking in that direction. "So you really were Gail Lampron," I said suddenly.

"Yes."

"I don't understand this body-changing bit at all."

"And I'm not about to tell you."

"Care to tell me why not?"

"Nope."

"Can't or won't?"

"Can't," she said.

"But if I already know something, would you be willing to add a bit?"

"Maybe. Try me."

"When you were Dan Martinez you took a shot at one of us. Which one was it?"

"Luke," she replied.

"Why?"

"I'd become convinced that he was not the one—that is, that he represented a threat to you—"

"—and you just wanted to protect me," I finished.

"Exactly."

"What did you mean 'that he was not the one'?"

"Slip of the tongue. That looks like a good tree over there."

I chuckled. "Too thick. Okay, be that way."

I headed on into the grove. There were a number of possibilities off to the right.

As I moved through the morning-lanced interstices, damp leaves and dew adhering to my boots, I became aware of some unusual scuffing along the way, a series of marks leading off farther to the right, where—

"What's that?" I said, kind of rhetorically, since I didn't think Vinta would know either, as I headed toward a dark mass at the shady foot of an old tree.

I reached it ahead of her. It was one of the Bayle dogs, a big brown fellow. Its throat had been torn open. The blood was dark and congealed. A few insects were crawling on it. Off farther to the right I saw the remains of a smaller dog. It had been disemboweled. I studied the area about the remains. The marks of very large paws were imprinted in the damp earth. At least they were not the three-toed prints of the deadly doglike creatures I had encountered in the past. They seemed simply to be those of a very large dog.

"This must be what I heard last night," I remarked. "I thought it sounded like a dogfight."

"When was that?" she asked.

"Some time after you left. I was drowsing."

Then she did a strange thing. She knelt, leaned and sniffed the track. When she recovered there was a slightly puzzled expression on her face.

"What did you find?" I asked.

She shook her head, then stared off to the northeast. "I'm not sure," she finally said, "but it went that way."

I studied the ground further, rising and finally moving along the trail it had left. It did run off in that direction, though I lost it after several hundred feet when it departed the grove. Finally, I turned away.

"One of the dogs attacked the others, I guess," I observed. "We'd better find that stick and head back if we want our breakfasts warm."

Inside, I learned that Luke's breakfast had been sent up to him. I was torn. I wanted to take mine upstairs, to join him and continue our conversation. If I did, though, Vinta would accompany me and the conversation would not be continued. Nor could I talk further with her under those circumstances. So I would have to join her down here, which meant leaving Luke alone for longer than I liked.

So I went along with her when she said, "We will eat in here," and led me into a large hall. I guessed she had chosen it because my room with its open window was above the patio, and Luke could have heard us talking if we ate out there.

We sat at the end of a long darkwood table, where we were served. When we were alone again, she asked, "What are you going to do now?"

"What do you mean?" I asked, sipping some grape juice.

She glanced upward. "With him," she said. "Take him back to Amber?"

"It would seem the logical thing to do," I replied.

"Good," she said. "You should probably transport him soon. They have decent medical facilities at the palace."

I nodded. "Yes, they do."

We ate a few mouthfuls, then she asked, "That *is* what you intend doing, isn't it?"

"Why do you ask?"

"Because anything else would be absolutely foolish, and obviously he is not going to want to do it. Therefore, he will try to talk you into something else, something that will give him some measure of freedom while he recovers. You know what a line of shit he has. He'll make it sound like a great idea, whatever it is. You must remember that he is an enemy of Amber, and when he is ready to move again you will be in the way."

"It makes sense," I said.

"I'm not finished."

"Oh?"

She smiled and ate a few more bites, to keep me wondering. Finally, "He came to you for a reason," she continued. "He could have crawled off to any of a number of places to lick his wounds. But he came to you because he wants something. He's gambling, but it's a calculated thing. Don't go for it, Merle. You don't owe him anything."

"I don't know why you think me incapable of taking care of myself," I replied.

"I never said that," she responded. "But some decisions are finely balanced things. A little extra weight this way or that sometimes makes the difference. You know Luke, but so do I. This is not a time to be giving him any breaks."

"You have a point there," I said.

"So you *have* decided to give him what he wants!"

I smiled and drank some coffee. "Hell, he hasn't been conscious long enough to give me the pitch," I said. "I've thought of these things, and I want to know what he's got in mind too."

"I never said you shouldn't find out as much as you can. I just wanted to remind you that talking with Luke can sometimes be like conversing with a dragon."

"Yeah," I acknowledged. "I know."

"And the longer you wait the harder it's going to be," she added.

I took a gulp of coffee; then, "Did you like him?" I asked.

"Like?" she said. "Yes, I did. And I still do. That is not material at this point, though."

"I don't know about that," I said.

"What do you mean?"

"You wouldn't harm him without good reason."

"No, I wouldn't."

"He is no threat to me at the moment."

"He does not seem to be."

"Supposing I were to leave him here in your care while I went off to Amber to walk the Pattern and to prepare them for the news?"

She shook her head vigorously. "No," she stated. "I will not— I cannot—take that responsibility at this time."

"Why not?"

She hesitated.

"And please don't say again that you cannot tell me," I went on. "Find a way to tell me as much as you can."

She spoke slowly then, as if choosing her words very carefully. "Because it is more important for me to watch you than Luke. There is still danger for you which I do not understand, even though it no longer seems to be proceeding from him. Guarding you against this unknown peril is of higher priority than keeping an eye on him. Therefore, I cannot remain here. If you are returning to Amber, so am I."

"I appreciate your concern," I said, "but I will not have you dogging my footsteps."

"Neither of us has a choice."

"Supposing I simply trump out of here to some distant shadow?"

"I will be obliged to follow you."

"In this form, or another?"

She looked away. She poked at her food.

"You've already admitted that you can be other persons. You locate me in some arcane fashion, then you take possession of someone in my vicinity."

She took a drink of coffee.

"Perhaps something prevents you from saying it," I continued, "but that's the case. I know it."

She nodded once, curtly, and resumed eating.

"Supposing I did trump out right now," I said, "and you followed after in your peculiar fashion." I thought back to my telephone conversations with Meg Devlin and Mrs. Hansen. "Then the real Vinta Bayle would wake up in her own body with a gap in her memory, right?"

"Yes," she answered softly.

"And that would leave Luke here in the company of a woman who would be happy to destroy him if she had any inkling who he really is."

She smiled faintly. "Just so," she said.

We ate in silence for a time. She had attempted to foreclose all my choices, to force me to trump back to Amber and take Luke with me. I do not like being manipulated or coerced. My reflexive attempt to do something other than what is desired of me then feels forced also.

I refilled our coffee cups when I had finished eating. I regarded a collection of dog portraits that hung on the wall across from me. I sipped and savored. I did not speak because I could think of nothing further to say.

Finally, she did. "So what are you going to do?" she asked me.

I finished my coffee and rose. "I am going to take Luke his stick," I said.

I pushed my chair back into place and headed for the corner of the room where I had leaned the stick.

"And then?" she said. "What will you do?"

I glanced back at her as I hefted the staff. She sat very erect, her hands palms down on the table. The Nemesis look overlay her features once again, and I could almost feel electricity in the air.

"Whatever I must," I replied, and I headed for the door.

I increased my pace as soon as I was out of sight. When I hit the stairs and saw that she was not following, I took the steps two at a time. On the way up, I withdrew my cards and located the proper one.

When I entered the room I saw that Luke was resting, his back against the bed's pillows. His breakfast tray was on the smaller chair, beside the bed. I dropped the latch on the door.

"What's the matter, man? We under attack or something?" Luke asked.

"Start getting up," I said.

I picked up his weapon then and crossed to the bed. I gave him a hand sitting up, thrust the staff and the blade at him.

"My hand has been forced," I said, "and I'm not about to turn you over to Random."

"That's a comfort," he observed.

"But we have to clear out—now."

"That's all right by me."

He leaned on the staff, got slowly to his feet. I heard a noise in the hall, but it was already too late. I'd raised the card and was concentrating.

There came a pounding on the door.

"You're up to something and I think it's the wrong thing," Vinta called out.

I did not reply. The vision was already coming clear.

The doorframe splintered from the force of a tremendous kick, and the latch was torn loose. There was a look of apprehension on Luke's face as I reached out and took hold of his arm.

"Come on," I said.

Vinta burst into the room as I led Luke forward, her eyes flashing, her hands extended, reaching. Her cry of "Fool!" seemed to change into a wail as she was washed by the spectrum, rippled and faded.

We stood in a patch of grass, and Luke let out a deep breath he had been holding.

"You believe in cutting things close, buddy-boy," he remarked, and then he looked around and recognized the place.

He smiled crookedly.

"What do you know," he said. "A crystal cave."

"From my own experience," I said, "the time flow here should be about what you were asking for."

He nodded and we began moving slowly toward the high blue hill.

"Still plenty of rations," I added, "and the sleeping bag should be where I left it."

"It will serve," he acknowledged.

He halted, panting, before we reached the foot. I saw his gaze drift toward a number of strewn bones off to our left. It would have been months since the pair who had removed the boulder had fallen there, long enough for scavengers to have done a thorough job. Luke shrugged, advanced a little, leaned against blue stone. He lowered himself slowly into a sitting position.

"Going to have to wait before I can climb," he said, "even with you helping."

"Sure," I said. "We can finish our conversation. As I recall, you were going to make me an offer I couldn't refuse. I was to bring you to a place like this, where you could recover fast *vis-à-vis* the time flow at the Keep. You, in turn, had a piece of information vital to the security of Amber."

"Right," he agreed, "and you didn't hear the rest of my story either. They go together."

I hunkered across from him. "You told me that your mother had fled to the Keep, apparently gotten into trouble there and called to you for help."

"Yes," he acknowledged. "So I dropped the business with Ghostwheel and tried to help her. I got in touch with Dalt, and he agreed to come and attack the Keep."

"It's always good to know a band of mercenaries you can get hold of in a hurry," I said.

He gave me a quick, strange look but I was able to maintain an innocent expression.

"So we led them through Shadow and we attacked the place," he said then. "It had to be us that you saw when you were there."

I nodded slowly. "It looked as if you made it over the wall. What went wrong?"

"I still don't know," he said. "We were doing all right. Their defense was crumbling and we were pushing right along, when suddenly Dalt turned on me. We'd been separated for a time; then he appeared again and attacked me. At first I thought he'd made a mistake—we were all grimy and bloody—and I shouted to him that it was me. But he just kept coming. That's how he was able to do a job like this on me. For a while I didn't want to strike back because I thought it was a misunderstanding and he'd realize his mistake in a few seconds."

"Do you think he sold you out? Or that it was something he'd been planning for a long time? Some grudge?"

"I don't like to think that."

"Magic, then?"

"Maybe. I don't know."

A peculiar thought occurred to me. "Did he know you'd killed Caine?" I asked.

"No, I make it a point never to tell anybody everything I'm about."

"You wouldn't kid me, would you?"

He laughed, moved as if to clap me on the shoulder, winced and thought better of it.

"Why do you ask?" he said then.

"I don't know. Just curious."

"Sure," he said. Then, "What say you give me a hand up and inside, so I can see what kind of supplies you've left me?"

"Okay."

I got to my feet and helped him to his. We moved around to

the right to the slope of easiest ascent, and I guided him slowly to the top.

Once we'd achieved the summit he leaned on his staff and stared down into the opening.

"No really easy way down in," he said, "for me. At first I was thinking you could roll up a barrel from the larder, and I could get down to it and then down to the floor. But now I look at it, it's an even bigger drop than I remembered. I'd tear something open, sure."

"Mm-hm," I said. "Hang on. I've got an idea."

I turned away from him and climbed back down. Then I made my way along the base of the blue rise to my right until I had rounded two shiny shoulders and was completely out of Luke's line of sight.

I did not care to use the Logrus in his presence if I did not have to. I did not wish for him to see how I went about things, and I did not want to give him any idea as to what I could or could not do. I'm not that comfortable letting people know too much about me, either.

The Logrus appeared at my summons, and I reached into it, extended through it. My desire was framed, became the aim. My sending extending sought the thought. Far, far. . . .

I kept extending for the damnedest long time. We really had to be out in the Shadow boonies. . . .

Contact.

I did not jerk, but rather exerted a slow and steady pressure. I felt it move toward me across the shadows.

"Hey, Merle! Everything okay?" I heard Luke call.

"Yeah," I answered, and I did not elaborate.

Closer, closer. . . .

There!

I staggered when it arrived, because it came to me too near to one end. The far end bounced on the ground. So I moved to the middle and took a new grip. I hefted it and carried it back.

I set it against a steep area of the rise a bit in advance of Luke's position and I mounted quickly. I began drawing it up behind me then.

"Okay, where'd you get the ladder?" he asked.

"Found it," I said.

"Looks like wet paint on the side there."

"Maybe someone lost it just recently."

I began lowering it into the opening. Several feet protruded after it reached the bottom. I adjusted it for stability.

"I'll start down first," I said, "and stay right under you."

"Take my stick and my blade down first, will you?"

"Sure."

I did that thing. By the time I climbed back he had caught hold and gotten onto it, had begun his descent.

"You'll have to teach me that trick one of these days," he said, breathing heavily.

"Don't know what you're talking about," I answered.

He descended slowly, pausing to rest at each rung, and he was flushed and panting when he reached the bottom. He slumped to the floor immediately, pressing his right palm against his lower rib cage. After a time, he inched backward a bit and rested against the wall.

"You okay?" I asked.

He nodded. "Will be," he said, "in a few minutes. Being stabbed takes a lot out of you."

"Want a blanket?"

"No, thanks."

"Well, you rest here and I'll go check the larder and see whether anything's gotten at the supplies. Want me to bring you anything?"

"Some water," he said.

The supplies proved to be in good order, and the sleeping bag was still where I'd left it. I returned with a drink for Luke and a few ironic memories of the occasion when he'd done the same for me.

"Looks as if you're in business," I told him. "There's still plenty of stuff."

"You didn't drink all the wine, did you?" he asked between sips.

"No."

"Good."

"Now, you said you have a piece of information vital to the interests of Amber," I said. "Care to tell me about it?"

He smiled. "Not yet," he said.

"I thought that was our deal."

"You didn't hear the whole thing. We were interrupted."

I shook my head. But, "All right, we were interrupted," I acknowledged. "Tell me the rest."

"I've got to get back on my feet, so I can take the Keep and free my mother. . . ."

I nodded.

"The information is yours after we rescue her."

"Hey! Wait a minute! You're asking a hell of a lot!"

"Not for what I'm paying."

"Sounds like I'm buying a pig in a poke."

"Yes, I guess you are. But believe me, it'll be worth knowing."

"What if it becomes worth knowing while I'm waiting?"

"No, I've figured the timing on this. My recovery is only going to take a couple of days, Amber time. I can't see the matter coming up that fast."

"Luke, this is starting to sound like some sort of trick."

"It is," he said, "but it will benefit Amber as well as myself."

"That's another thing. I can't see you giving something like this away to the enemy."

He sighed. "It might even be enough to get me off the hook," he added.

"You're thinking of calling off your feud?"

"I don't know. But I've been doing a lot of thinking, and if I did decide to go that route it would make for a real good opener."

"And if you decided not to, you'd be screwing yourself. Wouldn't you?"

"I could live with it, though. It might make my job harder, but not impossible."

"I don't know," I said. "If word of this gets out and I've got nothing to show for letting you get away like this, I'll be in real hot water."

"I won't tell anybody if you won't."

"There's Vinta."

"And she keeps insisting that her big aim in life is to protect you. Besides, she won't be there if you go back. Or rather, there will be the real Vinta, having awakened as from a troubled sleep."

"How can you be so sure?"

"Because you've left. She's probably already off seeking you."

"Do you know what she really is?"

"No, but I'll help you speculate sometime."

"Not now?"

"No, I've got to sleep some more. It's catching up with me again."

"Then let's go over this deal one more time. What are you going to do, how do you intend to do it and what are you promising me?"

He yawned. "I stay here till I'm back in shape," he said. "Then when I'm ready to attack the Keep I get in touch with you. Which reminds me, you still have my Trumps."

"I know. Keep talking. How do you intend taking the Keep?"

"I'm working on it. I'll let you know that too. Anyhow, you can help us or not at that point, as you see fit. I wouldn't mind having another sorcerer with me, though. Once we're in and she's freed, I'll tell you what I promised and you can take it back to Amber."

"What if you lose?" I asked.

He looked away. "I guess there's always that possibility," he finally agreed. "Okay, how's this? I'll write the whole thing out and keep it with me. I'll give it to you—by Trump or in person—before we attack. Win or lose, I'll have paid my way with you."

He extended his good hand and I clasped it.

"Okay," I said.

"Then let me have my Trumps back, and I'll be talking to you as soon as I get moving again."

I hesitated. Finally, I drew out my pack, which was now grown quite thick. I shuffled out my own then—along with a number of his—and passed him what remained.

"What about the rest?"

"I want to study them, Luke. Okay?"

He shrugged weakly. "I can always make more. But give me back my mother's."

"Here."

He accepted it, then said, "I don't know what you've got in mind, but I'll give you a piece of advice: Don't screw around with Dalt. He's not the nicest of guys when he's normal, and I think there's something wrong with him right now. Keep away from him."

I nodded, then got to my feet.

"You're going now?" he asked.

"Right."

"Leave me the ladder."

"It's all yours."

"What are you going to tell them back in Amber?"

"Nothing—yet," I said. "Hey, you want me to bring some food up here before I go? Save you a trip."

"Yeah. Good idea. Bring me a bottle of wine, too."

I went back and got him a load of provisions. I dragged in the sleeping bag also.

I started up the ladder, then paused. "You don't know your own mind on this yet," I said, "do you?"

He smiled. "Don't be too sure of that."

When I got to the top I stared at the big boulder that had once sealed me in. Earlier, I'd thought of returning the favor. I could keep track of the time, come get him when he was back on his feet. That way, he couldn't pull a disappearing act on me. I had decided against it, though, not only because I was the only one who knew he was here and if something happened to me he'd be dead. Mainly, it was because he wouldn't be able to reach me with my Trump when he was ready to move, if I kept him fully confined. That's what I told myself, anyhow.

I stooped and caught hold of the boulder, anyway, and pushed it nearer the opening.

"Merle! What are you doing?"—from below.

"Looking for fishing bait," I answered.

"Hey, come on! Don't. . . ."

I laughed and pushed it a little nearer.

"Merle!"

"Thought you might want the door closed, in case it rains," I said. "But it's too damned heavy. Forget it. Take it easy."

I turned and jumped. I thought the extra adrenaline might do him some good.

8

When I hit the ground I kept going, back to the place from which I had conjured the ladder, out of sight from several directions.

I withdrew one of the blank cards. Time was running. When I fished out the pencil, I discovered that its point had broken. I unsheathed my blade, which was about the length of my arm. I'd found another use for the thing.

A minute or so later I had the card before me on a flat rock, and I was sketching my room back at the Arbor House, the forces of the Logrus moving through my hands. I had to work deliberately, getting the proper feeling of the place into the drawing. Finally, when it was finished, I stood. It was right, it was ready. I opened my mind and regarded my work until it became reality. Then I walked forward into the room. Just as I did I thought of something I wanted to ask Luke, but it was too late.

Beyond the window, the shadows of the trees were stretching into the east. I had obviously been gone for most of the day.

When I turned I saw a sheet of paper upon the now made-up bed, secured against breezes by the edge of a pillow. I crossed to it and picked it up, removing the small blue button which lay atop it before I did so.

The writing was in English. It said: PUT THE BUTTON IN A SAFE PLACE TILL YOU NEED IT. I WOULDN'T CARRY IT AROUND TOO MUCH. I HOPE YOU DID THE RIGHT THING. I GUESS I'LL FIND OUT PRETTY SOON. SEE YOU AROUND.

It was unsigned.

Safe or not, I couldn't just leave it there. So I wrapped the button in the note and put it in my pocket. Then I fetched my cloak from the closet and slung it over my arm.

I departed the room. The latch being broken, I left the door standing wide. I stopped in the hallway and listened, but I heard no voices, no sounds of movement.

I made my way to the stairs and headed down. I was almost to the bottom before I noticed her, so still did she sit, there beside the window to my right, a tray of bread and cheese, a bottle and a goblet on a small table at her side.

"Merlin!" she said suddenly, half rising. "The servants said you were here, but when I looked I couldn't find you."

"I was called away," I said, descending the final stair and advancing. "How are you feeling?"

"How do you—what do you know about me?" she asked.

"You probably don't remember anything that happened during the past couple of days," I replied.

"You are right," she said. "Won't you sit down?"

She gestured at the empty chair at the other side of the small table.

"Please join me." She indicated the tray. "And let me get you some wine."

"That's all right," I said, seeing that she was drinking the white.

She rose and crossed the room to a cabinet, opened it and took out another goblet. When she returned she poured a healthy slug of Bayle's Piss into it and set it near my hand. I guessed it was possible they kept the good stuff for themselves.

"What can you tell me about my blackout?" she asked. "I'd been in Amber, and the next thing I knew I was back here and several days had gone by."

"Yes," I said, taking up a cracker and a bit of cheese. "About what time did you become yourself again?"

"This morning."

"It's nothing to worry about—now," I answered. "There shouldn't be a recurrence."

"But what was it?"

"Just something that's been going around," I said, trying the wine.

"It seems more like magic than the flu."

"Perhaps there was a touch of that too," I agreed. "You never know what might blow in out of Shadow. But almost everyone I know who's had it is okay now."

She furrowed her brow. "It was very strange."

I had a few more crackers and sips of the wine. They did keep the good stuff for themselves.

"There is absolutely nothing to worry about," I repeated.

She smiled and nodded. "I believe you. What are you doing here, anyhow?"

"Stopover. I'm on my way back to Amber," I said, "from elsewhere. Which reminds me—may I borrow a horse?"

"Certainly," she replied. "How soon will you be leaving?"

"As soon as I get the horse," I said.

She got to her feet. "I didn't realize you were in a hurry. I'll take you over to the stables now."

"Thanks."

I grabbed two more crackers and another piece of cheese on the way out and tossed off the rest of the wine. I wondered where the blue fog might be drifting now.

When I'd located a good horse, which she told me I could have delivered to their stable in Amber, I saddled him and fitted his bridle. He was a gray, named Smoke. I donned my cloak then and clasped Vinta's hands.

"Thanks for the hospitality," I said, "even if you don't recall it."

"Don't say good-bye yet," she told me. "Ride around to the kitchen door off the patio, and I'll give you a water bottle and some food for the road. We didn't have a mad affair that I don't remember, did we?"

"A gentleman never tells," I said.

She laughed and slapped my shoulder. "Come see me sometime when I'm in Amber," she told me, "and refresh my memory."

I grabbed a set of saddlebags, a bag of chow for Smoke and a longish tethering rope. I led him outside as Vinta headed back to the house. I mounted then and rode slowly after her, a few dogs capering about me. I circled the manor, taking the long way around, drew rein and dismounted near the kitchen. I considered the patio, wishing I had one just like it where I could sit and take coffee in the morning. Or had it just been the company?

After a time, the door opened and Vinta came out and passed me a bundle and a flask. As I was securing them, she said, "Let my father know that I'll be back in a few days, will you? Tell him that I came to the country because I wasn't feeling well, but that I'm all right now."

"Glad to," I said.

"I don't really know why you were here," she said. "But if it involves politics or intrigue I don't want to know."

"Okay," I said.

"If a servant took a meal to a big red-haired man who seemed to be pretty badly injured, this would be better forgotten?"

"I'd say."

"It will be, then. But one of these days I'd like the story."

"Me too," I said. "We'll see what we can do."

"So, have a good journey."

"Thanks. I'll try."

I clasped her hand, turned away and mounted.

"So long."

"See you in Amber," she said.

I mounted and continued my circuit of the house until I was back near the stables again. I headed past them then to a trail we had ridden that led off in the direction I wanted. Back toward the house, a dog began to howl and another joined it moments later. There was a breeze out of the south, and it carried a few leaves past me. I wanted to be on the road, far away and alone. I value my solitude because that is when I seem to do my best thinking, and right now I had many things to think over.

I rode to the northwest. About ten minutes later I came to a dirt road we had crossed the other day. This time I followed it westward, and it finally took me to the crossroads with the marker indicating that Amber lay straight ahead. I rode on.

It was a yellow dirt road that I traveled, showing the impress of many wagon wheels. It followed the contours of the land, passing between fallow fields bordered by low stone fences, a few trees at either hand. I could see the stark outlines of mountains far ahead, standing above the forested area I was soon to encounter. We moved along at an easy gait, and I let my mind drift over the events of the past few days.

That I had an enemy I did not doubt. Luke had assured me that it was no longer him, and I had found him to be more than a little persuasive. He need not have come to me to be patched up, as both he and Vinta had pointed out. And he could have found his own way to the crystal cave or some other sanctuary. And the business about my helping him to rescue Jasra could have waited. I was more than half convinced that he was trying to get back on better terms with me again quickly because I was his only contact with the Court of Amber, and his fortunes had taken a turn for the worse. I had a feeling that what he really wanted was an official determination as to his status with Amber, and that he had mentioned the piece of important information he would be willing to surrender both as a sign of good faith and as a bargaining chip. I was not at all certain that I, personally, would be very crucial to any plan he might have for rescuing Jasra. Not when he knew the Keep inside and out, was some kind of sorcerer himself and had a band of mercs he could transport from the shadow Earth. For all I knew, that fancy ammo of his would work there as well as in Amber. And whether that was true or not, why couldn't he just trump his attack force into the place? He wouldn't even really have to win a battle—just get in, grab Jasra and get out. No, I did not feel that I was really necessary to whatever operation he finally decided upon. I'd a feeling he'd waved a red herring at me, hoping that when the air cleared we would simply consider what he had and what he wanted and make him an offer.

I'd a feeling, too, that he might be willing to call it quits on the vendetta now that Caine was out of the way and family honor satisfied. And I'd a notion that Jasra was the stumbling block on his side. While I'd no idea what hold she might have over him, it had occurred to me that the piece of information to which he'd referred might represent some means of neutralizing her. If he got it to us quietly and it seemed to come from our side, he could save face with her as well as buying peace with us. Tantalizing. My problem now was to find the best way to present this at court without looking like a traitor for having let him go. Which meant I had to show that the profit would be worth the investment.

There were more trees at the roadside now, and the forest itself was nearer. I crossed a wooden bridge above a clear stream, and the gentle splashing sounds followed me for a time. There were brown fields and distant barns to my left, a wagon with a broken axle off to my right. . . .

And if I had read Luke wrong? Was there some way I might be able to pressure him and make my interpretation come out right anyway? A small idea began to form. I was not overjoyed with it, but I considered it nevertheless. Risk and speed were what it involved. It had its merits, though. I pushed it as far as I could, then put it aside and returned to my original train of thought.

Somewhere, there was an enemy. And if it wasn't Luke, who was it? Jasra seemed the most obvious candidate. She had made her feelings toward me pretty clear on the occasions of our two meetings. She could well be the one who had dispatched the assassins I had encountered in Death Alley. In that case, I was probably safe for a time—with her a prisoner back at the Keep—unless, of course, she had sent along a few more before she had been captured. That would have been redundant, though. Why waste all that manpower on me? I had only been a minor figure in the event she sought to avenge, and the men who came after me had been almost sufficient for the task.

And if it wasn't Jasra? Then I was still in jeopardy. The wizard in the blue mask, whom I assumed to be Sharu Garrul, had caused me to be pursued by a tornado, which seemed a far less friendly overture than the flowers that had followed. This latter, of course, identified him with the individual behind my peculiar experience at Flora's apartment back in San Francisco. In that instance, he had initiated the encounter, which meant that he had some designs on me. What was it he'd said? Something about the possibility of us being at cross-purposes at some future time. How interesting, in retrospect. For I could now see the possibility of such a situation's occurring.

But was it really Sharu Garrul who had sent the assassins? Despite his familiarity with the power of the blue stone that had guided them—as evidenced by the blue button in my pocket—it didn't seem to follow. For one thing, our purposes were not yet crossed. For another, it did not seem the proper style for a cryptic, flower-throwing master of elements. I could be dead wrong there, of course, but I expected something more in the nature of a sorcerous duel with that one.

The fields gave way to wilderness as I approached the verge of the forest. Something of twilight had already entered its bright-leafed domain. It did not seem a dense, ancient wood like Arden, however; from the distance I had seen numerous gaps within its higher reaches. The road continued wide and well-kept. I drew my cloak more fully about me as I entered the shadowed coolness. It seemed an easy ride, if it were all to be like this. And I was in no hurry. I had too many thoughts that wanted thinking. . . .

If only I had been able to learn more from that strange, nameless entity who had, for a time, controlled Vinta. What her true nature might be, I still had no idea. "Her," yes. I somehow felt the entity to be more feminine than masculine in nature, despite its having controlled George Hansen and Dan Martinez. Perhaps this was only because I had made love to her as Meg Devlin. Difficult to say. But I had known Gail for some time, and the Lady in the Lake had seemed a real lady. . . .

Enough. I'd decided on my pronoun. Other matters of greater importance were involved. Like, whatever she was, why was she following me about insisting that she wanted to protect me? While I appreciated the sentiment, I still had no insight into her motivation.

But there was something far more important to me than her motivation. Why she saw fit to guard me could remain her own business. The big question was: Against *what* did she feel I needed protection? She must have had a definite threat in mind, and she had not given me the slightest hint as to what it was.

Was this, then, the enemy? The real enemy? Vinta's adversary? I tried reviewing everything I knew or had guessed about her.

There is a strange creature who sometimes takes the form of a small blue mist. She is capable of finding her way to me through Shadow. She possesses the power to take control of a human body, completely suppressing its natural ego. She hung around in my vicinity for a number of years without my becoming aware of her. Her earliest incarnation that I know of was as Luke's former girl-friend, Gail.

Why Gail? If she were guarding me, why go around with Luke? Why not become one of the women I'd dated? Why not be Julia? But no. She had decided upon Gail. Was that because Luke was the threat, and she'd wanted to keep a close watch on him? But she'd actually let Luke get away with a few attempts on my life. And then Jasra. She'd admitted that she'd known Jasra was behind the later ones. Why hadn't she simply removed them? She could have taken over Luke's body, stepped in front of a speeding car, drifted away from the remains, then gone and done the same with Jasra. She wasn't afraid to die in a host body. I'd seen her do it twice.

Unless she'd somehow known that all their attempts on my life would fail. Could she have sabotaged the letter bomb? Could she, in some way, have been behind my premonition on the morn-ing of the opened gas jets? And perhaps something else with each of the others? Still, it would seem a lot simpler to go to the source and remove the problem itself. I knew that she had no compunc-tion about killing. She'd ordered the slaying of my final assailant in Death Alley.

What, then?

Two possibilities came to mind immediately. One was that she'd actually come to like Luke—and that she'd simply found ways to neutralize him without destroying him. But then I thought of her as Martinez, and it fell apart. She'd actually been shooting that night in Santa Fe. Okay. Then there was the other possibility: Luke was not the real threat, and she'd liked him enough to let him go on living once he'd quit the April 30 games and she saw that we'd gotten friendly. Something happened in New Mexico that made her change her mind. As to what it was, I had no idea. She had followed me to New York, then, and been George Hansen and Meg Devlin in quick succession. Luke was, by that time, out of the picture, following his disappearing act on the mountain. He no longer represented a threat, yet she was almost frantic in her efforts to get in touch with me. Was something else impending? The real threat?

I racked my brains, but I could not figure what that threat might have been. Was I following a completely false trail with this line of reasoning?

She certainly was not omniscient. Her reason for spiriting me to Arbor House was as much to pump me for information as it was to remove me from the scene of the attack. And some of the things she'd wanted to know were as interesting as some of the things she knew.

My mind did a backward flip. What was the first question she had asked me?

Landing adroitly on my mental feet, back at Bill Roth's place, I heard the question several times. As George Hansen she had asked it casually and I had lied; as a voice on the telephone she had asked it and been denied; as Meg Devlin, in bed, she had finally gotten me to answer it honestly: What was your mother's name?

When I'd told her that my mother was named Dara she had finally begun speaking freely. She had warned me against Luke. It seemed that she might have been willing to tell me more then, too, save that the arrival of the real Meg's husband had cut short our conversation.

To what was this the key? It placed my origin in the Courts of Chaos, to which she had at no time referred. Yet it had to be important, somehow.

I had a feeling that I already had the answer but that I would be unable to realize it until I had formulated the proper question.

Enough. I could go no further. Knowing that she was aware of my connection with the Courts still told me nothing. She was also obviously aware of my connection with Amber, and I could not see how that figured in the pattern of events either.

So I would leave it at that point and come back to it later. I had plenty of other things to think about. At least, I now had lots of new questions to ask her the next time we met, and I was certain that we would meet again.

Then something else occurred to me. If she'd done any real protecting of me at all, it had taken place offstage. She had given me a lot of information, which I thought was probably correct but which I had had no opportunity to verify. From her phoning and lurking back in New York to her killing of my one possible source of information in Death Alley, she had really been more a bother than a help. It was conceivable that she could actually show up and encumber me with aid again, at exactly the wrong moment.

So instead of working on my opening argument for Random, I spent the next hour or so considering the nature of a being capable of moving into a person and taking over the controls. There seemed only a certain number of ways it might be done, and I narrowed the field quickly, considering what I knew of her nature, by means of the technical exercises my uncle had taught me. When I thought I had it worked out I backtracked and mused over the forces that would have to be involved.

From the forces I worked my way through the tonic vibrations of their aspects. The use of raw power, while flashy, is wasteful and very fatiguing for the operator, not to mention aesthetically barbaric. Better to be prepared.

I lined up the spoken signatures and edited them into a spell. Suhuy would probably have gotten it down even shorter, but there is a point of diminishing returns on these things, and I had mine figured to where it should work if my main guesses were correct. So I collated it and assembled it. It was fairly long—too long to rattle off in its entirety if I were in the hurry I probably would be. Studying it, I saw that three linchpins would probably hold it, though four would be better.

I summoned the Logrus and extended my tongue into its moving pattern. Then I spoke the spell, slowly and clearly, leaving out the four key words I had chosen to omit. The woods grew absolutely still about me as the words rang out. The spell hung before me like a crippled butterfly of sound and color, trapped within the synesthetic web of my personal vision of the Logrus, to come again when I summoned it, to be released when I uttered the four omitted words.

I banished the vision and felt my tongue relax. Now she was not the only one capable of troublesome surprises.

I halted for a drink of water. The sky had grown darker and the small noises of the forest returned. I wondered whether Fiona or Bleys had been in touch, and how Bill was doing back in town. I listened to the rattling of branches. Suddenly, I had the feeling I was being watched—not the cold scrutiny of a Trump touch, but simply the sensation that there was a pair of eyes fixed upon me. I shivered. All those thoughts about enemies. . . .

I loosened my blade and rode on. The night was young, and there were more miles ahead than behind.

Riding through the evening I kept alert, but I neither heard nor saw anything untoward. Had I been wrong about Jasra, Sharu or even Luke? And was there a party of assassins at my back right now? Periodically, I drew rein and sat listening for a short while. But I heard nothing unusual on these occasions, nothing that could be taken as sounds of pursuit. I became acutely aware of the blue button in my pocket. Was it acting as a beacon for some sinister sending of the wizard's? I was loath to get rid of the thing because I could foresee a number of possible uses for it. Besides, if it had already attuned me—which it probably had—I could see no benefit in disposing of it now. I would secrete it someplace safe before I made my attempt to lose its vibes. Until such a time, I could see no percentage in doing anything else with it.

The sky continued to darken, and a number of stars had put in hesitant appearances. Smoke and I slowed even more in our course, but the road remained good and its pale surface stayed sufficiently visible to present no hazard. I heard the call of an owl from off to the right and moments later saw its dark shape rush at middle height among the trees. It would have been a pleasant night to be riding if I were not creating my own ghosts and haunting myself with them. I love the smells of autumn and the forest, and I resolved to burn a few leaves in my campfire later on for that pungency unlike any other I know.

The air was clean and cool. Hoof sounds, our breathing and the wind seemed to be the only noises in the neighborhood until we flushed a deer a bit later and heard the diminishing crashes of its retreat for some time afterward. We crossed a small but sturdy wooden bridge a little later, but no trolls were taking tolls. The road took a turn upward, and we wound our way slowly but steadily to a higher elevation. Now there were numerous stars visible through the weave of the branches, but no clouds that I could see. The deciduous trees grew barer as we gained a bit of altitude, and more evergreens began to occur. I felt the breezes more strongly now.

I began pausing more frequently, to rest Smoke, to listen, to nibble at my supplies. I resolved to keep going at least until moonrise—which I tried to calculate from its occurrence the other night, following my departure from Amber. If I made it to that point before I camped, the rest of the ride into Amber tomorrow morning would be pretty easy.

Frakir pulsed once, lightly, upon my wrist. But hell, that had often happened in traffic when I'd cut someone off. A hungry fox could have just passed, regarded me and wished itself a bear. Still, I waited there longer than I had intended, prepared for an attack and trying not to appear so.

But nothing happened, the warning was not repeated and after a time I rode on. I returned to my idea for putting the screws to Luke—and, for that matter, Jasra. I couldn't call it a plan yet, because it was lacking in almost all particulars. The more I thought of it, the crazier it seemed. For one thing, it was extremely tempting, as it held the potential for resolving a lot of problems. I wondered then why I had never created a Trump for Bill Roth. I felt a sudden need to talk to a good attorney. I might well want someone to argue my case before this was done. Too dark now to do any drawing, though . . . and not really necessary yet. Actually, I just wanted to talk with him, bring him up to date, get the views of someone not directly involved.

Frakir issued no further warnings during the next hour. We commenced a slightly downward course then, soon passing into a somewhat more sheltered area where the smell of pines came heavy. I mused on—about wizards and flowers, Ghostwheel and his problems, and the name of the entity who had recently occupied Vinta. There were lots of other musings, too, some of which went a long way back. . . .

Many stops later, with a bit of moonlight trickling through the branches behind me, I decided to call it quits and look for a place to bed down. I gave Smoke a brief drink at the next stream. About a quarter hour afterward, I thought I glimpsed what might be a promising spot off to the right, so I left the road and headed that way.

It turned out not to be as good a place as I'd thought, and I continued farther into the wood until I came across a small clear area that seemed adequate. I dismounted, unsaddled Smoke and tethered him, rubbed him down with his blanket and gave him something to eat. Then I scraped clear a small area of ground with my blade, dug a pit at its center and built a fire there. I used a spell to ignite it because I was feeling lazy, and I threw on several clumps of leaves as I recalled my earlier reflections.

I seated myself on my cloak, my back against the bole of a middle-sized tree, and ate a cheese sandwich and sipped water while I worked up the ambition to pull my boots off. My blade lay upon the ground at my side. My muscles began to unkink. The smell of the fire was a nostalgic thing. I toasted my next sandwich over it.

I sat and thought of nothing for a long while. Gradually, in barely perceptible stages, I felt the gentle disengagements lassitude brings to the extremities. I had meant to gather firewood before I took my ease. But I didn't really need it. It wasn't all that cold. I'd wanted the fire mainly for company.

However. . . . I dragged myself to my feet and moved off into the woods. I did a long, slow reconnaissance about the area once I got moving. Though to be honest, my main reason for getting up had been to go and relieve myself. I halted in my circuit when I thought that I detected a small flicker of light far off to the northeast. Another campfire? Moonlight on water? A torch? There had been only a glimpse and I could not locate it again, though I moved my head about, retraced my most recent few paces and even struck off a small distance in that direction.

But I did not wish to chase after some will-o'-the-wisp and spend my night beating the bushes. I checked various lines of sight back to my camp. My small fire was barely visible even from this distance. I circled my camp, entered and sprawled again. The fire was already dying and I decided to let it burn out. I wrapped my cloak about me and listened to the soft sounds of the wind.

I fell asleep quickly. For how long I slept, I do not know. There were no dreams that I can recall.

I was awakened by Frakir's frantic pulsing. I opened my eyes the barest slits and tossed, as if in sleep, so that my right hand fell near the haft of my blade. I maintained my slow breathing pattern. I heard and felt that the wind had risen, and I saw that it had fanned the embers to the point where my fire flared once again. I saw no one before me, however. I strained my hearing after any sounds, but all I heard was the wind and the popping of the fire.

It seemed as foolish to spring to my feet into a guard position when I did not know from which direction the danger was approaching as it did to remain a target. On the other hand, I had intentionally cast my cloak so that I lay with a large, low-limbed pine at my back. It would have been very difficult for someone to have approached me from the rear, let alone to have done so quietly. So it did not seem I was in danger of an imminent attack from that direction.

I turned my head slightly and studied Smoke, who had begun to seem a little uneasy. Frakir continued her now distracting warning till I willed her to be still.

Smoke was twitching his ears and moving his head about, nostrils dilated. As I watched, I saw that his attention seemed directed toward my right. He began edging his way across the camp, his long tether snaking behind him.

I heard a sound then, beyond the noise of Smoke's retreat, as of something advancing from the right. It was not repeated for a time, and then I heard it again. It was not a footfall, but a sound as of a body brushing against a branch which suddenly issued a weak protest.

I visualized the disposition of trees and shrubs in that direction and decided to let the lurker draw nearer before I made my move. I dismissed the notion of summoning the Logrus and preparing a magical attack. It would take a bit more time than I thought I had remaining. Also, from Smoke's behavior and from what I had heard, it seemed that there was only a single individual approaching. I resolved, though, to lay in a decent supply of spells the first chance I got, both offensive and defensive, on the order of the one I had primed against my guardian entity. The trouble is that it can take several days of solitude to work a really decent array of them out properly, enact them and rehearse their releases to the point where you can spring them at a moment's notice—and then they have a tendency to start decaying after a week or so. Sometimes they last longer and sometimes less long, depending both on the amount of energy you're willing to invest in them and on the magical climate of the particular shadow in which you're functioning. It's a lot of bother unless you're sure you're going to need them within a certain period of time. On the other hand, a good sorcerer should have one attack, one defense and one escape spell hanging around at all times. But I'm generally somewhat lazy, not to mention pretty easygoing, and I didn't see any need for that sort of setup until recently. And recently, I hadn't had much time to be about it.

So any use I might make of the Logrus now, were I to summon

it and situate myself within its ambit, would pretty much amount to blasting away with raw power—which is very draining on the operator.

Let him come a little nearer, that's all, and it would be cold steel and a strangling cord that he would face.

I could feel the presence advancing now, hear the soft stirring of pine needles. A few more feet, enemy. . . . Come on. That's all I need. Come into range. . . .

He halted. I could hear a steady, soft breathing.

Then, "You must be aware of me by now, Magus," came a low whisper, "for we all have our little tricks, and I know the source of yours."

"Who are you?" I asked, as I clasped the haft of my blade and rolled into a crouch, facing the darkness, the point of my weapon describing a small circle.

"I am the enemy," was the reply. "The one you thought would never come."

9

Power.

I remembered the day I had stood atop a rocky prominence. Fiona—dressed in lavender, belted with silver—stood in a higher place before me and somewhat to my right. She held a silver mirror in her right hand, and she looked downward through the haze to the place where the great tree towered. There was a total stillness about us, and even our own small sounds came muffled. The upper portions of the tree disappeared into a low-hanging fog bank. The light that filtered through limned it starkly against another pile of fog which hung at its back, rising to join with the one overhead. A bright, seemingly self-illuminated line was etched into the ground near the base of the tree, curving off to vanish within the fog. Far to my left, a brief arc of a similar intensity was also visible, emerging from and returning to the billowing white wall.

"What is it, Fiona?" I asked. "Why did you bring me to this place?"

"You've heard of it," she replied. "I wanted you to see it."

I shook my head. "I've never heard of it. I've no idea what I'm looking at."

"Come," she said, and she began to descend.

She disdained my hand, moving quickly and gracefully, and we came down from the rocks and moved nearer to the tree. There was something vaguely familiar there, but I could not place it.

"From your father," she said at last. "He spent a long time telling you his story. Surely he did not omit this part."

I halted as understanding presented itself, tentatively at first.

"That tree," I said.

"Corwin planted his staff when he commenced the creation of the new Pattern," she said. "It was fresh. It took root."

I seemed to feel a faint vibration in the ground.

Fiona turned her back on the prospect, raised the mirror she carried and angled it so that she regarded the scene over her right shoulder.

"Yes," she said, after several moments. Then she extended the mirror to me. "Take a look," she told me, "as I just did."

I accepted it, held it, adjusted it and stared.

The view in the mirror was not the same as that which had presented itself to my unaided scrutiny. I was able to see beyond the tree now, through the fog, to discern most of the strange Pattern which twisted its bright way about the ground, working its passages inward to its off-center terminus, the only spot still concealed by an unmoving tower of white, within which tiny lights like stars seemed to burn.

"It doesn't look like the Pattern back in Amber," I said.

"No," she answered. "Is it anything like the Logrus?"

"Not really. The Logrus actually alters itself somewhat, constantly. Still, it's more angular, whereas this is mostly curves and bends."

I studied it a little longer, then returned her looking glass.

"Interesting spell on the mirror," I commented, for I had been studying this also, while I held it.

"And much more difficult than you'd think," she responded, "for there's more than fog in there. Watch."

She advanced to the beginning of the Pattern, near the great tree, where she moved as if to set her foot upon the bright trail. Before it arrived, however, a small electrical discharge crackled upward and made contact with her shoe. She jerked her foot back quickly.

"It rejects me," she said. "I can't set foot on it. Try it."

There was something in her gaze I did not like, but I moved forward to where she had been standing.

"Why couldn't your mirror penetrate all the way to the center of the thing?" I asked suddenly.

"The resistance seems to go up the farther you go in. It is greatest there," she replied. "But as to why, I do not know."

I hesitated a moment longer. "Has anyone tried it other than yourself?"

"I brought Bleys here," she answered. "It rejected him too."

"And he's the only other one who's seen it?"

"No, I brought Random. But he declined to try. Said he didn't care to screw around with it right then."

"Prudent, perhaps. Was he wearing the Jewel at the time?"

"No. Why?"

"Just curious."

"See what it does for you."

"All right."

I raised my right foot and lowered it slowly toward the line. About a foot above it, I stopped.

"Something seems to be holding me back," I said.

"Strange. There is no electrical discharge for you."

"Small blessing," I responded, and I pushed my foot a couple of inches farther downward. Finally, I sighed. "Nope, Fi. I can't."

I read the disappointment in her features.

"I was hoping," she said as I drew back, "that someone other than Corwin might be able to walk it. His son seemed the most likely choice."

"Why is it so important that someone walk it? Just because it's there?"

"I think it's a menace," she said. "It has to be explored and dealt with."

"A menace? Why?"

"Amber and Chaos are the two poles of existence, as we understand it," she said, "housing as they do the Pattern and the Logrus. For ages there has been something of an equilibrium between them. Now, I believe, this bastard Pattern of your father's is undermining their balance."

"In what fashion?"

"There have always been wavelike exchanges between Amber and Chaos. This seems to be setting up some interference."

"It sounds more like tossing an extra ice cube into a drink," I said. "It should settle down after a while."

She shook her head. "Things are not settling. There have been far more shadow-storms since this thing was created. They rend the fabric of Shadow. They affect the nature of reality itself."

"No good," I said. "Another event a lot more important along these lines occurred at the same time. The original Pattern in Amber was damaged and Oberon repaired it. The wave of Chaos which came out of that swept through all of Shadow. Everything was affected. But the Pattern held and things settled again. I'd be more inclined to think of all those extra shadow-storms as being in the nature of aftershocks."

"It's a good argument," she said. "But what if it's wrong?"

"I don't think it is."

"Merle, there's some kind of power here—an immense amount of power."

"I don't doubt it."

"It has always been our way to keep an eye on power, to try to understand it, to control it. Because one day it might become a threat. Did Corwin tell you anything, anything at all, as to exactly what this represents and how we might get a handle on it?"

"No," I said. "Nothing beyond the fact that he made it in a hurry to replace the old one, which he'd figured Oberon might not have succeeded in repairing."

"If only we could find him."

"There still hasn't been any word?"

"Droppa claims that he saw him at the Sands, back on the shadow Earth you both favor. He said he was in the company of an attractive woman, and they were both having a drink and listening to a music group. He waved and headed toward them through a crowd, and he thought that Corwin saw him. When he got to their table, though, they were gone."

"That's all?"

"That's all."

"That's not much."

"I know. If he's the only one who can walk this damned thing, though, and if it *is* a menace, we could be in big trouble one day."

"I think you're being an alarmist, Aunty."

"I hope you're right, Merle. Come on, I'll take you home."

I studied the place once more, for details as well as feeling, because I wanted to be able to construct a Trump for it. I never told anyone that there had been no resistance as I had lowered my foot, because once you set foot into the Pattern or the Logrus there is no turning back. You either proceed to the end or are destroyed by it. And as much as I love mysteries, my break was at its end and I had to get back to class.

Power.

We were together in a wood within the Black Zone, that area of Shadow with which Chaos holds commerce. We were hunting *zhind*, which are horned, short, black, fierce and carnivorous. I do not much like hunting because I do not much like killing things I don't really have to. However, it was Jurt's idea, and since it was possibly also my last chance to work some reconciliation with my brother before I departed, I had decided to take him up on the offer. Neither of us was that great an archer, and *zhind* are pretty fast. So with any luck at all nothing would get dead and we'd have some chance to talk and perhaps come away on better terms at the end of the hunt.

On one occasion when we'd lost the trail and were resting, we talked for a long time about archery, court politics, Shadow and the weather. He had been much more civil to me of late, which I took for a good sign. He'd let his hair grow in such a fashion as to cover the area of his missing left ear. Ears are hard to regenerate. We did not speak of our duel, or of the argument that had led up to it. Because I would soon be out of his life, I felt perhaps he wished to close this chapter of his existence in a relatively friendly fashion, with both of us going our ways with a memory we could feel good about. I was half right, anyway.

Later, when we had halted for a cold trail lunch, he asked me, "So, what does it feel like?"

"What?" I said.

"The power," he answered. "The Logrus power—to walk in Shadow, to work with a higher order of magic than the mundane."

I didn't really want to go into detail, because I knew he'd prepared himself to traverse the Logrus on three different occasions and had backed down at the last moment each time, when he'd looked into it. Perhaps the skeletons of failures that Suhuy keeps around had troubled him also. I don't think Jurt was aware that I knew about the last two times he'd changed his mind. So I decided to downplay my accomplishment.

"Oh, you don't really feel any different," I said, "until you're actually using it. Then it's hard to describe."

"I'm thinking of doing it soon myself," he said. "It would be good to see something of Shadow, maybe even find a kingdom for myself somewhere. Can you give me any advice?"

I nodded. "Don't look back," I said. "Don't stop to think. Just keep going."

He laughed. "Sounds like orders to an army," he said.

"I suppose there is a similarity."

He laughed again. "Let's go kill us a *zhind*," he said.

That afternoon, we lost a trail in a thicket full of fallen branches. We'd heard the *zhind* crash through it, but it was not immediately apparent which way it had gone. I had my back to Jurt and was facing the forward edge of the place, searching for some sign, when Frakir constricted tightly about my wrist, then came loose and fell to the ground.

I bent over to retrieve her, wondering what had happened, when I heard a *thunk* from overhead. Glancing upward, I saw an arrow protruding from the bole of the tree before me. Its height above the ground was such that had I remained standing it would have entered my back.

I turned quickly toward Jurt, not even straightening from my crouch. He was fitting another arrow to his bow.

He said, "Don't look back. Don't stop to think. Just keep going," and he laughed.

I dove toward him as he raised the weapon. A better archer would probably have killed me. I think when I moved he panicked and released the arrow prematurely, though, because it caught in the side of my leather vest and I didn't feel any pain.

I clipped him above the knees, and he dropped the bow as he fell over backward. He drew his hunting knife, rolled to the side and swung the weapon toward my throat. I caught his wrist with my left hand and was cast onto my back by the force of his momentum. I struck at his face with my right fist while holding the blade away from me. He blocked the punch and kneed me in the balls.

The point of the blade dropped to within inches of my throat as this blow collapsed a big piece of my resistance. Still aching, I was able to turn my hip to prevent another ball-buster, simultaneous with casting my right forearm beneath his wrist and cutting my hand in the process. Then I pushed with my right, pulled with my left and rolled to the left with the force of the turn. His arm was jerked free from my still-weakened grasp, and he rolled off to the side and I tried to recover—and then I heard him scream.

Coming up onto my knees, I saw that he lay upon his left side where he had come to a stop and the knife was several feet beyond him, caught in a tangle of broken branches. Both hands were raised to his face, and his cries were wordless, animal-like bleats.

I made my way over to him to see what had happened, with Frakir held ready to wrap about his throat in case it were some sort of trick he was playing.

But it was not. When I reached him I saw that a sharp limb of a fallen branch had pierced his right eye. There was blood on his cheek and the side of his nose.

"Stop jerking around!" I said. "You'll make it worse. Let me get it out."

"Keep your damn hands off me!" he cried.

Then, clenching his teeth and grimacing horribly, he caught hold of the limb with his right hand and drew his head back. I had to look away. He made a whimpering noise several moments later and collapsed, unconscious. I ripped off my left shirt sleeve, tore a strip from it, folded it into a pad and placed it over his damaged eye. With another strip, I tied it into place there. Frakir found her way back about my wrist, as usual.

Then I dug out the Trump that would take us home and raised him in my arms. Mom wasn't going to like this.

Power.

It was a Saturday. Luke and I had been hang gliding all morning. Then we met Julia and Gail for lunch, and afterward we took the Starburst out and sailed all afternoon. Later, we'd hit the bar and grill at the marina where I bought the beers while we waited for steaks, because Luke had slammed my right arm flat against the tabletop when we'd wrist wrestled to see who paid for drinks.

Someone at the next table said, "If I had a million dollars, tax free, I'd . . ." and Julia had laughed as she listened.

"What's funny?" I asked her.

"His wish list," she said. "I'd want a closet full of designer dresses and some elegant jewelry to go with them. Put the closet in a really nice house, and put the house someplace where I'd be important. . . ."

Luke smiled. "I detect a shift from money to power," he said.

"Maybe so," she replied. "But what's the difference, really?"

"Money buys things," Luke said. "Power makes things happen. If you ever have a choice, take the power."

Gail's usual faint smile had faded, and she wore a very serious expression.

"I don't believe power should be an end in itself," she said. "One has it only to use it in certain ways."

Julia laughed. "What's wrong with a power trip?" she asked. "It sounds like fun to me."

"Only till you run into a greater power," Luke said.

"Then you have to think big," Julia answered.

"That's not right," Gail said. "One has duties and they come first."

Luke was studying her now, and he nodded.

"You can keep morality out of it," Julia said.

"No, you can't," Luke responded.

"I disagree," she said.

Luke shrugged.

"She's right," Gail said suddenly. "I don't see that duty and morality are the same thing."

"Well, if you've got a duty," Luke said, "something you absolutely must do—a matter of honor, say—then that becomes your morality."

Julia looked at Luke, looked at Gail. "Does that mean we just agreed on something?" she asked.

"No," Luke said, "I don't think so."

Gail took a drink. "You're talking about a personal code that need not have anything to do with conventional morality."

"Right," Luke said.

"Then it's not really morality. You're just talking duty," she said.

"You're right on the duty," Luke answered. "But it's still morality."

"Morality is the values of a civilization," she said.

"There is no such thing as civilization," Luke replied. "The word just means the art of living in cities."

"All right, then. Of a culture," she said.

"Cultural values are relative things," Luke said, smiling, "and mine say I'm right."

"Where do yours come from?" Gail asked, studying him carefully.

"Let's keep this pure and philosophical, huh?" he said.

"Then maybe we should drop the term entirely," Gail said, "and just stick with duty."

"What happened to power?" Julia asked.

"It's in there somewhere," I said.

Suddenly Gail looked perplexed, as if our discussion were not something which had been repeated a thousand times in different forms, as if it had actually given rise to some new turn of thought.

"If they are two different things," she said slowly, "which one is more important?"

"They're not," Luke said. "They're the same."

"I don't think so," Julia told him. "But duties tend to be clear-cut, and it sounds as if you can choose your own morality. So if I had to have one I'd go with the morality."

"I like things that are clear-cut," Gail said.

Luke chugged his beer, belched lightly. "Shit!" he said. "Philosophy class isn't till Tuesday. This is the weekend. Who gets the next round, Merle?"

I placed my left elbow on the tabletop and opened my hand.

While we pushed together, the tension building and building between us, he said through clenched teeth, "I was right, wasn't I?"

"You were right," I said, just before I forced his arm all the way down.

Power.

I removed my mail from the little locked box in the hallway and carried it upstairs to my apartment. There were two bills, some circulars and something thick and first class without a return address on it.

I closed the door behind me, pocketed my keys and dropped my briefcase onto a nearby chair. I had started toward the sofa when the telephone in the kitchen rang.

Tossing the mail toward the coffee table, I turned and started for the kitchen. The blast that occurred behind me might or might not have been strong enough to knock me over. I don't know, because I dove forward of my own volition as soon as it occurred. I hit my head on the leg of the kitchen table. It dazed me somewhat, but I was otherwise undamaged. All the damage was in the other room. By the time I got to my feet the phone had stopped ringing.

I already knew there were lots of easier ways to dispose of junk mail, but I wondered for a long time afterward who it was that had been on the telephone.

I sometimes remembered the first of the series, too, the truck that had come rushing toward me. I had only caught a glimpse of the driver's face before I'd moved—inert, he was completely expressionless, as if he were dead, hypnotized, drugged or somehow possessed. Choose any of the above, I decided, and maybe more than one.

And then there was the night of the muggers. They had attacked me without a word. When it was all over and I was heading away, I had glanced back once. I thought I'd glimpsed a shadowy figure draw back into a doorway up the street—a smart precaution, I'd say, in light of what had been going on. But of course it could have been someone connected with the attack, too. I was torn. The person was too far off to have been able to give a good description of me. If I went back and it turned out to be an innocent bystander, there would then be a witness capable of identifying me. Not that I didn't think it was an open-and-shut case of self-defense, but there'd be a lot of hassle. So I said the hell with it, and I walked on. Another interesting April 30.

The day of the rifle. There had been two shots as I'd hurried down the street. They'd both missed me before I'd realized what was going on, chipping brickbats from the side of the building to my left. There was no third shot, but there was a thud and a splintering sound from the building across the street. A third-floor window stood wide open.

I hurried over. It was an old apartment house and the front door was locked, but I didn't slow down for niceties. I located the stair and mounted it. When I came to what I thought was the proper room, I decided to try the door the old-fashioned way and it worked. It was unlocked.

I stood to the side and pushed it open and saw that the place was unfurnished and empty. Unoccupied, too, it seemed. Could I have been wrong? But then I saw that the window facing the street stood wide and I saw what lay upon the floor. I entered and closed the door behind me.

A broken rifle lay in the corner. From markings on the stock I guessed that it had been swung with great force against a nearby radiator before it had been cast aside. Then I saw something else on the floor, something wet and red. Not much. Just a few drops.

I searched the place quickly. It was small. The one window in its single bedroom also stood open and I went to it. There was a fire escape beyond it, and I decided that it might be a good way for me to make my exit, too. There were a few more drops of blood on the black metal, but that was it. No one was in sight below, or in either direction.

Power. To kill. To preserve. Luke, Jasra, Gail. Who was responsible for what?

The more I thought of it, the more it seemed possible that there might have been a telephone call on the morning of the open gas jets, too. Could that be what had roused me to an awareness of danger? Each time I thought of these matters there seemed to be a slight shifting of emphasis. Things stood in a different light. According to Luke and the pseudo-Vinta, I was not in great danger in the later episodes, but it seemed that any of those things could have taken me out. Who was I to blame? The perpetrator? Or the savior who barely saved? And who was which? I remembered how my father's story had been complicated by that damned auto accident which played like *Last Year at Marienbad*—though his had seemed simple compared to everything that was coming down on me. At least he knew what he had to do most of the time. Could I be the inheritor of a family curse involving complicated plotting?

Power.

I remembered Uncle Suhuy's final lesson. He had spent some time following my completion of the Logrus in teaching me things I could not have learned before then. There came a time when I thought I was finished. I had been confirmed in the Art and dismissed. It seemed I had covered all the basics and anything more would be mere elaboration. I began making preparations for my journey to the shadow Earth. Then one morning Suhuy sent for me. I assumed that he just wanted to say good-bye and give me a few friendly words of advice.

His hair is white, he is somewhat stooped and there are days when he carries a staff. This was one of them. He had on his yellow caftan, which I had always thought of as a working garment rather than a social one.

"Are you ready for a short trip?" he asked me.

"Actually, it's going to be a long one," I said. "But I'm almost ready."

"No," he said. "That was not the journey I meant."

"Oh. You mean you want to go somewhere right now?"

"Come," he said.

So I followed him, and the shadows parted before us. We moved through increasing bleakness, passing at last into places that bore no sign of life whatsoever. Dark, sterile rock lay all about us, stark in the brassy light of a dim and ancient sun. This final place was chill and dry, and when we halted and I looked about, I shivered.

I waited, to see what he had in mind. But it was a long while before he spoke. He seemed oblivious of my presence for a time, simply staring out across the bleak landscape.

Finally, "I have taught you the ways of Shadow," he said slowly, "and the composition of spells and their working."

I said nothing. His statement did not seem to require a reply.

"So you know something of the ways of power," he continued. "You draw it from the Sign of Chaos, the Logrus, and you invest it in various ways."

He glanced at me at last, and I nodded.

"I understand that those who bear the Pattern, the Sign of Order, may do similar things in ways that may or may not be similar," he went on. "I do not know for certain, for I am not an initiate of the Pattern. I doubt the spirit could stand the strain of knowing the ways of both. But you should understand that there is another way of power, antithetical to our own."

"I understand," I said, for he seemed to be expecting an answer.

"But you have a resource available to you," he said, "which those of Amber do not. Watch!"

His final word did not mean that I should simply observe as he leaned his staff against the side of a boulder and raised his hands before him. It meant that I should have the Logrus before me so I could see what he was doing at that level. So I summoned my vision and watched him through it.

Now the vision that hung before him seemed a continuation of my own, stretched and twisting. I saw and felt it as he joined his hands with it and extended a pair of its jagged limbs outward across the distance to touch upon a boulder that lay downhill of us.

"Enter the Logrus now yourself," he said, "remaining passive. Stay with me through what I am about to do. Do not, at any time, attempt to interfere."

"I understand," I said.

I moved my hands into my vision, shifting them about, feeling after congruity, until they became a part of it.

"Good," he said, when I had settled them into place. "Now all you need do is observe, on all levels."

Something pulsed along the limbs he controlled, passing down to the boulder. I was not prepared for what came after.

The image of the Logrus turned black before me, becoming a seething blot of inky turmoil. An awful feeling of disruptive power surged through me, an enormous destructive force that threatened to overwhelm me, to carry me into the blissful nothingness of ultimate disorder. A part of me seemed to desire this, while another part was screaming wordlessly for it to cease. But Suhuy maintained control of the phenomenon, and I could see how he was doing it, just as I had seen how he had brought it into being in the first place.

The boulder became one with the turmoil, joined it and was gone. There was no explosion, no implosion, only the sensation of great cold winds and cacophonous sounds. Then my uncle moved his hands slowly apart, and the lines of seething blackness followed them, flowing out in both directions from that area of chaos which had been the boulder, producing a long dark trench wherein I beheld the paradox of both nothingness and activity.

Then he stood still, arresting it at that point. Moments later, he spoke.

"I could simply release it," he stated, "letting it run wild. Or I could give it a direction and then release it."

As he did not continue, I asked, "What would happen then? Would it simply continue until it had devastated the entire shadow?"

"No," he replied. "There are limiting factors. The resistance of Order to Chaos would build as it extended itself. There would come a point of containment."

"And if you remained as you are, and kept summoning more?"

"One would do a great deal of damage."

"And if we combined our efforts?"

"More extensive damage. But that is not the lesson I had in mind. I will remain passive now while you control it."

So I took over the Sign of the Logrus and ran the line of disruption back upon itself in a great circle, like a dark moat surrounding us.

"Banish it now," he said, and I did.

Still, the winds and the sounds continued to rage, and I could not see beyond the dark wall which seemed to be advancing slowly upon us from all sides.

"Obviously, the limiting factor has yet to be achieved," I observed.

He chuckled. "You're right. Even though you stopped, you exceeded a certain critical limit, so that it is now running wild."

"Oh," I said. "How long till those natural limitations you mentioned dampen it?"

"Sometime after it has completely annihilated the area on which we stand," he said.

"It is receding in all directions as well as heading this way?"

"Yes."

"Interesting. What *is* the critical mass?"

"I'll have to show you. But we'd better find a new place first. This one is going away. Take my hand."

I did, and he conducted me to another shadow. This time I summoned the Chaos and conducted the operations while he observed. This time I did not let it run wild.

When I had finished and I stood, shaken, staring into a small crater I had caused, he placed his hand on my shoulder and told me, "As you knew in theory, that is the ultimate power behind your spells. Chaos itself. To work with it directly is dangerous. But, as you have seen, it can be done. Now you know it, your training is complete."

It was more than impressive. It was awesome. And for most situations I could visualize it was rather like using nukes for skeet shooting. Offhand, I couldn't think of any circumstances under which I would care to employ the technique, until Victor Melman really pissed me off.

Power, in its many shapes, varieties, sizes and styles, continues to fascinate me. It has been so much a part of my life for so long that I feel very familiar with it, though I doubt that I will ever understand it fully.

10

It's about time," I said, to whatever lurked in the shadows.

The sound that followed was not human. It was a low snarl. I wondered what manner of beast I confronted. I was certain an attack was imminent, but it did not come. Instead the growl died down, and whatever it was spoke again.

"Feel your fear," came the whisper.

"Feel your own," I said, "while you still can."

The sounds of its breathing came heavy. The flames danced at my back. Smoke had drawn as far away across the campsite as his lengthy tether permitted.

"I could have killed you while you slept," it said slowly.

"Foolish of you not to," I said. "It will cost you."

"I want to look at you, Merlin," it stated. "I want to see you puzzled. I want to see your fear. I want to see your anguish before I see your blood."

"Then I take it this is a personal rather than a business matter?"

There came a strange noise which it took me several moments to interpret as an inhuman throat trying to manage a chuckle.

Then, "Let us say that, magician," it responded. "Summon your Sign and your concentration will waver. I will know it and will rend you before you can employ it."

"Kind of you to warn me."

"I just wanted to foreclose that option in your thinking. The thing wound about your left wrist will not help you in time either."

"You have good vision."

"In these matters, yes."

"You wish perhaps to discuss the philosophy of revenge with me now?"

"I am waiting for you to break and do something foolish, to increase my pleasure. I have limited your actions to the physical, so you are doomed."

"Keep waiting, then," I said.

There was a sound of movement within the brush as something drew nearer. I still could not see it, though. I took a step to my left then, to allow firelight to reach that darkened area. At that, something shone, low. The light was reflected, yellow, from a single glaring eye.

I lowered the point of my weapon, directing it toward the eye. What the hell. Every creature I know of tries to protect its eyes.

"Banzai!" I cried, as I lunged. The conversation seemed to have stagnated, and I was anxious to get on to other matters.

It rose instantly and with great power and speed rushed toward me, avoiding my thrust. It was a large, black, lop-eared wolf, and it slipped past a frantic slash I managed and went straight for my throat.

My left forearm came up automatically and I thrust it forward into the open jaws. At the same time, I brought the hilt of my blade across and slammed it against the side of its head. At this, the clamping force of the bite loosened even as I was borne over backward, but the grip remained, penetrating shirt and flesh. And I was turning and pulling before I hit the ground, wanting to land on top, knowing I wouldn't.

I landed on my left side, attempting to continue the roll, and added another belt of the pommel to the side of the beast's skull. It was then that fortune favored me, for a change, when I realized that we lay near the lip of my fire pit and were still turning in that direction. I dropped my weapon and sought its throat with my right hand. It was heavily muscled, and there was no chance of crushing the windpipe in time. But that was not what I was after.

My hand went up high and back beneath the lower jaw, where I commenced squeezing with all my strength. I scrabbled with my feet until I found purchase and then pushed with my legs as well as my arms. Our movement continued the short distance necessary to push its snarling head back into the fire.

For a moment nothing happened save the steady trickle of blood from my forearm into its mouth and out again. The grip of its jaws was still strong and painful.

Seconds later, my arm was released as the fur of its neck and head caught fire and it struggled to draw away from the flames. I was thrust aside as it rose and pulled free, an ear-piercing howl rising from its throat. I rolled to my knees and raised my hands, but it did not come at me again. Instead, it rushed past me into the woods in the opposite direction from which it had come.

I snatched up my blade and took off after it. No time to pause and pull on my boots; I was able to shapeshift the soles of my feet a bit to toughen them against the litter and irregularity of the forest floor. My adversary was still in sight, for its head still smoldered; though I might have been able to follow just from the howling, which was almost continuous. And strangely, the tone and character of the howls was changing, sounding more and more like human cries and less like the complaint of a wolf. Strangely, too, the beast was fleeing with something less than the speed and guile I would have expected from one of its kind. I heard it crashing through the shrubbery and running into trees. On several of these latter occasions, it even emitted sounds that seemed to bear the pattern of human cursing. So I was able to stay closer to it than I had any reason to expect, even gaining on it somewhat after the first few minutes.

Then, suddenly, I realized its apparent destination. I saw again that pale light I had noted earlier—brighter now and its source larger, as we moved toward it. Roughly rectangular in shape, I judged it as being eight or nine feet in height, perhaps five in width. I forgot about tracking the wolf by ear and headed for the light. That had to be its goal, and I wanted to reach it first.

I ran on. The wolf was ahead of me and to my left. Its hair had ceased to blaze now, though it still snarled and yipped as it rushed along. Before us, the light grew brighter still, and I was able to see into it—through it—and distinguish some of its features for the first time. I saw a hillside with a low stone building upon it, approached by a flagged walkway and a series of stone steps—framed like a picture within the rectangle—hazy at first, but coming clearer with each step. It was a cloudy afternoon within the picture, and the thing stood about twenty meters away now, in the midst of a clearing.

I realized as I saw the beast burst into the clearing that I was not going to be able to reach the place in time to snatch up the thing I knew must lie nearby. Still, I thought I might have a chance of catching the creature and halting its passage.

But it put on additional speed once it was in the clear. I could see the scene toward which it was headed more clearly than anything else in the vicinity. I shouted to distract it, but that did not work. My final burst of speed was not good enough. Then, on the ground, near the threshold, I saw what I was looking for. Too late. Even as I watched, the beast lowered its head and caught up in its teeth a flat rectangular object, without even breaking stride.

I halted and turned away as it plunged ahead, dropping my blade as I dove, rolling, continuing to roll.

I felt the force of the silent explosion, followed by the implosion and the small series of shock waves. I lay there thinking nasty thoughts until the turmoil had ceased; then I rose and retrieved my weapon.

The night was normal about me once again. Starlight. The wind in the pines. There was no need for me to turn, though I did, to know that the thing toward which I had been racing but moments before was now gone, without leaving any sign that it had been there, bright doorway to another place.

I hiked back to my camp and spent a while talking to Smoke, calming him. I donned my boots and cloak then, kicked dirt over the embers in my pit, and led the horse back to the road.

I mounted there and we moved on up the road toward Amber for the better part of an hour, before I settled upon a new campsite under a bone-white piece of moon.

The rest of my night was untroubled. I was awakened by increased light and morning bird calls through the pines. I took care of Smoke, breakfasted quickly on the remains of my rations, put myself in the best order I could and was on my way within half an hour.

It was a cool morning, with banks of cumulus far off to my left, clear skies overhead. I did not hurry. My main reason for riding back rather than trumping home was to learn a little more of what this area near Amber was like, and the other was to gain a bit of solitude for thinking. With Jasra a prisoner, Luke in sick bay and Ghostwheel occupied it seemed that any major threats to Amber or myself were in abeyance, and a small breathing spell could be justified. I felt that I was actually near to a point where I could handle everything personally with regard to Luke and Jasra, as soon as I'd worked out a few more details. And I was certain I could deal with Ghost after that, as I'd found our most recent conversation somewhat encouraging.

That was the big stuff. I could worry about loose ends later. A two-bit wizard like Sharu Garrul was only a pain when considered in conjunction with everything else that was troubling me. Dueling with him would be no problem when I had a bit of leisure—though I had to admit I was puzzled as to why he should be interested in me at all.

Then there was the matter of the entity which had for a time been Vinta. While I saw no real threat in it, there was certainly a mystery which affected my peace of mind, and which seemed ultimately to have something to do with my security. This, too, was a matter to be dealt with when that bit of leisure finally came along.

And Luke's offer to reveal a piece of information vital to Amber's security, once Jasra was rescued, troubled me. Because I believed him, and I believed he'd keep his word. I had a hunch, though, that he wouldn't be giving it away unless it was too late to do much about it. Guesswork was, of course, futile; there was no way of knowing what preparations would be appropriate. Was the offer itself, no matter how authentic, also a bit of psychological warfare? Luke had always been more subtle than his bluff exterior seemed to indicate. It had taken me a long time to learn that, and I wasn't about to forget it now.

I felt I could discount the business of the blue stones for the moment, and I planned soon to be rid of all traces of their vibes. No problem there, other than a mental string around the finger for extra wariness, just in case—and I was already in that frame of mind, had been for some time.

That left the business of last night's wolf to be fitted into the bigger picture.

Obviously, it had been no normal beast, and its intent had been apparent enough. Other matters concerning its visit were less than clear, however. Who or what was it? Was it a principal or an agent? And, if the latter, who had sent it? And finally, finally, why?

Its clumsiness indicated to me—since I had tried that sort of business myself in the past—that it was a shapeshifted human rather than a true wolf magically gifted with speech. Most people who daydream of transforming themselves into some vicious beast and going about tearing people's throats out, dismembering them, disfiguring them and perhaps devouring them tend mainly to dwell upon how much fun it would be and generally neglect the practicalities of the situation. When you find yourself a quadruped, with a completely different center of gravity and a novel array of sensory input, it is not all that easy to get around for a time with any measure of grace. One is generally far more vulnerable than one's appearance would lead others to believe. And certainly one is nowhere near as lethal and efficient as the real thing with a lifetime of practice behind it. No. I've always tended to think of it more as a terrorist tactic than anything else.

Be that how it may, the manner of the beast's coming and going was actually the main cause of my trepidation concerning the entire affair. It had employed a Trump Gate, which is not a thing one does lightly—or at all, for that matter, if it can be avoided. It is a flashy and spectacular thing to make Trump contact with some distant place and then pour tons of power into the objectification of such a gateway as a form possessed for a time of an independent existence. It is exceedingly profligate of energy and effort— even a hellrun is much easier—to create one which will stand for even fifteen minutes. It can drain most of your resources for a long while. Yet this was what had occurred. The reason behind it did not trouble me, as much as the fact that it had happened at all. For the only people capable of the feat were genuine initiates of the Trumps. It couldn't be done by someone who just happened to come into possession of a card.

Which narrowed the field considerably.

I tried to picture the werebeast about its errand. First, it would have to locate me and—

Of course. I suddenly recalled the dead dogs in the grove near Arbor House and the large doglike tracks in the vicinity. The thing had spotted me sometime before, then, and had been watching, waiting. It had followed me when I set out yesterday evening, and when I made my camp it made its move. It set up—or was set up with—the Trump Gate, for a retreat that would brook no pursuit. Then it came to kill me. And I had no way of telling whether it involved Sharu Garrul, Luke's secret, the blue stones or the body-switching entity's mission. For now it would simply have to dangle as yet another loose end, while I concentrated on basics.

I overtook and passed a line of wagons headed for Amber. A few horsemen went by me headed in the other direction. No one I knew, though everyone waved. The clouds continued to mount to my left, but nothing resembling a storm took shape. The day remained cool and sunny. The road dipped and rose again, several times, though overall it rose more than it dipped. I stopped at a large, busy inn for lunch, had a quick, filling meal and did not linger. The road improved steadily after that, and it was not long before I caught distant glimpses of Amber atop Kolvir, sparkling in the noonday light.

Traffic grew heavier as the sun advanced through the heavens. I continued to make plans and indulge in whatever speculations came to mind as I rode on into afternoon. My uphill way took several turnings as the route passed through the heights, but Amber remained in sight most of the time.

I recognized no one along the way, and I reached the Eastern Gate—part of an ancient fortification—late in the afternoon. I made my way up East Vine and stopped at the Bayle town house, where I had once attended a party. I left Smoke with a groom at the stable in the rear, and they both seemed happy to see each other. I walked around to the front door then and knocked. A servant informed me that the Baron was out, so I identified myself and gave him Vinta's message, which he promised to deliver when his employer returned.

That duty out of the way, I proceeded up East Vine on foot. Near the top, but before the slope grew roughly level, I smelled food and discarded my plan of waiting to eat until I was back at the palace. I halted and cast about me for the source of the aromas. I located it up a side street to my right where the way widened into a large circle, a fountain at its center—in which a rearing copper dragon with a wonderful green patina pissed into a pink stone basin. The dragon faced a basement restaurant called the Pit, with ten outside tables enclosed by a low fence of copper pickets, potted plants along its inside perimeter. I crossed the circle. As I passed the fountain I saw a great number of exotic coins within its clear water, including a U.S. Bicentennial quarter. Crossing to the fenced area, I entered, made my way through and was about to descend the stair when I heard my name called.

"Merle! Over here!"

I looked about but did not see anyone I recognized at any of the four occupied tables. Then, as my eyes retraced their route, I realized that the older man at the corner table to my right was smiling.

"Bill!" I exclaimed.

Bill Roth rose to his feet—more a touch of display than any formality, I realized immediately. I hadn't recognized him at first because he now sported the beginnings of a grizzled beard and a mustache. Also, he had on brown trousers with a silver stripe running down their outside seams, vanishing into a pair of high brown boots. His shirt was silver with brown piping, and a black cloak lay folded upon the chair to his right. A wide black sword belt lay atop it and a sheathed blade of short-to-medium length was hung upon it.

"You've gone native. Also, you've lost some weight."

"True," he said, "and I'm thinking of retiring here. It agrees with me."

We seated ourselves.

"Did you order yet?" I asked him.

"Yes, but I see a waiter on the stair now," he said. "Let me catch him for you."

Which he did, and ordered for me too.

"Your Thari's much better," I said afterward.

"Lots of practice," he replied.

"What've you been doing?"

"I've sailed with Gérard. I've been to Deiga, and to one of Julian's camps in Arden. Visited Rebma, too. Fascinating place. I've been taking fencing lessons. And Droppa's been showing me around town."

"All the bars, most likely."

"Well, that's not all. In fact, that's why I'm here. He owns a half interest in the Pit, and I had to promise him I'd eat here a lot. A good place, though. When did you get back?"

"Just now," I said, "and I've another long story for you."

"Good. Your stories tend to be bizarre and convoluted," he said. "Just the thing for a cool autumn's eve. Let's hear it."

I talked throughout dinner and for a long while afterward. The day's-end chill began making it uncomfortable then, so we headed for the palace. I finally wound up my narrative over hot cider in front of the fireplace in one of the smaller rooms in the eastern wing.

Bill shook his head. "You do manage to stay busy," he finally said. "I have just one question."

"What?"

"Why didn't you bring Luke in?"

"I already told you."

"It wasn't much of a reason. For some nebulous piece of information he says is important to Amber? And you've got to catch him to get it?"

"It's not like that at all."

"He's a salesman, Merle, and he sold you a line of shit. That's what I think."

"You're wrong, Bill. I know him."

"For a long time," he agreed. "But how well? We've been all through this before. What you don't know about Luke far outweighs what you do know."

"He could have gone elsewhere, but he came to me."

"You're part of his plan, Merle. He intends to get at Amber through you."

"I don't think so," I said. "It's not his style."

"I think he'll use anything that comes to hand—or anyone."

I shrugged. "I believe him. You don't. That's all."

"I guess so," he said. "What are you going to do now, wait and see what happens?"

"I've a plan," I said. "Just because I believe him doesn't mean I won't take out insurance. But I've a question for you."

"Yes?"

"If I brought him back here and Random decided the facts weren't clear enough and he wanted a hearing, would you represent Luke?"

His eyes widened, and then he smiled. "What kind of hearing?" he asked. "I don't know how such things are conducted here."

"As a grandson of Oberon," I explained, "he'd come under House Law. Random is head of the House now. It would be up to him whether to forget about a thing, render a summary judgment or call a hearing. As I understand it, such a hearing could be as formal or informal as Random wanted. There are books on the subject in the library. But a person has always had the right to be represented at one if he wanted."

"Of course I'd take the case," Bill said. "It doesn't sound like a legal experience that comes along too often.

"But it might look like a conflict of interest," he added, "since I have done work for the Crown."

I finished my cider and put the glass on the mantelpiece. I yawned.

"I have to go now, Bill."

He nodded; then, "This is all just hypothetical, isn't it?" he asked.

"Of course," I said. "It might turn out to be *my* hearing. G'night."

He studied me. "Uh—this insurance you were talking about," he said. "It probably involves something risky, doesn't it?"

I smiled.

"Nothing anyone could help you with, I suppose?"

"Nope."

"Well, good luck."

"Thanks."

"See you tomorrow?"

"Later in the day, maybe. . . ."

I went to my room and sacked out. I had to get some rest before I went about the business I had in mind. I don't recall any dreams, pro or con, on the matter.

It was still dark when I woke. Good to know that my mental alarm was working.

It would have been very pleasant to turn over and go back to sleep, but I couldn't allow myself the luxury. The day that lay ahead was to be an exercise in timing. Accordingly, I got up, cleaned up and dressed myself in fresh clothes.

I headed for the kitchen then, where I made myself some tea and toast and scrambled a few eggs with chilis and onions and a bit of pepper. I turned up some melka fruit from the Snelters, too—something I hadn't had in a long while.

Afterward, I went out through the rear and made my way into the garden. Dark it was, moonless and damp, with a few wisps of mist exploring invisible paths. I followed a path to the northwest. The world was a very quiet place. I let my thoughts get that way, too. It was to be a one-thing-at-a-time day, and I wanted to start it off with that habit of mind in place.

I walked until I ran out of garden, passing through a break in a hedge and continuing along the rough trail my path had become. It mounted slowly for the first few minutes, took an abrupt turn and grew immediately steeper. I paused at one jutting point and looked back, from where I was afforded a view of the dark outline of the palace, a few lighted windows within it. Some scatters of cirrus high above looked like raked starlight in the celestial garden over which Amber brooded. I turned away moments later. There was still a good distance to travel.

When I reached the crest I was able to discern a faint line of lightening to the east, beyond the forest I had traversed so recently. I hurried past the three massive steps of song and story and began my descent to the north. Slow at first, the way I followed steepened abruptly after a time and led off to the northeast, then into a gentler decline. When it swung back to the northwest there was another steep area followed by another easy one, and I knew the going would be fine after that. The high shoulder of Kolvir at my back blocked all traces of the pre-dawn light I had witnessed earlier, and star-hung night lay before me and above, rubbing outlines to ambiguity on all but the nearest boulders. Still, I knew approximately where I was going, having been this way once before, though I'd only halted briefly at that time.

It was about two miles past the crest, and I slowed as I neared the area, searching. It was a large, somewhat horseshoe-shaped declivity, and when I finally located it I entered slowly, a peculiar feeling rising within me. I had not consciously anticipated all my reactions in this matter; but at some level I must have, I was certain.

As I moved into it, canyonlike walls of stone rising at either hand, I came upon the trail and followed it. It led me slightly downhill, toward a shadowy pair of trees, and then between them to where a low stone building stood, various shrubs and grasses grown wild about it. I understand that the soil was actually transported there to support the foliage, but afterward it was forgotten and neglected.

I seated myself on one of the stone benches in front of the building and waited for the sky to lighten. This was my father's tomb—well, cenotaph—built long ago when he had been presumed dead. It had amused him considerably to be able to visit the place later on. Now, of course, its status might well have changed. It could be the real thing now. Would this cancel the irony or increase it? I couldn't quite decide. It bothered me, though, more than I'd thought it would. I had not come here on a pilgrimage. I had come here for the peace and quiet a sorcerer of my sort needs in order to hang some spells. I had come here—

Perhaps I was rationalizing. I had chosen this spot because, real tomb or fake, it had Corwin's name on it, so it raised a sense of his presence, for me. I had wanted to get to know him better, and this might be as close as I could ever come. I realized, suddenly, why I had trusted Luke. He had been right, back at the Arbor House. If I learned of Corwin's death and saw that blame could be fixed for it, I knew that I would drop everything else, that I would go off to present the bill and collect it, that I would have to close the account, to write the receipt in blood. Even had I not known Luke as I did, it was easy to see myself in his actions and too uncomfortable a thing to judge him.

Damn. Why must we caricature each other, beyond laughter or insight, into the places of pain, frustration, conflicting loyalties?

I rose. There was enough light now to show me what I was doing.

I went inside and approached the niche where the empty stone sarcophagus stood. It seemed an ideal safe deposit box, but I hesitated when I stood before it because my hands were shaking. It was ridiculous. I knew that he wasn't in there, that it was just an empty box with a bit of carving on it. Yet it was several minutes before I could bring myself to take hold of the lid and raise it. . . .

Empty, of course, like so many dreams and fears. I tossed in the blue button and lowered the lid again. What the hell. If Sharu wanted it back and could find it here, let him have the message that he was walking close to the grave when he played his games.

I went back outside, leaving my feelings in the crypt. It was time to begin. I'd a mess of spells to work and hang, for I'd no intention of going gently to the place where the wild winds blew.

11

I stood on the rise above the garden, admiring the autumn foliage
below. The wind played games with my cloak. A mellow afternoon light bathed the palace. There was a chill in the air. A flock
of dead leaves rushed, lemming-like, past me and blew off the
edge of the trail, rattling, into the air.

I had not really stopped to admire the view, however. I had
halted while I blocked an attempted Trump contact—the day's
second. The first had occurred earlier, while I was hanging a spell
like a rope of tinsel on the image of Chaos. I figured that it was either Random—irritated that I was back in Amber and had not seen
fit to bring him up to date on my most recent doings and my
plans—or Luke, recovered now and wanting to request my assistance in his move against the Keep. They both came to mind because they were the two individuals I wished most to avoid;
neither of them would much like what I was about to do, though
for different reasons.

The call faded, was gone, and I descended the trail, passed
through the hedge and entered the garden. I did not want to waste
a spell to mask my passage, so I took a trail to the left, which led
through a series of arbors where I was less exposed to the gaze of
anyone who happened to glance out of a window. I could have
avoided this by trumping in, but that card always delivers one to
the main hall, and I had no idea who might be there.

Of course, I was headed that way. . . .

I went back in the way I had come out, through the kitchen,
helping myself to a sandwich and a glass of milk on the way.

Then I took the back stairs up a flight, lurked a bit and made it to my rooms without being spotted. There, I buckled on the sword belt I had left hanging at the head of my bed, checked the blade, located a small dagger I had brought with me from Chaos—a gift from the Pit-diver Borquist, whom I'd once fixed up with an introduction that led to a patronage (he was a middling-good poet)—and hung it on the other side of my belt. I pinned a Trump to the inside of my left sleeve. I washed my hands and face and brushed my teeth, too. But then I couldn't think of any other ways to stall. I had to go and do something I feared. It was necessary to the rest of my plan. I was overwhelmed by a sudden desire to be off sailing. Just lying on the beach would do, actually. . . .

Instead, I departed my quarters and made my way back downstairs, returning the way I had come. I headed west along the back corridor, listening for footsteps and voices, retreating once into a closet to let some nameless parties pass. Anything to avoid official notice for just a little longer. Finally, I turned left, walked a few paces and waited the better part of a minute before entering the major corridor, which led past the large marble dining hall. No one in sight. Good. I sprinted to the nearest entrance and peered within. Great. The place was not in use. It wasn't normally used every day, but I'd no way of knowing whether today was some state occasion—though this was not a normal dining hour either.

I entered and passed through. There is a dark, narrow corridor to its rear, with a guard normally posted somewhere near the passage's mouth or the door at its end. All members of the family have access there, though the guard would log our passage. His superior wouldn't have that information until the guard reported when he went off duty, though. By then it shouldn't matter to me.

Tod was short, stocky, bearded. When he saw me coming he presented arms with an ax that had been leaning against the wall moments before.

"At ease. Busy?" I asked.

"To tell the truth, no, sir."

"I'll be heading down. I hope there are some lanterns up here. I don't know that stairway as well as most."

"I checked a number inside when I came on duty, sir. I'll light you one."

Might as well save the energy that would have gone into the fire spell, I decided. Every little bit helps. . . .

"Thanks."

He opened the door, hefted, successively, three lanterns which stood inside to the right, selected the second one. He took it back outside, where he lit it from the massive candle in its stand partway up the corridor.

"I'll be awhile," I said as I accepted it from him. "You'll probably be off duty before I'm finished."

"Very good, sir. Watch your step."

"Believe me, I will."

The long spiraling stair turned round and round with very little visible in any direction but below, where a few chimneyed candles, sconced torches or hung lanterns flared along the central shaft, doing more for acrophobia than absolute blackness might, I suppose. There were just those little dots of light below me. I couldn't see the distant floor, or any walls. I kept one hand on the railing and held the lantern out in front with the other. Damp down here. Musty, too. Not to mention chilly.

Again, I tried counting the steps. As usual, I lost count somewhere along the way. Next time. . . .

My thoughts went back to that distant day when I had come this route believing I was headed for death. The fact that I hadn't died was small comfort now. It had still been an ordeal. And it was still possible that I could screw up on it this time and get fried or go up in a puff of smoke.

Around, around. Down, down. Night thoughts in the middle of the afternoon. . . .

On the other hand, I'd heard Flora say that it was easier the second time around. She'd been talking about the Pattern moments before, and I hoped that's what she was referring to.

The Grand Pattern of Amber, Emblem of Order. Matching in power the Great Logrus of the Courts, Sign of Chaos. The tensions between the two seem to generate everything that matters. Get involved with either, lose control—and you're done for. Just my luck to be involved with both. I've no one with whom to compare notes as to whether this makes things rougher, though it massages my ego to think that the mark of the one makes the other more difficult . . . and they do mark you, both of them. At some level you are torn apart and reassembled along the lines of vast cosmic principles when you undergo such an experience—which sounds noble, important, metaphysical, spiritual and lovely, but is mainly a pain in the ass. It is the price we pay for certain powers, but there is no cosmic principle requiring me to say I enjoy it.

Both the Pattern and the Logrus give to their initiates the ability to traverse Shadow unassisted—Shadow being the generic term for the possibly infinite collection of reality variations we play about in. And they also give us other abilities. . . .

Around and down. I slowed. I was feeling slightly dizzy, just like before. At least I wasn't planning on coming back this way. . . .

When the bottom finally came into sight I speeded up again. There was a bench, a table, a few racks and cases, a light to show them all. Normally, there was a guard on duty there, but I didn't see one. Could be off making rounds, though. There were cells somewhere to the left in which particularly unfortunate political prisoners might sometimes be found scrabbling about and going slowly out of their minds. I didn't know whether there were any such individuals doing time at the moment. I kind of hoped not. My father had once been one, and from his description of the experience it did not sound like easy time to do.

I halted when I reached the floor and called out a couple of times. I got back a suitably eerie echo, but no answer.

I moved to the rack and took up a filled lantern with my other hand. An extra one might come in handy. It was possible I would lose my way. I headed to the right then. The tunnel I wanted lay in that direction. After a long while, I stopped and raised a light, as it almost seemed I had come too far. There was still no tunnel mouth in sight. I looked back. The guard post was still in sight. I continued on, searching my memories of that last time.

Finally, there was a shifting of sounds—abrupt echoes of my footfalls. It would seem I was nearing a wall, an obstacle. I raised a lantern again.

Yes. Pure darkness ahead. Gray stone about it. I went that way.

Dark. Far. There was a continuous shadow-show as my light slid over rocky irregularities, as its beams glanced off specks of brightness in the stone walls. Then there was a side passage to my left. I passed it and kept going. It seemed there should be another fairly soon. Yes. Two. . . .

The third was farther along. Then there was a fourth. I wondered idly where they all led. No one had ever said anything about them to me. Maybe they didn't know either. Bizarre grottoes of indescribable beauty? Other worlds? Dead ends? Storerooms? One day, perhaps, when time and inclination came together. . . .

Five. . . .

And then another.

It was the seventh one I wanted. I halted when I came to it. It didn't go back all that far. I thought of the others who'd passed this way, and then I strode ahead, to the big, heavy, metal-bound door. There was a great key hanging from a steel hook that had been driven into the wall to my right. I took it down, unlocked the door and hung it back up again, knowing that the downstairs guard would check it and re-lock it at some point in his rounds; and I wondered—not for the first time—why it should be locked that way in the first place if the key was kept right there. It made it seem as if there were danger from something that might emerge from within. I had asked about that, but no one I'd questioned seemed to know. Tradition, I'd been told. Gérard and Flora had suggested, respectively, that I ask Random or Fiona. And *they* had both thought Benedict might know, but I'd never remembered to ask him.

I pushed hard and nothing happened. I put down the lanterns and tried again, harder. The door creaked and moved slowly inward. I recovered the lanterns and entered.

The door closed itself behind me, and Frakir—child of Chaos—pulsed wildly. I recalled my last visit and remembered why no one had brought an extra lantern upon that occasion: The bluish glow of the Pattern within the smooth, black floor lit the grotto well enough for one to see one's way about.

I lit the other lantern. I set the first one down at the near end of the Pattern and carried the other one with me about the periphery of the thing, setting it down at a point on its farther side. I did not care that the Pattern provided sufficient illumination to take care of the business at hand. I found the damned thing spooky, cold and downright intimidating. Having an extra natural light near at hand made me feel a lot better in its presence.

I studied that intricate mass of curved lines as I moved to the corner where they began. I had quieted Frakir but I had not entirely subdued my own apprehensions. If it were a response of the Logrus within me, I wondered whether my reaction to the Logrus itself would be worse were I to go back and essay it again, now that I bore the Pattern as well. Fruitless speculation. . . .

I tried to relax. I breathed deeply. I shut my eyes for a moment. I bent my knees. I lowered my shoulders. No use waiting any longer. . . .

I opened my eyes and set my foot upon the Pattern. Immediately, sparks rose about my foot. I took another step. More sparks. A tiny crackling noise. Another step. A bit of resistance as I moved again. . . .

It all came back to me—everything I had felt the first time through: the chill, the small shocks, the easy areas and the difficult ones. There was a map of the Pattern somewhere inside me, and it was almost as if I read from it as I moved along that first curve, resistance rising, sparks flying, my hair stirring, the crackling, a kind of vibration. . . .

I reached the First Veil, and it was like walking in a wind tunnel. Every movement involved heavy effort. Resolve, though; that was all that it really took. If I just kept pushing I would advance, albeit slowly. The trick was not to stop. Starting again could be horrible, and in some places impossible. Steady pressure was all that was required just now. A few moments more and I would be through. The going would be easier. It was the Second Veil that was the real killer. . . .

Turn, turn. . . .

I was through. I knew the way would be easy now for a time. I began to stride with a bit of confidence. Perhaps Flora had been right. This part seemed a little less difficult than it had the first time. I negotiated a long curve, then a sharp switchback. The sparks reached up to my boottops now. My mind was flooded with April thirtieths, with family politics in the Courts, where people dueled and died as the succession to the succession to the succession wound and shifted its intricate way through blood rituals of status and elevation. No more. I was done with all that. Push it away. They might be a lot politer about it, but more blood was spilled there than in Amber, and for the damnedest small advantages over one's fellows. . . .

I gritted my teeth. It was hard to keep my mind focused on the task at hand. Part of the effect, of course. I remembered that too, now. Another step. . . . Tingling sensations all the way up my legs. . . . The crackling sounds as loud as a storm to me. . . . One foot in front of the other. . . . Pick them up, put them down. . . . Hair standing on end now. . . . Turn. . . . Push. . . . Bringing the Starburst in before an autumn squall, Luke running the sails, wind like the breath of dragons at our back. . . . Three more steps and resistance rises. . . .

I am upon the Second Veil, and it is suddenly as if I am trying to push a car out of a muddy ditch. . . . All my strength goes forward, and the return on it is infinitesimal. I move with glacial slowness and the sparks are about my waist. I am blue flame. . . .

My mind is abruptly stripped of distraction. Even Time goes away and leaves me alone. There is only this pastless, nameless thing I am become, striving with its entire being against the inertia of all its days—an equation so finely balanced that I should be frozen here in mid-stride forever, save that this cancellation of masses and forces leaves the will unimpaired, purifies it in a way, so that the process of progress seems to transcend the physical striving. . . .

Another step, and another, and I am through, and ages older and moving again, and I know that I am going to make it despite the fact that I am approaching the Grand Curve, which is tough and tricky and long. Not at all like the Logrus. The power here is synthetic, not analytic. . . .

The universe seemed to wheel about me. Each step here made me feel as if I were fading and coming back into focus, being broken down and reassembled, scattered and gathered, dying and reviving. . . .

Outward. Onward. Three more curves then, followed by a straight line. I pushed ahead. Dizzy, nauseated. Soaking wet. End of the line. A series of arcs. Turn. Turn. Turn again. . . .

I knew that I was coming up to the Final Veil when the sparks rose to become a cage of lightnings and my feet began to drag again. The stillness and the terrible pushing. . . .

But this time I felt somehow fortified, and I drove onward knowing that I would win through. . . .

I made it, shaking, and only a single short arc remained. Those final three steps may well be the worst, however. It is as if, having gotten to know you this well, the Pattern is reluctant to release you. I fought it here, my ankles sore as at any race's end. Two steps. . . . Three—

Off. Standing still. Panting and shuddering. Peace. Gone the static. Gone the sparks. If that didn't wash off the blue stones' vibes I didn't know what would.

Now—well, in a minute—I could go anywhere. From this point, in this moment of empowerment, I could command the Pattern to transport me anywhere and I would be there delivered. Hardly a thing to waste to, say, save myself a walk up the spiral staircase and back to my rooms. No. I had other plans. In a minute. . . .

I adjusted my apparel, ran my hand through my hair, checked my weapons and my hidden Trump, waited for the pounding of my pulse to subside.

Luke had sustained his injuries in a battle at the Keep of the Four Worlds, fighting with his former friend and ally Dalt, the mercenary, son of the Desacratrix. Dalt meant little to me save as a possible obstacle, in that he now seemed in the employ of the keeper of the Keep. But even allowing for any time differential—which was probably not that great—I had seen him fairly soon following his fight with Luke. Which seemed to indicate that he was at the Keep when I had reached him via his Trump.

Okay.

I tried to recall it, my memory of the room where I had reached Dalt. It was pretty sketchy. What was the minimum amount of data the Pattern required in order to operate? I recalled the texture of the stone wall, the shape of the small window, a bit of worn tapestry upon the wall, strewn rushes on the floor; a low bench and a stool had come into view to his rear when Dalt had moved, a crack in the wall above them—and a bit of cobweb. . . .

I formed the image as sharply as I could. I willed myself there. I wanted to be in that place. . . .

And I was.

I turned around quickly, my hand on the hilt of my blade, but I was alone in the chamber. I saw a bed and an armoire, a small writing table, a storage chest, none of which had been in my line of sight during my brief view of the place. Daylight shone through the small window.

I crossed the room to its single door and stood there for a long while, listening. There was only silence on the other side. I opened it a crack—it swung to the left—and looked upon a long, empty hallway. I eased the door farther open. There was a stairway directly across from me, leading down. To my left was a blank wall. I stepped outside and closed the door. Go down or go right? There were several windows on both sides of the hallway. I moved to the nearest one, which was to my right, and looked out.

I saw that I was near to the lower corner of a rectangular courtyard, more buildings across the way and to my right and left, all of them connected at the corners save for an opening to the upper right which seemed as if it led to another courtyard where a very large structure rose beyond the buildings directly across from me. There were perhaps a dozen troops in the courtyard below, disposed near various entranceways, though not giving the appearance of being formally on guard—that is, they were engaged in cleaning and repairing their gear. Two of them were heavily bandaged. Still, most seemed in such a state that they could leap to service fairly quickly.

At the yard's far end was a strange bit of flotsam, looking like a large broken kite, which seemed somehow familiar. I decided to head along the hallway, which paralleled the courtyard, for it seemed that this would take me into those buildings along the farther edge of the perimeter and probably give me a view into the next yard.

I moved along the hallway, alert to any sounds of activity. There was nothing but silence as I advanced to the corner. I waited there for a long while, listening.

In that I heard nothing, I rounded the corner then, and froze. So did the man seated on the windowsill to the right. He wore a chain mail shirt, a leather cap, leather leggings and boots. There was a heavy blade at his side, but it was a dagger that he held in his hand, apparently giving himself a manicure. He looked as surprised as I felt when his head jerked in my direction.

"Who are you?" he asked.

His shoulders straightened and he lowered his hands as if to push himself from his perch and into a standing position.

Embarrassing to both of us. He seemed to be a guard. Whereas alertness or attempted stealth might have betrayed him to Frakir or myself, sloth had provided him with excellent concealment and me with a small dilemma. I was sure I couldn't bluff him, or trust to the result if I seemed to. I did not wish to attack him and create a lot of noise. This narrowed my choices. I could kill him quickly and silently with a neat little cardiac-arrest spell I had hanging in front of me. But I value life too highly to waste it when there is no need. So, as much as I hated to spend another spell that I carried this soon, I spoke the word that caused my hand to move reflexively through an accompanying gesture, and I had a glimpse of the Logrus as its force pulsed through me. The man closed his eyes and slumped back against the casement. I adjusted his position against slippage and left him snoring peacefully, the dagger still in his hand. Besides, I might have a greater need for the cardiac-arrest spell later.

The corridor entered some sort of gallery ahead, which seemed to bulge in both directions. In that I could not see what lay at either hand beyond a certain point, I knew that I would have to expend another spell sooner than I might wish. I spoke the word for my invisibility spell, and the world grew several shades darker. I had been hoping to get a little farther before I had to use it, since it was only good for about twenty minutes and I had no idea where my prize might lie. But I couldn't afford to take chances. I hurried along and passed into the gallery, which proved empty.

I learned a little more geography in that place, though. I had a view from there into the next courtyard, and it was gigantic. It contained the massive structure I had glimpsed from the other side. It was a huge, solidly built fortress; it appeared to have only one entrance, and that well guarded. From the opposite side of the gallery, I saw that there was also an outer courtyard, leading up to high, well-fortified walls.

I departed the gallery and sought a flight of stairs, almost certain that that hulking gray-stone structure was the place I should be searching. It had an aura of magic about it that I could feel down to my toes.

I jogged along the hallway, took a turn and saw a guard at the head of a stairway. If he felt anything of my passage it was only the breeze stirred by my cloak. I rushed down the stairs. There was an adit at its foot, leading to another corridor—a dark one—off to the left; and there was a heavy ironbound door directly before me, in the wall facing the inner courtyard.

I pushed the door open, passed through and stepped aside quickly, for a guard had turned, stared and was beginning to approach. I avoided him and moved toward the citadel. A focus of powers, Luke had said. Yes. I could feel this more strongly the closer I got to the place. I did not have time to try to figure out how to deal with them, to channel them. Anyway, I'd brought along my private stock.

When I neared the wall I cut to the left. A quick circuit was in order, for informational purposes. Partway around it, I saw that my guess that there was only one apparent entrance was correct. Also, there were no windows in its walls lower than about thirty feet. There was a high, spiked metal fence about the place, and a pit on the inside of the fence. The thing that most surprised me was not a feature of the structure, however. On its far side, near the wall, were two more of the large broken kites and three relatively intact ones. The matter of context no longer clouded my perception—not with the unbroken ones before me. They were hang gliders. I was eager to take a closer look at them, but time was running on my invisibility and I couldn't afford the detour. I hurried the rest of the way around and studied the gate.

The gate to the fence was closed and flanked by two guards. Several paces beyond it was a removable wooden bridge, reinforced with metal strapping, in place across the ditch. There were large eye bolts at its corners, and there was a winch built into the wall above the gate; the winch bore four chains terminating in hooks. I wondered how heavy the bridge was. The door to the citadel was recessed about three feet into the stone wall, and it was high, wide and plated, looking as if it could withstand a battering ram's pounding for a good long while.

I approached the gate to the fence and studied it. No lock on it—just a simple hand-operated latching mechanism. I could open it, run through, dash across the span and be at the big door before the guards had any idea as to what might be going on. On the other hand, considering the nature of the place, they might well have had some instruction as to the possibility of an unnatural attack. If so, it would not be necessary for them to see me if they responded quickly and cornered me in the alcove. And I'd a feeling the heavy door inside was not unlocked.

I mused for several moments, sorting through my spells. I also checked again on the position of the six or eight other people in the yard. None were too near, none moving in this direction. . . .

I advanced upon the guards quietly and placed Frakir on the shoulder of the man to my left with an order for a quick choke. Three rapid steps to the right, then, and I struck the other guard on the left side of his neck with the edge of my hand. I caught him beneath the armpits, to prevent the rattling a fall would produce, and lowered him to his rump, back against the fence, to the right of the gate. Behind me, though, I heard the clatter of the other man's scabbard against the fence as he slumped, clutching at his throat. I hurried to him, guided him the rest of the way to the ground and removed Frakir. A quick glance about showed me that two other men across the courtyard were now looking in this direction. Damn.

I unlatched the gate, slipped within, closed it and latched it behind me. I hurried across the bridge then and looked back. The two men I had noticed were now headed in this direction. Therefore, I was immediately presented with another choice. I decided to see how arduous the more strategically sound one might be.

Squatting, I caught hold of the nearest corner of the bridge— to my right. The ditch it spanned seemed something like twelve feet in depth, and it was almost twice that in width.

I began straightening my legs. Damned heavy, but the thing creaked and my corner rose several inches. I held it there for a moment, got control of my breathing and tried again. More creaking and a few more inches. Again.... My hands hurt where the edges pressed into them. My arms felt as if they were being slowly wrenched from their sockets. As I straightened my legs and strained upward with even greater exertion, I wondered how many people fail in robust undertakings because of sudden lower back problems. I guess they're the ones you don't hear about. I could feel my heart pounding as if it filled my entire chest. My corner was now about a foot above the ground, but the edge to my left was still touching. I strained again, feeling the perspiration appear as if by magic across my brow and under my arms. Breathe.... Up!

It went to knee level, then above. The corner to my left was finally raised. I heard the voices of the two approaching men— loud, excited—they were hurrying now. I began edging to my left, dragging the whole structure with me. The corner directly across from me moved outward as I did so. Good. I kept moving. The corner to my left was now a couple of feet out over the chasm. I felt fiery pains all the way up my arms and into my shoulders and neck. Farther....

The men were at the gate now, but they paused to examine the fallen guards. Good, again. I still wasn't certain that the bridge might not catch and hold if I were to drop it. It had to slip into the chasm, or I was making myself a candidate for disk surgery for nothing. Left....

It began swaying in my grip, tipping to the right. I could tell that it was going to slip from my control in a few moments. Left again, left ... almost.... The men had turned their attention from the fallen guards to the moving bridge now and were fumbling at the latch. Two more were rushing to join them from across the way, and I heard a series of shouts. Another step. The thing was really slipping now. I wasn't going to be able to hold it.... One more step....

Let go and get back!

My corner crashed against the edge of the chasm, but the wood splintered and the edge gave way and I kept retreating. The span flopped over as it fell, struck against the far side twice and hit the bottom with a terrific crash. My arms hung at my sides, useless for the moment.

I turned and headed for the doorway. My spell was still holding, so at least I was not a target for any hurled missiles from the other side of the moat.

When I got to the door it took all that I had of effort to raise my arms to the big ring on the right-hand side and catch hold of it. But nothing happened when I pulled. The thing was secured. I had expected that, though, and was prepared. I'd had to try first, however. I do not spend my spells lightly.

I spoke the words, three of them this time—less elegant because it was a sloppy spell, though it possessed immense force.

My entire body shook as the door exploded inward as if kicked by a giant wearing a steel-toed boot. I entered immediately and was immediately confused as my eyes adjusted to the dimness. I was in a two-story-high hall. Stairways rose to the right and the left ahead of me, curving inward toward a railed landing, the terminus of a second-floor hallway. There was another hallway below it, directly across from me. Two stairways also headed downward, to the rear of those which ascended. Decisions, decisions....

In the center of the room was a black stone fountain, spraying flames—not water—into the air; the fire descended into the font's basin, where it swirled and danced. The flames were red and orange in the air, white and yellow below, rippling. A feeling of power filled the chamber. Anyone who could control the forces loose in this place would be a formidable opponent indeed. With luck, I might not have to discover how formidable.

I almost wasted a special attack when I became aware of the two figures in the corner, off to my right. But they hadn't stirred at all. They were unnaturally still. Statues, of course....

I was trying to decide whether to go up, go down or move straight ahead, and I'd just about decided to descend, on the theory that there is some sort of instinct to imprison enemies in dank, below-ground quarters, when something about the two statues drew my attention again. My vision having adjusted somewhat, I could now make out that one was a white-haired man, the other a dark-haired woman. I rubbed my eyes, not realizing for several seconds that I had seen the outline of my hand. My invisibility spell was dissipating. . . .

I moved toward the figures. The fact that the old man was holding a couple of cloaks and hats should have been the tipoff. But I raised the skirt of his dark blue robe anyway. In the suddenly brighter light from the fountain I saw where the name RINALDO had been carved into his right leg. Nasty little kid, that.

The woman at his side was Jasra, saving me the problem of seeking her amid rodents below. Her arms were also outstretched, as in a warding gesture, and someone had hung a pale blue umbrella upon the left and a light gray London Fog raincoat upon the right; the matching rain hat was on her head, at a lopsided angle. Her face had been painted like a clown's and someone had pinned a pair of yellow tassels to the front of her green blouse.

The light behind me flared even more brightly, and I turned to see what was going on. The fountain, it turned out, was now spewing its liquid-like fires a full twenty feet into the air. They descended to overflow the basin and spread outward across the flagged floor. A major rivulet was headed in my direction. At that point, a soft chuckle caused me to look upward.

Wearing a dark robe, cowl and gauntlets, the wizard of the cobalt mask stood on the landing above me, one hand on the railing, the other pointed toward the fountain. In that I had anticipated our meeting on this expedition, I was not unprepared for the encounter. As the flames leaped even higher, forming a great bright tower that almost immediately began to bend and then topple toward me, I raised my arms in a wide gesture and spoke the word for the most appropriate of the three defensive spells I had hung earlier.

Air currents began to stir, powered by the Logrus, almost immediately achieving gale force and sending the flames back away from me. I adjusted my position then so that they were blown toward the wizard upstairs. Instantly, he gestured, and the flames fell back within the fountain, subsiding to the barest glowing trickle.

Okay. A draw. I had not come here to have it out with this guy. I had come to finesse Luke by rescuing Jasra on my own. Once she was my prisoner, Amber would sure as hell be safe from anything Luke had in mind. I found myself wondering, though, about this wizard, as my winds died down and the chuckle came again: Was he using spells, as I was? Or, living in the midst of a power source such as this, was he able to control the forces directly and shape them as he chose? If it were the latter, which I suspected, then he had a virtually inexhaustible source of tricks up his sleeve, so that in any full-scale competition on his turf I would eventually be reduced to flight or to calling in the nukes—that is, summoning Chaos itself to utterly reduce everything in the area—and this was a thing I was not about to do, destroying all the mysteries, including that of the wizard's identity, rather than solving them for answers that might be essential to Amber's well-being.

A shining metallic spear materialized in midair before the wizard, hung a moment, then flashed toward me. I used my second defensive spell, summoning a shield that turned it aside.

The only alternative I could see to my dueling with spells or blasting the place with Chaos would be for me to learn to control the forces here myself and try beating this guy at his own game. No time for practice now, though; I'd a job to do as soon as I could buy a few moments in which to get it done. Sooner or later, however, it seemed that we would have to have a full confrontation—since he seemed to have it in for me, and may well even have been the motive force behind the attack by the clumsy werewolf in the woods.

And I was not hot on taking chances to explore the power here further at this point—not if Jasra had been good enough to beat the original master of this place, Sharu Garrul, and then this guy had been good enough to beat Jasra. I'd give a lot, though, to know why he had it in for me. . . .

So, "What do you want, anyway?" I called out.

Immediately, that metallic voice replied, "Your blood, your soul, your mind and your body."

"What about my stamp collection?" I hollered back. "Do I get to keep the First Day Covers?"

I moved over beside Jasra and threw my right arm about her shoulders.

"What do you want with that one, funny man?" the wizard asked. "She is the most worthless property in this place."

"Then why should you object to my taking her off your hands?"

"You collect stamps. I collect presumptuous sorcerers. She's mine, and you're next."

I felt the power rising against me again even as I shouted, "What have you got against your brothers and sisters in the Art?" There was no reply, but the air about me was suddenly filled with sharp, spinning shapes—knives, ax blades, throwing stars, broken bottles. I spoke the word for my final defense, the Curtain of Chaos, raising a chittering, smoky screen about us. The sharp items hurtling in our direction were instantly reduced to cosmic dust on coming into contact with it.

Above the din of this engagement I cried out, "By what name shall I call you?"

"Mask!" was the wizard's immediate reply—not very original, I thought. I'd half expected a John D. MacDonald appellation—Nightmare Mauve or Cobalt Casque, perhaps. Oh, well.

I had just used my last defensive spell. I had also just raised my left arm so that that portion of my sleeve bearing the Amber Trump now hung within my field of vision. I had cut things a bit fine, but I had not yet played my full hand. So far, I had run a completely defensive show, and I was rather proud of the spell I had kept in reserve.

"She'll do you no good, that one," Mask said, as both our spells subsided and he prepared to strike again.

"Have a nice day, anyway," I said, and I rotated my wrists, pointed my fingers to direct the flow and spoke the word that beat him to the punch.

"An eye for an eye!" I called out, as the contents of an entire florist shop fell upon Mask, completely burying him in the biggest damned bouquet I'd ever seen. Smelled nice, too.

There was silence and a subsidence of forces as I regarded the Trump, reached through it. Just as the contact was achieved there was a disturbance in the floral display and Mask rose through it, like the Allegory of Spring.

I was probably already fading from his view as he said, "I'll have you yet."

"And sweets to the sweet," I replied, then spoke the word that completed the spell, dropping a load of manure upon him.

I stepped through into the main hall of Amber, bearing Jasra with me. Martin stood near a sideboard, a glass of wine in his hand, talking with Bors, the falconer. He grew silent at Bors's wide-eyed stare in my direction, then turned and stared himself.

I set Jasra on her feet beside the doorway. I was not about to screw around with the spell on her right now—and I was not at all sure what I'd do with her if I released her from it. So I hung my cloak on her, went over to the sideboard and poured myself a glass of wine, nodding to Bors and Martin as I passed.

I drained the glass, put it down, then said to them, "Whatever you do, don't carve your initials on her." Then I went and found a sofa in a room to the east, stretched out on it and closed my eyes. Like a bridge over troubled waters. Some days are diamonds. Where have all the flowers gone?

Something like that.

12

There was a lot of smoke, a giant worm and many flashes of colored light. Every sound was born into form, blazed to its peak, faded as it waned. Lightninglike stabs of existence, these—called from, returning to, Shadow. The worm went on forever. The dog-headed flowers snapped at me but later wagged their leaves. The flowing smoke halted before a skyhooked traffic light. The worm—no, caterpillar—smiled. A slow, blinding rain began, and all the drifting drops were faceted. . . .

What is wrong with this picture? something within me asked.

I gave up, because I couldn't be sure. Though I'd a vague feeling the occasional landscape shouldn't be flowing the way that it did. . . .

"Oh, man! Merle. . . ."

What did Luke want now? Why wouldn't he get off my case? Always a new problem.

"Look at that, will you?"

I watched where a series of bright bounding balls—or maybe they were comets—wove a tapestry of light. It fell upon the forest of umbrellas.

"Luke—" I began, but one of the dog-headed flowers bit a hand I'd forgotten about, and everything nearby cracked as if it were painted on glass through which a shot had just passed. There was a rainbow beyond—

"Merle! Merle!"

It was Droppa shaking my shoulder, my suddenly opened eyes showed me. And there was a damp place on the sofa where my head was resting.

I propped myself on an elbow. I rubbed my eyes.

"Droppa.... What—?"

"I don't know," he told me.

"What don't you know? I mean. . . . Hell! What happened?"

"I was sitting in that chair," he said, with a gesture, "waiting for you to wake up. Martin had told me you were here. I was just going to tell you that Random wanted to see you when you got back."

I nodded, then noticed that my hand was oozing blood—from the place where the flower had bitten me.

"How long was I out?"

"Twenty minutes, maybe."

I swung my feet to the floor, sat up. "So why'd you decide to wake me?"

"You were trumping out," he said.

"Trumping out? While I was asleep? It doesn't work that way. Are you sure—"

"I am, unfortunately, sober at the moment," he said. "You got that rainbow glow and you started to soften around the edges and fade. Thought I'd better wake you then and ask if that's what you really had in mind. What've you been drinking, spot remover?"

"No," I said.

"I tried it on my dog once. . . ."

"Dreams," I said, massaging my temples, which had begun throbbing. "That's all. Dreams."

"The kind other people can see, too? Like DTs *à deux?*"

"That's not what I meant."

"We'd better go see Random." He started to turn toward the doorway.

I shook my head. "Not yet. I'm just going to sit here and collect myself. Something's wrong."

When I glanced at him I saw that his eyes were wide, and he was staring past me. I turned.

The wall at my back seemed to be melting, as if it were cast of wax and had been set too near a fire.

"It appears to be alarums and excursions time," Droppa remarked. "Help!"

And he was across the room and out of the door, screaming.

Three eyeblinks later the wall was normal again in every way, but I was trembling. What the hell was going on? Had Mask managed to lay a spell on me before I'd cut out? If so, where was it headed?

I rose to my feet and turned in a slow circle. Everything seemed to be in place now. I knew that it could not have been anything as simple as hallucination born of all my recent stresses, since Droppa had seen it too. So I was not cracking up. This was something else—and whatever it was, I felt that it was still lurking nearby. There was a certain unnatural clarity to the air now, and every object seemed unusually vivid within it.

I made a quick circuit of the room, not knowing what I was really seeking. Not surprisingly, therefore, I did not find it. I stepped outside then. Whatever the problem, could it spring from something I had brought back with me? Might Jasra, stiff and gaudy, have been a Trojan horse?

I headed for the main hall. A dozen steps along the way, a lopsided gridwork of light appeared before me. I forced myself to continue, and it receded as I advanced, changing shape as it did so.

"Merle, come on!" Luke's voice, Luke himself nowhere in sight.

"Where?" I called out, not slowing.

No answer, but the gridwork split down the middle and its two halves swung away from me like a pair of shutters. They opened onto a near-blinding light; within it, I thought I glimpsed a rabbit. Then, abruptly, the vision was gone, and the only thing that saved me from believing everything was normal again was several seconds' worth of Luke's sourceless laughter.

I ran. Was it really Luke who was the enemy, as I had been warned repeatedly? Had I somehow been manipulated through everything which had happened recently, solely for the purpose of freeing his mother from the Keep of the Four Worlds? And now that she was safe had he the temerity to invade Amber herself and summon me to a sorcerous duel the terms of which I did not even understand?

No, I could not believe it. I was certain he did not possess that sort of power. But even if he did, he wouldn't dare try it—not with Jasra my hostage.

As I rushed along I heard him again—from everywhere, from nowhere. This time he was singing. He had a powerful baritone voice, and the song was "Auld Lang Syne." What sort of irony did this represent?

I burst into the main hall. Martin and Bors had departed. I saw their empty glasses on the sideboard near which they had been standing. And near the other door—? Yes, near the other door Jasra remained, erect, unchanged, still holding my cloak.

"Okay, Luke! Let's have it out!" I cried. "Cut the crap and let's settle this business!"

"Huh?"

The singing stopped abruptly.

I crossed slowly to Jasra, studying her as I went. Completely unchanged, save for a hat someone had added to her other hand. From somewhere else in the palace, I heard a shout. Maybe it was Droppa still alaruming.

"Luke, wherever you are," I said, "if you can hear me, if you can see me, take a good look and listen: I've got her here. See? Whatever you're planning, bear that in mind."

The room rippled violently, as if I were standing in the midst of an unframed painting someone had just decided to give a shake, to crinkle and then draw taut.

"Well?"

Nothing.

Then, a chuckle.

"My mother the hat rack. . . . Well, well. Hey, thanks, buddy. Good show. Couldn't reach you earlier. Didn't know you'd gone in. They slaughtered us. Took some mercs in on hang gliders, rode the thermals. They were ready, though. Took us out. Don't remember exactly then. . . . Hurts!"

"You okay?"

There came something like a sob, just as Random and Droppa entered the hall, the lank form of Benedict silent as death at their back.

"Merle!" Random called to me. "What's going on?"

I shook my head. "Don't know," I said.

"Sure, I'll buy you a drink," Luke's voice came very faintly.

A fiery blizzard swept through the center of the hall. It lasted only a moment, and then a large rectangle appeared in its place.

"You're the sorcerer," Random said. "Do something!"

"I don't know what the hell it is," I replied. "I've never seen anything like it. It's like magic gone wild."

An outline began to appear within the rectangle, human. Its form settled and took on features, garments. . . . It was a Trump—a giant Trump—hanging in the middle of the air, solidifying. It was—

Me. I regarded my own features and they looked back at me. I noted that I was smiling.

"C'mon, Merle. Join the party," I heard Luke say, and the Trump began to rotate slowly upon its vertical axis.

Sounds, as of glass bells, filled the hall.

The huge card turned until I viewed it edge-on, a black slash. Then the dark line widened with a ripple, like parting curtains, and I saw colored patches of intense light sliding beyond it. I also saw the caterpillar, puffing on a hookah, and fat umbrellas and a bright, shiny rail—

A hand emerged from the slit. "Right this way."

I heard a sharp intake of breath from Random.

Benedict's blade was suddenly pointed at the tableau. But Random laid his hand on his shoulder and said, "No."

There was a strange, disconnected sort of music hanging in the air now; it seemed somehow appropriate.

"C'mon, Merle."

"You coming or going?" I asked.

"Both."

"You made me a promise, Luke: a piece of information for your mother's rescue," I said. "Well, I've got her here. What's the secret?"

"Something vital to your well-being?" he asked slowly.

"Vital to the safety of Amber is what you'd said."

"Oh, *that* secret."

"I'd be glad to have the other one too."

"Sorry. One secret is all I'm selling. Which will it be?"

"The safety of Amber," I answered.

"Dalt," he replied.

"What of him?"

"Deela the Desacratrix was his mother—"

"I already know that."

"—and she'd been Oberon's prisoner nine months before he was born. He raped her. That's why Dalt's got it in for you guys."

"Bullshit!" I said.

"That's what I told him when I'd heard the story one time too many. I dared him to walk the Pattern in the sky then."

"And?"

"He did."

"Oh."

"I just learned that story recently," Random said, "from an emissary I'd sent to Kashfa. I didn't know about his taking the Pattern, though."

"If you knew, I still owe you," Luke said slowly, almost distractedly. "Okay, here's more: Dalt visited me on the shadow Earth after that. He's the one who raided my warehouse, stole a stock of weapons and special ammo. Burnt the place after that to cover the theft. I found witnesses, though. He'll be along—any time. Who knows when?"

"Another relative coming to visit," Random said. "Why couldn't I have been an only child?"

"Make what you will of it," Luke added. "We're square now. Give me a hand!"

"You coming through?"

He laughed, and the whole hall seemed to lurch. The opening in the air hung before me and the hand clasped my own. Something felt very wrong.

I tried to draw him to me, but felt myself drawn toward him instead. There was a mad power I could not fight, and the universe seemed to twist as it took hold of me. Constellations parted before me and I saw the bright railing again. Luke's booted foot rested upon it.

From some distant point to the rear I heard Random shouting, "B-twelve! B-twelve! And out!"

. . . And then I couldn't recall what the problem had been. It seemed a wonderful place. Silly of me to have mistaken the mushrooms for umbrellas, though. . . .

I put my own foot up on the rail as the Hatter poured me a drink and topped off Luke's. Luke gestured to his left and the March Hare got a refill too. Humpty was fine, balanced there near the end of things. Tweedledum, Tweedledee, the Dodo and the Frog Footman kept the music moving. And the Caterpillar just kept puffing away.

Luke clapped me on the shoulder, and there was something I wanted to remember but it kept slipping out of sight.

"I'm okay now," Luke said. "Everything's okay."

"No, there's something. . . . I can't recall. . . ."

He raised his tankard, clanked it against my own. "Enjoy!" he said. "Life is a cabaret, old chum!"

The cat on the stool beside me just kept grinning.

SIGN
OF
CHAOS

To Phil Cleverley
and our seasons in the sun:
Thanks for all the kokyu nages.

1

I felt vaguely uneasy, though I couldn't say why. It did not seem all that unusual to be drinking with a White Rabbit, a short guy who resembled Bertrand Russell, a grinning Cat, and my old friend Luke Raynard, who was singing Irish ballads while a peculiar landscape shifted from mural to reality at his back. Well, I was impressed by the huge blue Caterpillar smoking the hookah atop the giant mushroom because I know how hard it is to keep a water pipe lit. Still, that wasn't it. It was a convivial scene, and Luke was known to keep pretty strange company on occasion. So why should I feel uneasy?

The beer was good and there was even a free lunch. The demons tormenting the red-haired woman tied to the stake had been so shiny they'd hurt to look at. Gone now, but the whole thing had been beautiful. Everything was beautiful. When Luke sang of Galway Bay it had been so sparkling and lovely that I'd wanted to dive in and lose myself there. Sad, too.

Something to do with the feeling. . . . Yes. Funny thought. When Luke sang a sad song I felt melancholy. When it was a happy one I was greatly cheered. There seemed an unusual amount of empathy in the air. No matter, I guess. The light show was superb. . . .

I sipped my drink and watched Humpty teeter, there at the end of the bar. For a moment I tried to remember when I'd come into this place, but that cylinder wasn't hitting. It would come to me, eventually. Nice party. . . .

I watched and listened and tasted and felt, and it was all great.

Anything that caught my attention was fascinating. Was there something I'd wanted to ask Luke? It seemed there was, but he was busy singing and I couldn't think of it now, anyway.

What had I been doing before I'd come into this place? Trying to recall just didn't seem worth the effort either. Not when everything was so interesting right here and now.

It seemed that it might have been something important, though. Could that be why I felt uneasy? Might it be there was business I had left unfinished and should be getting back to?

I turned to ask the Cat but he was fading again, still seeming vastly amused. It occurred to me then that I, too, could do that. Fade, I mean, and go someplace else. Was that how I had come here and how I might depart? Possibly. I put down my drink and rubbed my eyes and my temples. Things seemed to be swimming inside my head, too.

I suddenly recalled a picture of me. On a giant card. A Trump. Yes. That was how I'd gotten here. Through the card. . . .

A hand fell upon my shoulder and I turned. It belonged to Luke, who grinned at me as he edged up to the bar for a refill.

"Great party, huh?" he said.

"Yeah, great. How'd you find this place?" I asked him.

He shrugged. "I forget. Who cares?"

He turned away, a brief blizzard of crystals swirling between us. The Caterpillar exhaled a purple cloud. A blue moon was rising.

What is wrong with this picture? I asked myself.

I had a sudden feeling that my critical faculty had been shot off in the war, because I couldn't focus on the anomalies I felt must be present. I knew that I was caught up in the moment, but I couldn't see my way clear.

I was caught up. . . .

I was caught. . . .

How?

Well. . . . It had all started when I'd shaken my own hand. No. Wrong. That sounds like Zen and that's not how it was. The hand I shook emerged from the space occupied by the image of myself on the card that went away. Yes, that was it. . . . After a fashion.

I clenched my teeth. The music began again. There came a soft scraping sound near to my hand on the bar. When I looked I saw that my tankard had been refilled. Maybe I'd had too much already. Maybe that's what kept getting in the way of my thinking. I turned away. I looked off to my left, past the place where the mural on the wall became the real landscape. Did that make me a part of the mural? I wondered suddenly.

No matter. If I couldn't think here. . . . I began running . . . to the left. Something about this place was messing with my head, and it seemed impossible to consider the process while I was a part of it. I had to get away in order to think straight, to determine what was going on.

I was across the bar and into that interface area where the painted rocks and trees became three-dimensional. I pumped my arms as I dug in. I heard the wind without feeling it.

Nothing that lay before me seemed any nearer. I was moving, but—

Luke began singing again.

I halted. I turned, slowly, because it sounded as if he were standing practically beside me. He was. I was only a few paces removed from the bar. Luke smiled and kept singing.

"What's going on?" I asked the Caterpillar.

"You're looped in Luke's loop," it replied.

"Come again?" I said.

It blew a blue smoke ring, sighed softly, and said, "Luke's locked in a loop and you're lost in the lyrics. That's all."

"How'd it happen?" I asked.

"I have no idea," it replied.

"Uh, how does one get unlooped?"

"Couldn't tell you that either."

I turned to the Cat, who was coalescing about his grin once again.

"I don't suppose you'd know—" I began.

"I saw him come in and I saw you come in later," said the Cat, smirking. "And even for this place your arrivals were somewhat . . . unusual—leading me to conclude that at least one of you is associated with magic."

I nodded.

"Your own comings and goings might give one pause," I observed.

"I keep my paws to myself," he replied. "Which is more than Luke can say."

"What do you mean?"

"He's caught in a contagious trap."

"How does it work?" I asked.

But he was gone again, and this time the grin went too.
Contagious trap? That seemed to indicate that the problem
was Luke's, and that I had been sucked into it in some fashion.
This felt right, though it still gave me no idea as to what the problem was or what I might do about it.

I reached for my tankard. If I couldn't solve my problem, I
might as well enjoy it. As I took a slow sip I became aware of a
strange pair of pale, burning eyes gazing into my own. I hadn't noticed them before, and the thing that made them strange was that
they occupied a shadowy corner of the mural across the room
from me—that, and the fact that they were moving, drifting
slowly to my left.

It was kind of fascinating, when I lost sight of the eyes but was
still able to follow whatever it was from the swaying of grasses as
it passed into the area toward which I had been headed earlier.
And far, far off to my right—beyond Luke—I now detected a slim
gentleman in a dark jacket, palette and brush in hand, who was
slowly extending the mural. I took another sip and returned my attention to the progress of whatever it was that had moved from flat
reality to 3-D. A gunmetal snout protruded from between a rock
and a shrub; the pale eyes blazed above it; blue saliva dripped
from the dark muzzle and steamed upon the ground. It was either
quite short or very crouched, and I couldn't make up my mind
whether it was the entire crowd of us that it was studying or me in
particular. I leaned to one side and caught Humpty by the belt or
the necktie, whichever it was, just as he was about to slump to the
side.

"Excuse me," I said. "Could you tell me what sort of creature
that is?"

I pointed just as it emerged—many—legged, long-tailed,
dark-scaled, undulating, and fast. Its claws were red, and it raised
its tail as it raced toward us.

Humpty's bleary eyes moved toward my own, drifted past.

"I am not here, sir," he began, "to remedy your zoological
ignor—My God! It's—"

It flashed across the distance, approaching rapidly. Would it
reach a spot shortly where its running would become a treadmill
operation—or had that effect only applied to me on trying to get
away from this place?

The segments of its body slid from side to side, it hissed like
a leaky pressure cooker, and steaming slaver marked its trail

from the fiction of paint. Rather than slowing, its speed seemed to increase.

My left hand jerked forward of its own volition and a series of words rose unbidden to my lips. I spoke them just as the creature crossed the interface I had been unable to pierce earlier, rearing as it upset a vacant table and bunching its members as if about to spring.

"A Bandersnatch!" someone cried.

"A frumious Bandersnatch!" Humpty corrected.

As I spoke the final word and performed the ultimate gesture, the image of the Logrus swam before my inner vision. The dark creature, having just extended its foremost talons, suddenly drew them back, clutched with them against the upper left quadrant of its breast, rolled its eyes, emitted a soft moaning sound, exhaled heavily, collapsed, fell to the floor, and rolled over onto its back, its many feet extended upward into the air.

The Cat's grin appeared above the creature. The mouth moved.

"A *dead* frumious Bandersnatch," it stated.

The grin drifted toward me, the rest of the Cat occurring about it like an afterthought.

"That was a cardiac arrest spell, wasn't it?" it inquired.

"I guess so," I said. "It was sort of a reflex. Yeah, I remember now. I did still have that spell hanging around."

"I thought so," it observed. "I was sure that there was magic involved in this party."

The image of the Logrus which had appeared to me during the spell's operation had also served the purpose of switching on a small light in the musty attic of my mind. Sorcery. Of course.

I—Merlin, son of Corwin—am a sorcerer, of a variety seldom encountered in the areas I have frequented in recent years. Lucas Raynard—also known as Prince Rinaldo of Kashfa—is himself a sorcerer, albeit of a style different than my own. And the Cat, who seemed somewhat sophisticated in these matters, could well have been correct in assessing our situation as the interior of a spell. Such a location is one of the few environments where my sensitivity and training would do little to inform me as to the nature of my predicament. This, because my faculties would also be caught up in the manifestation and subject to its forces, if the thing were at all self-consistent. It struck me as something similar to color blindness. I could think of no way of telling for certain what was going on, without outside help.

As I mused over these matters, the King's horses and men arrived beyond the swinging doors at the front of the place. The men entered and fastened lines upon the carcass of the Bandersnatch. The horses dragged the thing off. Humpty had climbed down to visit the rest room while this was going on. Upon his return he discovered that he was unable to achieve his former position atop the barstool. He shouted to the King's men to give him a hand, but they were busy guiding the defunct Bandersnatch among tables and they ignored him.

Luke strolled up, smiling.

"So that was a Bandersnatch," he observed. "I'd always wondered what they were like. Now, if we could just get a Jabberwock to stop by—"

"Sh!" cautioned the Cat. "It must be off in the mural somewhere, and likely it's been listening. Don't stir it up! It may come whiffling through the tulgey wood after your ass. Remember the jaws that bite, the claws that catch! Don't go looking for troub—"

The Cat cast a quick glance toward the wall and phased into and out of existence several times in quick succession. Ignoring this, Luke remarked, "I was just thinking of the Tenniel illustration."

The Cat materialized at the far end of the bar, downed the Hatter's drink, and said, "I hear the burbling, and eyes of flame are drifting to the left."

I glanced at the mural, and I, too, saw the fiery eyes and heard a peculiar sound.

"It could be any of a number of things," Luke remarked.

The Cat moved to a rack behind the bar and reached high up on the wall to where a strange weapon hung, shimmering and shifting in shadow. He lowered the thing and slid it along the bar; it came to rest before Luke.

"Better have the Vorpal Sword in hand, that's all I can say."

Luke laughed, but I stared fascinated at the device which looked as if it were made of moth wings and folded moonlight.

Then I heard the burbling again.

"Don't just stand there in uffish thought!" said the Cat, draining Humpty's glass and vanishing again.

Still chuckling, Luke held out his tankard for a refill. I stood there in uffish thought. The spell I had used to destroy the Bandersnatch had altered my thinking in a peculiar fashion. It seemed for a small moment in its aftermath that things were beginning to come clear in my head. I attributed this to the image of the Logrus which I had regarded briefly. And so I summoned it again.

The Sign rose before me, hovered. I held it there. I looked upon it. It seemed as if a cold wind began to blow through my mind. Drifting bits of memory were drawn together, assembled themselves into an entire fabric, were informed with understanding. Of course. . . .

The burbling grew louder and I saw the shadow of the Jabberwock gliding among distant trees, eyes like landing lights, lots of sharp edges for biting and catching. . . .

And it didn't matter a bit. For I realized now what was going on, who was responsible, how and why.

I bent over, leaning far forward, so that my knuckles just grazed the toe of my right boot.

"Luke," I said, "we've got a problem."

He turned away from the bar and glanced down at me.

"What's the matter?" he asked.

Those of the blood of Amber are capable of terrific exertions. We are also able to sustain some pretty awful beatings. So, among ourselves, these things tend to cancel out to some degree. Therefore, one must go about such matters just right if one is to attend to them at all. . . .

I brought my fist up off the floor with everything I had behind it, and I caught Luke on the side of the jaw with a blow that lifted him above the ground as it turned him and sent him sprawling across a table which collapsed, to continue sliding backward the length of the entire serving area where he finally came to a crumpled halt at the feet of the quiet Victorian-looking gentleman—who had dropped his paintbrush and stepped away quickly when Luke came skidding toward him. I raised my tankard with my left hand and poured its contents over my right fist, which felt as if I had just driven it against a mountainside. As I did this the lights grew dim and there was a moment of utter silence.

Then I slammed the mug back onto the bartop. The entire place chose that moment in which to shudder, as if from an earth tremor. Two bottles fell from a shelf, a lamp swayed, the burbling grew fainter. I glanced to my left and saw that the eerie shadow of the Jabberwock had retreated somewhat within the tulgey wood. Not only that, the painted section of the prospect now extended a good deal farther into what had seemed normal space, and it looked to be continuing its advance in that direction, freezing that corner of the world into flat immobility. It became apparent from whiffle to whiffle that the Jabberwock was now moving away, to the left, hurrying ahead of the flatness. Tweedledum, Tweedledee, the Dodo, and the Frog began packing their instruments.

I started across the bar toward Luke's sprawled form. The Caterpillar was disassembling his hookah, and I saw that his mushroom was tilted at an odd angle. The White Rabbit beat it down a hole to the rear, and I heard Humpty muttering curses as he swayed atop the bar stool he had just succeeded in mounting.

I saluted the gentleman with the palette as I approached.

"Sorry to disturb you," I said. "But believe me, this is for the better."

I raised Luke's limp form and slung him over my shoulder. A flock of playing cards flew by me. I drew away from them in their rapid passage.

"Goodness! It's frightened the Jabberwock!" the man remarked, looking past me.

"What has?" I asked, not really certain that I wished to know.

"That," he answered, gesturing toward the front of the bar.

I looked and I staggered back and I didn't blame the Jabberwock a bit.

It was a twelve-foot Fire Angel that had just entered—russet-colored, with wings like stained-glass windows—and, along with intimations of mortality, it brought me recollections of a praying mantis, with a spiked collar and thornlike claws protruding through its short fur at every suggestion of an angle. One of these, in fact, caught on and unhinged a swinging door as it came inside. It was a Chaos beast—rare, deadly, and highly intelligent. I hadn't seen one in years, and I'd no desire to see one now; also, I'd no doubt that I was the reason it was here. For a moment I regretted having wasted my cardiac arrest spell on a mere Bandersnatch— until I recalled that Fire Angels have three hearts. I glanced quickly about as it spied me, gave voice to a brief hunting wail, and advanced.

"I'd like to have had some time to speak with you," I told the artist. "I like your work. Unfortunately—"

"I understand."

"So long."

"Good luck."

I stepped down into the rabbit hole and ran, bent far forward because of the low overhead. Luke made my passage particularly awkward, especially on the turns. I heard a scrabbling noise far to the rear, with a repetition of the hunting wail. I was consoled, however, by the knowledge that the Fire Angel would actually have to enlarge sections of the tunnel in order to get by. The bad news was that it was capable of doing it. The creatures are incredibly strong and virtually indestructible.

I kept running till the floor dipped beneath my feet. Then I began falling. I reached out with my free hand to catch myself, but there was nothing to catch hold of. The bottom had fallen out. Good. That was the way I'd hoped and half-expected it would be. Luke uttered a single soft moan but did not stir.

We fell. Down, down, down, like the man said. It was a well, and either it was very deep or we were falling very slowly. There was twilight all about us, and I could not discern the walls of the shaft. My head cleared a bit further, and I knew that it would continue to do so for as long as I kept control of one variable: Luke. High in the air overhead I heard the hunting wail once again. It was followed immediately by a strange burbling sound. Frakir began pulsing softly upon my wrist again, not really telling me anything I didn't already know. So I silenced her again.

Clearer yet. I began to remember. . . . My assault on the Keep of the Four Worlds and my recovery of Luke's mother, Jasra. The attack of the werebeast. My odd visit with Vinta Bayle, who wasn't really what she seemed. . . . My dinner in Death Alley. . . . The Dweller, San Francisco, the crystal cave. . . . Clearer and clearer.

. . . And louder and louder the hunting wail of the Fire Angel above me. It must have made it through the tunnel and be descending now. Unfortunately, it possessed wings, while all I could do was fall.

I glanced upward. Couldn't make out its form, though. Things seemed darker up that way than down below. I hoped this was a sign that we were approaching something in the nature of a light at the end of the tunnel, as I couldn't think of any other way out. It was too dark to view a Trump or to distinguish enough of the passing scene to commence a shadow shift.

I felt we were drifting now, rather than falling, at a rate that might permit us to land intact. Should it seem otherwise when we neared the bottom, then a possible means of further slowing our descent came to mind—an adaptation of one of the spells I still carried with me. However, these considerations were not worth much should we be eaten on the way down—a distinct possibility, unless of course our pursuer were not all that hungry, in which case it might only dismember us. Consequently, it might become necessary to try speeding up to stay ahead of the beast—which of course would cause us to smash when we hit.

Decisions, decisions.

Luke stirred slightly upon my shoulder. I hoped he wasn't about to come around, as I didn't have time to mess with a sleep-spell and I wasn't really in a good position to slug him again. That pretty much left Frakir. But if he were borderline, then choking might serve to rouse him rather than send him back—and I did want him in decent shape. He knew too many things I didn't, things I now needed.

We passed through a slightly brighter area, and I was able to distinguish the walls of the shaft for the first time and to note that they were covered with graffiti in a language that I did not understand. I was reminded of a strange short story by Jamaica Kincaid, but it bore me no clues for deliverance. Immediately following our passage through that band of illumination, I distinguished a small spot of light far below. At almost the same moment I heard the wail once again, this time very near.

I looked up in time to behold the Fire Angel passing through the glow. But there was another shape close behind it, and it wore a vest and burbled. The Jabberwock was also on the way down, and it seemed to be making the best time of any of us. The question of its purpose was immediately prominent; as it gained, the circle of light grew and Luke stirred again. This question was quickly answered, however, as it caught up with the Fire Angel and attacked.

The whiffling, the wailing, and the burbling suddenly echoed down the shaft, along with hissing, scraping, and occasional snarls. The two beasts came together and tore at each other, eyes like dying suns, claws like bayonets, forming a hellish mandala in the pale light which now reached them from below. While this produced a round of activity too near at hand for me to feel entirely at ease, it did serve to slow them to the point where I felt I need not risk an ill-suited spell and an awkward maneuver to emerge from the tunnel in one piece.

"Argh!" Luke remarked, turning suddenly within my grasp.

"I agree," I said. "But lie still, will you? We're about to crash—"

"—and burn," he stated, twisting his head upward to regard the combatant monsters, then downward when he realized that we were falling, too. "What kind of trip is this?"

"A bad one," I answered, and then it hit me: That was exactly what it was.

The opening was even larger now, and our velocity sufficient for a bearable landing. Our reaction to the spell that I called the Giant's Slap would probably slow us to a standstill or even propel us backward. Better to collect a few bruises than become a traffic obstruction at this point.

A bad trip indeed. I was thinking of Random's words as we passed through the opening at a crazy angle, hit dirt, and rolled.

We had come to rest within a cave, near to its mouth. Tunnels ran off to the right and the left. The cave mouth was at my back. A quick glance showed it as opening upon a bright, possibly lush, and more than a little out-of-focus valley. Luke was sprawled unmoving beside me. I got to my feet immediately and caught hold of him beneath the armpits. I began dragging him back away from the dark opening from which we had just emerged. The sounds of the monstrous conflict were very near now.

Good that Luke seemed unconscious again. His condition was bad enough for any Amberite, if my guess were correct. But for one of sorcerous ability it represented a highly dangerous wild card of a sort I'd never encountered before. I wasn't at all certain how I should deal with it.

I dragged him toward the righthand tunnel because it was the smaller of the two and would theoretically be a bit easier to defend. We had barely achieved its shelter when the two beasts fell through the opening, clutching and tearing at each other. They commenced rolling about the floor of the cave, claws clicking, uttering hisses and whistles as they tore at each other. They seemed to have forgotten us entirely, and I continued our retreat until we were well back in the tunnel.

I could only assume Random's guess to be correct. After all, he was a musician and he'd played all over Shadow. Also, I couldn't come up with anything better.

I summoned the Sign of the Logrus. When I had it clear and had meshed my hands with it, I might have used it to strike at the fighting beasts. But they were paying me no heed whatsoever, and I'd no desire to attract their attention. Also, I'd no assurance that the equivalent of being hit by a two-by-four would have much effect on them. Besides, my order was ready, and filling it took precedence.

So I reached.

It took an interminable time. There was an extremely wide area of Shadow to pass through before I found what I was looking for. Then I had to do it again. And again. There were a number of things I wanted, and none of them near.

In the meantime, the combatants showed no sign of slackening, and their claws struck sparks from the cave's walls. They had cut each other in countless places and were now covered with dark gore. Luke had awakened during all of this, propped himself, and was staring fascinated at the colorful conflict. How long it might hold his attention I could not tell. It would be important for me to have him awake very soon now, and I was pleased that he had not started thinking of other matters yet.

I was cheering, by the way, for the Jabberwock. It was just a nasty beast and need not have been homing in on me in particular when it was distracted by the arrival of its exotic nemesis. The Fire Angel had been playing an entirely different game. There was no reason for a Fire Angel to be stalking about this far from Chaos unless it had been sent. They're devilish hard to capture, harder to train, and dangerous to handle. So they represent a considerable expense and hazard. One does not invest in a Fire Angel lightly. Their main purpose in life is killing, and to my knowledge no one outside the Courts of Chaos has ever employed one. They've a vast array of senses—some of them, apparently, paranormal—and they can be used as Shadow bloodhounds. They don't wander through Shadow on their own, that I know of. But a Shadow-walker can be tracked, and Fire Angels seem to be able to follow a very cold trail once they've been imprinted with the victim's identity. Now, I had been trumped to that crazy bar, and I didn't know they could follow a Trump jump, but several other possibilities occurred to me—including someone's locating me, transporting the thing to my vicinity, and turning it loose to do its business. Whatever the means, though, the attempt had the mark of the Courts upon it. Hence, my quick conversion to Jabberwock fandom.

"What's going on?" Luke asked me suddenly, and the walls of the cave faded for a moment and I heard a faint strain of music.

"It's tricky," I said. "Listen, it's time for your medicine."

I dumped out a palmful of the vitamin B12 tabs I had just brought in and uncapped the water bottle I had also summoned.

"What medicine?" he asked as I passed them to him.

"Doctor's orders," I said. "Get you back on your feet faster."

"Well, okay."

He threw all of them into his mouth and downed them with a single big drink.

"Now these."

I opened the bottle of Thorazine. They were 200 milligrams each and I didn't know how many to give him, so I decided on three. I gave him some tryptophan, too, and some phenylalanine.

He stared at the pills. The walls faded again, the music returned. A cloud of blue smoke drifted past us. Suddenly the bar came into view, back to whatever passed for normal in that place. The upset tables had been righted, Humpty still teetered, the mural went on.

"Hey, the club!" Luke exclaimed. "We ought to head back. Looks like the party's just getting going."

"First, you take your medicine."

"What's it for?"

"You got some bad shit somewhere. This is to let you down easy."

"I don't feel bad. In fact, I feel real good—"

"Take it!"

"Okay! Okay!"

He tossed off the whole fistful.

The Jabberwock and the Fire Angel seemed to be fading now—and my latest exasperated gesture in the vicinity of the bartop had encountered some resistance, though the thing was not fully solid to me yet. Suddenly, then, I noticed the Cat, whose games with substantiality somehow at this point made it seem more real than anything else in the place.

"You coming or going?" it asked.

Luke began to rise. The light grew brighter, though more diffuse.

"Uh, Luke, look over there," I said, pointing.

"Where?" he asked, turning his head.

I slugged him again.

As he collapsed, the bar began to fade. The walls of the cave phased back into focus. I heard the Cat's voice. "Going . . ." it said.

The noises returned full blast, only this time the dominant sound was a bagpipelike squeal. It was coming from the Jabberwock, who was pinned to the ground and being slashed at. I decided then to use the Fourth of July spell I had left over from my assault on the citadel. I raised my hands and spoke the words. I moved in front of Luke to block his view as I did so, and I looked away and squeezed my eyes shut as I said them. Even through closed eyes I could tell there followed a brilliant flash of light. I heard Luke say, "Hey!" but all other sounds ceased abruptly. When I looked again I saw that the two creatures lay as if stunned, unmoving, toward the far side of the small cave.

I grabbed hold of Luke's hand and drew him up and over my shoulders in a fireman's carry. Then I advanced quickly into the cave, slipping only once on monster blood as I edged my way along the nearest wall, heading for the cave mouth. The creatures began to stir before I made it out, but their movements were more reflexive than directed. I paused at the opening where I beheld an enormous flower garden in full bloom. All of the flowers were at least as tall as myself, and a shifting breeze bore me an overpowering redolence.

Moments later I heard a more decisive movement at my back and I turned. The Jabberwock was drawing itself to its feet. The Fire Angel was still crouched and was making small piping noises. The Jabberwock staggered back, spreading its wings, then suddenly turned, beat the air, and fled back up the high hole in the cleft at the rear of the cave. Not a bad idea, I decided, as I hurried out into the garden.

Here the aromas were even stronger, the flowers, mostly in bloom, a fantastic canopy of colors as I rushed among them. I found myself panting after a short while, but I jogged on nevertheless. Luke was heavy, but I wanted to put as much distance as I could between ourselves and the cave. Considering how fast our pursuer could move, I wasn't sure there was sufficient time to fool with a Trump yet.

As I hurried along I began feeling somewhat woozy, and my extremities seemed extremely distant. It occurred to me immediately that the flower smells might be a bit narcotic. Great. That was all I needed, to get caught up in a drug high while trying to bring Luke back from one. I could make out a small, slightly elevated clearing in the distance, though, and I headed for it. Hopefully, we could rest there for a bit while I regained my mental footing and decided what to do next. So far, I could detect no sounds of pursuit.

Rushing on, I could feel myself beginning to reel. My equilibrium was becoming impaired. I suddenly felt a fear of falling, almost akin to acrophobia. For it occurred to me that if I fell I might not be able to rise again, that I might succumb to a drugged sleep and be discovered and dispatched by the creature of Chaos while I dozed. Overhead, the colors of the flowers ran together, flowing and tangling like a mass of ribbons in a bright stream. I tried to control my breathing, to take in as little of the effluvia as possible. But this was difficult, as winded as I was becoming.

But I did not fall, though I collapsed beside Luke at the center of the clearing after I'd lowered him to the ground. He remained unconscious, a peaceful expression on his face. A wind swept our hillock from the direction of its far side, where nasty-looking, spiked plants of a nonflowering variety grew. Thus, I no longer smelled the seductive odors of the giant flower field, and after a time my head began to clear. On the other hand, I realized that this meant that our own scents were being borne back in the direction of the cave. Whether the Fire Angel could unmask them within the heady perfumes, I did not know, but providing it with even that much of an opportunity made me feel uncomfortable.

Years ago, as an undergraduate, I had tried some LSD. It had scared me so badly that I'd never tried another hallucinogen since. It wasn't simply a bad trip. The stuff had affected my shadow-shifting ability. It is kind of a truism that Amberites can visit any place they can imagine, for everything is out there, somewhere, in Shadow. By combining our minds with motion we can tune for the shadow we desire. Unfortunately, I could not control what I was imagining. Also unfortunately, I was transported to those places. I panicked, and that only made it worse. I could easily have been destroyed, for I wandered through the objectified jungles of my subconscious and passed some time in places where the bad things dwell. After I came down I found my way back home, turned up whimpering on Julia's doorstep, and was a nervous wreck for days. Later, when I told Random about it, I learned that he had had some similar experiences. He had kept it to himself at first as a possible secret weapon against the rest of the family; but later, after they'd gotten back onto decent terms with each other, he had decided to share the information in the interest of survival. He was surprised to learn then that Benedict, Gérard, Fiona, and Bleys knew all about it— though their knowledge had come from other hallucinogens and, strangely, only Fiona had ever considered its possibility as an infamily weapon. She'd shelved the notion, though, because of its unpredictability. This had been sometime back, however, and in the press of other business in recent years it had slipped his mind; it simply had not occurred to him that a new arrival such as myself should perhaps be cautioned.

Luke had told me that his attempted invasion of the Keep of the Four Worlds, by means of a glider-borne commando team, had been smashed. Since I had seen the broken gliders at various points within the walls during my own visit to that place, it was logical to assume that Luke had been captured. Therefore, it seemed a fairly strong assumption that the sorcerer Mask had done whatever had been done to him to bring him to this state. It would seem that this simply involved introducing a dose of a hallucinogen to his prison fare and turning him loose to wander and look at the pretty lights. Fortunately, unlike myself, his mental travelings had involved nothing more threatening than the brighter aspects of Lewis Carroll. Maybe his heart was purer than mine. But the deal was weird any way you looked at it. Mask might have killed him or kept him in prison or added him to the coatrack collection. Instead, while what had been done was not without risk, it was something which would wear off eventually and leave him chastened but at liberty. It was more a slap on the wrist than a real piece of vengeance. This, for a member of the House which had previously held sway in the Keep and would doubtless like to do so again. Was Mask supremely confident? Or did he not really see Luke as much of a threat?

And then there is the fact that our shadow-shifting abilities and our sorcerous abilities come from similar roots—the Pattern or the Logrus. It had to be that messing with one also messed with the other. That would explain Luke's strange ability to summon me to him as by a massive Trump sending, when in actuality there was no Trump: His drug-enhanced abilities of visualization must have been so intense that the card's physical representation of me was unnecessary. And his skewed magical abilities would account for all of the preliminary byplay, all of the odd, reality-distorting experiences I'd had before he actually achieved contact. This meant that either of us could become very dangerous in certain drugged states. I'd have to remember that. I hoped he wouldn't wake up mad at me for hitting him, before I could talk to him a bit. On the other hand, the tranquilizer would hopefully keep him happy while the other stuff worked at detoxing him.

I massaged a sore muscle in my left leg and rose to my feet. I caught hold of Luke beneath the armpits and dragged him about twenty paces farther along into the clearing. Then I sighed and returned to the spot where I had rested. There was not sufficient time to flee farther. And as the wailing increased in volume and the giant flowers swayed in a line heading directly toward me— glimpses of a darker form becoming visible amid the stalks—I knew that with the Jabberwock fled the Fire Angel was back on the job, and since this confrontation seemed inevitable, this clearing was as good a place to meet it as any, and better than most.

2

I unfastened the bright thing at my belt and began to unfold it. It made a series of clicking noises as I did so. I was hoping that I was making the best choice available to me rather than, say, a bad mistake.

The creature took longer than I'd thought to pass among the flowers. This could mean it was having trouble following my trail amid its exotic surroundings. I was hoping, though, that it meant it had been sufficiently injured in its encounter with the Jabberwock that it had lost something of its strength and speed.

Whatever, the final stalks eventually swayed and were crushed. The angular creature lurched forward and halted to stare at me with unblinking eyes. Frakir panicked, and I calmed her. This was a little out of her league. I had a Fire Fountain spell left, but I didn't even bother with it. I knew it wouldn't stop the thing, and it might make it behave unpredictably.

"I can show you the way back to Chaos," I shouted, "if you're getting homesick!"

It wailed softly and advanced. So much for sentimentality.

It came on slowly, oozing fluids from a dozen wounds. I wondered if it were still capable of rushing me or if its present pace were the best it could manage. Prudence dictated I assume the worst, so I tried to stay loose and ready to match anything it attempted.

It didn't rush, though. It just kept coming, like a small tank with appendages. I didn't know where its vital spots were located. Fire Angel anatomy had not been high on my list of interests back home. I gave myself a crash course, however, in the way of gross observation as it approached. Unfortunately, this gave me to believe that it kept everything important well protected. Too bad.

I did not want to attack in case it was trying to sucker me into something. I was not aware of its combat tricks, and I did not care to expose myself unduly in order to learn them. Better to stay on the defense and let it make the first move, I told myself. But it just kept moving nearer and nearer. I knew that I'd be forced to do something soon, even if it were only to retreat. . . .

One of those long, folded front appendages flashed out toward me, and I spun to the side and cut. Snicker-snack! The limb lay on the ground, still moving. So I kept moving, also. One-two, one-two! Snicker-snack!

The beast toppled slowly to its left, for I had removed all of the limbs on that side of its body.

Then, overconfident, I passed too near in racing to round its head to reach the other side and repeat the performance while it was still traumatized and collapsing. Its other extensor flashed out. But I was too near and it was still toppling. Instead of catching me with its clawed extremity, it hit me with the equivalent of shin or forearm. The blow struck me across the chest and I was knocked backward.

As I scrambled away and drew my feet beneath me to rise, I heard Luke say, groggily, "Now what's going on?"

"Later," I called, without looking back.

Then, "Hey! You hit me!" he added.

"All in good fun," I answered. "Part of the cure," and I was up and moving again.

"Oh," I heard him say.

The thing was on its side now and that big limb struck wildly at me, several times. I avoided it and was able to guage its range and striking angle.

Snicker-snack. The limb fell to the ground and I moved in.

I swung three blows which passed all the way through its head from different angles before I was able to sever it. It kept making clicking noises, though, and the torso kept pitching and scrabbling about on the remaining limbs.

I don't know how many times I struck after that. I just kept at it until the creature was literally diced. Luke had begun shouting "Olé!" each time that I struck. I was perspiring somewhat by then, and I noticed that heat waves or something seemed to be causing my view of the distant flowers to ripple in a disturbing fashion. I felt foresighted as all hell, though—the Vorpal Sword I'd appropriated back in the bar had proved a fine weapon. I swung it through a high arc, which I'd noted seemed to cleanse it entirely, and then I began folding it back into its original compact form. It was as soft as flower petals, and it still gave off a faint dusty glow. . . .

"Bravo!" said a familiar voice, and I turned until I saw the smile followed by the Cat, who was tapping his paws lightly together. "Callooh! Callay!" he added. "Well done, beamish boy!"

The background wavering grew stronger, and the sky darkened. I heard Luke say "Hey!" and when I glanced back I saw him getting to his feet, moving forward. When I looked again I could see the bar forming at the Cat's back, and I caught a glimpse of the brass rail. My head began to swim.

"There's normally a deposit on the Vorpal Sword," the Cat was saying. "But since you're returning it intact—"

Luke was beside me. I could hear music again, and he was humming along with it. Now it was the clearing, with its butchered Fire Angel, that seemed the superimposition, as the bar increased in solidity, taking on nuances of color and shading.

But the place seemed somehow smaller—the tables closer together, the music softer, the mural more compressed and its artist out of sight. Even the Caterpillar and his mushroom had retreated to a shadowy nook, and both seemed shrunken, the blue smoke less dense. I took this as a vaguely good sign, for if our presence there were a result of Luke's state of mind then perhaps the fixation was losing its hold on him.

"Luke?" I said.

He moved up to the bar beside me.

"Yeah?" he answered.

"You know you're on a trip, don't you?"

"I don't. . . . I'm not sure what you mean," he said.

"When Mask had you prisoner I think he slipped you some acid," I said. "Is that possible?"

"Who's Mask?" he asked me.

"The new head honcho at the Keep."

"Oh, you mean Sharu Garrul," he said. "I do remember that he had on a blue mask."

I saw no reason to go into an explanation as to why Mask wasn't Sharu. He'd probably forget, anyway. I just nodded and said, "The boss."

"Well . . . yes, I guess he could have given me something," he replied. "You mean that all this . . . ?" He gestured toward the room at large.

I nodded.

"Sure, it's real," I said. "But we can transport ourselves into hallucinations. They're all real somewhere. Acid'll do it."

"I'll be damned," he said.

"I gave you some stuff to bring you down," I told him. "But it may take a while."

He licked his lips and glanced about.

"Well, there's no hurry," he said. Then he smiled as a distant screaming began and the demons started in doing nasty things to the burning woman off in the mural. "I kind of like it here."

I placed the folded weapon back upon the bartop. Luke rapped on the surface beside it and called for another round of brews. I backed away, shaking my head.

"I've got to go now," I told him. "Someone's still after me, and he just came close."

"Animals don't count," Luke said.

"The one I just chopped up does," I answered. "It was sent."

I looked at the broken doors, wondering what might come through them next. Fire Angels have been known to hunt in pairs.

"But I've got to talk to you . . . ," I continued.

"Not now," he said, turning away.

"You know it's important."

"I can't think right," he answered.

I supposed that had to be true, and there was no sense trying to drag him back to Amber or anywhere else. He'd just fade away and show up here again. His head would have to clear and his fix-ation dissipate before we could discuss mutual problems.

"You remember that your mother is a prisoner in Amber?" I asked.

"Yes."

"Call me when you've got your head together. We have to talk."

"I will."

I turned away and walked out the doors and into a bank of fog. In the distance I heard Luke begin singing again, some mournful ballad. Fog is almost as bad as complete darkness when it comes to shadow-shifting. If you can't see any referents while you're moving, there is no way to use the ability that allows you to slip away. On the other hand, I just wanted to be alone for a time to think, now my head was clear. If I couldn't see anybody in this stuff, nobody could see me either. And there were no sounds other than my own footfalls on a cobbled surface.

So what had I achieved? When I was awakened from a brief nap to attend Luke's unusual sending to Amber, I'd been dead tired following extraordinary exertions. I was transported into his presence, learned that he was tripping, fed him something I hoped would bring him off it sooner, hacked up a Fire Angel, and left Luke back where he had started.

I'd gotten two things out of it, I mused, as I strolled through the cottony mist: I'd stalemated Luke in any designs he might still have upon Amber. He was now aware that his mother was our prisoner, and I couldn't see him bringing any direct action against us under the circumstances. Aside from the technical problems involved in transporting Luke and keeping him in one place, this was the reason I was willing to leave him as I just had. I'm sure Random would have preferred him unconscious in a cell in the basement, but I was certain he would settle for a defanged Luke at large; especially so, when it was likely that Luke would be getting in touch with us sooner or later regarding Jasra. I was willing to let him come down and come around in his own good time. I had problems of my own in the waiting room, like Ghostwheel, Mask, Vinta . . . and the new specter which had just taken a number and a seat.

Maybe it had been Jasra who had been using the homing power of the blue stones to send assassins after me. She had the ability as well as a motive. It could also have been Mask, though, who I'd judge had the ability—and who seemed to have a motive, though I didn't understand it. Jasra was out of the way now, however; and while I intended to have things out with Mask eventually, I believed that I had succeeded in detuning myself from the blue stones. I also believed that I might have scared Mask somewhat in our recent encounter at the Keep. Whatever, it was extremely unlikely that Mask or Jasra, whatever their powers, would have had access to a trained Fire Angel. No, there's only one place Fire Angels come from, and shadow-sorcerers aren't on the customer list.

A puff of wind parted the fog for a moment and I caught sight of dark buildings. Good. I shifted. The fog moved again almost immediately, and they were not buildings but dark rock formations. Another parting and a piece of dawn or evening sky came into view, a foam of bright stars spilled across it. Before too long a wind whipped the fog away and I saw that I walked in a high rocky place, the heavens a blaze of starry light bright enough to read by. I followed a dark trail leading off to the edge of the world. . . .

The whole business with Luke, Jasra, Dalt, and Mask was somehow of a piece—completely understandable in some places and clouded in others. Given some time and legwork it would all hang together. Luke and Jasra seemed to be nullified now. Mask, an enigma of sorts, seemed to have it in for me personally but did not appear to represent any particular threat to Amber. Dalt, on the other hand, did, with his fancy new weaponry—but Random was aware of this situation and Benedict was back in town. So I was confident that everything possible was being done to deal with this.

I stood at the edge of the world and looked down into a bottomless rift full of stars. My mountain did not seem to grace the surface of a planet. However, there was a bridge to my left, leading outward to a dark, star-occluding shape—another floating mountain, perhaps. I strolled over and stepped out onto the span. Problems involving atmosphere, gravitation, temperature, meant nothing here, where I could, in a sense, make up reality as I went along. I walked out onto the bridge, and for a moment the angle was right and I caught a glimpse of another bridge on the far side of the dark mass, leading off to some other darkness.

I halted in the middle, able to see along it for a great distance in either direction. It seemed a safe and appropriate spot. I withdrew my packet of Trumps and riffled through them until I located one I hadn't used in a long, long time.

I held it before me and put the others away, studying the blue eyes and the young, hard, slightly sharp features beneath a mass of pure white hair. He was dressed all in black, save for a bit of white collar and sleeve showing beneath the glossy tight-fitting jacket. He held three dark steel balls in his gloved hand.

Sometimes it's hard to reach all the way to Chaos, so I focused and extended, carefully, strongly. The contact came almost immediately. He was seated on a balcony beneath a crazily stippled sky, the Shifting Mountains sliding to his left. His feet were propped on a small floating table and he was reading a book. He lowered it and smiled faintly.

"Merlin," he said softly. "You look tired."

I nodded.

"You look rested," I said.

"True," he answered, as he closed the book and set it on the table. Then, "There is trouble?" he asked.

"There is trouble, Mandor."

He rose to his feet.

"You wish to come through?"

I shook my head. "If you have any Trumps handy for getting back, I'd rather you came to me."

He extended his hand.

"All right," he said.

I reached forward, our hands clasped; he took a single step and stood beside me on the bridge. We embraced for a moment and then he turned and looked out and down into the rift.

"There is some danger here?" he asked.

"No. I chose this place because it seems very safe."

"Scenic, too," he replied. "What's been happening to you?"

"For years I was merely a student, and then a designer of certain sorts of specialized machinery," I told him. "Things were pretty uneventful until fairly recently. Then all hell broke loose—but most of it I understand, and much of it seems under control. That part's complicated and not really worth your concern."

He rested a hand on the bridge's side-piece.

"And the other part?" he asked.

"My enemies up until this point had been from the environs of Amber. But suddenly, when it seemed that most of that business was on its way to being settled, someone put a Fire Angel on my trail. I succeeded in destroying it just a little while ago. I've no idea why, and it's certainly not an Amber trick."

He made a clicking noise with his lips as he turned away, paced a few steps, and turned back.

"You're right, of course," he said. "I'd no idea it had come anywhere near this, or I'd have spoken with you some time ago. But let me differ with you as to orders of importance before I indulge in certain speculations on your behalf. I want to hear your entire story."

"Why?"

"Because you are sometimes appallingly naive, little brother, and I do not yet trust your judgment as to what is truly important."

"I may starve to death before I finish," I answered.

Smiling crookedly, my step-brother Mandor raised his arms. While Jurt and Despil are my half-brothers, borne by my mother, Jasra, to Prince Sawall the Rim Lord, Mandor was Sawall's son by an earlier marriage. Mandor is considerably older than I, and as a result he reminds me much of my relatives back in Amber. I'd always felt a bit of an outsider among the children of Dara and Sawall. In that Mandor was—in a more stable sense—not part of that particular grouping either, we'd had something in common. But whatever the impulse behind his early attentions, we'd hit it off and become closer, I sometimes think, than full blood brothers. He had taught me a lot of practical things over the years, and we had had many good times together.

The air was distorted between us, and when Mandor lowered his arms a dinner table covered with embroidered white linen came into sudden view between us, soundlessly, followed a moment later by a pair of facing chairs. The table bore numerous covered dishes, fine china, crystal, silverware; there was even a gleaming ice bucket with a dark twisted bottle within it.

"I am impressed," I stated.

"I've devoted considerable time to gourmet magic in recent years," he said. "Pray, be seated."

We made ourselves comfortable there on the bridge between two darknesses. I muttered appreciatively as I tasted, and it was some minutes before I could begin a summary of the events that had brought me to this place of starlight and silence.

Mandor listened to my entire tale without interruption, and when I'd finished he nodded and said, "Would you care for another serving of dessert?"

"Yes," I agreed. "It's quite nice."

When I glanced up a few moments later, I saw that he was smiling.

"What's funny?" I asked.

"You," he replied. "If you recall, I told you before you left for that place to be discriminating when it came to giving your trust."

"Well? I told no one my story. If you're going to lecture me on being friendly with Luke without learning his, I've already heard it."

"And what of Julia?"

"What do you mean? She never learned. . . ."

"Exactly. And she seems like one you could have trusted. Instead, you turned her against you."

"All right! Maybe I used bad judgment there, too."

"You designed a remarkable machine, and it never occurred to you it might also become a potent weapon. Random saw that right away. So did Luke. You might have been saved from disaster on that front only by the fact that it became sentient and didn't care to be dictated to."

"You're right. I was more concerned with solving technical problems. I didn't think through all the consequences."

He sighed.

"What am I going to do with you, Merlin? You take risks when you don't even know you're taking risks."

"I didn't trust Vinta," I volunteered.

"I think you could have gotten more information out of her," he said, "if you hadn't been so quick to save Luke, who already appeared to be out of danger. She seemed to be loosening up considerably at the end of your dialogue."

"Perhaps I should have called you."

"If you encounter her again, do it, and I'll deal with her."

I stared. He seemed to mean it.

"You know what she is?"

"I'll unriddle her," he said, swirling the bright orange beverage in his glass. "But I've a proposal for you, elegant in its simplicity. I've a new country place, quite secluded, with all the amenities. Why not return to the Courts with me rather than bouncing around from hazard to hazard? Lie low for a couple of years, enjoy the good life, catch up on your reading. I'll see that you're well protected. Let everything blow over, then go about your business in a more peaceful climate."

I took a small sip of the fiery drink.

"No," I said. "What happened to those things you indicated earlier that you knew and I didn't?"

"Hardly important, if you accept my offer."

"Even if I were to accept, I'd want to know."

"Bag of worms," he said.

"You listened to my story. I'll listen to yours."

He shrugged and leaned back in his chair, looked up at stars.

"Swayvill is dying," he said.

"He's been doing that for years."

"True, but he's gotten much worse. Some think it has to do with the death curse of Eric of Amber. Whatever, I really believe he hasn't much longer."

"I begin to see. . . ."

"Yes, the struggle for the succession has become more intense. People have been falling over left and right—poison, duels, assassinations, peculiar accidents, dubious suicides. A great number have also departed for points unknown. Or so it would seem."

"I understand, but I don't see where it concerns me."

"One time it would not have."

"But?"

"You are not aware that Sawall adopted you, formally, after your departure?"

"What?"

"Yes. I was never certain as to his exact motives. But you are a legitimate heir. You follow me but take precedence over Jurt and Despil."

"That would still leave me way in hell down on the list."

"True," he said slowly. "Most of the interest lies at the top. . . ."

"You say 'most.' "

"There are always exceptions," he answered. "You must realize that a time such as this is also a fine occasion for the paying off of old debts. One death more or less hardly rouses an eyebrow the way it would have in more placid times. Even in relatively high places."

I shook my head as I met his eyes.

"It really doesn't make sense in my case," I said.

He continued to stare until I felt uncomfortable.

"Does it?" I finally asked.

"Well . . ." he said. "Give it some thought."

I did. And just as the notion came to me, Mandor nodded as if he viewed the contents of my mind.

"Jurt," he said, "met the changing times with a mixture of delight and fear. He was constantly talking of the latest deaths and of the elegance and apparent ease with which some of them were accomplished. Hushed tones interspersed with a few giggles. His fear and his desire to increase his own capacity for mischief finally reached a point where they became greater than his other fear—"

"The Logrus. . . ."

"Yes. He finally tried the Logrus, and he made it through."

"He should be feeling very good about that. Proud. It was something he'd wanted for years."

"Oh, yes," Mandor answered. "And I'm sure he felt a great number of other things as well."

"Freedom," I suggested. "Power," and as I studied his half-amused expression, I was forced to add, "and the ability to play the game himself."

"There may be hope for you," he said. "Now, would you care to carry that through to its logical conclusion?"

"Okay," I responded, thinking of Jurt's left ear as it floated away following my cut, a swarm of blood-beads spreading about it. "You think Jurt sent the Fire Angel."

"Most likely," he replied. "But would you care to pursue that a little further?"

I thought of the broken branch piercing Jurt's eyeball as we wrestled in the glade. . . .

"All right," I said. "He's after me. It could be a part of the succession game, because I'm slightly ahead of him on that front, or just plain dislike and revenge—or both."

"It doesn't really matter which," Mandor said, "in terms of results. But I was thinking of that crop-eared wolf that attacked you. Only had one eye, too, it seemed. . . ."

"Yes," I said. "What does Jurt look like these days?"

"Oh, he's grown about half the ear back. It's pretty ragged and ugly-looking. Generally, his hair covers it. The eyeball is regenerated, but he can't see out of it yet. He usually wears a patch."

"That might explain recent developments," I said. "Hell of a time for it, though, with everything else that's been going on. Muddies the waters considerably."

"It's one of the reasons I suggest you simply drop out and let everything cool down. Too busy. With as many arrows as there seem to be in the air, one may well find your heart."

"I can take care of myself, Mandor."

"You could have fooled me."

I shrugged, got up, walked over to the rail, and looked down at the stars.

After a long while he called out to me, "Have you got any better ideas?" but I didn't answer him because I was thinking about that very matter. I was considering what Mandor had said about my tunnel vision and lack of preparedness and had just about concluded that he was right, that in nearly everything that had happened to me up to this point—with the exception of my going after Jasra—I had mainly been responding to circumstance. I had been far more acted upon than acting. Admittedly, it had all happened very quickly. But still, I had not formed any real plans for covering myself, learning about my enemies or striking back. It seemed that there were some things I might be doing. . . .

"If there is that much to worry about," he said, "you are probably better off playing it safe."

He was probably right, from the standpoints of reason, safety, caution. But he was strictly of the Courts, while I possessed an additional set of loyalties in which he did not participate. It was possible—if only through my connection with Luke—that I might be able to come up with some personal course of action that would further the security of.Amber. So long as such a chance existed, I felt obliged to pursue matters. And beyond this, from a purely personal standpoint, my curiosity was too strong to permit me to walk away from the unanswered questions which abounded when I could be actively seeking some answers.

As I was considering how I might best phrase these matters in my reply to Mandor, I was again acted upon. I became aware of a faint feeling of inquiry, as of a cat scratching at the doors of my mind. It grew in force, thrusting aside other considerations, until I knew it as a Trump sending from some very distant place. I guessed that it might be from Random, anxious to discover what had transpired since my absence from Amber. So I made myself receptive, inviting the contact.

"Merlin, what's the matter?" Mandor asked, and I raised my hand to indicate I was occupied. At that, I saw him place his napkin upon the tabletop and rise to his feet.

My vision cleared slowly and I beheld Fiona, looking stern, rocks at her back, a pale green sky above her.

"Merlin," she said. "Where are you?"

"Far away," I answered. "It's a long story. What's going on? Where are you?"

She smiled bleakly.

"Far away," she replied.

"We seem to have chosen very scenic spots," I observed. "Did you pick the sky to compliment your hair?"

"Enough!" she said. "I did not call you to compare travel notes."

At that moment Mandor came up beside me and placed his hand upon my shoulder, which was hardly in keeping with his character, as it is considered a gauche thing to do when a Trump communication is obviously in progress—on the order of intentionally picking up an extension phone and breaking in on someone's call. Nevertheless. . . .

"My! My!" he said. "Will you please introduce me, Merlin?"

"Who," Fiona asked, "is that?"

"This is my brother Mandor," I told her, "of the House of Sawall in the Courts of Chaos. Mandor, this is my Aunt Fiona, Princess of Amber."

Mandor bowed.

"I have heard of you, Princess," he said. "It is indeed a pleasure." Her eyes widened for a moment.

"I know of the house," she replied, "but I'd no idea of Merlin's relationship with it. I am pleased to know you."

"I take it there's some problem, Fi?" I asked.

"Yes," she answered, glancing at Mandor.

"I will retire," he said. "Honored to have met you, Princess. I wish you lived a bit nearer the Rim."

She smiled.

"Wait," she said. "This does not involve any state secrets. You are an initiate of the Logrus?"

"I am," he stated.

". . . And I take it you two did not get together to fight a duel?"

"Hardly," I answered.

"In that case, I would welcome his view of the problem, also. Are you willing to come to me, Mandor?"

He bowed again, which I thought was hamming it a bit.

"Anyplace, Madam," he responded.

She said, "Come then," and she extended her left hand and I clasped it. Mandor reached out and touched her wrist. We stepped forward.

We stood before her in the rocky place. It was breezy and a bit chill there. From somewhere distant there came a muted roar, as of a muffled engine.

"Have you been in touch with anyone in Amber recently?" I asked her.

"No," she stated.

"Your departure was somewhat abrupt."

"There were reasons."

"Such as your recognizing Luke?"

"His identity is known to you now?"

"Yes."

"And to the others?"

"I told Random," I answered, "and Flora."

"Then everyone knows," she said. "I departed quickly and took Bleys with me because we had to be next on Luke's list. After all, I tried killing his father and almost succeeded. Bleys and I were Brand's closest relatives, and we'd turned against him."

She turned a penetrating gaze upon Mandor, who smiled.

"I understand," he stated, "that right now Luke drinks with a Cat, a Dodo, a Caterpillar, and a White Rabbit. I also understand that with his mother a prisoner in Amber he is powerless against you."

She regarded me again.

"You *have* been busy," she said.

"I try."

". . . So that it is probably safe for you to return," Mandor continued.

She smiled at him, then glanced at me.

"Your brother seems well informed," she observed.

"He's family, too," I said, "and we've a lifelong habit of looking out for each other."

"His life or yours?" she asked.

"Mine," I replied. "He *is* my senior."

"What are a few centuries this way or that?" Mandor offered.

"I thought I felt a certain maturity of spirit," she noted. "I've a mind to trust you further than I'd intended."

"That's very sporting of you," he replied, "and I treasure the sentiment. . . ."

". . . But you'd rather I didn't overdo it?"

"Precisely."

"I've no intention of testing your loyalties to home and throne," she said, "on such short acquaintance. It does concern both Amber and the Courts, but I see no conflict in the matter."

"I do not doubt your prudence. I merely wanted to make my position clear."

She turned back toward me.

"Merlin," she said then, "I think you lied to me."

I felt myself frowning as I tried to recall an occasion when I might have misled her about something. I shook my head.

"If I did," I told her, "I don't remember."

"It was some years ago," she said, "when I asked you to try walking your father's Pattern."

"Oh," I answered, feeling myself blush and wondering whether it was apparent in this strange light.

"You took advantage of what I had told you—about the Pattern's resistance," she continued. "You pretended it was preventing you from setting your foot upon it. But there was no visible sign of the resistance, such as there was when I tried stepping onto it."

She looked at me, as if for confirmation.

"So?" I said.

"So," she replied, "it has become more important now than it was then, and I have to know: Were you faking it that day?"

"Yes," I said.

"Why?"

"Once I took one step upon it," I explained, "I'd have been committed to walking it. Who knows where it might have led me and what situation might have followed? I was near the end of my holiday and in a hurry to get back to school. I didn't have time for what might have turned into a lengthy expedition. Telling you there were difficulties seemed the most graceful way of begging off."

"I think there's more to it than that," she said.

"What do you mean?"

"I think Corwin told you something about it that the rest of us do not know—or that he left you a message. I believe you know more than you let on concerning the thing."

I shrugged.

"Sorry, Fiona. I have no control over your suspicions," I said. "Wish I could be of more help."

"You can," she replied.

"Tell me how."

"Come with me to the place of the new Pattern. I want you to walk it."

I shook my head.

"I've got a lot more pressing business," I told her, "than satisfying your curiosity about something my dad did years ago."

"It's more than just curiosity," she said. "I told you once before that I think it's what is behind the increased incidence of shadow storms."

"And I gave you a perfectly good reason for something else being the cause. I believe it's an adjustment to the partial destruction and recreation of the old Pattern."

"Would you come this way?" she asked, and she turned from me and began to climb.

I glanced at Mandor, shrugged, and followed her. He came along.

We mounted toward a jagged screen of rock. She reached it

first and made her way onto a lopsided ledge which ran partway along it. She traversed this until she came to a place where the rock wall had broken down into a wide V-shaped gap. She stood there with her back to us then, the light from the green sky doing strange things to her hair.

I came up beside her and followed the direction of her gaze. On a distant plain, far below us and to the left, a large black funnel spun like a top. It seemed the source of the roaring sound we had been hearing. The ground appeared to be cracked beneath it. I stared for several minutes, but it did not change in form or position. Finally, I cleared my throat.

"Looks like a big tornado," I said, "not going anyplace."

"That's why I want you to walk the new Pattern," she told me. "I think it's going to get us unless we get it first."

3

If you had a choice between the ability to detect falsehood and the ability to discover truth, which one would you take? There was a time when I thought they were different ways of saying the same thing, but I no longer believe that. Most of my relatives, for example, are almost as good at seeing through subterfuge as they are at perpetrating it. I'm not at all sure, though, that they care much about truth. On the other hand, I'd always felt there was something noble, special, and honorable about seeking truth—a thing I'd attempted with Ghostwheel. Mandor had made me wonder, though. Had this made me a sucker for truth's opposite?

Of course, it's not as cut and dried as all that. I know that it is not a pure either/or situation with the middle excluded, but is rather a statement of attitude. Still, I was suddenly willing to concede that I might have gone to an extreme—to the point of foolhardiness—and that I had let certain of my critical faculties doze for far too long.

So I wondered about Fiona's request.

"What makes it such a threat?" I asked her.

"It is a shadow storm in the form of a tornado," she said.

"There have been such things before," I answered.

"True," she responded, "but they tend to move through Shadow. This one does have extension through an area of Shadow, but it is totally stationary. It first appeared several days ago, and it has not altered in any way since then."

"What's that come to in Amber-time?" I asked.

"Half a day, perhaps. Why?"

I shrugged. "I don't know. Just curious," I said. "I still don't see why it's a threat."

"I told you that such storms had proliferated since Corwin drew the extra Pattern. Now they're changing in character as well as frequency. That Pattern has to be understood soon."

A moment's quick reflection showed me that whoever gained control of Dad's Pattern could become master of some terrible forces. Or mistress.

So, "Supposing I walk it," I said. "Then what? As I understand it from Dad's story, I'd just wind up in the middle, the same as with the Pattern back home. What's to be learned from that?"

I studied her face for some display of emotion, but my relatives tend to have too much control for such simple self-betrayal.

"As I understand it," she said, "Brand was able to trump in when Corwin was at the middle."

"That's the way I understand it, too."

". . . So, when you reach the center, I can come in on a Trump."

"I suppose so. Then there will be two of us standing at the middle of the Pattern."

". . . And from there we will be in a position to go someplace we could not reach from any other point in existence."

"That being?" I asked.

"The primal Pattern which lies behind it."

"You're sure there is one?"

"There must be. It is in the nature of such a construct to be scribed at a more basic level of reality as well as the mundane."

"And our purpose in traveling to that place?"

"That is where its secrets dwell, where its deepest magics might be learned."

"I see," I told her. "Then what?"

"Why, there we might learn how to undo the trouble the thing is causing," she answered.

"That's all?"

Her eyes narrowed.

"We will learn whatever we can, of course. Power is power, and represents a threat until it is understood."

I nodded slowly.

"But right now there are a number of powers that are more pressing in the threat department," I said. "That Pattern is going to have to wait its turn."

"Even if it may represent the forces you need to deal with your other problems?" she asked.

"Even so," I said. "It might turn into a lengthy enterprise, and I don't believe I have the time for that."

"But you don't know that for certain."

"True. But once I set foot on it, there's no turning back."

I did not add that I'd no intention of taking her to the primal Pattern, then leaving her there on her own. After all, she had tried her hand at king-making once. And if Brand had made it to the throne of Amber in those days, she would have been standing right behind him, no matter what she had to say about it now. I think she was about to ask me to deliver her to the primal Pattern then but realized that I'd already considered it and rejected it. Not wanting to lose face by asking and being refused, she returned to her original argument.

"I suggest you make time now," she said, "if you do not wish to see worlds torn up about you."

"I didn't believe you the first time you told me that," I answered, "and I don't believe you now. I still think the increased shadow-storm activity is probably an adjustment to the damage and repair of the original Pattern. I also think that if we mess around with a new Pattern we don't know anything about, we stand a chance of making things worse, not better—"

"I don't want to mess around with it," she said. "I want to study—"

The Sign of the Logrus flashed between us suddenly. She must have seen it or felt it somehow, too, because she drew back at the same instant I did.

I turned my head with sure knowledge as to what I would see.

Mandor had mounted the battlementlike wall of stone. He stood as still as if he were a part of it, his arms upraised. I suppressed my first impulse, which was to shout to him to stop. He knew what he was doing. And I was certain that he would not pay me the slightest heed, anyway.

I advanced to the notch in which he had taken his position, and I looked past him at the swirling thing on the cracked plain far below. Through the image of the Logrus, I felt the dark, awful rush of power that Suhuy had revealed to me in his final lesson. Mandor was calling upon it now and pouring it into the shadow-storm. Did he not realize that the force of Chaos he was unleashing must spread until it had run a terrible course? Could he not see that if the storm were indeed a manifestation of Chaos then he was turning it into a truly monstrous thing?

It grew larger. Its roaring increased in volume. It became frightening to watch it.

From behind me, I heard Fiona gasp.

"I hope you know what you're doing," I called to him.

"We'll know in about a minute," he replied, lowering his arms.

The Sign of the Logrus winked out before me.

We watched the damned thing spin for some time, bigger and noisier.

Finally, "What have you proved?" I asked him.

"That you have no patience," he answered.

There was nothing particularly instructive to the phenomenon, but I continued to watch it anyway. Abruptly, the sound became a stutter. The dark apparition jerked about suddenly, shaking off bits of accumulated debris as it contracted. Soon it was restored to its former size, and it hit its earlier pitch and the sound grew steady once more.

"How did you do that?" I asked him.

"I didn't," he said. "It adjusted itself."

"It shouldn't have," Fiona stated.

"Exactly," he replied.

"You've lost me," I said.

"It should have gone roaring right on, stronger than ever, after he'd augmented it that way," Fiona said. "But whatever is controlling it had other plans. So it was readjusted."

". . . And it is a Chaos phenomenon," Mandor continued. "You could see that in the way it drew upon Chaos when I provided the means. But that pushed it past some limit, and there was a correction. Someone is playing with the primal forces themselves out there. Who or what or why, I cannot say. But I think it's strong testimony that the Pattern isn't involved. Not with Chaos games. So Merlin is probably correct. I think that this business has its origin elsewhere."

"All right," Fiona conceded. "All right. What does that leave us with?"

"A mystery," he said. "But hardly, I think, an imminent threat."

A faint firefly of an idea flitted through my mind. It could easily be dead wrong, though that was not the reason I decided against sharing it. It led into an area of thought I could not explore in an instant, and I don't like giving away pieces of things like that.

Fiona was glaring at me now, but I maintained a bland expression. Abruptly then, seeing that her cause was fruitless, she decided to change the subject:

"You said that you left Luke under somewhat unusual circumstances. Just where is he now?"

The last thing I wanted to do was to get her really mad at me. But I couldn't see turning her loose on Luke in his present condition. For all I knew, she might actually be up to killing him, just as a form of life insurance. And I did not want Luke dead. I'd a feeling he might be undergoing something of a change of attitude, and I wanted to give him every break I could. We still owed each other a few, even though it was hard keeping score; and there is something to be said for old times' sake. Considering what I'd judged his condition to be when I'd left him, it was going to be a while before he was in decent shape again. And then I had a number of things I wanted to talk to him about.

"Sorry," I said. "He's my province at the moment."

"I believe I have some interest in the matter," she replied levelly.

"Of course," I said, "but I feel that mine is greater and that we may get in each other's ways."

"I can judge these things for myself," she said.

"Okay," I told her. "He's on an acid trip. Any information you'd get out of him might be colorful, but it would also be highly disappointing."

"How did this happen?" she asked.

"A wizard named Mask apparently slipped him some chemicals when he had him prisoner."

"Where was this? I've never heard of Mask."

"A place called the Keep of the Four Worlds," I told her.

"It's been a long time since I heard the Keep mentioned," she said. "A sorcerer named Sharu Garrul used to hold it."

"He's a coatrack now," I stated.

"What?"

"Long story, but Mask has the place these days."

She stared at me, and I could tell she was just realizing that there was a lot she didn't know in the way of recent developments. I'd judge she was deciding which of several obvious questions to ask next when I decided to beat her to the punch while she was still off-balance.

"So how's Bleys?" I asked.

"He's much improved. I treated him myself and he's recovering quickly."

I was about to ask her where he was, which I knew she would refuse to answer, and hopefully we would both smile when she saw what I was driving at: no address for Bleys, no address for Luke; we keep our secrets and stay friends.

"Hello!" I heard Mandor say, and we both turned in the direction he was facing—back out through the notch.

The dark tornado-form had collapsed to half its former size, and even as we watched, it continued to diminish. It fell steadily in upon itself, shrinking and shrinking, and in about a half minute it was gone, completely.

I could not suppress a smile, but Fiona did not even notice. She was looking at Mandor.

"Do you think it was because of what you did?" she asked him.

"I have no way of knowing," he replied, "but it may well be."

"But does it tell you anything?" she said.

"Perhaps whoever was responsible did not like having me tinker with his experiment."

"You really believe there's an intelligence behind it?"

"Yes."

"Someone from the Courts?"

"It seems more likely than someone from your end of the world."

"I suppose so . . . ," she agreed. "Have you any guesses as to the person's identity?"

He smiled.

"I understand," she said quickly. "Your business is your business. But a general threat is everybody's business. That's what I was really getting at."

"True," he acknowledged. "This is why I propose investigating it. I'm at loose ends at the moment. It might be amusing."

"It is awkward asking you to communicate your findings to me," she said, "when I do not know what interests might be involved."

"I appreciate your position," he replied, "but to the best of my knowledge the treaty provisions still hold and no one in the Courts is promoting any special designs against Amber. In fact. . . . If you like, we might pursue the matter together, at least part of the way."

"I've got the time," she said.

"I don't," I injected quickly. "I've some pressing business to attend to."

Mandor shifted his attention to me.

"About my offer . . . ," he said.

"I can't," I told him.

"Very well. Our conversation is not concluded, however. I'll be in touch later."

"Okay."

Fiona looked my way then, also.

"You will keep me posted on Luke's recovery, and his intentions," she stated.

"Of course."

"Good day, then."

Mandor gave me a small half-salute and I returned it. I began walking then, and as soon as I was out of sight I began shifting.

I found my way to a rocky slope, where I halted and withdrew my Trump for Amber. I raised it, focused my awareness, and transported myself as soon as I felt my way through. I was hoping the main hall would be empty, but at this point I didn't really care that much.

I came through near Jasra, who was holding an extra cloak over her outstretched left arm. I ducked out the doorway to my left into an empty corridor and made my way to the back stair. Several times I heard voices and I detoured to avoid the speakers. I was able to make it to my rooms without being discovered.

The only rest I had had in what seemed an age and a half had been a fifteen-minute nap before Luke's spaced-out sorcerous faculty had caused him to summon me to the Looking Glass Bar via a hallucinatory Trump. When? For all I knew, it could have been yesterday—which had been a very full day before that incident.

I barred the door and staggered to the bed, flinging myself down upon it without even removing my boots. Sure, there were all sorts of things I should be doing, but I was in no condition for any of them. I'd returned home because I still felt safest in Amber, despite the fact that Luke had reached me here once.

Someone with a high-powered subconscious might have had a brilliantly revelatory dream following as much crap as I'd been through recently, and then have awakened with a wonderful series of insights and answers detailing appropriate courses of action. I didn't. I woke once, in a small panic, not knowing where I was. But I opened my eyes and satisfied myself on that count, then went back to sleep. Later—much later, it seemed—I returned by degrees, like some piece of flotsam being pushed higher and higher onto a beach by wave following wave, until finally I was there. I saw no reason for going any further until I realized that my feet hurt. Then I sat up and pulled my boots off, which might have been one of the six greatest pleasures in my life. I removed my socks in a hurry then and threw them into the corner of the room. Why doesn't anyone else in my line of work seem to get sore feet? I filled the basin and soaked them for a time, then resolved to go barefoot for the next few hours.

Finally I rose, stripped, cleaned up, and put on a pair of Levi's and a purple flannel shirt of which I am fond. The hell with swords, daggers, and cloaks for a time. I opened the shutters and looked outside. It was dark. Because of clouds, I couldn't even guess from the stars whether it might be early evening, late night, or almost morning.

It was very quiet in the hall, and there were no sounds as I made my way down the back stair. The kitchen was deserted also, the big fires banked and smoldering low. I didn't want to stir things up beyond hanging a pot of water to warm for tea while I located some bread and fruit preserves. I turned up a jug of something like grapefruit juice, too, in one of the walk-in ice boxes.

As I sat warming my feet and working my way through the loaf, I began to feel uneasy. I was sipping my tea before I realized what it was. There seemed a great necessity that I be doing something, yet I had no idea what. Now I had something of a breather, and it felt strange. So I decided to start thinking again.

By the time I'd finished eating, I had a few small plans. The first thing I did was to make my way to the main hall, where I removed all of the hats and cloaks from Jasra and swept her off her feet. Later, as I was bearing her stiff form along the upstairs hallway in the direction of my room, a door opened partway and a bleary-eyed Droppa watched me go by.

"Hey, I'll take two!" he called after me.

"Reminds me of my first wife," he added then, and closed the door.

Once I had her installed in my quarters, I drew up a chair and seated myself before her. Garishly clad as part of a savage joke, her hard sort of beauty was not really diminished. She had placed me in extreme peril on one occasion, and I had no desire to free her at a time like this for a possible repeat performance. But the spell that held her claimed my attention for more than one reason, and I wanted to understand it fully.

Carefully then, I began exploring the construct which held her. It was not overcomplicated, but I could see that tracing all of its byways was going to take a while. All right. I wasn't about to stop now. I pushed on ahead into the spell, taking mental notes as I went.

* * *

I was busy for hours. After I had solved the spell, I decided to hang some more of my own, times being what they were. The castle came awake about me as I worked. I labored steadily as the day progressed, until everything was in place and I was satisfied with my work. I was also famished.

I moved Jasra off into a corner, pulled on my boots, departed my quarters, and headed for the stair. In that it seemed about lunchtime I checked out the several dining rooms in which the family generally ate. But all of them were deserted and none of them were set up for a meal yet to come. Nor did any of them show signs of a meal having recently been dispatched.

I suppose it was possible my time sense was still skewed and I was much too late or too early, but it did seem that it had been daylight long enough to bring me into the vicinity of the proper hour. Nobody, however, seemed to be eating, so something had to be wrong with this assumption. . . .

Then I heard it—the faint click of cutlery upon plate. I headed in the apparent direction of the sound. Obviously, the meal was taking place in a less frequented setting than usual. I turned right, then left. Yes, they had decided to set up in a drawing room. No matter.

I entered the room, where Llewella was seated with Random's wife, Vialle, on the red divan, dinner laid on a low table before them. Michael, who worked in the kitchen, stood nearby behind a cart loaded with dishes. I cleared my throat.

"Merlin," Vialle announced with a sensitivity that always gives me a small chill—she being completely blind. "How pleasant!"

"Hello," Llewella said. "Come and join us. We're anxious to hear what you've been doing."

I drew a chair up to the far side of the table and seated myself. Michael came over and laid a fresh setting before me. I thought about it quickly. Anything Vialle heard would doubtless get back to Random. So I gave them a somewhat edited version of recent events—leaving out all references to Mandor, Fiona, and anything having to do with the Courts. It made for a considerably shorter story and let me get to my food sooner.

"Everybody's been so busy lately," Llewella remarked when I'd finished talking. "It almost makes me feel guilty."

I studied the delicate green of her more-than-olive complexion, her full lips, her large catlike eyes.

"But not quite," she added.

"Where are they all, anyway?" I asked.

"Gérard," she said, "is down seeing to harbor fortifications, and Julian is in command of the army, which has now been equipped with some firearms and is set to defend the approaches to Kolvir."

"You mean Dalt has something in the field already? Coming this way?"

She shook her head. "No, it was a precautionary measure," she replied, "because of that message from Luke. Dalt's force had not actually been sighted."

"Does anyone even know where he is?" I asked.

"Not yet," she answered, "but we're expecting some intelligence on that soon." She shrugged. Then, "Perhaps Julian already has it," she added.

"Why is Julian in command?" I asked between nibbles. "I'd have thought Benedict would take charge of something like this."

Llewella looked away, glancing at Vialle, who seemed to feel the shifting of focus.

"Benedict and a small force of his men have escorted Random to Kashfa," Vialle said, softly.

"Kashfa?" I said. "Why would he want to do that? In fact, Dalt usually hangs out around Kashfa. The area could be dangerous right now."

She smiled faintly.

"That is why he wanted Benedict and his guard for escort," she said. "They may even be the intelligence-gathering expedition themselves, though that's not their reason for going right now."

"I don't understand," I said, "why the trip should be necessary at all."

She took a sip of water.

"A sudden political upheaval," she replied. "Some general had taken over in the absence of the queen and the crown prince. The general was just assassinated recently, and Random has succeeded in obtaining agreement for placing his own candidate—an older nobleman—on the throne."

"How'd he do that?"

"Everyone with an interest in the matter was even more interested in seeing Kashfa admitted to the Golden Circle of privileged trade status."

"So Random bought them off to see his own man in charge," I observed. "Don't these Golden Circle treaties usually give us the right to move troops through a client kingdom's territory with very little in the way of preliminaries?"

"Yes," she said.

I suddenly recalled that tough-looking emissary of the Crown I'd met at Bloody Bill's, who had paid his tab in Kashfan currency. I decided I did not really want to know how close in point of time that was to the assassination that had made this recent arrangement possible. What struck me with more immediate force was the picture that now emerged: It looked as if Random had just blocked Jasra and Luke from recovering their usurped throne—which, to be fair, I guess Jasra had usurped herself, years ago. With all that usurping going on, the equities of the thing were more than a little hazy to me. But if Random's ethics were no better than those which had gone before, they were certainly no worse. It looked now, though, as if any attempt on the part of Luke to regain his mother's throne would be met by a monarch who possessed a defense alliance with Amber. I suddenly felt willing to bet that the terms of the defense provisions of the alliance included Amber's assistance in internal troubles as well as help against outside aggressors.

Fascinating. It sounded as if Random were going to an awful lot of trouble to isolate Luke from his power base and any semblance of legitimacy as a head of state. I supposed the next step could be to get him outlawed as a pretender and a dangerous revolutionary, and to put a price on his head. Was Random overreacting? Luke didn't seem all that dangerous now, especially with his mother in our custody. On the other hand, I didn't really know how far Random intended to go. Was he just foreclosing all of the threatening options, or was he actually out to get Luke? The latter possibility bothered me in that Luke seemed on halfway good behavior at the moment and possibly in the throes of reconsidering his position. I did not want to see him needlessly thrown to the wolves as a result of overkill on Random's part.

So, "I suppose this has a lot to do with Luke," I said to Vialle.

She was silent for a moment, then replied, "It was Dalt that he seemed concerned about."

I shrugged mentally. It seemed that it would come down to the same thing in Random's mind, since he would see Dalt as the military force Luke would turn to, to recover the throne. So I said, "Oh," and went on eating.

There were no new facts to be had beyond this, and nothing to clarify Random's thinking any further, so we lapsed into small talk while I considered my position once again. It still came down to a feeling that urgent action was necessary and uncertainty as to what form it should take. My course was determined in an unexpected fashion sometime during dessert.

A courtier named Randel—tall, thin, dark, and generally smiling—came into the room. I knew something was up because he was not smiling and he was moving faster than usual. He swept us with his gaze, fixed upon Vialle, advanced quickly and cleared his throat.

"M'lady Majesty . . . ?" he began.

Vialle turned her head slightly in his direction.

"Yes, Randel?" she said. "What is it?"

"The delegation from Begma has just arrived," he answered, "and I find myself without instructions as to the nature of their welcome and any special arrangements that would be suitable."

"Oh dear!" Vialle said, laying aside her fork. "They weren't due until the day after tomorrow, when Random will be back. He's the one they'll be wanting to complain to. What have you done with them?"

"I seated them in the Yellow Room," he replied, "and told them I would go and announce their arrival."

She nodded.

"How many of them are there?"

"The prime minister, Orkuz," he said, "his secretary, Nayda—who is also his daughter—and another daughter, Coral. There are also four servants—two men and two women."

"Go and inform the household staff, and be sure that appropriate quarters are made ready for them," she directed, "and alert the kitchen. They may not have had lunch."

"Very good, Your Highness," he said, beginning to back away.

". . . Then report to me in the Yellow Room, to let me know it's been done," she continued, "and I'll give you additional instructions at that time."

"Consider it done," he replied, and he hurried off.

"Merlin, Llewella," Vialle said, beginning to rise, "come help me entertain them while arrangements are being made."

I gulped my last bite of dessert and got to my feet. I did not really feel like talking to a diplomat and his party, but I was handy and it was one of life's little duties.

"Uh. . . . What are they here for, anyway?" I asked.

"Some sort of protest over what we've been doing in Kashfa," she replied. "They've never been friendly with Kashfa, but I'm not sure now whether they're here to protest Kashfa's possible admission to the Golden Circle or whether they're upset about our interfering in Kashfa's domestic affairs. It could be they're afraid they'll lose business with such a close neighbor suddenly enjoying the same preferred trade status they have. Or it may be they had different plans for Kashfa's throne and we just foreclosed them. Maybe both. Whatever. . . . We can't tell them anything we don't know."

"I just wanted to know what subjects to avoid," I said.

"All of the above," she answered.

"I was wondering the same thing myself," Llewella said. "I was also wondering, though, whether they might have any useful information on Dalt. Their intelligence service must keep a close eye on doings in and about Kashfa."

"Don't pursue that topic," Vialle said, moving toward the door. "If they let something slip or want to give something away, fine. Bring it home. But don't show them you'd like to know."

Vialle took my arm and I guided her out, heading toward the Yellow Room. Llewella produced a small mirror from somewhere and inspected her features. Obviously pleased, she put it away, then remarked, "Lucky you showed up, Merlin. An extra smiling face is always useful at times like this."

"Why don't I feel lucky?" I said.

We made our way to the room where the prime minister and his daughters waited. Their servants had already retired to the kitchen for refreshments. The official party was still hungry, which says something about protocol, especially since it seemed to take a long while before some trays of provender could be attractively assembled. Orkuz was of medium stature and stocky, his black hair tastefully streaked, the lines on his broad face seeming to indicate that he did a lot more frowning than smiling—a practice in which he indulged most of the while that afternoon. Nayda's was a more pleasingly sculpted version of his face, and though she showed the same tendency toward corpulence, it was held firmly in check at an attractive level of roundedness. Also, she smiled a lot and she had pretty teeth. Coral, on the other hand, was taller than either her father or sister, slender, her hair a reddish brown. When she smiled it seemed less official. Also, there was something vaguely familiar about her. I wondered whether I had met her at some boring reception years before. If I had, though, I felt I might have remembered.

After we had been introduced and wine had been poured,

Orkuz made a brief comment to Vialle about "recent distressing news" concerning Kashfa. Llewella and I quickly moved to her side for moral support, but she simply said that such matters would have to be dealt with fully upon Random's return, and that for the moment she wished merely to see to their comfort. He was completely agreeable to this, even to the point of smiling. I had the impression he just wanted the purpose of his visit on the record immediately. Llewella quickly turned the conversation to the matter of his journey, and he graciously allowed the subject to be changed. Politicians are wonderfully programmed.

I learned later that the Begman ambassador wasn't even aware of his arrival, which would seem to indicate that Orkuz had come so quickly he had preceded any notification to their embassy. And he hadn't even bothered dropping in there, but had come straight to the palace and had a message sent over. I learned this a little later, when he asked to have the message delivered. Feeling somewhat supernumerary to Llewella's and Vialle's graceful cascades of neutral talk, I dropped back a pace to plan my escape. I was not at all interested in whatever game was being set up.

Coral backed off also and sighed. Then she glanced at me and smiled, surveyed the room quickly and came closer.

"I've always wanted to visit Amber," she said then.

"Is it the way you imagined it?" I asked.

"Oh, yes. So far. Of course, I haven't seen that much of it yet. . . ."

I nodded, and we withdrew a little farther from the others.

"Have I met you somewhere before?" I asked.

"I don't think so," she said. "I haven't traveled that much, and I don't believe you've been out our way. Have you?"

"No, though I've grown curious about it recently."

"I do know something of your background, though," she went on, "just from general gossip. I know you're from the Courts of Chaos, and I know you went to school on that Shadow world you Amberites seem to visit so frequently. I've often wondered what it was like."

I took the bait and I began telling her about school and my job, about a few places I'd visited and things I'd enjoyed doing. We made our way to a sofa across the room as I spoke, and we got more comfortable. Orkuz, Nayda, Llewella, and Vialle didn't seem to miss us, and if I had to be here I found talking with Coral more enjoyable than listening to them. Not to monopolize things, though, I asked her about herself.

She began telling me of a girlhood spent in and around Begma, of her fondness for the outdoors—of horses and of boating on the many lakes and rivers in that region—of books she had read, and of relatively innocent dabblings in magic. A member of the household staff came in just as she was getting around to a description of some interesting rites performed by members of the local farming community to insure the fertility of the crops, and she approached Vialle and told her something. Several more staff members were in view outside the doorway. Vialle then said something to Orkuz and Nayda, who nodded and moved toward the entrance. Llewella departed the group and came our way.

"Coral," she said, "your suite is ready. One of the staff will show you where it is. Perhaps you'd like to freshen up or rest after your journey."

We got to our feet.

"I'm not really tired," Coral said, looking at me rather than Llewella, a hint of a smile at the corners of her mouth.

What the hell. I suddenly realized I had been enjoying her company, so, "If you'd care to change into something simpler," I said, "I'll be glad to show you a bit of the town. Or the palace."

It became a full smile worth seeing.

"I'd much rather do that," she said.

"Then I'll meet you back here in about half an hour," I told her.

I saw her out, and accompanied her and the others as far as the foot of the big stairway. In that I still had on my Levi's and purple shirt, I wondered whether I should change into something more in keeping with local fashion. The hell with it, I decided then. We were just going to be knocking around. I'd simply add my swordbelt and weapons, a cloak, and my best boots. Might trim my beard, though, since I had a little time. And maybe a quick manicure. . . .

"Uh, Merlin. . . ."

It was Llewella, her hand on my elbow, steering me toward an alcove. I allowed myself to be steered.

Then, "Yes?" I said. "What's up?"

"Hm . . . ," she said. "Kind of cute, isn't she?"

"I suppose so," I replied.

"You got the hots for her?"

"Jeez, Llewella! I don't know. I just met the lady."

". . . And made a date with her."

"Come on! I deserve a break today. I enjoyed talking with her. I'd like to show her around a bit. I think we'd have a good time. What's wrong with that?"

"Nothing," she answered, "so long as you keep things in perspective."

"What perspective did you have in mind?"

"It strikes me as faintly curious," she said, "that Orkuz brought along his two good-looking daughters."

"Nayda *is* his secretary," I said, "and Coral's wanted to see the place for some time."

"Uh-huh, and it would be a very good thing for Begma if one of them just happened to latch onto a member of the family."

"Llewella, you're too damned suspicious," I said.

"It comes of having lived a long time."

"Well, I hope to live a long time myself, and I hope it doesn't make me look for an ulterior motive in every human act."

She smiled. "Of course. Forget I said anything," she told me, knowing I wouldn't. "Have a good time."

I growled politely and headed for my room.

4

And so, in the midst of all manner of threats, intrigues, menaces, and mysteries, I decided to call a holiday and stroll about town with a pretty lady. Of all possible choices I might have made, it was certainly the most attractive. Whoever the enemy, whatever the power I faced, the ball was now in its court. I had no desire to hunt for Jurt, duel with Mask, or follow Luke about until he came down and told me whether or not he still wanted the family's scalps. Dalt was not my problem, Vinta was gone, Ghostwheel was silent, and the matter of my father's Pattern could await my leisure. The sun was shining and the breeze was gentle, though these could change quickly at this season. It was a shame to waste what could well be the year's last good day on anything less than enjoyment. I hummed as I repaired myself, and I headed downstairs early for our meeting.

Coral had moved more quickly than I'd guessed, however, and was waiting for me. I approved of her sensible dark green breeches, heavy coppery shirt, and warm brown cloak. Her boots looked fine for walking, and she had on a dark hat that covered most of her hair. There were gloves and a dagger at her belt.

"All ready," she said when she saw me.

"Great," I replied, smiling, and I led her out into the hallway.

She started to turn in the direction of the main doorway, but I led her off to the right, then later to the left.

"Less conspicuous to use one of the side doors," I said.

"You people are certainly secretive," she said.

"Habit," I replied. "The less that outsiders know of your business the better."

"What outsiders? What are you afraid of?"

"Just now? A great number of things. But I don't really want to spend a nice day like this making lists."

She shook her head in what I took to be a mixture of awe and disgust.

"It's true what they say then?" she asked. "That your affairs are so complex you all carry scorecards?"

"Haven't had time for any affairs recently," I told her, "or even a simple score." Then, "Sorry," I added, when I saw her blush. "Life *has* been a bit complicated for me lately."

"Oh," she said, glancing at me, clearly asking for elaboration.

"Some other time," I said, forcing a laugh, flipping my cloak, and greeting a guard.

She nodded and, diplomatically, changed the subject:

"I guess I came at the wrong time of year to see your famous gardens."

"Yeah, they've pretty much had it for the season," I said, "except for Benedict's Japanese garden which is kind of far out back. Perhaps we can go and have a cup of tea there one day, but I thought we'd go into town now."

"Sounds fine," she agreed.

I told the postern guard to tell Henden, Amber's steward, that we were heading into town and weren't sure when we'd be back. He said that he would as soon as he got off duty, which would be pretty soon. My experience at Bloody Bill's had taught me the lesson of leaving such messages—not that I thought we were in any danger, or that Llewella's knowing wouldn't be sufficient.

Leaves crunched beneath our feet as we took one of the walks toward a side gate. With only a few strands of cirrus high overhead, the sun shone brightly. To the west, a flock of dark birds flapped its way toward the ocean, south.

"It's already snowed back home," she told me. "You're lucky."

"There's a warm current that gives us a break," I said, remembering something Gérard had once told me. "It moderates the climate considerably, compared to other places at equal latitude."

"You travel a lot?" she asked me.

"I've been traveling more than I care to," I said, "recently. I'd like to sit down and go to seed for about a year."

"Business or pleasure?" she asked me, as a guard let us out the gate and I quickly surveyed the environs for lurkers.

"Not pleasure," I answered as I took her elbow for a moment and steered her toward the way I had chosen.

When we reached civilized precincts, we followed the Main Concourse for a time. I pointed out a few landmarks and notable residences, including the Begman Embassy. She showed no inclination to visit the latter, though, saying she'd have to see her countrymen officially before she left, anyway. She did stop in a shop we found later, however, to buy a couple of blouses, having the bill sent to the embassy and the garments to the palace.

"My father promised me some shopping," she explained. "And I know he'll forget. When he hears about this, he'll know that I didn't."

We explored the streets of the various trades and stopped for a drink at a sidewalk cafe, watching pedestrians and horsemen pass. I had just turned toward her to relate an anecdote concerning one of the riders when I felt the beginning of a Trump contact. I waited for several seconds as the feeling grew stronger, but no identity took shape beyond the reaching. I felt Coral's hand upon my arm.

"What's the matter?" she asked.

I reached out with my mind, attempting to assist in the contact, but the other seemed to retreat as I did so. It was not the same as that lurking scrutiny when Mask had regarded me at Flora's place in San Francisco, though. Could it just be someone I knew trying to reach me and having trouble focusing? Injured, perhaps? Or—

"Luke?" I said. "Is that you?"

But there was no response and the feeling began to fade. Finally, it was gone.

"Are you all right?" Coral asked.

"Yeah, it's okay," I said. "I guess. Someone tried to reach me and then decided otherwise."

"Reach? Oh, you mean those Trumps you use?"

"Yes."

"But you said 'Luke' . . ." she mused. "None of your family is named—"

"You might know him as Rinaldo, Prince of Kashfa," I said.

She chuckled.

"Rinny? Sure I know him. He didn't like us to call him Rinny, though. . . ."

"You really *do* know him? Personally, I mean?"

"Yes," she replied, "though it's been a long time. Kashfa's pretty close to Begma. Sometimes we were on good terms, sometimes not so good. You know how it is. Politics. When I was little there were long spells when we were pretty friendly. There were lots of state visits, both ways. We kids would often get dumped together."

"What was he like in those days?"

"Oh, a big, gawky, red-haired boy. Liked to show off a lot—how strong he was, how fast he was. I remember how mad he got at me once because I beat him in a footrace."

"You beat Luke in a race?"

"Yes. I'm a very good runner."

"You must be."

"Anyway, he took Nayda and me sailing a few times, and on some long hikes. Where is he now, anyway?"

"Drinking with a Cheshire cat."

"What?"

"It's a long story."

"I'd like to hear it. I've been worried about him since the coup."

Mm. . . . I thought quickly about how to edit this so as not to tell the daughter of the Begman prime minister any state secrets, such as Luke's relationship to the House of Amber. . . . So, "I've known him for quite some time," I began. "He recently incurred the wrath of a sorcerer who drugged him and saw him banished to this peculiar bar. . . ."

I went on for a long while then, partly because I had to stop and summarize Lewis Carroll. I also had to promise her the loan of one of the Thari editions of *Alice* from the Amber library. When I finally finished, she was laughing.

"Why don't you bring him back?" she said then.

Ouch. I couldn't very well say that his shadow-shifting abilities would work against this until he came down. So, "It's part of the spell; it's working on his own sorcerous ability," I said. "He can't be moved till the drug wears off."

"How interesting," she observed. "Is Luke really a sorcerer himself?"

"Uh . . . yes," I said.

"How did he gain that ability. He showed no signs of it when I knew him."

"Sorcerers come by their skills in various ways," I explained. "But you know that," and I suddenly realized that she was smarter than that smiling, innocent expression indicated. I'd a strong feeling she was trying to steer this toward an acknowledgment of Pattern magic on Luke's part, which of course would say interesting things about his paternity. "And his mother, Jasra, is something of a sorceress herself."

"Really? I never knew that."

Damn! Coming and going. . . .

"Well, she'd learned it somewhere."

"What about his father?"

"I can't really say," I replied.

"Did you ever meet him?"

"Only in passing," I said.

A lie could make the matter seem really important if she had even a small idea as to the truth. So I did the only other thing I could think of. There was no one seated at the table behind her, and there was nothing beyond the table but a wall. I wasted one of my spells, with an out-of-sight gesture and a single mutter.

The table flipped over as it flew back and crashed against the wall. The noise was spectacular. There were loud exclamations from several other patrons, and I leaped to my feet.

"Is everyone all right?" I said, looking about as if for casualties.

"What happened?" she asked me.

"Freak gust of wind or something," I said. "Maybe we'd better be moving on."

"All right," she said, regarding the debris. "I'm not looking for trouble."

I tossed some coins onto our table, rose, and headed back outside, talking the while of anything I could think of to put some distance between us and the subject. This had the desired effect, because she did not attempt to retrieve the question.

Continuing our stroll, I headed us in the general direction of West Vine. When we reached it I decided to head downhill to the harbor, recalling her fondness for sailing. But she put her hand on my arm and halted me.

"Isn't there a big stairway up the face of Kolvir?" she asked. "I believe your father once tried to sneak troops up it and got caught and had to fight his way along."

I nodded. "Yes, that's true," I said. "Old thing. It goes way back. It's not used very much these days. But it's still in decent shape."

"I'd like to see it."

"All right."

I turned to the right and we headed back, uphill, toward the Main Concourse. A pair of knights wearing Llewella's livery passed us, headed in the other direction, saluting as they went by. I could not help but wonder whether they were on a legitimate errand or were following some standing order to keep an eye on my movements. The thought must have passed through Coral's mind, also, because she quirked an eyebrow at me. I shrugged and kept going. When I glanced back a bit later, they were nowhere to be seen.

We passed people in the garb of a dozen regions as we strolled, and the air was filled with the smells of cooking from open stalls, to satisfy a multitude of tastes. At various points in our career up the hill, we stopped for meat pies, yogurts, sweets. The stimuli were too overpowering for any but the most sated to ignore.

I noticed the lithe way she moved about obstacles. It wasn't just gracefulness. It was more a state of being—preparedness, I guess. Several times I noticed her glancing back in the direction from which we had come. I looked myself, but there was nothing unusual to see. Once, when a man stepped suddenly from a door-way we were approaching, I saw her hand flash toward the dagger at her belt, then drop away.

"There is so much activity, so much going on here . . . ," she commented after a time.

"True. Begma is less busy, I take it?"

"Considerably."

"Is it a pretty safe place to stroll about?"

"Oh, yes."

"Do the women as well as the men take military training there?"

"Not ordinarily. Why?"

"Just curious."

"I've had some training in armed and unarmed combat, though," she said.

"Why was that?" I asked.

"My father suggested it. Said it could come in handy for a rel-ative of someone in his position. I thought he might be right. I think he really wanted a son."

"Did your sister do it, too?"

"No, she wasn't interested."

"You planning on a diplomatic career?"

"No. You're talking to the wrong sister."

"A wealthy husband?"

"Probably stodgy and boring."

"What, then?"

"Maybe I'll tell you later."

"All right. I'll ask if you don't."

We made our way southward along the Concourse, and the breezes picked up as we neared Land's End. It was a winter ocean that came into view across the distance, slate-gray and white-capped. Many birds wheeled far out over the waves, and one very sinuous dragon.

We passed through the Great Arch and came at last to the landing and looked downward. It was a vertiginous prospect, out across a brief, broad stair—the steep drop to the tan-and-black beach far below. I regarded the ripples in the sand left by the retreating tide, wrinkles in an old man's brow. The breezes were stronger here, and the damp, salty smell, which had been increasing as we approached, seasoned the air to a new level of intensity. Coral drew back for a moment, then advanced again.

"It looks a little more dangerous than I'd thought," she said, after a time. "Probably seems less so once you're on it."

"I don't know," I replied.

"You've never climbed it?"

"Nope," I said. "Never had any reason to."

"I'd think you'd have wanted to, after your father's doomed battle along it."

I shrugged. "I get sentimental in different ways."

She smiled. "Let's climb down to the beach. Please."

"Sure," I said, and we moved forward and started.

The broad stair took us down for perhaps thirty feet, then terminated abruptly where a much narrower version turned off to the side. At least the steps weren't damp and slippery. Somewhere far below, I could see where the stair widened again, permitting a pair of people to go abreast. For now, though, we moved single file, and I was irritated that Coral had somehow gotten ahead of me.

"If you'll scrunch over, I'll go past," I told her.

"Why?" she asked.

"So I can be ahead of you in case you slip."

"That's all right," she replied. "I won't."

I decided it wasn't worth arguing and let her lead.

The landings where the stairway switched back were haphazard affairs, hacked wherever the contours of the rock permitted such a turning. Consequently, some descending stretches were longer than others and our route wandered all over the face of the mountain. The winds were much stronger now than they were above, and we found ourselves staying as close to the mountain's side as its contours permitted. Had there been no wind, we probably would have done the same. The absence of any sort of guard railing made us shy back from the edge. There were places where the mountain's wall overhung us for a cavelike effect; other places, we followed a bellying of the rock and felt very exposed. My cloak blew up across my face several times and I cursed, recalling that natives seldom visit historical spots in their own neighborhoods. I began to appreciate their wisdom. Coral was hurrying on ahead, and I increased my pace to catch up with her. Beyond her, I could see that there was a landing which signaled the first turning of the way. I was hoping she'd halt there and tell me she'd reconsidered the necessity for this expedition. But she didn't. She turned and kept right on going. The wind stole my sigh and bore it to some storybook cave reserved for the plaints of the imposed-upon.

Still, I couldn't help but look down upon occasion; and whenever I did I thought of my father fighting his way up along these steps. It was not something I'd care to try—at least, not until I'd exhausted all of the more sneaky alternatives. I began to wonder how far we were below the level of the palace itself. . . .

When we finally came to the landing from which the stairway widened, I hurried to catch up with Coral so that we could walk abreast. In my haste, I snagged my heel and stumbled as I rounded the turn. It was no big deal. I was able to reach out and stabilize myself against the cliff's face as I jolted forward and swayed. I was amazed, though, at Coral's perception of my altered gait just on the basis of its sound, and by her reaction to it. She cast herself backward suddenly and twisted her body to the side. Her hands came in contact with my arm as she did this, and she thrust me to the side, against the rock.

"All right!" I said, from rapidly emptying lungs. "I'm okay."

She rose and dusted herself off as I recovered.

"I heard—" she began.

"I gather. But I just caught my heel. That's all."

"I couldn't tell."

"Everything's fine. Thanks."

We started down the stair side by side, but something was changed. I now harbored a suspicion I did not like but could not dispel. Not yet, anyway. What I had in mind was too dangerous, if I should prove correct.

So instead, "The rain in Spain stays mainly in the plain," I said.

"What?" she asked. "I didn't understand. . . ."

"I said, 'It's a fine day to be walking with a pretty lady.' "

She actually blushed.

Then, "What language did you say it in . . . the first time?"

"English," I replied.

"I've never studied it. I told you that when we were talking about *Alice*."

"I know. Just being whimsical," I answered.

The beach, nearer now, was tiger-striped and shiny in places. A froth of foam retreated along its slopes while birds cried and dipped to examine the waves' leavings. Sails bobbed in the offing, and a small curtain of rain rippled in the southeast, far out at sea. The winds had ceased their noise-making, though they still came upon us with cloak-wrapping force.

We continued in silence until we had reached the bottom. We stepped away then, moving a few paces onto the sand.

"The harbor's in that direction," I said, gesturing to my right, westward, "and there's a church off that way," I added, indicating the dark building where Caine's service had been held and where seamen sometimes came to pray for safe voyages.

She looked in both directions and also glanced behind us and upward.

"More people headed down," she remarked.

I looked back up and saw three figures near the top of the stairway, but they were standing still, as if they'd only come down a short distance to try the view. None of them wore Llewella's colors. . . .

"Fellow sightseers," I said.

She watched them a moment longer, then looked away.

"Aren't there caves along here somewhere?" she asked.

I nodded to my right.

"That way," I answered. "There's a whole series. People get lost in them periodically. Some are pretty colorful. Others just wander through darkness. A few are simply shallow openings."

"I'd like to see them," she said.

"Sure, easily done. Let's go."

I began walking. The people on the stair had not moved. They still appeared to be looking out to sea. I doubted they were smugglers. It doesn't seem like a daytime occupation for a place where anyone might wander by. Still, I was pleased that my faculty for suspicion was growing. It seemed appropriate in light of recent events. The object of my greatest suspicion, of course, was walking beside me, turning driftwood with the toe of her boot, scuffing bright pebbles, laughing—but there was nothing I was ready to do about it at the moment. Soon. . . .

She took my arm suddenly.

"Thanks for bringing me," she said. "I'm enjoying this."

"Oh, I am, too. Glad we came. You're welcome."

This made me feel slightly guilty, but if my guess were wrong no harm would be done.

"I think I would enjoy living in Amber," she remarked as we went along.

"Me, too," I replied. "I've never really done it for any great length of time."

"Oh?"

"I guess I didn't really explain how long I'd spent on the shadow Earth where I went to school, where I had that job I was telling you about . . . ," I began, and suddenly I was pouring out more autobiography to her—a thing I don't usually do. I wasn't certain why I was telling it at first, and then I realized that I just wanted someone to talk to. Even if my strange suspicion was correct, it didn't matter. A friendly-seeming listener made me feel better than I had in a long while. And before I realized it, I was telling her about my father—how this man I barely knew had rushed through a massive story of his struggles, his dilemmas, his decisions, as if he were trying to justify himself to me, as if that were the only opportunity he might have to do it, and how I had listened, wondering what he was editing, what he had forgotten, what he might be glossing over or dressing up, what his feelings were toward me. . . .

"Those are some of the caves," I told her, as they interrupted my now embarrassing indulgence in memory. She started to say something about my monologue, but I simply continued, "I've only seen them once."

She caught my mood and simply said, "I'd like to go inside one."

I nodded. They seemed a good place for what I had in mind.

I chose the third one. Its mouth was larger than the first two, and I could see back into it for a good distance.

"Let's try that one. It looks well lighted," I explained.

We walked into a shadow-hung chill. The damp sand followed us for a while, thinning only slowly to be replaced by a gritty stone floor. The roof dipped and rose several times. A turn to the left joined us with the passage of another opening, for looking back along it I could see more light. The other direction led more deeply into the mountain. We could still feel the echoing pulse of the sea from where we stood.

"These caves could lead back really far," she observed.

"They do," I replied. "They twist and cross and wind. I wouldn't want to go too far without a map and a light. They've never been fully charted, that I know of."

She looked about, studying areas of blackness within the darkness where side tunnels debouched into our own.

"How far back do you think they go?" she inquired.

"I just don't know."

"Under the palace?"

"Probably," I said, remembering the series of side tunnels I'd passed on my way to the Pattern. "It seems possible they cut into the big caves below it—somewhere."

"What's it like down there?"

"Under the palace? Just dark and big. Ancient. . . ."

"I'd like to see it."

"Whatever for?"

"The Pattern's down there. It must be pretty colorful."

"Oh, it is—all bright and swirly. Rather intimidating, though."

"How can you say that when you've walked it?"

"Walking it and liking it are two different things."

"I'd just thought that if it were in you to walk it, you'd feel some affinity, some deep resonant kinship with it."

I laughed, and the sounds echoed about us.

"Oh, while I was walking it I knew it was in me to do it," I said. "I didn't feel it beforehand, though. I was just scared then. And I never liked it."

"Strange."

"Not really. It's like the sea or the night sky. It's big and it's powerful and it's beautiful and it's there. It's a natural force and you make of it what you will."

She looked back along the passageway leading inward.

"I'd like to see it," she said.

"I wouldn't try to find my way to it from here," I told her. "Why do you want to see it, anyhow?"

"Just to see how I'd respond to something like that."

"*You're* strange," I said.

"Will you take me when we go back? Will you show it to me?"

This was not going at all the way I'd thought it would. If she were what I thought, I didn't understand the request. I was half-tempted to take her to it, to find out what she had in mind. However, I was operating under a system of priorities, and I'd a feeling she represented one concerning which I'd made myself a promise and some elaborate preparations.

"Perhaps," I mumbled.

"Please. I'd really like to see it."

She seemed sincere. But my guess felt near-perfect. Sufficient time had passed for that strange body-shifting spirit, which had dogged my trail in many forms, to have located a new host and then to have zeroed in on me again and be insinuating itself into my good graces once more. Coral was perfect for the role, her arrival appropriately timed, her concern for my physical welfare manifest, her reflexes fast. I'd have liked to keep her around for questioning, but I knew that she would simply lie to me in the absence of proof or an emergency situation. And I did not trust her. So I reviewed the spell I had prepared and hung on my way home from Arbor House, a spell I had designed to expel a possessing entity from its host. I hesitated a moment, though. My feelings toward her were ambivalent. Even if she were the entity, I might be willing to put up with her if I just knew her motive.

So, "What is it that you want?" I asked.

"Just to see it. Honestly," she answered.

"No, I mean that if you are what I think you really are, I'm asking the big question: Why?"

Frakir began to pulse upon my wrist.

Coral was silent for the space of an audible deep breath, then, "How could you tell?"

"You betrayed yourself in small ways discernible only to one who has recently become paranoid," I responded.

"Magic," she said. "Is that it?"

"It's about to be," I replied. "I could almost miss you, but I can't trust you."

I spoke the guide words to the spell, letting them draw my hands smoothly through the appropriate gestures.

There followed two horrible shrieks, and then a third. But they weren't hers. They came from around the corner in the passageway we had recently quitted.

"What—?" she began.

"—the hell!" I finished, and I rushed past her and rounded the corner, drawing my blade as I went.

Backlighted by the distant cavemouth I beheld three figures on the floor of the cave. Two of them were sprawled and unmoving.

The third was seated and bent forward, cursing. I advanced slowly, the point of my weapon directed toward the seated one. His shadowy head turned in my direction, and he climbed to his feet, still bent forward. He clutched his left hand with his right, and he backed away until he came into contact with the wall. He halted there, muttering something I could not quite hear. I continued my cautious advance, all of my senses alert. I could hear Coral moving at my back, then I glimpsed her accompanying me on my left when the passage widened. She had drawn her dagger, and she held it low and near to her hip. No time now to speculate as to what my spell might have done to her.

I halted as I came to the first of the two fallen forms. I prodded it with the toe of my boot, ready to strike instantly should it spring into an attack. Nothing. It felt limp, lifeless. I used my foot to turn it over, and the head rolled back in the direction of the cavemouth. In the light that then fell upon it I beheld a half-decayed human face. My nose had already been informing me that this state was no mere illusion. I advanced upon the other one and turned him, also. He, too, bore the appearance of a decomposing corpse. While the first one clutched a dagger in his right hand, the second was weaponless. Then I noted another dagger—on the floor, near the live man's feet. I raised my eyes to him. This made no sense whatsoever. I'd have judged the two figures upon the floor to have been dead for several days, at least, and I had no idea as to what the standing man had been up to.

"Uh. . . . Mind telling me what's going on?" I inquired.

"Damn you, Merlin!" he snarled, and I recognized the voice.

I moved in a slow arc, stepping over the fallen ones. Coral stayed near to my side, moving in a similar fashion. He turned his head to follow our progress, and when the light finally fell upon his face, I saw that Jurt was glaring at me out of his one good eye—a patch covered the other—and I saw, too, that about half of his hair was missing, the exposed scalp covered with welts or scars, his half-regrown ear-stub plainly visible. From this side I could also see that a bandana suitable for covering most of this damage had slipped down around his neck. Blood was dripping from his left hand, and I suddenly realized that his little finger was missing.

"What happened to you?" I asked.

"One of the zombies hit my hand with his dagger as he fell," he said, "when you expelled the spirits that animated them."

My spell—to evict a possessing spirit. . . . They had been within range of it. . . .

"Coral," I asked, "are you all right?"

"Yes," she replied. "But I don't understand. . . ."

"Later," I told her.

I did not ask him about his head, as I recalled my struggle with the one-eyed werewolf in the wood to the east of Amber—the beast whose head I had forced into the campfire. I had suspected for some time that it had been Jurt in a shape-shifted form, even before Mandor had offered sufficient information to confirm it.

"Jurt," I began, "I have been the occasion of many of your ills, but you must realize that you brought them on yourself. If you would not attack me, I would have no need to defend myself—"

There came a clicking, grinding sound. It took me several seconds to realize that it was a gnashing of teeth.

"My adoption by your father meant nothing to me," I said, "beyond the fact that he honored me by it. I was not even aware until recently that it had occurred."

"You lie!" he hissed. "You tricked him some way, to get ahead of us in the succession."

"You've got to be kidding," I said. "We're all so far down on the list that it doesn't matter."

"Not for the Crown, you fool! For the House! Our father isn't all that well!"

"I'm sorry to hear that," I said. "But I'd never even thought of it that way. And Mandor's ahead of all of us, anyhow."

"And now you're second."

"Not by choice. Come on! I'll never see the title. You know that!"

He drew himself upright, and when he moved I became aware of a faint prismatic nimbus that had been clinging to his outline.

"That isn't the real reason," I continued. "You've never liked me, but you're not after me because of the succession. You're hiding something now. It's got to be something else, for all this activity on your part. By the way, you did send the Fire Angel, didn't you?"

"It found you that fast?" he said. "I wasn't even sure I could count on that. I guess it was worth the price after all. But. . . . What happened?"

"It's dead."

"You're very lucky. Too lucky," he replied.

"What is it that you want, Jurt? I'd like to settle this once and for all."

"Me, too," he answered. "You betrayed someone I love, and only your death will set things right."

"Who are you talking about? I don't understand."

He grinned suddenly.

"You will," he said. "In the last moments of your life I'll let you know why."

"I may have a long wait, then," I answered. "You don't seem to be very good at this sort of thing. Why not just tell me now and save us both a lot of trouble?"

He laughed, and the prism effect increased, and it occurred to me in that instant what it was.

"Sooner than you think," he said, "for shortly I will be more powerful than anything you ever met."

"But no less clumsy," I suggested, both to him and to whomever held his Trump, watching me through it, ready to snatch him away in an instant. . . .

"That *is* you, Mask, isn't it?" I said. "Take him back. You don't have to send him again either and watch him screw up. I'll promote you on my list of priorities and come calling soon, if you'll just give me an assurance that it's really you."

Jurt opened his mouth and said something, but I couldn't hear it because he faded fast and his words went away with him. Something flew toward me as this occurred; there was no need to parry it, but I couldn't stop the reflex.

Along with two moldering corpses and Jurt's little finger, a dozen or so roses lay scattered on the floor at my feet, there at the rainbow's end.

5

As we walked along the beach in the direction of the harbor, Coral finally spoke:

"Does that sort of thing happen around here very often?"

"You should come by on a bad day," I said.

"If you don't mind telling me, I'd like to hear what it was all about."

"I guess I owe you an explanation," I agreed, "because I wronged you back there, whether you know it or not."

"You're serious."

"Yep."

"Go on. I'm really curious."

"It's a long story . . . ," I began again.

She looked ahead to the harbor, then up to Kolvir's heights.

". . . A long walk, too," she said.

". . . And you're a daughter of the prime minister of a country with which we have somewhat touchy relations at the moment."

"What do you mean?"

"Some of the things that are happening may represent kind of sensitive information."

She put her hand on my shoulder and halted. She stared into my eyes.

"I can keep a secret," she told me. "After all, you know mine."

I congratulated myself on having finally learned my relatives' trick of controlling facial expression even when puzzled as all hell. She *had* said something back in the cave when I had addressed her as if she were the entity, something that sounded as if she believed I had discovered a secret concerning her.

So I gave her a wry smile and nodded.

"Just so," I said.

"You're not planning on ravaging our country or anything like that, are you?" she asked.

"To my knowledge, no. And I don't think it likely either."

"Well, then. You can only speak from your knowledge, can't you?"

"True," I agreed.

"So let's hear the story."

"All right."

As we walked along the strand and I spoke, to the accompaniment of the waves' deep notes, I could not help but remember again my father's long narrative. Was it a family trait, I wondered, to go autobiographical at a time of troubles if the right listener turned up? For I realized I was elaborating my telling beyond the bounds of necessity. And why should she be the right listener, anyhow?

When we reached the port district, I realized I was hungry, anyway, and I still had a lot of telling to do. In that it was still daylight and doubtless considerably safer than when I'd made my nighttime visit, I found my way over to Harbor Road—which was even dirtier in strong light—and, having learned that Coral was hungry, too, I took us on around to the rear of the cove, pausing for a few minutes to watch a many-masted vessel with golden sails round the sea wall and head in. Then we followed the curving way to the western shore, and I was able to locate Seabreeze Lane without any trouble. It was still early enough that we passed a few sober sailors. At one point a heavy, black-bearded man with an interesting scar on his right cheek began to approach us, but a smaller man caught up with him first and whispered something in his ear. They both turned away.

"Hey," I said. "What did he want?"

"Nothin'," the smaller man said. "He don't want nothin'." He studied me for a moment and nodded. Then, "I saw you here the other night," he added.

"Oh," I said, as they continued to the next corner, turned it, and were gone.

"What was that all about?" Coral said.

"I didn't get to that part of the story yet."

But I remembered it vividly when we passed the place where it had occurred. No signs of that conflict remained.

I almost passed what had been Bloody Bill's, though, because a new sign hung above the door. It read "Bloody Andy's," in fresh green letters. The place was just the same inside, however, except for the man behind the counter, who was taller and thinner than the shaggy, crag-faced individual who had served me last time. His name, I learned, was Jak, and he was Andy's brother. He sold us a bottle of Bayle's Piss and put in our order for two fish dinners through the hole in the wall. My former table was vacant and we took it. I laid my sword belt on the chair to my right, with the blade partly drawn, as I had been taught etiquette required here.

"I like this place," she said. "It's . . . different."

"Uh . . . yes," I agreed, glancing at two passed-out drunks—one to the front of the establishment, one to the rear—and three shifty-eyed individuals conversing in low voices off in one corner. A few broken bottles and suspicious stains were upon the floor, and some not-too-subtle artwork of an amorous nature hung on the far wall. "The food's quite good," I added.

"I've never been in a restaurant like this," she continued, watching a black cat, who rolled in from a rear room, wrestling with an enormous rat.

"It has its devotees, but it's a well-kept secret among discriminating diners."

I continued my tale through a meal even better than the one I remembered. When the door opened much later to admit a small man with a bad limp and a dirty bandage about his head I noticed that daylight was beginning to wane. I had just finished my story and it seemed a good time to be leaving.

I said as much, but she put her hand on mine.

"You know I'm not your entity," she said, "but if you need any kind of help I can give you, I'll do it."

"You're a good listener," I said. "Thanks. We'd better be going now."

We passed out of Death Alley without incident and made our way along Harbor Road over to Vine. The sun was getting ready to set as we headed upward, and the cobbles passed through a variety of bright earth tones and fire colors. Street and pedestrian traffic was light. Cooking smells drifted on the air; leaves rattled along the road; a small yellow dragon rode the air currents high overhead; curtains of rainbow light rippled high in the north beyond the palace. I kept waiting, expecting more questions from Coral than the few she had asked. They never came. If I'd just heard my story, I think I'd have a lot of questions, unless I were totally overpowered by it or somehow understood it thoroughly.

"When we get back to the palace . . . ?" she said then.

"Yes?"

". . . You *will* take me to see the Pattern, won't you?" I laughed.

. . . Or unless something else were occupying my mind.

"Right away? First thing in the door?" I asked.

"Yes."

"Sure," I said.

Then, that off her mind, "Your story changes my picture of the world," she said, "and I wouldn't presume to advise you. . . ."

"But—" I continued.

". . . It seems that the Keep of the Four Worlds holds the answers you want. Everything else may fall into place when you learn what's going on there. But I don't understand why you can't just do a card for it and trump in."

"Good question. There are parts of the Courts of Chaos to which no one can trump because they change constantly and cannot be represented in a permanent fashion. The same applies to the place where I situated Ghostwheel. Now, the terrain around the Keep fluctuates quite a bit, but I'm not positive that's the reason for the blockage. The place is a power center, and I think it possible that someone diverted some of that power into a shielding spell. A good enough magician might be able to drill through it with a Trump, but I've a feeling that the force required would probably set off some psychic alarm and destroy any element of surprise."

"What does the place look like, anyway?" she asked.

"Well . . . ," I began. "Here." I took my notebook and Scripto from my shirt pocket and sketched. "See, all of this area is volcanic." I scribbled in a few fumaroles and wisps of smoke. "And this part is Ice Age." More scribbles. "Ocean here, mountains here. . . ."

"Then it sounds as if your best bet is to use the Pattern again," she said, studying the drawing and shaking her head.

"Yes."

"Do you think you'll be doing it soon?"

"Possibly."

"How will you attack them?"

"I'm still working on that."

"If there's any sort of way that I can help you, I meant what I said."

"There isn't."

"Don't be so sure. I'm well trained. I'm resourceful. I even
know a few spells."

"Thanks," I said. "But no."

"No discussion?"

"Nope."

"If you change your mind. . . ."

"I won't."

". . . Let me know."

We reached the Concourse, moved along it. The winds grew
more blustery here and something cold touched my cheek. Then
again. . . .

"Snow!" Coral announced, just as I realized that a few middle-
sized flakes were drifting past us, vanishing immediately when
they hit the ground.

"If your party had arrived at the proper time," I observed, "you
might not have had your walk."

"Sometimes I'm lucky," she said.

It was snowing fairly hard by the time we reached the palace
grounds. We used the postern gate again, pausing on the walkway
to gaze back down over the light-dotted town, half-screened by
falling flakes. I knew she kept looking longer than I did, because I
turned to gaze at her. She appeared—happy, I guess—as if she
were pasting the scene in a mental scrapbook. So I leaned over
and kissed her cheek, because it seemed like a good idea.

"Oh," she said, turning to face me. "You surprised me."

"Good," I told her. "I hate to telegraph these things. Let's get
the troops in out of the cold."

She smiled and took my arm.

Inside, the guard told me, "Llewella wants to know whether
you two will be joining them all for dinner."

"When *is* dinner?" I asked him.

"In about an hour and a half, I believe."

I glanced at Coral, who shrugged.

"I guess so," I said.

"Front dining room, upstairs," he told me. "Shall I pass the
word to my sergeant—he's due by soon—and have him deliver it?
Or do you want to—"

"Yes," I said. "Do that."

"Care to wash up, change clothes . . . ?" I began, as we walked
away.

"The Pattern," she said.

"It would involve a lot more stairs," I told her.

She turned toward me, her face tightening, but saw that I was smiling.

"This way," I said, leading her to the main hall and through it. I didn't recognize the guard at the end of the brief corridor that led up to the stair. He knew who I was, though, glanced curiously at Coral, opened the door, found us a lantern, and lit it.

"I'm told there's a loose step," he remarked as he passed me the light.

"Which one is it?"

He shook his head.

"Prince Gérard's reported it several times," he said, "but no one else seems to notice it."

"Okay," I said. "Thanks."

This time Coral didn't object to my going first. Of the two, this was more intimidating than the stairway on the cliff face, mainly because you can't see bottom and after a few paces you can't see much of anything beyond the shell of light within which you move as you wind your way down. And there's a heavy sense of vastness all about you. I've never seen the place illuminated, but I gather that the impression is not incorrect. It's a very big cavern, and you go round and round and down in the middle of it, wondering when you'll reach the bottom.

After a time, Coral cleared her throat, then, "Could we stop for a minute?" she asked.

"Sure," I said, halting. "Out of breath?"

"No," she said. "How much farther?"

"I don't know," I replied. "It seems a different distance each time I come this way. If you want to go back and have dinner, we can see it tomorrow. You've had a busy day."

"No," she answered. "But I wouldn't mind your holding me for a minute."

It seemed an awkward place to get romantic, so I cleverly deduced that there was another reason, said nothing, and obliged.

It took me a long while to realize that she was crying. She was very good at concealing it.

"What's the matter?" I finally asked.

"Nothing," she replied. "Nervous reaction, maybe. Primitive reflex. Darkness. Claustrophobia. Like that."

"Let's go back."

"No."

So we started down again.

About a half minute later I saw something white near the side
of a lower step. I slowed. Then I realized that it was only a handkerchief. A little nearer, however, and I saw that it was held in
place by a dagger. Also, there were markings upon it. I halted,
reached out, flattened it, and read. "THIS ONE, DAMN IT!—
GÉRARD," it said.

"Careful here," I said to Coral.

I prepared to step over it, but on an impulse I tested it lightly
with one foot. No squeaks. I shifted more weight onto it. Nothing.
It felt firm. I stood on it. The same. I shrugged.

"Careful, anyway," I said.

Nothing happened when she stepped on it either, and we kept
going. A little later, I saw a flicker in the distance below. It was
moving, and I guessed someone was doing a patrol. What for? I
wondered. Were there prisoners to be tended and watched? Were
certain cave mouths considered vulnerable points? And what
about the business of locking the chamber of the Pattern and
hanging the key on the wall near the door? Was there some possible danger from that quarter? How? Why? I realized that I ought
to pursue these questions one of these days.

When we reached the bottom the guard was nowhere in sight,
however. The table, the racks, and a few foot lockers—which con-
stituted the guard station—were illuminated by a number of
lanterns, but the guard was not at his post. Too bad. It would be interesting to ask what the orders called for in the event of an
emergency—hopefully also specifying the possible natures of
various emergencies. For the first time, though, I noticed a rope
hanging down from the darkness into the dimness beside a
weapons rack. I drew upon it ever so gently and it yielded, to be
followed a moment later by a faint metallic sound from somewhere high overhead. Interesting. Obviously, this was the alarm.

"Which . . . way?" Coral asked.

"Oh, come on," I said, taking her hand, and I led her off to the
right.

I kept waiting for echoes as we moved, but none came. Periodically, I raised the light. The darkness would recede a bit then,
but nothing came into view beyond an additional area of floor.

Coral seemed to be slowing now, and I felt a certain tension in
her arm as she hung back. I plodded on and she kept moving,
however.

Finally, "It shouldn't be too much longer," I said, as the
echoes began, very faintly.

"Good," she replied, but she did not increase her pace.

At last the gray wall of the cavern came into view, and far off to my left was the dark opening of the tunnel mouth I sought. I changed course and headed toward it. When we finally reached it and entered, I felt her flinch.

"If I'd known it would bother you this much—" I began.

"I'm really all right," she answered, "and I do want to see it. I just didn't realize that getting there would be this . . . involved."

"Well, the worst of it is over. Soon now," I said.

We came to the first side passage to the left fairly quickly and went on by. There was another shortly thereafter, and I slowed and extended the lantern toward it.

"Who knows?" I commented. "That could take you through some strange route back to the beach."

"I'd rather not check it out."

We walked for some time before we passed the third opening. I gave it a quick glance. There was a vein of some bright mineral partway back in it.

I speeded up and she kept pace, our footsteps ringing loudly now. We passed the fourth opening. The fifth. . . . From somewhere, it seemed I heard faint strains of music.

She glanced at me inquiringly when we neared the sixth passageway, but I just kept going. It was the seventh that I wanted, and when we finally came to it I turned, took a few paces, halted, and raised the lantern. We stood before a big metal-bound door.

I took the key down from the hook on the wall to my right, inserting it in the lock, turned it, withdrew it, and rehung it. Then I put my shoulder against the door and pushed hard. There followed a long moment of resistance, then slow movement accompanied shortly by a complaint from a tight hinge. Frakir tightened upon my wrist, but I kept pushing till the door was opened wide. Then I stood to the side and held it for Coral.

She moved a few steps past me into that strange chamber and halted. I stepped away and let the door swing shut, then came up beside her.

"So that's it," she remarked.

Roughly elliptical, the intricately wound oval form of the Pattern glowed blue-white within the floor. I set the lantern aside. It wasn't really necessary, the glow from the Pattern providing more than sufficient illumination. I stroked Frakir, calming her. A jet of sparks rose at the far end of the great design, subsided quickly, occurred again nearer to us. The chamber seemed filled with a half-familiar pulsing I had never consciously noted before. On an impulse—to satisfy a long-held point of curiosity—I summoned the Sign of the Logrus.

This was a mistake.

Immediately the image of the Logrus flared before me, sparks erupted along the entire length of the Pattern, and a high-pitched banshee wail rose from somewhere. Frakir went wild, my ears felt as if icicles had been driven into them, and the brightness of the writhing Sign hurt my eyes. I banished the Logrus in that instant, and the turmoil began to subside.

"What," she asked me, "was that?"

I tried to smile, didn't quite manage it.

"A little experiment I'd always meant to try," I told her.

"Did you learn anything from it?"

"Not to do it again, perhaps," I answered.

"Or at least not till the company's left," she said. "That hurt."

"Sorry."

She moved nearer to the edge of the Pattern, which had calmed itself again.

"Eerie," she observed. "Like a light in a dream. But it's gorgeous. And all of you have to walk it to come into your heritage?"

"Yes."

She moved slowly to the right, following its perimeter. I followed her as she strolled, her gaze roving across the bright expanse of arcs and turns, short straight lines, long sweeping curves.

"I assume it is difficult?"

"Yes. The trick is to keep pushing and not to stop trying even if you stop moving," I replied.

We walked on, to the right, circling slowly around to the rear. The design seemed to be within the floor rather than upon it, seen as through a layer of glass. But nowhere was the surface slippery.

We paused for a minute or so while she took its measure from a new angle.

"So how are you responding to it?" I finally asked.

"Esthetically," she said.

"Anything else?"

"Power," she said. "It seems to radiate something." She leaned forward and waved her hand above the nearest line. "It's almost a physical pressure," she added then.

We moved farther, passing along the back length of the grand design. I could see across the Pattern, to the place where the lantern glowed on the floor near to the entranceway. Its light was negligible beside the greater illumination we regarded now.

Shortly, Coral halted again. She pointed.

"What is this single line, which seems to end right here?" she asked.

"It's not the end," I said. "It's the beginning. That is the place where one commences the walking of the Pattern."

She moved nearer, passing her hand above it also.

"Yes," she said after a moment. "I can feel that it starts here."

For how long we stood there, I am uncertain. Then she reached out, took hold of my hand and squeezed it.

"Thanks," she said, "for everything."

I was about to ask her why that had such a final sound about it, when she moved forward and set her foot upon the line.

"No!" I cried. "Stop!"

But it was too late. Her foot was already in place, brightness outlining the sole of her boot.

"Don't move!" I said. "Whatever you do, stay still!"

She did as I said, holding her position. I licked my lips, which suddenly seemed very dry.

"Now, try to raise the foot you placed upon the line and draw it back. Can you do it?"

"No," she replied.

I knelt beside her and studied it. Theoretically, once you'd set foot upon the Pattern there was no turning back. You had no choice but to continue and either make it through or be destroyed somewhere along the way. On the other hand, she should already be dead. Theoretically, again, anyone not of the blood of Amber shouldn't be able to set foot upon it and live. So much for theory.

"Hell of a time to ask," I said. "But why'd you do it?"

"You indicated to me back in the cave that my guess was correct. You said that you knew what I was."

I recalled what I'd said, but that was with reference to my guess at her being the body-shifting entity. What could she have taken it to mean that had to do with the Pattern? But even as I sought after a spell that might free her from the Pattern's hold, the obvious answer to things drifted into my mind.

"Your connection with the House . . . ?" I said softly.

"King Oberon supposedly had an affair with my mother before I was born," she said. "The timing would have been right. It was only a rumor, though. I couldn't get anyone to provide details. So I was never certain. But I dreamed of it being true. I wanted it to be true. I hoped to find some tunnel that would bring me to this place. I wanted to sneak in and walk the Pattern and have the shadows unfold before me. But I was afraid, too, because I knew that if I were wrong I would die. Then, when you said what you said, you answered my dream. But I did not stop being afraid. I am still afraid. Only now I'm afraid that I won't be strong enough to make it."

That sense of familiarity I had felt when I first met her. . . . I suddenly realized that it was a general family resemblance that had caused it. Her nose and brow reminded me a bit of Fiona, her chin and cheekbones something of Flora. Her hair and eyes and height and build were her own, though. But she certainly did not resemble her nominal father or sister.

I thought again of a faintly leering portrait of my grandfather which I had often studied, in an upstairs hallway, to the west. The lecherous old bastard really got around. Giving him his due, though, he was a very good-looking man. . . .

I sighed and rose to my feet. I laid a hand upon her shoulder.

"Listen, Coral," I said. "All of us were well briefed before we tried it. I am going to tell you about it before you take another step, and while I speak you may feel energy flowing from me into you. I want you to be as strong as possible. When you take your next step I do not want you to stop again until you have reached the middle. I may call out instructions to you as you move along, also. Do whatever I say immediately, without thinking about it.

"First I will tell you about the Veils, the places of resistance. . . ."

For how long I spoke, I do not know.

I watched as she approached the First Veil.

"Ignore the chill and the shocks," I said. "They can't hurt you. Don't let the sparks distract you. You're about to hit major resistance. Don't start breathing rapidly."

I watched her push her way through.

"Good," I said, as she came onto an easier stretch, deciding against telling her that the next Veil was far worse. "By the way, don't think that you're going crazy. Shortly, it will begin playing head games with you—"

"It already has," she responded. "What should I do?"

"It's probably mostly memories. Just let them flow, and keep your attention on the path."

She continued, and I talked her through the Second Veil. The sparks reached almost to her shoulders before she was out of it. I watched her struggle through arc after arc, then tricky curves and long, sweeping ones, turns, reversals. There were times when she moved quickly, times when she was slowed almost to a standstill. But she kept moving. She had the idea, and it seemed she had the will. I did not think that she really needed me now. I was certain that I had nothing left to offer, that the outcome was entirely in her own hands.

So I shut up and watched, irritated with but unable to prevent my own leaning and turning, shifting and pressing, as if I were out there myself, anticipating, compensating.

When she came to the Grand Curve she was a living flame. Her progress was very slow, but there was a relentless quality to it. Whatever the outcome, I knew that she was being changed, had been changed already, that the Pattern was inscribing itself upon her, and that she was very near to the end of its statement. I almost cried out as she seemed to stop for a moment, but the words died in my throat as she shuddered once, then continued. I wiped my brow on my sleeve as she approached the Final Veil. Whatever the outcome, she had proved her suspicions. Only a child of Amber could have survived as she had.

I do not know how long it took her to pierce the last Veil. Her effort became timeless, and I was caught up in that protracted moment. She was a burning study in extreme slow motion, the nimbus that enshrouded her lighting up the entire chamber like a great blue candle.

And then she was through and onto that final short arc, the last three steps of which may well be the most difficult part of the entire Pattern. Some sort of psychic surface tension seems joined with the physical inertia one encounters just before the point of emergence.

Again, I thought she had stopped, but it was only an appearance. It was like watching someone doing tai chi, the painful slowness of that trio of paces. But she completed it and moved again. If the final step didn't kill her, then she was home free. Then we could talk. . . .

That final moment went on and on and on. Then I saw her foot move forward and depart the Pattern. Shortly, the other foot followed and she stood panting at the center.

"Congratulations!" I shouted.

She waved weakly with her right hand while slowly raising her left to cover her eyes. She stood thus for the better part of a minute, and one who has walked the Pattern understands the feeling. I did not call out again, but let her recover, giving her the silence in which to enjoy her triumph.

The Pattern seemed to be glowing more brightly just then, as it often does immediately after being traversed. This gave a fairyland quality to the grotto—all blue light and shadow—and made a mirror of that small, still pool in the far corner where blind fish swim. I tried to think ahead to what this act might mean, for Coral, for Amber. . . .

She straightened suddenly.

"I'm going to live," she announced.

"Good," I replied. "You have a choice now, you know."

"What do you mean?" she asked.

"You are now in a position to command the Pattern to transport you anywhere," I explained. "So you could just have it deposit you back here again, or you could save yourself a long walk by having it return you to your suite right now. As much as I enjoy your company, I'd recommend the latter since you're probably pretty tired. Then you can soak in a nice warm bath and take your time dressing for dinner. I'll meet you in the dining room. Okay?"

I saw that she was smiling as she shook her head.

"I'm not going to waste an opportunity like this," she said.

"Listen, I know the feeling," I told her. "But I think you should restrain yourself. Rushing off someplace weird could be dangerous, and coming back could be tricky when you haven't had any training in shadow walking."

"It's just sort of a will and expectation thing, isn't it?" she asked. "You kind of impose images on the environment as you go along, don't you?"

"It's trickier than that," I said. "You have to learn to capitalize on certain features as points of departure. Normally, one is accompanied on one's first shadow walk by someone with experience—"

"Okay, I get the idea."

"Not enough," I said. "Ideas are fine, but there's feedback, too. There's a certain feeling you get when it begins working. That can't be taught. It has to be experienced—and until you're sure of it, you should have someone along for a guide."

"Seems like trial and error would do."

"Maybe," I answered. "But supposing you wound up in danger? That'd be a hell of a time to start learning. Kind of distracting—"

"All right. You made your point. Fortunately, I'm not planning on anything that would put me in such a position."

"What are you planning?"

She straightened and gestured widely.

"Ever since I learned about the Pattern, there's been something I wanted to try if I got this far," she said.

"What might that be?"

"I'm going to ask it to send me where I should go."

"I don't understand."

"I'm going to leave the choice up to the Pattern."

I shook my head.

"It doesn't work that way," I told her. "You have to give it an order to transport you."

"How do you know that?"

"It's just the way it works."

"Have you ever tried what I'm saying?"

"No. Nothing would happen."

"Has anyone you know of ever tried it?"

"It would be a waste of time. Look, you're talking as if the Pattern is somehow sentient, is capable of coming to a decision on its own and executing it."

"Yes," she replied. "And it must know me real well after what I've just been through with it. So I'm just going to ask its advice and—"

"Wait!" I said.

"Yes?"

"On the off chance that something happens, how do you plan on getting back?"

"I'll walk, I guess. So you're admitting that something *could* happen?"

"Yes," I said. "It's conceivable that you have an unconscious desire to visit a place, and that it will read that and take you there if you give a transport order. That won't prove that the Pattern is sentient—just that it's sensitive. Now, if it were me standing there, I'd be afraid to take a chance like that. Supposing I have suicidal tendencies I'm not aware of? Or—"

"You're reaching," she answered. "You're really reaching."

"I'm just counseling you to play it safe. You have your whole life to go exploring. It would be silly to—"

"Enough!" she said. "My mind's made up, and that's it. It feels right. See you later, Merlin."

"Wait!" I cried again. "All right. Do it if you must. But let me give you something first."

"What?"

"A means of getting out of a tight spot in a hurry. Here."

I withdrew my Trumps, shuffled out my own card. Then I unfastened my dagger and sheath from my belt. I wrapped my card around the haft and tied it there with my handkerchief.

"You have an idea how to use a Trump?"

"You just stare and think of the person till there's contact, don't you?"

"That'll do," I said. "Here's mine. Take it with you. Call me when you want to come home, and I'll bring you back."

I tossed it out across the Pattern, underhand. She caught it easily and hung it on her belt on the side opposite her own.

"Thanks," she said, straightening. "I guess I'll give it a try now."

"Just in case it really works, don't stay long. Okay?"

"Okay," she answered, and she closed her eyes.

An instant later she was gone. Oh, my.

I moved to the edge of the Pattern and held my hand above it until I could feel the forces stirring there.

"You'd better know what you're doing," I said. "I want her back."

A spark shot upward and tickled my palm.

"You trying to tell me you're really sentient?"

Everything swirled about me. The dizziness passed in an instant, and the first thing I noticed then was that the lantern was beside my right foot. When I looked about I realized that I was standing on the other side of the Pattern from where I had been and was now near the door.

"I was within your field and I'm already attuned," I said. "It was just my unconscious desire to get out."

Then I hefted the lantern, locked the door behind me, and hung the key back on its hook. I still didn't trust the thing. If it had really wanted to be helpful, it would have sent me directly to my quarters and saved me all those stairs.

I hurried along the tunnel. It was by far the most interesting first date I'd ever had.

6

As I passed out of the main hall and headed along the back hallway which would take me to any of a number of stairs, a fellow in black leathers and various pieces of rusty and shiny chain emerged from a corridor to my right, halted, and stared at me. His hair was of an orange Mohawk cut and there were several silver rings in his left ear near what looked like an electrical outlet of some sort.

"Merlin?" he said. "You okay?"

"For the moment," I replied as I drew nearer, trying to place him, there in the dimness.

"Martin!" I said. "You're . . . changed."

He chuckled.

"I'm just back from a very interesting shadow," he said. "Spent over a year there—one of those places where time runs like hell."

"I'd judge—just guessing—that it was high-tech, urban. . . ."

"Right."

"I thought you were a country boy."

"I got over it. Now I know why my dad likes cities and noise."

"You a musician, too?"

"Some. Different sounds, though. You going to be at dinner?"

"I was planning on it. As soon as I get cleaned up and changed."

"See you there, then. We've a lot of things to talk about."

"Sure thing, Cousin."

He clasped my shoulder and released it as I passed. His grip was still strong.

I walked on. Before I'd gone very far, I felt the beginning of a Trump contact. I halted and reached quickly, figuring it was Coral wanting to return. Instead, my eyes met those of Mandor, who smiled faintly.

"Ah, very good," he said. "You are alone and apparently safe."

As things came clearer I saw that Fiona was standing beside him, standing very close as a matter of fact.

"I'm okay," I said. "I'm back in Amber. You all right?"

"Intact," he said, looking past me, though there was not much to see beyond wall and a bit of tapestry.

"Would you care to come through?" I asked.

"I'd love to see Amber," he replied. "But that pleasure will have to await another occasion. We are somewhat occupied at the moment."

"You've discovered the cause of the disturbances?" I asked.

He glanced at Fiona, then back at me.

"Yes and no," he said. "We've some interesting leads but no certainty at the moment."

"Uh, what can I do for you then?" I asked.

Fiona extended her index finger and suddenly became much clearer. I realized that she must have reached out and touched my Trump for better contact.

"We've had an encounter with a manifestation of that machine you built," she said. "Ghostwheel."

"Yes?" I said.

"You're right, it's sentient—social AI as well as technical."

"I was already certain it could pass the Turing test."

"Oh, no doubt about that," she responded, "since by definition the Turing test requires a machine capable of lying to people and misleading them."

"What are you getting at, Fiona?" I asked.

"It's not just social AI. It's downright antisocial," she replied. "I think your machine is crazy."

"What did it do?" I asked. "Attack you?"

"No, nothing physical. It's wacky and mendacious and insulting, and we're too busy to go into details right now. I'm not saying it couldn't get nasty, though. I don't know. We just wanted to warn you not to trust it."

I smiled.

"That's it? End of message?" I said.

"For now," she answered, lowering her finger and growing dim.

I shifted my gaze to Mandor and was about to explain that I

had built a host of safeguards into the thing, so that not just any-body could access it. Mainly, though, I wanted to tell him about Jurt. But our communication was suddenly severed, as I felt another presence reaching toward me.

I was intrigued by the sensation. I had occasionally wondered what would occur if someone tried for a Trump contact when I was already in touch with someone else via a Trump. Would it turn into a conference call? Would someone get a busy signal? Would it put the other party on hold? I'd doubted I'd ever find out, though. It just seemed statistically unlikely. However. . . .

"Merlin, baby. I'm okay."

"Luke!"

Mandor and Fiona were definitely gone.

"I'm really okay now, Merle."

"You sure?"

"Yeah, as soon as I started coming down I switched to a fast lane. In this shadow it's been several days since I've seen you."

He was wearing sunglasses and green swim trunks. He was seated at a small table beside a swimming pool in the shade of a great umbrella, the remains of a large lunch spread before him. A lady in a blue bikini dived into the pool and passed from my line of sight.

"Well, I'm glad to hear about that and—"

"So what happened to me, anyhow? I remember you said something about someone slipping me some acid when I was a prisoner back at the Keep. Is that how it went?"

"It seems very likely."

"I guess that's what happens when you drink the water," he mused. "Okay. What's been going on while I've been out of it?"

Knowing how much to tell him was always a problem. So, "Where do we stand?" I asked.

"Oh. That," he said.

"Yeah."

"Well, I've had a chance to do a lot of thinking," he replied, "and I'm going to call it quits. Honor has been satisfied. It's point-less to keep pushing this thing against everybody else. But I'm not about to put myself in Random's hands for a kangaroo trial. Now it's your turn: Where do I stand so far as Amber's concerned? Should I be looking over my shoulder?"

"Nobody's said anything yet, one way or the other. But Random is out of town now and I just got back myself. I haven't really had a chance to learn what the others' feelings might be on this thing."

He removed his sunglasses and studied me.

"The fact that Random's out of town. . . ."

"No, I know he's not after you," I said, "because he's in Kash—" and I tried to stop it just a syllable too late.

"Kashfa?"

"So I understand."

"What the hell's he doing there? Amber was never interested in the place before."

"There's been a . . . death," I explained. "Some kind of shake-up going on."

"Ha!" Luke remarked. "That bastard finally bought it. Good! But. . . . Hey! Why's Amber moving in so suddenlike, huh?"

"Don't know," I said.

He chuckled. "Rhetorical question," he said. "I can see what's going on. I've got to admit Random's got style. Listen, when you find out who he puts on the throne let me know, will you? I like to keep abreast of doings in the old hometown."

"Oh, sure," I said, trying unsuccessfully to determine whether such information could be harmful. It would become public knowledge very soon, if it wasn't already.

"So what else is going on? That other person who was Vinta Bayle . . . ?"

"Gone," I said. "I don't know where."

"Very strange," he mused. "I don't think we've seen the last of her. She *was* Gail, too. I'm sure. Let me know if she comes back, will you?"

"Okay. You want to ask her out again?"

He shrugged, then smiled. "I could think of worse ways to spend some time."

"You're lucky she didn't try to take *you* out, literally."

"I'm not so sure she would've," he replied. "We always got along pretty well. Anyhow, none of this is the main reason I called. . . ."

I nodded, having already guessed as much.

"How's my mother doing?" he asked.

"Hasn't stirred," I answered. "She's safe."

"That's something," he said. "You know, it's kind of undigni-fied for a queen to be in that position. A coatrack. Jeez!"

"I agree," I agreed. "But what's the alternative?"

"Well, I'd sort of like to . . . get her freed," he said. "What'll it take?"

"You raise a very thorny issue," I stated.

"I sort of figured that."

"I've a strong feeling she's the one behind this revenge business, Luke, that she's the one who put you up to going after everybody. Like with that bomb. Like encouraging you to set up that private army with modern weapons, to use against Amber. Like trying for a hit on me every spring. Like—"

"Okay, okay. You're right. I don't deny it. But things have changed—"

"Yeah. Her plans fell through and we've got her."

"That's not what I meant. I'm changed. I understand her now, and I understand myself better. She can't push me around that way anymore."

"Why is that?"

"That trip I was on. . . . It shook loose my thinking quite a bit. About her and me. I've had several days now to mull over what some of it meant, and I don't think she can pull the same crap on me that she used to."

I recalled the red-haired woman tied to the stake, tormented by demons. There was a resemblance, now I thought of it.

"But she's still my mother," he went on, "and I don't like leaving her in the position she's in. What kind of deal might be possible for turning her loose?"

"I don't know, Luke," I answered. "The matter hasn't come up yet."

"Well, she's *your* prisoner, actually."

"But her plans were directed against all of us."

"True, but I won't be helping her with them anymore. She really needs someone like me for carrying them out."

"Right. And if she doesn't have you to help, what's to prevent her from finding someone like you, as you put it? She'd still be dangerous if we let her go."

"But you know about her now. That would crimp her style quite a bit."

"It might just make her more devious."

He sighed. "I suppose there's some truth in that," he admitted. "But she's as venal as most people. It's just a matter of finding the right price."

"I can't see Amber buying someone off that way."

"I can."

"Not when that person is already a prisoner here."

"That does complicate matters a little," he acknowledged.

"But I hardly think it's an insurmountable barrier. Not if she's more useful to you free than as a piece of furniture."

"You've lost me," I said. "What are you proposing?"

"Nothing yet. I'm just sounding you out."

"Fair enough. But offhand, I can't see a situation such as you describe arising. More valuable to us free than a prisoner. . . . I guess we'd go where the value lies. But these are just words."

"Just trying to plant a seed or two while I work on it. What is your greatest concern right now?"

"Me? Personally? You really want to know?"

"You bet."

"Okay. My mad brother Jurt has apparently allied himself with the sorcerer Mask back at the Keep. The two of them are out to get me. Jurt made an attempt just this afternoon, but I can see it's really a challenge from Mask. I'm going to take them on soon."

"Hey, I didn't know you had a brother!"

"Half-brother. I have a couple of others, too. But I can get along with them. Jurt's been after me for a long time."

"That's really something. You never mentioned them."

"We never talked family. Remember?"

"Yeah. But you've got me puzzled now. Who's this Mask? I seem to remember your mentioning him before. It's really Sharu Garrul, isn't it?"

I shook my head.

"When I brought your mother out of the citadel she left the company of a similarly stricken old guy with RINALDO carved on his leg. I was trading spells with Mask at the time."

"Most strange," Luke said. "Then he's a usurper. And he's the one slipped me the acid?"

"That seems most likely."

"Then I have a score to settle with him, too—apart from what he did to my mother. How tough is Jurt?"

"Well, he's nasty. But he's kind of clumsy, too. At least, he's screwed up whenever we've fought and left a piece of himself behind."

"He could also be learning from his mistakes, you know."

"That's true. And he said something kind of cryptic today, now you mention it. He talked as if he were about to become very powerful."

"Uh-oh," Luke said. "Sounds as if this Mask is using him as a guinea pig."

"For what?"

"The Fount of Power, man. There's a steady, pulsing source of pure energy inside the Citadel, you know. Inter-Shadow stuff. Comes from the four worlds jamming together there."

"I know. I've seen it in action."

"I've got a feeling that this Mask is still in the process of getting a handle on it."

"He had a pretty good grip when we met."

"Yeah, but there's more to it than plugging into a wall outlet. There are all sorts of subtleties he's probably just becoming aware of and exploring."

"Such as?"

"Bathing a person in it will, if he's properly protected, do wonders for strength, stamina, and magical abilities. That part's easy for a person with some training to learn. I've been through it myself. But old Sharu's notes were in his lab, and there was something more in them—a way of replacing part of the body with energy, really packing it in. Very dangerous. Easily fatal. But if it works you get something special, a kind of superman, a sort of living Trump."

"I've heard that term before, Luke. . . ."

"Probably," he replied. "My father undertook the process, with himself as the subject—"

"That's it!" I said. "Corwin claimed that Brand had become some sort of living Trump. Made it almost impossible to nail him."

Luke gritted his teeth.

"Sorry," I said. "But that's where I heard about it. So *that* was the secret of Brand's power. . . ."

Luke nodded.

"I get the impression this Mask thinks he knows how it was done and is getting ready to try it on your brother."

"Shit!" I observed. "That's all I need. Jurt as a magical being or a natural force—or whatever the hell. This is serious. How much do you know about the process?"

"Oh, I know most of it, in theory. I wouldn't mess with it, though. I think it takes away something of your humanity. You don't much give a shit about other people or human values afterward. I think that's part of what happened to my father."

What could I say? Maybe that part was true and maybe it wasn't. I was sure Luke wanted to believe in some external cause for his father's treachery. I knew I'd never contradict him on it, even if I learned differently. And so I laughed.

"With Jurt," I said, "there'd be no way of telling the difference."

Luke smiled. Then, "You could get dead going up against a guy like that, along with a sorcerer, on their own turf."

"What choice have I got?" I asked. "They're after me. Better to move now. Jurt hasn't had the treatment yet. Does it take long?"

"Well, there are fairly elaborate preliminaries, but the subject doesn't have to be present for some of them. It all depends on how far along Mask is with the work."

"I'd better move pretty fast then."

"I won't have you going in there alone," he said. "It could be suicide. I know the place. I also have a small force of mercs bivouacked in Shadow and ready for action on short notice. If we can get them in, they can hold off the guards, maybe even take them out."

"Will that fancy ammo work there?"

"No. We tried it when I pulled the glider attack. It'll have to be hand to hand. Body armor and machetes, maybe. I'll have to work it out."

"*We* could use the Pattern to get in, but the troops can't . . . and Trumps aren't reliable for that place."

"I know. I'll have to work on that, too."

"Then it would be you and me against Jurt and Mask. If I tell any of the others here, they'll try to stop me till Random gets back, and that may be too late."

He smiled. "You know, my mother would really be useful in there," he said. "She knows more about the Fount than I do."

"No!" I said. "She tried to kill me."

"Easy, man. Easy," he said. "Hear me out."

"Besides, she lost to Mask last time they met. That's why she's a coatrack."

"All the more reason for her to be wary now. Anyway, it had to be trickery, not skill. She's good. Mask must have surprised her. She'd be a real asset, Merle."

"No! She wants all of us dead!"

"Details," he explained. "After Caine, the rest of you are just symbolic enemies. Mask is a real one, who took something away from her and still has it. Given the choice, she'll go after Mask."

"And if we're successful, she'll turn on Amber afterward."

"Not at all," he said. "That's the beauty of my plan."

"I don't want to hear about it."

"Because you already know you'll agree, right? I just figured a way to solve all your problems. Give her the Keep after it's liberated, as a kind of peace offering, to forget her differences with you guys."

"Just hand her this terrible power?"

"If she were going to use it against you, she'd have done it a long time ago. She's afraid to employ it in the extreme. With Kashfa down the tubes, she'll grab at the chance to salvage something. That's where the value lies."

"You really think so?"

"Better Queen of the Keep than a coatrack in Amber."

"Damn you, Luke. You always make the stupidest things sound sort of attractive."

"It's an art," he replied. "What do you say?"

"I've got to think about it," I said.

"Better think fast, then. Jurt may be bathing in that glow right now."

"Don't pressure me, man. I said I'll think about it. This is only one of my problems. I'm going to eat dinner now and mull things over."

"Want to tell me about your other problems, too? Maybe I can work them into the package some way."

"No, damn it! I'll call you back . . . soon. Okay?"

"Okay. But I'd better be around when you snap Mom out of it, to kind of smooth things over. You *have* figured out how to break the spell, haven't you?"

"Yes."

"Glad to know that. I wasn't sure how to do it, and I can stop working on it now. I'm going to finish here and go shape up the troops," he said, eyeing the lady in the bikini who had just emerged from the pool. "Call me."

"Okay," I said, and he was gone.

Damn. Amazing. No wonder Luke kept winning those sales awards. I had to admit it was a good pitch, despite my feelings about Jasra. And Random had not ordered me to keep her a prisoner. Of course, he had not had much opportunity to tell me anything the last time we had been together. Would she really behave as Luke said, though? It made a sort of sense, but then people seldom keep company with rationality at times when they should.

I passed along the hallway and decided to use the back stair. As I made the turn, I saw that there was a figure standing near the top. It was a woman, and she was looking the other way. She had on a full-length red-and-yellow gown. Her hair was very dark and she had lovely shoulders. . . .

She turned when she heard my tread, and I saw that it was Nayda. She studied my face.

"Lord Merlin," she said, "can you tell me where my sister is? I understand she went off with you earlier."

"She was admiring some art, and then she had a little errand she wanted to run afterward," I replied. "I'm not sure exactly where she was going, but she gave the impression she'd be back pretty soon."

"All right," she said. "It's just that it's getting near to dinnertime, and we'd expected her to be joining us. Did she enjoy her afternoon?"

"I believe she did," I said.

"She's been a bit moody recently. We were hoping this trip would cheer her up. She was looking forward to it quite a bit."

"She seemed pretty cheerful when I left her," I admitted.

"Oh, where was that?"

"Near here," I said.

"Where all did you go?"

"We had a long walk in and about town," I explained. "I showed her a bit of the palace, also."

"Then she's in the palace right now?"

"She was the last time I saw her. But she might have stepped out."

"I see," she said. "I'm sorry I didn't really get to talk to you at any length earlier. I feel as if I've known you for a long while."

"Oh?" I said. "Why is that?"

"I read through your file several times. It's kind of fascinating."

"File?"

"It's no secret that we keep files on people we're likely to encounter in our line of work. There's a file on everyone in the House of Amber, of course, even those who don't have much to do with diplomacy."

"I'd never thought about it," I said, "but it figures."

"Your early days are glossed over, of course, and your recent troubles are very confusing."

"They're confusing to me, too," I said. "You trying to update the file?"

"No, just curious. If your problems have ramifications that may involve Begma, we have an interest in them."

"How is it that you know of them at all?"

"We have very good intelligence sources. Small kingdoms often do."

I nodded.

"I won't press you on your sources, but we're not having a fire sale on classified data."

"You misunderstand me," she said. "I'm not trying to update that file either. I was trying to discover whether I might be able to offer you assistance."

"Thank you. I appreciate that," I told her. "I can't really think of any way you could help me, though."

She smiled, showing what seemed a set of perfect teeth.

"I can't be more precise without knowing more," she said. "But if you decide that you do want help—or if you just want to talk—come and see me."

"Well taken," I said. "I'll see you at dinner."

"Later, too, I hope," she said, as I passed her and turned down the hall.

What had she meant by that last bit? I wondered. Was she talking assignation? If so, her motives seemed awfully transparent. Or was she merely expressing her desire for information? I was not certain.

As I passed along the hallway in the direction of my rooms I noted an odd lighting phenomenon ahead of me: A bright white band about six or eight inches in width ran up both walls, across the ceiling, and over the floor. I slowed as I neared it, wondering whether someone had introduced a new method of illuminating the place in my absence.

As I stepped over the band on the floor, everything disappeared, except for the light itself, which resolved into a perfect circle, flipped once about me and settled on a level with my feet, myself at its center. The world appeared beyond the circle, suddenly, and it looked as if it were made of green glass formed into a dome. The surface on which I stood was reddish, irregular and moist in the pale light. It was not until a large fish swam by that I realized I might be underwater, standing on a ridge of coral.

"This is pretty as all hell," I said, "but I was trying to get to my apartment."

"Just showing off a bit," came a familiar voice which sounded eerily all about my magic circle. "Am I a god?"

"You can call yourself whatever you want," I said. "Nobody will disagree with you."

"It might be fun being a god."

"Then what does that make me?" I asked.

"That's a difficult theological question."

"Theological, my ass. I'm a computer engineer, and you know I built you, Ghost."

A sound like a sigh filled my submarine cell.

"It's hard to get away from one's roots."

"Why try? What's wrong with roots? All of the best plants have them."

"Pretty bloom above, mire and muck below."

"In your case it's metal and an interesting cryogenic setup—and quite a few other things—all of them very clean."

"Maybe it's mire and muck that I need, then."

"You feeling all right, Ghost?"

"I'm still trying to find myself."

"Everyone goes through phases like that. It'll pass."

"Really?"

"Really."

"When? How? Why?"

"It would be cheating to tell. Besides, it's different for everyone."

A whole school of fish swam by—little black-and-red-striped guys.

"I can't quite swing the omniscience business . . ." Ghost said after a time.

"That's okay. Who needs it?" I said.

". . . And I'm still working on omnipotence."

"That one's hard, too," I agreed.

"You're very understanding, Dad."

"I try. You got any special problems?"

"You mean, apart from the existential?"

"Yeah."

"No. I brought you here to warn you about a fellow named Mandor. He's—"

"He's my brother," I said.

There was silence.

Then, "That would make him my uncle, wouldn't it?"

"I guess so."

"How about the lady with him? She—"

"Fiona's my aunt."

"*My* great-aunt. Oh, my!"

"What's wrong?"

"It's bad form to speak ill of relatives, isn't it?"

"Not in Amber," I said. "In Amber we do it all the time."

The circle of light flipped again. We were back in the hallway.

"Now that we're in Amber," he said, "I want to speak ill of them. I wouldn't trust them if I were you. I think they're a little crazy. Also insulting and mendacious."

I laughed. "You're becoming a true Amberite."

"I am?"

"Yes. That's the way we are. Nothing to worry about. What came down between you, anyhow?"

"I'd rather work it out on my own, if you don't mind."

"Whatever you think is best."

"I don't really need to warn you about them?"

"No."

"Okay. That was my main concern. I guess I'll go and try the mire and muck bit now—"

"Wait!"

"What?"

"You seem pretty good at transporting things through Shadow these days."

"I seem to be improving, yes."

"What about a small band of warriors and their leader?"

"I think I could manage that."

"And me."

"Of course. Where are they and where do you want to go?"

I fished in my pocket, found Luke's Trump, held it up before me.

"But . . . He's the one you warned me not to trust," Ghost said.

"It's okay now," I told him. "Just for this matter. Nothing else, though. Things have changed a bit."

"I don't understand. But if you say so."

"Can you run him down and set things up?"

"I should be able to. Where do you want to go?"

"Do you know the Keep of the Four Worlds?"

"Yes. But that's a dangerous place, Dad. Very tricky coming and going. And that's where the red-haired lady tried to lay a power lock on me."

"Jasra."

"I never knew her name."

"She's Luke's mother," I explained, waving his Trump.

"Bad blood," Ghost stated. "Maybe we shouldn't have anything to do with either of them."

"She might be coming with us," I said.

"Oh, no. That's a dangerous lady. You don't want her along. Especially not in a place where she's strong. She might try to grab me again. She might succeed."

"She'll be too occupied with other matters," I said, "and I may need her. So start thinking of her as part of the package."

"Are you sure you know what you're doing?"

"I'm afraid so."

"When do you want to go there?"

"That depends in part on when Luke's troops will be ready. Why don't you go and find out?"

"All right. But I still think you might be making a mistake, going into that place with those people."

"I need someone who can help, and the die is damned well cast," I said.

Ghost coalesced to a point and winked out.

I drew a deep breath, changed my mind about sighing, and moved on toward my nearest door, which was not that much farther up the hall. As I was reaching for it I felt the movement of a Trump contact. Coral?

I opened myself to it. Mandor appeared before me again.

"Are you all right?" he asked immediately. "We were cut off in such an odd fashion."

"I'm fine," I told him. "We were cut off in a once-in-a-lifetime fashion. Not to worry."

"You seem a trifle agitated."

"That's because it's an awfully long walk from downstairs to upstairs with all the powers of the universe converging to slow me."

"I don't understand."

"It's been a rough day," I said. "See you later."

"I did want to talk with you some more, about those storms and the new Pattern and—"

"Later," I said. "I'm waiting on an incoming call."

"Sorry. No rush. I'll check back."

He broke the contact and I reached for the latch. I wondered whether it would solve everybody's problems if I could turn Ghost into an answering service.

7

I hung my cloak on Jasra and my weapons belt on the bedpost. I cleaned my boots, washed my hands and face, hunted up a fancy ivory shirt—all ruffled, brocaded, frogged—and put it on, along with a pair of gray trousers. Then I brushed off my deep purple jacket, the one on which I'd once laid a spell to make the wearer seem a little more charming, witty, and trustworthy than is actually the case. It seemed a good occasion for getting some use out of it.

As I was brushing my hair there came a knock on the door.

"Just a minute," I called.

I finished up—which left me ready to go and also, probably, running late—then went to the door, unbarred it, and opened it.

Bill Roth stood there in browns and reds, looking like an aging condottiere.

"Bill!" I said, clasping his hand, arm, and shoulder and leading him in. "Good to see you. I'm just back from some troubles and about to take off after more. I didn't know whether you were here in the palace now or what. I was going to look you up again as soon as things slowed a bit."

He smiled and punched my shoulder lightly.

"I'll be at dinner," he replied, "and Hendon said you'd be there, too. I thought I'd come up and walk over with you, though, since those Begman people will be there."

"Oh? You got some news?"

"Yes. Any fresh word on Luke?"

"I was just talking to him. He says the vendetta's off."

"Any chance of his wanting to justify himself at that hearing you asked me about?"

"Not from the way he sounded."

"Too bad. I've been doing a lot of research, and there are some good precedents for the vendetta defense—like, there was your uncle Osric, who took on the whole House of Karm over the death of a relative on his mother's side. Oberon was particularly friendly with Karm in those days, too, and Osric offed three of them. Oberon acquitted him at a hearing, though, basing his decision on earlier cases, and he even went further by stating a kind of general rule—"

"Oberon also sent him off to the front lines in a particularly nasty war," I interrupted, "from which he did not return."

"I wasn't aware of that part," Bill said, "but he did come off well in court."

"I'll have to mention it to Luke," I said.

"Which part?" he asked.

"Both," I answered.

"That wasn't the main thing I came to tell you," he went on. "There's something going on at a military level."

"What are you talking about?"

"It's even easier to show you," he explained. "It should only take a minute."

"Okay. Let's go," I agreed, and I followed him out into the hall.

He led the way down the back stair and turned left at its foot. We moved on past the kitchen and followed another hallway which turned off toward the rear. As we did, I heard some rattling sounds from up ahead. I glanced at Bill, who nodded.

"That's what I heard earlier," he told me, "when I was passing by. That's why I took a walk up this way. Everything around here makes me curious."

I nodded, understanding the feeling. Especially when I knew that the sounds were coming from the main armory.

Benedict stood in the midst of activity, peering at his thumbnail through a rifle barrel. He looked up immediately and our eyes met. Perhaps a dozen men moved about him, carrying weapons, cleaning weapons, stacking weapons.

"I thought you were in Kashfa," I said.

"Was," he replied.

I gave him a chance to continue, but nothing was forthcoming. Benedict has never been noted for loquacity.

"Looks like you're getting ready for something close to home," I remarked, knowing that gunpowder was useless here and that the special ammo we had only worked in the area of Amber and certain adjacent kingdoms.

"Always best to be safe," he said.

"Would you care to elaborate on that?" I asked.

"Not now," he answered, a reply twice as long as I'd anticipated and holding out hope of future enlightenment.

"Should we all be digging in?" I asked. "Fortifying the town? Arming ourselves? Raising—"

"It won't come to that," he said. "Just go on about your business."

"But—"

He turned away. I'd a feeling the conversation was over. I was sure of it when he ignored my next several questions. I shrugged and turned back to Bill.

"Let's go eat," I said.

As we walked back up the hall, Bill said softly, "Any idea what it means?"

"Dalt's in the neighborhood," I told him.

"Benedict was in Begma with Random. Dalt could be causing trouble there."

"I've a feeling he's nearer."

"If Dalt were to capture Random. . . ."

"Impossible," I said, feeling a slight chill at the idea. "Random can trump back here anytime he wants. No. When I talked about defending Amber, and Benedict said, 'It won't come to that,' I got the impression he was talking about something close at hand. Something he feels he can control."

"I see what you mean," he agreed. "But then he told you not to bother fortifying."

"If Benedict feels we don't need to fortify, then we don't need to fortify."

"Waltz and drink champagne while the cannons boom?"

"If Benedict says it's okay."

"You really trust that guy. What would you do without him?"

"Be more nervous," he said.

He shook his head. "Excuse me," he said. "I'm not used to being acquainted with legends."

"You don't believe me?"

"I shouldn't believe you, but I do believe you. That's the trouble." He was silent as we turned the corner and headed back toward the stair. Then he added, "It was that way whenever I was around your father, too."

"Bill," I said, as we began to climb. "You knew my dad back before he regained his memory, when he was just plain old Carl Corey. Maybe I've been going about this thing wrong. Is there anything you can recall about that phase of his life which might explain where he is now?"

He halted a moment and looked at me.

"Don't think I haven't thought about that angle, Merle. Many a time I've wondered whether he might have been involved in something as Corey that he'd have felt obliged to follow through on once his business here was finished. But he was a very secretive man, even in that incarnation. Paradoxical, too. He'd done a lot of hitches in a lot of different varieties of military, which seems logical enough. But he sometimes wrote music, which goes against that hard-ass image."

"He'd lived a long time. He'd learned a lot, felt a lot."

"Exactly, and that's what makes it hard to guess what he might have been involved in. Once or twice when he'd had a few drinks he'd mention people in the arts and sciences I'd never have guessed him to be acquainted with. He was never just plain Carl Corey. He had a few centuries' worth of Earth memory when I knew him. That makes for a character too complex to be easily predictable. I just don't know what he might have gone back to—if he went back."

We continued on up the stairway. Why did I feel that Bill knew more than he was telling me?

I heard music as we neared the dining room, and when we entered, Llewella gave me a nasty look. I saw that food was being kept warm at a serving table off against the far wall, and no one was seated yet. People stood about talking, drinks in hand, and most of them glanced in our direction as we entered. Three musicians were playing, off to my right. The dining table was to my left, near the big window in the south wall, providing a glorious view across the town below. It was still snowing lightly, casting a spectral veil over the entire bright prospect.

Llewella approached quickly.

"You've kept everybody waiting," she whispered. "Where's the girl?"

"Coral?"

"Who else?"

"I'm not sure where she's gotten off to," I said. "We parted company a couple of hours ago."

"Well, is she coming or isn't she?"

"I'm not sure."

"We can't keep things waiting any longer," she said. "And now the seating arrangement's screwed. What did you do, wear her out?"

"Llewella. . . ."

She muttered something I didn't understand in some lisping Rebman dialect. Just as well, probably. She turned away then and moved off toward Vialle.

"You in a heap of trouble, boy," Bill commented at my side. "Let's hit the bar while she's reassigning places."

But the wine steward was already approaching with a couple of drinks on a tray.

"Bayle's Best," he observed as we took them.

I sipped and saw that he was right, which heartened me a bit.

"I don't recognize all of these people," Bill said. "Who's that fellow with the red sash, over by Vialle?"

"That's Orkuz, the Begman prime minister," I told him, "and the rather attractive lady in the yellow-and-red dress who's talking to Martin is his daughter Nayda. Coral—the one I just got chewed out about—is her sister."

"Uh-huh. And who's the husky blond lady batting her eyes at Gérard?"

"I don't know," I said. "And I don't know that lady and the guy over to the right of Orkuz either."

We drifted inward, and Gérard, looking perhaps a trifle uncomfortable in layers of ruffled finery, introduced us to the lady he was with as Dretha Gannell, assistant to the Begman ambassador. The ambassador, it turned out, was the tall lady standing near Orkuz—and her name, I gathered, was Ferla Quist. The fellow with her was her secretary, whose name sounded something like Cade. While we were looking in that direction, Gérard tried slipping off and leaving us with Ferla. But she caught his sleeve and asked him something about the fleet. I smiled and nodded and moved away. Bill came along.

"Goodness! Martin's changed!" he announced suddenly. "He looks like a one-man rock video. I almost didn't recognize him. Just last week—"

"It's been over a year," I said, "for him. He's been off finding himself on some street scene."

"I wonder if he's finished?"

"Didn't get a chance to ask him that," I replied, but a peculiar thought occurred to me. I shelved it.

The music died just then, and Llewella cleared her throat and indicated Hendon, who announced the new seating arrangement. I was at the foot of the table, and I learned later that Coral was to have been seated to my left and Cade to my right. I also learned later that Llewella had tried to get hold of Flora at the last minute, to sit in Coral's place, but Flora wasn't taking any calls.

As it was, Vialle, at the head, had Llewella seated to her right and Orkuz to her left, with Gérard, Dretha, and Bill below Llewella, and Ferla, Martin, Cade, and Nayda below Orkuz. I found myself escorting Nayda to the table and seating her to my right, while Bill settled himself at my left.

"Fuss, fuss, fuss," Bill muttered softly, and I nodded, then introduced him to Nayda as counsel to the House of Amber. She looked impressed and asked him about his work. He proceeded to charm her with a story about once having represented the interests of a dog in an estate settlement, which had nothing to do with Amber but was a good story. Got her to laughing a bit, and also Cade, who was listening in.

The first course was served and the musicians began playing again, softly, which shortened the distance our voices carried and reduced conversation to a more intimate level. At this, Bill signaled he had something he wanted to tell me, but Nayda had beaten him by a second or two and I was already listening to her.

"About Coral," she said softly. "Are you sure she's all right? She wasn't feeling ill when you parted—or anything like that—was she?"

"No," I answered. "She seemed healthy enough."

"Strange," she said. "I had the impression she was looking forward to things like this dinner."

"She's obviously taking longer than she'd intended in whatever she's about," I observed.

"What exactly was she about?" Nayda asked. "Where did you part?"

"Here in the palace," I replied. "I was showing her around. She wanted to spend more time with certain features of the place than I could spare. So I came on ahead."

"I don't think she could have forgotten dinner."

"I think she got caught up by the power of an artistic piece."

"So she's definitely on the premises?"

"Now, that's hard to say. As I said before, a person can always step out."

"You mean you're not sure exactly where she is?"

I nodded.

"I'm not certain where she is at this moment," I said. "She could well be back in her room changing her clothes."

"I'll check after dinner," she said, "if she hasn't shown up by then. If that should be the case, will you help me find her?"

"I was planning on looking for her anyway," I answered, "if she doesn't put in an appearance soon."

She nodded and continued eating. Very awkward. Beyond the fact that I didn't want to distress her, I couldn't very well tell her what had happened without its becoming apparent that her sister was indeed an illegitimate daughter of Oberon. At a time such as this, when I had been cautioned about saying anything that might strain relations between Amber and Begma, I was not about to confirm to the daughter of the Begman prime minister the rumor that her mother had had an affair with the late king of Amber. Maybe it was an open secret back in Begma and nobody gave a damn. But maybe it wasn't. I didn't want to disturb Random for advice, partly because he might be extremely occupied in Kashfa just now, but mainly because he might also start asking me about my own immediate plans and problems, and I would not lie to him. That could get me into too much trouble. Such a conversation might well also result in his forbidding my attack on the Keep. The only other person I could tell about Coral and get some sort of official response from, as to how far I might go in informing her family, was Vialle. Unfortunately, Vialle was completely occupied as hostess at the moment.

I sighed and returned to my dinner.

Bill caught my attention and leaned a little in my direction. I leaned a little, too.

"Yes?" I said.

"There were some things I wanted to tell you," he began. "I was hoping for some leisure, some quiet, and some privacy, though."

I chuckled.

"Exactly," he continued. "I believe this is the best we're going to get for a time. Fortunately, voices don't seem to be carrying if one keeps them down. I couldn't make out what you and Nayda were talking about. So it's probably okay, so long as the musicians keep playing."

I nodded, took a few more bites.

"Thing is, the Begmans shouldn't hear about it, on the one hand. But on the other, I feel that perhaps you ought to know, because of your involvement with Luke and Jasra. So what's your schedule? I'd rather tell you later, but if you're going to be tied up, I can give you the gist of it now."

I glanced at Nayda and Cade. They seemed totally occupied with their food, and I didn't think they could overhear us. Unfortunately, I didn't have any sort of sheltering spells hung.

"Go ahead," I whispered from behind my wine glass.

"First," he said, "Random sent me a whole slew of papers to go over. They're the draft of an agreement whereby Amber will grant Kashfa privileged trade status, the same as Begma. So they'll definitely be coming into the Golden Circle."

"I see," I said. "That doesn't come as a complete surprise. But it's good to know for sure what's going on."

He nodded.

"There's a lot more to it, though," he said.

Just then the musicians stopped playing and I could hear voices from all around the table again. I glanced off to the right and saw that a steward had just taken the players a food tray and some wine. They were setting their instruments aside and taking a break. They had probably been playing for some time before I'd arrived and were doubtless due a rest.

Bill chuckled.

"Later," he said.

"Right."

There followed a funny little fruit dish with an amazing sauce. As I spooned it away, Nayda caught my attention with a gesture and I leaned toward her again.

"So what about tonight?" she whispered.

"What do you mean? I said I'd look for her if she doesn't show up."

She shook her head. "I wasn't referring to that," she said. "I meant later. Will you have time to stop by and talk?"

"About what?"

"According to your file you've been in a bit of trouble recently, with someone trying to get you."

I began wondering about that damned file. But, "It's out of date," I said. "Whatever's in there has already been cleared up."

"Really? Then nobody's after you just now?"

"I wouldn't say that," I replied. "The cast of characters keeps changing."

"So somebody still has you marked?"

I studied her face.

"You're a nice lady, Nayda," I said, "but I've got to ask, What is it to you? Everybody has problems. I just have more than usual at the moment. I'll work them out."

"Or die trying?"

"Maybe. I hope not. But what's your interest?"

She glanced at Cade, who seemed busy with his food.

"It is possible that I could help you."

"In what fashion?"

She smiled.

"A process of elimination," she stated.

"Oh? That refers to a person or persons?"

"Indeed."

"You have some special means of going about this sort of business?"

She continued to smile.

"Yes, it's good for removing problems caused by people," she continued. "All I'll need are their names and locations."

"Some sort of secret weapon?"

She glanced at Cade again, since I had raised my voice a bit.

"You might call it that," she answered.

"An interesting proposal," I said. "But you still haven't answered my first question."

"Refresh my memory."

We were interrupted by the wine steward, who came around topping off goblets, and then by another toast. The first had been to Vialle, led by Llewella. This one was proposed by Orkuz, to "the ancient alliance between Amber and Begma." I drank to that, and I heard Bill mutter, "It's going to get a bit more strained."

"The alliance?" I said.

"Yep."

I glanced at Nayda, who was staring at me, clearly expecting a resumption of our sotto voces. Bill noted this, too, and turned away. Just then Cade began talking to Nayda, however, so I finished what was on my plate and took a sip of wine while I waited. In a little while the plate was whisked away, to be replaced shortly by another.

I glanced at Bill who glanced at Nayda and Cade, then said, "Wait for the music."

I nodded. In a sudden moment of silence I overheard Dretha say, "Is it true that King Oberon's ghost is sometimes seen?" Gérard grunted something that sounded like an affirmative just as they were drowned out again. My mind being a lot fuller than my stomach, I kept eating. Cade, trying to be diplomatic or just conversational, turned my way a little later, addressed me and asked my views on the Eregnor situation. He jerked suddenly then and looked at Nayda. I'd a strong feeling she'd just kicked him under the table, which was fine with me because I didn't know what the hell the Eregnor situation was. I muttered something about there being things to be said for both sides of most matters, which seemed diplomatic enough for anything. If it were something barbed, I suppose I could have countered with an innocent-sounding observation about the Begman party's early arrival, but Eregnor might actually be some tedious conversation piece that Nayda didn't want to get into because it would cut off our own discussion. Also, I'd a feeling that Llewella might suddenly materialize and kick me under the table.

A thought hit suddenly then. Sometimes I'm a little slow. Obviously, they had known Random wasn't here, and from what I already knew and from what Bill had just said, they weren't too happy with whatever Random was about in the neighboring kingdom. Their early arrival seemed intended to embarrass us in some fashion. Did that mean that whatever Nayda was offering me was part of some scheme that fitted in with their general diplomatic strategy on this matter? If so, why me? I was a very poor choice, in that I had no say whatsoever concerning Amber's foreign policy. Were they aware of this? They must be, if their intelligence service were as good as Nayda had indicated. I was baffled, and I was half-tempted to ask Bill his views on the Eregnor situation. But then, he might have kicked me under the table.

The musicians, having finished snacking, resumed the entertainment with "Greensleeves," and Nayda and Bill both leaned toward me simultaneously, then glanced up, their gazes meeting. Both smiled.

"Ladies first," Bill said loudly.

She nodded to him.

Then, "Have a chance to think about my offer?" she asked me.

"Some," I said, "but I had a question. Remember?"

"What was it?"

"It's kind of you to want to do me a favor," I said, "but at times such as this, one must be excused for checking the price tag."

"What if I were to say that your good will would be sufficient?"

"What if I were to say that my good will isn't worth much at the policy level here?"

She shrugged. "Small price for a small return. I already knew that. But you're related to everybody in this place. Nothing may ever happen, but it's conceivable that someone might ask your opinion of us. I'd like you to know you have friends in Begma and to feel kindly disposed toward us if that occurred."

I studied her very serious expression. There was more to it than that, and we both knew it. Only I didn't know what might be on the horizon, and she obviously did.

I reached out and stroked her cheek once with the back of my hand.

"I am expected to say something nice about you folks if someone should ask me, that's all, and for this you will go out and kill someone for me if I just supply the particulars. Right?"

"In a word, yes," she replied.

"It makes me wonder why you think you can manage an assassination better than we could. We're old hands at it."

"We have, as you put it, a secret weapon," she said. "But I was thinking that this is a personal matter for you, not a state matter—and that you might not want any of the others involved. Also, I can provide a service that will not be traceable."

Bag of worms time again. Was she implying that she thought I did not trust all of the others here—or that I should not? What did she know that I didn't? Or was she just guessing, based on Amber's history of intrigue within the family? Or was she intentionally trying to stir up a generational conflict? Would that suit Begma's purpose in some fashion? Or. . . . Was she guessing that such a situation existed and offering to remove a family member for me? And if so, did she think I'd be stupid enough to get someone else to do the job? Or even to discuss such a notion and thereby give Begma a shot at sufficient evidence to have some kind of hold over me? Or. . . .

I drew back from the view. It pleased me that my thought processes were finally working properly for the company my family keeps. (Both my families, actually.) It had taken me a long while to get the hang of it. It felt good.

A simple refusal would foreclose all of the above. But, on the other hand, if I were to string her along a bit, she might prove a tantalizing source of information.

So, "Would you go after anyone I would name?" I said. "Anyone?"

She studied my face very carefully. Then, "Yes," she answered.

"You must excuse me again," I responded, "but doing it for such an intangible as my good will causes me to wonder about your good faith."

Her face reddened. Whether it was a simple blush or anger I

could not be certain, because she looked away immediately. This didn't bother me, though, because I was certain it was a buyer's market.

I returned my attention to my food and was able to put away several mouthfuls before she was back again.

"Does this mean you won't be stopping by tonight?" she asked.

"I can't," I said. "I am going to be completely occupied."

"I can believe you are very busy," she said. "But does that mean we will not be able to talk at all?"

"It depends entirely on how things break," I said. "I have an awful lot going on just now, and I may be leaving town soon."

She started slightly. I was certain she considered asking me where I was going, but thought better of it.

Then, "This is awkward," she said. "Have you refused my offer?"

"Is the deal only good for this evening?" I asked.

"No, but it was my understanding you were in some peril. The sooner you move against your enemy, the sooner your sleep is untroubled."

"You feel I am in danger here in Amber?"

She hesitated a moment, then said, "No one is safe, anywhere, from an enemy of sufficient determination and skill."

"Do you feel the threat to be a local one?" I inquired.

"I asked you to name the party," she stated. "You are in the best position to know."

I drew back immediately. It was too simple an entrapment, and obviously she'd already smelled it.

"You've given me much to think about," I answered, and I returned to my food.

After a time, I saw that Bill was looking at me as if he wanted to say something. I gave him a minuscule shake of my head, which he seemed to understand.

"Breakfast, then?" I heard her say. "This trip you spoke of could represent a time of vulnerability. It would be good to settle this before you depart."

"Nayda," I said, as soon as I had swallowed, "I would like to be clear on the matter of my benefactors. If I were to discuss this with your father—"

"No!" she interrupted. "He knows nothing about it!"

"Thank you. You must admit my curiosity as to the level at which this plan originates."

"There is no need to look any further," she stated. "It is entirely my idea."

"Some of your earlier statements cause me to infer that you have special connections within the Begman intelligence community."

"No," she said, "only the ordinary ones. The offer is my own."

"But someone would have to . . . effectuate this design."

"That is the province of the secret weapon."

"I would have to know more about it."

"I've offered you a service and I've promised you total discretion. I will go no further as to means."

"If this idea is wholly your own, it would seem that you stand to benefit from it personally. How? What's in it for you?"

She looked away. She was silent for a long time.

"Your file," she said at last. "It was . . . fascinating reading it. You're one of the few people here close to my own age, and you've led such an interesting life. You can't imagine how dull most of the things I have to read are—agricultural reports, trade figures, appropriations studies. I have no social life whatsoever. I am always on call. Every party I attend is really a state function in one form or another. I read your file over and over and I wondered about you. I . . . I have something of a crush on you. I know it sounds silly, but it's true. When I saw some of the recent reports and realized that you might be in great danger, I decided I would help you if I could. I have access to all sorts of state secrets. One of them would provide me with the means of helping you. Using it would benefit you without damaging Begma, but it would be disloyal of me to discuss it further. I've always wanted to meet you, and I was very jealous of my sister when you took her out today. And I still wish you'd stop by later."

I stared at her. Then I raised my wineglass to her and took a drink.

"You are . . . amazing," I said. I couldn't think of anything else to say. It was either an on-the-spot fabrication or it was true. If it were true, it was somewhat pathetic; if not, I thought it a rather clever bit of quick thinking, calculated to hit me in that wonderfully vulnerable place, the ego. She deserved either my sympathy or my wariest admiration. So I added, "I'd like to meet the person who wrote the reports. There may be a great creative talent going to waste in a government office."

She smiled, raised her own glass and touched it to mine.

"Think about it," she said.

"I can honestly say I won't forget you," I told her.

We both returned to our food, and I spent the next five minutes or so catching up. Bill decently allowed me to do this. Also, I think, he was waiting to be certain that my conversation with Nayda was finally concluded.

At last he winked at me.

"Got a minute?" he asked.

"Afraid so," I said.

"I won't even ask whether it was business or pleasure going on on the other side."

"It was a pleasure," I said, "but a strange business. Don't ask or I'll miss dessert."

"I'll summarize," he said. "The coronation in Kashfa will take place tomorrow."

"Not wasting any time, are we?"

"No. The gentleman who will be taking the throne is Arkans, Duke of Shadburne. He's been in and out of various Kashfan governments in fairly responsible positions any number of times over the years. He actually knows how things work, and he's distantly related to one of the earlier monarchs. Didn't get along well with Jasra's crowd and pretty much stayed at his country place the whole time she was in power. He didn't bother her and she didn't bother him."

"Sounds reasonable."

"In fact, he actually shared her sentiments on the Eregnor situation, as the Begmans are well aware—"

"Just what," I asked, "is the Eregnor situation?"

"It's their Alsace-Lorraine," he said, "a large, rich area between Kashfa and Begma. It has changed hands back and forth so many times over the centuries that both countries make reasonable-sounding claims to it. Even the inhabitants of the area aren't all that firm on the matter. They have relatives in both directions. I'm not even sure they care which side claims them, so long as their taxes don't go up. I think Begma's claim might be a little stronger, but I could argue the case either way."

"And Kashfa holds it now, and Arkans says they'll damn well keep it."

"Right. Which is the same thing Jasra said. The interim ruler, however—Jaston was his name, military man—was actually willing to discuss its status with the Begmans, before his unfortunate fall from the balcony. I think he wanted to repair the treasury and was considering ceding the area in return for the settlement of some ancient war damage claims. Things were actually well along and headed in that direction."

"And . . . ?" I said.

"In the papers I got from Random, Amber specifically recognizes Kashfa as including the area of Eregnor. Arkans had insisted that go into the treaty. Usually—from everything I've been able to find in the archives—Amber avoids getting involved in touchy situations like this between allies. Oberon seldom went looking for trouble. But Random seems to be in a hurry, and he let this guy drive a hard bargain."

"He's overreacting," I said, "not that I blame him. He remembers Brand too well."

Bill nodded.

"I'm just the hired help," he said. "I don't want to have an opinion."

"Well, anything else I should know about Arkans?"

"Oh, there are lots of other things the Begmans don't like about him, but that's the big one—right when they thought they were making some headway on an issue that's been a national pastime for generations. They've even gone to war over the matter in the past. Don't doubt that that's why they came rushing to town. Govern yourself accordingly."

He raised his goblet and took a drink.

A little later Vialle said something to Llewella, rose to her feet, and announced that she had to see to something, that she'd be right back. Llewella started to get up also, but Vialle put a hand on her shoulder, whispered something, and departed.

"Wonder what that could be?" Bill said.

"Don't know," I answered.

He smiled.

"Shall we speculate?"

"My mind's on cruise control," I told him.

Nayda gave me a long stare. I met it and shrugged.

Another little while, and plates were cleared and more were coming. Whatever it was looked good. Before I could find out for certain, though, a member of the general house staff entered and approached.

"Lord Merlin," she said, "the queen would like to see you."

I was on my feet immediately.

"Where is she?"

"I'll take you to her."

I excused myself from my companions, borrowing the line that I'd be right back, wondering if it were true. I followed her out and around the corner to a small sitting room, where she left me with Vialle, who was seated in an uncomfortable-looking high-backed chair of dark wood and leather, held together with cast iron studs. If she'd wanted muscle, she'd have sent for Gérard. If she'd wanted a mind full of history and political connivance, Llewella would be here. So I was guessing it involved magic, since I was the authority in residence.

But I was wrong.

"I'd like to speak to you," she said, "concerning a small state of war in which we seem about to become engaged."

8

After a pleasant time with a pretty lady, a series of stimulating hallway conversations, and a relaxing dinner with family and friends, it seemed almost fitting that it be time for something different and distracting. The idea of a small war seemed, at least, better than a big one, though I did not say that to Vialle. A moment's careful thought, and I shaped the query:

"What's going on?"

"Dalt's men are dug in near the western edge of Arden," she said. "Julian's are strung out facing them. Benedict has taken Julian additional men and weapons. He says he can execute a flanking movement that will take Dalt's line apart. But I told him not to."

"I don't understand. Why not?"

"Men will die," she said.

"That's the way it is in war. Sometimes you have no choice."

"But we do have a choice, of sorts," she said, "one that I don't understand. And I do want to understand it before I give an order that will result in numerous deaths."

"What is the choice?" I asked.

"I came here to respond to a Trump message from Julian," she said. "He had just spoken with Dalt under a flag of truce. Dalt told him that his objective was not, at this time, the destruction of Amber. He pointed out that he could conduct an expensive attack, though, in terms of our manpower and equipment. He said he'd rather save himself and us the expense, however. What he really wants is for us to turn two prisoners over to him—Rinaldo and Jasra."

"Huh?" I said. "Even if we wanted to, we can't give him Luke. He's not here."

"That is what Julian told him. He seemed very surprised. For some reason, he believed we had Rinaldo in custody."

"Well, we're not obliged to provide the man with an education. I gather he's been something of a pain for years. I think Benedict has the right answer for him."

"I did not call you in for advice," she said.

"Sorry," I told her. "It's just that I don't like seeing someone trying to pull a stunt like this and actually believing he has a chance of success."

"He has no chance of success," Vialle stated. "But if we kill him now, we learn nothing. I would like to find out what is behind this."

"Have Benedict bring him in. I have spells that will open him up."

She shook her head.

"Too risky," she explained. "Once bullets start flying, there's the chance one might find him. Then we lose even though we win."

"I don't understand what it is that you want of me."

"He asked Julian to get in touch with us and relay his demand. He's promised to hold the truce until we give him some sort of official answer. Julian says he has the impression that Dalt would settle for either one of them."

"I don't want to give him Jasra either."

"Neither do I. What I do want very badly is to know what is going on. There would be small point in releasing Jasra and asking her, since this is a recent development. I want to know whether you have means of getting in touch with Rinaldo. I want to talk to him."

"Well, uh . . . yes," I said. "I have a Trump for him."

"Use it."

I got it out. I regarded it. I moved my mind into that special area of alertness and calling. The picture changed, came alive. . . .

It was twilight, and Luke stood near a campfire. He had on his green outfit, a light brown cloak about his shoulders clasped with that Phoenix pin.

"Merle," he said. "I can move the troops pretty fast. When do you want to hit the place and—"

"Put it on hold," I interrupted. "This is something different."

"What?"

"Dalt's at the gates, and Vialle wants to talk to you before we take him apart."

"Dalt? There? Amber?"

"Yes, yes, and yes. He says he'll go and play someplace else if we give him the two things he wants most in the world: you and your mother."

"That's crazy."

"Yeah. We think so, too. Will you talk to the queen about it?"

"Sure. Bring me thr—" He hesitated and looked into my eyes. I smiled.

He extended his hand. I reached forward and took it. Suddenly, he was there. He looked about, saw Vialle. Immediately, he unclasped his sword belt and passed it to me. He approached her, dropped to his right knee, and lowered his head.

"Your Majesty," he said. "I've come."

She reached forward and touched him.

"Raise your head," she said.

He did, and her sensitive fingers slid over the planes and arches of his face.

"Strength," she said, "and sorrow. . . . So you're Rinaldo. You've brought us some grief."

"It works both ways, Your Majesty."

"Yes, of course," she replied. "Wrongs done and wrongs avenged have a way of spilling over on the innocent. How far will it go this time?"

"This thing with Dalt?" he asked.

"No. This thing with you."

"Oh," he said. "It's over. I've done with it. No more bombs or ambushes. I've already told Merlin that."

"You've known him for several years?"

"Yes."

"You've become friends?"

"He's one of the reasons I'm calling it off."

"You must trust him, to come here. I respect that," she said. "Take this."

She removed a ring she wore upon her right forefinger. The band was of gold, the stone a milky green; the prongs of its setting caught it in a fashion to suggest some mantic spider guarding dreamland treasures against the daybreak world.

"Your Majesty. . . ."

"Wear it," she said.

"I will," he replied, slipping it upon the little finger of his left hand. "Thank you."

"Rise. I want you to know exactly what has occurred."

He got to his feet, and she began telling him what she had told me, concerning Dalt's arrival, his forces' disposition, his demands, while I stood stunned at the implications of what she had done. She had just placed Luke under her protection. Everyone in Amber knew that ring. I wondered what Random would think. I realized then that there would not be a hearing. Poor Bill. I believe he was really looking forward to arguing Luke's case.

"Yes, I know Dalt," I heard him saying. "Once we shared . . . certain goals. But he's changed. He tried to kill me the last time we met. I'm not sure why. At first I thought the wizard of the Keep had taken control of him."

"And now?"

"Now, I just don't understand. I've a feeling he's on a leash, but I don't know who holds it."

"Why not the wizard?"

"It makes no sense to go to these lengths to claim me when he had me and let me go just a few days ago. He could simply have left me in my cell."

"True," she replied. "What is this wizard's name?"

"Mask," he answered. "Merlin knows more about him than I do."

"Merlin," she said. "Who is this Mask?"

"He's the wizard who took the Keep of the Four Worlds away from Jasra," I explained, "who, in turn, had taken it away from Sharu Garrul, who is now also a coatrack. Mask wears a blue mask and seems to draw power from a strange fountain in the citadel there. Doesn't seem to like me much either. That's about all I can tell you."

I'd omitted mentioning my plan to head that way for a showdown soon, because of Jurt's involvement, for the same reason I hadn't wanted Random to know about it. I was certain Luke had tossed me the question because he wasn't sure how far I wanted it taken.

"That doesn't really tell us much," she decided, "as to Dalt's involvement."

"There may not be a connection," I said. "I gather Dalt is a mercenary, and their relationship could have been a one-time thing. He could either be working for someone else now or pulling something on his own."

"I can't see why anybody wants us badly enough to go to such dramatic lengths," Luke said. "But I've a score to settle with that guy, and I'm going to combine business with pleasure."

"What do you mean?" she asked.

"I assume there's a way to get down there in a hurry," he said.

"One could always trump through to Julian," I said, "but what have you got in mind, Luke?"

"I want to talk to Dalt."

"It's too dangerous," she said, "since you're what he wants."

Luke grinned. "It could be a bit dangerous for Dalt, too," he replied.

"Wait a minute," I said. "If you've got more in mind than just talking, you could blow this truce. Vialle's trying to avoid a conflict here."

"There won't be any conflict," Luke said. "Look, I've known Dalt since we were kids, and I think he's bluffing. He does that sometimes. He hasn't got the kind of force to risk another attack on Amber. Your guys would slaughter him. If he wants Mom or me, I think he'd be willing to tell me why, and that's what we want to find out, isn't it?"

"Well, yes," I said. "But—"

"Let me go," he said to Vialle, "and I'll find a way to get him off your back. I promise."

"You tempt me," she told him. "But I don't like your talk of settling accounts with him at this time. As Merlin said, I want to avoid this conflict—for more than one reason."

"I promise not to let it go that far," he stated. "I can read the dice. I'm good at playing things by ear. I'm willing to postpone gratification."

"Merlin . . . ?" she said.

"He's right, in that," I answered. "He's the deadliest salesman in the southwest."

"I'm afraid I don't understand the concept."

"It's a highly specialized art, back on that Shadow Earth we both inhabited. In fact, he's using it on you right now."

"Do you think he can do what he says?"

"I think he's very good at getting what he wants."

"Exactly," Luke observed. "And since we both want the same thing here, I think the future looks bright for all of us."

"I see what you mean," she said. "How much danger would this put you near, Rinaldo?"

"I'll be as safe as I am right here in Amber," he said.

She smiled.

"All right, I'll speak to Julian," she agreed, "and you can go to him and see what you can learn from Dalt."

"A moment," I requested. "It's been snowing on and off, and that's a pretty nasty wind out there. Luke just came in from a more temperate clime, and it's a pretty flimsy-looking cloak he has on. Let me get him something warmer. I've a nice heavy one he can take, if he finds it suitable."

"Go ahead," she said.

"We'll be right back."

She pursed her lips, then nodded.

I passed Luke his weapons belt and he buckled it on. I knew that she knew I just wanted to talk to him alone for a few minutes. And she was certainly aware that I knew it. And we both knew she trusted me, which brightens my existence, as well as complicating it.

As we passed along the hallway toward my rooms, I'd intended to fill Luke in concerning the upcoming coronation in Kashfa, as well as a few other matters. I waited, however, till we were well away from the sitting room, because Vialle has inordinately acute hearing. This, though, gave Luke a foot in the door, and he began to speak first.

"What a strange development," he said. Then, "I like her, but I've a feeling she knows more than she's telling."

"Probably true," I answered. "I guess we're all like that."

"You, too?"

"These days, yes. It's gotten that way."

"You know anything more about this situation that I should be aware of?"

I shook my head. "This is very new, and she gave you the whole story I know. Would you, perchance, know something about it that we don't?"

"Nope," he said. "It came as a surprise to me, too. But I've got to pursue it."

"I guess so."

We were nearing my stretch of corridor now, and I felt obliged to prepare him.

"We'll be to my rooms in a minute," I said, "and I just wanted you to know your mother's in there. She's safe, but you won't find her too talkative."

"I'm familiar with the results of that spell," he said. "I also recall that you said you know how to lift it. So. . . . That leads into the next topic. I've been thinking. This interlude is slowing us down a bit in our plan for going after Mask and your brother."

"Not all that much," I responded.

"We don't really know how long this is going to take me, though," he went on. "Supposing it drags out a bit? Or supposing something happens to really slow me down?"

I gave him a quick glance.

"Like, what have you got in mind?" I asked.

"I don't know. I'm just supposing. Okay? I like to plan ahead. Say we get delayed on this attack. . . ."

"All right. Say that," I said, as we neared my door.

"What I'm getting at," he continued, "is, what if we get there too late? Supposing we arrive and your brother has already undergone the ritual that turns him into hell on wheels?"

I unlocked my door, opened it, and held it for him. I did not like entertaining the possibility he had just described, because I recalled my father's stories of the times he'd encountered Brand and faced that uncanny power.

Luke stepped inside. I snapped my fingers and a number of oil lamps came to life, their flames dancing for a moment before settling to a glowing steadiness.

Jasra was there in plain sight before him, holding a number of my garments on outstretched arms. I was concerned for a moment as to what his reaction might be.

He halted, studying her, then advanced, his speculations concerning Jurt forgotten. He regarded her for perhaps ten seconds, and I found myself growing uncomfortable. Then he chuckled.

"She always liked being decorative," he said, "but to combine it with being useful was generally beyond her. You've got to hand it to Mask, even though she probably won't catch the moral of it."

He turned away and faced me.

"No, she'll probably wake up mean as cat piss and looking for trouble," he reflected. Then, "She doesn't seem to be holding that cloak you mentioned."

"I'll get it."

I moved to an armoire, opened it, and fetched out a dark fur one. As we traded, he ran his hand over it.

"Manticore?" he asked.

"Dire wolf," I said.

I hung his within and closed the door while he donned mine.

"As I was saying when we came in here," he offered, "supposing I don't come back?"

"You weren't saying that," I corrected.

"Not in so many words," he admitted. "But whether it's a small delay or the big one, what difference does it make? The point is, what if Jurt goes through with the ritual and succeeds in obtaining the powers he's after before we can do anything about it? And supposing I'm not around right then to give you a hand?"

"That's a lot of supposing," I said.

"That's what separates us from the losers, man. Nice cloak."

He moved toward the door, glanced back at me, at Jasra.

"Okay," I said. "You go down there, Dalt cuts off your head and uses it for a football, then Jurt shows up ten feet tall and farting fire. I'm supposing. How does that separate us from the losers?"

He stepped out into the hall. I followed him, snapping my fingers again, leaving Jasra to the darkness.

"It's a matter of knowing your options," he told me, as I secured the door.

I fell into step beside him as he headed back down the hall.

"A person who acquires that kind of power also picks up a vulnerability, by way of its source," he said.

"What does that mean?" I asked.

"Specifically, I don't know," he told me. "But the power in the Keep can be used against a person who is empowered by the Keep. I learned that much in Sharu's notes. But Mom took them away before I read them all, and I never saw them again. Never trust—that's her motto, I think."

"You're saying . . . ?"

"I'm saying that if something happens to me and he comes up a winner in this game, I believe she knows some special way of destroying him."

"Oh."

"I'm also pretty sure that she'll have to be asked very nicely."

"Somehow, I think I already knew that."

He gave a humorless chuckle.

"So you tell her that I've ended the vendetta, that I'm satisfied, and then offer her the citadel in return for her help."

"What if she says that's not enough?"

"Hell! Turn her back into a coatrack then! It's not as if the guy can't be killed. My dad still died with an arrow through his throat, despite his fancy powers. A deathstroke is still a deathstroke. It's just that delivering it to a guy like that is a lot harder."

"You really think that'll be enough?" I said.

He halted and looked at me, frowning.

"She'll argue, but of course she'll agree," he said. "It'll be a step up in the world. And she'll want revenge on Mask as much as that piece of her former holdings. But to answer your question, don't trust her. No matter what she promises, she'll never be happy with less than she had before. She'll be scheming. She'll be a good ally till the job's done. Then you've got to think about protecting yourself against her. Unless. . . ."

"Unless what?"

"Unless I come up with something to sweeten the pot."

"Like what?"

"I don't know yet. But don't lift that spell until things are definitely settled between Dalt and me. Okay?"

He resumed walking.

"Wait a minute," I said. "What are you planning?"

"Nothing special," he answered. "Like I told the queen, I'm just going to play things by ear."

"I sometimes get the feeling you're as devious as you make her out to be," I said.

"I hope so," he replied. "But there's a difference. I'm honest."

"I don't know that I'd buy a used car from you, Luke."

"Every deal I make is special," he said, "and for you it's always top of the line."

I glanced at him, saw that he kept his expression under control.

"What else can I say?" he added, indicating the sitting room with a quick gesture.

"Nothing, now," I answered, and we entered there.

Vialle turned her head in our direction as we came in, her expression as unreadable as Luke's.

"I take it you are properly attired now?" she asked.

"I am indeed," he answered.

"Then let's be about this," she said, raising her left hand, which I saw to contain a Trump. "Come over here, please."

Luke approached her and I followed him. I could see then that it was Julian's Trump that she held.

"Place your hand upon my shoulder," she told him.

"All right."

He did, and she reached, found Julian and began speaking to him. Shortly, Luke was party to the conversation, explaining what he intended to do. I overheard Vialle saying that the plan had her approval.

Moments later I saw Luke raise his free hand and extend it. I also saw the shadowy figure of Julian reaching forward, though I

was not part of the Trump nexus. This was because I had sum-
moned my Logrus Sight and had become sensitive to such things.
I needed it for the timing, not wanting Luke whisked away before
I could move.

I let my hand fall upon his shoulder and I moved forward as
he did.

"Merlin! What are you doing?" I heard Vialle call.

"I'd like to see what happens," I said. "I'll come right home
when things are concluded," and the rainbow gate closed behind me.

We stood within the flickering light of oil lamps inside a large
tent. From outside, I could hear the wind and the sounds of stirring branches. Julian stood facing us. He let Luke's hand fall and
regarded him without expression.

"So you are Caine's killer," he said.

"I am," Luke replied.

And I was remembering that Caine and Julian had always
been particularly close. If Julian were to kill Luke and cry
vendetta, I was certain that Random would merely nod and agree.
Perhaps he'd even smile. Hard to say. If I were Random, I would
greet Luke's removal with a sigh of relief. In fact, that was one of
the reasons I'd come along. Supposing this whole deal were a
setup? I couldn't picture Vialle as a part of it, but she could easily
have been deceived by Julian and Benedict. Supposing Dalt
wasn't even out there?

Or suppose he were—and that what he'd really asked for was
Luke's head? After all, he had tried to kill Luke fairly recently. I
had to admit the possibility now, and I also had to admit that Julian was the most likely candidate to be a willing party to such a
design. For the good of Amber.

Julian's gaze met mine, and I wore as affectless a mask as
his own.

"Good evening, Merlin," he said. "Do you have a special part
in this plan?"

"I'm an observer," I answered. "Anything else I may do will
be dictated by circumstance."

From somewhere outside I heard the growling of a hellhound.

"So long as you keep out of the way," Julian said.

I smiled.

"Sorcerers have special ways of avoiding notice," I replied.

He studied me again, wondering, I am certain, whether that
involved some sort of threat—to defend Luke or to avenge him.
Then he shrugged and turned away to where a small table

held an unrolled map, weighted in place with a rock and a dagger. He indicated that Luke should join him there, and I followed when he did.

It was a map of the western fringe of Arden, and he pointed out our position on it. Garnath lay to our south-southwest, Amber to the southeast.

"Our troops are situated here," he said, with a movement of his finger. "And Dalt's are here." He described another line, roughly paralleling our own.

"What about Benedict's force?" I inquired.

He glanced at me, showing the slightest of frowns.

"It is good for Luke to know that there is such a force," he stated, "but not its size, location, or objective. That way, if Dalt were to capture and question him, he'd have a lot to worry about and nothing to act upon."

Luke nodded. "Good idea," he said.

Julian pointed again, to a spot midway between the lines. "This is the place where I met with him when we spoke earlier," he explained. "It is a clear, level area, in view of both sides during daylight. I'd suggest we use it again, for your meeting."

"All right," Luke said, and I noticed that as he spoke, Julian's fingertips caressed the handle of the dagger that lay before him. Then I saw that Luke's right hand, in casual movement, had come to rest upon his belt, slightly to the left and near to his own dagger.

Simultaneously, then, Luke and Julian smiled at each other, and held it several seconds too long. Luke was bigger than Julian, and I knew he was fast and strong. But Julian had centuries of experience with weapons behind him. I wondered how I would intervene if either made a move toward the other, because I knew that I would try to stop them. But they let their hands fall to their sides then, as if by sudden agreement, and Julian said, "Let me offer you a glass of wine."

"Don't mind if I do," Luke replied, and I wondered whether my presence had kept them from fighting. Probably not. I'd the feeling that Julian had just wanted to make his feelings clear, and Luke had wanted to let him know he didn't give a damn. I really don't know which one I'd have bet on.

Julian placed three cups upon the table, filled them with Bayle's Best, gestured for us to help ourselves as he corked the bottle, then picked up the remaining cup and took a swallow before either of us could do more than sniff ours. A quick assurance that we weren't being poisoned and that he wanted to talk business.

"When I met with him we each brought two retainers along," he said.

"Armed?" I asked.

He nodded.

"More for show, really."

"Were you mounted or on foot?" Luke asked.

"On foot," he replied. "We each left our lines at the same time and proceeded at the same pace till we met there in the middle, several hundred paces from either side."

"I see," Luke said. "No hitches?"

"None. We talked and returned."

"When was this?"

"Around sundown."

"Did he seem to be a man in a normal state of mind?"

"I'd say. I count a certain arrogant posturing and a few insults toward Amber as normal for Dalt."

"Understandable," Luke said. "And he wanted me or my mother, or both? And failing to get us, he threatened to attack?"

"Yes."

"Did he give any indication as to why he wants us?"

"None," Julian replied.

Luke took a sip of his wine.

"Did he specify whether he wanted us dead or alive?" he asked.

"Yes. He wants you alive," Julian answered.

"What are your impressions?"

"If I give you to him, I'm rid of you," Julian said. "If I spit in his eye and take him on in battle, I'm rid of him. Either way, I come out ahead. . . ."

Then his gaze moved to the wine cup, which Luke had picked up with his left hand, and for an instant his eyes widened. I realized he had just then noticed that Luke was wearing Vialle's ring.

"It looks as if I get to kill Dalt, anyway," he concluded.

"By impressions," Luke went on, unperturbed, "I meant, do you believe he will really attack? Do you have any idea where he came from? Any indication where he might be headed when he leaves here—if he leaves?"

Julian swirled his wine in his cup.

"I have to go under the assumption that he means what he says and plans to attack. When we first became aware of his troop movements, he was advancing from the general direction of Begma and Kashfa—probably Eregnor, since he hangs out there a lot. Your guess is as good as anyone's as to where he wants to go if he leaves here."

Luke took a quick swallow of wine a fraction of a second too late for it to conceal what appeared to be a sudden smile. No, I realized right then, Luke's guess was not as good as anyone else's. It was probably a hell of a lot better. I took a quick drink myself, though I'm not sure what expression I might have been concealing.

"You can sleep here," Julian said. "If you're hungry, I'll have some food brought in. We'll set up this meeting for you at daybreak."

Luke shook his head.

"Now," Luke said, with another subtle but obvious display of the ring. "We want it set up right away."

Julian studied him for several pulsebeats. Then, "You'll not be in the clearest sight of either side in the dark, especially with snow coming down," he said. "Some little misunderstanding could result in an attack, from either side."

"If both of my companions bore large torches—and if both of his did the same—" he suggested, "we ought to be visible to both sides at a few hundred yards."

"Possibly," Julian said. "All right. I'll have the message sent to his camp, and I'll choose two retainers to accompany you."

"I already know who I want to have with me," Luke said. "Yourself and Merlin here."

"You are a curious individual," Julian observed. "But yes, I agree. I would like to be there when whatever happens, happens."

Julian moved to the front of his tent, opened the flap, and summoned an officer with whom he spoke for several minutes. In this space, I asked, "You know what you're doing, Luke?"

"Certainly," he replied.

"I've a feeling this is a little more than playing it by ear," I said. "Any reason why you can't tell me your plan?"

He appraised me for a moment, then said, "I only recently realized that I, too, am a son of Amber. We've met, and we've seen that we're too much like each other. Okay. That's good. It means we can do business, right?"

I allowed myself to frown. I wasn't sure what he was trying to say.

He clasped my shoulder lightly.

"Don't worry," he said. "You can trust me. Not that you have a great deal of choice at this point. But you may a bit later. I want you to remember then that, whatever happens, you must not interfere."

"What do you think is going to happen?"

"We haven't the time or the privacy to speculate," he said. "So let it go, and remember everything I said this evening."

"As you said, I haven't much choice at this point."

"I want you to remember it later," he said, as Julian lowered the flap and turned toward us.

"I'll take you up on that meal," Luke called to him. "How about you, Merle? Hungry?"

"Lord, no!" I replied. "I just sat through a state dinner."

"Oh?" he inquired almost too casually. "What was the occasion?"

I began to laugh. It was too much for one day. I was about to tell him that we hadn't the time or the privacy. But Julian had just reopened the tent flap and was calling for an orderly, and I wanted to throw a few curve balls through Luke's broken field just to see what they did to his composure.

"Oh, it was for the Begman prime minister, Orkuz, and some of his staff," I explained.

He waited while I pretended to take a long drink of wine. Then I lowered it and said, "That's all."

"Come on, Merlin. What's it about? I've been relatively square with you recently."

"Oh?" I said.

For a minute I didn't think he'd see the humor in it, but then he began to laugh, too.

"Sometimes the mills of the gods grind too damned fast and we get buried in grist," he observed. "Look, how about giving me this one for free. I don't have anything brief to trade right now. What's he want?"

"You'll bear in mind that this is classified until tomorrow?"

"Okay. What happens tomorrow?"

"Arkans, Duke of Shadburne, gets crowned in Kashfa."

"Holy shit!" Luke said. He glanced at Julian, then back at me. "That was a damned clever choice on Random's part," he said after a time. "I didn't think he'd move this fast."

He stared off into some vanishing point for a long while. Then he said, "Thanks."

"Well, does it help or hurt?" I asked.

"Me, or Kashfa?" he said.

"I hadn't split it down that fine."

"That's okay, because I'm not sure how to take this. I need to do some thinking. Get the big picture."

I stared at him and he smiled again.

"It *is* interesting," he added. "You got anything else for me?"

"That's enough," I said.

"Yeah, probably you're right," he agreed. "Don't want to overload the systems. Think we're losing touch with the simple things, old buddy?"

"Not so long as we know each other," I said.

Julian dropped the flap, returned to us, and sought his wine cup.

"Your food will be along in a few minutes," he told Luke.

"Thanks."

"According to Benedict," he said, "you told Random that Dalt is a son of Oberon."

"I did," Luke acknowledged. "One who's walked the Pattern, at that. Does it make a difference?"

Julian shrugged.

"Won't be the first time I've wanted to kill a relative," he stated. "By the way, you're my nephew, aren't you?"

"Right . . . uncle."

Julian swirled the contents of his cup again.

"Well, welcome to Amber," he said. "I heard a banshee last night. I wonder if there's any connection?"

"Change," Luke said. "They mean things are changing and they wail for what's being lost."

"Death. They mean death, don't they?"

"Not always. Sometimes they just show up at turning points for dramatic effect."

"Too bad," Julian said. "But one can always hope."

I thought Luke was going to say something else, but Julian began again before he could.

"How well did you know your father?" he asked.

Luke stiffened slightly, but answered, "Maybe not as well as most. I don't know. He was like a salesman. Always coming and going. Didn't usually stay with us long."

Julian nodded.

"What was he like, near the end?" he inquired.

Luke studied his hands.

"Well, he wasn't exactly normal, if that's what you mean," he finally said. "Like I was telling Merlin earlier, I think the process he undertook to gain his powers might have unbalanced him some."

"I never heard that story."

Luke shrugged.

"The details aren't all that important—just the results."

"You're saying he wasn't a bad father before that?"

"Hell, I don't know. I never had another father to compare him to. Why do you ask?"

"Curiosity. It's a part of his life I knew nothing about."

"Well, what kind of brother was he?"

"Wild," Julian said. "We didn't get along all that well. So we pretty much stayed out of each other's ways. He was smart, though. Talented, too. Had a flare for the arts. I was just trying to figure how much you might take after him."

Luke turned his hands palms upward.

"Beats me," he said.

"Well, no matter," Julian replied, setting down his cup and turning toward the front of the tent again. "I believe your food is about to arrive."

He moved off in that direction. I could hear the tiny crystals of ice rattling against the canvas overhead, and a few growls from outside: concerto for wind and hellhound. No banshees, though. Not yet.

9

I walked a pace or so behind Luke, a couple of yards off to his left, trying to keep even with Julian, who was over to the right. The torch I bore was a big thing, about six tapering feet of pitchy wood, sharpened at its terminus to make it easy to drive into the ground. I held it at arm's distance, because the oily flames licked and lashed in all directions in accord with vagaries of the wind. Sharp, icy flakes fell upon my cheek, my forehead, my hands, with a few catching in my eyebrows and lashes. I blinked vigorously as the heat of the torch melted them and they ran into my eyes. The grasses beneath my feet were sufficiently cold to give a brittle, crunching sensation every time I took a step. Directly ahead I could see the slow advance of two other torches toward us, and the shadowy figure of a man who walked between them. I blinked and waited for the flow from one or the other of his torches to give me a better look. I'd only seen him once, very briefly, via Trump, back at Arbor House. His hair looked golden, or even coppery, by what light there was upon it; but I remembered it as a kind of dirty blond by natural light. His eyes, I recalled, were green, though there was no way I could see that now. I did begin to realize for the first time, however, that he was pretty big—either that or he had chosen fairly short torchbearers. He had been alone that one time I'd seen him, and I had had no standard for comparison. As the light from our torches reached him I saw that he had on a heavy, green sleeveless doublet without a collar, over something black and also heavy, with sleeves that extended down his arms to vanish within green gauntlets. His trousers were black, as were the high boots they entered; his cloak was black and lined with an emerald green that caught our light as the cloak furled about him in shifting, oily landscapes of yellow and red. He wore a heavy circular medallion, which looked to be gold, on a chain about his neck; and though I could not make out the details of its device, I was certain that it bore a Lion rending a Unicorn. He came to a halt about ten or twelve paces from Luke, who stopped an instant later. Dalt gestured, and his retainers drove the butts of their torches into the ground. Julian and I immediately did the same, and we remained near them, as Dalt's men were doing. Then Dalt nodded to Luke, and they both advanced again, meeting at the center of the box formed by the lights, clasping right forearms, staring into each other's eyes. Luke's back was to me, but I could see Dalt's face. He showed no signs of emotion, but his lips were already moving. I couldn't hear a word that was being said, between the wind and the fact that they seemed intentionally to be keeping it low. At least, I finally had a point of reference for Dalt's size. Luke is about six three, and I could see that Dalt was several inches taller. I glanced at Julian, but he was not looking my way. I wondered how many eyes regarded us from both sides of the field.

Julian is always a bad person to check for reactions. He was simply watching the two of them, expressionless, stolid. I cultivated the same attitude, and the minutes passed, the snow kept falling.

After a long while Luke turned away and headed back toward us. Dalt moved off toward one of his torchbearers. Luke stopped midway between us, and Julian and I moved to join him.

"What's up?" I asked him.

"Oh," he said, "I think I found a way of settling this without a war."

"Great," I said. "What did you sell him?"

"I sold him on the idea of fighting a duel with me to determine how this thing goes," he explained.

"God damn it, Luke!" I said. "That guy's a pro! And I'm sure he's got our genetic package for strength. And he's been living in the field all this time. He's probably in top shape. And he outweighs you and outreaches you."

Luke grinned.

"So, I might get lucky," he said. He looked at Julian. "Anyway, if you can get a message back to the lines and tell them not to attack when we start this thing, Dalt's side will be holding still for it, too."

Julian looked over to where one of Dalt's torchbearers had started back toward his lines. He turned toward his own side then and executed a number of hand signals. Shortly, a man emerged from cover and began jogging toward us.

"Luke," I said. "This is crazy. The only way you're going to win is to get Benedict for a second and then break a leg."

"Merle," he said, "let it go. This is between Dalt and me. Okay?"

"I've got a bunch of fairly fresh spells," I said. "We can let this thing start, and then I'll hit him with one at the right time. It'll look as if you did it."

"No!" he said. "This really is a matter of honor. So you've got to stay out of it."

"Okay," I said, "if that's how you want it."

"Besides, nobody's going to die," he explained. "Neither of us wants that right now, and it's part of the deal. We're too valuable to each other alive. No weapons. Strictly *mano a mano*."

"Just what," Julian inquired, "*is* the deal?"

"If Dalt whips my ass," Luke replied, "I'm his prisoner. He'll withdraw his force and I'll accompany him."

"Luke, you're crazy!" I said.

Julian glared at me.

"Continue," he said.

"If I win, he's my prisoner," he went on. "He goes back with me to Amber, or anywhere else I care to transport him, and his officers withdraw his troops."

"The only way of assuring such a withdrawal," Julian said, "is to let them know that if they don't they're doomed."

"Of course," Luke said. "That's why I told him that Benedict is waiting in the wings to roll down on him. I'm sure it's the only reason he's agreed to do this."

"Most astute," Julian observed. "Either way, Amber wins. What are you trying to buy with this, Rinaldo, for yourself?"

Luke smiled.

"Think about it," he said.

"There is more to you than I'd thought, Nephew," he replied. "Move over there to my right, would you?"

"Why?"

"To block his view of me, of course. I've got to let Benedict know what's going on."

Luke moved while Julian located his Trumps and shuffled out the proper one. In the meantime the runner from our lines had come up and stood waiting. Julian put away all of the cards but one then, and commenced his communication. It lasted for a minute or so, then Julian paused to speak with the runner and send him back. Immediately, he continued the conversation with the card. When he finally stopped talking or seeming to listen, he did not restore the Trump to the inner pocket where he kept the others, but retained it in his hand out of sight. I realized then that the contact would not be broken, that he would stay in touch with Benedict until this business was finished, so that Benedict would know in an instant what it was that he must do.

Luke unfastened the cloak I'd lent him, came over, and handed it to me.

"Hold this till I'm done, will you?" he said.

"Yes," I agreed, accepting it. "Good luck."

He smiled briefly and turned away. Dalt was already moving toward the center of the square.

Luke advanced, also. He and Dalt both halted, facing each other, while there were still several paces separating them. Dalt said something I could not hear, and Luke's reply was lost to me, also.

Then they raised their arms. Luke struck a boxer's stance, and Dalt's hands came up in a wrestler's defense. Luke threw the first punch—or maybe it was just a feint; either way, it didn't land—toward Dalt's face. Dalt brushed at it and stepped back, and Luke moved in quickly and landed two blows on his midsection. Another shot at his face was blocked, though, and Luke began to circle, jabbing. Dalt tried rushing twice then and got clipped both times, a little trickle of blood coming from his lip after the second one. On his third rush, though, he sent Luke sprawling but was unable to crash down on top of him, as Luke was able to twist partly away and roll when he hit. He tried kicking Dalt in the right kidney, though, as soon as he'd scrambled to his feet, and Dalt caught his ankle and rose, bearing him over backward. Luke landed a kick on the side of his knee with his other foot as he went down, but Dalt kept hold of the foot, bearing down and beginning to twist. Luke bent forward then, grimmacing, and managed to catch Dalt's right wrist with both hands and tear his foot free of the larger man's grip. He doubled and moved forward then, still holding the wrist, regaining his feet and straightening as he advanced, passing under Dalt's arm on his right side, turning, and dragging him face downward to the ground. He moved quickly then, bending the arm up into a hammerlock, holding it with his right hand

and seizing a handful of Dalt's hair with his left. But as he drew
Dalt's head backward—preparatory, I was certain, to slamming it
a few times against the ground—I saw that it wasn't going to
work. Dalt stiffened, and his arm started to move downward. He
was straightening it against Luke's lock. Luke tried pushing Dalt's
head forward several times then, without effect. It became apparent that if he released either hand he was in trouble, and he wasn't
able to maintain the hold. Dalt was just too damned strong. Seeing
this, Luke threw all of his weight against Dalt's back, pushed, and
sprang up. He wasn't quite fast enough, however, because Dalt's
freed arm swung around and clipped him across the left calf as he
moved away. Luke stumbled. Dalt was up and swinging immediately. He caught Luke with a wild haymaker that knocked him
over backward. This time, when he threw himself upon Luke,
Luke was unable to roll free; he only managed to turn his body
partly. Dalt landed with considerable force, twisting past a slow
knee aimed toward his groin. Luke did not get his hands free in
time to defend against a punch that caught him on the left side of
the jaw. He turned with it and fell completely flat. Then his right
hand snapped upward, its heel striking the point of Dalt's chin,
fingers hooking toward the eyes. Dalt jerked his head back and
slapped the hand away. Luke threw a hammer blow toward his
temple with the other hand, and though it connected, Dalt was already moving his head to the side, and I couldn't see that it had
any effect. Luke dropped both elbows to the ground and pushed
himself up and forward, bowing. His forehead struck Dalt's
face—where, I am not precisely certain—before he fell back. Moments later, Dalt's nose began bleeding as he reached out with his
left hand to grasp Luke by the neck. His right hand, open, slapped
Luke hard on the side of the head. I saw Luke's teeth just before it
landed, as he tried biting at the incoming hand, but the grip on his
neck prevented this. Dalt moved to repeat the blow, but this time
Luke's left arm came up and blocked it, while his right hand
caught hold of Dalt's left wrist in an effort to pull it away from his
neck. Dalt's right hand snaked in past Luke's left then, to take
hold, creating a two-handed grip on Luke's neck, thumbs moving
to depress the windpipe.

   I thought that might well be it. But Luke's right hand suddenly
moved to Dalt's left elbow, his left hand crossed both of Dalt's
arms to seize the left forearm, and Luke twisted his body and
cranked the elbow skyward. Dalt went over to the left and Luke
rolled to the right and regained his footing, shaking his head as he

did so. This time he did not try kicking Dalt, who was already recovering. Dalt again extended his arms, Luke raised his fists, and they began circling once more.

The snow continued to fall, the wind to slacken and surge, sometimes driving the icy flakes hard against faces, other times permitting the snow to descend like a troubled curtain. I thought of all the troops about me and wondered for a moment whether I would find myself in the middle of a battlefield when this thing was finally over. The fact that Benedict was ready to swoop down from somewhere and wreak extra havoc did not exactly comfort me, even though it meant that my side would probably win. I remembered then that my being there was my own choice.

"Come on, Luke!" I yelled. "Flatten him!"

This produced a very odd effect. Immediately, Dalt's torchbearers began shouting encouragement to him. Our voices must have carried through the wind's lulls, for shortly there came waves of sound, which I at first took to be some distant part of the storm and only later realized to be shouting coming from both lines. Only Julian remained silent, inscrutable.

Luke continued to circle Dalt, throwing jabs and trying occasional combinations, and Dalt kept swatting away at them and trying to catch an arm. Both of them had blood on their faces and both seemed a bit slower than they had been earlier. I'd a feeling they'd both been hurt, though it was impossible to guess to what extent. Luke had opened a small cut high on Dalt's left cheek. Both of their faces were beginning to look puffy.

Luke connected with another body combination, but it was hard to say how much force there was behind the blows. Dalt took them stoically and found extra energy somewhere to rush forward and attempt to grapple. Luke was slow in withdrawing and Dalt managed to draw him into a clinch. Both tried kneeing the other; both turned their hips and avoided it. They kept tangling arms and twisting as Dalt continued reaching after a better grip and Luke kept defeating the efforts while attempting to free an arm and get in a punch. Both tried several forehead bashes and instep stompings, but all of these were avoided by the other. Finally, Luke succeeded in hooking Dalt's leg, driving him backward to the ground.

Half kneeling atop him then, Luke caught him with a left cross and followed it immediately with a right. He tried for another left then, and Dalt caught his fist, surged upward and threw him back to the ground. As Dalt hurled himself upon him again, his face a half mask of blood and dirt, Luke was somehow able to strike him beneath the heart, but this did not stop Dalt's right fist which came down like a falling rock on the side of Luke's jaw. Dalt followed it with a weak left to the other side, a weak right, paused to suck in a great breath, then landed a solid left. Luke's head rolled to the side and he did not move.

Dalt crouched there atop him, panting like a dog, studying his face as if suspecting some trick, his right hand twitching as if he were contemplating striking again.

But nothing happened. They remained in that position for ten or fifteen seconds before Dalt slowly drew himself erect, eased off of Luke to Luke's left, then rose carefully to his feet, swayed for a second and straightened fully.

I could almost taste the death spell I had hung earlier. It would only take a few seconds to nail him, and no one would be certain how he had died. But I wondered what would happen if he were to collapse now, too. Would both sides attack? It was neither this nor humanitarian considerations that finally restrained me, however. Instead, it was Luke's words, "This really is a matter of honor. So you've got to stay out of it," and, "Nobody's going to die. . . . We're too valuable to each other alive."

Okay. There was still no sound of trumpets. No rush of men to combat. It seemed that things might actually go as had been agreed. This was the way Luke had wanted it. I was not going to interfere.

I watched as Dalt knelt and began to raise Luke from the ground. Immediately, he lowered him, then called to his two torchmen to come and carry him. Dalt rose again and faced Julian as the men advanced.

"I call upon you to observe the rest of our agreement," he said loudly.

Julian inclined his head slightly.

"We will, provided you do," he answered. "Have your men out of here by daybreak."

"We leave now," Dalt replied, and he began to turn away.

"Dalt!" I called out.

He turned back and regarded me.

"My name is Merlin," I said. "We've met, though I don't know whether you remember."

He shook his head.

I raised my right arm and pronounced my most useless and at the same time flashiest spell. The ground erupted before him, showering him with dirt and gravel. He stepped back and wiped his face, then looked down into the rough trench that had appeared.

"That is your grave," I said, "if Luke's death comes of this."

He studied me again.

"Next time I'll remember you," he said, and he turned and followed the men who were carrying Luke back to his lines.

I looked over at Julian, who was watching me. He turned away and uprooted his torch. I did the same. I followed him back the way we had come.

Later, in his tent, Julian observed, "That solves one problem. Possibly two."

"Maybe," I said.

"It takes care of Dalt for the moment."

"I guess."

"Benedict tells me the man is already breaking camp."

"I don't think we've seen the last of him."

"If that's the best he can manage for an army these days, it won't matter."

"Don't you get the impression this was an impromptu mission?" I asked. "I'd guess he pulled his force together very fast. It makes me think he had a tight schedule."

"You may be right there. But he really gambled."

"And he won."

"Yes, he did. And you shouldn't have shown him your power, there at the end."

"Why not?"

"You'll have a wary enemy if you ever go after him."

"He needed warning."

"A man like that lives with risks. He calculates and he acts. However he figures you, he won't change his plans at this point. Besides, you haven't seen the last of Rinaldo either. He's the same way. Those two understand each other."

"You may be right."

"I am."

"If the fight had gone the other way, do you think his army would have stood for it?" I asked.

Julian shrugged. "He knew mine would if he won, because he knew I stood to gain by it. That was sufficient."

I nodded.

"Excuse me," he said. "I have to report this business to Vialle now. I assume you'll want to trump through when I've finished?"

"Yes."

He produced a card and set about the business. And I found myself wondering, not for the first time, just what it was that

Vialle sensed when it came to a Trump contact. I always see the other person myself, and all of the others say that they do, too. But Vialle, as I understood it, had been blind from birth. I've always felt it would be impolite to ask her, and for that matter it's occurred to me that her answer probably wouldn't make much sense to a sighted person. I'll probably always wonder, though.

As Julian addressed her shadowy presence, I turned my mind to the future. I was going to have to do something about Mask and Jurt soon, and it looked now as if I'd be doing it without Luke. Did I really want to follow his advice and try to talk Jasra into an alliance against them? Would the benefits really be worth the risk? And if I didn't, how would I manage the thing? Maybe I should make my way back to that strange bar and see about renting the Jabberwock. Or the Vorpal Sword. Or both. Maybe—

I heard my name mentioned, and I drifted back to the present moment, present problems. Julian was explaining something to Vialle, but I knew there wasn't all that much to explain. So I got to my feet, stretched, and summoned the Logrus Sight.

I saw her ghostly form clearly when I directed my vision toward the area before Julian. She was in that same stiff chair where I had last seen her. I wondered whether she had remained there the entire while or had just returned. I hoped she'd had a chance to go back and eat that dessert I hadn't had a shot at.

Julian glanced at me, then, "If you're ready to go, she's ready to take you through," he said.

I crossed over and stood beside him, dropping the Logrus vision as I did so. I had decided it was not a good idea to bring the forces of the Logrus and the Pattern into too great a proximity. I reached out and touched the card, and Vialle's image sprang into full focus. A moment, and it was no longer an image.

"Anytime," she said, extending a hand.

I reached out and took hold of it gently.

"So long, Julian," I said, as I stepped forward.

He did not reply. Or if he did, I didn't catch it.

"I did not mean for things to go this way," she told me immediately, not releasing my hand.

"There was no way of foreseeing what happened," I said.

"Luke knew," she replied. "It makes sense now, doesn't it? Some of those little remarks he made? He planned the challenge all along."

"I guess so," I said.

"He's gambling on something. I wish I knew what."

"I can't help you on that," I answered. "He didn't say anything to me about it."

"But you will be the one with whom he will get in touch, eventually," she said. "I want to know immediately when you hear from him."

"All right," I agreed.

She released my hand.

"It would seem there is nothing more to say, for the moment."

"Well," I began, "there is another matter I think you ought to know about."

"Oh?"

"It concerns Coral's not being present at dinner this evening."

"Go on," she said.

"You are aware that we took a long walk about town today?"

"I am," she said.

"We wound up below," I continued, "in the chamber of the Pattern. She'd expressed a desire to see it."

"Many visitors do. It is pretty much a matter of judgment whether to take them. Often they lose interest, though, when they learn about the stairway."

"I did tell her about it," I said, "but it didn't discourage her. When she got there, she set foot upon the Pattern—"

"No!" she cried. "You should have watched her more closely! All that other trouble with Begma . . . and now this! Where is her body?"

"Good question," I responded. "I don't know. But she was alive the last time I saw her. You see, she claimed Oberon was her father, and then she proceeded to walk the Pattern. When she'd finished, she had it transport her somewhere. Now, her sister—who is aware that we went off together—is concerned. She was pestering me through dinner as to where Coral might be."

"What did you tell her?"

"I told her that I'd left her sister enjoying some of the beauties of the palace and that she might be a bit late to dinner. As things wore on, though, she seemed to grow more concerned and made me promise to search for her tonight if she didn't turn up. I didn't want to talk about what had really happened because I didn't want to go into the business of Coral's parentage."

"Understandable," she replied. "Oh, my."

I waited, but she said nothing more. I continued to wait.

Finally, "I was not aware of the late king's affair in Begma," she said, "so it is difficult to assess the impact of this revelation.

Did Coral give you any indication as to how long she intended to stay away? And for that matter, did you provide her with any means of return?"

"I gave her my Trump," I said, "but she hasn't been in touch. I got the impression she didn't intend to be away for too long, though."

"This could be serious," Vialle decided, "for reasons other than the obvious. How does Nayda strike you?"

"She seemed quite sensible," I said. "Also, I believe she rather likes me."

Vialle brooded a moment, then said, "If word of this gets to Orkuz, he could well get the impression that we are holding her hostage against his proper performance in any negotiations which might arise out of the situation in Kashfa."

"You're right. I hadn't thought of that."

"He will. People tend to think of such matters when dealing with us. So what we need to do is buy some time and try to turn her up before this begins looking suspicious."

"I understand," I said.

"Most likely, he will send to her quarters soon—if he hasn't already done so—to discover why she was not present at dinner. If he can be satisfied now, you will have the entire night in which to try to locate her."

"How?"

"You're the magician. You figure it out. In the meantime, you say that Nayda is sympathetic?"

"Very much so."

"Good. It seems to me that the best course of action then would be to attempt to enlist her aid. I trust you to be tactful and do this in the least distressing manner possible, of course—"

"Naturally—" I began.

"—because of her recent illness," she went on. "All we need to do now is give the second daughter a heart attack."

"Illness?" I inquired. "She hadn't mentioned anything about that."

"I'd imagine the memory is still distressing. She was apparently quite close to death until very recently, then rallied suddenly and insisted on accompanying her father on this mission. He's the one who told me about it."

"She seemed fine at dinner," I said lamely.

"Well, try to keep her that way. I want you to go to her immediately, tell her what happened as diplomatically as possible, and try to get her to cover for her sister while you search for her. There is, of course, the risk that she will not believe you and that she will go directly to Orkuz. Perhaps you might employ a spell to prevent this. But we have no other choice that I can see. Tell me whether I'm wrong."

"You're not wrong," I said.

"Then I suggest you be about it . . . and report back to me immediately if there are any problems, or any progress, no matter what the hour."

"I'm on my way," I said.

I departed the room in a hurry but shortly came to a halt. It occurred to me that while I knew the general area of the palace in which the Begman party was quartered, I did not really know where Nayda's rooms were located. I did not want to go back and ask Vialle because it would make me look stupid for not having found out during dinner.

It took me the better part of ten minutes to turn up a member of the palace staff able to give me directions—along with a smirk—and then to follow them at a jog until I stood before Nayda's door.

I ran my hand through my hair, brushed off my trousers and jacket, wiped my boots on the backs of my pants legs, took a deep breath, smiled, exhaled, and knocked.

The door opened a few moments later. It was Nayda. She returned my smile and stepped aside.

"Come in," she said.

"I was expecting the maid," I told her as I entered. "You surprised me."

"Since I was expecting you, I sent her off to bed early," she replied.

She had changed into an outfit that looked like a gray sweat suit with a black sash. She also had on a pair of black slippers, and she had removed most of her makeup. Her hair was now drawn back severely and tied with a black ribbon. She gestured toward a couch, but I did not move to seat myself.

I clasped her shoulder lightly and stared into her eyes. She moved nearer.

"How are you feeling?" I asked.

"Find out," she said softly.

I could not even permit myself a sigh. Duty called. I slipped my arms around her, drew her to me, and kissed her. I held the pose for several seconds, then drew away, smiled again, and said,

"You feel fine to me. Listen, there are some things I did not tell you—"

"Shall we sit down?" she said, taking my hand and leading me toward the couch.

Vialle had told me to be diplomatic, so I followed her. Immediately, she continued our embrace and began to add refinements. Damn! And me constrained to rush her out to cover for Coral. If she would, I'd be happy to cover her afterward. Or any other interesting position Begmans might go in for. I'd better ask quickly, though, I decided. A couple of minutes more and it would be very undiplomatic to begin talking about her sister. Today was just a bad day when it came to timing.

"Before we get too involved here," I said, "I've got to ask a favor of you."

"Ask me anything," she said.

"I think there's going to be a delay in turning up your sister," I explained, "and I'd hate to worry your father. Do you know whether he's sent to her rooms yet, or been by them, to check on her?"

"I don't believe so. He strolled off with Gérard and Mr. Roth after dinner. I don't think he's returned to his apartment yet."

"Could you possibly find a way of giving him the impression that she hasn't strayed? Buy me some time to find out where she's off to?"

She looked amused.

"And those things you haven't told me . . . ?"

"I'll give you the whole story if you'll do this for me."

She traced my jawline with her index finger.

"All right," she said then. "We have a deal. Don't go away."

She rose, crossed the room, and passed out into the hall, leaving the door a few inches ajar. Why hadn't I had a nice normal affair since Julia? The last woman I'd made love to had actually been under the control of that strange body-shifting entity. Now . . . Now there was the faintest of shadows across the couch, as I realized that I'd rather be holding Coral than her sister. That was ridiculous. I'd only known her for half a day. . . .

There had simply been too much activity since my return. I was getting punchy. That had to be it.

When she returned she seated herself on the couch again, but this time with a couple of feet separating us. She seemed cheerful enough, though she made no move to resume our earlier occupation.

"It's taken care of," she said. "He will be misled, if he asks."

"Thanks," I told her.

"Now it's your turn," she stated. "Tell me things."

"All right," I began, and I launched into the story of Coral and the Pattern.

"No," she interrupted. "Start at the beginning, would you?"

"What do you mean?"

"Give me your whole day, from the time you left the palace together until you parted."

"That's silly," I protested.

"Humor me," she said. "You owe me one, remember?"

"Very well," I agreed, and I started again. I was able to skip over the bit about blasting the table in the cafe, but when I glossed over the business in the sea caves by saying that we'd looked around in them and found them pretty, she interrupted me.

"Stop," she said. "You're leaving something out. What occurred in the caves?"

"What makes you say that?" I asked.

"That is a secret I do not care to share just now," she explained. "Suffice it to say I have a means of spot-checking your veracity."

"It's not relevant," I said. "It will just confuse the issue. That's why I omitted it."

"You said you'd give me the whole afternoon."

"All right, lady," I agreed, and I did.

She bit her lip while I told her about Jurt and the zombies, and she licked idly at the beads of blood that appeared thereafter.

"What are you going to do about him?" she asked suddenly.

"That's my problem," I said then. "I promised you the afternoon, not my memoirs and survival plans."

"It's just that. . . . Remember, I offered to try to help you?"

"What do you mean? Do you think you can nail Jurt for me? I've got news for you: He's practically a candidate for godhood at the moment."

"What do you mean by 'godhood'?" she asked.

I shook my head.

"It would take most of the night to tell you this story properly, and we don't have the time, not if I'm going to start looking for Coral soon. Just let me finish with the business about the Pattern, will you?"

"Go ahead."

I did, and she showed no surprise whatsoever at the matter of her sister's paternity. I was going to question her as to her lack of reaction. Then I said, the hell with it. She's done what I wanted, and I did what I promised. She hasn't had a heart attack. And now it's time to go.

"That's it," I said, and I added, "Thanks."

I began to rise, and she moved quickly and was hugging me again.

I returned her embrace for a moment, then said, "I'd really better be going. Coral could be in danger."

"The hell with her," she said. "Stay with me. We have more important things to talk about."

I was surprised by her callousness, but I tried not to show it.

"I've a duty to her," I said, "and I've got to see to it now."

"All right," she said, sighing. "I'd better come along and give you a hand."

"How?" I asked.

"You'd be surprised," she told me, and she was on her feet and smiling a twisted smile.

I nodded, feeling that she was probably right.

10

We hiked back along the hallway to my apartment. When I opened the door and summoned the lights, Nayda did a fast survey of the first room. She froze when she saw my coatrack.

"Queen Jasra!" she said.

"Yep. She had a disagreement with a sorcerer named Mask," I explained. "Guess who won?"

Nayda raised her left hand and moved it in a slow pattern—behind Jasra's neck and down her back, across her chest, then downward again. I did not recognize any of the movements she was performing.

"Don't tell me that you're a sorceress, too," I said. "It seems that everyone run into these days has had some training in the Art."

"I am not a sorceress," she answered, "and I've had no such training. I have only one trick and it is not sorcery, but I use it for everything."

"And what is that trick?" I asked.

She ignored the question, then said, "My, she's certainly tightly bound. The key lies somewhere in the region of her solar plexus. Did you know that?"

"Yes," I replied. "I understand the spell fully."

"Why is she here?"

"Partly because I promised her son Rinaldo I'd rescue her from Mask, and partly as an assurance against his good behavior."

I pushed the door shut and secured it. When I turned back, she was facing me.

"Have you seen him recently?" she said in a conversational tone.

"Yes. Why?"

"Oh, no special reason."

"I thought we were trying to help each other," I said.

"I thought we were looking for my sister."

"It can wait another minute if you know something special about Rinaldo."

"I was just curious where he might be right now."

I turned away and moved to the chest where I keep art supplies. I removed the necessary items and took them to my drawing board. While I was about it, I said, "I don't know where he is."

I set up the piece of pasteboard, seated myself and closed my eyes, summoning a mental image of Coral, preliminary to beginning her sketch. Again, I half wondered whether the picture in my mind, along with the appropriate magical endorsement, would be sufficient for contact. But now was not the time to mess around being experimental. I opened my eyes and began to draw. I used the techniques I'd learned in the Courts, which are different yet similar to those employed in Amber. I was qualified to execute them in either fashion, but I'm faster with the style I learned first.

Nayda came over and stood near, watching, not asking whether I minded. As it was, I did not.

"When did you see him last?" she asked.

"Who?"

"Luke."

"This evening," I answered.

"Where?"

"He was here earlier."

"Is he here now?"

"No."

"Where did you last see him?"

"In the forest of Arden. Why?"

"It seems a strange place to part."

I was working on Coral's eyebrows.

"We parted under strange circumstances," I said.

A little more work about the eyes, a bit on the hair. . . .

"Strange? In what way?" she asked.

More color to the cheeks. . . .

"Never mind," I told her.

"All right," she said. "It's probably not that important."

I decided against rising to that bait, because I was suddenly getting something. As had occasionally happened in the past, my concentration on the Trump as I put the final touches to it was sufficiently intense to reach through and. . . .

"Coral!" I said, as the features moved, perspectives shifted.

"Merlin . . . ?" she answered. "I . . . I'm in trouble."

Oddly, there was no background whatever. Just blackness. I felt Nayda's hand upon my shoulder.

"Are you all right?" I asked.

"Yes. . . . It's dark here," she said. "Very dark."

Of course. One cannot manipulate Shadow in the absence of light. Or even see to use a Trump.

"That's where the Pattern sent you?" I asked.

"No," she answered.

"Take my hand," I said. "You can tell me about it afterward."

I extended my hand and she reached toward it.

"They—" she began.

And with a stinging flash the contact was broken. I felt Nayda stiffen beside me.

"What happened?" she asked.

"I don't know. We were suddenly blocked. I can't tell what forces were involved."

"What are you going to do?"

"Try again in a little bit," I said. "If it were a reaction thing, resistance will probably be high just now, and it may ease up later. At least she says she's all right."

I withdrew the packet of Trumps I normally carry, shuffled out Luke's. Now seemed as good a time as any to see how he was faring. Nayda glanced at the card and smiled.

"I thought you just saw him a little while ago," she said.

"A lot can happen in a little while."

"I'm certain a lot *has* happened."

"You think you know something about what's going on with him?" I asked.

"Yes. I do."

I raised the Trump.

"What?" I said.

"I'd be willing to wager, you won't get through to him."

"We'll see."

I concentrated and I reached. I reached again. A minute or so later I wiped my brow.

"How'd you know?" I asked.

"Luke's blocking you. I would, too . . . under the circumstances."

"What circumstances?"

She gave me a quirked smile, crossed to a chair, and sat down.

"Now I have something to trade with you again," she said.

"Again?"

I studied her. Something jiggled and fell into place.

"You've been calling him 'Luke' rather than 'Rinaldo,' " I said.

"So I have."

"I'd been wondering when you'd show up again."

She continued to smile.

"I went and shot my eviction-notice spell," I observed. "Can't complain, though. It probably saved my life. Do I owe you that one, in some roundabout fashion?"

"I'm not proud. I'll take it."

"I'm going to ask you again what you want, and if you say it's to help me or to protect me, I'm going to turn you into a coatrack."

She laughed.

"I'd have guessed you'd take whatever help you could get right now," she said.

"A lot depends on what you mean by 'help.' "

"If you'll tell me what you have in mind, I'll tell you whether I can be of any assistance."

"All right," I said. "I'm going to change clothes while I talk, though. I don't feel like storming a citadel dressed like this. May I lend you something tougher than a sweat suit?"

"I'm fine. Start at Arbor House, okay?"

"Okay," I said, and I proceeded to fill her in while I garbed myself in tougher fare. She was no longer a pretty lady to me, but rather a nebulous entity in human form. She seated herself while I was talking and stared at the wall, or through it, over steepled fingers. When I was finished, she kept staring, and I went over to my drawing board, took up Coral's Trump, tried again, but couldn't get through. I tried Luke's card, also, with the same results.

As I was about to replace Luke's Trump, square the deck, and case it, I glimpsed the next lower card and a lightning chain of recollections and speculations flashed through my mind. I removed the card and focused on it. I reached. . . .

"Yes, Merlin?" he said moments later, seated at a small table on a terrace—evening skyline of a city behind him—lowering what appeared to be a cup of espresso to a tiny white saucer.

"Right now. Hurry," I said. "Come to me."

Nayda had begun to make a low growling sound just as the contact occurred, and she was on her feet and moving toward me, her eyes fixed upon the Trump, just as Mandor took my hand and stepped through. She halted when the tall, black-garbed figure appeared before her. They regarded each other without expression for a moment, and then she took a long sliding step toward him, her hands beginning to rise. Immediately, from the depth of some inner cloak pocket where his right hand was thrust, there came a single, sharp, metallic click.

Nayda froze.

"Interesting," Mandor said, raising his left hand and passing it in front of her face. Her eyes did not follow it. "This is the one you told me about earlier—Vinta, I believe, you called her?"

"Yes, only now she's Nayda."

He produced a small, dark metal ball from somewhere and held it upon the palm of his left hand, which he extended before her. Slowly, the ball began to move, describing a counterclockwise circle. Nayda emitted a single sound, something halfway between a cry and a gasp, and she dropped forward to her hands and knees, head lowered. From where I stood I could see saliva dripping from her mouth.

He said something very fast, in an archaic form of Thari which I could not follow. She responded in the affirmative.

"I believe I've solved your mystery," he said then. "Do you recall your lessons on Respondances and High Compellings?"

"Sort of," I said. "Academically. I was never exactly swept away by the subject."

"Unfortunate," he stated. "You should report back to Suhuy for a postgraduate course sometime."

"Are you trying to tell me . . . ?"

"The creature you see before you, inhabiting a not unattractive human form, is a *ty'iga,*" he explained.

I stared. The *ty'iga* were a normally bodiless race of demons that dwelled in the blackness beyond the Rim. I recalled being told that they were very powerful and very difficult to control.

"Uh . . . can you make this one stop slobbering on my carpet?" I said.

"Of course," he replied, and he released the sphere, which fell to the floor before her. It did not bounce, but began immediately to roll, describing a rapid circuit about her.

"Stand up," he said, "and stop releasing bodily fluids upon the floor."

She did as he ordered, climbing to her feet, her expression vacant.

"Seat yourself in that chair," he directed, indicating the one she had occupied but minutes earlier.

She complied, and the rolling ball adjusted itself to her progress and continued its circle, about the chair now.

"It cannot vacate that body," he said then, "unless I release it. And I can cause it any amount of torment within my sphere of power. I can get you your answers now. Tell me what the questions are."

"Can she hear us right now?"

"Yes, but it cannot speak unless I permit it."

"Well, there's no point to causing unnecessary pain. The threat itself may be sufficient. I want to know why she's been following me about."

"Very well," he said. "That is the question, *ty'iga*. Answer it!"

"I follow him to protect him," she said, her voice flat.

"I've already heard that one," I said. "I want to know why."

"Why?" Mandor repeated.

"I must," she answered.

"Why must you?" he asked.

"I. . . ." Her teeth raked her lower lip and the blood began to flow again.

"Why?"

Her face grew flushed and beads of perspiration appeared upon her brow. Her eyes were still unfocused, but they brimmed with tears. A thin line of blood trickled down her chin. Mandor extended a clenched fist and opened it, revealing another metal ball. He held this one about ten inches before her brow, then released it. It hung in the air.

"Let the doors of pain be opened," he said, and he flicked it lightly with a fingertip.

Immediately, the small sphere began to move. It passed about her head in a slow ellipse, coming close to her temples on each orbit. She began to wail.

"Silence!" he said. "Suffer in silence!"

The tears ran down her cheeks, the blood ran down her chin. . . .

"Stop it!" I said.

"Very well." He reached over and squeezed the ball for a moment between the thumb and middle finger of his left hand. When he released it, it remained stationary, a small distance before her right ear. "Now you may answer the question," he said. "That was but the smallest sample of what I can do to you. I can push this to your total destruction."

She opened her mouth but no words came forth. Only a gagging sound.

"I think we may be going about this wrong," I said. "Can you just have her speak normally, rather than this question-and-answer business?"

"You heard him," Mandor said. "It is my will, also."

She gasped, then said, "My hands. . . . Please free them."

"Go ahead," I said.

"They are freed," Mandor stated.

She flexed her fingers.

"A handkerchief, a towel . . . ," she said softly.

I drew open a drawer in a nearby dresser, took out a handkerchief. As I moved to pass it to her, Mandor seized my wrist and took it from me. He tossed it to her and she caught it.

"Don't reach within my sphere," he told me.

"I wouldn't hurt him," she said, as she wiped her eyes, her cheeks, her chin. "I told you, I mean only to protect him."

"We require more information than that," Mandor said, as he reached for the sphere again.

"Wait," I said. Then, to her, "Can you at least tell me why you can't tell me?"

"No," she answered. "It would amount to the same thing."

Suddenly I saw it as a strange sort of programming problem, and I decided to try a different tack.

"You must protect me at all costs?" I said. "That is your primary function?"

"Yes."

"And you are not supposed to tell me who set you this task, or why?"

"Yes."

"Supposing the only way you could protect me would be by telling me these things?"

Her brow furrowed.

"I . . . ," she said. "I don't. . . . The *only* way?"

She closed her eyes and raised her hands to her face.

"I. . . . Then I would have to tell you."

"Now we're getting somewhere," I said. "You would be willing to violate the secondary order in order to carry out the primary one?"

"Yes, but what you have described is not a real situation," she said.

"I see one that is," Mandor said suddenly. "You cannot follow that order if you cease to exist. Therefore, you would be violating it if you permit yourself to be destroyed. I will destroy you unless you answer those questions."

She smiled.

"I don't think so," she said.

"Why not?"

"Ask Merlin what the diplomatic situation would be if a daughter of the Begman prime minister were found dead in his room under mysterious circumstances—especially when he's already responsible for the disappearance of her sister."

Mandor frowned and looked at me.

"I don't understand what that's all about," he said.

"It doesn't matter," I told him. "She's lying. If something happens to her, the real Nayda simply returns. I saw it happen with George Hansen, Meg Devlin, and Vinta Bayle."

"That is what would normally occur," she said, "except for one thing. They were all alive when I took possession of their bodies. But Nayda had just died, following a severe illness. She was exactly what I needed, though, so I took possession and healed the body. She is not here anymore. If I depart, you'll be left either with a corpse or a human vegetable."

"You're bluffing," I said, but I remembered Vialle's saying that Nayda had been ill.

"No," she said. "I'm not."

"It doesn't matter," I told her.

"Mandor," I said, turning to him, "you said you can keep her from vacating that body and following me?"

"Yes," he replied.

"Okay, Nayda," I said. "I am going somewhere and I am going to be in extreme danger there. I am not going to permit you to follow me and carry out your orders."

"Don't," she answered.

"You give me no choice but to keep you pent while I go about my business."

She sighed.

"So you've found a way to get me to violate one order in order to get me to carry out the other. Very clever."

"Then you'll tell me what I want to know?"

She shook her head.

"I am physically unable to tell you," she said. "It is not a matter of will. But . . . I think I've found a way around it."

"What is that?"

"I believe I could confide in a third party who also desires your safety."

"You mean—"

"If you will leave the room for a time, I will try to tell your brother those things I may not explain to you."

My eyes met Mandor's. Then, "I'll step out in the hall for a bit," I said.

And I did. A lot of things bothered me as I studied a tapestry on the wall, not the least being that I had never told her that Mandor was my brother.

When my door opened after a long while, Mandor looked in both directions. He raised his hand when I began to move toward him. I halted, and he stepped outside and came toward me. He continued to glance about as he advanced.

"This is Amber palace?" he inquired.

"Yes. Not the most fashionable wing, perhaps, but I call it home."

"I'd like to see it under more relaxed circumstances," he said.

I nodded. "It's a date. So tell me, what happened in there?"

He looked away, discovered the tapestry, studied it.

"It's very peculiar," he said. "I can't."

"What do you mean?"

"You still trust me, don't you?"

"Of course."

"Then trust me in this. I've a good reason for not telling you what I learned."

"Come on, Mandor! What the hell's going on?"

"The *ty'iga* is not a danger to you. It really does care about your welfare."

"So what else is new? I want to know why."

"Leave it," he said, "for now. It's better that way."

I shook my head. I made a fist and looked around for something to hit.

"I know how you feel, but I'm asking you to drop it," he said.

"You mean the knowledge would hurt me in some way?"

"I didn't say that."

"Or do you mean that you're afraid to tell me?"

"Drop it!" he said.

I turned away and got control of myself.

"You must have a good reason," I finally decided.

"I do."

"I'm not going to give up on this," I told him. "But I haven't the time to pursue it further against this kind of resistance. Okay, you have your reasons and I have pressing business elsewhere."

"She mentioned Jurt and Mask and the Keep where Brand gained his powers," he said.

"Yes, that's where I'll be heading."

"She expects to accompany you."

"She is wrong."

"I would counsel against taking her, too."

"You'll keep her for me until I've taken care of things?"

"No," he said, "because I'm coming with you. I'll put her into a very deep trance, though, before we depart."

"But you don't know what's been going on since our dinner. A lot has happened, and I just haven't the time to bring you up to date."

"It doesn't matter," he said. "I know that it involves an unfriendly sorcerer, Jurt, and a dangerous place. That's enough. I'll come along and give you a hand."

"But that may not be enough," I countered. "*We* may not be enough."

"Even so, I think the *ty'iga* could turn into a hindrance."

"I wasn't referring to her. I was thinking about the stiff lady near the door."

"I'd meant to ask you about her. Some enemy you're punishing?"

"She had been an enemy, yes. And she's nasty, untrustworthy, and has a poisonous bite. She's also a deposed queen. I didn't freeze her, though. The sorcerer who's after me did it. She's the mother of a friend, and I rescued her and brought her back here for safekeeping. I had no reason for releasing her, until now."

"Ah, as an ally against her old enemy."

"Exactly. She's well acquainted with the place I'm going. But she doesn't like me and she's not easy to deal with—and I don't really know whether her son gave me enough ammunition to make her trustworthy."

"Do you feel she'd be a real asset?"

"Yes. I'd like to have all of that animus on my side. And I understand she's an accomplished sorceress."

"If additional persuading is needed, there are only threats and bribes. I've a few private hells I've designed and furnished—for purely esthetic reasons. She might find a quick tour very impressive. On the other hand, I could send for a pot of jewels."

"I don't know," I said. "Her motivations are somewhat complex. Let me handle this, as far as I'm able."

"Of course. Those were only suggestions."

"As I see it, the next order of business is to rouse her, put the proposition to her, and attempt to judge her response."

"There is no one else you might bring along, from among your kinsmen here?"

"I'm afraid to let any of them know I'm going. It could easily result in an order not to, until Random gets back. I haven't the time to wait around."

"I might summon some reinforcement from the Courts."

"Here? To Amber? I'd really be up shit creek if Random ever got wind of that. He might start suspecting subversion."

He smiled.

"This place reminds me a bit of home," he remarked, turning back toward my door.

When we entered, I saw that Nayda was still seated, her hands upon her knees, staring at a metal ball that hovered about a foot before her. The other continued its slow circuit down on the floor.

Seeing the direction of my gaze, Mandor remarked, "Very light trance state. She can hear us. You can rouse her in an instant if you wish."

I nodded and turned away. Now it was Jasra's turn.

I removed all of the garments I'd hung upon her and placed them on a chair across the room. Then I fetched a cloth and the basin and washed the clown makeup off her face.

"Am I forgetting anything?" I said, half to myself.

"A glass of water and a mirror," Mandor stated.

"What for?"

"She may be thirsty," he replied, "and I can just tell she'll want to look at herself."

"You may have a point there," I said, drawing up a small table. I placed a pitcher and a goblet upon it; also, a hand mirror.

"I'd also suggest you support her, in case she collapses when the spell is removed."

"True."

I placed my left arm about her shoulders, thought of her deadly bite, stepped back, and held her at arm's distance with the one hand.

"If she bites me, it will knock me out almost instantly," I said. "Be ready to defend yourself quickly if this occurs."

Mandor tossed another metal ball into the air. It hung there for an unnaturally long moment at the top of its arc, then dropped back to his hand.

"All right," I said, and then I spoke the words that raised the spell.

Nothing as dramatic as I'd feared ensued. She slumped and I supported her. "You're safe," I said, and added, "Rinaldo knows you're here," to invoke the most familiar. "Here's a chair. Do you want some water?"

"Yes," she replied, and I poured some and passed it to her.

Her eyes were darting, taking in everything as she drank. I wondered whether she'd recovered instantly and might not now be stalling for time as she sipped, her mind racing, spells dancing at her fingertips. Her eyes returned more than once to Mandor, appraising, though she gave Nayda a long, hard stare.

Finally, she lowered the goblet and smiled.

"I take it, Merlin, that I am your prisoner," she said, choking slightly. She took another sip.

"Guest," I replied.

"Oh? How did this come about? Accepting the invitation escapes my mind."

"I brought you here from the citadel at the Keep of the Four Worlds in a somewhat cataleptic condition," I said.

"And where might 'here' be?"

"My apartment in the Palace of Amber."

"Prisoner, then," she stated.

"Guest," I repeated.

"In that case, I should be introduced, should I not?"

"Excuse me. Mandor, I introduce Her Highness Jasra, Queen of Kashfa." (I intentionally omitted the "Most Royal" part.) "Your Majesty, I request leave to present my brother, Lord Mandor."

She inclined her head, and Mandor approached, dropped to one knee, and raised her hand to his lips. He's better at such courtly gestures than I am, not even sniffing the back of her hand for the scent of bitter almonds. I could tell that she liked his manner—and she continued to study him afterward.

"I was not aware," she observed, "that the royal house here contained an individual named Mandor."

"Mandor is heir to the dukedom of Sawall in the Courts of Chaos," I replied.

Her eyes widened.

"And you say he is your brother?"

"Indeed."

"You've succeeded in surprising me," she stated. "I had forgotten your double lineage."

I smiled, nodded, stepped aside and gestured.

"And this—" I began.

"I am acquainted with Nayda," she said. "Why is the girl . . . preoccupied?"

"That represents a matter of great complexity," I said, "and there are other things I am certain you will find to be of much greater interest."

She cocked an eyebrow at me.

"Ah! That fragile, perishable item—the truth," she said. "When it surfaces so quickly there is usually a claustrophobia of circumstance. What is it that you want of me?"

I held my smile.

"It is good to appreciate circumstance," I said.

"I appreciate the fact that I am in Amber and alive and not occupying a cell, with two gentlemen behaving in a conciliatory fashion. I also appreciate the fact that I am not in the straits my most recent memories indicate I should occupy. And I have you to thank for my deliverance?"

"Yes."

"Somehow I doubt it was a matter of altruism on your part."

"I did it for Rinaldo. He tried getting you out once and got clobbered. Then I figured a way that might work, and I tried it. It did."

Her facial muscles tightened at the mention of her son's name. I'd decided she'd prefer hearing the one she'd given him, rather than "Luke."

"Is he all right?" she asked.

"Yes," I said, hoping it were so.

"Then why is he not present?"

"He's off somewhere with Dalt. I'm not sure as to his location. But—"

Nayda made a small noise just then, and we glanced her way.

But she did not stir. Mandor gave me an inquiring look, but I shook my head slightly. I did not want her roused just then.

"Bad influence, that barbarian," Jasra observed, choking again and taking another drink. "I'd so wanted Rinaldo to acquire more of the courtly graces, rather than doing rude things on horseback much of the time," she continued, glancing at Mandor and granting him a small smile. "In this, I was disappointed. Do you have something stronger than water?"

"Yes," I replied, and I uncorked a bottle of wine and poured some into a goblet for her. I glanced at Mandor and at the bottle then, but he shook his head. "But you have to admit he did well in that track meet against UCLA, in his sophomore year," I said, not to let her put him down completely. "A certain amount of that comes from the more vigorous side of life."

She smiled as she accepted the drink.

"Yes. He broke a world record that day. I can still see him passing over the final hurdle."

"You were there?"

"Oh, yes. I attended all of your meets. I even watched you run," she said. "Not bad."

She sipped the wine.

"Would you like me to send for a meal for you?" I asked.

"No, I'm not really hungry. We were talking about truth a little while ago. . . ."

"So we were. I gather there had been some sorcerous exchange back at the Keep, between you and Mask—"

"Mask?" she said.

"The blue-masked sorcerer who rules there now."

"Oh, yes. Quite."

"I do have the story right, don't I?"

"Yes, but the encounter was more than a little traumatic. Forgive my hesitation. I was surprised and did not get my defenses up in time. That was really all there was to it. It will not happen again."

"I'm sure. But—"

"Did you spirit me away?" she interrupted. "Or did you actually fight with Mask to get me free?"

"We fought," I said.

"In what condition did you leave Mask?"

"Buried under a pile of manure," I said.

She chuckled.

"Wonderful! I like a man with a sense of humor."

"I have to go back," I added.

"Oh? Why is that?"

"Because Mask is now allied with an enemy of mine—a man named Jurt, who desires my death."

She shrugged slightly.

"If Mask is no match for you, I fail to see where Mask and this man should represent a great problem."

Mandor cleared his throat.

"Begging your leave," he said. "But Jurt is a shape shifter and minor sorcerer from the Courts. He also has power over Shadow."

"I suppose that would make something of a difference," she said.

"Not as much as what the two of them apparently plan to accomplish," I told her. "I believe that Mask intends running Jurt through the same ritual your late husband undertook—something involving the Fount of Power."

"No!" she cried, and she was on her feet, the rest of the wine mixing with Nayda's spittle and a few old bloodstains on the Tabriz I'd purchased for its delicately detailed pastoral scene. "It must not happen again!"

A storm came and went behind her eyes. Then, for the first time, she looked vulnerable.

"I lost him because of that . . . ," she said.

Then the moment was gone. The hardness returned.

"I had not finished my wine," she said then, reseating herself.

"I'll get you another glass," I told her.

"And is that a mirror on the table?"

11

I waited till she was finished primping, glancing out of the window at the snow and surreptitiously trying again to reach Coral or Luke while my back was turned to her. No luck, though. When she put down the comb and brush she'd borrowed from me and laid the mirror beside them, I gathered she'd finished organizing her thoughts as well as her hair and was ready to talk again. I turned back slowly and strolled over.

We studied each other while practicing expressionlessness, then she asked, "Is anyone else in Amber aware that you have awakened me?"

"No," I replied.

"Good. That means I've a chance of leaving here alive. Presumably, you want my assistance against Mask and this Jurt?"

"Yes."

"Exactly what sort of help do you desire, and what are you prepared to pay for it?"

"I intend to penetrate the Keep and neutralize Mask and Jurt," I said.

" 'Neutralize'? That's one of those little euphemisms for 'kill,' isn't it?"

"I suppose so," I replied.

"Amber has never been noted for its squeamishness," she said. "You have been exposed to too much American journalism. So, you are aware of my familiarity with the Keep, and you want my help in killing the two of them. Correct?"

I nodded.

"Rinaldo has told me that if we were to arrive too late and Jurt had already undergone the transformational ritual, you might know a way to use that same power against him," I explained.

"He'd gotten further into those notes than I'd realized," she said. "I am going to have to be frank with you then, since our lives may depend on it: Yes, there is such a technique. But no, it won't be of any help to us. Some preparations are required to turn the power to such an end. It is not something I could simply reach out and do at a moment's notice."

Mandor cleared his throat.

"I'd rather not see Jurt dead," he stated, "if there's a possibility I could take him back to the Courts as a prisoner. He could be disciplined. There might be a way of neutralizing him without really . . . neutralizing him, as you put it."

"And if there isn't?" I asked.

"Then I'll help you to kill him," he said. "I have no illusions about him, but I feel obliged to try something. I'm afraid that the news of his death could push our father over the edge."

I looked away. He could be right, and even though old Sawall's death would mean his own succession to the title and control of considerable holdings, I was certain he was not anxious to acquire them at that price.

"I understand," I said. "I hadn't thought of that."

"So give me a chance to subdue him. If I fail, I'll join you in whatever must be done."

"Agreed," I said, watching to see how Jasra was taking this.

She was studying us, a curious expression on her face.

" 'Our father'?" she said.

"Yes," I replied. "I wasn't going to mention that, but since it got out, Jurt's our younger brother."

Her eyes were alight now, at the scent of connivance.

"This is a family power struggle, isn't it?" she asked.

"I suppose you could put it that way," I said.

"Not really," Mandor said.

"And yours is an important family in the Courts?"

Mandor shrugged. So did I. I'd a feeling she was trying to figure a way to cash in on that end of it, too, and I decided to stonewall her.

"We were discussing the task at hand," I said. "I want to take us in there and accept Mask's challenge. We stop Jurt if he gets in the way and give him to Mandor. If it is impossible simply to subdue him, we go the rest of the way. Are you with us?"

"We have not yet discussed the price," she said.

"All right," I acknowledged. "I've talked about this with Rinaldo, and he told me to tell you that he's called the vendetta off. He feels things were settled with Amber when Caine died. He asked me to release you if you would go along with this, and he suggested that in return for your help against the new lord of the citadel we restore the Keep of the Four Worlds to your sovereignty. Bottom line, as he put it. What do you say?"

She picked up the goblet and took a long, slow sip. She'd stall, I knew, trying to figure a way to squeeze more out of this deal.

"You've spoken with Rinaldo very recently?" she said.

"Yes."

"I am not clear as to why he is running about with Dalt, rather than being here with us, if he is so much in agreement with this plan."

I sighed.

"Okay, I'll tell you the story," I said. "But if you're with us, I do want to get moving soon."

"Proceed," she said.

So I recounted the evening's adventure in Arden, omitting only the fact that Vialle had placed Luke under her protection. Nayda seemed to grow progressively distressed as I told the tale, uttering small whimpering sounds at odd intervals.

When I was finished, Jasra placed her hand upon Mandor's arm and rose, brushing him lightly with her hip as she passed, and she went to stand before Nayda.

"Now tell me why the daughter of a high Begman official is restrained here," she said.

"She is possessed of a demon that enjoys interfering in my affairs," I explained.

"Really? I've often wondered what hobbies demons might pursue," she observed. "But it seems this particular demon has been trying to say something in which I might be interested. If you would be so good as to free it for a moment's conversation I promise to consider your offer afterward."

"Time is running," I said.

"In that case my answer is no," she told me. "Lock me up someplace and go to the Keep without me."

I glanced at Mandor.

"In that I have not yet agreed to accept your offer," Jasra continued, "Rinaldo would call this an entertainment expense."

"I see no harm in it," Mandor said.

"Then let her speak," I told him.

"You may talk, *ty'iga*," he said.

Her first words were not addressed to Jasra, however, but to me: "Merlin, you have to let me accompany you."

I moved around to where I could see her face.

"No way," I told her.

"Why not?" she asked.

"Because your penchant for protecting me will actually hinder me in a situation where I will probably have to take some chances."

"That is my nature," she responded.

"And my problem," I said. "I mean you no ill. I'll be glad to talk to you when this is all over, but you're going to have to sit this one out."

Jasra cleared her throat.

"Is that the entire message? Or is there something you wished to tell me, also?" Jasra asked.

There followed a long silence, then, "Will you be accompanying them or not?" Nayda inquired.

Jasra took just as long to respond, obviously weighing her words:

"This is a clandestine, personal operation," she said. "I am not at all certain it would be countenanced by Merlin's seniors here in Amber. While it is true that I stand to gain if I cooperate, I will also undergo considerable risk. Of course, I want my freedom and the restoration of the Keep. It is almost a fair trade. But he also asks a quitclaim on the vendetta. What assurance have I that this means anything here, and that the hierarchy of Amber will not hunt me down as a troublemaker afterward? He cannot speak for the others when he operates on the sly this way."

Somehow, it had become a question addressed to me, and since it was a very good question to which I did not really have an answer, I was glad that the *ty'iga* had something to say:

"I believe that I can persuade you that it would be in your best interest to agree to accompany them and to render every assistance you can," she offered.

"Pray, begin," Jasra told her.

"I would have to speak with you in private on this matter."

Jasra smiled, out of her love for intrigue, I am certain.

"It is agreeable to me," she said.

"Mandor, force her to say it now," I said.

"Wait!" Jasra declared. "I will have this private conversation or you can forget about my help."

I began wondering just how much help Jasra really represented if she couldn't call upon the Fount to dispose of Jurt, should that become our biggest problem. True, she knew the Keep. But I didn't even know for certain how accomplished a sorceress she might be.

On the other hand, I wanted this thing settled now, and one more adept could make the difference.

"Nayda," I said, "are you planning something that could be damaging to Amber?"

"No," she replied.

"Mandor, what do *ty'iga* swear by?" I inquired.

"They don't," he said.

"What the hell," I said. "How much time do you want?"

"Give us ten minutes," she told me.

"Let's take a walk," I said to Mandor.

"Surely," he agreed, tossing another metal ball toward Nayda. It joined the others in orbit about her, a little above waist level.

I fetched a key from my desk drawer before departing. And as soon as we were in the hall I asked him, "Is there any way Jasra could free her?"

"Not with the additional circuit of confinement I established on the way out," he replied. "Not many could figure a way past it, and certainly not in ten minutes."

"She's just full of secrets, that damned *ty'iga*," I said. "Kind of makes me wonder who's really the prisoner here."

"She's only trading some bit of knowledge for Jasra's cooperation," he said. "She wants the lady to accompany us if she can't go herself, since it will mean extra protection for you."

"Then why can't we be present?"

"Nothing that I learned from her sheds any light on this," he said.

"Well, since I have a few minutes, there is a small errand I want to run. Would you keep an eye on things here and take charge if she calls us in before I get back?"

He smiled.

"If one of your relatives strolls by, should I introduce myself as a lord of Chaos?"

"I thought you were also a lord of deception."

"Of course," he said, and he clapped his hands and vanished.

"I'll hurry," I said.

"Cheerio," came his voice, from somewhere.

I hurried off up the hall. It was a little pilgrimage, I suppose—

one that I had not made in a long while. On the brink of an enterprise such as this, it seemed somehow appropriate.

When I reached the door, I stood outside it for a moment, my eyes closed, visualizing the interior as last I had seen it. It was my father's apartment. I had wandered through it on many occasions, trying to judge from the furnishings, the layout, his bookshelves, and his curious collections something more than I already knew about the man. There was always some little thing that caught my attention, that answered a question or raised a new one—an inscription on the flyleaf of a book or a note in a margin, a silver hairbrush bearing the wrong set of initials, a daguerrotype of an attractive brunette signed "To Carl, Love, Carolyn," a snapshot of my father shaking hands with General MacArthur. . . .

I unlocked the door and pushed it open.

I did not move for several seconds, however, as a light glowed inside the place. For more long moments I listened, but there were no sounds from within. Slowly then, I entered. A number of candles burned upon the dresser set against the far wall. There was no one in sight.

"Hello?" I called out. "It's me. Merlin."

There came no answer.

I drew the door closed behind me and moved forward. A bud vase stood upon the dresser amid the candles. It contained a single rose, and it appeared to be silver in color. I drew nearer. Yes, it was real, not artificial. And it *was* silver. In what shadow did such flowers grow?

I picked up one of the candles by its holder and moved away with it, shielding its flame with my hand. I crossed to my left and entered the next room. Immediately, on opening the door, I saw that there was no need to have brought the candle. More of them were burning here.

"Hello?" I repeated.

Again, no answer. No sounds of any sort.

I set the candle upon a nearby table and crossed to the bed. I raised a sleeve and let it fall. A silvery shirt was laid out upon the counterpane beside a black pair of trousers—my father's colors. They had not been there when last I had visited.

I seated myself beside them and stared across the room into a shadowy corner. What was going on? Some bizarre household ritual? A haunting? or. . . .

"Corwin?" I said.

In that I'd hardly expected a reply, I was not disappointed.

When I rose, however, I bumped against a heavy object hung upon the nearest bedpost. I reached out and raised it for a better view. A belt with a sheathed weapon hung upon it. These had not been present last time either. I gripped the haft and drew the blade.

A portion of the Pattern, contained within the gray metal, danced in the candlelight. This was Grayswandir, sword of my father. What it was doing back here now, I had no idea.

And I realized with a pang that I could not stick around to see what might be going on. I had to get back to my own problems. Yes, timing was definitely against me today.

I resheathed Grayswandir.

"Dad?" I said. "If you can hear me, I want to get together again. But I have to go now. Good luck on whatever you're about."

Then I departed the room, touched the silver rose as I passed and locked the door behind me. As I turned away, I realized that I was shaking.

I passed no one on the walk back, and when I approached my own door I wondered whether I should enter, knock, or wait. Then something touched my shoulder, and I turned around but no one was there. When I turned forward once again Mandor stood before me, his brow slightly creased.

"What's the matter?" he asked. "You appear more troubled than when you left."

"Something totally different," I told him, "I think. Any word from inside yet?"

"I heard a shriek from Jasra while you were gone," he said, "and I hurried to the door and opened it. But she was laughing and she asked me to close it."

"Either ty'igas know some good stories or the news is favorable."

"So it would seem."

A little later the door opened and Jasra nodded to us.

"Our conversation is concluded," she said.

I studied her as I entered the room. She looked a lot more cheerful than she had seemed when we'd left. There was a bit more of a crinkling about the outer edges of her eyes, and she seemed almost to be fighting the corners of her mouth down into place.

"I hope it was a fruitful interview," I said.

"Yes. On the whole, I'd say it was that," she answered.

A glance at Nayda showed me that nothing had changed in terms of her position or expression.

"I'll have to be asking you for a decision now," I said. "I can't afford to cut things much closer than this."

"What happens if I say no?" she asked.

"I'll have you conducted to your quarters and inform the others that you're up and about," I said.

"As a guest?"

"As a very well-protected guest."

"I see. Well, I do not really care to inspect those quarters. I have decided to accompany you and assist you under the terms we discussed."

I bowed to her.

"Merlin!" Nayda said.

"No!" I answered, and I looked to Mandor.

He approached and stood before Nayda.

"It is best that you sleep now," he told her, and her eyes closed, her shoulders slumped. "Where is a good place for her to rest deeply?" he asked me.

"Through there," I said, indicating the doorway to the next room.

He took her by the hand and led her away. After a time, I heard him speaking softly, and then there was only silence. He emerged a little later, and I went to the door and glanced inside. She was stretched out on my bed. I did not see any of his metal spheres in the neighborhood.

"She's out of it?" I said.

"For a long time," he replied.

I looked at Jasra, who was glancing down into the mirror.

"Are you ready?" I inquired.

She regarded me through lowered lashes.

"How do you propose transporting us?" she asked.

"Do you have an especially tricky means of getting us in?"

"Not at the moment."

"Then I will be calling upon the Ghostwheel to take us there."

"Are you certain it is safe? I've conversed with that . . . device. I am not sure it is trustworthy."

"It's fine," I said. "Any spells you want to prime first?"

"Not necessary. My . . . resources should be in good order."

"Mandor?"

I heard a clicking sound from somewhere within his cloak.

"Ready," he said.

I withdrew the Ghostwheel Trump and studied it. I began my

meditation. Then I reached. Nothing happened. I tried again, re-calling, tuning, expanding. I reached again, calling, feeling. . . .

"The door . . . ," Jasra said.

I glanced at the door to the hallway, but there was nothing un-usual about it. Then I looked at her and realized the direction of her gaze.

The doorway to the next room, where Nayda slept, had begun to glow. It shone with a yellow light, and even as I watched, it grew in intensity. A spot of greater brightness then occurred at its center. Abruptly, the spot began a slow up-and-down movement.

Then came music, from where I was not certain, and Ghost's voice announced, "Follow the bouncing ball."

"Stop it!" I said. "It's distracting!"

The music went away. The circle of light grew still.

"Sorry," Ghost said. "I thought you'd find a little comic relief relaxing."

"You guessed wrong," I replied. "I just want you to take us to the citadel at the Keep of the Four Worlds."

"Do you want the troops, also? I can't seem to locate Luke."

"Just the three of us," I answered.

"What about the one who sleeps next door? I've met her be-fore. She doesn't scan right."

"I know. She's not human. Let her sleep."

"Very well, then. Pass through the door."

"Come on," I said to the others, picking up my weapons belt and buckling it on, adding my spare dagger, grabbing my cloak off a chair, and drawing it over my shoulders.

I walked toward the portal and Mandor and Jasra followed. I stepped through, but the room was no longer there. Instead, there came a moment of blurring, and when my senses cleared, I was staring down and outward across a great distance beneath a heav-ily overcast sky, a cold wind whipping at my garments.

I heard an exclamation from Mandor and, a moment later, an-other from Jasra—behind me and to the left. The great ice field lay bone-white to my right, and in the opposite direction a slate-gray sea tossed whitecaps like serpents in a bucket of milk. Far below, before me, the dark ground simmered and steamed.

"Ghost!" I cried. "Where are you?"

"Here," came a soft response, and I looked down to behold a tiny ring of light near the toe of my left boot.

Directly ahead and below, the Keep stood stark in the distance. There were no signs of life outside its walls. I realized that I must be in the mountains, standing somewhere near the place where I had held my lengthy colloquy with the old hermit named Dave.

"I wanted you to take us into the citadel within the Keep," I explained. "Why did you bring us up here?"

"I told you I don't like that place," Ghost answered. "I wanted to give you a chance to look it over and decide exactly where you wished to be sent within. That way I can move very fast on the delivery, and not expose myself overlong to forces I find distressing."

I continued to study the Keep. A pair of twisters were again circling the outer walls. If there had not been a moat, they would probably have done a good job of creating one. They stayed almost exactly 180 degrees apart, and they took turns at illumination. The nearest one grew spark-shot with bolts of lightning, acquiring an eerie incandescence; then, as it began to fade, the other brightened. They passed through this cycle several times as I watched.

Jasra made a small noise, and I turned and asked her, "What's going on?"

"The ritual," she responded. "Someone is playing with those forces right now."

"Can you tell how far along they might be?" I asked.

"Not really. They could just be starting, or they could be finished already. All the poles of fire tell me is that everything is in place."

"You call it then, Jasra," I told her. "Where should we put in our appearance?"

"There are two long hallways leading to the chamber of the fountain," she said. "One is on the same level and the other a floor above it. The chamber itself is several stories high."

"I recall that," I acknowledged.

"If they are working directly with the forces and we simply appear within the chamber," she continued, "the advantage of surprise will only be momentary. I can't say for certain what they might hit us with. Better to approach along one of the two hallways and give me a chance to assess the situation. Since there is a possibility that they could note our approach along the lower hallway, the upper one would be best for all our purposes."

"All right," I agreed. "Ghost, can you put us back a distance in that upper hallway?"

The circle spread, tilted, rose, stood high above us for a moment, then dropped.

"You are . . . already . . . there," Ghost said, as my vision swam and the circle of light passed over us, head to toe. "Goodbye."

He was right. We were on target this time. We stood in a long, dim corridor, its walls of dark, hewn stone. Its one end was lost in darkness. Its other led into an area of illumination. The ceiling was of rough timbers, the heavy cross-beams softened by curtains and plumes of spider-webbing. A few blue wizard globes flickered within wall brackets, shedding a pale light that indicated they were near the ends of their spells. Others had already gone dead. Near the brighter end of the hallway some of these had been re-placed by lanterns. From overhead came the sounds of small things scurrying within the ceiling. The place smelled damp, musty. But the air had an electric quality to it, as though we were breathing ozone, with an edge-of-event jitteriness permeating everything.

I shifted to Logrus Sight, and immediately there was a consid-erable brightening. Lines of force like glowing yellow cables ran everywhere. They provided the additional illumination I now per-ceived. And every time my movements intersected one, it height-ened the overall tingling effect I experienced. I could see now that Jasra was standing at the intersection of several of these and seemed to be drawing energy from them into her body. She was acquiring a glowing quality I was not certain my normal vision would have detected. When I glanced at Mandor I saw the Sign of the Logrus hovering before him also, which meant that he was aware of everything I was seeing.

Jasra began moving slowly along the corridor toward the lighted end. I fell in behind her and slightly to her left. Mandor followed me, moving so silently I had to glance back occasionally to assure myself he was still with us. As we advanced I became aware of a certain throbbing sensation, as of the beating of a vast pulse. Whether this was being transmitted through the floor or along those vibrating lines we continually encountered, I could not say.

I wondered whether our disturbing this net of forces was betray-ing our presence, and even our position, to the adept working with the stuff down at the Fount. Or was his concentration on the task at hand sufficiently distracting to permit us to approach undetected?

"It *has* started?" I whispered to Jasra.

"Yes," she replied.

"How far along?"

"The major phase could be completed."

A few paces more, and then she asked me, "What is your plan?"

"If you're right, we attack immediately. Perhaps we should try to take out Jurt first—all of us, I mean—if he's become that high-powered, that dangerous."

She licked her lips.

"I'm probably best equipped to deal with him, because of my connection with the Fount," she said then. "Better you don't get in my way. I'd rather see you dealing with Mask while I'm about it. It might be better to keep Mandor in reserve, to lend his aid to whichever of us might need it."

"I'll go along with your judgment," I said. "Mandor, did you hear all that?"

"Yes," he replied softly. "I'll do as she says."

Then, "What happens if I destroy the Fount itself?" he asked Jasra.

"I don't believe it can be done," she answered.

He snorted, and I could see the dangerous lines along which his thoughts were running.

"Humor me and suppose," he said.

She was silent for a time, then, "If you were able to shut it down, even for a little while," she offered, "the citadel would probably fall. I've been using its emanations to help hold this place up. It's old, and I never got around to buttressing it where it needs it. The amount of energy required to attack the Fount successfully, though, would be much better invested elsewhere."

"Thanks," he said.

She halted, extending a hand into one of the lines of force and closing her eyes as if she were taking a pulse.

"Very strong," she said a little later. "Someone is tapping it at deep levels now."

She began moving again. The light at the end of the hallway grew brighter, then dimmer, brighter, dimmer. The shadows retreated and flowed back repeatedly as this occurred. I became aware of a sound something like the humming of high wires. There was also an intermittent crackling noise coming from that direction. I increased my pace as Jasra began to hurry. At about that time there came a sound of laughter from up ahead. Frakir tightened upon my wrist. Flakes of fire flashed past the corridor's mouth.

"Damn, damn, damn," I heard Jasra saying.

She raised her hand as we came into sight of the landing where Mask had stood at the time of our encounter. I halted as she moved very slowly, approaching the railing. There were stairs both to the right and the left, leading downward to opposite sides of the chamber.

She looked down for only an instant; then she threw herself back and to the right, rolling when she hit the floor. Taking out a piece of railing, a ball of orange flame fled upward like a slow comet, passing through the area she had just quitted. I rushed to her side, slipped an arm beneath her shoulders, began to raise her.

I felt her stiffen, as her head jerked slightly to the left. Somehow, I already knew what I would see when I turned that way.

Jurt stood there, stark naked save for his eye patch, glowing, smiling, a pulse away from substantiality.

"Good of you to drop by, brother," he said. "Sorry you can't stay."

Sparks danced at his fingertips as he swung his arm in my direction. I doubted that shaking hands was foremost in his mind.

The only response I could think of was, "Your shoelace is untied," which of course didn't stop him, but it actually had him looking puzzled for a second or two.

12

Jurt had never played football. I do not believe he expected me to come up fast and rush him; and when it happened, I don't think he anticipated my coming in as low as I did.

And as for clipping him just above the knees and knocking him back through the opening in the railing, I'm sure he was surprised. At least he looked surprised as he went over backward and plummeted, sparks still dancing at his fingertips.

I heard Jasra chuckle, even as he faded in mid-fall and vanished before the floor got to spread him around a bit. Then, from the corner of my eye, I saw her rise.

"I'll deal with him now," she said, and, "No problem. He's clumsy," even as he appeared at the head of the stair to her right. "You take care of Mask!"

Mask was on the opposite side of the black stone fountain, staring up at me through an orange and red geyser of flames. Below, in the basin, the fires rippled yellow and white. When he scooped up a handful and worked them together as a child might shape a snowball, they became an incandescent blue. Then he threw it at me.

I sent it past with a simple parry. This was not Art, it was basic energy work. But it served as a reminder, even as I saw Jasra perform the preliminary gestures to a dangerous spell purely as a feint, bringing her near enough to Jurt to trip him, pushing him backward down the stair.

Not Art. Whoever enjoyed the luxury of living near and utilizing a power source such as this would doubtless get very sloppy as time went on, only using the basic frames of spells as guides, running rivers of power through them. One untutored, or extremely lazy, might possibly even dispense with that much after a time and play directly with the raw forces, a kind of shamanism, as opposed to the Higher Magic's purity—like that of a balanced equation—producing a maximum effect from a minimum of effort.

Jasra knew this. I could tell she'd received formal training somewhere along the line. That much was to the good anyway, I decided as I parried another ball of fire and moved to my left.

I began descending the stair—sideways—never taking my gaze off Mask. I was ready to defend or to strike in an instant.

The railing began to glow before me, then it burst into flame. I retreated a pace and continued my descent. Hardly worth wasting a spell to douse it. It was obviously meant for show rather than damage. . . .

Well. . . .

There was another possibility, I realized then, as I saw that Mask was simply watching me, was making no move to throw anything else in my direction.

It could also be a test. Mask might simply be attempting to discover whether I was limited to whatever spells I had brought with me—or whether I had learned to tap the power source here directly and would shortly be slugging things out with him as Jurt and Jasra were now obviously preparing to do. Good. Let him wonder. A finite number of spells against a near-limitless source of energy?

Jurt suddenly appeared upon a windowsill, high and to my left. He had time only for a brief frown before a curtain of fire was rung down upon him. Both he and the curtain were gone a moment later, and I heard Jasra's laughter and his curse, followed by a crashing noise off to the other side of the chamber.

As I moved to descend another step, the stairway faded from view. Suspecting illusion, I continued the slow downward movement of my foot. I encountered nothing, though, and finally extended my stride to pass over the gap and on down to the next stair. It also vanished, however, as I shifted my weight. There came a chuckle from Mask as I turned my movement into a leap to avoid the area. Once I was committed to jumping, the stairs winked out one by one as I passed over them.

I was certain Mask's thinking must be that if I had a handle on the local power, reflex would cause me to betray that connection here. And if I didn't it might still cause me to waste an escape spell.

But I judged the distance to the now-visible floor. If no more stairs vanished I might be able to catch a handhold on the next one, hang a moment, then drop. That would be perfectly safe. And if I missed, or if another stair vanished . . . I still felt I would land reasonably intact. Better to use an entirely different sort of spell on the way down.

I caught the rearward edge of the farthest stair, dangled and dropped, turning my body and speaking the words of a spell I call the Falling Wall.

The fountain shuddered. The fires sloshed and splashed, overflowing the basin on the side nearest Mask. And then Mask himself was thrown backward to the floor as my spell continued its course of descent.

Mask's arms rose before him as his body seemed to sop up the swirling glow, his hands to expel it. There was a bright arc between his hands, then a shieldlike dome. He held it above him, warding off the final collapsive force of my spell. I was already moving quickly in his direction. Even as I did so, Jurt appeared before me, standing on the far lip of the fountain just above Mask, glaring at me. Before I could draw my blade, throw Frakir, or utter another spell, however, the fountain welled up, a great wave toppling Jurt from its side, sending him sprawling upon the floor, washing him past Mask and across the chamber toward the foot of the other stair, down which I now saw that Jasra was slowly descending.

"It means nothing to be able to transport yourself anywhere," I heard her say, "if you are a fool in all places."

Jurt snarled and sprang to his feet. Then he looked upward, past Jasra. . . .

"You, too, brother?" he said.

"I am here to preserve your life, if at all possible," I heard Mandor reply. "I would suggest you return with me now—"

Jurt cried out—no recognizable words, just an animal-like bleat. Then, "I do not need your patronage!" he screamed. "And you are the fool, to trust Merlin! You stand between him and a kingdom!"

A series of glowing circles drifted like glowing smoke rings from between Jasra's hands, dropping as if to settle about his body. Jurt immediately vanished, though moments later I heard him shouting to Mandor from a different direction.

I continued to advance upon Mask, who had guarded successfully against my Falling Wall and was now beginning to rise. I spoke the words of the Icy Path, and his feet went out from beneath him. Yes, I was going to throw a finite number of spells against his power source. I call it confidence. Mask had power. I had a plan, and the means to execute it.

A flagstone tore itself loose from the floor, turned into a cloud of gravel amid a grating, crunching noise, then flew toward me like a charge of shot. I spoke the words of the Net and gestured.

All of the fragments were collected before they could reach me. Then I dumped them upon Mask, who was still struggling to rise.

"Do you realize that I still don't know why we're fighting?" I said. "This was your idea. I can still—"

For the moment, Mask had given up on trying to rise. He had placed his left hand in a simmering puddle of light and had extended his right, palm toward me. The puddle vanished, and a shower of fire emerged from the right hand and sped at me, like drops from a lawn sprinkler. I was ready for this, though. If the Fount could contain the fire, then it had to be insulated against it.

I threw myself flat on the other side of the dark structure, using its base as a shield.

"It is likely one of us is going to die," I called out, "since we are not pulling our punches. Either way, I won't have a chance to ask you later: What's your bitch? What am I to you?"

The only reply was a chuckling sound from the other side of the Fount, as the floor began to move beneath me.

From somewhere off to my right, near the foot of the undamaged stair, I heard Jurt say, "A fool in all places? What about close quarters?" and I looked up in time to see him appear before Jasra and seize hold of her.

A moment later he screamed, as Jasra lowered her head and her lips touched his forearm. She pushed him away then, and he fell down the remaining steps, landing stiffly, not moving.

I crept to the right of the Fount, over the sharp edges of the broken flooring, which jiggled and sawed at me within the matrix of Mask's power.

"Jurt is out of it," I commented, "and you stand alone now, Mask, against the three of us. Call it quits, and I'll see that you go on living."

"Three of you," came that flat, distorted voice. "You admit that you cannot beat me without help?"

" 'Beat'?" I said. "Perhaps you consider it a game. I do not. I will not be bound by any rules you choose to recognize. Call it quits or I'll kill you, with or without help, any way I can."

A dark object suddenly appeared overhead, and I rolled back away from the Fount as it came to rest in the basin. It was Jurt. Unable to move normally because of the paralytic effect of Jasra's bite, he had trumped away from the foot of the stair and into the Fount.

"You have your friends, Lord of Chaos, and I have mine," Mask replied, as Jurt moaned softly and began to glow.

Suddenly Mask went spinning into the air, as I heard the flooring shatter. The Fount itself died down, grew weaker, as a flaming tower twisted ceilingward, rising from a new opening in the floor, bearing Mask with it on the crest of its golden plume.

"And enemies," Jasra stated, moving nearer.

Mask spread his arms and legs and wheeled slowly through the middle air, suddenly in control of his trajectory. I got to my feet and backed away from the Fount. I'm seldom at my best at centers of geological catastrophes.

A rushing, rumbling sound now came from the doubled fountain, and a high-pitched, sourceless-seeming note accompanied it. A small wind sighed among the rafters. The tower of fire atop which Mask rode continued its slow spiraling, and the spray in the lowered fountain began a similar movement. Jurt stirred, moaned, raised his right arm.

"And enemies," Mask acknowledged, beginning a series of gestures I recognized immediately because I'd spent a lot of time figuring them out.

"Jasra!" I cried. "Watch out for Sharu!"

Jasra took three quick steps to her left and smiled. Something very much like lightning then fell from the rafters, blackening the area she had just departed.

"He always starts with a lightning stroke," she explained. "He's very predictable."

She spun once and vanished redly, with a sound like breaking glass.

I looked immediately to where the old man had stood, RINALDO carved upon his right leg. He was leaning against the wall now, one hand to his forehead, the other implementing a simple but powerful shielding spell.

I was about to scream for Mandor to take the old boy out, when Mask hit me with a Klaxon spell which temporarily deafened me while bursting blood vessels in my nose.

Dripping, I dove and rolled, interposing the now-rising Jurt between myself and the sorcerer in the air. Jurt actually appeared to be throwing off the effects of Jasra's bite. So I drove my fist into his stomach as I rose and turned him into an even better position to serve as my shield. A mistake. I received a jolt from his body, not unlike a nasty electrical shock, and he even managed a brief laugh as I fell.

"He's all yours," I heard him gasp then.

From the corner of my eye, I saw where Jasra and Sharu Garrul stood, each of them seemingly holding one end of a great long piece of macramé work woven of cables. The lines were pulsing and changing colors, and I knew they represented forces rather than material objects, visible only by virtue of the Logrus Sight, under which I continued to operate. The pulse increased in tempo, and both sank slowly to their knees, arms still extended, faces glistening. A quick word, a gesture, and I could break that balance. Unfortunately, I had problems of my own just then. Mask was swooping toward me like some huge insect—expressionless, shimmering, deadly. A succession of brittle snapping sounds occurred within the front wall of the Keep, where a series of jagged cracks raced downward like black lightning. I was aware of falling dust beyond the spiraling lights, of the growling and the whining sounds—faint now within my ringing ears—of the continuing vibration of the floor beneath my half-numbed legs. But that was all right. I raised my left hand as my right slid within my cloak.

A fiery blade appeared in Mask's right hand. I did not stir, but waited a second longer before speaking the guide words to my Fantasia-for-Six-Acetylene-Torches spell as I snapped my forearm back to cover my eyes and rolled to the side.

The stroke missed me, passing through broken stone. Mask's left arm fell across my chest, however, elbow connecting with my lower ribs. I did not stop to assess damages, though, as I heard the sword of fire crackle and come free of the stone. And so, turning, I struck with my own more mundane dagger of steel, driving its full length up into Mask's left kidney.

There followed a scream as the sorcerer stiffened and slumped beside me. Almost immediately thereafter I was kicked with considerable force behind my right hip. I twisted away and another blow landed upon my right shoulder. I am sure it was aimed for my head. As I covered my neck and temples and rolled away, I heard Jurt's voice, cursing.

Drawing my longer blade, I rose to my feet, and my gaze met Jurt's. He was rising at the same time, and he held Mask cradled in his arms.

"Later," he said to me, and he vanished, bearing the body away with him. The blue mask remained on the floor, near to a long smear of blood.

Jasra and Sharu were still facing each other from kneeling positions, panting, bodies completely drenched, their life forces twisting about each other like mating serpents.

Then, like a surfacing fish, Jurt appeared within the tower of forces beyond the Fount. Even as Mandor hurled two of his spheres—which seemed to grow in size as they fled down the chamber, to crash into the Fount and reduce it to rubble—I saw what I believed I would never see again.

As the reverberation of the Fount's collapse spread and the groaning and grinding within the walls was replaced by a snapping and swaying, and dust, gravel and timbers fell about me, I was moving forward, skirting the wreckage, sidestepping new geysers and rivulets of glowing forces, cloak raised to protect my face, blade extended.

Jurt cursed me roundly as I came on. Then, "Pleased, brother? Pleased?" he said. "May death be the only peace between us."

But I ignored the predictable sentiment, for I had to get a better look at what I thought I had seen moments before. I leaped over a piece of broken masonry and beheld the fallen sorcerer's face within the flames, head cradled against his shoulder.

"Julia!" I cried.

But they vanished even as I moved forward, and I knew it was time for me to do the same.

Turning, I fled through the fire.

KNIGHT
OF
SHADOWS

This book is for John Douglas

1

Her name was Julia, and I'd been damn certain she was dead back on April 30 when it all began. My finding her grisly remains and destroying the doglike creature which I'd thought had killed her were pretty much the way it started. And we had been lovers, which I suppose was how things had really commenced. Long before.

Perhaps I could have trusted her more. Perhaps I should never have taken her on that shadow-walk which led to denials that took her away from me, down dark ways and into the studio of Victor Melman, a nasty occultist I later had to kill—the same Victor Melman who was himself the dupe of Luke and Jasra. But now, perhaps—just barely—I might have been in a position to forgive myself for what I'd thought I'd done, for it seemed that I hadn't really done it after all. Almost.

That is to say, I learned that I hadn't been responsible for it while I was in the act of doing it. It was when I drove my knife into the side of the mysterious sorcerer Mask, who had been on my case for some time, that I discovered that Mask was really Julia. My half brother Jurt, who's been trying to kill me longer than anyone else in the business, snatched her away, and they vanished then, immediately following his transformation into a kind of living Trump.

As I fled the burning, crumbling Keep there at the Citadel of the Four Worlds, a falling timber caused me to dodge to my right, trapping me in a cul-de-sac of crashed masonry and burning beams. A dark metal ball flashed past me then, seeming to grow as it moved. It struck the wall and passed through it, leaving a hole one could dive through—a hint I was not slow in taking. Outside I jumped the moat, using my Logrus extensions to knock aside a section of fence and a score of troops, before I turned back and shouted, "Mandor!"

"Right here," came his soft voice from behind my left shoulder.

I turned in time to see him catch a metal ball, which bounced once before us and dropped into his extended hand.

He brushed ashes from his black vest and ran a hand through his hair. Then he smiled and turned back toward the burning Keep.

"You've kept your promise to the Queen," he remarked, "and I don't believe there's anything more for you here. Shall we go now?"

"Jasra's still inside," I answered, "having it out with Sharu."

"I thought you were done with her."

I shook my head.

"She still knows a lot of things I don't. Things I'll be needing."

A tower of flame began to rear itself above the Keep, halted and hovered a moment, heaved itself higher.

"I didn't realize," he said. "She does seem to want control of that fountain fairly badly. If we were to snatch her away now, that fellow Sharu will claim it. Does that matter?"

"If we don't snatch her away, he may kill her."

Mandor shrugged.

"I've a feeling she'll take him. Would you care to place a small wager?"

"Could be you're right," I said, watching the fountain continue its climb skyward, following another pause. I gestured toward it. "Thing looks like an oil gusher. I hope the winner knows how to cap it—if there is a winner. Neither one of them may last much longer, the way the place is coming apart."

He chuckled.

"You underestimate the forces they've generated to protect themselves," he said. "And you know it isn't all that easy for one sorcerer to do in another by sorcerous means. However, you've a point there when it comes to the inertia of the mundane. With your permission . . . ?"

I nodded.

With a quick underhand toss he cast the metal ball across the ditch toward the burning building. It struck the ground and with each bounce thereafter it seemed to increase in size. It produced a cymballike crash each time it hit, entirely out of proportion with its apparent mass and velocity, and this sound increased in volume on each successive bounce. It passed then into the burning, tottering ruin that was the near end of the Keep and for several moments was gone from sight.

I was about to ask him what was going on when I saw the shadow of a large ball pass before the opening through which I had fled. The flames—save for the central tower from the broken Fount—began to subside, and a deep rumbling sound came from within. Moments later an even larger circular shadow passed, and I began to feel the rumbling through the soles of my boots.

A wall tumbled. Shortly thereafter part of another wall fell. I could see inside fairly clearly. Through the dust and smoke the image of the giant ball passed again. The flames were snuffed. My Logrus vision still granted me glimpses of the shifting lines of power which flowed between Jasra and Sharu.

Mandor extended a hand. A minute or so later a small metal ball came bouncing our way, and he caught it.

"Let's head back," he said. "It would be a shame to miss the end."

We passed through one of the many gaps in the fence, and sufficient rubble filled the ditch at one point for us to walk across on it. I spent a barrier spell then, to keep the re-forming troops off the premises and out of our way for a time.

Entering through the broken wall, I saw that Jasra stood with her back to the tower of fire, her arms upraised. Streaks of sweat lined her face zebra through a mask of soot, and I could feel the pulsing of the forces which passed through her body. About ten feet above her, face purple and head twisted to one side as if his neck were broken. Sharu hung in the middle of the air. To the untutored he might have seemed magically levitated. My Logrus sight gave me view of the line of force from which he hung suspended, however, victim of what might, I suppose, be termed a magical lynching.

"Bravo," Mandor stated, clapping his hands slowly and softly together. "You see, Merlin? I'd have won that bet."

"You always were a better judge of talent than I was," I acknowledged.

". . . and swear to serve me," I overheard Jasra saying.

Sharu's lips moved.

"And swear to serve you," he gasped.

She lowered her arms slowly, and the line of force which held him began to lengthen. As he descended toward the Keep's cracked floor, her left hand executed a gesture similar to one I had once seen an orchestra conductor employ in encouraging the woodwinds, and a great gout of fire came loose from the Fountain, fell upon him, washed over him, and passed on down into the ground. Flashy, though I didn't quite see the point . . .

His slow descent continued, as if someone in the sky were trolling for crocodiles. I discovered myself holding my breath as his feet neared the ground, in sympathetic anticipation of the eased pressure on his neck. This, however, did not come to pass. When his feet reached the ground, they passed on into it, and his descent continued, as if he were an occulted hologram. He sank past his ankles and up to his knees and kept going. I could no longer tell whether he was breathing. A soft litany of commands rolled from Jasra's lips, and sheets of flame periodically separated themselves from the Fountain and splashed over him. He sank past his waist and up to his shoulders and slightly beyond. When only his head remained visible, eyes open but unfocused, she executed another hand movement, and his journey into the earth was halted.

"You are now the guardian of the Fount," she stated, "answerable only to me. Do you acknowledge this?"

The darkened lips writhed.

"Yes," came a whispered reply.

"Go now and bank the fires," she ordered. "Commence your tenure."

The head seemed to nod at the same time it began sinking again. After a moment only a cottony tuft of hair remained, and an instant later the ground swallowed this, too. The line of force vanished.

I cleared my throat. At the sound Jasra let her arms fall and turned toward me. She was smiling faintly.

"Is he alive or dead?" I asked, and then added, "Academic curiosity."

"I'm not really certain," she responded. "But a little of both, I think. Like the rest of us."

" 'Guardian of the Fount,' " I reflected. "Interesting existence."

"Beats being a coatrack," she observed.

"I daresay."

"I suppose you feel I owe you some gratitude now, for my restoration," she stated.

I shrugged.

"To tell you the truth, I've other things to think about," I said.

"You wanted an end to the feud," she said, "and I wanted this place back. I still have no kind thoughts toward Amber, but I am willing to say we're even."

"I'll settle for that," I told her. "And there is a small loyalty I may share with you."

She studied me through narrowed eyes for a moment, then smiled.

"Don't worry about Luke," she said.

"But I must. That son of a bitch Dalt—"

She continued to smile.

"Do you know something I don't?" I asked.

"Many things," she replied.

"Anything you'd care to share?"

"Knowledge is a marketable commodity," she observed, as the ground shook slightly and the fiery tower swayed.

"I'm offering to help your son and you're offering to sell me the information on how to go about it?" I inquired.

She laughed.

"If I thought Rinaldo needed help," she said, "I'd be at his side this moment. I suppose it makes it easier to hate me if you feel I lack even maternal virtues."

"Hey, I thought we were calling things even," I said.

"That doesn't preclude hating each other," she replied.

"Come on, lady! Outside of the fact that you tried to kill me year after year, I've got nothing against you. You happen to be the mother of someone I like and respect. If he's in trouble, I want to help him, and I'd as soon be on good terms with you."

Mandor cleared his throat as the flames dropped ten feet, shuddered, dropped again.

"I've some fine culinary spells," he remarked, "should recent exertions have roused some appetites."

Jasra smiled almost coquettishly, and I'd swear she batted her eyelashes at him. While he makes a striking appearance with that shock of white hair, I don't know that you'd exactly call Mandor handsome. I've never understood why women are as attracted to him as they usually seem to be. I've even checked him out for spells on that particular count, but he doesn't wear one. It must be some different order of magic entirely.

"A fine idea," she responded. "I'll provide the setting if you'll take care of the rest."

Mandor bowed; the flames collapsed the rest of the way to the ground and were damped therein. Jasra shouted an order to Sharu, the Invisible Guardian, telling him to keep them that way. Then she turned and led us toward the downward stair.

"Underground passage," she explained, "to more civilized shores."

"It occurs to me," I remarked, "that anyone we encounter will probably be loyal to Julia."

Jasra laughed.

"As they were to me before her and to Sharu before me," she replied. "They are professionals. They come with the place. They are paid to defend the winners, not to avenge the losers. I will put in an appearance and make a proclamation after dinner, and I will enjoy their unanimous and heartfelt loyalty until the next usurpation. Mind that third step. There's a loose flagstone."

So she led us on, through a section of fake wall and into a dark tunnel, heading in what I believed to be a northwesterly direction toward the area of the Citadel which I had investigated somewhat on my previous journey this way. That was the day I had rescued her from Mask/Julia and taken her back to Amber to be a coatrack in *our* citadel for a while. The tunnel we entered was totally dark, but she conjured a darting dot, bright in its will-o'-the-wispiness, which preceded us through the gloom and the damp. The air was stale and the walls were cobwebby. The floor was of bare earth, save for an irregular patch of flagstones down its middle; there were occasional fetid puddles at either hand; and small dark creatures flashed past us—both on the ground and in the air—every now and then.

Actually, I did not need the light. Probably none of us did. I held to the Sign of the Logrus, which provided a magical way of seeing, granting a silvery, directionless illumination. I maintained it because it would also give me a warning against magical effects—which might include booby trap spells about the premises or, for that matter, a bit of treachery on Jasra's part. One effect of this seeing was to note that the Sign also hovered before Mandor, who, to my knowledge, has never been much into trust either. Something cloudy and vaguely Pattern-like also occupied a similar position vis-à-vis Jasra, completing the circle of wariness. And the light danced on before us.

We emerged from behind a stack of barrels into what appeared to be a very well-stocked wine cellar. Mandor paused after six paces and carefully removed a dusty bottle from the rack to our left. He drew a corner of his cloak across its label.

"Oh, my!" he observed.

"What is it?" Jasra inquired.

"If this is still good, I can build an unforgettable meal around it."

"Really? Better bring several to be sure then," she said. "These go back before my time—perhaps before Sharu's time even."

"Merlin, you bring these two," he said, passing me a pair. "Carefully, now."

He studied the rest of the rack before selecting two more, which he carried himself.

"I can see why this place is often under siege," he remarked to Jasra. "I'd have been inclined to have a go at it myself had I known about this part."

She reached out and squeezed his shoulder.

"There are easier ways to get what you want," she said, smiling.

"I'll remember that," he replied.

"I hope you'll hold me to it."

I cleared my throat.

She gave me a small frown, then turned away. We followed her out a low doorway and up a creaking flight of wooden stairs. We emerged in a large pantry and passed through it into an immense, deserted kitchen.

"Never a servant around when you need one," she remarked, casting her gaze about the room.

"We won't be needing one," Mandor said. "Find me a congenial dining area and I'll manage."

"Very well," she replied. "This way then."

She led us through the kitchen; then we passed through a series of rooms till we came to a stairway, which we mounted.

"Ice fields?" she asked. "Lava fields? Mountains? Or a storm-tossed sea?"

"If you are referring to a choice of views," Mandor responded, "give me the mountains."

He glanced at me, and I nodded.

She conducted us to a long, narrow room, where we unfastened a series of shutters to behold a dappled range of round-topped peaks. The room was cool and a bit dusty with shelves running the length of the near wall. These held books, writing implements, crystals, magnifying glasses, small pots of paint, a few simple magical instruments, a microscope, and a telescope. There was a trestle table at the room's middle, a bench on either side of it.

"How long will it take to prepare this?" Jasra asked.

"A minute or two," Mandor said.

"In that case," she said, "I would like to repair myself somewhat first. Perhaps you would also."

"Good idea," I said.

"Indeed," Mandor acknowledged.

She led us to what must have been guest quarters, not too far away, and left us with soap, towels, and water. We agreed to meet back in the narrow room in half an hour.

"Think she's planning something nasty?" I asked as I drew off my shirt.

"No," Mandor replied. "I like to flatter myself in thinking that she would not want to miss this meal. Nor, do I feel, would she want us to miss seeing her at her best, having so far seen her at something less than that. And a possibility of gossip, confidences . . ." He shook his head. "You may never have been able to trust her before and may never again. But this meal will be a Timeout if I'm any judge."

"I'll hold you to that," I said as I splashed and lathered.

Mandor gave me a crooked smile, then conjured a corkscrew and opened the bottles—"to let them breathe a little"—before he tended to himself. I trusted his judgment, but I hung on to the Sign of the Logrus in case I had to duel with a demon or avoid a falling wall.

No demons sprang; no masonry toppled. I entered the dining room behind Mandor and watched him transform it with a few words and gestures. The trestle table and the benches were replaced by a round table and comfortable-looking chairs—the chairs so situated as to provide a good view of the mountains from each. Jasra had not yet arrived, and I was carrying the two wine bottles whose respiration Mandor found most appealing. Before I could even set them down, Mandor conjured an embroidered tablecloth and napkins; delicate china, which looked as if it had been hand decorated by Miró; finely wrought silverware. He studied the tableau a moment, banished the silverware, summoned a set with a different pattern. He hummed as he paced and regarded the layout from various angles. Just as I moved forward to place the bottles on the table, he summoned a crystal bowl filled with floating flowers as a centerpiece. I took a step backward then as crystal goblets appeared.

I made a small growling noise, and he seemed to notice me for the first time in a while.

"Oh, set them there. Set them there, Merlin," he said, and an ebony tray appeared on the table to my left.

"We'd better check to see how the wine is holding up, before the lady arrives," he said then, pouring some of the ruby fluid into two of the goblets.

We sampled these, and he nodded. It was better than Bayle's. By far.

"Nothing wrong there," I said.

He rounded the table, went to the window, and looked out. I followed. Somewhere up in those mountains, I supposed, was Dave in his cave.

"I feel almost guilty," I said, "taking a break like this. There are so many things I should be tending to—"

"Possibly even more than you suspect," he said. "Look upon this less as a break than a retrenchment. And you may learn something from the lady."

"True," I replied. "I wonder what, though."

He swirled his wine in his glass, took another small sip, and shrugged.

"She knows a lot. She may let something slip, or she may feel expansive at the attention and grow generous. Take things as they're dealt."

I took a drink, and I could be nasty and say my thumbs began to prickle. But it was actually the Logrus field that warned me of Jasra's approach along the hall outside. I did not remark upon it to Mandor, since I was certain he felt it, too. I simply turned toward the door, and he matched my movement.

She had on a low over-one-shoulder (the left) white dress, fastened at the shoulder with a diamond pin, and she wore a tiara, also of diamonds, which seemed almost to be radiating in the infrared range amidst her bright hair. She was smiling, and she smelled good, too. Involuntarily I felt myself standing straighter, and I glanced at my fingernails to be certain they were clean.

Mandor's bow was more courtly than mine, as usual. And I felt obliged to say something pleasant. So, "You're looking quite . . . elegant," I observed, letting my eyes wander to emphasize the point.

"It is seldom that I dine with two princes," she remarked.

"I'm Duke of the Western Marches," I said, "not a prince."

"I was referring to the House of Sawall," she replied.

"You've been doing homework," Mandor noted, "recently."

"I'd hate to commit a breach of protocol," she said.

"I seldom use my Chaos title at this end of things," I explained.

"A pity," she told me. "I find it more than a little . . . elegant. Aren't you about thirtieth in the line of succession?"

I laughed.

"Even that great a distance is an exaggeration," I said.

"No, Merle, she's about right," Mandor told me. "Give or take the usual few."

"How can that be?" I asked. "The last time I looked—"

He poured a goblet of wine and offered it to Jasra. She accepted it with a smile.

"You haven't looked recently," Mandor said. "There have been more deaths."

"Really? So many?"

"To Chaos," Jasra said, raising her goblet. "Long may she wave."

"To Chaos," Mandor replied, raising his.

"Chaos," I echoed, and we touched the goblets together and drank.

A number of delightful aromas came to me suddenly. Turning, I saw that the table now bore serving dishes. Jasra had turned at the same moment, and Mandor stepped forward and gestured, causing the chairs to slide back to accommodate us.

"Be seated, please, and let me serve you," he said.

We did, and it was more than good. Several minutes passed, and apart from compliments on the soup nothing was said. I did not want to be the first with a conversational gambit, though it had occurred to me that the others might feel the same way.

Finally, Jasra cleared her throat, and we both looked at her. I was surprised that she suddenly seemed slightly nervous.

"So, how are things in Chaos?" she asked.

"At the moment, chaotic," Mandor replied, "not to be facetious." He thought a moment, then sighed and added, "Politics."

She nodded slowly, as if considering asking him for the details he did not seem to care to divulge, then deciding against it. She turned toward me.

"Unfortunately, I'd no opportunity to sight-see while I was in Amber," she said. "From what you told me, though, life seems a bit chaotic there also."

I nodded.

"It's good that Dalt's gone," I said, "if that's what you mean. But he was never a real threat, just a nuisance. Speaking of whom—"

"Let's not," she interrupted, smiling sweetly. "What I really had in mind was anything else."

I smiled back.

"I forgot. You're not a fan of his," I said.

"It's not that," she responded. "The man has his uses. It's just"—she sighed—"politics," she finished.

Mandor laughed, and we joined him. Too bad I hadn't thought to use that line about Amber. Too late now.

"I bought a painting awhile back," I said, "by a lady named Polly Jackson. It's of a red '57 Chevy. I like it a lot. It's in storage in San Francisco right now. Rinaldo liked it, too."

She nodded, stared out the window.

"You two were always stopping in some gallery or other," she said. "Yes, he dragged me to a lot of them, too. I always thought he had good taste. No talent, but good taste."

"What do you mean, 'no talent'?"

"He's a very good draftsman, but his own paintings were never that interesting."

I had raised the subject for a very special reason, and this wasn't it. But I was fascinated by a side of Luke I'd never known, and I decided to pursue the matter.

"Paintings? I never knew he painted."

"He's tried any number of times, but he never shows them to anyone because they're not good enough."

"Then how do you know about them?"

"I'd check out his apartment periodically."

"When he wasn't around?"

"Of course. A mother's privilege."

I shuddered. I thought again of the burning woman down the Rabbit Hole. But I didn't want to say what I felt and spoil the flow now that I had her talking. I decided to return to my original trail.

"Was it in connection with any of this that he met Victor Melman?" I asked.

She studied me for a moment through narrowed eyes, then nodded and finished her soup.

"Yes," she said then, laying her spoon aside. "He took a few lessons from the man. He'd liked some of his paintings and looked him up. Perhaps he bought something of his, too. I don't know. But at some point he mentioned his own work and Victor asked to see it. He told Rinaldo he liked it and said he thought he could teach him a few things that might be of help."

She raised her goblet and sniffed it, sipped her wine, and stared at the mountains.

I was about to prompt her, hoping she'd go on, when she began to laugh. I waited it out.

"A real asshole," she said then. "But talented. Give him that."

"Uh, what do you mean?" I asked.

"After a time he began speaking of the development of personal power, using all those circumlocutions the half-enlightened love to play with. He wanted Rinaldo to know he was an occultist with something pretty strong going for him. Then he began to hint that he might be willing to pass it along to the right person."

She began laughing again. I chuckled myself, at the thought of that trained seal addressing the genuine article in such a fashion.

"It was because he realized Rinaldo was rich, of course," she continued. "Victor was, as usual, broke himself at the time. Rinaldo showed no interest, though, and simply stopped taking painting lessons from him shortly after that—as he felt he'd learned all he could from him. When he told me about it later, however, I realized that the man could be made into a perfect cat's-paw. I was certain such a person would do anything for a taste of real power."

I nodded.

"Then you and Rinaldo began the visitation business? You took turns clouding his mind and teaching him a few real things?"

"Real enough," she said, "though I handled most of his training. Rinaldo was usually too busy studying for exams. His point average was generally a little higher than yours, wasn't it?"

"He usually had pretty good grades," I conceded. "When you talk of empowering Melman and turning him into a tool, I can't help thinking about the reason: You were priming him to kill me, in a particularly colorful fashion."

She smiled.

"Yes," she said, "though probably not as you think. He knew of you, and he had been trained to play a part in your sacrifice. But he acted on his own the day he tried it, the day you killed him. He had been warned against such a solo action, and he paid the price. He was anxious to possess all of the powers he thought would come of it, rather than share them with another. As I said— an asshole."

I wanted to appear nonchalant, to keep her going. Continuing my meal seemed the best measure to indicate such poise. When I glanced down, however, I discovered that my soup bowl had vanished. I picked up a roll, broke it, was about to butter it when I saw that my hand was shaking. A moment later I realized that this was because I wanted to strangle her.

So I took a deep breath and let it go, had another drink of wine. An appetizer plate appeared before me, and a faint aroma of garlic and various tantalizing herbs told me to be calm. I nodded thanks to Mandor, and Jasra did the same. A moment later I buttered the roll.

Several mouthfuls after that, I said, "I confess that I do not understand. You say that Melman was to play a part in my ritual slaying—but only a part?"

She continued eating for a half minute or so, then found another smile.

"It was too appropriate an opportunity to pass up," she told me then, "when you broke up with Julia and she grew interested in the occult. I saw that I would have to get her together with Victor, to have him train her, to teach her a few simple effects, to capitalize on her unhappiness at your parting, to turn it into a full-blown hatred so intense that she would be willing to cut your throat when the time came for the sacrifice."

I choked on something which otherwise tasted wonderful.

A frosty crystal goblet of water appeared beside my right hand. I raised it and washed everything down. I took another sip.

"Ah, that reaction is worth something, anyhow," Jasra remarked. "You must admit that having someone you once loved as executioner adds spice to vengeance."

Out of the corner of my eye I saw that Mandor was nodding. And I, also, had to agree that she was right.

"I must acknowledge it as a well-conceived bit of revenge," I said. "Was Rinaldo in on this part?"

"No, you two had grown too chummy by then. I was afraid he'd warn you."

I thought about it for another minute or so, then, "What went wrong?" I asked.

"The one thing I'd never have guessed," she said. "Julia really had talent. A few lessons from Victor, and she was better than he was at anything he could do—except painting. Hell! Maybe she paints, too. I don't know. I'd dealt myself a wild card, and it played itself."

I shuddered. I thought of my conversation with the *ty'iga* at

Arbor House, back when it was possessing Vinta Bayle. "Did Julia develop the abilities she sought?" it had asked me. I'd told it that I didn't know. I'd said that she'd never shown any signs. . . . And shortly thereafter I'd remembered our meeting in the supermarket parking lot and the dog she told to sit that may never have moved again. . . . I'd recalled this, but—

"And you never noticed any indication of her talent?" Jasra ventured.

"I wouldn't say that," I replied as I began to realize why things were as they were. "No, I wouldn't say that."

. . . Like that time at Baskin-Robbins when she caused a change of flavors 'twixt cone and lip. Or the storm she'd stayed dry in without an umbrella . . .

She frowned a puzzled frown and narrowed her eyes as she stared. "I don't understand," she said. "If you knew, you could have trained her yourself. She was in love with you. You would have been a formidable team."

I writhed internally. She was right, and I *had* suspected, had probably even known, but I'd been suppressing it. I'd possibly even triggered its onset myself, with that shadow walk, with my body energies. . . .

"It's tricky," I said, "and very personal."

"Oh. Matters of the heart are either very simple or totally inscrutable to me," she said. "There doesn't seem to be a middle ground."

"Let's stipulate simple," I told her. "We were already breaking up when I noticed the signs, and I'd no desire to call up the power in an ex-lover who might one day want to practice on me."

"Understandable," Jasra said. "Very. And ironic in the extreme."

"Indeed," Mandor observed, and with a gesture he caused more steaming dishes to appear before us. "Before you get carried away with a narrative of intrigue and the underside of the psyche, I'd like you to try a little breast of quail drowned in Mouton Rothschild, with a bit of wild rice and a few amusing asparagus tips."

I had driven her to her studies by showing her another layer of reality, I realized. And I had driven her away from me because I had not really trusted her enough to tell her the truth about myself. I suppose this said something about my capacity for love as well as trust. But I had felt this all along. There was something else. There was more. . . .

"This is delicious," Jasra announced.

"Thank you." He rose, rounded the table, and refilled her glass manually rather than use a levitation trick. As he did, I noticed that the fingers of his left hand lightly brushed her bare shoulder. He sloshed a little into my glass as an afterthought then and went back and sat down.

"Yes, excellent," I observed as I continued my quick introspect through the dark glass suddenly cleared.

I had felt something, had suspected something from the beginning, I knew now. Our shadow walk was only the most spectacular of a series of small, off-the-cuff tests I had occasionally thrown her way, hoping to catch her off guard, hoping to expose her as— what? Well, a potential sorceress. So?

I set my utensils aside and rubbed my eyes. It was near, though I'd been hiding it from myself for a long while. . . .

"Is something the matter, Merlin?" I heard Jasra asking.

"No. Just realized I was a little tired," I said. "Everything's fine."

A sorceress. Not just a potential sorceress. There had been the buried fear, I now understood, that she was behind the April 30 attempts on my life—and I had suppressed this and kept on caring for her. Why? Because I knew and did not care? Because she was my Nimue? Because I had cherished my possible destroyer and hidden evidence from myself? Because I'd not only loved unwisely but had had one big death wish following me around, grinning, and any time now I might cooperate with it to the utmost?

"I'll be okay," I said. "It's really nothing."

Did it mean that I was, as they say, my own worst enemy? I hoped not. I didn't really have time to go through therapy, not when my life depended on so many external things as well.

"A penny for your thoughts," Jasra said sweetly.

2

"They're priceless," I answered. "Like your jokes. I must applaud you. Not only did I know nothing of this at the time, but I didn't make any correct guesses when I did have a few facts to rub together. Is that what you wanted to hear?"

"Yes," she said.

"I'm pleased there came a point where things went wrong for you," I added.

She sighed, nodded, took a drink of wine.

"Yes, it came," she acknowledged. "I was hardly expecting any recoil from such a simple bit of business. I still find it hard to believe that there's that much irony running around loose in the world."

"If you want me to appreciate the whole thing, you're going to have to be a little more explicit," I suggested.

"I know. In a way, I hate trading that vaguely puzzled expression you're wearing for one of delight at my own discomfort. On the other hand, there may still be material able to distress you in some fresh fashion on the other side of it."

"Win a few, lose a few," I said. "I'm willing to bet there are still features of those days that puzzle you."

"Such as?" she asked.

"Such as why none of those April thirtieth attempts on my life succeeded."

"I assume Rinaldo sabotaged me some way, tipped you off."

"Wrong."

"What, then?"

"The *ty'iga*. She's under a compulsion to protect me. You

might recall her from those days, as she resided in the body of Gail Lampron."

"Gail? Rinaldo's girlfriend? My son was dating a demon?"

"Let's not be prejudiced. He'd done a lot worse his freshman year."

She thought a moment, then nodded slowly.

"You've got a point there," she admitted. "I'd forgotten Carol. And you still have no idea—beyond what the thing admitted back in Amber—as to why this was going on?"

"I still don't know," I said.

"It casts that entire period in an even stranger light," she mused, "especially since our paths have crossed again. I wonder . . . ?"

"What?"

"Whether she was there to protect you or to thwart me—your bodyguard or my curse?"

"Hard to say, since the results came to the same thing."

"But she's apparently been hanging around you most recently, which would seem to indicate the former."

"Unless, of course, she knows something we don't."

"Such as?"

"Such as the possibility of a conflict developing between us again."

She smiled.

"You should have gone to law school," she said. "You're as devious as your relatives back in Amber. I can be truthful, though, in saying I have nothing planned that could be taken that way."

I shrugged.

"Just a thought. Please continue with Julia's story."

She proceeded to eat several mouthfuls. I kept her company, then discovered I could not stop eating. I glanced at Mandor, but he remained inscrutable. He'll never admit to magically enhancing a flavor or laying a compulsion on diners to clean their plates. Either way, we did finish the course before she spoke again. And I could hardly complain, considering.

"Julia studied with a variety of teachers after you two broke up," she began. "Once I hit upon my plan, it was a simple matter to cause them to do or say things which would disillusion or discourage her and set her to looking for someone else. It was not long before she came to Victor, who was already under our tutelage. I ordered him to sweeten her stay and to skip many of the usual preliminaries and to proceed to teaching her about an initiation I had chosen for her—"

"That being?" I interrupted. "There are an awful lot of initiations around, with a variety of specialized ends."

She smiled and nodded, breaking a roll and buttering it.

"I led her myself through a version of my own—the Way of the Broken Pattern."

"Sounds like something dangerous from the Amber end of Shadow."

"I can't fault your geography," she said. "But it is not all that dangerous if you know what you're doing."

"It is my understanding," I said, "that those Shadow worlds which contain shadows of the Pattern can only hold imperfect versions and that this always represents a hazard."

"It is a hazard only if one does not know how to deal with it."

"And you had Julia walk this—Broken Pattern?"

"My knowledge of what you refer to as walking the Pattern is restricted to what my late husband and Rinaldo have told me of it. I believe that you follow the lines from a definite external beginning to an interior point where the power comes to you?"

"Yes," I acknowledged.

"In the Way of the Broken Pattern," she explained, "you enter through the imperfection and make your way to the center."

"How can you follow the lines if they are broken or imperfect? The real Pattern would destroy you if you departed the design."

"You don't follow the lines. You follow the interstices," she said.

"And when you emerge . . . wherever?" I asked.

"You bear the image of the Broken Pattern within you."

"And how do you conjure with this?"

"Through the imperfection. You summon the image, and it is like a dark well from which you draw power."

"And how do you travel among shadows?"

"Much as you do—as I understand it," she said. "But the break is always with you."

"The break? I don't understand."

"The flaw in the Pattern. It follows you through Shadow. It is always there beside you as you travel, sometimes as a hair-fine crack, sometimes a great chasm. It shifts about; it may appear suddenly, anywhere—a lapse in reality. This is the hazard for those of the Broken Way. To fall into it is the final death."

"It must lie within all of your spells then also, like a booby trap."

"All occupations have their hazards," she said. "Avoiding them is a part of the art."

"And this is the initiation through which you took Julia?"

"Yes."

"And Victor?"

"Yes."

"I understand what you are saying," I replied, "but you must realize that the broken Patterns are drawing their power from the real one."

"Of course. What of it? The image is almost as good as the real thing, if you're careful."

"For the record, how many useful images are there?"

"Useful?"

"They must degenerate from shadow to shadow. Where do you draw the line and say, 'Beyond this broken image I will not risk breaking my neck'?"

"I see what you mean. You can work with perhaps the first nine. I've never gone farther out. The first three are best. The circle of the next three is still manageable. The next three are a lot riskier."

"A bigger chasm for each?"

"Exactly."

"Why are you giving me all this esoteric information?"

"You're a higher-level initiate, so it doesn't matter. Also, there is nothing you could do to affect the setup. And finally, you need to know this to appreciate the rest of the story."

"All right," I said.

Mandor tapped the table, and small crystal cups of lemon sherbet appeared before us. We took the hint and cleared our palates before resuming the conversation. Outside, the shadows of clouds slid across the mountain slopes. A faint music drifted into the room from somewhere far back along the corridor. Clinking and scraping noises, sounding like distant pick-and-shovel work, came to us from somewhere outside—most likely at the Keep.

"So you initiated Julia," I prompted.

"Yes," Jasra said.

"What happened then?"

"She learned to summon the image of the Broken Pattern and use it for magical sight and the hanging of spells. She learned to draw raw power through the break in it. She learned to find her way through Shadow—"

"While minding the chasm?" I suggested.

"Just so, and she had a definite knack for it. She'd a flair for everything, as a matter of fact."

"I'm amazed that a mortal can traverse even a broken image of the Pattern and live."

"Only a few of them do," Jasra said. "The others step on a line or die mysteriously in the broken area. Ten percent make it, maybe. That isn't bad. Keeps it somewhat exclusive. Of them, only a few can learn the proper mantic skills to amount to anything as an adept."

"And you say that she was actually better than Victor, once she knew what she was about?"

"Yes. I didn't appreciate just how good until it was too late."

I felt her gaze upon me, as if she were checking for a reaction. I glanced up from my food and cocked an eyebrow.

"Yes," she went on, apparently satisfied. "You didn't know that was Julia you were stabbing back at the Fount, did you?"

"No," I admitted. "I'd been puzzled by Mask all along. I couldn't figure any motive for whatever was going on. The flowers were an especially odd touch, and I never really understood whether it was you or Mask behind the bit with the blue stones."

She laughed.

"The blue stones, and the cave they come from, are something of a family secret. The material is a kind of magical insulator, but two pieces—once together—maintain a link, by which a sensitive person can hold one and track the other—"

"Through Shadow?"

"Yes."

"Even if the person doing the tracking otherwise has no special abilities along these lines?"

"Even so," she said. "It's similar to following a shadow shifter while she's shifting. Anyone can do it if she's quick enough, sensitive enough. This just extends the practice a little further. It's following the shifter's trail rather than the shifter herself."

"Herself, herself . . . You trying to tell me it's been pulled on you?"

"That's right."

I looked up in time to see her blush.

"Julia?" I said.

"You begin to understand."

"No," I said. "Well, maybe a little. She was more talented than you'd anticipated. You already told me that. I get the impression she suckered you on something. But I'm not sure where or how."

"I brought her here," Jasra said, "to pick up some equipment I wanted to take along to the first circle of shadows near Amber. She did have a look at my workroom in the Keep at that time. And perhaps I was overly communicative then. But how was I to know she was making mental notes and probably formulating a plan? I'd felt her too cowed to entertain such thoughts. I must admit she was a pretty good actress."

"I read Victor's diary," I said. "I take it you were masked or hooded and possibly using some sort of voice-distorting spell the whole time?"

"Yes, but rather than awe Julia into submission, I think I roused her cupidity for things magical. I believe she picked up one of my tragoliths—the blue stones—at that time. The rest is history."

"Not for me."

A bowl of totally unfamiliar but delicious-smelling vegetables appeared, steaming, before me.

"Think about it."

"You took her to the Broken Pattern and conducted her initiation . . ." I began.

"Yes."

"The first chance she had," I continued, "she used the . . . tragolith to return to the Keep and learn some of your other secrets."

Jasra applauded softly, sampled the veggies, quickly ate more. Mandor smiled.

"Beyond that I draw a blank," I admitted.

"Be a good boy and eat your vegetables," she said.

I obeyed.

"Basing my conclusions concerning this remarkable tale solely upon my experience of human nature," Mandor suddenly observed, "I would say that she wished to test her talons as well as her wings. I'd guess she went back and challenged her former master—this Victor Melman—and fought a sorcerous duel with him."

I heard Jasra's intake of breath.

"Is that truly only a guess?" she asked.

"Truly," he answered, swirling his wine in his goblet. "And I would guess further that you had once done something similar with your own teacher."

"What devil told you that?" she asked.

"It is only a guess that Sharu was your teacher—and perhaps more than that," he said. "But it would explain both your acquisition of this place and your ability to catch its former lord off guard. He might even have had a stray moment before his defeat for a wishful curse that the same fate attend you one day. And even if not, these things do sometimes have a way of running full circle with people in our trade."

She chuckled.

"The devil called Reason, then," she said, a note of admiration in her voice. "Yet you summon him by intuition, which makes it an art."

"It is good to know he still comes when I call. I take it Julia was surprised, however, by Victor's ability to thwart her."

"True. She did not anticipate that we tend to wrap apprentices in a layer or two of protection."

"Yet her own defenses obviously proved adequate—at least."

"True. Though that, of course, was tantamount to defeat. For she knew that I would learn of her rebellion and come soon to discipline her."

"Oh," I observed.

"Yes," she stated. "That is why she faked her death, which I must admit had me completely fooled for a long while."

I recalled the day I had visited Julia's apartment, found the body, been attacked by the beast. The corpse's face had been partly destroyed, the remaining features gory. But the lady had been the right size, and general resemblances had jibed. And she had been in the right place.

And then I had become the object of the lurking doglike creature's attention, which had distracted me more than a little from the minutiae of identity. By the time my struggle for my life was concluded, to the accompaniment of approaching sirens, I was more interested in flight than in further investigation. Thereafter, whenever I had returned in memory to that scene, it was Julia dead whom I beheld.

"Incredible," I said. "Then whose body was it that I found?"

"I've no idea," she replied. "It could have been one of her own shadow selves or some stranger off the street. Or a corpse stolen from the morgue. I've no way of knowing."

"It was wearing one of your blue stones."

"Yes. And its mate was on the collar of the beast you slew—and she opened the way for it to come through."

"Why? And why all that business with the Dweller on the Threshold as well?"

"Red herring of the first water. Victor thought I'd killed her, and I thought he had. He assumed I'd opened a way from the Keep and sent the hunting beast after her. I guessed he'd done it, and I was irritated he'd hidden his rapid development from me. Such things seldom bode well."

I nodded.

"You breed those creatures around here?"

"Yes," she replied, "and I show them, too, in several adjacent shadows. I've a number who've taken blue ribbons."

"I'll stick with pit bulls," I said. "They're a lot cuter and better behaved. So, she left a body and a hidden corridor to this place, and you thought Victor had done her in and was setting things up for a raid on your sanctum sanctorum."

"More or less."

"And he thought she'd become sufficiently dangerous to you—as with the corridor—that you'd killed her?"

"I don't really *know* that he ever found the corridor. It was fairly well hidden, as you learned. Either way, neither of us was aware of what she'd really done."

"That being?"

"She'd also planted a piece of tragolith on me. Later, after the initiation, she used its mate to track me through Shadow to Begma."

"Begma? What the hell were you doing there?"

"Nothing important," she said. "I mention it only to show her subtlety. She did not approach me at that time. I know of it, in fact, only because she told me of it later. She trailed me then from the perimeter of the Golden Circle back here to the Citadel. The rest you know."

"I'm not sure that I do."

"She had designs on this place. When she surprised me, I was surprised indeed. It was how I became a coatrack."

"And she took over here, donning a goalie mask for public relations purposes. She dwelled here for a time, building her powers, increasing her skills, hanging umbrellas on you—"

Jasra growled softly, and I remembered that her bite was worse. I hastened into a fresh area of speculation. "I still don't understand why she spied on me on occasion and sometimes threw flowers."

"Men are exasperating," Jasra said, raising her wineglass and draining it. "You've managed to understand everything but her motive."

"She was on a power trip," I said. "What's to understand past that? I even recall a long discussion we once had concerning power."

I heard Mandor chuckle. When I glanced at him, he looked away, shaking his head.

"Obviously," Jasra said, "she still cared about you. Most likely, a great deal. She was playing games with you. She wanted to rouse your curiosity. She wanted you to come after her, to find her, and she probably wanted to try her power against your own. She wanted to show you that she was worthy of all those things you'd denied her when you denied her your confidence."

"So you know about that, too."

"There were times when she spoke freely to me."

"So she cared for me so well that she sent men with tragoliths to track me to Amber and try to slay me. They almost succeeded, too."

Jasra looked away, coughed. Mandor immediately rose, circled the table, and refilled her goblet, interposing himself between us. At that time, while she was wholly blocked from my sight, I heard her say softly, "Well, not exactly. The assassins were . . . mine. Rinaldo wasn't around to warn you, as I'd guessed he was doing, and I thought I'd have one more shot at you."

"Oh," I observed. "Any more wandering around out there?"

"They were the last," she said.

"That's a comfort."

"I'm not apologizing. I'm just explaining, to clear our differences. Are you willing to cancel this account, too? I've got to know."

"I already said I was willing to call things even. It still goes. Where does Jurt come into all this? I don't understand how they got together and what they are to each other."

Mandor added a touch of wine to my own glass before returning to his seat. Jasra met my eyes.

"I don't know," she said. "She had no allies when we fought. It had to have happened while I was rigid."

"Have you any idea where she and Jurt might have fled?"

"No."

I glanced at Mandor, and he shook his head.

"Neither have I," he said. "However, a peculiar thought has occurred to me."

"Yes?"

"Besides the fact that he has negotiated the Logrus and come into his powers, is it necessary for me to point out that Jurt—apart from his scars and missing pieces—bears you a strong resemblance?"

"Jurt? Me? You've got to be kidding!"

He glanced at Jasra.

"He *is* right," she said. "It's obvious that the two of you are related."

I put down my fork and shook my head.

"Preposterous," I said, more in self-defense than as a matter of certainty. "I never noticed."

Mandor shrugged, very slightly.

"You want a lecture on the psychology of denial?" Jasra asked me.

"No," I said. "I want a little while in which to let this sink in."

"Time for another course anyway," Mandor announced, and he gestured widely and it was delivered.

"Will you be in trouble with your relatives for having released me?" Jasra asked after a while.

"By the time they realize you're gone, I hope to have a good story ready," I answered.

"In other words, you will be," she said.

"Maybe a little."

"I'll see what I can do."

"What do you mean?"

"I don't like to be obligated to anyone," she said, "and you've done more for me than I have for you in this. If I come upon a means of turning their wrath away from you, I'll employ it."

"What could you possibly have in mind?"

"Let it go at that. Sometimes it's better not to know too much."

"I don't like the sound of this at all."

"An excellent reason for changing the subject," she said. "How great an enemy has Jurt become?"

"To me?" I asked. "Or are you wondering whether he'll be returning here for second helpings?"

"Both, when you put it that way."

"I believe he'll kill me if he can," I said, glancing at Mandor, who nodded.

"I fear that is so," he stated.

"As for whether he'll be back here for more of whatever it is that he got," I continued, "you're the best judge. How close did he seem to be to possessing the full powers one might gain from that ritual at the Fountain?"

"It's hard to say exactly," she said, "as he was testing them under very chaotic conditions. Fifty percent, maybe. Just a guess. Will that satisfy him?"

"Perhaps. How dangerous does that make him?"

"Very. When he gets the full hang of things. Still, he must realize that this place will be heavily guarded—even against someone such as himself—should he decide to return. I suspect he'll stay away. Just Sharu—in his present circumstances—would be a formidable obstacle."

I went on eating.

"Julia will probably advise him not to try it," she continued, "familiar as she is with the place."

I nodded my acceptance of the notion. We would meet when we met. Nothing much I could do now to forestall it.

"Now may I ask you a question?" she said.

"Go ahead."

"The *ty'iga* . . ."

"Yes?"

"Even in the body of the duke Orkuz's daughter, I am certain that she did not just walk into the palace and wander on up to your apartments."

"Hardly," I replied. "She's with an official party."

"May I ask when the party arrived?"

"Earlier in the day," I answered. "I'm afraid, though, that I can't go into any detail as to—"

She flipped her well-ringed hand in a gesture of denial.

"I'm not interested in state secrets," she said, "though I know Nayda usually accompanies her father in a secretarial capacity."

"So?"

"Did her sister come along or did she stay home?"

"That would be Coral, wouldn't it?" I asked.

"Yes."

"She did," I replied.

"Thank you," she said, and returned to her food.

Damn. What was that about? Did she know something concerning Coral that I didn't? Something that might bear on her present, indeterminate state? If so, what might it cost me to find out?

"Why?" I said then.

"Just curious," she replied. "I knew the family in . . . happier times."

Jasra sentimental? Never. What then?

"Supposing the family had a problem or two?" I asked.

"Apart from Nayda's possession by the *ty'iga?*"

"Yes," I said.

"I would be sorry to hear that," she said. "What problem?"

"Just a little captivity thing involving Coral."

There came a small clatter as she dropped her fork and it fell upon her plate.

"What *are* you talking about?" she asked.

"A misplacement," I said.

"Of Coral? How? Where?"

"It depends partly on how much you really know about her," I explained.

"I'm fond of the girl. Don't toy with me. What happened?"

More than a little puzzling. But not the answer I was after.

"You knew her mother pretty well?"

"Kinta. I'd met her, at diplomatic functions. Lovely lady."

"Tell me about her father."

"Well, he's a member of the royal house, but of a branch not in the line of succession. Before he was prime minister, Orkuz was the Begman ambassador to Kashfa. His family was in residence with him, so naturally I saw him at any number of affairs—"

She looked up when she realized I was staring at her—through the Sign of the Logrus, across her Broken Pattern. Our eyes met, and she smiled.

"Oh. You did ask about her *father,*" she said. Then she paused, and I nodded. "So there's truth in that rumor," she observed at last.

"You didn't really know?"

"There are so many rumors in the world, most of them impossible to check. How am I to know which of them hold truth? And why should I care?"

"You're right, of course," I said. "Nevertheless . . ."

"Another of the old boy's by-blows," she said. "Does anyone keep score? It's a wonder he had any time for affairs of state."

"Anyone's guess," I said.

"To be frank then, in addition to knowing the rumor I'd heard, there was indeed a family resemblance. I couldn't judge on that count, though, not being personally acquainted with most of the family. You're saying there's truth in it?"

"Yes."

"Just because of the resemblance, or is there something more?"

"Something more."

She smiled sweetly and retrieved her fork.

"I've always enjoyed that fairy-tale revelation which sees one rise in the world."

"I also," I said, and I resumed eating.

Mandor cleared his throat.

"It seems hardly fair," he said, "to tell only part of a story."

"You're right," I agreed.

Jasra returned her gaze to me and sighed.

"All right," she said, "I'll ask. How did you know for cer—Oh. Of course. The Pattern."

I nodded.

"Well, well, well. Little Coral, Mistress of the Pattern. This was a fairly recent occurrence?"

"Yes."

"I suppose she is off somewhere in Shadow now—celebrating."

"I wish I knew."

"What do you mean?"

"She's gone, but I don't know where. And it's the Pattern that did it to her."

"How?"

"Good question. I don't know."

Mandor cleared his throat.

"Merlin," he said, "perhaps there are some matters"—he rotated his left hand—"that on reflection you may wish—"

"No," I said. "Ordinarily discretion would rule—perhaps even with you, my brother, as a Lord of Chaos. And certainly in the case of Your Highness"—I nodded to Jasra—"save that you are acquainted and may even have a touch of affection for the lady." I decided against laying it on too thick and quickly added, "Or at least no malice toward her."

"As I said, I'm very fond of the girl," Jasra stated, leaning forward.

"Good," I replied, "for I feel at least partly responsible for what happened, even though I was duped in the matter. So I feel obliged to try to set things right. Only I don't now how."

"What happened?" she asked.

"I was entertaining her when she expressed a desire to see the Pattern. So I obliged her. On the way she asked me questions about it. It seemed harmless conversation, and I satisfied her curiosity. I was not familiar with the rumors concerning her parentage, or I would have suspected something. As it was, when we got there, she set foot upon the Pattern and commenced walking it."

Jasra sucked in her breath.

"It would destroy one not of the blood," she said. "Correct?"

I nodded.

"Or even one of us," I said then, "if any of a number of mistakes be made."

Jasra chuckled.

"Supposing her mother'd really been carrying on with a footman or the cook?" she remarked.

"She's a wise daughter," I said. "At any rate, once one begins the Pattern, one may not turn back. I was obliged to instruct her as she went along. That, or be a very poor host and doubtless damage Begman-Amber relations."

"And spoil all sorts of delicate negotiations?" she asked, half-seriously.

I'd a feeling just then that she'd welcome a digression concerning the exact nature of the Begman visit, but I wasn't biting.

"You might say that," I said. "At any rate, she completed the Pattern, and then it took her away."

"My late husband told me that from its center one can command the Pattern to deliver one anywhere."

"True," I said, "but it was the nature of her command that was a bit unusual. She told the Pattern to send her wherever it wanted."

"I'm afraid I don't understand."

"Neither do I, but she did, and it did."

"You mean she just said, 'Send me wherever you want to send me,' and she was instantly dispatched for points unknown?"

"You've got it."

"That would seem to imply some sort of intelligence on the part of the Pattern."

"Unless, of course, it was responding to an unconscious desire on her part to visit some particular locale."

"True. I suppose there is that possibility. But have you no means of tracing her?"

"I'd a Trump I'd done of her. When I tried it, I reached her. She seemed pent in a dark place. Then we lost touch, and that's it."

"How long ago was this?"

"A matter of hours by my subjective reckoning," I said. "Is this place on anything near Amber time?"

"Close enough, I believe. Why didn't you try again?"

"I've been somewhat occupied ever since. Also, I've been casting about for some alternate way of approaching this."

There came a clinking, rattling sound, and I smelled coffee.

"If you're asking whether I'll help you," Jasra said, "the answer is yes. Only I don't really know how to go about it. Perhaps if you were to try her Trump again—with me backing you—we might reach her."

"All right," I said, lowering my cup and fumbling forth the cards. "Let's give it a try."

"I will assist you also," Mandor stated, rising to his feet and coming to stand to my right.

Jasra came over and stood to my left. I held the Trump so that we all had a clear view.

"Let us begin," I said, and I moved forward with my mind.

3

A patch of light I had taken to be a stray sunbeam drifted from its position on the floor to a spot beside my coffee cup. It was ring-shaped, and I decided not to remark upon it since neither of the others seemed to take note of it.

I reached after Coral and found nothing. I felt Jasra and Mandor reaching also, and I tried again, joining forces with them. Harder.

Something?

Something . . . I recalled wondering what Vialle felt when she used the Trumps. It had to be something other than the visual cues with which the rest of us were familiar. It might be something like this.

Something.

What I felt was a sense of Coral's presence. I regarded her form upon the card, but it would not come alive. The card itself had grown perceptibly cooler, but it was not the same ice-edged chill I normally felt on achieving communication with one of the others. I tried harder. I felt Mandor and Jasra increasing their efforts also.

Then Coral's image on the card faded, but nothing came to replace it. I sensed her presence, however, as I regarded the void. The feeling came closest to that of attempting to make contact with someone who was asleep.

"I cannot tell whether it's simply a difficult place to reach," Mandor began, "or—"

"I believe she is under a spell," Jasra announced.

"That could account for a part of it," Mandor said.

"But only part," came a soft, familiar voice from near at hand. "There are awesome powers holding her, Dad. I've never seen anything like this before."

"The Ghostwheel is right," Mandor said. "I'm beginning to feel it."

"Yes," Jasra began, "there is something. . . ."

And suddenly the veil was pierced, and I beheld the slumped form of Coral, apparently unconscious, lying upon a dark surface in a very dark place, the only illumination coming from what seemed a circle of fire drawn about her. She couldn't have brought me through if she wanted to, and—

"Ghost, can you take me to her?" I asked.

Her image faded before he could reply, and I felt a cold draft. It was several seconds before I realized that it seemed to be blowing upon me from the now-icy card.

"I don't think so, I wouldn't want to, and it may be that there is no need," he answered. "The force that holds her has become aware of your interest and even now is reaching toward you. Is there some way you can turn off that Trump?"

I passed my hand across its face, which is usually sufficient. Nothing happened. The cold breeze even seemed to increase in intensity. I repeated the gesture along with a mental order. I began to feel whatever it was, focusing upon me.

Then the Sign of the Logrus fell upon the Trump, and the card was torn from my hand as I was cast backward, striking my shoulder against the edge of the door. Mandor lurched to his right as this occurred, catching hold of the table to steady himself. In my Logrus vision I had seen wild lines of light flash outward from the card before it fell away.

"Did that do the trick?" I called out.

"It broke the connection," Ghost replied.

"Thanks, Mandor," I said.

"But the power that was reaching for you through the Trump knows where you are now," Ghost said.

"What makes you privy to its awareness?" I inquired.

"It is a surmise, based upon the fact that it's still reaching for you. It is coming the long way round—across space—though. It could take as long as a quarter of a minute before it reaches you."

"Your use of the pronoun is a little indefinite," Jasra said. "Is it just Merlin that it wants? Or is it coming for all of us?"

"Uncertain. Merlin is the focus. I've no idea what it will do to you."

I lurched forward during this exchange and retrieved Coral's Trump.

"Can you protect us?" she asked.

"I've already begun transferring Merlin to a distant place. Shall I do this for you also?"

As I looked up from pocketing the Trump, I noted that the chamber had become something less than substantial—translucent, as if everything were made of colored glass.

"Please," the cathedral-window form of Jasra said softly.

"Yes," came my fading brother's faint echo.

Then I was passed through a fiery hoop into a place of darkness. I stumbled against a stone wall, felt my way along it. A quarter turn, a lighter area before me dotted with bright points . . .

"Ghost?" I asked.

No answer.

"I don't appreciate these interrupted conversations," I continued.

I moved forward until I came to what was obviously a cave mouth. A clear night sky hung before me, and when I stepped outside a cold wind rubbed up against me. I retreated several paces, shivering.

I had no idea where I might be. Not that it really mattered if it brought me a breathing spell. I reached through the Logrus Sign for a great distance before I located a heavy blanket. Wrapping it about myself, I sank to a seated position upon the cave's floor. Then I reached again. It was easier to find a stack of wood and no trick at all to ignite a portion of it. I'd also been looking forward to one more cup of coffee. I wondered. . . .

Why not? I reached again, and the bright circle rolled into view before me.

"Dad! Please stop!" came the offended voice. "I've gone to a lot of trouble to tuck you away in this obscure corner of Shadow. Too many sendings, though, and you'll call attention to yourself."

"Come on!" I said. "All I want is a cup of coffee."

"I'll get one for you. Just don't use your own powers for a while."

"Why won't your action draw just as much attention?"

"I'm using a roundabout route. There!"

A steaming mug of some dark stoneware stood on the floor of the cave near my right hand.

"Thanks," I said, taking it up and sniffing it. "What did you do with Jasra and Mandor?"

"I sent each of you off in a different direction amidst a horde of fake images flitting hither and yon. All you have to do now is lie low for a while. Let its attention subside."

"Whose attention? What's attention?"

"The power that has Coral. We don't want it to find us."

"Why not? I seem to recall your wondering earlier whether you were a god. What's for you to fear?"

"The real thing. It seems to be stronger than I am. On the other hand, I seem to be faster."

"That's something, anyway."

"Get a good night's sleep. I'll let you know in the morning whether it's still hunting you."

"Maybe I'll find out for myself."

"Don't go manifesting unless it's a matter of life or death."

"That wasn't what I meant. Supposing it finds me?"

"Do whatever seems appropriate."

"Why do I have a feeling you're keeping things from me?"

"I guess you're just suspicious by nature, Dad. It seems to run in your family. I've got to go now."

"Where?" I asked.

"Check on the others. Run a few errands. See to my personal development. Check my experiments. Things like that. Bye."

"What about Coral?"

But the circle of light which had hovered before me spun from brightness to dimness and vanished. An unarguable end to the conversation. Ghost was getting more and more like the rest of us—sneaky and misleading.

I sipped the coffee. Not as good as Mandor's, but acceptable. I began wondering where Jasra and Mandor had been sent. I decided against trying to reach them. In fact, it might not be a bad idea, I decided, to fortify my own position against magical intrusion.

I resummoned the Sign of the Logrus, which I had let slip while Ghost was transporting me. I used it to set wards at the cave mouth and about my situation within. Then I released it and took another sip. As I did, I realized that this coffee could not possibly keep me awake. I was coming off a nervous jag, and the weight of all my activities was suddenly heavy upon me. Two more sips, and I could hardly hold the cup. Another, and I noticed that each time I blinked my eyelids were closing a lot more easily than they opened.

I set the cup aside, drew my blanket more tightly about me, and found a relatively comfortable position on the stone floor, having become something of an expert on the activity back in the crystal cave. The flickering flames mustered shadow armies behind my eyelids. The fire popped like a clash of arms; the air smelled of pitch.

I went away. Sleep is perhaps the only among life's great pleasures which need not be of short duration. It filled me, and I drifted. How far and for how long, I cannot say.

Nor can I say what it was that roused me. I know only that I was somewhere else and the next moment I had returned. My position had changed slightly, my toes were cold, and I felt that I was no longer alone. I kept my eyes closed, and did not alter my breathing pattern. It could be that Ghost had simply decided to look in on me. It could also be that something was testing my wards.

I raised my eyelids but the smallest distance, peering outward and upward through a screen of eyelashes. A small misshaped figure stood outside the cave mouth, the fire's remaining glow faintly illuminating his strangely familiar face. There was something of myself in those features and something of my father.

"Merlin," he said softly. "Come awake now. You've places to go and things to do."

I opened my eyes wide and stared. He fitted a certain description. . . . Frakir throbbed, and I stroked her still.

"Dworkin . . . ?" I said.

He chuckled.

"You've named me," he replied.

He paced, from one side of the cave mouth to the other, occasionally pausing to extend a hand partway toward me. Each time he hesitated and drew it back.

"What is it?" I asked. "What's the matter? Why are you here?"

"I've come to fetch you back to the journey you abandoned."

"And what journey might that be?"

"Your search for the lady somewhere astray who walked the Pattern t'other day."

"Coral? You know where she is?"

He raised his hand, lowered it, gnashed his teeth.

"Coral? Is that her name? Let me in. We must discuss her."

"We seem to be talking just fine the way we are."

"Have you no respect for an ancestor?"

"I do. But I also have a shapeshifting brother who'd like to mount my head and hang it on the wall of his den. And he might just be able to do it real quick if I give him half a chance." I sat up and rubbed my eyes, my wits finishing the job of reassembling themselves. "So where's Coral?"

"Come. I will show you the way," he said, reaching forward. This time his hand passed my ward and was immediately outlined in fire. He did not seem to notice. His eyes were a pair of dark stars, drawing me to my feet, pulling me toward him. His hand began to melt. The flesh ran and dripped away like wax. There were no bones within, but rather an odd geometry—as if someone had sketched a hand quickly in a three-dimensional medium, then molded some fleshlike cover for it. "Take my hand."

I found myself raising my hand against my will, reaching toward the fingerlike curves, the swirls of the knuckles. He chuckled again. I could feel the force that drew me. I wondered what would happen if I took hold of that strange hand in a special way.

So I summoned the Sign of the Logrus and sent it on ahead to do my handclasping for me.

This may not have been my best choice of actions. I was momentarily blinded by the brilliant, sizzling flash that followed. When my vision cleared, I saw that Dworkin was gone. A quick check showed that my wards still held. I perked up the fire with a short, simple spell, noted that my coffee cup was half full, and warmed its tepid contents with an abbreviated version of the same rendering. I reshrouded myself then, settled, and sipped. Analyze as I might, I couldn't figure what had just happened.

I knew of no one who had seen the half-mad demiurge in years, though according to my father's tale, Dworkin's mind should have been largely mended when Oberon repaired the Pattern. If it had really been Jurt, seeking to trick his way into my presence and finish me off, it was an odd choice of form for him to assume. Come to think of it, I wasn't at all certain that Jurt even knew what Dworkin looked like. I debated the wisdom of calling for Ghostwheel to solicit an inhuman opinion on the matter. Before I could decide, however, the stars beyond the cave mouth were occulted by another figure, much larger than Dworkin's— heroically proportioned even.

A single step brought it within range of the firelight, and I spilled coffee when I beheld that face. We had never met, but I had seen his likeness in many places in Castle Amber.

"I understand that Oberon died in redrawing the Pattern," I said.

"Were you present at the time?" he asked.

"No," I replied, "but coming as you do, on the heels of a rather bizarre apparition of Dworkin, you must excuse my suspicions as to your bona fides."

"Oh, that was a fake you encountered. I'm the real thing."

"What was it then that I saw?"

"It was the astral form of a practical joker—a sorcerer named Jolos from the fourth circle of Shadow."

"Oh," I responded. "And how am I to know you're not the projection of someone named Jalas from the fifth?"

"I can recite the entire genealogy of the royal House of Amber."

"So can any good scribe back home."

"I'll throw in the illegitimates."

"How many were there, anyway?"

"Forty-seven, that I know of."

"Aw, come on! How'd you manage?"

"Different time streams," he said, smiling.

"If you survived the reconstruction of the Pattern, how come you didn't return to Amber and continue your reign?" I asked. "Why'd you let Random get crowned and muddy the picture even further?"

He laughed.

"But I didn't survive it," he said. "I was destroyed in the process. I am a ghost, returned to solicit a living champion for Amber against the rising power of the Logrus."

"Granted, *arguendo,* that you are what you say you are," I replied, "you're still in the wrong neighborhood, sir. I am an initiate of the Logrus and a son of Chaos."

"You are also an initiate of the Pattern and a son of Amber," the magnificent figure answered.

"True," I said, "and all the more reason for me not to choose sides."

"There comes a time when a man must choose," he stated, "and that time is now. Which side are you on?"

"Even if I believed that you are what you say, I do not feel obliged to make such a choice," I said. "And there is a tradition in the Courts that Dworkin himself was an initiate of the Logrus. If that is true, I'm only following in the footsteps of a venerable ancestor."

"But he renounced Chaos when he founded Amber."

I shrugged.

"Good thing I haven't founded anything," I said. "If there is something specific that you want of me, tell me what it is, give me a good reason for doing it and maybe I'll cooperate."

He extended his hand.

"Come with me, and I will set your feet upon the new Pattern you must follow, in a game to be played out between the Powers."

"I still don't understand you, but I am certain that the real Oberon would not be stopped by these simple wards. You come to me and clasp my hand, and I will be glad to accompany you and take a look at whatever it is you want me to see."

He drew himself up to an even greater height.

"You would test me?" he asked.

"Yes."

"As a man, it would hardly have troubled me," he stated. "But being formed out of this spiritual crap now, I don't know. I'd rather not take the chance."

"In that case, I must echo your sentiment with respect to your own proposal."

"Grandson," he said levelly, a ruddy light entering his eyes, "even dead, none of my spawn may address me so. I come for thee now in a less than friendly fashion. I come for thee now, and this journey shall I hale thee amid fires."

I took a step backward as he advanced.

"No need to take it personally . . ." I began.

I shaded my eyes as he hit my wards, and the flashbulb effect began. Squinting through it, I saw something of a repetition of the flensing of Dworkin's flesh by fire. Oberon became transparent in places; other places he melted. Within him, through him, as the outward semblance of the kind passed away, I saw the swirls and curves, the straits and channels—black-lined, geometrizing abstractly inside the general outline of a large and noble figure. Unlike Dworkin, however, the image did not fade. Having passed my wards, its movement slowed, it continued toward me nevertheless, reaching. Whatever its true nature, it was one of the most frightening things I had ever encountered. I continued to back away, raising my hands, and I called again upon the Logrus.

The Sign of the Logrus occurred between us. The abstract version of Oberon continued to reach, scribbled spirit hands encountering the writhing limbs of Chaos.

I was not reaching through the Logrus's image to manipulate it against that apparition. I felt an unusual dread of the thing, even at our distance. What I did was more on the order of thrusting the Sign against the image of the king. Then I dived past them both, out the cave mouth, and I rolled, scrabbling for handholds and toeholds when I struck a slope, coming up hard against a boulder and hugging it as the cave erupted with the noise and flash of an ammo dump that had taken a hit.

I lay there shuddering, my eyes squeezed shut, for perhaps half a minute. Any second, I felt, and something would be on my ass—unless, perhaps, I crouched perfectly still and tried hard to look like another rock. . . .

The silence was profound, and when I opened my eyes, the light had vanished and the shape of the cave mouth was unaltered. I rose slowly to my feet, advanced even more slowly. The Sign of the Logrus had departed, and for reasons I did not understand I was loath to call it back. When I looked within the cave, there were no signs that anything at all had occurred, save for the fact that my wards were blown.

I stepped inside. The blanket still lay where it had fallen. I put out a hand and touched the wall. Cold stone. That blast must have taken place at some other level than the immediate. My small fire was still flickering feebly. I recalled it yet again to life. But the only thing I saw in its glow which I had not seen previously was my coffee cup, broken where it had fallen.

I let my hand remain upon the wall. I leaned. After a time, there came an uncontrollable tightening of my diaphragm. I began laughing. I am not sure why. The weight of everything which had transpired since April 30 was upon me. It just happened that laughter had edged out the alternative of beating my breast and howling.

I thought I knew who all the players were in this complex game. Luke and Jasra seemed to be on my side now, along with my brother Mandor, who'd always looked out for me. My mad brother Jurt wanted me dead, and he was now allied with my old lover Julia, who didn't seem too kindly disposed toward me either. There was the *ty'iga*—an overprotective demon inhabiting the body of Coral's sister, Nayda, whom I'd left sleeping in the midst of a spell back in Amber. There was the mercenary Dalt—who, now I thought of it, was also my uncle—who'd made off with Luke for points and purposes unknown after kicking Luke's ass in Arden with two armies watching. He had nasty designs on Amber but lacked the military muscle to provide more than occasional guerrilla-style annoyance. And then there was Ghostwheel, my cybernetic Trump dealer and minor-league mechanical demigod, who seemed to have evolved from rash and manic to rational and paranoid—and I wasn't at all sure where he was headed from here, but at least he was showing some filial respect mixed in with the current cowardice.

And that had been pretty much it.

But these latest manifestations seemed evidence that there was something else at play here also, something that wanted to drag me off in yet another direction. I had Ghost's testimony that it was strong. I had no idea what it really represented. And I had no desire to trust it. This made for an awkward relationship.

"Hey, kid!" came a familiar voice from down the slope. "You're a hard man to find. You don't stay put."

I turned quickly, moved forward, stared downward.

A lone figure was toiling up the slope. A big man. Something flashed in the vicinity of his throat. It was too dark to make out his features.

I retreated several paces, commencing the spell which would restore my blasted wards.

"Hey! Don't run off!" he called. "I've got to talk to you."

The wards fell into place, and I drew my blade and held it, point lowered, at my right, entirely out of sight from the cave mouth when I turned my body. I ordered Frakir to hang invisible from my left hand also. The second figure had been stronger than the first, to make it past my wards. If this third one should prove stronger than the second, I was going to need everything I could muster.

"Yeah?" I called out. "Who are you and what do you want?"

"Hell!" I heard it say. "I'm no one in particular. Just your old man. I need some help, and I like to keep things in the family."

I had to admit, when it reached the area of firelight, that it was a very good imitation of Prince Corwin of Amber, my father, complete with black cloak, boots, and trousers, gray shirt, silver studs, and buckle—and even a silver rose—and he was smiling that same quirky sort of smile the real Corwin had sometimes worn on telling me his story, long ago. . . . I felt a kind of wrenching in my guts at the sight. I'd wanted to get to know him better, but he'd disappeared, and I'd never been able to find him again. Now, for this thing—whatever it was—to pull this impersonation . . . I was more than a little irritated at such a patent attempt to manipulate my feelings.

"The first fake was Dworkin," I said, "and the second was Oberon. You're climbing right down the family tree, aren't you?"

He squinted and cocked his head in puzzlement as he advanced, another realistic mannerism.

"I don't know what you're talking about, Merlin," he responded. "I—"

Then it entered the warded area and jerked as if touching a hot wire.

"Holy shit!" it said. "You don't trust anybody, do you?"

"Family tradition," I replied, "backed up by recent experience."

I was puzzled, though, that the encounter had not involved more pyrotechnics. Also, I wondered why the thing's transformation into scrollwork had not yet commenced.

With another oath, it swirled its cloak to the left, wrapping it about its arm; its right hand crossed toward an excellent facsimile of my father's scabbard. A silver-chased blade sighed as it arced upward, then fell toward the eye of the ward. When they met, the sparks rose in a foot-high splash and the blade hissed as if it had been heated and were now being quenched in water. The design on the blade flared, and the sparks leaped again—this time as high as a man—and in that instant I felt the ward break.

Then it entered, and I turned my body, swinging my blade. But the blade that looked like Grayswandir fell and rose again, in a tightening circle, drawing my own weapon's point to the right and sliding straight in toward my breast. I did a simple parry in quarte, but he slipped under it and was still coming in from the outside. I parried sixte, but he wasn't there. His movement had been only a feint. He was back inside and coming in low now. I reversed myself and parried again as he slid his entire body in to my right, dropping his blade's point, reversing his grip, fanning my face with his left hand.

Too late I saw the right hand rising as the left slid behind my head. Grayswandir's pommel was headed straight for my jaw.

"You're really . . ." I began, and then it connected.

The last thing I remember seeing was the silver rose.

That's life: Trust and you're betrayed; don't trust and you betray yourself. Like most moral paradoxes, it places you in an untenable position. And it was too late for my normal solution. I couldn't walk away from the game.

I woke in a place of darkness. I woke wondering and wary. As usual when wondering and wary, I lay perfectly still and let my breathing continue its natural rhythm. And I listened.

Not a sound.

I opened my eyes slightly.

Disconcerting patterns. I closed them again.

I felt with my body for vibrations within the rocky surface upon which I was sprawled.

No vibes.

I opened my eyes entirely, fought back an impulse to close them. I raised myself onto my elbows, then gathered my knees beneath me, straightened my back, turned my head. Fascinating. I hadn't been this disoriented since I'd gone drinking with Luke and the Cheshire Cat.

There was no color anywhere about me. Everything was black, white, or some shade of gray. It was as if I had entered a photographic negative. What I presumed to be a sun hung like a black hole several diameters above the horizon to my right. The sky was a very dark gray, and ebon clouds moved slowly within it. My skin was the color of ink. The rocky ground beneath me and about me shone an almost translucent bone-white, however. I rose slowly to my feet, turning. Yes. The ground seemed to glow, the sky was dark, and I was a shadow between them. I did not like the feeling at all.

The air was dry, cool. I stood in the foothills to an albino mountain range, so stark in appearance as to rouse comparison with the Antarctic. These stretched off and up to my left. To the right—low and rolling—toward what I guessed to be a morning sun, lay a black plain. Desert? I had to raise my hand and "shade" against its . . . what? Antiglow?

"Shit!" I tried saying, and I noticed two things immediately.

The first was that my word remained unvoiced. The second was that my jaw hurt where my father or his simulacrum had slugged me.

I repeated my silent observation and withdrew my Trumps. All bets were off when it came to messing with sendings. I shuffled out the Trump for the Ghostwheel and focused my attention upon it.

Nothing. It was completely dead to me. But, then, it was Ghost who'd told me to lie low, and maybe he was simply refusing to entertain my call. I thumbed through the others. I paused at Flora's. She was usually willing to help me out of a tight spot. I studied that lovely face, sent out my call to it. . . .

Not a golden curl stirred. Not a degree's drop in temperature. The card remained a card. I tried harder, even muttering an enhancement spell. But there was nobody home.

Mandor, then. I spent several minutes on his card with the same result. I tried Random's. Ditto. Benedict's, Julian's. No and no. I tried for Fiona, Luke, and Bill Roth. Three more negatives. I even pulled a couple of the Trumps of Doom, but I couldn't reach the Sphinx either, or a building of bones atop a green glass mountain.

I squared them, cased them, and put them away. It was the first time I had encountered a phenomenon of this sort since the Crystal Cave. Trumps can be blocked in any of a number of ways, however, and so far as I was concerned, the matter was, at the moment, academic. I was more concerned about removing myself to a more congenial environment. I could save the research for some future bit of leisure.

I began walking. My footsteps were soundless. When I kicked a pebble and it bounced along before me, I could detect nothing of sound to its passage.

White to the left of me, black to the right. Mountains or desert. I turned left, walking. Nothing else in motion that I could see except for the black, black clouds. To the lee side of every outcrop a near-blinding area of enhanced brightness: crazy shadows across a crazy land.

Turn left again. Three paces, then round the boulder. Upward. Over the ridge. Turn downhill. Turn right. Soon a streak of red amid rocks to the left . . .

Nope. Next time then . . .

Brief twinge in the frontal sinus. No red. Move on.

Crevice to the right, next turn . . .

I massaged my temples when they began to ache as no crevice was delivered. My breath came heavy, and I felt moisture upon my brow.

Textures of gray to green and brittle flowers, slate-blue, low on the next talus slope . . .

A small pain in my neck. No flowers. No gray. No green.

Then let the clouds part and the darkness pour down from the sun . . .

Nothing.

. . . and a sound of running water from a small stream, next gully.

I had to halt. My head was throbbing; my hands were shaking. I reached out and touched the rock wall to my left. It felt solid enough. Rampant reality. Why was it treading all over me?

And how had I gotten here?

And where was here?

I relaxed. I slowed my breathing and adjusted my energies. The pains in my head subsided, ebbed, were gone.

Again I began walking.

Birdsong and gentle breeze . . . Flower in a crannied nook . . .

No. And the first twinge of returning resistance . . .

What sort of spell might I be under, that I had lost my power to walk in Shadow? I had never understood it to be something that could be taken away.

"It's not funny," I tried saying. "Whoever you are, whatever you are, how did you do it? What do you want? Where are you?"

Again I heard nothing; least of all an answer.

"I don't know how you did it. Or why," I mouthed, and thought. "I don't feel as if I'm under a spell. But I must be here for a reason. Get on with your business. Tell me what you want."

Nada.

I walked on, continuing in a halfhearted fashion my attempts to shift away through Shadow. As I did, I pondered my situation. I'd a feeling there was something elementary that I was overlooking in this entire business.

. . . And a small red flower behind a rock, next turn.

I made the turn, and there was the small red flower I had half-consciously conjured. I rushed toward it to touch it, to confirm that the universe was a benign, essentially Merlin-loving place.

I stumbled in my rush, kicking up a cloud of dust. I caught myself, raised myself, looked about. I must have searched for the next ten or fifteen minutes, but I could not locate the flower. Finally, I cursed and turned away. No one likes to be a butt of the universe's jokes.

On a sudden inspiration I sought through all my pockets, should I have even a chip of the blue stones upon my person. Its odd vibrational abilities might just somehow conduct me through Shadow back toward its source. But no. Not even a speck of blue dust remained. They all were in my father's tomb, and that was it. It would have been too easy an out for me, I guess.

What was I missing?

A fake Dworkin, a fake Oberon, and a man who'd claimed to be my father all had wanted to conduct me to some strange place—to compete in some sort of struggle between the Powers, the Oberon figure had indicated, whatever that meant. The Corwin figure had apparently succeeded, I reflected as I rubbed my jaw. Only what sort of game was it? And what were the Powers?

The Oberon thing had said something about my choosing between Amber and Chaos. But, then, it had lied about other things during the same conversation. The devil with both of them! I didn't ask to get involved in their power game. I had enough problems of my own. I didn't even care to learn the rules to whatever was going on.

I kicked a small white stone, watched it roll away. This didn't feel like something of Jurt's or Julia's doing. It seemed either a new factor or an old one which had transformed itself considerably. Where had it first seemed to enter the picture? I guessed it had something to do with the force which had come rushing after me on our attempt to reach Coral. I could only assume that it had located me and this was the result. But what might it be? It would first, I supposed, be necessary that I learn where Coral lay in her circle of fire. Something in that place, I presumed, was behind my current situation. Where then? She had asked the Pattern to send her where she ought to go. . . . I had no way now of asking the Pattern where that might be—and no way at the moment of walking it, to have it send me after her.

It was time, therefore, to resign the game and employ different means to solve the problem. My Trumps having blown a circuit and my ability to traverse Shadow having encountered a mysterious blockage, I decided it was time to up the power factor by an order of magnitude in my favor. I would summon the Sign of the Logrus and continue my shadow walk, backing every step that I took with the power of Chaos.

Frakir cut into my wrist. I sought about quickly after any approaching menaces, but I saw nothing. I remained wary for several minutes longer, exploring the vicinity. Nothing occurred, though, and Frakir grew still.

It was hardly the first time her alarm system had been improperly cued—whether by some stray astral current or some odd thought of my own. But in a place like this, one could not afford to take chances. The highest stand of stone in the vicinity stood at about fifteen to twenty meters, perhaps a hundred paces uphill, to my left. I made my way over to it and commenced climbing.

When I finally reached its chalky peak, I commanded a view over a great distance in every direction. I did not behold another living thing in this strange silent yinyang universe.

So I decided that it had indeed been a false alarm, and I climbed back down. I reached once again to summon the Logrus and Frakir practically behanded me. Hell. I ignored her, and I sent out my call.

The Sign of the Logrus rose and rushed toward me. It danced like a butterfly, hit like a truck. My newsreel world went away, black and white to black.

4

Recovering.

My head ached, and there was dirt in my mouth. I was sprawled face down. Memory made its way home through the traffic, and I opened my eyes. Still black and white and gray all about. I spit sand, rubbed my eyes, blinked. The Logrus Sign was not present, and I could not account for my recent experience with it.

I sat up and hugged my knees. I seemed to be stranded, all of my extramundane means of travel and communication blocked. I couldn't think of anything to do other than get up, pick a direction, and start walking.

I shuddered. Where would that take me? Just through more of the same—more of this monotonous landscape?

There came a soft sound, as of a throat being gently cleared.

I was on my feet in an instant, having inspected every direction on the way up.

Who's there? I inquired, having given up on articulation.

I seemed to hear it again, very near at hand.

Then, *I've a message for you,* something seemed to say within my head.

What? Where are you? Message? I tried asking.

Excuse me, came the muffled voice, *but I'm new at this business. To take things in order, I am where I've always been—on your wrist—and when the Logrus blasted through here, it enhanced me additionally, so that I could deliver the message.*

Frakir?

Yes. My first enhancement, that day you bore me through the Logrus, involved sensitivity to danger, mobility, combat reflexes, and a limited sentience. This time the Logrus added direct mental communication and expanded my awareness to the point where I could deliver messages.

Why?

It was in a hurry, could stay in this place for only an instant, and this was the only way for it to let you know what is going on.

I didn't realize the Logrus was sentient.

Something like a chuckle followed.

Then, *It is hard to classify an intelligence of that order, and I suppose it doesn't really have much to say most of the time,* came Frakir's reply. *Its energies are mainly expended in other areas.*

Well, why did it come through here and blitz me?

Unintentional. It was a by-product of my enhancement, once it saw that I was the only means of reaching you with more than a few words or images.

Why was its time here so limited? I asked.

It is the nature of this land, which lies between the shadows, that it be mainly inaccessible both to the Pattern and the Logrus.

A sort of demilitarized zone?

No, it is not a matter of truce. It is simply that it is extremely difficult for either of them to manifest here at all. This is why the place is pretty much unchanging.

This is a place they can't *reach?*

That's about the size of it.

How come I never heard of it before?

Probably because no one else can reach it too readily either.

So what's the message?

Basically, that you not try calling upon the Logrus again while you're here. The place represents such a distorting medium that there's no assurance how any projected energy might manifest outside some convenient vessel. It could be dangerous for you.

I massaged my throbbing temples. At least it got my mind off my sore jaw.

All right, I agreed. *Any hints as to what I'm supposed to be doing here?*

Yes, this is a trial. Of what, I can't say.

Do I have a choice?

What do you mean?

May I refuse to participate?

I suppose. But then I don't know how you get out of here.

So I do get released from this place at the end, if I play?
If you're still living, yes. Even if you're not, I'd imagine.
Then I really have no choice.
There will be a choice.
When?
Somewhere along the way. I don't know where.
Why don't you just repeat all of your instructions to me?
Can't. I don't know what all is here. It will surface only in response to a question or a situation.
Will any of this interfere with your strangling function?
It shouldn't.
That's something, anyway. Very well. Have you any idea what I'm supposed to do next?
Yes. You should begin climbing the highest hill to your left.
Which—Okay, I guess that's the one, I decided, my gaze settling upon a broken fang of blazing white stone.

And so I walked toward it, up a gradually steepening slope. The black sun mounted higher into the grayness. The eerie silence continued.

Uh, do you know exactly what we will find whenever we get to wherever we're going? I tried to say in Frakir's direction.

I am certain that the information is present, came the reply, *but I do not believe that it will be available until we reach the appropriate locale.*

I hope you're right.

Me, too.

The way continued to steepen. While I had no way to measure the time exactly, it seemed that more than an hour passed before I left the foothills and was climbing the white mountain itself. While I observed no footprints nor saw any other sign of life, I did, on several occasions, encounter long stretches of natural-seeming trail, shelflike, leading up that high bleached face. Several more hours must have passed as I negotiated this, the dark sun riding to mid-heaven and beginning its descent toward a west that lay beyond this peak. It was annoying not to be able to curse aloud.

How can I be sure we're on the proper side of the thing? Or heading for the right area? I asked.

You're still going in the proper direction, Frakir answered.

But you don't know how much farther it'll be?

Nope. I'll know when I see it, though.

The sun is going to slip behind the mountain fairly soon. Will you be able to see it to know it then?

*I believe the sky actually brightens here when the sun goes
away. Negative space is funny that way. Whatever, something is always bright here and something is always dark. There'll be the
wherewithal for detection.*
 Any idea what we're actually doing?
 One of those damned quest-things, I think.
 Vision? Or practical?
 *It was my understanding that they all partake of both, though
I feel this one is heavily weighted toward the latter. On the other
wrist, anything you encounter between shadows is likely to par-
take of the allegorical, the emblematic—all that crap people bury
in the nonconscious parts of their beings.*
 In other words, you don't know either.
 Not for sure, but I make my living as a sensitive guesser.

I reached high, grabbed handholds, drew myself up to another
ledge. I followed it for a time, climbed again.

At length the sun went away, and it made no difference in my
ability to see. Darkness and light changed places.

I scaled a five- or six-meter irregularity and halted when I finally
got a look into the recessed area it rose to. There was an opening in
the face of the mountain to its rear. I hesitated to label it a cave because it appeared artificial. It looked as if it had been carved in the
form of an arch, and it was big enough to ride through on horseback.

What do you know, Frakir commented, twitching once upon
my wrist. *This is it.*

What? I asked.

The first station, she replied. *You stop here and go through a
bit of business before moving on.*

That being?

It's easier just to go and look.

I hauled myself up over the edge, got to my feet, and walked
forward. The big entranceway was filled with that sourceless light.
I hesitated on the threshold, peered within.

It looked to be a generic chapel. There was a small altar, a pair
of candles upon it sporting flickering coronas of blackness. There
were stone benches carved along the walls. I counted five doorways apart from the one by which I stood: three in the wall across
from me; one in that to the right; another to the left. Two piles of
battle gear lay in the middle of the room. There were no symbols
of whatever religion might be represented.

I entered.

What am I supposed to do here? I asked.

You are supposed to sit vigil, guarding your armor overnight.

Aw, come on, I said, moving forward to inspect the stuff. *What's the point?*

That's not a part of the information I've been given.

I picked up a fancy white breastplate which would have made me look like Sir Galahad. Just my size, it seemed. I shook my head and lowered the piece. I moved over to the next pile and picked up a very odd-looking gray gauntlet. I dropped it immediately and rooted through the rest of the stuff. More of the same. Contoured to fit me, also. Only—

What is the matter, Merlin?

The white stuff, I said, *looks as if it would fit me right now. The other armor appears to be of a sort used in the Courts. It looks as if it would fit me just right when I'm shifted into my Chaos form. So either set would probably do for me, depending on circumstances. I can use only one outfit at a time, though. Which am I supposed to guard?*

I believe that's the crux of the matter. I think you're supposed to choose.

Of course! I snapped my fingers, heard nothing. *How slow of me, that I need to have things explained by my strangling cord!*

I dropped to my knees, swept both sets of armor and weapons together into one nasty-looking heap.

If I have to guard them, I said, *I'll guard both sets. I don't care to take sides.*

I've a feeling something isn't going to like that, Frakir answered.

I stepped back and regarded the pile,.

Tell me about this vigil business again, I said. *What all's involved?*

You're supposed to sit up all night and guard it.

Against what?

Against anything that tries to misappropriate it, I guess. The powers of Order—

—or Chaos.

Yeah, I see what you mean. Heaped up together that way, anything might come by to grab off a piece.

I seated myself on the bench along the rear wall, between two doorways. It was good to rest for a bit after my long climb. But something in my mind kept grinding away. Then, after a time, *What's in it for me?* I asked.

What do you mean?

Say I sit here all night and watch the stuff. Maybe something even comes along and makes a pass at it. Say I fight it off. Morning comes, the stuff is still here, I'm still here. Then what? What have I gained?

Then you get to don your armor, pick up your weapons, and move on to the next stage of affairs.

I stifled a yawn.

You know, I don't think I really want any of that stuff, I said then. *I don't like armor, and I'm happy with the sword I've got.* I clapped my hand to its hilt. It felt strange, but then so did I. *Why don't we just leave the whole pile where it is and move on to the next stage now? What is the next stage anyway?*

I'm not sure. The way the Logrus threw information at me it just seems to surface at the appropriate time. I didn't even know about this place till I saw the entrance.

I stretched and folded my arms. I leaned my back against the wall. I extended my legs and crossed them at the ankles.

Then we're stuck here till something happens or you get inspired again?

Right.

Wake me when it's over, I said, and I closed my eyes.

The wrist twitch that followed was almost painful.

Hey! You can't do that! Frakir said. *The whole idea is that you sit up all night and watch.*

And a very half-assed idea it is, I said. I refuse to play such a stupid game. If anything wants the stuff, I'll give it a good price on it.

Go ahead and sleep if you want. But what if something comes along and decides you had better be taken out of the picture first?

To begin with, I replied, *I don't believe that anything could care about that pile of medieval junk, let alone lust after it—and in closing, it's your job to warn me of danger.*

Aye, aye, Captain. But this is a weird place. What if it limits my sensitivity some way?

You're really reaching now, I said. *I guess you'll just have to improvise.*

I dozed. I dreamed that I stood within a magic circle and various things tried to get at me. When they touched the barrier, though, they were transformed into stick figures, cartoon characters which rapidly faded. Except for Corwin of Amber, who smiled faintly and shook his head.

"Sooner or later you'll have to step outside," he said.

"Then let it be later," I replied.

"And all your problems will still be there, right where you left them."

I nodded.

"But I'll be rested," I answered.

"Then it's a trade-off. Good luck."

"Thanks."

The dream fell apart into random images then. I seem to remember standing outside the circle a little later, trying to figure a way to get back in. . . .

I wasn't certain what woke me. It couldn't have been a noise. But suddenly I was alert and rising, and the first thing I beheld was a dwarf with a mottled complexion, his hands clasped at his throat, lying unmoving in a twisted position near the armor pile.

"What's going on?" I tried saying.

But there was no reply.

I crossed and knelt beside the short big-shouldered guy. With my fingertips, I felt after a carotid pulse but couldn't locate one. At that moment, however, I felt a tickling sensation about my wrist, and Frakir—phasing into and out of visibility—made her way back into touch with with me.

You took that guy out? I asked.

There came a soft pulsation then. *Suicides don't strangle themselves,* she replied.

Why didn't you alert me?

You needed your rest, and it wasn't anything I couldn't handle. Our empathy is too strong, though. Sorry I woke you.

I stretched.

How long was I asleep?

Several hours, I'd judge.

I feel kind of sorry about this, I said. *That scrap heap isn't worth somebody's life.*

It is now, Frakir answered.

True. Now that someone's died for the stuff have you gotten the word as to what we do next?

Things are a little clearer, but not enough to act on. We must remain until morning for me to be certain.

Does the information you have include anything on whether there's food or drink available in the neighborhood?

Yes. There's supposed to be a jug of water behind the altar. Also a loaf of bread. But that's for morning. You're supposed to be fasting throughout the night.

That's only if I take this whole business seriously, I said, turning toward the altar.

I took two steps, and the world started to come apart. The floor of the chapel trembled, and I heard my first sounds since my arrival; a deep growling, grating noise came from somewhere far beneath me. A horde of colors flashed through the air of this colorless place, half blinding me with their intensity. Then the colors fled, and the room divided itself. The whiteness grew intense in the vicinity of the archway by which I had entered. I had to raise my hand to shield my eyes against it. Across from this, a profound darkness occurred, masking the three doorways in that wall.

What . . . is it? I asked.

Something terrible, Frakir replied, *beyond my ability to assess.*

I clasped the hilt of the blade I wore and reviewed the spells I still had hanging. Before I could do any more than that, an awful sense of presence pervaded the place. So potent did it seem that I did not feel that drawing my blade or reciting a spell was the most politic action I might take.

Ordinarily I'd have summoned the Sign of the Logrus by then, but that way was barred to me also. I tried clearing my throat, but no sound came forth. Then there came a movement at the heart of the light, a coalescing. . . .

The shape of a Unicorn, like Blake's Tyger, burning bright, took form, so painful to behold that I had to look away.

I shifted my gaze to the deep, cool blackness, but there was no rest for my eyes in that place either. Something stirred within the darkness, and there came another sound—a grating, as of metal being scraped on stone. This was followed by a powerful hissing. The ground trembled again. Curved lines flowed forward. Even before the brightness of the Unicorn etched its lineaments within that mighty gloom, I realized it was the head of a one-eyed serpent which had come partway into the chapel. I shifted my gaze to a point between them, catching each within my peripheral vision. Far better than any attempt to behold either directly. I felt their gazes upon me, the Unicorn of Order and the Serpent of Chaos. It was not a pleasant feeling, and I retreated until the altar was at my back.

Both came slightly farther into the chapel. The Unicorn's head was lowered, horn pointed directly at me. The Serpent's tongue darted in my direction.

"Uh, if either of you want this armor and stuff," I ventured, "I certainly have no object—"

The Serpent hissed and the Unicorn raised a hoof and let it fall, cracking the floor of the chapel, the fracture line racing toward me like a streak of black lightning and halting just at my feet.

"On the other hand," I observed, "no insult is intended by the offer, Your Eminences—"

Wrong thing to say—again, Frakir interjected, weakly.

Tell me what's right, I said, trying for a mental sotto voce.

I don't—Oh!

The Unicorn reared; the Serpent drew itself upward. I dropped to my knees and looked away, their gazes having somehow become physically painful. I was trembling, and all of my muscles had begun to ache.

It is suggested, Frakir recited, *that you play the game the way it is set up.*

What metal entered my backbone I know not. But I raised my head and turned it, looking first to the Serpent, then to the Unicorn. Though my eyes watered and ached as if I were trying to stare down the sun, I managed the gesture.

"You can make me play," I said, "but you cannot make me choose. My will is my own. I will guard this armor all night, as is required of me. In the morning I will go on without it because I do not choose to wear it."

Without it you may die, Frakir stated, as if translating.

I shrugged.

"If it is my choice to make, I choose not to place one of you before the other."

A rush of wind blew hot and cold past me, seemed a cosmic sigh.

You will choose, Frakir relayed, *whether you become aware of it or not. Everyone does. You are simply being asked to formalize your choice.*

"What's so special about my case?" I asked.

Again that wind.

Yours is a dual heritage, combined with great power.

"I never wanted either of you for an enemy," I stated.

Not good enough, came the reply.

"Then destroy me now."

The game is already in progress.
"Then let's get on with it," I answered.
We are not pleased with your attitude.
"Vice versa," I answered.
The thunderclap that followed left me unconscious. The reason I felt I could afford total honesty was a strong hunch that players for this game might be hard to come by.

I woke sprawled across the pile of greaves, cuirasses, gauntlets, helms, and other good things of a similar nature, all of them possessed of corners or protuberances, most of which were jabbing into me. I became aware of this only by degrees, for I had gone numb in lots of important places.
Hi, Merlin.
Frakir, I responded. *Have I been out for long?*
I don't know. I just came around myself.
I didn't know a piece of rope could be knocked out.
Neither did I. It never happened to me before.
Let me amend my question then: Any idea how long we've been out?
Fairly long, I feel. Get me a glimpse out the doorway, and I may be able to give you a better idea.
I pushed myself slowly to my feet, could not remain standing, dropped. I crawled to the entranceway, noting in passing that nothing on the heap seemed to be missing. The floor was indeed cracked. There really was a dead dwarf to the rear of the chamber.
I looked outside, beheld a bright sky, black points disposed within it.
Well? I asked after a time.
If I figure right, it should be morning soon.
Always brightest before the dawn, eh?
Something like that.
My legs burned as their circulation was restored. I pushed myself upright, stood leaning against the wall.
Any new instructions?
Not yet. I've a feeling they're due with the dawn.
I staggered to the nearest bench, collapsed upon it.
If anything comes in now, all I've got to hit it with is an odd assortment of spells. Sleeping on armor leaves a few kinks. Almost as bad as sleeping in it.
Throw me at the enemy and the least I can do is buy you time.

Thanks.

How far back does your memory go?

To when I was a little kid, I guess. Why?

I recall sensations from when I was first enhanced, back in the Logrus. But everything up until we got here is kind of dreamlike. I just sort of used to react to life.

A lot of people are that way, too.

Really? I couldn't think, or communicate this way before.

True.

Do you think it will last?

What do you mean?

Might this just be a temporary condition? Might I just have been enhanced to deal with the special circumstances in this place?

I don't know, Frakir, I answered, massaging my left calf. *I suppose it's possible. Are you getting attached to the state?*

Yes. Silly of me, I guess. How can I care about something I won't miss when it's gone?

Good question, and I don't know the answer. Maybe you would have achieved this state anyway eventually.

I don't think so. But I don't know for certain.

You afraid to regress?

Yes.

Tell you what. When we find a way out of here, you stay behind.

I couldn't do that.

Why not? You've come in handy on occasion, but I can take care of myself. Now you're sentient you should have a life of your own.

But I'm a freak.

Aren't we all? I just want you to know I understand, and it's okay with me.

She pulsed once and shut up.

I wished I weren't afraid to drink the water.

I sat there for perhaps the better part of an hour, going over everything that had happened to me recently, looking for patterns, clues.

I can sort of hear you thinking, Frakir said suddenly, *and I can offer you something in one area.*

Oh? What might that be?

The one who brought you here—

The thing that looked like my father?

Yes.

What of him?

He was different from your other two visitors. He was human. They weren't.

You mean it might actually have been Corwin?

I never met him, so I can't say. He wasn't one of those constructs, though.

Do you know what they were?

No. I only know one peculiar thing about them, and I don't understand it at all.

I leaned forward and rubbed my temples. I took several deep breaths. My throat was very dry, and my muscles ached.

Go ahead. I'm waiting.

I don't quite know how to explain it, Frakir said. *But back in my presentient days you inconsiderately wore me about your wrist when you walked the Pattern.*

I recall. I had a scar for a long time after, from your reaction to it.

Things of Chaos and things of Order do not mix well. But I survived. And the experience is recorded within me. Now the Dworkin and the Oberon figures that visited you back at the cave—

Yes?

Beneath their apparent humanity they were pulsing energy fields within geometrical constructs.

Sounds sort of like computer animation.

Maybe it is something like that. I couldn't say.

And my father wasn't one of these?

Nope. But that wasn't what I was getting at. I recognized the source.

I was suddenly alert.

What do you mean?

The swirls—the geometrical constructs on which the figures were based—they reproduced sections of the Pattern at Amber.

You must be mistaken.

No. What I lacked in sentience I made up in memory. Both figures were three-dimensional twistings of Pattern segments.

Why would the Pattern be creating simulacra to bug me?

I'm just a humble killing aid. Reasoning is not one of my strong points yet.

If the Unicorn and the Serpent are involved, I suppose the Pattern might be also.

We know that the Logrus is.

And it seemed to me that the Pattern demonstrated sentience the day Coral walked it. Say that's true and add on the ability to manufacture constructs—Is this the place it wanted them to bring me? Or did Corwin transport me someplace else? And what does the Pattern want of me? And what does my father want of me?

I envy your ability to shrug, Frakir answered. *Those are what I take it you call rhetorical questions?*

I guess so.

Information of another sort is beginning to come to me, so I assume the night is ending.

I sprang to my feet.

Does that mean I can eat—and drink? I asked.

I believe so.

I moved quickly then.

While I am new to these things, I cannot help wondering whether it might be considered disrespectful to vault over an altar that way, Frakir commented.

The black flames flickered as I passed between them.

Hell, I don't even know what it's an altar to, I answered, *and I've always thought of disrespect as something that had to be identity-specific.*

The ground trembled slightly as I seized the jug and took a deep swallow.

Then, again, perhaps you have a point there, I said, choking.

I carried the jug and the loaf around the altar, past the stiffening dwarf and over to the bench which ran along the back wall. Seating myself, I commenced eating and drinking more slowly.

What comes next? I asked. *You said that the information was flowing again.*

You have kept vigil successfully, she said. *Now you must select what you need from among the armor and weapons you watched, then pass through one of the three doorways in this wall.*

Which one?

One is the door of Chaos, one the door of Order, and I know not the nature of the third.

Uh, how does one make an informed decision in these matters?

I think your way may be barred by all but the one you're supposed to pass.

Then one does not really have a choice, does one?

I believe that the matter of the doorways may be predicated upon the choice one makes in the hardware department.

I finished the bread, washed it down with the rest of the water. I got to my feet then.

Well, I said, *let's see what they'll do if I don't make a choice. Too bad about the dwarf.*

He knew what he was doing, what chances he was taking.

That's more than I can say.

I approached the right-hand door since it was the nearest. It let into a bright corridor which grew brighter and brighter as it receded until sight of it was lost to me beyond a few paces' distance. I kept walking. Damn near broke my nose, too. It was as if I'd encountered a wall of glass. It figures. I couldn't picture myself walking off into the light that way.

You're actually getting more cynical as I watch, Frakir observed. *I caught that thought.*

Good.

I approached the middle one more carefully. It wore gray and seemed to let into a long corridor also. I could see down it perhaps a little farther than the first, though no features other than walls, roof, and floor presented themselves. I extended my arm and discovered that my way was not barred.

Seems to be the one, Frakir observed.

Maybe.

I moved over to the left-hand doorway, its passage black as the inside of God's pocket. Again there was no resistance when I explored for hidden barriers.

Hm. It appears I do have a choice.

Odd. I haven't any instructions to cover this.

I returned to the middle one, took a step forward. Hearing a sound behind me, I turned. The dwarf had sat up. He was holding his sides and laughing. I tried to turn back then, but now something barred my return. Suddenly then the scene dwindled, as if I were accelerating to the rear.

I thought the little guy was dead, I said.

So did I. He gave every indication.

I turned away, back to the direction I'd been headed. There was no feeling of acceleration. Perhaps it was the chapel that was receding while I stood still.

I took a step forward, then another. Not a sound from my footfalls. I began walking. After a few paces I put out my hand to touch the left-hand wall. It encountered nothing. I tried again with the right. Again nothing. I took a step to the right and reached again. Nope. I still seemed approximately equidistant from two shadowy walls. Growling, I ignored them and strode forward.

What's the matter, Merle?

Do you or do you not sense walls to the right and left of us? I asked.

Nope, Frakir replied.

Any idea at all where we are?

We are walking between shadows.

Where are we headed?

Don't know yet. We're following the Way of Chaos, though.

What? How do you know that? I thought we had to pick something Chaosian for the pile to be admitted here.

At this I gave myself a quick search. I found the dagger tucked into my right boot sheath. Even in the dim light I could recognize the workmanship as something from back home.

We were set up somehow, I said. *Now I know why the dwarf was laughing. He planted this on me while we were passed out.*

But you still had a choice—between this and the dark corridor.

True.

So why'd you pick this one?

The light was better.

5

A half dozen steps later even the impression of walls had vanished. Ditto the roof, for that matter. Looking back, I saw no sign of the corridor or its entrance. There was only a vast dismal area. Fortunately the floor or ground remained firm underfoot. The only manner in which I could distinguish the way I traveled from the surrounding gloom had to do with visibility. I walked a pearl-gray trail through a valley of shadow, though, technically, I supposed, I walked between shadows. Picky-picky. Someone or something had grudgingly spilled a minimum of light to mark my way.

I trudged through the eerie silence, wondering how many shadows I passed among, then wondering whether that was too linear a way of considering the phenomenon. Probably.

At that moment, before I could invoke mathematics, I thought I saw something move off to my right. I halted. A tall ebon pillar had come into view, barely, at the edge of vision. But it was not moving. I concluded that it was my own movement which had given it the appearance of motion. Thick, still, smooth—I ran my gaze up that dark shaft until I lost sight of it. There seemed no way of telling how high the thing stood.

I turned away. I took a few more paces. I noted another pillar then—ahead of me, to the left. I gave this one only a glance as I continued. Shortly more came into view at either hand. The darkness into which they ascended held nothing resembling stars, positive or negative; my world's canopy was a simple, uniform blackness. A little later, the pillars occurred in odd groupings, some very near at hand, and their respective sizes no longer seemed uniform.

I halted, reached toward a stand of them to my left which

seemed almost within touching range. It wasn't, though. I took a step in that direction.

There came a quick squeeze at my wrist.

I wouldn't do that if I were you, Frakir observed.

Why not? I inquired.

It might be easy to get lost and into a lot of trouble.

Maybe you're right.

I broke into a jog. Whatever was going on, my only real desire concerning it was to have it over with as soon as possible, so that I could get back to matters I considered important—like locating Coral, springing Luke, finding a way to deal with Jurt and Julia, looking for my father. . . .

The pillars, at varying distances, slid by, and items which were not pillars began occurring among them. Some were squat, asymmetrical; others were tall, tapered; some leaned upon neighbors, bridged them, or lay broken at their bases. It was something of a relief to see that monotonous regularity destroyed, in a way that showed that forces played upon forms.

The ground lost its flatness then, though it retained a stylized geometric quality in the stacked, step, and shelflike appearance of its various levels. My own way remained flat and vaguely lighted as I jogged amid the ruins of a thousand Stonehenges.

I increased my pace, and soon I was running past galleries, amphitheaters, forestlike stands of stone. I seemed to glimpse movement within several of these, but again it could easily have been a function of velocity and poor lighting.

Sense anything alive in the neighborhood? I asked Frakir.

No, came the answer.

Thought I saw something move.

Maybe you did. Doesn't mean it's there.

Talking for less than a day, and you've already learned sarcasm.

I hate to say it, boss, but anything I learn I pick up from your vibes. Ain't no one else around to teach me manners and like that.

Touché, I said. *Maybe I'd better warn you if there's trouble.*

Touché, boss. Hey, I like these combat metaphors.

Moments later I slowed my pace. Ahead something was flickering off to the right. There were moments of blue and red within the changing light intensities. I halted. These glimpses lasted only a few moments but were more than sufficient to make me wary. I regarded their apparent source for a long while.

Yes, Frakir said after a time. *Caution is in order. But don't ask me what to expect. It is only a general feeling of menace that I have.*

Perhaps there's some way I could just sneak by whatever it is.

You'd have to leave the trail to do that, Frakir replied, *and since the trail does run through the circle of stones where it's coming from, I'd say no.*

Nobody told me I couldn't leave the trail. Do you have any instructions to that effect?

I know you are supposed to follow the trail. I've nothing specific concerning the consequences of leaving it, though.

Hm.

The way curved to the right, and I followed it. It ran directly into the massive circle of stones, and though I slowed my pace, I did not deviate I studied it as I drew near, however, and noted that while the trail entered there, it did not emerge again.

You're right, Frakir observed. *Like the den of the dragon.*

But we're supposed to go this way.

Yes.

Then we will.

I'd slowed to a walk by then, and I followed the shining way between two gray plinths.

The lighting was different within the circle from without. There was more of it, though the place was still a study in black and white, with a fairyland sparkle to it. For the first time here I saw something that appeared to be living. There was something like grass underfoot; it was silver and seemed to be studded with dewdrops.

I halted, and Frakir constricted in a very odd fashion—less a warning, it seemed, than a statement of interest. Off to my right was an altar—not at all like the one over which I had vaulted back in the chapel. This one was a rude slab of stone set atop a couple of boulders. No candles, linens, or other ecclesiastical niceties kept company with the lady who lay atop it, her wrists and ankles bound. Because I recalled a similar bothersome situation in which I had once found myself, my sympathies were all with the lady— white-haired, black-skinned, and somehow familiar—my animus with the peculiar individual who stood behind the altar, faced in my direction, blade upraised in his left hand. The right half of his body was totally black; the left, blindingly white. Immediately galvanized by the tableau, I moved forward. My Concerto for Cuisinart and Microwave spell would have minced him and parboiled him in an instant, but it was useless to me when I could not speak the guide words.

I seemed to feel his gaze upon me as I raced toward him, though one side of him was too dark and the other too bright for me to know for certain. And then the knife hand descended and the blade entered her breast beneath the sternum with an arcing movement. At that instant she screamed, and the blood spurted and it was red against all those blacks and whites, and I realized as it covered the man's hand that had I tried, I might have uttered my spell and saved her.

Then the altar collapsed, and a gray whirlwind obliterated my view of the entire tableau. The blood swirled through it to a barber pole-like effect, gradually spreading and attenuating to turn the funnel rosy, then pink, then faded to silver, then gone. When I reached the spot, the grasses sparkled, sans altar, sans priest, sans sacrifice.

I drew up short, staring.

"Are we dreaming?" I asked aloud.

I do not believe I am capable of dreaming, Frakir replied.

"Then tell me what you saw."

I saw a guy stab a lady who was tied up on a stone surface. Then the whole thing collapsed and blew away. The guy was black and white, the blood was red, the lady was Deirdre—

"What? By God, you're right! It did look like her—in negative. But she's already dead—"

I must remind you that I saw whatever you thought you saw. I don't know what the raw data were, just the mixing job your nervous system did on them. My own special perceptions told me that these were not normal people but were beings on the order of the Dworkin and Oberon figures that visited you back in the cave.

An absolutely terrifying thought occurred to me just then. The Dworkin and Oberon figures had had me thinking briefly of three-dimensional computer simulations. And the Ghostwheel's shadow-scanning ability was based on digitized abstractions of portions of the Pattern I believed to be particularly concerned with this quality. And Ghost had been wondering—almost wistfully, it now seemed—concerning the qualifications for godhood.

Could my own creation be playing games with me? Might Ghost have imprisoned me in a stark and distant shadow, blocked all my efforts at communication, and set about playing an elaborate game with me? If he could beat his own creator, for whom he seemed to feel something of awe, might he not feel he had achieved personal elevation—to a level beyond my status in his private cosmos? Maybe. If one keeps encountering computer simulations, *cherchez le deus ex machina.*

It made me wonder just how strong Ghost really was. Though

his power was, in part, an analogue of the Pattern, I was certain it did not match that of the Pattern—or the Logrus. I couldn't see him blocking this place off from either.

On the other hand, all that would really be necessary would be to block me. I suppose he could have impersonated the Logrus in our flash encounter on my arrival. But that would have required Ghost's actually enhancing Frakir, and I didn't believe he could do it. And what about the Unicorn and the Serpent?

"Frakir," I asked, "are you sure it was really the Logrus that enhanced you this time and programmed you with all the instructions you're carrying?"

Yes.

"What makes you certain?"

It had the same feeling as our first encounter back within the Logrus, when I was enhanced initially.

"I see. Next question: Could the Unicorn and the Serpent we saw back in the chapel have been the same sort of things as the Oberon or Dworkin figures back at the cave?"

No. I'd have known. They weren't like them at all. They were terrible and powerful and very much what they seemed.

"Good," I said. "I was worried this might be some elaborate charade on the part of the Ghostwheel."

I see that in your mind. Though I fail to see why the reality of the Unicorn and the Serpent defeats the thesis. They could simply have entered the Ghost's construct to tell you to stop horsing around because they want to see this thing played out.

"I hadn't thought of that."

And maybe the Ghost was able to locate and penetrate a place that is pretty much inaccessible to the Pattern and the Logrus.

"I suppose you've a point there. Unfortunately this pretty much puts me back where I started."

No, because this place is not something Ghost put together. It's always been around. I learned that much from the Logrus.

"I suppose there's some small comfort in knowing that, but—"

I never completed the thought because a sudden movement called my attention to the opposite quadrant of the circle. There I beheld an altar I had not noted before, a female figure standing behind it, a man dappled in shadow and light lying, bound, upon it. They looked very similar to the first pair. . . .

"No!" I cried. "Let it end!"

But the blade descended even as I moved in that direction. The ritual was repeated, and the altar collapsed, and everything again swirled away. When I reached the site, there was no indication that anything unusual had occurred upon it.

"What do you make of that one?" I asked Frakir.

Same forces as before, but somehow reversed.

"Why? What's going on?"

It is a gathering of powers. The Pattern and the Logrus are both attempting to force their way into this place, for a little while. Sacrifices, such as those you just witnessed, help provide the openings they need.

"Why do they wish to manifest here?"

Neutral ground. Their ancient tension is shifting in subtle ways. You are expected in some fashion to tip the balance of power one way or another.

"I haven't the faintest idea how to go about such a thing."

When the time comes, you will.

I returned to the trail and walked on.

"Did I pass by just as the sacrifices were due?" I said. "Or were the sacrifices due because I was passing by?"

They were marked to occur in your vicinity. You are a nexus.

"Then do you think I can expect—"

A figure stepped out from behind a stone to my left and chuckled softly. My hand went to my sword, but his hands were empty, and he moved slowly.

"Talking to yourself. Not a good sign," he remarked.

The man was a study in black, white, and gray. In fact, from the cast of the darkness upon his right-hand side and the lay of the light on his left, he might have been the first wielder of the sacrificial dagger. I'd no real way of telling. Whoever or whatever he or it was, I'd no desire to become acquainted.

So I shrugged.

"The only sign I care about here has 'exit' written on it," I told him as I brushed past him.

His hand fell upon my shoulder and turned me back easily in his direction.

Again the chuckle.

"You must be careful what you wish for in this place," he told me in low and measured tones, "for wishes are sometimes granted here, and if the granter be depraved and read 'quietus' for your 'exit'—why, then, poof! You may cease to be. Up in smoke. Downward to the earth. Sideways to hell and gone."

"I've already been there," I answered, "and lots of points along the way."

"What ho! Look! Your wish *has* been granted," he remarked, his left eye catching a flash of light and reflecting it, tapetumlike, in my direction. No matter how I turned or squinted, however, could I find sight of his right eye. "Over there," he finished, pointing.

I turned my head in the direction he indicated, and there upon the top stone of a dolmen shone an exit sign exactly like the one above the emergency door at a theater I used to frequent near campus.

"You're right," I said.

"Will you go through it?"

"Will you?"

"No need," he replied. "I already know what's there."

"What?" I inquired.

"The other side."

"How droll," I answered.

"If one gets one's wish and spurns it, one might piss off the Powers," he said then.

"You have firsthand knowledge of this?"

I heard a grinding, clicking noise then, and it was several moments before I realized he was gnashing his teeth. I walked away then toward the exit sign, wanting to inspect whatever it represented at nearer range.

There were two standing stones with a flat slab across the top. The gateway thus formed was large enough to walk through. It was shadowy, though. . . .

You going through it, boss?

"Why not? This is one of the few times in my life that I feel indispensable to whoever is running the show."

I wouldn't get too cocky . . . Frakir began, but I was already moving.

Three quick paces were all that it took, and I was looking outward across a circle of stones and sparkling grass past a black-and-white man toward another dolmen bearing an exit sign, a shadowy form within it. Halting, I took a step backward and turned. There was a black-and-white man regarding me, a dolmen to his rear, dark Form within it. I raised my right hand above my head. So did the shadowy figure. I turned back in the direction I had initially been headed. The shadowy figure across from me also had his hand upraised. I stepped on through.

"Small world," I observed, "but I'd hate to paint it."

The man laughed.

"Now you are reminded that your every exit is also an entrance," he said.

"Seeing you here, I am reminded even more of a play by Sartre," I responded.

"Unkind," he answered, "but philosophically cogent. I have always found that hell is other people. Only I have done nothing to rouse your distrust, have I?"

"Were you or were you not the person I saw sacrifice a woman in this vicinity?" I asked.

"Even if I were, what is that to you? You were not involved."

"I guess I have peculiar feelings about little things—like the value of life."

"Indignation is cheap. Even Albert Schweitzer's reverence for life didn't include the tapeworm, the tsetse fly, the cancer cell."

"You know what I mean. Did you or did you not sacrifice a woman on a stone altar a little while ago?"

"Show me the altar."

"I can't. It's gone."

"Show me the woman."

"She is, too."

"Then you haven't much of a case."

"This isn't a court, damn it! If you want to converse, answer my question. If you don't, let's stop making noises at each other."

"I have answered you."

I shrugged.

"All right," I said. "I don't know you, and I'm very happy that way. Good day."

I took a step away from him, back in the direction of the trail. As I did, he said, "Deirdre. Her name was Deirdre, and I did indeed kill her," and he stepped into the dolmen from which I had just emerged, and there he disappeared. Immediately I looked across the way, but he did not exit beneath the exit sign. I did an about-face and stepped into the dolmen myself. I did emerge from the other side, across the way, catching sight of myself entering the opposite one as I did so. I did not see the stranger anywhere along the way.

"What do you make of that?" I asked Frakir as I moved back toward the trail.

A spirit of place, perhaps? A nasty spirit for a nasty place? she ventured. *I don't know, but I think he was one of those damned constructs, too—and they're stronger here.*

I headed down to the trail, set foot upon it, and commenced following it once again.

"Your speech patterns have altered enormously since your enhancement," I remarked.

Your nervous system's a good teacher.

"Thanks. If that guy puts in an appearance again and you sense him before I see him, give me the high sign."

Right. Actually, this entire place has the feeling of one of those constructs. Every stone here has a bit of Pattern scribble to it.

"When did you learn this?"

Back when we first tried the exit. I scanned it for dangers then.

As we came to the periphery of the outer circle, I slapped a stone. It felt solid enough.

He's here! Frakir warned suddenly.

"Hey!" came a voice from overhead, and I looked up. The black-and-white stranger was seated atop the stone, smoking a thin cigar. He held a chalice in his left hand. "You interest me, kid," he went on. "What's your name?"

"Merlin," I answered. "What's yours?"

Instead of replying, he pushed himself outward, fell in slow motion, landed on his feet beside me. His left eye squinted as he studied me. The shadows flowed like dark water down his right side. He blew silvery smoke into the air.

"You're a live one," he announced then, "with the mark of the Pattern and the mark of Chaos upon you. You bear the blood of Amber. What is your lineage, Merlin?"

The shadows parted for a moment, and I saw that his right eye was hidden by a patch.

"I am the son of Corwin," I told him, "and you are— somehow—the traitor Brand."

"You have named me," he said, "but I never betrayed what I believed in."

"That being your own ambition," I said. "Your home and your family and the forces of Order never mattered to you, did they?"

He snorted.

"I will not argue with a presumptuous puppy."

"I've no desire to argue with you either. For whatever it's worth, your son Rinaldo is probably my best friend."

I turned away and began walking. His hand fell upon my shoulder.

"Wait!" he said. "What is this talk? Rinaldo is but a lad."

"Wrong," I answered. "He's around my age."

His hand fell away, and I turned. He had dropped his cigar, which lay smoking upon the trail, and he'd transferred the chalice to his shadow-clad hand. He massaged his brow.

"That much time has passed in the mainlines . . ." he remarked.

On a whim, I withdrew my Trumps, shuffled out Luke's, held it up for him to see.

"That's Rinaldo," I said.

He reached for it, and for some obscure reason I let him take it. He stared at it for a long while.

"Trump contact doesn't seem to work from here," I said.

He looked up, shook his head, and handed the card back to me.

"No, it wouldn't," he stated. "How . . . is he?"

"You know that he killed Caine to avenge you?"

"No, I didn't know. But I'd expect no less of him."

"You're not exactly Brand, are you?"

He threw back his head and laughed.

"I am entirely Brand, and I am not Brand as you might have known him. Anything more than that will cost you."

"What will it cost me to learn what you really are?" I inquired as I cased my cards.

He raised the chalice, held it before him with both hands, like a begging bowl.

"Some of your blood," he said.

"You've become a vampire?"

"No, I'm a Pattern-ghost," he replied. "Bleed for me, and I'll explain."

"All right," I said. "It'd better be a good story, though," and I drew my dagger and pricked my wrist, which I'd extended to a position above his cup.

Like a spilled oil lamp, the flames came forth. I don't really have fire flowing around inside me, of course. But the blood of a Chaosite is highly volatile in certain places, and this, apparently, was such a place.

It spewed forth, half into and half past the cup, splashing over his hand, his forearm. He screamed and seemed to collapse in upon himself. I stepped backward as he was transformed into a vortex—not unlike those following the sacrifices I had witnessed, only this one of the fiery variety—which rose into the air with a roar and vanished a moment later, leaving me startled, staring upward and applying direct pressure to my smoking wrist.

Uh, colorful exit, Frakir remarked.

"Family specialty," I responded, "and speaking of exits . . ."

I stepped past the stone, departing the circle. The darkness moved in again, intensified. Reflexively my trail seemed to brighten. I released my wrist, saw that it had stopped smoking. I broke into a jog then, anxious to be away from that place. When I looked back a little later, I no longer saw the standing stones. There was only a pale, fading vortex, drawing itself upward, upward, then gone.

I jogged on, and the trail began, gradually, to slope until I was running downhill with an easy, loping gait. The trail ran like a bright ribbon downward and off into a great distance before it faded from view. I was puzzled, however, to see that it intersected another glowing line not too far below. These lines quickly faded off to my right and my left.

"Any special instructions pertaining to crossroads?" I inquired.

Not yet, Frakir answered. *Presumably, it's a decision point, with no way of knowing what to base one on till you get there.*

It seemed a vast, shadowy plain that was spread below, with here and there a few isolated dots of light, some of them constant, others appearing, then fading, all of them stationary. There were no other lines, however, than my trail and the one which intersected it. There were no sounds other than my breathing and that of my footfalls. There were no breezes, no peculiar odors, and the temperature was so clement that it claimed no notice. Again there were dark shapes at either hand, but I'd no desire to investigate them. All I wanted was to conclude whatever business was in progress and get the hell out and be about my own affairs as soon as possible.

Hazy patches of light then began occurring at irregular intervals, both sides of the trail, wavery, sourceless, blotchy, popping into and out of existence. These seemed like gauzy, dappled curtains hung beside the trail, and I did not pause to examine them at first, not till the obscure areas grew fewer and fewer, being replaced by shadings of greater and greater distinction. It was almost as if a tuning process were in operation, with increasing clarity of outline indicating familiar objects: chairs; tables; parked cars; store windows. Before long, faded colors began to occur within these tableaus.

I halted beside one and stared. It was a red '57 Chevy with some snow on it, parked in a familiar-looking driveway. I advanced and reached toward it.

My left hand and arm faded as they entered the dim light. I

reached to touch the left fin. There followed a vague sensation of contact and a faint coolness. I swept my hand to the right then, brushing away some of the snow. When I withdrew my hand, there was snow upon it. Immediately the prospect faded to black.

"I intentionally used my left hand," I said, "with you on the wrist. What was there?"

Thanks a lot. It seemed a red car with snow on it.

"It was a construct of something picked from my mind. That's my Polly Jackson painting, upscaled to life size."

Then things are getting worse, Merle. I couldn't tell it was a construct.

"Conclusions?"

Whatever's doing it is getting better at it, or stronger. Or both.

"Shit," I observed, and I turned away and jogged on.

Perhaps something wants to show you that it can baffle you completely now.

"Then it's succeeded," I acknowledged. "Hey, Something!" I shouted. "You hear that? You win! You've baffled me completely. Can I go home now? If it's something else you're trying to do, though, you've failed! I'm missing the point completely!"

The dazzling flash which followed cast me down upon the trail and blinded me for several long moments. I lay there tense and twitching, but no thunderclap followed. When my vision cleared and my muscles stopped their spasms, I beheld a giant regal figure posed but a few paces before me: Oberon.

Only it was a statue, a duplicate of one which occupied the far end of the Main Concourse back in Amber, or possibly even the real thing, for on closer inspection I noted what appeared to be bird droppings upon the great man's shoulder.

"Real thing or construct?" I said aloud.

Real, I'd say, Frakir replied.

I rose slowly.

"I understand this to be an answer," I said. "I just don't understand what it means."

I reached out to touch it, and it felt like canvas rather than bronze. In that instant my perspective somehow shifted, and I felt myself touching a larger than life-size painting of the Father of His Country. Then its borders began to waver, it faded, and I saw that it was part of one of those hazy tableaux I had been passing. Then it rippled and was gone.

"I give up," I said, walking through the space it had occupied but moments before. "The answers are more confusing than the situations that cause the questions."

Since we are passing between shadows, could this not be a statement that all things are real—somewhere?

"I suppose. But I already knew that."

And that all things are real in different ways, at different times, in different places?

"Okay, what you are saying could well be the message. I doubt that something is going to these extremes, however, just to make philosophical points that may be new to you but are rather well worn elsewhere. There must be a special reason, one that I still don't grasp."

Up until now the scenes I'd passed had been still lifes. Now, however, a number occurrred which contained people; some, other creatures. In these, there was action—some of it violent, some amorous, some simply domestic.

Yes, it seems to be a progression. It may be leading up to something.

"When they leap out and attack me, I'll know I've arrived."

Who knows? I gather that art criticism is a complex area.

But the sequences faded shortly thereafter, and I was left jogging on my bright trail through darkness once again. Down, down the still gentle slope toward the crossroads. Where was the Cheshire Cat when rabbit hole logic was what I really needed?

One moment I was watching the crossroads as I advanced upon it. An eye blink later I was still watching the crossroads, only now the scene was altered. There was now a lamppost on the near right-hand corner. A shadowy figure stood beneath it, smoking.

"Frakir, how'd they pull that one?" I asked.

Very quickly, she replied.

"What do the vibes read?"

Attention focused in your direction. No vicious intent, yet.

I slowed as I drew near. The trail became pavement, curbs at either hand, sidewalks beyond them. I stepped out of the street onto the right-hand walk. As I moved along it, a damp fog blew past me, hung between me and the light. I slowed my pace even more. Shortly I saw that the pavement had grown damp. My footsteps echoed as if I walked between buildings. By then the fog had grown too dense for me to discern whether buildings had actually occurred beside me. It felt as if they had, for there were darker areas here and there within the gloom. A cold wind began to blow against my back, and droplets of moisture fell upon me at random intervals. I halted. I turned up the collar of my cloak. From somewhere entirely out of sight, high overhead, came the faint buzzing sound of an airplane. I began walking again after it had gone by. Tinily then, and muffled, from across the street perhaps, came the sound of a piano playing a half-familiar tune. I drew my cloak about me. The fog swirled and thickened.

Three paces more, and then it cleared, and she was standing before me, back against the lamppost. A head shorter than I was, she had on a trench coat and a black beret, her hair glossy, inky. She dropped her cigarette and slowly ground it out beneath the toe of a high-heeled black patent-leather shoe. I glimpsed something of her leg as she did so, and it was perfectly formed. She removed from within her coat then a flat silver case, the raised outline of a rose upon it, opened it, took out a cigarette, placed it between her lips, closed the case, and put it away. Then, without looking at me, she asked, "Have you a light?"

I hadn't any matches, but I wasn't about to let a little thing like that deter me.

"Of course," I said, extending my hand slowly toward those delicate features. I kept it turned slightly away from her so that she could not see that it was empty. As I whispered the guide word which caused the spark to leap from my fingertip to the tip of the cigarette, she raised her hand and touched my own, as if to steady it. And she raised her eyes—large, deep blue, long-lashed—and met mine as she drew upon it. Then she gasped, and the cigarette fell away.

"*Mon Dieu!*" she said, and she threw her arms about me, pressed herself against me, and began to sob. "Corwin!" she said. "You've found me! It has been forever!"

I held her tightly, not wanting to speak, not wanting to break her happiness with something as cloddish as truth. The hell with truth. I stroked her hair.

After a long while she pulled away, looked up at me. A moment or so more, and she would realize that it was only a resemblance and that she was seeing but what she wanted to see. So, "What's a girl like you doing in a place like this?" I asked.

She laughed softly.

"Have you found a way?" she said, and then her eyes narrowed. "You're not—"

I shook my head.

"I hadn't the heart," I told her.

"Who are you?" she asked, taking a half step backward.

"My name is Merlin, and I'm on a crazy quest I don't understand."

"Amber," she said softly, her hands still on my shoulders, and I nodded.

"I don't know you," she said then. "I feel that I should, but . . . I . . . don't. . . ."

Then she came to me again and rested her head on my chest. I started to say something, to try to explain, but she placed a finger across my lips.

"Not yet, not now, maybe never," she said. "Don't tell me. Please don't tell me more. But *you* ought to know whether you're a Pattern-ghost."

"Just what is a Pattern-ghost?" I said.

"An artifact created by the Pattern. It records everyone who walks it. It can call us back whenever it wants, as we were at one of the times we walked it. It can use us as it would, send us where it will with a task laid upon us—a *geas,* if you like. Destroy us, and it can create us over again."

"Does it do this sort of thing often?"

"I don't know. I'm not familiar with its will, let alone its operations with any other than myself." Then, "You're not a ghost! I can tell!" she announced suddenly, taking hold of my hand. "But there is something different about you—different from others of the blood of Amber. . . ."

"I suppose," I answered. "I trace my lineage to the Courts of Chaos as well as to Amber."

She raised my hand to her mouth as if she were about to kiss it. But her lips moved by, to the place on my wrist where I had cut myself at Brand's request. Then it hit me: Something about the blood of Amber must hold a special attraction for Pattern-ghosts.

I tried to draw my hand away, but the strength of Amber was hers also.

"The fires of Chaos sometimes flow within me," I said. "They may do you harm."

She raised her head slowly and smiled. There was blood on her mouth. I glanced down and saw that my wrist was wet with it, too.

"The blood of Amber has power over the Pattern," she began, and the fog rolled, churned about her ankles. "No!" she cried then, and she bent forward once more.

The vortex rose to her knees, her calves. I felt her teeth upon my wrist, tearing. I knew of no spell to fight this thing, so I laid my arm across her shoulder and stroked her hair. Moments later she dissolved within my embrace, becoming a bloody whirlwind.

"Go right," I heard her wail as she spun away from me, her cigarette still smoldering upon the pavement, my blood dripping beside it.

I turned away. I walked away. Faintly, faintly, through the night and the fog I could still hear the piano playing some tune from before my time.

6

I took the road to the right, and everywhere my blood fell reality melted a little. I heal fast, though, and I stopped bleeding soon. Even stopped throbbing before too long.

You got blood all over me, boss.

"Could have been fire," I observed.

I got singed a little, too, back at the stones.

"Sorry about that. Figure out what's going on yet?"

No new instructions, if that's what you mean. But I've been thinking, now I know how to do it, and this place gets more and more fascinating. This whole business of Pattern-ghosts, for instance. If the Pattern can't penetrate here directly, it can at least employ agents. Wouldn't you think the Logrus might have some way of doing the same?

"I suppose it's possible."

I get the impression there's some sort of duel going on between them here, on the underside of reality, between shadows. What if this place came first? Before Shadow, even? What if they've been fighting here since the very beginning, in some strange metaphysical way?

"What if they have?"

That could almost make Shadow an afterthought, a by-product of the tension between the poles.

"I'm afraid you've lost me, Frakir."

What if Amber and the Courts of Chaos were created only to provide agents for this conflict?

"And what if this idea were placed within you by the Logrus during your recent enhancement?"

Why?

"Another way to make me think that the conflict is more important than the people. Another pressure to make me choose a side."

I don't feel manipulated.

"As you pointed out, you're new to this thinking business. And that's a pretty damned abstract line of thought for you to be following this early in the game."

Is it?

"Take my word for it."

What does that leave us with?

"Unwelcome attention from On High."

Better watch your language if this is their war zone.

"A pox on both their houses. For some reason I don't understand, they need me for this game. They'll put up with it."

From somewhere up ahead I heard a roll of thunder.

See what I mean?

"It's a bluff," I replied.

Whose?

"The Pattern's, I believe. Its ghosts seem in charge of reality in this sector."

You know, we could be wrong on all of this. Just shooting in the dark.

"I also feel shot at out of the dark. That's why I refuse to play by anybody else's rules."

Have you got a plan?

"Hang loose. And if I say 'kill,' do it. Let's get to where we're going."

I began to run again, leaving the fog, leaving the ghosts to play at being ghosts in their ghost city. Bright road through dark country, me running, reverse shadow-shifting, as the land tried to change me. And there ahead a flare and more thunder, virtual street scene flashing into and out of existence beside me.

And then it was as if I raced myself, dark figure darting along a bright way—till I realized it was indeed, somehow, a mirror effect. The movements of the figure to my right which paralleled my own mimicked mine; fleeting scenes to my left were imaged to the other's right.

What's going on, Merle?

"Don't know," I said. "But I'm not in the mood for symbolism, allegory, and assorted metaphorical crap. If it's supposed to mean that life is a race with yourself, then it sucks—unless they're real platitudinizing Powers that are running this show. Then I guess it would be in character. What do you think?"

I think you might still be in danger of being struck by lightning.
The lightning did not follow, but my reflection did. The imaging effect continued for much longer than any of the previous beside-the-road sequences I'd witnessed. I was about to dismiss it, to ignore it completely, when my reflection put on a burst of speed and shot ahead of me.

Uh-oh.

"Yeah," I agreed, stepping up my own pace to close the gap with and match the stride of that dark other.

We were parallel for no more than a few meters after I caught up. Then it began to pull ahead again. I stepped up my pace and caught up once more. Then, on an impulse, I sucked air, bore down, and moved ahead.

My double noted it after a time, moved faster, began to gain. I pushed harder, held my lead. What the hell were we racing for anyway?

I looked ahead. In the distance I could see an area where the trail widened. There appeared to be a tape stretched across it at that point. Okay. Whatever the significance, I decided to go for it.

I held my lead for perhaps a hundred meters before my shadow began to gain on me again. I leaned into it and was able to hold that shortened distance for a time. Then it moved again, coming up on me at a pace I suspected might be hard to hold the rest of the way to the tape. Still, it was not the sort of thing one waited around to find out. I poured it on. I ran all out.

The son of a bitch gained on me, kept gaining, caught me, drew ahead, faltered for an instant. I was back beside it in that instant. But the thing did not flag again. It held the terrible pace at which we were now moving, and I had no intention of stopping unless my heart exploded.

We ran on, damn near side by side. I didn't know whether I had a finishing spurt in me or not. I couldn't tell whether I was slightly ahead, just abreast, or slightly to the rear of the other. We pounded our parallel gleaming trails toward the line of brightness when abruptly the sensation of a glass interface vanished. The two narrow-seeming trails became one wide one. The other's arms and legs were moving differently from my own.

We drew closer and closer together as we entered the final stretch—close enough, finally, for recognition. It was not an image of myself that I was running against, for its hair streamed back and I saw that its left ear was missing.

I found a final burst of speed. So did the other. We were awfully close together when we came to the tape. I think that I hit it first, but I could not be certain.

We went on through and collapsed, gasping. I rolled quickly, to keep him under surveillance, but he just lay there, panting. I rested my right hand on the hilt of my weapon and listened to the sound of my blood in my ears.

When I'd caught my breath somewhat, I remarked, "Didn't know you could run a race like that, Jurt."

He gave a brief laugh.

"There're a lot of things you don't know about me, brother."

"I'm sure," I said.

Then he wiped his brow with the back of his hand, and I noted that the finger he'd lost in the caves of Kolvir was back in place. Either this was the Jurt of a different time line or—

"So how's Julia?" I asked him. "Is she going to be all right?"

"Julia?" he said. "Who's that?"

"Sorry," I said. "You're the wrong Jurt."

"Now what else does that mean?" he asked, propping himself on an elbow and glaring at me with his good eye.

"The real Jurt was never anywhere near the Pattern of Amber—"

"I *am* the real Jurt!"

"You've got all your fingers. He lost one very recently. I was there."

He looked away suddenly.

"You must be a Logrus-ghost," I continued. "It must pull the same stunt the Pattern does—recording those who make it through it."

"Is that . . . what happened?" he asked. "I couldn't quite recall . . . why I was here—except to race with you."

"I'll bet your most recent memories before this place involve negotiating the Logrus."

He looked back. He nodded.

"You're right. What does it all mean?" he asked.

"I'm not sure," I said. "But I've got some ideas about it. This place is a kind of eternal underside to Shadow. It's damn near off limits for both the Pattern and the Logrus. But both can apparently penetrate here by means of their ghosts—artificial constructs from the recordings they made of us back when we passed through them—"

"You mean that all I am is some sort of recording?" He looked as if he were about to cry. "Everything seemed so glorious just a little while ago. I'd made it through the Logrus. All of Shadow lay at my feet." He massaged his temples. Then, "You!" he spat. "I was somehow brought here because of you—to compete with you, to show you up in this race."

"You did a pretty good job, too. I didn't know you could run like that."

"I started practicing when I learned you were doing it in college. Wanted to get good enough to take you on."

"You got good," I acknowledged.

"But I wouldn't be in this damned place if it weren't for you. Or—" He gnawed his lip. "That's not exactly right, is it?" he asked. "*I* wouldn't be anywhere. I'm just a recording. . . ." Then he stared directly at me. "How long do we last?" he said. "How long is a Logrus-ghost good for?"

"I've no idea," I said, "what goes into creating one or how it's maintained. But I've met a number of Pattern-ghosts, and they gave me the impression that my blood would somehow sustain them, give them some sort of autonomy, some independence of the Pattern. Only one of them—Brand—got the fire instead of the blood, and it dissolved. Deirdre got the blood but was taken away then. I don't know whether she got enough."

He shook his head.

"I've a feeling—I don't know where it comes from—that something like that would work for me, too, and that it's blood for the pattern, fire for the Logrus."

"I don't know how to tell in what regions my blood is volatile," I said.

"It'd flame here," he answered. "Depends on who's in control. I just seem to know it. I don't know how."

"Then why did Brand show up in Logrus territory?"

He grinned.

"Maybe the Pattern sought to use a traitor for some sort of subversion. Or maybe Brand was trying to pull something on his own—like double-crossing the Pattern."

"That would be in character," I agreed, my breath finally slowing.

I whipped the Chaos blade out of my boot, slashed my left forearm, saw that it spouted fire, and held it toward him.

"Quick! Take it if you can!" I cried. "Before the Logrus calls you back!"

He seized my arm and seemed almost to inhale the fire that fountained from me. Looking down, I saw his feet become transparent, then his legs. The Logrus seemed anxious to reclaim him, just as the Pattern had Deirdre. I saw the fiery swirls begin within the haze that had been his legs. Then, suddenly, they flickered out, and the outline of those limbs became visible once again. He continued to draw my volatile blood from me, though I could no longer see flames as he was drinking now as Deirdre had, directly from the wound. His legs began to solidify.

"You seem to be stabilizing," I said. "Take more."

Something struck me in the right kidney, and I jerked away, turning as I fell. A tall dark man stood beside me, withdrawing his boot from having kicked me. He had on green trousers and a black shirt, a green bandanna tied about his head.

"Now what perverse carrying-on is this?" he asked. "And in a sacred spot?"

I rolled to my knees and continued on up to my feet, my right arm bending, its wrist turning over, coming in to hold the dagger beside my hip. I raised my left arm, extended it before me. Blood rather than fire now fell from my latest wound.

"None of your damn business," I said, then added his name, having grown certain on the way up, "Caine."

He smiled and bowed, and his hands crossed and came apart. They'd been empty going in, but the right one held a dagger coming out. It must have come from a sheath strapped to his left forearm, inside the billowy sleeve. He had to have practiced the move a lot, too, to be that fast at it. I tried to remember things I'd heard about Caine and knives, and then I did and wished I hadn't. He was supposed to have been a master knife fighter. Shit.

"You have the advantage of me," he stated. "You look very familiar, but I do not believe I know you."

"Merlin," I said. "Corwin's son."

He had begun circling me slowly, but he halted.

"Excuse me if I find that difficult to believe."

"Believe as you wish. It is true."

"And this other one—his name is Jurt, isn't it?"

He gestured toward my brother, who had just gotten to his feet.

"How do you know that?" I asked.

He halted, furrowing his brow, narrowing his eyes.

"I—I'm not certain," he said then.

"I am," I told him. "Try to remember where you are and how you got here."

He backed away, two paces. Then he cried, "He's the one!" just as I saw it coming and shouted, "Jurt! Watch out!"

Jurt turned and bolted. I threw the dagger—always a bad thing to do, save that I was wearing a sword with which I could reach Caine before Caine could reach me now.

Jurt's speed was still with him, and he was out of range in an instant. The dagger, surprisingly, struck at the side of Caine's right shoulder point first, penetrating perhaps an inch or so into muscle. Then, even before he could turn back toward me, his body erupted in a dozen directions, emitting a series of vortices which sucked away all semblance of humanity in an instant, producing high-pitched whistling sounds as they orbited one another, two of them merging into a larger entity, which quickly absorbed the others then, its sound falling lower with each such acquisition. Finally there was but the one. For a moment it swayed toward me, then shot skyward and blew apart. The dagger was blown back in my direction, landing a pace to my right. When I recovered it, I found it to be warm, and it hummed faintly for several seconds before I sheathed it in my boot.

"What happened?" Jurt asked, turning back, approaching.

"Apparently Pattern-ghosts react violently to weapons from the Courts," I said.

"Good thing you had it handy. But why did he turn on me like that?"

"I believe that the Pattern sent him to stop you from gaining autonomy—or to destroy you if you already had. I've a feeling it doesn't want agents of the other side gaining strength and stability in this place."

"But I'm no threat. I'm not on anybody's side but my own. I just want to get the hell out of here and be about my own business."

"Perhaps that of itself constitutes a threat."

"How so?" he asked.

"Who knows what your unusual background may fit you for as an independent agent—in light of what's going on? You may disturb the balance of the Powers. You may possess or have access to information which the principals do not wish to see bruited about the streets. You may be like the gipsy moth. Nobody could see what its effect on the environment would be when it escaped from the lab. You may—"

"Enough!" He raised a hand to silence me. "I don't care about any of those things. If they let me go and leave me alone, I'll stay out of their way."

"I'm not the one you have to convince," I told him.

He stared at me for a moment, then turned, describing a full circle. Darkness was all that I could see beyond the light of the roadway, but he called out in a large voice to anything, I suppose, "Do you hear me? I don't want to be involved in all this. I just want to go away. Live and let live, you know? Is that okay with you?"

I reached forward, caught hold of his wrist, and jerked him toward me. I did this because I had seen a small, ghostly replica of the Sign of the Logrus begin to take form in the air above his head. An instant later it fell, flashing like a lightning stroke, to the accompaniment of a sound like the cracking of a whip, passing through the space he had been occupying, opening a gap in the trail as it vanished.

"I guess it's not that easy to resign," he said. He glanced overhead. "It could be readying another of those right now. It could strike again anytime, when I least expect it."

"Just like real life," I agreed. "But I think you may take it as a warning shot and let it go at that. They have a hard time reaching here. More important, since I was led to believe that this is my quest, do you know offhand whether you're supposed to be helping me or hindering me?"

"Now that you mention it," he said, "I remember suddenly being where I was with a chance to race you and a feeling that we'd fight or something afterward."

"What're your feelings on that now?"

"We've never gotten along all that well. But I don't like the idea of being used like this either."

"You willing to call a truce till I can see my way through this game and out of here?"

"What's in it for me?" he asked.

"I *will* find a way out of this damned place, Jurt. Come along and give me a hand—or at least don't get in the way—and I'll take you with me when I go."

He laughed.

"I'm not sure there is a way out of here," he said, "unless the Powers release us."

"Then you've nothing to lose," I told him, "and you'll probably even get to see me die trying."

"Do you really know both kinds of magic—Pattern and Logrus?" he asked.

"Yeah. But I'm a lot better at Logrus."

"Can you use either against its source?"

"That's a very intriguing metaphysical point, and I don't know the answer," I said, "and I'm not sure I'll find out. It's dangerous to invoke the Powers here. So all I'm left with is a few hung spells. I don't think it's magic that'll get us out of here."

"What, then?"

"I'm not certain. I am sure that I won't see the full picture till I get to the end of this trail, though."

"Well, hell—I don't know. This doesn't seem the healthiest place for me to spend my time. On the other hand, what if it's the only place something like me can have an existence? What if you find me a door and I step through it and melt?"

"If the Pattern-ghosts can manifest in Shadow, I'd guess you can, too. Those of Dworkin and Oberon came to me on the outside before I came to this place."

"That's encouraging. Would you try it if it were you?"

"You bet your life," I said.

He snorted.

"I get the point. I'll go a ways with you and see what happens. I'm not promising to help, but I won't sabotage you."

I held out my hand, and he shook his head.

"Let's not get carried away," he told me. "If my word's no good without a handshake, it's no good with one, is it?"

"I guess not."

"And I've never had a great desire to shake hands with you."

"Sorry I asked," I said. "Would you mind telling me why, though? I've always wondered."

He shrugged.

"Why does there always have to be a reason?" he said.

"The alternative is irrationality," I replied.

"Or privacy," he responded, turning away.

I commenced walking the trail once more. Shortly Jurt fell into step beside me. We walked for a long while in silence. One day I may learn when to keep my mouth shut or to quit when I'm ahead. Same thing.

The trail ran straight for a time but seemed to vanish not too far ahead. When we neared the point of vanishment, I saw why: The trail curved behind a low prominence. We followed this turning and met with another shortly thereafter. Soon we had entered upon a regular series of switchbacks, realizing quickly that they were mitigating a fairly steep descent. As we proceeded down this turning way, I suddenly became aware of a bright squiggle, hanging in the middle distance. Jurt raised his hand, pointing at it, and began, "What . . . ?" just as it became apparent that it was the continuation of our trail, rising. At this, an instant reorientation occurred, and I realized that we were descending into what seemed a massive pit. And the air seemed to have grown somewhat cooler.

We continued our descent, and after a time something cold and moist touched the back of my right hand. I looked down in time to see a snowflake melting in the twilight glow which surrounded us. Moments later several more breezed by. A little after that we became aware of a larger brightness, far below.

I don't know what it is either, Frakir pulsed into my mind.

Thanks, I thought strongly back at her, having decided against advising Jurt of her presence.

Down. Down and around. Back. Back and forth. The temperature continued to decline. Snowflakes flitted. Arrays of rocks in the wall we now descended took on a bit of glitter.

Oddly, I didn't realize what it was until the first time I slipped.

"Ice!" Jurt announced suddenly, half toppling and catching himself up against the stone.

A distant sighing sound occurred, and it grew and grew, nearing us. It was not until it arrived, with a great buffeting gust, that we knew it to be a wind. And cold. It fled past like the breath of an ice age, and I raised my cloak against it. It followed us, softer thereafter, yet persistent, as we continued our descent.

By the time we reached the bottom it was damn cold, and the steps were either fully frosted over or carved of ice. The wind blew a steady, mournful note, and flakes of snow or pellets of ice came and went.

"Miserable climate!" Jurt growled, teeth chattering.

"I didn't think ghosts were susceptible to the mundane," I said.

"Ghost, hell!" he observed. "I feel the same as I always did. You'd think whatever sent me fully dressed to cross your trail might at least have provided for this eventuality.

"And this place isn't that mundane," he added. "They want us somewhere, you'd think they might have provided a shortcut. As it is, we'll be damaged merchandise by the time we get there."

"I don't really believe that either the Pattern or the Logrus has that much power in this place," I told him. "I'd just as soon they stayed out of our way entirely."

Our trail led outward across a gleaming plain—so flat and so gleaming that I feared it to consist entirely of ice. Nor was I incorrect.

"Looks slippery," Jurt said. "I'm going to shapeshift my feet, make them broader."

"It'll destroy your boots and leave you with cold feet," I said. "Why not just shift some of your weight downward, lower your center of gravity?"

"Always got an answer," he began sullenly. Then, "But this time you're right," he finished.

We stood there for several minutes as he grew shorter, more squat.

"Aren't you going to shift yourself?" he asked.

"I'll take my chances holding my center. I can move faster this way," I said.

"You can fall on your ass that way, too."

"We'll see."

We started out. We held our balance. The winds were stronger away from the wall we had descended. The surface of our icy trail, however, was not so slick as it had appeared on distant inspection. There were small ripples and ridges to it, adequate to provide some traction. The air burned its way into my lungs; flakes were beaten into swirling snow devil towers which fled like eccentric tops across our way. It was a bluish glow which emanated from the trail, tinting those flakes which came within its ambit. We hiked for perhaps a quarter mile before a new series of ghostly images began. The first appeared to be myself, sprawled across a heap of armor back at the chapel; the second was Deirdre beneath a lamppost, looking at her watch.

"What?" Jurt asked, as they came and went in a matter of instants.

"I didn't know the first time I saw them, and I still don't know," I answered, "though I thought you might be one of them when we first began our race. They come and go—at random, it would seem—with no special reason that I can figure."

The next was what appeared to be a dining room, a bowl of flowers on the table. There were no people in the room. There and gone—

No. Not entirely. It went away, but the flowers remained, there on the surface of the ice. I halted, then walked out toward them.

Merle, I don't know about leaving the trail. . . .

Oh, shit, I responded, moving toward a slab of ice which reminded me of the Stonehenge-like area back where I'd come aboard, incongruous flashes of color near its base.

There were a number of them—roses of many sorts. I stooped and picked one up. Its color was almost silver. . . .

"What *are* you doing here, dear boy?" I heard a familiar voice say.

I straightened immediately, to see that the tall dark figure which had emerged from behind the block of ice was not addressing me. He was nodding to Jurt, smiling.

"A fool's errand, I'm sure," Jurt replied.

"And this must be the fool," the other responded, "plucking that damnable flower. Silver rose of Amber—Lord Corwin's, I believe. Hello, Merlin. Looking for your father?"

I removed one of the spare clasp pins I keep pinned to the inside of my cloak. I used it to fasten the rose at my left breast. The speaker was Lord Borel, a duke of the royal House of Swayvill and reputedly one of my mother's lovers of long ago. He was also deemed to be one of the deadliest swordsmen in the Courts. Killing my father or Benedict or Eric had been an obsession with him for years. Unfortunately it had been Corwin whom he'd met, at a time when Dad was in a hurry—and they'd never crossed blades. Dad had suckered him instead and killed him in what I supposed was technically a somewhat less than fair fight. Which is okay. I'd never much liked the guy.

"You're dead, Borel. You know that?" I told him. "You're just a ghost of the man you were the day you took the Logrus. Out in the real world there is no Lord Borel anymore. You want to know why? Because Corwin killed you the day of the Patternfall War."

"You lie, you little shit!" he told me.

"Uh, no," Jurt offered. "You're dead all right. Run through, I heard. Didn't know it was Corwin did it, though."

"It was," I said.

He looked away, and I saw his jaw muscles bunching and relaxing, bunching and relaxing.

"And this place is some sort of afterlife?" he asked a little later, still not looking back at us.

"I suppose you could call it that," I said.

"Can we die yet again here?"

"I think so," I told him.

"What is that?"

His gaze had suddenly dropped, and I followed it. Something lay upon the ice nearby, and I took a step toward it.

"An arm," I replied. "It appears to be a human arm."

"What's it doing there?" Jurt asked, walking over and kicking it.

It moved in a fashion which showed us that it was not simply lying there but rather was extended up out of the ice. In fact, it twitched and continued to flex spasmodically for several seconds after Jurt kicked it. Then I noted another, some distance away, and what appeared to be a leg. Farther on, a shoulder, arm attached, a hand . . .

"Some cannibal's deep freeze," I suggested.

Jurt chuckled.

"Then you're dead, too," Borel stated.

"Nope," I replied. "I'm the real thing. Just passing through, on my way to a far, far better place."

"What of Jurt?"

"Jurt's an interesting problem, both physically and theologically," I explained. "He's enjoying a peculiar kind of bilocation."

"I'd hardly say I'm enjoying it," Jurt observed. "But considering the alternative, I suppose I'm glad I'm here."

"That's the sort of positive thinking that's worked so many wonders for the Courts over the years," I said.

Jurt chuckled again.

I heard that metallic sighing sound one does not easily forget. I knew that I could not possibly draw my blade, turn, and parry in time if Borel wished to run me through from the rear. On the other hand, he took great pride in observing every punctilio when it came to killing people. He always played fair because he was so damned good that he never lost anyway. Might as well go for the reputation, too. I immediately raised both hands, to irritate him by acting as if he had just threatened me from the rear.

Stay invisible, Frakir. When I turn and snap my wrist, let go. Stick to him when you hit, find your way to his throat. You know what to do when you get there.

Right, boss, she replied.

"Draw your blade and turn, Merle."

"Doesn't sound too sporting to me, Borel," I replied.

"You dare to accuse me of anything less than propriety?" he said.

"Hard to tell when I can't see what you're up to," I answered.

"Then draw your weapon and turn around."

"I'm turning," I said. "But I'm not touching the thing."

I turned quickly, snapping my left wrist, feeling Frakir depart. As I did, my feet went out from under me. I'd moved too fast on a very smooth patch of ice. Catching myself, I felt a shadow drift into place before me. When I looked up, I beheld the point of Borel's blade, about six inches from my right eye.

"Rise slowly," he said, and I did.

"Draw your weapon now," he ordered.

"And if I refuse?" I inquired, trying to buy time.

"You will prove yourself unworthy to be considered a gentleman, and I will act accordingly."

"By attacking me anyway?" I asked.

"The rules permit this," he said.

"Shove your rules," I replied, crossing my right foot behind my left and springing backward as I drew my blade and let it fall into a guard position.

He was on me in an instant. I continued my retreat, backing past the big slab of ice from behind which he had appeared. I had no desire to stand and trade techniques with him, especially now that I could see the speed of those attacks. Parrying them took a lot less effort while I was backing off. My blade did not feel quite right, however, and as I scanned it quickly I saw why. It was *not* my weapon.

In the glittering light from the trail, bounced off the ice, I saw the swirling inlay along part of the blade. There was only one weapon like this that I knew of, and I had only just seen it recently, in what might have been my father's hand. It was Grayswandir that moved before me. I felt myself smile at the irony. This was the weapon which had slain the real Lord Borel.

"You smile at your own cowardice?" he asked. "Stand and fight, bastard!"

As if in answer to his suggestion, I felt my rearward movement arrested. I was not run through when I ventured a quick downward glance, however, for I realized from his expression that something similar had happened to my attacker.

Our ankles had been seized by several of those hands which extended up through the ice, holding us firmly in place. And this made it Borel's turn to smile, for though he could not lunge, I could no longer retreat. Which meant—

His blade flashed forward, and I parried in quarte, attacked in sixte. He parried and feinted. Then quarte again, and the next attack. Riposte. Parry sixte—No, that was a feint. Catch him in four. Feint. Feint again. Hit—

Something white and hard passed over his shoulder and struck my forehead. I fell back, though the grasping hands kept me from collapsing completely. Good thing I sagged, actually, or his thrust might have punctured my liver. My reflexes or some touch of the magic I've heard may dwell in Grayswandir threw my arm forward as my knees buckled. I felt the blade strike something, though I was not even looking in that direction, and I heard Borel grunt surprisedly, then utter an oath. I heard Jurt mouthing an oath of his own about then, too. He was out of my line of sight.

Then came a bright flash, even as I flexed my legs, stabilizing, parried a head cut, and began rising. I saw then that I had succeeded in cutting Borel's forearm, and fire spurted fountainlike from the wound. His body began to glow, his lower outline to blur.

"It was by no skill you bested me!" he cried.

I shrugged.

"It isn't the Winter Olympics either," I told him.

He changed his grip on his blade, drew back his arm, and hurled the weapon at me—right before he dissolved into a tower of sparks and was drawn upward and vanished above.

I parried the blade, and it passed me to the left, buried itself partway in the ice and stood vibrating there, like something in a Scandinavian's version of Arthurian legend. Jurt rushed toward me, kicked at the hands which held my ankles until they released me, and squinted at my brow.

I felt something fall upon me.

Sorry, boss. I hit around his knee. By the time I reached his throat he was already on fire, Frakir said.

All's well that ends well, I replied. *You weren't singed, were you? Didn't even feel the heat.*

"Sorry I hit you with that piece of ice," Jurt said. "I was aiming at Borel."

I moved away from the plain of hands, heading back toward the trail.

"Indirectly it helped," I said, but I didn't feel like thanking him. How could I know where he'd really been aiming? I glanced back once, and several of the hands Jurt had kicked were giving us the finger.

Why had I been wearing Grayswandir? Would another weapon have affected a Logrus-ghost as strongly? Had it really been my father, then, who had brought me here? And had he felt I might need the extra edge his weapon could provide? I wanted to think so, to believe that he had been more than a Pattern-ghost. And if he was, I wondered at his part in the entire affair. What might he know about all this? And which side might he be on?

The winds died down as we moved along the trail, and the only arms we saw extended above the ice bore torches which brightened our way for a great distance—to the foot of the far escarpment, actually. Nothing untoward occurred as we crossed that frozen place.

"From what you've told me and what I've seen," Jurt said, "I get the impression it's the Pattern that's sponsoring this trip and the Logrus that's trying to punch your ticket."

Just then the ice cracked in a number of places. Fracture lines rushed toward us from several directions, both sides. They slowed, however, as they neared our trail, causing me to notice for the first time that it had risen above the general level of the plain. We now occupied something of a causeway, and the ice shattered itself harmlessly along its sides.

"Like that," Jurt observed with a gesture. "How'd you get into this mess anyway?"

"It all started on April thirtieth," I began.

7

Some of the arms seemed to be waving good-bye to us as we commenced our climb after reaching the wall. Jurt thumbed his nose at them.

"Can you blame me for wanting to escape this place?" he asked.

"Not in the least," I replied.

"If that transfusion you gave me really placed me beyond control of the Logrus, then I might dwell here for some indefinite period of time."

"Sounds possible."

"That's why you must realize I threw the ice at Borel, not you. Besides the fact that you're smarter than he was and might be able to find a way out of here, he was a creature of the Logrus, too, and wouldn't have had enough fire if the need arose."

"That had occurred to me also," I said, withholding a possible out I'd guessed at, to keep myself indispensable. "But what are you getting at?"

"I'm trying to say that I'll give you any kind of help you need, just so you don't leave me behind when you go. I know we never got along before, but I'm willing to put that aside if you are."

"I always was," I said. "You were the one who started all our fights and kept me in trouble."

He smiled.

"I never did, and I won't do it again," he said. "Yeah, okay, you're right. I didn't like you, and maybe I still don't. But I won't mess you up when we need each other this way."

"The way I see it, you need me a hell of a lot more than I need you."

"I can't argue with that, and I can't make you trust me," he said. "Wish I could." We climbed a little more before he continued, and I fancied the air had already grown a trifle warmer. Then, "But look at it this way," he finally continued, "I resemble your brother Jurt, and I come close to representing something he once was—close, but not a perfect fit. I began diverging from his model beginning with our race. My circumstances are uniquely my own, and I've been thinking steadily since I gained my autonomy. The real Jurt knows things I do not and has powers I don't possess. But I have his memories up through his taking the Logrus, and I'm the second greatest authority there is on the way he thinks. Now, if he's become such a threat as you've indicated, you might find me more than a little useful when it comes to second-guessing him."

"You have a point," I acknowledged. "Unless, of course, the two of you were to throw in together."

He shook his head.

"He wouldn't trust me," he said, "and I wouldn't trust him. We'd both know better. A matter of introspection. See what I mean?"

"It means neither one of you is trustworthy."

His brow furrowed; then he nodded.

"Yeah, I guess so," he said.

"So why should I trust you?"

"Right now because you've got me by the balls. Later on because I'll be so damn useful."

After several more minutes' ascending, I told him, "The thing that bothers me the most about you is that it was not all that long ago that Jurt took the Logrus. You are not an older, milder version of my least favorite relative. You are a very recent model. As for your divergence from the original, I can't see this short while as making that much difference."

He shrugged.

"What can I say that I haven't said already?" he asked. "Let's just deal in terms of power and self-interest then."

I smiled. We both knew that that was the way it was anyway. The conversation helped pass the time, though.

A thought came to me as we climbed.

"Do you think you could walk through Shadow?" I asked him.

"I don't know," he answered after a time. "My last memory

from before I came to this place was of completing the Logrus. I guess the recording was completed at that time, too. So I have no recollection of Suhuy instructing me in shadow-walking, no memory of trying it. I'd guess I could do it, wouldn't you think?"

I paused to catch my breath.

"It's such an arcane matter that I don't even feel qualified to speculate on it. I thought maybe you'd come equipped with ready-made answers for things like that—some sort of preternatural awareness of your limits and abilities."

"Afraid not. Unless you'd call a hunch preternatural."

"I suppose I would if you were right often enough."

"Shit. It's too soon to tell."

"Shit. You're right."

Soon we'd climbed above the line of haze from which the flakes seemed to fall. A little farther, and the winds died to breezes. Farther still, and these subsided to nothing. The rim was in sight by then, and shortly thereafter we achieved it.

I turned and looked back down. All I could see was a bit of glitter through the mist. In the other direction our trail ran on in a zigzag fashion, here and there looking like a series of Morse dashes—regular interruptions, possibly rock formations. We followed it to the right until it turned left.

I reserved some attention for Jurt, looking for signs of recognition at any feature of the terrain. A talk is only words, and he was still some version of the Jurt I'd grown up with. And if he became responsible for my falling into any sort of trap, I was going to pass Gray-swandir through his personal space as soon as I became aware of it.

Flicker . . .

Formation to the left, cavelike, as if the hole in the rock opened into another reality. An oddly shaped car driving up a steep city street . . .

"What . . . ?" Jurt began.

"I still don't know their significance. A whole mess of sequences like this were with me earlier, though. In fact, at first I thought you were one of them."

"Looks real enough to walk into."

"Maybe it is."

"It might be our way out of here."

"Somehow that just seems a little too easy."

"Well, let's give it a try."

"Go ahead," I told him.

We departed the trail, advanced upon the reality window, and kept going. In a moment he was on the sidewalk next to the street up which the car was passing. He turned and waved. I saw his mouth working, but no words came to me.

If I could brush snow off the red Chevy, why couldn't I enter entirely into one of these sequences? And if I could do that, mightn't it be possible that I could shadow-walk from there, wending my way to some more congenial spot, leaving this dark world behind? I moved forward.

Suddenly I was there, and the sound had been turned on for me. I looked about at the buildings, at the sharply inclined street. I listened to the traffic sounds, and I sniffed the air. This place could almost be one of San Francisco's shadows. I hurried to catch up with Jurt, who was moving toward the corner.

I reached him quickly, fell into step beside him. We came to the corner. We turned. We froze.

There was nothing there. We faced a wall of blackness. That is, not just darkness but an absolute emptiness, from which we immediately drew back.

I put my hand forth slowly. A tingling began as it neared the blackness, then a chill, followed by a fear. I drew back. Jurt reached for it, did the same. Abruptly he stopped, picked up the bottom of a broken bottle from the gutter, turned, and hurled it through a nearby window. Immediately he began running in that direction.

I followed. I joined him before the broken pane, stared within.

Again the blackness. There was nothing at all on the other side of the window.

"Kind of spooky," I remarked.

"Uh-huh," Jurt said. "It's as if we're being granted extremely limited access to various shadows. What do you make of it?"

"I'm beginning to wonder whether there isn't something we're supposed to be looking for in one of these places," I said.

Suddenly the blackness beyond the window was gone, and a candle flickered on a small table beyond it. I began to reach through the broken glass toward it. Immediately it vanished. Again there was only blackness.

"I'd take that as an affirmative response to your question," Jurt said.

"I believe you're right. But we can't be looking for something in every one of these things we pass."

"I think maybe something's just been trying to get your attention, to get you to realize that you should be watching what appears, that something probably will be presented once you begin noticing."

Brightness. A whole tableful of candles now blazed beyond the window.

"Okay," I hollered. "If that's all you want, I'll do it. Is there anything else I should be looking for here?"

The darkness came. It crept around the corner and moved slowly toward us. The candles vanished, and it flowed from the window. The buildings across the street disappeared behind an ebon wall.

"I take it the answer is no," I cried. Then I turned and beat it back along our narrowing black tunnel toward the trail. Jurt was right behind me.

"Good thinking," I told him when we stood back on the glowing way, watching that rising street get squeezed out of existence beside us. "Do you think it was just pulling these sequences at random till I finally entered one?"

"Yes."

"Why?"

"I think it has more control in those places and could respond to your questions more readily in one of them."

" 'It' being the Pattern?"

"Probably."

"Okay. The next one it opens to me, I'm going in. I'll do whatever it wants there if it means I get out of here sooner."

"We, brother. We."

"Of course," I answered.

We commenced walking again. Nothing new and intriguing appeared beside us, though. The road zigged and zagged, and we walked along it, and I got to wondering whom we might meet next. If I were indeed on the Pattern's turf and on the verge of doing something it wanted, then it seemed that the Logrus might send along someone I knew to attempt to dissuade me. No one appeared at all, though, and we took the final turn, followed a trail suddenly grown straight for some time, then saw it end abruptly within a dark mass far ahead.

Continuing, I saw that it plunged on into a great, dark, mountainous mass. I felt vaguely claustrophobic, just considering the implications, and I heard Jurt mutter an obscenity as we trudged toward it. Before we reached it, there came a flickering to my right. Turning, I beheld Random and Vialle's bedroom, back in

Amber. I was looking from the southern side of the room, between the sofa and a bedside table, past a chair, across the rug and the cushions toward the fireplace, the windows which flanked it admitting a soft daylight. No one was present in the bed or occupying any other piece of furniture, and the logs on the grate had burned themselves down to red embers, smoking fitfully.

"What now?" Jurt asked.

"This is it," I replied. "It has to be, don't you see? Once I got the message as to what was going on, it presented the real thing. I've got to act fast, too, I think—as soon as I figure just what—"

One of the stones beside the fireplace began to glow redly. It increased in intensity as I watched. There was no way that those embers could be doing it. Therefore . . .

I rushed forward under the influence of a powerful imperative. I heard Jurt shout something behind me, but his voice was cut off as I entered the room. I caught a whiff of Vialle's favorite perfume as I passed beside the bed. This was really Amber, I was certain, not just some shadowy facsimile thereof. I moved quickly to the right of the fireplace.

Jurt burst into the room behind me.

"Better come out fighting!" he cried.

I whirled to face him, shouted, "Shut up!" then raised a finger to my lips.

He crossed to my side, caught hold of my arm, and whispered hoarsely, "Borel's trying to materialize again! He might be solid and waiting by the time you leave!"

From the sitting room I heard Vialle's voice.

"Is someone there?" she called.

I jerked my arm free of Jurt's grasp, knelt upon the hearth, and seized hold of the glowing stone. It appeared to be mortared in place but came loose easily when I drew upon it.

"How'd you know that one came free?" Jurt whispered.

"The glow," I replied.

"What glow?" he asked.

I did not answer him but thrust my right hand into the opened area, hoping offhandedly there were no booby traps. The opening extended back for a good distance beyond the length of the stone. And there I felt it, suspended from peg or hook: a length of chain. I caught hold of it and drew it forth. I heard Jurt catch his breath beside me.

The last time I had seen it was when Random had worn it at Caine's funeral. It was the Jewel of Judgment that I held in my hand. I raised it quickly and slipped the chain over my head, letting that red stone fall upon my breast, just as the door to the sitting room was opened.

Placing my finger to my lips, once more I reached forward, caught hold of Jurt's shoulders, and turned him back toward the opened wall which let upon our trail. He began to protest, but I propelled him with a sharp push, and he moved off in that direction.

"Who's there?" I heard Vialle ask, and Jurt glanced back at me, looking puzzled.

I did not feel we could afford the time for my explaining by sign language or whisper that she was blind. So I gave him another push. Only this time he stepped to the side, extended his leg, slipped a hand behind my back, and pushed me forward. A brief expletive escaped my lips, and then I was falling. From behind me, I heard Vialle's "Who—" before her voice was cut off.

I tumbled onto the trail, managing to draw the dagger from my right boot as I fell. I rolled and came up with the point extended toward the figure of Borel, which seemed to have found its form once more.

He was smiling, his weapon yet undrawn, as he regarded me.

"There is no field of arms here," he stated, "to provide you with a lucky accident such as you enjoyed when last we met."

"Too bad," I said.

"If I but gain that bauble you wear about your neck and deliver it to the place of the Logrus, I will be granted a normal existence, to replace my living counterpart—he who was treacherously slain by your father, as you pointed out."

The vision of Amber's royal apartments had vanished. Jurt stood off the trail, near what had been its interface with this odd realm. "I knew I couldn't beat him," he called out when he felt my glance, "but you took him once."

I shrugged.

At this Borel turned toward Jurt.

"You would betray the Courts and the Logrus?" he asked him.

"On the contrary," Jurt responded. "I may be saving them from a serious mistake."

"What mistake might that be?"

"Tell him, Merlin. Tell him what you told me while we were climbing out of the deep freeze," he said.

Borel glanced back at me.

"There's something funny about this entire setup," I said. "I've a feeling it's all a duel between the Powers—the Logrus and the

Pattern. Amber and the Courts may be secondary to the entire affair. You see—"

"Ridiculous!" he interrupted, drawing his weapon. "This is just made-up nonsense to avoid *our* duel."

I tossed the dagger into my left hand and drew Gray-swandir with my right.

"The hell with you then!" I said. "Come and get it!"

A hand fell upon my shoulder. And it kept right on falling with a sort of twist to it, spinning me into a downward spiral which threw me off to the left of the trail. From the corner of my eye, I saw that Borel had taken a step backward.

"You've a resemblance to Eric or to Corwin," came a soft, familiar voice, "though I know you not. But you wear the Jewel, which makes your person too important to risk in a petty squabble."

I came to a stop and turned my head. It was Benedict whom I beheld—a Benedict with two normal hands.

"My name is Merlin and I'm Corwin's son," I said, "and this is a master duelist from the Courts of Chaos."

"You appear to be on a mission, Merlin. Be about it then," Benedict said.

The point of Borel's blade flicked into a position about ten inches from my throat. "You are going nowhere," he stated, "not with that jewel."

There was no sound as Benedict's blade was drawn and moved to beat Borel's off its line.

"As I said, be on your way, Merlin," Benedict told me.

I got to my feet, moved quickly out of range, passed them both cautiously.

"If you kill him," Jurt said, "he can rematerialize after a period of time."

"How interesting," Benedict remarked, flicking off an attack and retreating slightly. "How long a time?"

"Several hours."

"And how much time will you need to complete whatever you're about?"

Jurt looked at me.

"I'm not certain," I answered.

Benedict executed an odd little parry, followed by a strange shuffling step and a brief slashing attack. A button flew from Borel's shirt front.

"In that case I'll make this last for a time," Benedict said. "Good luck, lad."

He gave me a quick salute with the weapon, at which moment Borel attacked. Benedict used an Italianate sixte which threw both their points off to the side, advancing as he did so. He reached forward quickly then with his left hand and pulled the other's nose. Then he pushed him away, stepped back a pace, and smiled.

"What do you usually charge for lessons?" I overheard him asking as Jurt and I hurried down the path.

"I wonder how long it does take for one of the Powers to materialize a ghost," Jurt said as we jogged toward the mountainous mass the trail entered.

"Several hours for Borel alone," I said, "and if the Logrus wants the Jewel as badly as I'd guess, I'd think it would have summoned an army of ghosts if it could. I'm certain now that this place is very difficult for both Powers to reach. I get the feeling they can only manifest via the barest trickles of energy. If that weren't the case, I'd never have gotten this far."

Jurt reached out as if to touch the Jewel, apparently thought better of it, withdrew his hand.

"It seems you've definitely aligned yourself with the Pattern now," he observed.

"Looks as if you have, too. Unless you're planning on stabbing me in the back at the last moment," I said.

He chuckled. Then, "Not funny," he said. "I've got to be on your side. I can see that the Logrus just created me as a disposable tool. I'd wind up on the scrap heap when the job's done. I've a feeling I might have dissipated already had it not been for the transfusion. So I'm with you, like it or not, and your back is safe."

We ran on along the now-straight way, its terminus finally grown near. Jurt finally asked, "What is the significance of that pendant? The Logrus seems to want it badly."

"It's called the Jewel of Judgment," I answered. "It is said to be older than the Pattern itself and to have been instrumental in its creation."

"Why do you think you were led to it and obtained it with such ease?"

"I have no idea whatsoever," I said. "If you get one before I do, I'll be glad to hear it."

Soon we reached the place where the trail plunged into the greater darkness. We halted and regarded it.

"No signs posted," I said, checking above and to either side of that entranceway.

Jurt gave me an odd look.

"You've always had a weird sense of humor, Merlin," he said. "Who'd put up a sign in a place like this?"

"Someone else with a weird sense of humor," I replied.

"Might as well go on," he said, turning back toward the entrance.

A bright red exit sign had appeared above the opening. Jurt stared for a moment, then shook his head slowly. We entered.

We took our way down a wandering tunnel—a thing which puzzled me a bit. The artificial quality of most of the rest of this place had led me to expect a ruler-straight trail through a smooth-walled shaft, geometrically precise in all its features. Instead, it seemed as if we were traversing a series of natural caverns—stalactites, stalagmites, pillars, and pools displayed at either hand.

The Jewel cast a baleful light over any features I turned to scrutinize.

"Do you know how to use that stone?" Jurt asked me.

I thought back over my father's story.

"When the time comes, I believe that I will," I said, raising the Jewel and studying it for a moment, then letting it fall again. I was less concerned with it than with the route we were following.

I kept turning my head as we made our way from damp grotto to high cathedral chamber, along narrow passages, down stony waterfalls. There was something familiar here, though I couldn't put my finger on it.

"Anything about this place bring back memories?" I asked him.

"Not for me," Jurt replied.

We kept going, at one point passing a side cave containing three human skeletons. These being, in their fashion, the first real signs of life I had seen since the onset of this journey, I remarked on it.

Jurt nodded slowly.

"I am beginning to wonder whether we are still walking between shadows," he said, "or whether we might actually have departed that place and entered Shadow—perhaps when we came into these caves."

"I could find out by trying to summon the Logrus," I said, causing Frakir immediately to pulse sharply upon my wrist. "But considering the metaphysical politics of the situation, I'd rather not."

"I was just going by the colors of all the minerals in the walls," he said. "The place we left behind kind of favored monochrome. Not that I give a shit about the scenery. What I'm saying is that if we have, it's a kind of victory."

I pointed at the ground.

"So long as that glowing trail is there, we're not off the hook."

"What if we simply walked away from it now?" he asked, turning to the right and taking a single step in that direction.

A stalactite vibrated and crashed to the ground before him. It missed him by about a foot. He was back beside me in an instant.

"Of course, it would be a real shame not to find out where we're headed," he said.

"Quests are that way. It'd be bad form to miss the fun."

We hiked on. Nothing allegorical happened around us. Our voices and our footfalls echoed. Water dripped in some of the danker grots. Minerals flashed. Our way seemed a gradual descent.

For how long we walked I could not tell. After a time stony chambers took on a generic appearance—as if we passed regularly through a teleportation device which rerouted us back through the same caves and corridors. This had the effect of blurring my sense of time. Repetitious actions have a lulling effect and—

Suddenly our trail debouched into a larger passage, turned left. Finally, some variation. Only this way, too, looked familiar. We followed our line of light through the darkness. After a time we went by a side passage to the left. Jurt glanced up it and hurried past.

"Any damned thing might be lurking around here," he observed.

"True," I acknowledged. "But I wouldn't worry about it."

"Why not?"

"I think I'm beginning to understand."

"Mind telling me what's going on?"

"It'd take too long. Just wait. We'll be finding out pretty soon."

We went by another side passage. Similar, yet different. Of course.

I increased my pace, anxious to learn the truth. Another sideway. I broke into a run . . .

Another . . .

Jurt pounded along beside me, the echoes falling about us. Up ahead. Soon.

Another turning.

And then I slowed, for the passage continued ahead but our trail didn't. It curved to the left, vanishing beneath a big metal-bound door. I reached out to my right to where the hook was supposed to be, located it, removed the key that hung there. I inserted it, turned it, withdrew it, rehung it.

I don't like this place, boss, Frakir noted.

I know.

"Seems as if you know what you're doing," Jurt remarked.

"Yep," I said, then added, "Up to a point," as I realized that this door opened outward rather than inward.

I caught hold of the large handle to the left and began to pull upon it.

"Mind telling me where we've wound up?" he asked.

The big door creaked, commenced a slow movement as I walked backward.

"These are amazingly like a section of caverns in Kolvir beneath Amber Castle," I replied.

"Great," he said. "And what's behind the door?"

"This is much like the entrance to the chamber which houses the Pattern in Amber."

"Wonderful," he said. "I'll probably go up in a puff of smoke if I set foot inside."

"But it is not quite the same," I continued. "We had Suhuy come and look at the Pattern itself before I walked it. He didn't suffer any ill effects from the proximity."

"Our mother walked the Pattern."

"Yes, that's true."

"Frankly, I think anyone of proper consanguinity in the Courts could walk the Pattern—and vice versa for my relatives in Amber with the Logrus. Tradition has it we're all related from back somewhere in the dim and misty."

"Okay. I'll go in with you. There's room to move around inside without touching the thing, isn't there?"

"Yes."

I drew the door the rest of the way open, braced my shoulder against it, and stared. This was it. I saw that our glowing trail ended a few inches beyond the threshold.

I drew a deep breath and muttered some expletive as I let it go.

"What is it?" Jurt asked, trying to see past me.

"Not what I expected," I told him.

I moved aside and let him have a look.

He stared for several seconds, then said, "I don't understand."

"I am not certain that I do either," I said, "but I intend to find out."

I entered the chamber, and he followed me. This was not the Pattern that I knew. Or rather, it was and it wasn't. It conformed to the same general configuration as the Pattern in Amber, only it was broken. There were several places where the lines had been erased, destroyed, removed in some fashion—or perhaps never properly executed in the first place. The ordinarily dark interlinear areas were bright, blue-white, the lines themselves black. It was as if some essence had drained from the diagram to permeate the field. The lighted area seemed to ripple slowly as I viewed it.

And beyond all of this was the big difference: The Pattern in Amber did not contain a circle of fire at its center, a woman dead, unconscious, or under a spell within it.

And the woman, of course, had to be Coral. I knew that immediately, though I had to wait for more than a minute before I got a glimpse of her face beyond the flames.

The big door shut itself behind us while I stood staring. Jurt stood unmoving for a long time also before he said, "That Jewel is certainly busy at something. You should see your face in its light right now."

I glanced downward and observed its ruddy pulsations. Between the blue-white flux in which the Pattern was grounded and the flickering of that circle of flame I had not noted the sudden activity on the part of the stone.

I moved a step nearer, feeling a wave of coldness similar to that of an activated Trump. This had to be one of the Broken Patterns of which Jasra had been speaking—representative of one of the Ways in which she and Julia were initiates. This placed me in one of the early shadows, near Amber herself. Thoughts began to race through my mind at a ferocious pace.

I had only recently become aware of the possibility that the Pattern might actually be sentient. Its corollary, that the Logrus was sentient, seemed likely also. The notion of its sentiency had been presented to me when Coral had succeeded in negotiating the Pattern and then had asked it to send her where she should go. It had done so, and this was the place to which she had been transported, and her condition was obviously the reason I couldn't reach her by means of her Trump. When I had addressed the Pattern following her disappearance, it had—almost playfully, it seemed at the time—shifted me from one end of its chamber to the other, apparently to satisfy me on the matter of its sentience.

And it wasn't merely sentient, I decided, as I raised the Jewel of Judgment and stared into its depths. It was clever. For the images that I saw within the stone, showing me what it was that was desired of me, represented something I would not have been willing to do under other circumstances. Having come away from that strange realm through which I had been led on this quest, I would have shuffled out a Trump and called someone for a fast exit—or even summoned the image of the Logrus and let the two of them slug it out while I slipped away through Shadow. But Coral slept in a circle of flame at the heart of the Broken Pattern. . . . She was the authentic Pattern's hold over me. It had to have understood something back when she was walking it, laid its plan, and set me up at that time.

It wanted me to repair this particular image of itself, to mend this Broken Pattern, by walking it, bearing the Jewel of Judgment with me. This was how Oberon had repaired the damage to the original. Of course, the act had been sufficiently traumatic to kill him . . .

On the other hand, the King had been dealing with the real thing, and this was only one of its images. Also, my father had survived the creation of his own ersatz Pattern from scratch.

Why me? I wondered then. Was it because I was the son of the man who had succeeded in creating another Pattern? Did it involve the fact that I bore the image of the Logrus within me as well as that of the Pattern? Was it simply because I was handy and coercible? All of the above? None of them?

"How about it?" I called out. "Have you got an answer for me?"

There was a quick pang in my stomach and a wave of dizziness as the chamber spun, faded, stood still, and I regarded Jurt across the expanse of the Pattern, the big door at his back.

"How'd you do that?" he hollered.

"I didn't," I replied.

"Oh."

He edged his way to his right till he came to the wall. Maintaining contact with it, he began moving about the Pattern's periphery, as if afraid to approach any nearer to it than he had to or to remove his gaze from it.

From this side I could see Coral a bit more clearly, within the fiery hedge. Funny. It was not as if there were a large emotional investment here. We were not lovers, not even terrifically close friends. We had become acquainted only the other day, shared a long walk about, around, and under the town and palace, had a meal together, a couple of drinks, a few laughs. If we became better acquainted, perhaps we would discover that we couldn't stand each other. Still, I had enjoyed her company, and I realized that I did want to take the time to get to know her better. And in some ways I felt responsible for her present condition, through a kind of contributory negligence. In other words, the Pattern had me by the balls. If I wanted to free her, I had to repair it.

The flames nodded in my direction.

"It's a dirty trick," I said aloud.

The flames nodded again.

I continued to study the Broken Pattern. Almost everything I knew about the phenomenon had come to me by way of my conversation with Jasra. But I recalled her telling me that initiates of the Broken Pattern walked it in the areas between the lines, whereas the image in the Jewel was instructing me to walk the lines, as one normally would the Pattern itself. Which made sense, as I recalled my father's story. It should serve to inscribe the proper path across the breaks. I wasn't looking for any half-assed between-the-lines initiation.

Jurt made his way about the far end of the Pattern, turned, and began to move toward me. When he came abreast of a break in the outer line, the light flowed from it across the floor. The look on his face was ghastly as it touched his foot. He screamed and began to melt.

"Stop!" I cried. "Or you can find another Pattern repairman! Restore him and leave him alone or I won't do it! I mean it!"

Jurt's collapsing legs lengthened again. The rush of blue-white incandescence which had fled upward through his body was withdrawn as the light retreated from him. The expression of pain left his face.

"I know he's a Logrus-ghost," I said, "and he's patterned on my least favorite relative, but you leave him alone, you son of a bitch, or I won't walk you! You can keep Coral and you can stay broken!"

The light flowed back through the imperfection, and things stood as they had moments before.

"I want a promise," I said.

A gigantic sheet of flame rose from the Broken Pattern to the top of the chamber, then fell again.

"I take it that is an affirmative," I said.

The flames nodded.

"Thanks," I heard Jurt whisper.

8

And so I commenced my walk. The black line did not have the same feeling to it as the blazing ones back under Amber. My feet came down as if on dead ground, though there was a tug and a crackle when I raised them.

"Merlin!" Jurt called out. "What should I do?"

"What do you mean?" I shouted back.

"How do I get out of here?"

"Go out the door and start shadow-shifting," I said, "or follow me through this Pattern and have it send you wherever you want."

"I don't believe you can shadow-shift this close to Amber, can you?"

"Maybe we are too close. So get away physically and then do it."

I kept moving. There came small crackling sounds whenever I raised my feet now.

"I'd get lost in the caves if I tried that."

"Then follow me."

"The Pattern will destroy me."

"It's promised not to."

He laughed harshly.

"And you believe it?"

"If it wants this job done properly, it has no choice."

I came to the first break in the Pattern. A quick consultation of the Jewel showed me where the line should lie. With some trepidation I took my first step beyond the visible marking. Then another. And another. I wanted to look back when I finally crossed the gap. Instead, I waited until the natural curving of my route granted me that view. I saw then that the entire line I had walked thus far had begun to glow, just like the real thing. The spilled luminescence seemed to have been absorbed within it, darkening the interstitial ground area. Jurt had moved to a position near that beginning.

He caught my gaze.

"I don't know, Merlin," he said. "I just don't know."

"The Jurt I knew wouldn't have had guts enough to try it," I told him.

"Neither do I."

"As you pointed out, our mother did it. Odds are you've got the genes. What the hell. If I'm wrong, it'll be over before you know it."

I took another step. He gave a mirthless laugh.

Then, "What the hell," he said, and he set his foot upon it.

"Hey, I'm still alive," he called out. "What now?"

"Keep coming," I said. "Follow me. Don't stop. And don't leave the line or all bets are off."

There followed another turning of the way, and I followed it and lost sight of him. As I continued along, I became aware of a pain in my right ankle—product of all the hiking and climbing I had done, I supposed. It began increasing with each step. It was hot and soon grew to be quite terrible. Had I somehow torn a ligament? Had I—

Of course. I could smell the burning leather now.

I plunged my hand into the sheath area of my boot and withdrew the Chaos dagger. It was radiating heat. This proximity to the Pattern was affecting it. I couldn't keep it about me any longer.

I drew my arm back and cast the weapon across the Pattern in the direction I was facing, toward the end of the room where the doorway was situated. Automatically my gaze followed its passage. There was a small movement in the shadows toward which it flew. A man was standing there, watching me. The dagger struck the wall and fell to the floor. He leaned over and picked it up. I heard a chuckle. He made a sudden movement, and the dagger came arcing back across the Pattern in my direction.

It landed ahead and to the right of me. As soon as it made contact with the Pattern, a fountain of blue flame engulfed it, rising well above the level of my head, splattering, sizzling. I flinched and I slowed, though I knew it would do me no permanent harm, and I kept walking. I had reached the long frontal arc where the going was slow.

"Stay on the line," I yelled to Jurt. "Don't worry about things like that."

"I understand," he said. "Who's that guy?"

"Damned if I know."

I pushed ahead. I was nearer to the circle of flame now. I wondered what the *ty'iga* would think of my present predicament. I made my way around another turn and was able to see back over a considerable section of my trail. It was glowing evenly, and Jurt was coming on strongly, moving as I had, the flames rising above his ankles now. They were almost up to my knees. From the corner of my eye I saw a movement from that area of the chamber where the stranger stood.

The man moved forth from his shadowy alcove, slowly, carefully, flowing along the far wall. At least he did not seem interested in walking the Pattern. He moved to a point almost directly opposite its beginning.

I had no choice but to continue my course, which took me through curves and turns that removed him from my sight. I came to another break in the Pattern and felt it knit as I crossed it. A barely audible music seemed to occur as I did so. The tempo of the flux within the lighted area seemed to increase also, as it flowed into the lines, etching a sharp, bright trail behind me. I called an occasional piece of advice to Jurt, who was several laps back, though his course sometimes brought him abreast of me and close enough to touch had there been any reason to.

The blue fires were higher now, reaching up to mid-thigh, and my hair was rising. I began a slow series of turns. Above the crackling and the music, I asked, *How're you doing, Frakir?* There was no reply.

I turned, kept moving through an area of high impedance, emerged from it, beholding the fiery wall of Coral's prison there at the Pattern's center. As I took my way around it, the opposite side of the Pattern slowly came into view.

The stranger stood waiting, the collar of his cloak turned high. Within the shadows which lay upon his face, I could see that his teeth were bared in a grin. I was startled by the fact that he stood in the midst of the Pattern itself—watching my advance, apparently waiting for me—until I realized that he had entered by way of a break in the design which I was headed to repair.

"You are going to have to get out of my way," I called out. "I can't stop, and I can't let you stop me!"

He didn't stir, and I recalled my father's telling me of a fight which had occurred on the primal Pattern. I slapped the hilt of Grayswandir.

"I'm coming through," I said.

The blue-white fires came up even higher with my next step, and in their light I saw his face. It was my own.

"No," I said.

"Yes," he said.

"You are the last of the Logrus-ghosts to confront me."

"Indeed," he replied.

I took another step.

"Yet," I observed, "if you are a reconstruction of myself from the time I made it through the Logrus, why should you oppose me here? The self I recall being in those days wouldn't have taken a job like this."

His grin went away.

"I am not you in that sense," he stated. "The only way to make this happen as it must, as I understand it, was to synthesize my personality in some fashion."

"So you're me with a lobotomy and orders to kill."

"Don't say that," he replied. "It makes it sound wrong, and what I'm doing is right. We even have many of the same memories."

"Let me through and I'll talk to you afterward. I think the Logrus may have screwed itself by trying this stunt. You don't want to kill yourself, and neither do I. Together we could win this game, and there's room in Shadow for more than one Merlin."

I'd slowed, but I had to take another step then. I couldn't afford to lose momentum at this point.

His lips tightened to a thin line, and he shook his head.

"Sorry," he said. "I was born to live one hour—unless I kill you. If I do, your life will be given to me."

He drew his blade.

"I know you better than you think I do," I said, "whether you've been restructured or not. I don't think you'll do it. Furthermore, I might be able to lift that death sentence. I've learned some things about how it works for you ghosts."

He extended his blade, which resembled one I'd had years ago, and its point almost reached me.

"Sorry," he repeated.

I drew Grayswandir for purposes of parrying it. I'd have been a fool not to. I didn't know what sort of job the Logrus had done on his head. I racked my memories for fencing techniques I'd studied since I'd become an initiate of the Logrus.

Yes. Benedict's game with Borel had reminded me. I'd taken some lessons in Italian-style fencing since then. It gave one wider, more careless-seeming parries, compensated by greater extension. Grayswandir went forth, beat his blade to the outside, and extended. His wrist bent into a French four, but I was already under it, arm still extended, wrist straight, sliding my right foot forward along the line as the forte of my blade beat heavily against the forte of his from the outside, and I immediately stepped forward with my left foot, driving the weapon across his body till the guards locked and continuing its drop in that direction.

And then my left hand fell upon the inside of his right elbow, in a maneuver a martial artist friend had taught me back in college—*zenponage,* I think he called it. I lowered my hips as I pressed downward. I turned my hips then, counterclockwise. His balance broke, and he fell toward my left. Only I could not permit that. If he landed on the Pattern proper, I'd a funny feeling he'd go off like a fireworks display. So I continued the drop for several more inches, shifted my hand to his shoulder, and pushed him, so that he fell back into the broken area.

Then I heard a scream, and a blazing form passed on my left side.

"No!" I cried, reaching for it.

But I was too late. Jurt had stepped off the line, springing past me, driving his blade into my double even as his own body swirled and blazed. Fire also poured from my double's wound. He tried unsuccessfully to rise and fell back.

"Don't say that I never served you, brother," Jurt stated, before he was transformed into a whirlwind, which rose to the chamber's roof, where it dissipated.

I could not reach far enough to touch my doppelgänger, and moments later I did not wish to, for he was quickly transformed into a human torch.

His gaze was directed upward, following Jurt's spectacular passing. He looked at me then and smiled crookedly.

"He was right, you know," he said, and then he, too, was engulfed.

It took awhile to overcome my inertia, but after a time I did, continuing my ritual dance about the fire. The next time around there was no trace of either of their persons, though their blades remained where they had fallen, crossed, across my path. I kicked them off the Pattern as I went by. The flames were up to my waist by then.

Around, back, over. I glanced into the Jewel periodically, to avoid missteps, and piece by piece I stitched the Pattern together. The light was drawn into the lines, and save for the central blaze, it came more and more to resemble the thing we kept in the basement back home.

The First Veil brought painful memories of the Courts and of Amber. I stayed aloof, shivering, and these things passed. The Second Veil mixed memory and desire in San Francisco. I controlled my breathing and pretended I was only a spectator. The flames danced about my shoulders, and I thought of a series of half-moons as I traversed arc after arc, curve upon reverse curve. The resistance grew till I was drenched with sweat as I struggled against it. But I had been this way before. The Pattern was not just around me but inside me as well.

I moved, and I reached the point of diminishing returns, of less and less distance gained for the effort expended. I kept seeing dissolving Jurt and my own dying face amid flames, and it didn't matter a bit that I knew the memory rush was Pattern-induced. It still bothered me as I drove myself forward.

I swept my gaze around me once as I neared the Grand Curve, and I saw that this Pattern had now been fully repaired. I had bridged all of the breaks with connecting lines, and it burned now like a frozen Catherine wheel against a black and starless sky. Another step . . .

I patted the warm Jewel that I wore. Its ruddy glow came up to me even more strongly now than it had earlier. I wondered whether there was an easy way to get it back where it belonged. Another step . . .

I raised the Jewel and stared into it. There was an image of me completing the walking of the Grand Curve and continuing right on through the wall of flames as if this represented no problem whatsoever. While I took the vision as a piece of advice, I was reminded of a David Steinberg routine which Droppa had once appropriated. I hoped that the Pattern was not into practical jokes.

The flames enveloped me fully as I commenced the Curve. I continued to slow as my efforts mounted. Step after painful step I drew nearer to the Final Veil. I could feel myself being transformed into an expression of pure will, as everything that I was became focused upon a single end. Another step . . . It felt as if I were weighted down with heavy armor. It was the final three steps that pushed one near despair's edge.

Again . . .

Then came the point where even movement became less important than the effort. It was no longer the results but the attempt that mattered. My will was the flame; my body, smoke or shadow. . . .

And again . . .

Seen through my risen blue light, the orange flames which surrounded Coral became silver-gray spikes of incandescence. Within the crackling and the popping I heard something like music once again—low, adagio, a deep, vibrant thing, like Michael Moore playing bass. I tried to accept the rhythm, to move with it. Somehow, then, it seemed that I succeeded—that, or my time sense became distorted—as I moved with a feeling of something like fluidity through the next steps.

Or maybe the Pattern felt it owed me a favor and had eased up for a few beats. I'll never know.

I passed through the Final Veil, faced the wall of flame, suddenly orange again, and kept going. I drew my next breath in the heart of fire.

Coral lay there at the Pattern's center, looking pretty much as she had when last I had seen her—in a copper shirt and dark green breeches—save that she appeared to be sleeping, sprawled there upon her heavy brown cloak. I dropped to my right knee beside her and laid my hand upon her shoulder. She did not stir. I brushed a strand of her reddish hair off her cheek, stroked that cheek a few times.

"Coral?" I said.

No response.

I returned my hand to her shoulder, shook her gently.

"Coral?"

She drew a deep breath and sighed it out, but she did not awaken.

I shook her a bit harder. "Wake up, Coral."

I slipped my arm beneath her shoulders, raised her partway. Her eyes did not open. Obviously she was under some sort of spell. The middle of the Pattern was hardly the place to summon the Sign of the Logrus if one wished to remain unincinerated. So I tried the storybook remedy. I leaned forward and kissed her. She made a small, deep noise, and her eyelids fluttered. But she did not come around. I tried again. Same result.

"Shit!" I remarked. I wanted a little elbowroom for working on a spell like this, a place where I had access to some of the tools of my trade and could call upon the source of my powers with impunity.

I raised her higher and commanded the Pattern to transport us back to my apartment in Amber, where her *ty'iga*-possessed sister lay in a trance of her own—one of my brother's doing, for purposes of protecting me from her.

"Take us home," I said aloud, for emphasis.

Nothing happened.

I employed a strong visualization then and backed it once more with the mental command.

We didn't stir.

I lowered Coral gently, rose, and looked out across the Pattern through the faintest area of the flames.

"Look," I said, "I just did you a big favor, involving a lot of exertion and considerable risk. Now I want to get the hell out of here and take the lady with me. Will you please oblige?"

The flames died down, were gone, for several beats. In the diminished light which followed I became aware that the Jewel was pulsing, like the message light on a hotel phone. I raised it and stared into it.

I hardly expected an X-rated short feature, but that's what was playing.

"I believe I'm receiving the wrong channel," I said. "If you've got a message, let's have it. Otherwise, I just want to go home."

Nothing changed, save that I became aware of a strong resemblance between the two figures in the Jewel and Coral and myself. They were going at it on a cloak at what appeared to be the center of a Pattern, flagrante ad infinitum—rather like a spicier version of the old salt box label, it seemed, if they could be seeing into the Jewel the guy was wearing and watching. . . .

"Enough!" I cried. "This is fucking ridiculous! You want a Tantric ritual I'll send you some professionals! The lady isn't even awake—"

The Jewel pulsed again, with such intensity that it hurt my eyes. I let it fall. I knelt then, scooped Coral up, and stood.

"I don't know whether anyone's ever walked you backwards before," I said, "but I don't see why it shouldn't work."

I took a step in the direction of the Final Veil. Immediately the wall of flame sprang up before me. I stumbled in drawing away from it, fell back upon the outspread cloak. I held Coral to me that she not be cast into the fire. She came down on top of me. She seemed almost awake. . . .

Her arms went around my neck, and she sort of nuzzled my

cheek. She seemed more drowsy than comatose now. I held her tightly and thought about it.

"Coral?" I tried again.

"Mm," she said.

"Seems the only way we can get out of here is by making love."

"Thought you'd never ask," she mumbled, eyes still closed.

That made it seem somewhat less like necrophilia, I told myself as I turned us onto our sides so I could get at those coppery buttons. She muttered a little more while I was about things, but it didn't exactly turn into a conversation. Still, her body was not unresponsive to my attentions, and the encounter quickly took on all the usual features, too commonplace to be of much concern to the sophisticated. It seemed an interesting way to break a spell. Maybe the Pattern did have a sense of humor. I don't know.

The fires died down at about the same time that the fires died down, so to speak. Coral's eyes finally opened.

"That seems to have taken care of the circle of flames," I said.

"When did this cease being a dream?" she asked.

"Good question," I replied, "and only you can answer it."

"Did you just rescue me from something?"

"That seems the easiest way to put it," I answered as she drew away somewhat and cast her gaze about the chamber. "See where it got you when you asked the Pattern to send you where you should go?" I said.

"Screwed," she replied.

"Precisely."

We drew apart. We adjusted our apparel.

"It's a good way to get to know each other better . . ." I had begun when the cavern was shaken by a powerful earth tremor.

"The timing is really off here," I observed as we were rocked together and clung to each other for comfort, if not support.

It was over in an instant, and the Pattern was suddenly blazing more brilliantly than I'd ever seen it before. I shook my head. I rubbed my eyes. Something was wrong, even though it felt very right. Then the great metal-bound door opened—inward!—and I realized that we had come back to Amber, the real Amber. My glowing trail still led up to the threshold, though it was fading fast, and a small figure stood upon it. Before I could even squint against the corridor's gloom, I felt a familiar disorientation, and we were in my bedroom.

"Nayda!" Coral exclaimed when she viewed the figure reclined upon my bed.

"Not exactly," I said. "I mean, it's her body. But the spirit that
moves it is of a different order."

"I don't understand."

I was busy thinking of the person who had been about to invade the precincts of the Pattern. I was also a mass of aching muscles, screaming nerves, and assorted fatigue poisons. I crossed to
the table where the wine bottle I'd opened for Jasra—how long
ago?—still stood. I found us two clean glasses. I filled them. I
passed one to Coral.

"Your sister was very ill awhile back, wasn't she?"

"Yes," she replied.

I took a big swallow.

"She was near death. At that time her body was possessed by a
ty'iga spirit—a kind of demon—as Nayda no longer had any use
for it."

"What do you mean by that?"

"I understand that she actually died."

Coral stared into my eyes. She didn't find whatever she
sought, and she took a drink instead.

"I'd known something was wrong," she said. "She hasn't really been herself since the illness."

"She became nasty? Sneaky?"

"No, a lot nicer. Nayda was always a bitch."

"You didn't get along?"

"Not till recently. She's not in any pain, is she?"

"No, she's just sleeping. She's under a spell."

"Why don't you release her? She doesn't look like much of a
danger."

"I don't think she is now. Just the opposite, in fact," I said.
"And we will release her, soon. My brother Mandor will have to
undo it, though. It's his spell."

"Mandor? I don't really know much about you—or your
family—do I?"

"Nope," I said, "and vice versa. Listen, I don't even know
what day it is." I crossed the room and peered out the window.
There was daylight. It was cloudy, though, and I couldn't guess
the time. "There's something you should do right away. Go see
your father and let him know you're all right. Tell him you got lost
in the caverns or took a wrong turn into the Corridor of Mirrors

and wound up on some other plane of existence or something. Anything. To avoid a diplomatic incident. Okay?"

She finished her drink and nodded. Then she looked at me and blushed and looked away.

"We'll get together again before I leave, won't we?"

I reached out and patted her shoulder, not really knowing what my feelings were. Then I realized that wouldn't do, and I stepped forward and embraced her.

"You know it," I said as I stroked her hair.

"Thanks for showing me around town."

"We'll have to do it again," I told her, "as soon as the pace slackens."

"Uh-huh."

We walked to the door.

"I want to see you soon," she said.

"I'm fading fast," I told her, as I opened it. "I've been through hell and back."

She touched my cheek.

"Poor Merlin," she said. "Sleep tight."

I gulped the rest of my wine and withdrew my Trumps. I wanted to do just what she said, but certain unavoidables came first. I riffled my way to the Ghostwheel's card, removed it, and regarded it.

Almost immediately, following the faintest drop in temperature and the barest formation of desire on my part, Ghostwheel appeared before me—a red circle turning in the middle of the air.

"Uh, hello, Dad," it stated. "I was wondering where you'd gotten to. When I checked back at the cave, you were gone, and none of my shadow-indexing procedures could turn you up. It never even occurred to me that you might simply have come home. I—"

"Later," I said. "I'm in a hurry. Get me down to the chamber of the Pattern fast."

"There's something I'd better tell you first."

"What?"

"That force that followed you to the Keep—the one I hid you from in the cave . . . ?"

"Yes?"

"It was the Pattern itself that was seeking you."

"I guessed that," I said, "later. We've had our encounter and sort of come to terms for now. Get me down there right away. It's important."

"Sir, I am afraid of that thing."

"Then take me as close as you dare and step aside. I have to check something out."

"Very well. Come this way."

I took a step forward. Ghost rose into the air, rotated ninety degrees toward me, and dropped quickly, passing my head, shoulders, torso and vanishing beneath my feet. The lights went out as he did so, and I called up my Logrus vision immediately. It showed me that I stood in the passageway outside the big door to the chamber of the Pattern.

"Ghost?" I said softly.

There was no reply.

I moved forward, turned the corner, advanced to the door, and leaned upon it. It was still unlocked, and it yielded to my pushing. Frakir pulsed once upon my wrist.

Frakir? I inquired.

There came no answer from that quarter either.

Lose your voice, lady?

She pulsed twice. I stroked her.

As the door opened before me, I was certain that the Pattern had grown brighter. The observation was quickly pushed aside, however. A dark-haired woman stood at the Pattern's center, her back to me, her arms upraised. I almost shouted the name I thought she might answer to, but she was gone before my vocal mechanism responded. I slumped against the wall.

"I really feel used," I said aloud. "You've run my ass ragged, you placed my life in jeopardy more than once, you got me to perform to satisfy your metaphysical voyeurism, then you kicked me out after you got the last thing you wanted—a slightly brighter glow. I guess that gods or powers or whatever the hell you are don't have to say 'Thank you' or 'I'm sorry' or 'Go to hell' when they've finished using someone. And obviously you feel no need to justify yourself to me. Well, I'm not a baby carriage. I resent being pushed around by you and the Logrus in whatever game you're playing. How'd you like it if I opened a vein and bled all over you?"

Immediately there was a great coalescence of energies at my side of the Pattern. With a heavy whooshing sound a tower of blue flame built itself before me, widened, assumed genderless features of an enormous inhuman beauty. I had to shade my eyes against it.

"You do not understand," came a voice modulated of the roaring of flames.

"I know. That's why I'm here."

"Your efforts are not unappreciated."

"Glad to hear it."

"There was no other way to conduct matters."

"Well, were they conducted to your satisfaction?"

"They were."

"Then you are welcome, I guess."

"You are insolent, Merlin."

"The way I feel right now I've nothing to lose. I'm just too damned tired to care what you do to me. So I came down here to tell you that I think you owe me a big one. That's all."

I turned my back on it then.

"Not even Oberon dared address me so," it said.

I shrugged and took a step toward the door. When I set my foot down, I was back in my apartment.

I shrugged again, then went and splashed water in my face.

"You still okay, Dad?"

There was a ring around the bowl. It rose into the air and followed me about the room."

"I'm all right," I acknowledged. "How about yourself?"

"Fine. It ignored me completely."

"Do you know what it's up to?" I asked.

"It seems to be dueling with the Logrus for control of Shadow. And it just won a round. Whatever happened seems to have strengthened it. You were involved, right?"

"Right."

"Where were you after you left the cave I'd put you in?"

"You know of a land that lies between the shadows?"

"*Between?* No. That doesn't make sense."

"Well, that's where I was."

"How'd you get there?"

"I don't know. With considerable difficulty, I'd guess. Are Mandor and Jasra all right?"

"The last time I looked they were."

"How about Luke?"

"I'd no reason to seek him out. Do you want me to?"

"Not just now. Right now I want you to go upstairs and look in on the royal suite. I want to know whether it is, at the moment, occupied. And if so, by whom. I also want you to check the fireplace in the bedroom. See whether a loose stone which was removed from an area to the right of it has been replaced or is still lying upon the hearth."

He vanished, and I paced. I was afraid to sit down or to lie down. I'd a feeling that I'd go to sleep instantly if I did and that I'd be difficult to awaken. But Ghost spun back into existence before I chalked up much mileage.

"The Queen, Vialle, is present," he said, "in her studio, the loose stone has been replaced, and there is a dwarf in the hall knocking on doors."

"Damn," I said. "Then they know it's missing. A dwarf?"

"A dwarf."

I sighed.

"I guess I'd better walk on upstairs, return the Jewel, and try to explain what happened. If Vialle likes my story, she might just forget to mention it to Random."

"I'll transfer you up there."

"No, that would not be too politic. Or polite either. I'd better go knock on the door and get admitted properly this time."

"How do people know when to knock and when to go on in?"

"In general, if it's closed, you knock on it."

"As the dwarf is doing?"

I heard a faint knocking from somewhere outside.

"He's just going along, indiscriminately banging on doors?" I asked.

"Well, he's trying them in sequence, so I don't know that you could say it's indiscriminate. So far all of the doors he's tried have been to rooms which are empty. He should reach yours in another minute or so."

I crossed to my door, unlocked it, opened it, and stepped out into the hallway.

Sure enough, there was a short guy moving along the hallway. He looked in my direction at the opening of my door, and his teeth showed within his beard as he smiled and headed toward me.

It quickly became apparent that he was a hunchback.

"My God!" I said. "You're Dworkin, aren't you? The real Dworkin!"

"I believe so," he replied in a not unpleasant voice. "And I do hope that you are Corwin's son, Merlin."

"I am," I said. "This is an unusual pleasure, coming at an unusual time."

"It is not a social call," he stated, drawing near and clasping my hand and shoulder. "Ah! These are your quarters!"

"Yes. Won't you come in?"

"Thank you."

I led him in. Ghost did a fly-on-the-wall imitation, became about a half inch in diameter, and took up residence on the armoire as if the result of a stray sunbeam. Dworkin did a quick turn about the sitting room, glanced into the bedroom, stared at Nayda for a time, muttered, "Always let sleeping demons lie," touched the Jewel as he passed me on his return, shook his head forebodingly, and sank into the chair I'd been afraid I'd go to sleep in.

"Would you care for a glass of wine?" I asked him.

He shook his head.

"No, thank you," he replied. "It was you who repaired the nearest Broken Pattern in Shadow, was it not?"

"Yes, it was."

"Why did you do it?"

"I didn't have much choice in the matter."

"You had better tell me all about it," the old man said, tugging at his grisly, irregular beard. His hair was long and could have used a trim also. Still, there seemed nothing of madness in his gaze or his words.

"It is not a simple story, and if I am to stay awake long enough to tell it, I am going to need some coffee," I said.

He spread his hands, and a small, white-clothed table appeared between us, bearing service for two and a steaming silvery carafe set above a squat candle. There was also a tray of biscuits. I couldn't have summoned it all that fast. I wondered whether Mandor could.

"In that case, I will join you," Dworkin said.

I sighed and poured. I raised the Jewel of Judgment.

"Perhaps I'd better return this thing before I start," I told him. "It may save me a lot of trouble later."

He shook his head as I began to rise.

"I think not," he stated. "If you take it off now, you will probably die."

I sat down again.

"Cream and sugar?" I asked him.

9

I came around slowly. That familiar blueness was a lake of prebeing in which I drifted. Oh, yes, I was here because . . . I was here, as the song said. I turned over onto my other side within my sleeping bag, drew my knees up to my chest, and went back to sleep.

The next time I came around and gave it a quick glance the world was still a blue place. Fine. There is much to be said for the tried, the true. Then I recalled that Luke might be by at any time to kill me, and my fingers wrapped themselves around the hilt of the weapon beside me, and I strained my hearing after signs of anything's approach.

Would I spend the day chipping at the wall of my crystal cave? I wondered. Or would Jasra come and try again to kill me?

Again?

Something was wrong. There'd been an awful lot of business involving Jurt and Coral and Luke and Mandor, even Julia. Had it all been a dream?

The moment of panic came and went, and then my wandering spirit returned, bringing along the rest of my memories, and I yawned and everything was all right again.

I stretched. I sat up. I knuckled my eyes.

Yes, I was back in the crystal cave. No, everything that had happened since Luke imprisoned me had not been a dream. I had returned here by choice (a) because a good night's sleep in this time line amounted to only a brief span back in Amber, (b) because nobody could bother me here with a Trump contact, and (c) because it was possible that even the Pattern and the Logrus couldn't track me down here.

I brushed my hair out of my eyes, rose, and headed back to the john. It had been a good idea, having Ghost transport me here following my colloquy with Dworkin. I was certain I had slept for something like twelve hours—deep, undisturbed stuff, the best kind. I drained a quart water bottle. I washed my face with more of the stuff.

Later, after I had dressed and stowed the bedclothes in the storeroom, I walked to the entrance chamber and stood in the light beneath the overhead adit. What I could see of the sky through it was clear. I could still hear Luke's words the day he had imprisoned me here and I'd learned we were related.

I drew the Jewel of Judgment up from within my shirt, removed it, held it high so that the light shone from behind it, stared into its depths. No messages this time.

Just as well. I wasn't in the mood for two-way traffic.

I lowered myself into a comfortable cross-legged position, still regarding the stone. Time to do it and be done with it, now that I felt rested and somewhat alert. As Dworkin had suggested, I sought the Pattern within that red pool.

After a time it began to take shape. It did not appear as I had been visualizing it, but this was not an exercise in visualization. I watched the structure come clear. It was not as if it were suddenly coming into existence, however, but rather as if it had been there all along and my eyes were just now adjusting to perceive it properly. Likely this was actually the case, too.

I took a deep breath and released it. I repeated the process. Then I began a careful survey of the design. I couldn't recall everything my father had said about attuning oneself to the Jewel. When I had mentioned this to Dworkin, he had told me not to worry about it, that I needed but to locate the three-dimensional edition of the Pattern within the stone, find its point of entry, and traverse it. When I pressed him for details, he had simply chuckled and told me not to worry.

All right.

Slowly I turned it, drawing it nearer. A small break appeared, high, to the right. As I focused upon it, it seemed to rush toward me.

I went to that place, and I went in there. It was a strange roller coaster of an experience, moving along Pattern-like lines within the gemstone. I went where it drew me, sometimes with a near-eviscerating feeling of vertigo, other times pushing with my will against the ruby barriers till they yielded and I climbed, fell, slid, or pushed my way onward. I lost most of the awareness of my body, hand holding the chain high, save that I knew I was sweating profusely, as it stung my eyes with some regularity.

I've no idea how much time passed in my attunement to the Jewel of Judgment, the higher octave of the Pattern. Dworkin felt that there were reasons other than my having pissed off the Pattern for its wanting me dead immediately following my completion of my bizarre quest and repairing of the nearest of the Broken Patterns. But Dworkin refused to elaborate, feeling that my knowing the reason could influence a possible future choice which should be made freely. All of which sounded like gibberish to me, save that everything else he said struck me as eminently sane, in contrast with the Dworkin I knew of from legend and hearsay.

My mind plunged and reared through the pool of blood that was the Jewel's interior. The Pattern segments I had traversed and those I had yet to travel moved about me, flashing like lightning. I'd a feeling my mind was going to crash against some invisible Veil and shatter. My movement was out of control now, accelerating. There was no way, I knew, for me to withdraw from this thing until I had run its course.

Dworkin felt that I had been protected from the Pattern during our confrontation, when I had gone back to check on the figure I had seen, because I was wearing the Jewel. I could not keep wearing it for too long, though, because this also had a tendency to prove fatal. He decided that I must become attuned to the Jewel—as were my father and Random—before I let it out of my possession. I would thereafter bear the higher-order image within me, which should function as well as the Jewel in defending me against the Pattern. I could hardly argue with the man who had supposedly created the Pattern, using the Jewel. So I agreed with him. Only I was too tired to do what he suggested. That was why I had had Ghost return me to my crystal cave, my sanctuary, to rest first.

Now, now . . . I flowed. I spun. Occasionally I stalled. The Jewel's equivalents of the Veils were no less formidable because I had left my body behind. Each such passage left me as wrung out as running a mile in Olympic time. Though I knew at one level that I stood holding the Jewel through which I took my initiatory way, at another I could feel my heart pounding, and at another I recalled parts of a guest lecture by Joan Halifax for an anthropology course I was taking, years before. The medium swirled like Geyser Peak Merlot 1985 in a goblet—and whom was I looking across the table at that night? No matter. Onward, down and around. The blood-brightened tide was loosed. A message was being inscribed upon my spirit. In the beginning was a word I cannot spell . . . Brighter, brighter. Faster, faster. Collision with a ruby wall, I a smear upon it. Come now, Schopenhauer, to the final game of will. An age or two came and went; then, suddenly, the way was opened. I was spilled forth into the light of an exploding star. Red, red, red, shifting me onward, away, like my little boat *Starburst,* driven, expanding, coming home . . .

I collapsed. Though I did not lose consciousness, my state of mind was not normal either. There was a hypnagogia I could have passed through at any time I chose, in either direction. But why? I am seldom the recipient of such a delivery of euphoria. I felt I'd earned it, so I drifted, right there, for a long, long time.

When it finally subsided below the level that made indulgence worthwhile, I climbed to my feet, swayed, leaned against the wall, made my way to the storeroom for another drink of water. I was also ravenous, but none of the tinned or freeze-dried foods appealed to me that greatly. Especially when fresher things were not that hard to come by.

I walked back through those familiar chambers. So I had followed Dworkin's advice. It was a pity I'd turned my back before I recalled a long list of questions I wished to ask him. When I turned back again, he was gone.

I climbed. Coming up out of my cave, I stood atop the blue prominence which held the only entranceway I knew of. It was a breezy, balmy, springlike morning with only a few small puffs of cloud to the east. I drew a deep breath for pleasure and expelled it. Then I stooped and moved the blue boulder to block the opening. I'd hate to be surprised by a predator should I come this way again in need of sanctuary.

I took off the Jewel of Judgment and hung it on a spur of the boulder. Then I moved off about ten paces.

"Hi, Dad."

The Ghostwheel was a golden Frisbee, come sailing out of the west.

"Good morning, Ghost."

"Why are you abandoning that device? It's one of the most powerful tools I've ever seen."

"I'm not abandoning it, but I'm about to summon the Sign of the Logrus, and I don't think they'd get on too well. I'm even a little leery over how the Logrus will take to me with this higher-order Pattern attunement I'm wearing."

"Perhaps I'd better move along and check back with you later."

"Stick around," I said. "Maybe you can bail me out if this turns into a problem."

I summoned the Sign of the Logrus then, and it came and hovered before me, and nothing happened. I shifted a part of my awareness into the Jewel, there on the side of the boulder, and through it I was able to perceive the Logrus from another perspective. Eerie. Also painless.

I centered myself within my own skull once again, extended my arms into the Logrus limbs, reached. . . .

In less than a minute I had a plate of buttermilk pancakes, a side order of sausages, a cup of coffee, and a glass of orange juice.

"I could have gotten them for you faster than that," Ghost remarked.

"I'm sure you could have," I said. "I was just testing systems."

As I ate, I tried to sort my priorities. When I finished, I sent the dishes back where they had come from, retrieved the Jewel, hung it about my neck, and stood.

"Okay, Ghost. Time to head back to Amber," I said.

He expanded and opened and sank, so that I stood before a golden arch. I stepped forward—

—and back into my apartment.

"Thanks," I said.

"*De nada,* Dad. Listen, I've a question: When you summoned breakfast, did you notice anything at all unusual in the way the Logrus Sign behaved?"

"How do you mean that?" I asked as I moved to wash my hands.

"Let's start with physical sensations. Did it seem . . . sticky?"

"That's an odd way to put it," I said. "But as a matter of fact, it did seem to take slightly longer than usual to disengage. Why do you ask?"

"A peculiar notion has just occurred to me. Can you do Pattern magic?"

"Yeah, but I'm better at the Logrus variety."

"You might want to try them both and compare them if you get a chance."

"Why?"

"I'm actually starting to get hunches. I'll tell you as soon as I've checked this one out."

Ghostwheel was gone.

"Shit," I said, and I washed my face.

I looked out the window, and a handful of snowflakes blew by. I fetched a key from my desk drawer. There were a couple of things I wanted to get out of the way immediately.

I stepped into the corridor. I had not gone more than a few paces before I heard the sound. I halted and listened. Then I continued, past the stairway, the sound growing steadily in volume as I advanced. By the time I reached the long corridor which ran past the library I knew that Random was back because I didn't know of anyone else around here who could drum like that—or would dare to use the King's drums if he could.

I continued on past the half-opened door to the corner, where I turned right. My first impulse had been to enter, give him back the Jewel of Judgment, and try to explain what had happened. Then I recalled Flora's advice that anything honest, straightforward, and aboveboard would always get you in trouble here. While I hated to give her credit for having enunciated a general rule, I could see that in this particular instance it would certainly tie me up with a lot of explaining when there were other things I wanted to be about—and, for that matter, it might also get me ordered not to do some of them.

I continued to the far entrance to the dining room, where I checked quickly and determined the place to be deserted. Good. Inside and to the right, as I recalled, there was a sliding panel which would get me into a hollow section of wall beside the library, furnished with pegs or a ladder that would take me up to a hidden entrance to the library's balcony. It could also take me down through the spiral stair's shaft and into the caverns below, if memory served. I hoped I never had reason to check that part out, but I was sufficiently into family tradition these days that I wanted to do a little spying, as several muttered exchanges as I'd passed the opened door led me to believe that Random was not alone in there. If knowledge really is power, then I needed all I could get my hands on, as I'd felt especially vulnerable for some time now.

Yes, the panel slid, and I was through it in a trice, sending my spirit-light on ahead. I hand-over-handed my way quickly to the top and opened the panel there slowly and quietly, feeling grateful to whoever had thought to conceal its space with a wide chair. I was able to see around the chair's right arm with comparative safety from detection—a good view of the room's north end.

And there was Random, drumming, and Martin, all chains and leather, was seated before him, listening. Random was doing something I'd never seen done before. He was playing with five sticks. He had one in each hand, one under each arm, and he held one in his teeth. And he was revolving them as he played, moving the one in his mouth to replace the one under his right arm, which replaced the one in his right hand, which he had switched over to his left hand, the left-hand one going up beneath his left arm, the left arm one going to his teeth, all without missing a beat. It was hypnotic. I stared until he wound out the number. His old set of traps was hardly the fusion drummer's dreamworld of translucent plastic with tipped cymbals the size of battle shields set around the snares, a mess of tomtoms, and a couple of basses, all lit up like Coral's circle of fire. Random's set went back to a time before snares grew thin and nervous, basses shrank, and cymbals caught acromegaly and began to hum.

"Never saw that done before," I heard Martin say.

Random shrugged.

"Bit of horsing around," he said. "Learned it from Freddie Moore, in the thirties, either at the Victoria or the Village Vanguard, when he was with Art Hodes and Max Kaminsky. I forget which place. It goes back to vaudeville, when they didn't have any mikes and the lighting was bad. Had to do show-off things like that, or dress funny, he told me, to keep the audience paying attention."

"Shame they had to cater to the crowd that way."

"Yeah, none of you guys would dream of dressing funny or throwing your instruments around."

There followed a silence, and there was no way I could see the expression on Martin's face. Then, "I meant it different from that," Martin said.

"Yeah, me, too," Random replied. Then he tossed three of the sticks down and began to play again.

I leaned back and listened. A moment later I was startled to hear an alto sax come in. When I looked again, Martin was standing, his back still to me, and playing the thing. It must have been on the floor on the other side of his chair. There was a Richie Cole flavor to it that I rather liked, and it kind of surprised me. As much as I enjoyed it, I felt that I did not belong in this room right now, and I edged back, opened the panel, passed through, and closed it. After I'd climbed down and let myself out, I decided to cut through the dining room rather than pass the library entrance again. The music carried for some distance thereafter, and I wished I'd learned a spell of Mandor's for capturing sounds in precious stones, though I'm not sure how the Jewel of Judgment would have taken to containing "Wild Man Blues."

I was planning on walking up the east corridor to the point where it intersected with the north one in the vicinity of my apartment, turning left there, and taking the stairs up to the royal suite, knocking on the door, and returning the Jewel to Vialle, whom I hoped I could get to take a rain check on explanations. And if not, I'd rather explain to her than to Random anyway. I could leave out a lot that she wouldn't know to ask me. Of course, Random would catch up with me with questions eventually. But the later, the better.

But then I was going right past my father's rooms. I'd brought along the key so that I could stop in later, for what I considered obvious reasons. Still, since I was already on the spot, it would be more time-effective. I unlocked the door, opened it, and stepped inside.

The silver rose was gone from the bud vase on the dresser. Odd. I took a step toward it. There came a sound of voices from the other room, too soft for me to distinguish words. I froze. He might well be in there. But you don't just go bursting into someone's bedroom, especially when it's likely there's company present—particularly when it's your father's room and you had to unlock an outer door to get where you were. Suddenly I was extremely self-conscious. I wanted to get out of there, fast. I unbuckled my sword belt, from which Grayswandir depended in its not-quite-perfect fit of a sheath. I did not dare bear it any farther but hung it from one of the garment pegs on the wall near the door next to a short trench coat I hadn't noticed before. I slipped out then and locked the door as quietly as I could.

Awkward. Was he really coming and going with some regularity, somehow managing to avoid notice? Or was some sort of phenomenon of an entirely different order in progress within his quarters? I'd heard an occasional rumor that some of the older chambers had *sub specie spatium* doorways, if one could but figure how to activate them, providing considerable extra closet space as well as private means of entry and egress. Something else I should have asked Dworkin about. Maybe I've got a pocket universe under my bed. I'd never looked.

I turned and walked quickly away. As I neared the corner, I slowed. Dworkin had felt that the presence of the Jewel of Judgment on my person was the thing that had protected me from the Pattern, had it really been tempted to harm me earlier. On the other hand, the Jewel, worn too long, could itself do damage to the wearer. Therefore, he had counseled me to get some rest and then pass my mind through the stone's matrix, in effect creating a recording of a higher power of the Pattern within me along with some measure of immunity to assaults by the Pattern itself. Interesting conjecture. And that's all it was, of course: conjecture.

When I reached the cross corridor where a left would take me to the stairway or a right back to my rooms, I hesitated. There was a sitting room diagonally across the way, to the left, across from Benedict's seldom used rooms. I headed for it, entered, sank into a heavy chair in the corner. All I wanted to do was deal with my enemies, help my friends, get my name off any shit lists it currently occupied, locate my father, and come to some sort of terms with the sleeping *ty'iga*. Then I could see about the continuance of my interrupted *Wanderjahr.* All of which, I realized, required that I now reask myself the now near-rhetorical question, How much of my business did I want Random to know?

I thought of him in the library, playing a duet with his near-estranged son. I understood that he had once been pretty wild and footloose and nasty, that he hadn't really wanted the job of ruling this archetypal world. But parenthood, marriage, and the Unicorn's choice seemed to have laid a lot on him—deepening his character, I suppose, at the price of a lot of the fun things in his life. Right now he seemed to have a lot of problems with this Kashfa-Begma business, possibly having just resorted to an assassination and agreed to a less than favorable treaty to maintain the complex political forces of the Golden Circle at an even level. And who knew what might be going on elsewhere to add to his troubles? Did I really want to draw this man into something I might well be able to handle myself with his never being any the wiser, or ever even bothered, concerning it? Conversely, if I did draw him into my affairs, it seemed likely that he might well lay restrictions on me which could hamper my ability to respond to what seemed the daily exigencies of my life. It could also raise another matter which had been shunted aside years ago.

I had never sworn allegiance to Amber. Nobody had ever asked me to. After all, I was Corwin's son, and I had come to Amber willingly and made my home here for some time before going off to the shadow Earth, where so many of the Amberites had gone to school. I returned often, and I seemed to be on good terms with everyone. I didn't really see why the concept of dual citizenship shouldn't apply.

I'd rather the matter did not come up at all, though. I did not like the thought of being forced to choose between Amber and the Courts. I wouldn't do it for the Unicorn and the Serpent, the Pattern and the Logrus, and I didn't care to do it for the royalty of either court.

All of which indicated that Vialle should not have even a sketchy edition of my story. Any version at all would require an eventual accounting. However, if the Jewel were returned without an explanation of where it had been, then no one would know to come after me on the matter, and things would still be set right. How could I lie if I were not even asked questions?

I mulled that along a little further. What I would actually be doing would be to save a tired, troubled man the burden of additional problems. There was nothing he could or should do about most of my affairs. Whatever was going on between the Pattern and the Logrus seemed mainly important as a metaphysical affair. I couldn't see where much good or bad might come out of it on a practical level. And if I saw something coming, I could always tell Random then.

Okay. That's one nice thing about reasoning abilities. You can use them to make yourself feel virtuous rather than, say, guilty. I stretched and cracked my knuckles.

"Ghost?" I said softly.

No response.

I reached for my Trumps, but even as I touched them, a wheel of light flashed on across the room.

"You did hear me," I said.

"I felt your need," came the reply.

"Whatever," I said, drawing the Jewel's chain up over my head and holding the stone out before me. "Do you think you could return this to its secret compartment beside the fireplace in the royal suite without anyone's being any wiser?" I asked.

"I'm leery about touching that thing," Ghost responded. "I don't know what its structure might do to my structure."

"Okay," I said. "I guess I'll find a way to do it myself then. But the time has come to test a hypothesis. If the Pattern attacks me, try to whisk me to safety, please."

"Very well."

I set the Jewel on a nearby table.

After about a half minute I realized that I had braced myself against the Pattern's death stroke. I relaxed my shoulders. I drew a deep breath. I remained intact. Could be that Dworkin was right and the Pattern would leave me alone. Also, I should be able to summon the Pattern in the Jewel now, he told me, as I do the Sign of the Logrus. There were Pattern-magics which could only be wrought via this route, though Dworkin hadn't taken the time to instruct me in their employment. He'd suggested that a sorcerer should be able to figure the system out. I decided that this could wait. I was in no mood just now for commerce of any sort with the Pattern in any of its incarnations.

"Hey, Pattern," I said. "Want to call it even?"

There came no reply.

"I believe it is aware of you here and what you just did," Ghost said. "I feel its presence. Could be you're off the hook."

"Could be," I responded, taking out my Trumps and sorting through them.

"Whom would you like to get in touch with?" Ghost asked.

"I'm curious about Luke," I said. "I want to see whether he's okay. And I'm wondering about Mandor. I assume you sent him to a safe place."

"Oh, nothing but the best," Ghost replied. "Same for Queen Jasra. Did you want her, too?"

"Not really. In fact, I don't *want* any of them. I just wanted to see—"

Ghost winked out while I was still talking. I wasn't at all certain that his eagerness to please was an improvement over his earlier belligerence.

I withdrew Luke's card and went inside it.

I heard someone passing along the corridor. The footsteps went on by.

I felt Luke's awareness, though no vision of his circumstances reached me.

"Luke, you hear me?" I inquired.

"Yep," he answered. "You okay, Merle?"

"I'm all right," I said. "How about yourself? That was quite a fight you—"

"I'm fine."

"I hear your voice, but I can't see a thing."

"Got a blackout on the Trumps. You don't know how to do that?"

"Never looked into the matter. Have to get you to teach me sometime. Uh, why are they blacked out anyway?"

"Somebody might get in touch and figure what I'm up to."

"If you're about to lead a commando raid on Amber, I'm going to be highly pissed."

"Come on! You know I swore off! This is something entirely different."

"Thought you were a prisoner of Dalt's."

"My status is unchanged."

"Well, he damn near killed you once and he just beat the shit out of you the other day."

"The first time he'd stumbled into an old berserker spell Sharu'd left behind for a trap; the second time was business. I'll be okay. But right now everything I'm up to is hush-hush, and I've got to run. G'bye."

Gone Luke, the presence.

The footsteps had halted, and I'd heard a knocking on a nearby door. After a time I heard a door being opened, then closed. I had not overheard any exchange of words. In that it had been nearby and that the two nearest apartments were Benedict's and my own, I began to wonder. I was fairly certain that Benedict was not in his, and I recalled not having locked my own door when I had stepped out. Therefore . . .

Picking up the Jewel of Judgment, I crossed the room and stepped out into the hall. I checked Benedict's door. Locked. I looked down the north-south hallway and walked back to the stairway and checked around in that area. There was no one in sight. I strode up to my own place then and stood listening for a time outside each of my doors. No sounds from within. The only alternatives I could think of were Gérard's rooms, back down the side corridor, and Brand's, which lay behind my own. I had thought of knocking out a wall—in keeping with the recent spirit of remodeling and redecorating Random had gotten into—adding Brand's rooms to my own, for a very good-size apartment. The rumor that his were haunted, though, and the wailings I sometimes heard through the walls late at night dissuaded me.

I took a quick walk then, knocking on and finally trying both Brand's and Gérard's doors. No response, and both were locked. Odder and odder.

Frakir had given a quick pulse when I'd touched Brand's door, and while I'd gone on alert for several moments, nothing untoward had approached. I was about to dismiss it as a disturbing reaction to the remnants of eldritch spells I had occasionally seen drifting about the vicinity when I noticed that the Jewel of Judgment was pulsing.

I raised the chain and stared into the gem. Yes, an image had taken form. I beheld the hallway around the corner, my two doors, and intervening artwork on the wall in plain view. The doorway to the left—the one that let upon my bedroom—seemed to be outlined in red and pulsing. Did that mean I was supposed to avoid it or rush in there? That's the trouble with mystical advice.

I walked back and turned the corner again. This time the gem—perhaps having felt my query and decided some editing was in order—showed me approaching and opening the door it was indicating. Of course, of the two, that door was locked. . . .

I fumbled for my key, reflecting that I could not even rush in with a drawn blade, having just disposed of Grayswandir. I did have a couple of tricky spells hung, though. Maybe one of them would save me if the going got too rough. Maybe not, too.

I turned the key and flung the door open.

"Merle!" she shrieked, and I saw that it was Coral. She stood beside my bed, where her putative sister the *ty'iga* was reclined. She quickly moved one hand behind her back. "You, uh, surprised me."

"Vice versa," I replied, for which there *is* an equivalent in Thari. "What's up, lady?"

"I came back to tell you that I located my father and gave him a soothing story about that Corridor of Mirrors you told me about. Is there really such a place here?"

"Yes. You won't find it in any guides, though. It comes and goes. So, he's mollified?"

"Uh-huh. But now he's wondering where Nayda is."

"This gets trickier."

"Yes."

She was blushing, and she did not meet my eyes readily. She seemed aware, too, that I was noting her discomfort.

"I told him that perhaps Nayda was exploring, as I'd been," she went on, "and that I'd ask after her."

"Mm-hm."

I shifted my gaze to Nayda. Coral immediately moved forward and brushed against me. She placed a hand on my shoulder, drew me toward her.

"I thought you were going to sleep," she said.

"Yes, I was. Did, too. I was running some errands just now."

"I don't understand," she said.

"Time lines," I explained. "I economized. I'm rested."

"Fascinating," she said, brushing my lips with her own. "I'm glad that you're rested."

"Coral," I said, embracing her briefly, "you don't have to bullshit me. You know I was dead tired when you left. You had no reason to believe that I'd be anything but comatose if you returned this soon."

I caught hold of her left wrist behind her back and drew her hand around to the front, raising it between us. She was surprisingly strong. And I made no effort to pry open her hand, for I could see between the fingers what it was that she held. It was one of the metal balls Mandor often used to create impromptu spells. I released her hand. She did not draw away from me, but rather, "I can explain," she said, finally meeting my gaze and holding it.

"I wish you would," I said. "In fact, I wish you'd done it a bit sooner."

"Maybe the story you heard about her being dead and her body the host for a demon is true," she said. "But she's been good to me recently. She's finally become the sister I'd always wished she'd been. Then you brought me back here and I saw her like that, not knowing what you really planned to do with her—"

"I want you to know that I wouldn't hurt her, Coral," I interrupted. "I owe her—it—for favors past. When I was young and naive on the shadow Earth, she probably saved my neck, several times. You have no reason to fear for her here."

She cocked her head to the right and narrowed one eye.

"I'd no way of knowing that," she said, "from what you told me. I came back, hoping to get in, hoping you were deeply asleep, hoping I could break the spell or at least lift it enough to talk with her. I wanted to find out for myself whether she was really my sister—or something else."

I sighed. I reached out to squeeze her shoulder and realized I was still clutching the Jewel of Judgment in my left hand. I squeezed her arm with my right hand instead and said, "Look, I understand. It was boorish of me to show you your sister laid out that way and not to have gone into a little more detail. I can only plead industrial fatigue and apologize. I promise you she's in no pain. But I really don't want to mess with this spell right now because it's not one of mine—"

Just then Nayda moaned softly. I studied her for several minutes, but nothing more followed.

"Did you pluck that metal ball out of the air?" I asked. "I don't recall seeing one for the final spell."

Coral shook her head.

"It was lying on her breast. One of her hands was over it," she said.

"What prompted you to check there?"

"The position looked unnatural, that's all. Here."

She handed me the ball. I took it and weighed it in the palm of my right hand. I had no idea how the things functioned. The metal balls were to Mandor what Frakir was to me—a piece of idiosyncratic personal magic, forged out of his unconscious in the heart of the Logrus.

"Are you going to put it back?" she asked.

"No," I told her. "Like I said, it wasn't one of my spells. I don't know how it works, and I don't want to fool around with it."

"Merlin . . . ?"—whispered, from Nayda, her eyes still closed.

"We'd better go talk in the next room," I said to Coral. "I'll lay a spell of my own on her first, though. Just a simple soporific—"

The air sparkled and spun behind Coral, and she must have guessed from my stare that something was going on, for she turned.

"Merle, what is it?" she asked, retreating toward me as a golden archway took form.

"Ghost?" I said.

"Right," came the reply. "Jasra was not where I left her. But I brought your brother."

Mandor, still clad mainly in black, his hair a great mass of silver-white, appeared suddenly, glancing at Coral and Nayda, focusing on me, beginning to smile, stepping forward. Then his gaze shifted, and he halted. He stared. I had never seen that frightened expression on his face before.

"Bloody Eye of Chaos!" he exclaimed, summoning up a protective screen with a gesture. "How did you come by it?"

He took a step backward. The arch immediately collapsed into a gold-leaf calligraphed letter *O,* and Ghost slid around the room to hover at my right side.

Suddenly Nayda sat up on my bed, darting wild glances.

"Merlin!" she cried. "Are you all right?"

"So far so good," I answered. "Not to worry. Take it easy. All's well."

"Who's been tampering with my spell?" Mandor asked as Nayda swung her legs over the side of the bed and Coral cringed.

"It was a sort of accident," I said.

I opened my right hand. The metal sphere immediately levitated and shot off in his direction, narrowly missing Coral, whose hands were now extended in a general martial arts defense pattern, though she seemed uncertain what or whom she should be defending against. So she kept turning—Mandor, Nayda, Ghost, repeat. . . .

"Cool it, Coral," I said. "You're in no danger."

"The left eye of the Serpent!" Nayda cried. "Free me, oh, Formless One, and I will pledge with mine!"

Frakir in the meantime was warning me that all was not well, in case I hadn't noticed.

"Just what the hell is going on?" I yelled.

Nayda sprang to her feet, lunged forward, and with that unnatural demon strength snatched the Jewel of Judgment from my hand, pushed me aside, and tore out into the hallway.

I stumbled, recovered.

"Hold that *ty'iga!*" I cried, and the Ghostwheel flashed past me followed by Mandor's balls.

10

I was the next thing out into the hallway. I turned left and started running. A *ty'iga* may be fast, but so am I.

"I thought you were supposed to be protecting me!" I shouted after her.

"This takes precedence," she answered, "over your mother's binding."

"What?" I said. "My mother?"

"She placed me under a *geas* to take care of you when you went off to school," she replied. "This breaks it! Free at last!"

"Damn!" I observed.

Then, as she neared the stairway, the Sign of the Logrus appeared before her, larger than any I'd ever summoned, filling the corridor from wall to wall, roiling, sprawling, fire-shot, tentacular, a reddish haze of menace drifting about it. It took a certain measure of chutzpah for it to manifest like that here in Amber on the Pattern's turf, so I knew the stakes were high.

"Receive me, oh, Logrus," she cried, "for I bear the Eye of the Serpent," and the Logrus opened, creating a fiery tunnel at its center. I could somehow tell that its other end was not a place farther along my hallway.

But then Nayda was halted, as if she had suddenly encountered a glass partition, and she stiffened into a position of attention. Three of Mandor's gleaming spheres were suddenly orbiting her cataleptic form.

I was thrown from my feet and pressed back against the wall. I raised my right arm to block whatever might be coming down on me, as I looked backward.

An image of the Pattern itself, as large as the Logrus Sign, had just put in an appearance only a few feet behind me, manifesting about as far in that direction from Nayda as the Logrus was before her, parenthesizing the lady or the *ty'iga* between the poles of existence, so to speak, and incidentally enclosing me along with her. The area about me near the Pattern grew bright as a sunny morning while that at the other end took on the aspect of a baleful twilight. Were they about to reenact the Big Bang/Crunch, I wondered, with me as an unwilling momentary witness?

"Uh, Your Honors," I began, feeling obliged to try talking them out of it and wishing I were Luke, who just might be able to swing such a feat. "This is a perfect time to employ an impartial arbitrator, and I just happen to be uniquely qualified if you will but reflect—"

The golden circlet that I knew to be Ghostwheel suddenly dropped over Nayda's head, lengthening itself downward into a tube. Ghost had fitted himself within the orbits of Mandor's spheres and must somehow have insulated himself against whatever forces they were exerting, for they slowed, wobbled, and finally dropped to the floor, two striking the wall ahead of me and one rolling down the stairway ahead and to the right.

The Signs of the Pattern and the Logrus began to advance then, and I crawled quickly to keep ahead of the Pattern.

"Don't come any closer, fellows," Ghostwheel suddenly announced. "There's no telling what I might do if you make me even more nervous than I already am."

Both Power Signs halted in their advances. From around the corner to the left, up ahead, I heard Droppa's drunken voice, raised in some bawdy ballad, coming this way. Then it grew silent. Several moments passed, and he began singing "Rock of Ages" in a far, far weaker voice. Then this, too, was cut off, followed by a heavy thud and the sound of breaking glass.

It occurred to me that I should be able, from a distance such as this, to extend my awareness into the Jewel. But I was uncertain what effects I might then be able to produce with the thing, considering the fact that none of the four principals involved in the confrontation was human.

I felt the beginnings of a Trump contact.

"Yes?" I whispered.

Dworkin's voice came to me then.

"Whatever control you may have over the thing," he said, "use it to keep the Jewel away from the Logrus."

Just then a crackly voice, shifting in pitch and gender from syllable to syllable, emerged from the red tunnel.

"Return the Eye of Chaos," it said. "The Unicorn took it from the Serpent when they fought, in the beginning. It was stolen. Return it. Return it."

The blue face I had seen above the Pattern did not materialize, but the voice I'd heard at that time responded, "It was paid for with blood and pain. Title passed."

"The Jewel of Judgment and the Eye of Chaos or Eye of the Serpent are different names for the same stone?" I said.

"Yes," Dworkin replied.

"What happens if the Serpent gets its eye back?" I inquired.

"The universe will probably come to an end."

"Oh," I observed.

"What am I bid for the thing?" Ghost asked.

"Impetuous construct," the voice of the Pattern intoned.

"Rash artifact," wailed the Logrus.

"Save the compliments," Ghost said, "and give me something I want."

"I could tear it from you," the Pattern responded.

"I could have you apart and it away in an instant," stated the Logrus.

"But neither of you will do it," Ghost answered, "because such a focusing of your attention and energies would leave either of you vulnerable to the other."

In my mind, I heard Dworkin chuckle.

"Tell me why this confrontation need take place at all," Ghost went on, "after all this time."

"The balance was tipped against me by recent actions of this turncoat," the Logrus replied—a burst of fire occurring above my head, presumably to demonstrate the identity of the turncoat in question.

I smelled burning hair, and I warded the flame.

"Just a minute!" I cried. "I wasn't given much choice in the matter!"

"But there was a choice," wailed the Logrus, "and you made it."

"Indeed, he did," responded the Pattern. "But it served only to redress the balance you'd tipped in your own favor."

"Redress? You overcompensated! Now it's tipped in your favor! Besides, it was accidentally tipped my way, by the traitor's father." Another fireball followed, and I warded again. "It was not my doing."

"You probably inspired it."

"If you can get the Jewel to me," Dworkin said, "I can put it out of reach of both of them until this matter is settled."

"I don't know whether I can get hold of it," I said, "but I'll remember that."

"Give it to me," the Logrus said to Ghost, "and I will take you with me as First Servant."

"You are a processor of data," said the Pattern. "I will give you knowledge such as none in all of Shadow possess."

"I will give you power," said the Logrus.

"Not interested," said Ghost, and the cylinder spun and vanished.

The girl, the Jewel, and everything were gone.

The Logrus wailed, the Pattern growled, and the Signs of both Powers rushed to meet, somewhere near Bleys's nearer room.

I raised every protective spell that I could. Behind me I could feel Mandor doing the same. I covered my head, I drew up my knees, I—

I was falling. Through a bright, soundless concussion. Bits of debris struck me. From several directions. I'd a hunch that I had just bought the farm and that I was about to die without opportunity to reveal my insight into the nature of reality: The Pattern did not care about the children of Amber any more than the Logrus did about those of the Courts of Chaos. The Powers cared, perhaps, about themselves, about each other, about heavy cosmic principles, about the Unicorn and the Serpent, of which they were very probably but geometric manifestations. They did not care about me, about Coral, about Mandor, probably not even about Oberon or Dworkin himself. We were totally insignificant or at most tools or sometimes annoyances, to be employed or destroyed as the occasion warranted—

"Give me your hand," Dworkin said, and I saw him, as in a Trump contact. I reached and—

—fell hard at his feet upon a colorful rug spread over a stone floor, in a windowless chamber my father had once described to me, filled with books and exotic artifacts, lit by bowls of light which hung without visible means of support high in the air.

"Thanks," I said, rising slowly, brushing myself off, massaging a sore spot in my left thigh.

"Caught a whiff of your thoughts," he said. "There's more to it."

"I'm sure. But sometimes I enjoy being bleak-minded. How much of that crap the Powers were arguing about was true?"

"Oh, all of it," Dworkin said, "by their lights. The biggest bar to understanding is the interpretation they put on each other's doings. That, and the fact that everything can always be pushed another step backward—such as the break in the Pattern having strengthened the Logrus and the possibility that the Logrus actively influenced Brand into doing it. But then the Logrus might claim this was in retaliation for the Day of the Broken Branches several centuries ago."

"I haven't heard about that one," I said.

He shrugged.

"I'm not surprised. It wasn't all that important a matter, except to them. What I'm saying is that to argue as they do is to head into an infinite regression—back to first causes, which are always untrustworthy."

"So what's the answer?"

"Answer? This isn't a classroom. There are no answers that would matter, except to a philosopher—that is, none with any practical applications."

He poured a small cup of green liquid from a silver flask and passed it to me.

"Drink this," he said.

"It's a little early in the day for me."

"It's not refreshment. It's medication," he explained. "You're in a state of near shock, whether you've noticed or not."

I tossed the thing off, and it burned like a liquor but didn't seem to be one. I did feel myself beginning to relax during the next few minutes, in places I had not even realized I was tense.

"Coral, Mandor . . ." I said.

He gestured, and a glowing globe descended, drew nearer. He signed the air with a half-familiar gesture, and something like the Logrus Sign without the Logrus came over me. A picture formed within the globe.

That long section of hallway where the encounter had occurred had been destroyed, along with the stairs, Benedict's apartment, and possibly Gérard's as well. Also, Bleys's rooms, portions of my own, the sitting room I had been occupying but a short time before, and the northeast corner of the library were missing, as were the floor and ceiling. Below, I could see that sections of the kitchen and armory had been hit, and possibly more across the way. Looking upward—magic globes being wondrous accommodating—I could see sky, which meant that the blast had gone through the third and fourth floors, possibly damaging the royal suite along with the upper stairways and maybe the laboratory—and who knew what all else.

Standing on the edge of the abyss near what had been a section of Bleys's or Gérard's quarters was Mandor, his right arm apparently broken, hand tucked in behind his wide black belt. Coral leaned heavily upon his left shoulder, and there was blood on her face. I am not sure that she was fully conscious. Mandor held her about the waist with his left arm, and a metal ball circled the two of them. Diagonally across the abyss, Random stood on a heavy crossbeam near the opening to the library. I believe Martin was standing atop a short stack, below and to the rear. He was still holding his sax. Random appeared more than a little agitated and seemed to be shouting.

"Voice! Voice!" I said.

Dworkin waved.

"—ucking Lord of Chaos blowing up my palace!" Random was saying.

"The lady is injured, Your Highness," Mandor said.

Random passed a hand across his face. Then he looked upward.

"If there's an easy way to get her to my quarters, Vialle is very skilled in certain areas of medicine," he said in a softer voice. "So am I, for that matter."

"Just where is that, Your Highness?"

Random leaned to his side and pointed upward.

"Looks as if you won't need the door to get in, but I can't tell whether there's enough stairway left to get up there or where you might cross to it if there is."

"I'll make it," Mandor said, and two more of the balls came rushing to him and set themselves into eccentric orbits about him and Coral. Shortly thereafter they were levitated and drifted slowly toward the opening Random had indicated.

"I'll be along shortly," Random called after them. He looked as if he were about to add something, but then regarded the devastation, lowered his head, and turned away. I did the same thing.

Dworkin was offering me another dose of the green medicine, and I took it. Some sort of trank, it seemed, in addition to whatever else it did.

"I have to go to her," I told him. "I like that lady, and I want to be sure she's all right."

"I can certainly send you there," Dworkin said, "though I cannot think of anything you could do for her which will not be done well by others. Perhaps the time were more profitably spent in pursuit of that errant construct of yours the Ghostwheel. It must be persuaded to return the Jewel of Judgment."

"Very well," I acknowledged. "But I want to see Coral first."

"Your appearance could cause considerable delay," he said, "because of explanations which may be required of you."

"I don't care," I told him.

"All right. A moment then."

He moved away and took down what appeared to be a sheathed wand from the wall, where it had hung suspended from a peg. He hung the sheath upon his belt, then crossed to a small cabinet and removed a flat leather-bound case from one of its drawers. It rattled with a faint metallic sound as he slipped it into a pocket. A small jewelry box vanished up a sleeve without any sound.

"Come this way," he told me, approaching and taking my hand.

He turned me and led me toward the room's darkest corner, where I had not noted that a tall, curiously framed mirror hung. It exhibited an odd reflective capacity in that it showed us and the room behind us with perfect clarity from a distance, but the closer we approached to its surface, the more indistinct all of its images became. I could see what was coming, coming. But I still tensed as Dworkin, a pace in advance of me by then, stepped through its foggy surface and jerked me after him.

I stumbled and regained my footing, coming to myself in the good half of the blasted royal suite in front of a decorative mirror. I reached back quickly and tapped it with my fingertips, but its surface remained solid. The short, stooped figure of Dworkin stood before me, and he still had hold of my right hand. Looking past that profile, which in some ways caricatured my own, I saw that the bed had been moved eastward, away from the broken corner and a large opening formerly occupied by a section of flooring. Random and Vialle stood on the near side of the bed, their backs to us. They were studying Coral, who was stretched out upon the counterpane and appeared to be unconscious. Mandor, seated in a heavy chair at the bed's foot, observing operations, was the first to notice our presence, which he acknowledged with a nod.

"How . . . is she?" I asked.

"Concussion," Mandor replied, "and damage to the right eye."

Random turned. Whatever he was about to say to me died on his lips when he realized who stood beside me.

"Dworkin!" he said. "It's been so long. I didn't know whether you were still alive. Are you . . . all right?"

The dwarf chuckled.

"I read your meaning, and I'm rational," he replied. "I would like to examine the lady now."

"Of course," Random answered, moving aside.

"Merlin," Dworkin said, "see whether you can locate that Ghostwheel device of yours, and ask it to return the artifact it borrowed."

"I understand," I said, reaching for my Trumps.

Moments later I was reaching, reaching . . .

"I felt your intent several moments ago, Dad."

"Well, do you have the Jewel or don't you?"

"Yes, I just finished with it."

" 'Finished'?"

"Finished utilizing it."

"In what fashion did you . . . utilize it?"

"As I understood from you that passing one's awareness through it would give some protection against the Pattern, I wondered whether it might work for an ideally synthesized being such as myself."

"That's a nice term, 'ideally synthesized.' Where'd it come from?"

"I coined it myself when seeking the most appropriate designation."

"I've a hunch it'll reject you."

"It didn't."

"Oh. You actually got all the way through the thing?"

"I did."

"What effect did it have upon you?"

"That's a hard thing to assess. My perceptions are altered. It's difficult to explain. . . . It's subtle, whatever it is."

"Fascinating. Can you move your awareness into the stone from a distance now?"

"Yes."

"When all of our present troubles have passed, I'm going to want to test you again."

"I'm curious myself to know what's changed."

"In the meantime, there is a need for the Jewel here."

"Coming through."

The air shimmered before me.

Ghostwheel appeared as a silver circlet, the Jewel of Judgment as its center. I cupped my hand and collected it. I took it to Dworkin, who did not even glance at me as he received it. I looked down at Coral's face and looked away quickly, wishing I hadn't.

I moved back near Ghost.

"Where's Nayda?" I asked.

"I'm not sure," he replied. "She asked me to leave her—there near the crystal cave—after I took the Jewel away from her."

"What was she doing?"

"Crying."

"Why?"

"I suppose because both of her missions in life have been frustrated. She was charged to guard you unless some wild chance brought her the opportunity of obtaining the Jewel, in which instance she was released from the first directive. This actually occurred; only I deprived her of the stone. Now she is bound to neither course."

"You'd think she'd be happy to be free at last. She wasn't on either job as a matter of choice. She can go back to doing whatever carefree demons do beyond the Rimwall."

"Not exactly, Dad."

"What do you mean?"

"She seems to be stuck in that body. Apparently she can't simply abandon it the way she could others she's used. It has something to do with there being no primary occupant."

"Oh. I suppose she could, uh, terminate and get loose that way."

"I suggested that, but she's not sure it would work that way. It might just kill her along with the body, now that she's bound to it the way she s."

"So she's still somewhere near the cave?"

"No. She retains her *ty'iga* powers, which make her something of a magical being. I believe she must simply have wandered off through Shadow while I was in the cave experimenting with the Jewel."

"Why the cave?"

"That's where you go to do clandestine things, isn't it?"

"Yeah. So how come I could reach you there with the Trump?"

"I'd already finished the experiment and departed. In fact, I was looking for her when you called."

"I think you'd better go and look some more."

"Why?"

"Because I owe her for favors past—even if my mother did sic her on me."

"Certainly. I'm not sure how successful I'll be, though. Magical beings don't track as readily as the more mundane sort."

"Give it a shot anyway. I'd like to know where she's gotten to and whether there's anything I can do for her. Maybe your new orientation will be of help—somehow."

"We'll see," he said, and he winked out.

I sagged. How was Orkus going to take it? I wondered. One daughter injured and the other possessed of a demon and wandering, off in Shadow. I moved to the foot of the bed and leaned against Mandor's chair. He reached up with his left hand and squeezed my arm.

"I don't suppose you learned anything about bonesetting off on that shadow-world, did you?" he inquired.

"Afraid not," I answered.

"Pity," he replied. "I'll just have to wait my turn."

"We can Trump you somewhere and get it taken care of right away," I said, reaching for my cards.

"No," he said. "I want to see things played out here."

While he was speaking, I noticed that Random seemed engaged in an intense Trump communication. Vialle stood nearby, as if shielding him from the opening in the wall and whatever might emerge therefrom. Dworkin continued to work upon Coral's face, his body blocking sight of exactly what he was doing.

"Mandor," I said, "did you know that my mother sent the *ty'iga* to take care of me?"

"Yes," he replied. "It told me that when you stepped out of the room. A part of the spell would not permit it to tell you this."

"Was she just there to protect me, or was she spying on me, too?"

"That I couldn't tell you. The matter didn't come up. But it does seem her fears were warranted. You were in danger."

"You think Dana knew about Jasra and Luke?"

He began to shrug, winced, thought better of it.

"Again, I don't know for certain. If she did, I can't answer the next one either: How did she know? Okay?"

"Okay."

Random completed a conversation, covering a Trump. Then he turned and stared at Vialle for some time. He looked as if he were about to say something, thought better of it, looked away. He looked at me. About then I heard Coral moan, and I looked away, rising.

"A moment, Merlin," Random said, "before you go rushing off."

I met his gaze. Whether it was angry or merely curious, I could not tell. The tightening of the brows, the narrowing of the eyes could indicate either.

"Sir?" I said.

He approached, took me by the elbow, and turned me away from the bed, leading me off toward the doorway to the next room.

"Vialle, I'm borrowing your studio for a few moments," he said.

"Surely," she replied.

He led me inside and closed the door behind us.

Across the room a bust of Gérard had fallen and broken. What appeared to be her current project—a multilimbed sea creature of a sort I'd never seen—occupied a work area at the studio's far end.

Random turned on me suddenly and searched my face.

"Have you been following the Begma-Kashfa situation?" he asked.

"More or less," I replied. "Bill briefed me on it the other night. Eregnor and all that."

"Did he tell you that we were going to bring Kashfa into the Golden Circle and solve the Eregnor problem by recognizing Kashfa's right to that piece of real estate?"

I didn't like the way he'd asked that one, and I didn't want to get Bill in trouble. It had seemed that that matter was still under wraps when we'd spoken. So, "I'm afraid I don't recall all the details on this stuff," I said.

"Well, that's what I planned on doing," Random told me. "We don't usually make guarantees like that—the kind that will favor one treaty country at the expense of another—but Arkans, the Duke of Shadburne, kind of had us over a barrel. He was the best possible head of state for our purposes, and I'd paved the way for his taking the throne now that that red-haired bitch is out of the picture. He knew he could lean on me a bit, though—since he'd be taking a chance accepting the throne following a double break in the succession—and he asked for Eregnor, so I gave it to him."

"I see," I said, "everything except how this affects me."

He turned his head and studied me through his left eye.

"The coronation was to be today. In fact, I was going to dress and Trump back for it in a little while. . . ."

"You use the past tense," I observed, to fill the silence he had left before me.

"So I do. So I do," he muttered, turning away, pacing a few steps, resting his foot on a piece of broken statuary, turning back. "The good Duke is now either dead or imprisoned."

"And there will be no coronation?" I said.

"*Au contraire,*" Random replied, still studying my face.

"I give up," I said. "Tell me what's going on."

"There was a coup, at dawn, this morning."

"Palace?"

"Possibly that, too. But it was backed by external military force."

"What was Benedict doing while this was going on?"

"I ordered him to pull the troops out yesterday, right before I came home myself. Things seemed stable, and it wouldn't have looked good to have combat troops from Amber stationed there during the coronation."

"True," I said. "So somebody moved right in, almost as soon as Benedict moved out and did away with the man who would be king, without the local constabulary even suggesting that that was not nice?"

Random nodded slowly.

"That's about the size of it," he said. "Now why do you think that might be?"

"Perhaps they were not totally displeased with the new state of affairs."

Random smiled and snapped his fingers.

"Inspired," he said. "One could almost think you knew what was going on."

"One would be wrong," I said.

"Today your former classmate Lukas Raynard becomes Rinaldo I, King of Kashfa."

"I'll be damned," I said. "I'd no idea he really wanted that job. What are you going to do about it?"

"I think I'll skip the coronation."

"I mean, over a slightly longer term."

Random sighed and turned away, kicking at the rubble.

"You mean, am I going to send Benedict back, to depose him?"

"In a word, yes."

"That would make us look pretty bad. What Luke just did is not above the Graustarkian politics that prevail in the area. We'd moved in and helped straighten out something that was fast becoming a political shambles. We could go back and do it again, too, if it were just some half-assed coup by a crazy general or some noble with delusions of grandeur. But Luke's got a legitimate claim, and it actually is stronger than Shadburne's. Also, he's popular. He's young, and he makes a good appearance. We'd have a lot less justification for going back than we had for going in initially. Even so, I was almost willing to risk being called an aggressor to keep that bitch's homicidal son off the throne. Then my man in Kashfa tells me that he's under Vialle's protection. So I asked her about it. She says that it's true and that you were present when it happened. She said she'd tell me about it after the operation Dworkin's doing now, in case he needs her empathic abilities. But I can't wait. Tell me what happened."

"You tell me one more thing first."

"What is it?"

"What military forces brought Luke to power?"

"Mercenaries."

"Dalt's?"

"Yes."

"Okay. Luke canceled his vendetta against the House of Amber," I said. "He did this freely, following a conversation with Vialle, just the other night. It was then that she gave him the ring. At the time I thought it was to keep Julian from trying to kill him, as we were on our way down to Arden."

"This was in response to Dalt's so-called ultimatum regarding Luke and Jasra?"

"That's right. It never occurred to me that the whole thing might be a setup—to get Luke and Dalt together so they could go off and pull a coup. That would mean that even that fight was staged, and now that I think of it, Luke did have a chance to talk with Dalt before it occurred."

Random raised his hand.

"Wait," he said. "Go back and tell me the thing from the beginning."

"Right."

And so I did. By the time I'd finished we had both paced the length of the studio countless times.

"You know," he said then, "the whole business sounds like

something Jasra might have set up before her career as a piece of furniture."

"The thought had occurred to me," I said, hoping he wasn't about to pursue the matter of her present whereabouts. And the more I thought of it, recalling her reaction to the information about Luke following our raid on the Keep, the more I began to feel not only that she had been aware of what was going on but that she'd even been in touch with Luke more recently than I had at that time.

"It was pretty smoothly done," he observed. "Dalt must have been operating under old orders. Not being certain how to collect Luke or locate Jasra for fresh instructions, he took a chance with that feint on Amber. Benedict might well have spitted him again, with equal skill and greater effect."

"True. I guess you have to give the devil his due when it comes to guts. It also means that Luke must have done a lot of fast plotting and laid that fixed fight out during their brief conference in Arden. So he was really in control there, and he conned us into thinking he was a prisoner, which precluded his being the threat to Kashfa that he really was—if you want to look at it that way."

"What other way is there to look at it?"

"Well, as you said yourself, his claim is not exactly without merit. What do you want to do?"

Random massaged his temples.

"Going after him, preventing the coronation, would be a very unpopular move," he said. "First, though, I'm curious. You say this guy's a great bullshitter. You were there. Did he con Vialle into placing him under her protection?"

"No, he didn't," I said. "He seemed as surprised as I was at her gesture. He called off the vendetta because he felt that honor had been satisfied, that he had to an extent been used by his mother, and out of friendship for me. He did it without any strings on it. I still think she gave him the ring so the vendetta would end there, so none of us would go gunning for him."

"That is very like her," Random said. "If I thought he'd taken advantage of her, I was going to go after him myself. The embarrassment for me is unintentional then, and I guess I can live with it. I prime Arkans for the throne, and then he's shunted aside at the last minute by someone under my wife's protection. Almost makes it look as if there's a bit of divisiveness here at the center of things—and I'd hate to give that impression."

"I've got a hunch Luke will be very conciliatory. I know him well enough to know he appreciates all of these nuances. I'd guess he'd be a very easy man for Amber to deal with, on any level."

"I'll bet he will. Why shouldn't he?"

"No reason," I said. "What's going to happen to that treaty now?"

Random smiled.

"I'm off the hook. I never felt right about the Eregnor provisions. Now, if there's to be a treaty at all, we go at it *ab initio*. I'm not even sure we need one, though. The hell with 'em."

"I'll bet Arkans is still alive," I said.

"You think Luke's holding him hostage, against my giving him Golden Circle status?"

I shrugged.

"How close are you to Arkans?"

"Well, I did set him up for this thing, and I feel I owe him. I don't feel I owe him that much, though."

"Understandable."

"There would be loss of face for Amber even to approach a second-rate power like Kashfa directly at a time like this."

"True," I said, "and for that matter, Luke isn't officially head of state yet."

"Arkans would still be enjoying life at his villa if it weren't for me, though, and Luke really does seem to be a friend of yours—a scheming friend, but a friend."

"You would like me to mention this during a forthcoming discussion of Tony Price's atomic sculpture?"

He nodded.

"I feel you should have your art discussion very soon. In fact, it would not be inappropriate for you to attend a friend's coronation—as a private individual. Your dual heritage will serve us well here, and he will still be honored."

"Even so, I'll bet he wants that treaty."

"Even if we were inclined to grant it, we would not guarantee him Eregnor."

"I understand."

"And you are not empowered to commit us to anything."

"I understand that, too."

"Then why don't you clean up a bit and go talk to him about it? Your room is just around the abyss. You can leave through the hole in the wall and shinny down a beam I noticed was intact."

"Okay, I will," I answered, moving in that direction. "But one question first, completely off the subject."

"Yes?"

"Has my father been back recently?"

"Not to my knowledge," he said, shaking his head slowly. "We're all pretty good at hiding our comings and goings if we wish, of course. But I think he'd have let me know if he were around."

"Guess so," I said, and I turned and exited through the wall, skirting the abyss.

11

No.

I hung from the beam, swung, and let go. I landed almost
gracefully in the middle of the hallway in an area that would have
been located approximately midway between my two doors, save
that the first door was missing, also the section of wall through
which it had provided entrance (or exit, depending on which side
you happened to be), not to mention my favorite chair and a display case which had held seashells I'd picked up from beaches
around the world. Pity.

I rubbed my eyes and turned away, for even the prospect of my
ruined apartment took second place just now. Hell, I'd had apartments ruined in the past. Usually around April 30 . . .

As in "Niagara Falls," slowly I turned. . . .

No . . .

Yes.

Across the hall from my rooms, where I had previously faced
a blank wall, there was now a hallway running to the north. I'd
gotten a glimpse up its sparkling length as I'd dropped from my
rafter. Amazing. The gods had just uptempoed my background
music yet again. I'd been in that hallway before, in one of its com-
moner locations up on the fourth floor, running east-west between
a couple of storerooms. One of Castle Amber's intriguing anomalies, the Corridor of Mirrors, in addition to seeming longer in one
direction than the other, contained countless mirrors. Literally
countless. Try counting them, and you never come up with the
same total twice. Tapers flicker in high, standing holders, casting
infinities of shadows. There are big mirrors, little mirrors, narrow

mirrors, squat mirrors, tinted mirrors, distorting mirrors, mirrors with elaborate frames—cast or carved—plain, simply framed mirrors, and mirrors with no frames at all; there are mirrors in multitudes of sharp-angled geometric shapes, amorphous shapes, curved mirrors.

I had walked the Corridor of Mirrors on several occasions, sniffing the perfumes of scented candles, sometimes feeling subliminal presences among the images, things which faded at an instant's sharp regard. I had felt the mixed enchantments of the place but had somehow never roused its sleeping genii. Just as well perhaps. One never knew what to expect in that place; at least that's what Bleys once told me. He was not certain whether the mirrors propelled one into obscure realms of Shadow, hypnotized one and induced bizarre dream states, cast one into purely symbolic realms decorated with the furniture of the psyche, played malicious or harmless head games with the viewer, none of the above, all of the above, or some of the above. Whatever, it was something less than harmless, though, as thieves, servants, and visitors had occasionally been found dead or stunned and mumbling along that sparkling route, oft-times wearing highly unusual expressions. And generally around the solstices and equinoxes— though it could occur at any season—the corridor moved itself to a new location, sometimes simply departing altogether for a time. Usually it was treated with suspicion, shunned, though it could as often reward as injure one or offer a useful omen or insight as readily as an unnerving experience. It was the uncertainty of it that roused trepidations.

And sometimes, I was told, it was almost as if it came looking for a particular person, bearing its ambiguous gifts. On such occasions it was said to be more dangerous to turn it down than to accept its invitation.

"Aw, come on," I said. "Now?"

The shadows danced along its length, and I caught a whiff of those intoxicating tapers. I moved forward. I extended my left hand past its corner and patted the wall. Frakir didn't stir.

"This is Merlin," I said, "and I'm kind of busy just now. You sure you wouldn't rather reflect someone else?"

The nearest flame seemed, for an instant, a fiery hand, beckoning.

"Shit," I whispered, and I strode forward.

There was no sense of transition as I entered. A long red-patterned runner covered the floor. Dust motes spun in the lights I passed. I was beside myself in many aspects, flickering flamelight harlequinading my garments, transforming my face within a dance of shadows.

Flicker.

For an instant it seemed that the stern visage of Oberon regarded me from a small high metal-framed oval—as easily a trick of the light as the shade of his late highness, of course.

Flicker.

I'd swear an animalistic travesty of my own face had leered at me for a moment, tongue lolling, from a mid-level rectangle of quicksilver to my left, framed in ceramic flowers, face humanizing as I turned, quickly, to mock me.

Walking. Footsteps muffled. Breathing slightly tight. I wondered whether I should summon my Logrus sight or even try that of the Pattern. I was loath to attempt either, though, memories of the nastier aspects of both Powers still too fresh within me for comfort. Something was about to happen to me, I was certain.

I halted and examined the one I thought must have my number—framed in black metal, with various signs from the magical arts inlaid in silver about it. The glass was murky, as if spirits swam just out of sight within its depths. My face looked leaner, its lines more heavily inscribed, the faintest of purple halos, perhaps, flickering about my head within it. There was something cold and vaguely sinister about that image, but though I studied it for a long while, nothing happened. There were no messages, enlightenments, changes. In fact, the longer I stared, the more all of the dramatic little touches seemed but tricks of the lighting.

I walked on, past glimpses of unearthly landscapes, exotic creatures, hints of memory, near subliminals of dead friends and relatives. Something within a pool even waved a rake at me. I waved back. Having so recently survived the traumas of my trek through the land between shadows, I was not as intimidated by these manifestations of strangeness and possible menace as I would likely have been at almost any other time. I thought I had sight of a gibbeted man, swinging as in a strong wind, hands tied behind his back, El Greco sky above him.

"I've had a rough couple of days," I said aloud, "and there's no sign of any letup. I'm sort of in a hurry, if you know what I mean."

Something punched me in the right kidney, and I spun around, but there was no one there. Then I felt a hand upon my shoulder, turning me. I cooperated quickly. No one there either.

"I apologize," I said, "if the truth requires it here."

Invisible hands continued to push and tug at me, moving me past a number of attractive mirrors. I was steered to a cheap-looking mirror in a dark-stained wooden frame. It looked as if it might have come from some discount house. There was a slight imperfection in the glass, in the vicinity of my left eye. Whatever forces had propelled me to this point released me here. It occurred to me that the powers that be here might actually have been attempting to expedite things per my request, rather than simply hustling me in a peevish spirit.

So, "Thanks," I said, just to be safe, and I continued to stare. I moved my head back and forth and from side to side, producing ripple effects across my image. I repeated the movements while waiting for whatever might occur.

My image remained unchanged, but on the third or fourth ripple my background was altered. It was no longer a wall of dimly lit mirrors that stood behind me. It flowed away and did not return with my next movement. In its place was a stand of dark shrubbery beneath an evening sky. I continued to move my head slightly several times more, but the ripple effect had vanished. The bushes seemed very real, though my peripheral vision showed me that the hallway was intact in both directions and still seemed to possess its right-hand wall at both ends.

I continued to search the seemingly reflected shrubbery, looking for portents, omens, signs, or just a little movement. None of these became apparent, though a very real sensation of depth was there. I could almost feel a cool breeze upon my neck. I must have stared for several minutes, waiting for the mirror to produce something new. But it did not. If this was the best the mirror had to offer, it was time to move on, I decided.

Something seemed to stir in the bushes at my back then, causing reflex to take over. I turned quickly, raising my hands before me.

It was only the wind that had rustled them, I saw. And then I realized that I was not in the hallway, and I turned again. The mirror and its wall were gone. I now faced a low hill, a line of broken masonry at its top. Light flickered from behind that shattered wall. Both curiosity and my sense of purpose roused, I began climbing slowly, my wariness yet present.

The sky seemed to grow darker even as I climbed, and it was cloudless, a profusion of stars pulsing in unfamiliar constellations across it. I moved with some stealth amid stones, grasses, shrubs, broken masonry. From beyond the vine-clad wall I now heard the sounds of voices. Though I could not distinguish the words being spoken, it did not seem conversation that I overheard, but rather a cacophony—as if a number of individuals, of both genders and various ages, were delivering simultaneous monologues.

Coming to the hill's top, I extended my hand until it made contact with the wall's irregular surface. I decided against going around it to see what sort of activity was in progress on the other side. It could make me visible to I knew not what. It seemed so much simpler to reach as high as I could, hook my fingers over the top of the nearest depressed area, and draw myself upward—as I did. I even located toeholds as my head neared the top, and I was able to ease some of the strain on my arms by resting part of my weight upon them.

I drew myself carefully up those final few inches, peering past fractured stone and down into the interior of the ruined structure. It appeared to have been some sort of church. The roof was fallen, and the far wall still stood, in much the same condition as the one I clung to. There was an altar in bad repair in a raised area off to my right. Whatever had happened here must have happened long ago, for shrubs and vines grew in the interior as well as without, softening the lines of collapsed pews, fallen pillars, fragments of the roof.

Below me, in a cleared area, a large pentagram was drawn. At each of the star's points stood a figure, facing outward. Inward from them, at the five points where the lines crossed, flared a torch, its butt driven into the earth. This seemed a somewhat peculiar variation on the rituals with which I was familiar, and I wondered at the summoning and why the five were not better protected and why they were not about the work in concert, rather than each seeming off on a personal trip and ignoring the others. The three whom I could see clearly had their backs to me. The two who faced in my direction were barely within my line of sight, their faces covered over with shadows. Some of the voices were male; some, female. One was singing; two were chanting; the other two seemed merely to be speaking, though in stagy, artificial tones.

I drew myself higher, trying for a glimpse of the faces of the nearer two. This because there was something familiar about the entire ensemble, and I felt that if I were to identify one, I might well realize all of their identities.

Another question high on my list was, What was it they were summoning? Was I safe up here on the wall, this close to the operation, if something unusual put in an appearance? It did not seem that the proper constraints were in place below. I drew myself higher still. I felt my center of gravity shifting just as my view of affairs improved yet again. Then I realized that I was moving forward without effort. An instant later I knew that the wall was toppling, carrying me forward and down right into the midst of their oddly choreographed ritual. I tried to push myself away from the wall, hoping to hit the ground rolling and run like hell. But it was already too late. My abrupt push-up raised me into the air but did not really halt my forward momentum.

No one beneath me stirred, though rubble rained about them all, and I finally caught some recognizable words as I fell.

". . . summon thee, Merlin, to fall into my power now!" one of the women was chanting.

A very effective ritual after all, I decided, as I landed on my back upon the pentagram, arms flopping out to my sides at shoulder level, legs spread. I was able to tuck my chin, protecting my head, and the slapping of my arms seemed to produce a break-fall effect so that I was not badly stunned by the impact. The five high towers of fire danced wildly about me for several seconds, then settled once again into steadier blazing. The five figures still faced outward. I attempted to rise and found that I could not. It was as if I were staked out in that position.

Frakir had warned me too late, as I was falling, and now I was uncertain to what employment I might put her. I could send her creeping off to any of the figures with orders to work her way upward and commence choking. But so far I had no way of knowing which one, if any, might deserve such treatment.

"I hate dropping in without notice," I said, "and I can see this is a private party. If someone will be good enough to turn me loose, I'll be on my way—"

The figure in the vicinity of my left foot did an about-face and stood staring down at me. She wore a blue robe, but there was no mask upon her fire-reddened face. There was only a tight smile, which went away when she licked her lips. It was Julia, and there was a knife in her right hand.

"Always the smartass," she said. "Ready with a flippant answer to any situation. It's a cover for your unwillingness to commit yourself to anything or anyone. Even those who love you."

"It could just be a sense of humor, too," I said, "a thing I'm beginning to realize you never possessed."

She shook her head slowly.

"You keep everyone at arms' distance. There is no trust in you."

"Runs in the family," I said. "But prudence does not preclude affection."

She had begun raising the blade, but she faltered for a second. "Are you saying that you still care about me?" she asked.

"I never stopped," I said. "It's just that you came on too strong all of a sudden. You wanted more of me than I was willing to give just then."

"You lie," she said, "because I hold your life in my hand."

"I could think of a lot worse reasons for lying," I said. "But, unfortunately, I'm telling the truth."

There came another familiar voice then, from off to my right.

"It was too early for us to speak of such things," she said, "but I begrudge her your affection."

Turning my head, I saw that this figure, too, now faced inward, and it was Coral and her right eye was covered by a black patch and she, too, held a knife in her right hand. Then I saw what was in her left hand, and I shot a glance back at Julia. Yes, they both held forks as well as knives.

"Et tu," I said.

"I told you I don't speak English," Coral replied.

"Et by two," Julia responded, raising her utensils. "Who says I don't have a sense of humor?"

They spit at each other across me, some of the spittle not quite going the distance.

Luke, it occurred to me, might have tried settling matters by proposing to both of them on the spot. I'd a feeling it wouldn't work for me, so I didn't.

"This is an objectification of marriage neurosis," I said. "It's a projective experience. It's a vivid dream. It's—"

Julia dropped to one knee, and her right hand flashed downward. I felt the blade enter my left thigh.

My scream was interrupted when Coral drove her fork into my right shoulder.

"This is ridiculous!" I cried as the other utensils flashed in their hands and I felt fresh stabs of pain.

Then the figure at the star's point near my right foot turned slowly, gracefully. She was wrapped in a dark brown cloak with a yellow border, her arms crossed before her holding it closed up to her eye level.

"Stop, you bitches!" she ordered, flinging the garment wide

and resembling nothing so much as a mourning cloak butterfly. It was, of course, Dara, my mother.

Julia and Coral had already raised their forks to their mouths and were chewing. There was a tiny bead of blood beside Julia's lip. The cloak continued to flow outward from my mother's fingertips as if it were alive, as if it were a part of her. Its wings blocked Julia and Coral completely from my sight, falling upon them as she continued to spread her arms, covering them, bearing them over backward to become body-size lumps upon the ground, growing smaller and smaller until the garment simply hung naturally and they were gone from their points of the star.

There came a slow, delicate clapping sound then, followed by a hoarse laugh from my left.

"Extremely well executed," came that painfully familiar voice, "but then you always liked him best."

"Better," she corrected.

"Isn't poor Despil even in the running?" Jurt said.

"You're being unfair," she told him.

"You liked that mad Prince of Amber more than you ever cared for our father, who was a decent man," he told her. "That's why Merlin was always your pet, isn't it?"

"That's just not true, Jurt, and you know it," she said.

He laughed again.

"We all summoned him because we all want him," he said, "for different reasons. But in the end our desires all come to this, do they not?"

I heard the growl, and I turned my head just in time to see his face slide along the projective curve wolfward, muzzle descending, fangs flashing as he fell to all fours and slashed at my left shoulder, gaining himself a gory taste of my person.

"Stop that!" she cried. "You little beast!"

He threw back his muzzle and howled, and it came out the way a coyote's cry does, as a kind of mad laughter.

A black boot struck his shoulder, knocking him over backward and sending him crashing into the uncollapsed section of wall behind him, which promptly collapsed upon him. He uttered but a brief whimper before being covered over completely by the falling rubble.

"Well, well, well," I heard Dara say, and looking that way, I saw that she also held a knife and fork. "What's a bastard like you doing in a nice place like this?"

"Keeping the last of the predators at bay, it would seem,"

replied the voice which had once told me a very long story containing multiple versions of an auto accident and a number of genealogical gaffes.

She lunged at me, but he stooped, caught me beneath the shoulders, and snatched me out of her way. Then his great black cloak swirled like a matador's, covering her. As she had done with Coral and Julia, she herself seemed to melt into the earth beneath it. He set me on my feet, stooped then, raised the cloak, and brushed it off. As he refastened it with a silver rose of a clasp, I studied him for fangs or at least cutlery.

"Four out of five," I said, brushing myself off. "No matter how real this seems, I'm sure it's only analogically or anagogically true. So how come you're not cannibalistically inclined in this place?"

"On the other hand," he said, drawing on a silver gauntlet, "I was never a real father to you. It's kind of difficult when you don't even know the kid exists. So I didn't really want anything from you either."

"That sure looks like Grayswandir you're wearing," I said.

He nodded.

"It seems to have served you, too."

"I suppose I should thank you for that. I also suppose you're the wrong . . . person to ask whether you really bore me from that cave to the land between shadows."

"Oh, it was me all right."

"Of course, you'd say that."

"I don't know why I should if I didn't. Look out! The wall!"

One quick glance showed me that another big section of wall was falling toward us. Then he pushed me, and I sprawled across the pentagram again. I heard the stones crashing behind me, and I half rose and threw myself even farther forward.

Something struck the side of my head.

I woke up in the Corridor of Mirrors. I was lying facedownward, my head resting on my right forearm, a rectangular piece of stone clutched in my hand, the aromas of the candles drifting about me. When I began to rise, I felt pains in both shoulders and in my left thigh. A quick investigation showed me that I bore cuts in all three of those places. Though there wasn't much I could do now to help demonstrate the veracity of my recent adventure beyond this, it wasn't something I felt like shrugging off either.

I got to my feet and limped back to the corridor that ran past my rooms.

"Where'd you go?" Random called down to me.

"Huh? What do you mean?" I responded.

"You walked back up the hall, but there's nothing there."

"How long was I gone?"

"Half a minute maybe," he answered.

I waved the stone I still carried.

"Saw this lying on the floor. Couldn't figure what it was," I said.

"Probably blown there when the Powers met," he said, "from one of the walls. There were a number of arches edged with stones like that at one time. Mostly plastered over on your floor now."

"Oh," I said. "See you in a bit, before I take off."

"Do that," he replied, and I turned and found my way through one of the day's many broken walls and on into my room.

The far wall had also been blasted, I noticed, creating a large opening into Brand's dusty chambers. I paused and studied it. Synchronicity, I decided. It appeared there had once been an archway connecting those rooms with these. I moved forward and examined the exposed curve along its left side. Yes, it had been rendered from stones similar to the one I held. In fact—

I brushed away plaster and slid mine into a broken area. It fitted perfectly. In fact, when I gave it a small tug, it refused to be removed. Had I really brought it back from the sinister father-mother-brother-lovers ritual dream beyond the mirror? Or had I half-consciously picked it up on my return, from wherever it had been blasted during the recent architectural distress?

I turned away, removing my cloak, stripping off my shirt. Yes. There were punctures like fork marks on my right shoulder, something like an animal bite on my left. Also, there was dried blood on my left trouser leg in the area of a tear beyond which my thigh was tender. I washed up and brushed my teeth and combed my hair, and I put a dressing on my leg and left shoulder. The family metabolism would see me healed in a day, but I didn't want some exertion tearing them open and getting fresh garments gory.

Speaking of which . . .

The armoire was undamaged, and I thought I'd wear my other colors, to give Luke a happy memory or two for his coronation: the golden shirt and royal blue trousers I'd found which approximated Berkeley's colors almost exactly; a leather vest dyed to match the pants; matching cloak with gold trim; black sword belt, black gloves tucked behind it, reminding me I needed a new blade. Dagger, too, for that matter. I was wondering about a hat when a series of sounds caught my attention. I turned.

Through a fresh screen of dust I now had a symmetrical view into Brand's quarters; rather than a jagged opening in the wall the archway stood perfect and entire, the wall intact at either hand and above. The wall to my right also seemed less damaged than it had been earlier.

I moved forward and ran my hand along the curve of stones. I inspected adjacent plastered areas, looking for cracks. There were none. All right. The stone had borne an enchantment. To what end?

I strode through the archway and looked around. The room was dark, and I summoned the Logrus sight reflexively. It came and served me, as usual. Perhaps the Logrus had decided against holding a grudge.

At this level I could see the residue of many magical experiments as well as a number of standing spells. Most sorcerers leave a certain amount of not normally visible magical clutter about, but Brand seemed to have been a real slob, though of course, he might have been rushed quite a bit near the end there when he was trying to take over control of the universe. It's not the sort of occupation wherein neatness counts the way it might in other endeavors. I passed on along my tour of inspection. There were mysteries here, unfinished bits of business and indications that he had gone farther along some magical routes than I had ever wished to go. Still, there was nothing here that I felt I could not handle and nothing representing grave and immediate danger. It was just possible, now I'd finally had an opportunity to inspect them, that I might want to leave the archway intact and add Brand's quarters to my own.

On the way out I decided to check Brand's armoire to see whether he had a hat to go with what I was wearing. I opened it and discovered a dark three-cornered one with a golden feather, which fitted me perfectly. The color was a little off, but I suddenly recalled a spell which altered it. As I was about to turn away, something to the rear of that top shelf which held the hats glinted for a moment within my Logrus vision. I reached in and withdrew it.

It was a long and lovely gold-chased sheath of dark green, and the hilt of the blade which protruded from it appeared to be gold-plated, with an enormous emerald set in its pommel. I took hold of it and drew it partway, half expecting it to wail like a demon on whom one has dropped a balloon filled with holy water. Instead, it merely hissed and smoked a little. And there was a bright design worked into the metal of its blade—almost recognizable. Yes, a section of the Pattern. Only this excerpting was from the Pattern's end, whereas Grayswandir's was from a point near the beginning. I sheathed it, and on an impulse I hung it from my belt. His old man's sword would make a neat coronation present for Luke, I decided. So I'd take it along for him. I let myself out into the side corridor then, made my way over a small section of collapsed wall from Gérard's quarters and back past Fiona's door to my dad's rooms. There was one thing more I wanted to check, and the sword had reminded me. I fished in my pocket for the key I'd transferred from my bloody trousers. Then I decided I'd better knock. What if . . .

I knocked and waited, knocked again and waited again. In that nothing but silence ensued I unlocked the door and entered. I went no farther than that first place. I'd just wanted to check the rack.

Grayswandir was gone from the peg where I'd hung it.

I backed out, closing and locking the door. The fact that the row of pegs had been empty was an instance of obtaining the knowledge one wanted and still not being certain what one had proved thereby. Yet it had been something I'd wished to know, and it did make me feel that final knowledge was nearer than it had been. . . .

I walked back, past Fiona's rooms. I reentered Brand's rooms through the door I had left ajar. I hunted around till I spotted a key in a nearby ashtray. I locked the door and pocketed the key; that was almost silly because anyone could walk in from my room now and my room was missing a wall. Still . . .

I hesitated before crossing back to my sitting room with its Tabriz stained with *ty'iga* spit and partly covered by fallen wall. There was something almost restful about Brand's quarters, a kind of peaceful quality I hadn't really noticed before. I wandered a bit, opening drawers and looking inside magic boxes, studying a folder of the man's drawings. The Logrus sight showed me that something small and potent and magical was secreted in a bedpost, radiating lines of force every which way. I unscrewed the knob, found the compartment within it. It contained a small velvet bag which bore a ring. The band was wide, possibly of platinum. It bore a wheel-like device of some reddish metal, with countless tiny spokes, many of them hair-fine. And each of these spokes extended a line of power leading off somewhere, quite possibly into

Shadow, where some power cache or spell source lay. Perhaps
Luke would rather have the ring than the sword. When I slipped it
on, it seemed to extend roots to the very center of my body. I
could feel my way back along them to the ring and then out along
those connections. I was impressed by the variety of energies it
reached and controlled—from simple chthonic forces to sophisticated constructs of High Magic, from elementals to things that
seemed like lobotomized gods. I wondered why he hadn't been
wearing it on the day of the Patternfall battle. If he had, I'd a feeling he might have been truly invincible. We could all have been
living on Brandenberg in Castle Brand. I wondered, too, why
Fiona, in the next room over, had not felt its presence and come
looking for it. On the other hand, I hadn't. For what it was, it
didn't register well at all, beyond a few feet. It was amazing the
treasures this place contained. Was it something about the private
universe effect said to obtain in some of these rooms? The ring
was a beautiful alternative to Pattern Power or Logrus Power,
hooked in as it was with so many sources. It must have taken centuries to empower the thing. Whatever Brand had wanted it for, it
had not been part of a short-range plan. I decided I could not surrender the thing to Luke—or to anyone with any familiarity with
the Arts. I didn't even think I should trust a nonmagician with it.
And I certainly didn't feel like returning it to the bedpost. What
was that throbbing at my wrist? Oh, yes, Frakir. It had been going
on for some small while, and I'd barely noticed.

"Sorry you lost your voice, old girl," I said, stroking her as I
explored the room for threats both psychic and physical. "I can't
find a damned thing here that I should be worried about."

Immediately she spiraled down from my wrist and tried to remove the ring from my finger.

"Stop!" I ordered. "I know the ring could be dangerous. But
only if you use it wrongly. I'm a sorcerer, remember? I'm into
these matters. There is nothing special about it for me to fear."

But Frakir disobeyed my order and continued her attack on the
ring, which I could now only attribute to some form of magical artifact jealousy. I tied her in a tight knot around the bedpost and left
her there, to teach her a lesson.

I began to search the apartment more diligently. If I were to
keep the sword *and* the ring, it would be nice to find something
else of his father's that I could take to Luke—

"Merlin! Merlin!" I heard bellowed from somewhere beyond
my room.

Rising from a tapping of the floor and lower walls, where I had been seeking hollow spots, I returned to my archway and passed through into my own sitting room. I halted then, despite another summons in what I now recognized to be Random's voice. The wall which faced upon the side corridor was more than half rebuilt since last I had viewed it—as if an invisible crew of carpenters and plasterers had been silently at work since I had positioned the dreamstone in the gateway to the kingdom of Brand. Amazing. I simply stood and stared, hoping for some betraying bit of business within the damaged area. Then I heard Random mutter, "I guess he's gone," and I called back, "Yeah? What is it?"

"Get your ass up here quick," he said. "I need your advice."

I stepped out into the corridor through the opening which remained in that wall, and I looked upward. Immediately I could feel the capabilities in the ring that I wore, responding like a musical instrument to my most immediate need. The appropriate line was activated as I assented to the suggestion, and I took the gloves from behind my belt and drew them on as I was levitated toward the opening in the ceiling. This, because it had occurred to me that Random might recognize the ring as having once been Brand's, and that could lead to a complicated discussion I'd no desire for at the moment.

I held my cloak close to my side as I came up through the hole into the studio, to keep the blade under wraps also.

"Impressive," Random said. "Glad you're keeping the magical muscle exercised. That's what I called you for."

I gave him a bow. Being dressed up made me feel vaguely courtly.

"How may I be of service?"

"Cut the crap and come on," he said, taking hold of my elbow and steering me back toward the demi-bedroom. Vialle stood at the door, holding it open.

"Merlin?" she said as I brushed by.

"Yes?" I answered.

"I wasn't certain," she said.

"Of what?" I asked.

"That it was you," she responded.

"Oh, it's me, all right," I said.

"It is indeed my brother," Mandor stated, rising from his chair and approaching us. His arm was splinted and slung, his face considerably relaxed. "If anything about him strikes you as strange," he continued, "it is likely because he has had a number of traumatic experiences since he left here."

"Is that true?" Random asked.

"Yes," I replied. "I didn't realize it was all that apparent."

"Are you all right?" Random asked.

"I seem to be intact," I said.

"Good. Then we'll save the particulars of your story for another time. As you can see, Coral is gone and Dworkin is, too. I didn't see them go. I was still in the studio when it happened."

"When what happened?" I asked.

"Dworkin finished his operation," Mandor said, "took the lady by the hand, drew her to her feet, and transported her away from here. It was most elegantly managed. One moment they stood at the bedside; the next their afterimages ran through the spectrum and winked out."

"You say that he transported them. How do you know that they weren't snatched away by Ghostwheel or one of the Powers?" I asked.

"Because I watched his face," he said, "and there was no surprise whatsoever upon it, only a small smile."

"I guess you're right," I admitted. "Then who set your arm, if Random was off in the studio and Dworkin occupied?"

"I did," Vialle said. "I've been trained in it."

"So you were the only eyewitness to their vanishment?" I said to Mandor.

He nodded.

"What I want of you," Random said, "is some idea where they flashed off to. Mandor said he couldn't tell. Here!"

He handed me a chain, from which a metal setting hung.

"What's this?" I asked.

"It was the most important of all the Crown Jewels," he said, "the Jewel of Judgment. This is what they left me. The Jewel part is what they took."

"Oh," I said. Then: "It must be secure if it's in Dworkin's care. He'd said something about putting it in a safe place, and he knows more about it than anyone else—"

"He may also have flipped out again," Random said. "I'm not interested in discussing his merits as its custodian, though. I just want to know where the hell he's gone with the thing."

"I don't believe he left any tracks," Mandor said.

"Where were they standing?" I asked.

"Over there," he said, with a gesture of the good arm, "to the right of the bed."

I moved to that area, feeling through the potencies I ruled after the most appropriate.

"A little nearer the foot."

I nodded, feeling it would not be all that difficult to look back a small distance through time within my personal space.

I felt the rainbow rush and saw their outlines. Freeze.

A power line moved forth from the ring, attached itself, ran rainbow with them, passed through the portal which closed with a mild implosion. Raising the back of my hand to my forehead, I seemed to look down the line—

—into a large hall hung with six shields to my left. To my right hung a multitude of flags and pennons. A fire blazed in an enormous hearth before me. . . .

"I see the place they went to," I said, "but I don't recognize it."

"Is there some way you can share the vision?" Random asked.

"Perhaps," I replied, realizing there was a way even as I said it. "Regard the mirror."

Random turned, moved nearer the looking glass through which Dworkin had brought me—how long ago? "By the blood of the beast on the pole and the shell that is cracked at the center of the world," I said, feeling the need to address two of the powers I controlled, "may the sight be cast!"

The mirror frosted over, and when it cleared, my vision of the hall lay within it.

"I'll be damned," Random said. "He took her to Kashfa. I wonder why."

"One day you'll have to teach me that trick, brother," Mandor commented.

"In that I was about to head for Kashfa," I said, "is there anything special I should do?"

"Do?" Random said. "Just find out what's going on and let me know, will you?"

"Of course," I said, uncasing my Trumps.

Vialle came up and took my hand as if in farewell.

"Gloves," she commented.

"Trying to look a little formal," I explained.

"There is something in Kashfa that Coral seems to fear," she whispered. "She muttered about it in her sleep."

"Thanks," I said. "I'm ready for anything now."

"You may say that for confidence," she said, "but never believe it."

I laughed as I held a Trump before me and pretended to study it while extending the force of my being along the line I had sent to Kashfa. I reopened the route Dworkin had taken and stepped through.

12

Kashfa.

I stood in the gray stone hall, flags and shields on the walls, rushes strewn about the floors, rude furniture about me, a fire before me which did not completely dispel the dampness of the place, cooking smells heavy on the air. I was the only person in the room, though I could hear voices from many directions; also the sounds of musicians tuning and practicing. So I had to be fairly near the action. The disadvantage of coming in the way I did rather than using a Trump was that there was no one on the spot to show me around and tell me what was going on. The advantage was the same—that is, if there were any spying I wanted to do, now was the time. The ring, a veritable encyclopedia of magics, found me an invisibility spell in which I quickly cloaked myself.

I spent the next hour or so exploring. There were four large buildings and a number of smaller ones within this central walled area. There was another walled sector beyond it and another beyond that—three roughly concentric zones of ivy-covered protection. I couldn't see any signs of heavy damage, and I got the feeling Dalt's troops hadn't met with much resistance. No indications of pillaging or burning, but then they'd been hired to deliver a property, and I'd a feeling Jasra had stipulated that it remain relatively intact. The troops occupied all three rings, and I got the impression from a bit of eavesdropping that they'd be around till after the coronation. There were quite a few in the large plaza in the central area, making fun of the local troops in their fancy livery as they waited for the coronation procession. None of this was in particular bad nature, however, possibly because Luke was popular with both groups, though it did also seem that many individuals on both sides seemed personally acquainted.

The First Unicornian Church of Kashfa, as one might translate its title, was across the plaza from the palace proper. The building in which I'd arrived was an ancillary, all-purpose adjunct, at this time being used to house a number of hastily summoned guests, along with servants, courtiers, and hangers-on.

I'd no idea exactly when the coronation was to take place, but I decided I'd better try to see Luke in a hurry, before he got too swept up into the course of events. He might even have an idea where Coral had been delivered, and why.

So I found me a niche with a blank-walled, neutral background even a native probably couldn't recognize out of context, dropped my invisibility spell, located Luke's Trump, and gave him a call. I didn't want him to think I was already in town because I didn't want him to know I possessed the power to drop in the way I had. This under the theory that you never tell anybody everything.

"Merlin!" he announced, studying me. "Is the cat out of the sack or what?"

"Yeah, the kittens, too," I said. "Congratulations on your coronation day."

"Hey! You're wearing the school colors!"

"What the hell. Why not? You won something, didn't you?"

"Listen. It's not as festive a thing as all that. In fact, I was about to call you. I need your advice before this goes any further. Can you bring me through?"

"I'm not in Amber, Luke."

"Where are you?"

"Well . . . downstairs," I admitted. "I'm on the side street between your palace and the building next door that's sort of like a hotel at the moment."

"That won't do," he said. "I'd get spotted too quick if you bring me down. Go on over to the Unicorn Temple. If it's relatively empty and there's a dark, quiet corner where we can talk, call me and bring me through. If there isn't, figure something else, okay?"

"Okay."

"Hey, how'd you get here anyway?"

"Advance scout for an invasion," I said. "One more take-over would be a coup-coup, wouldn't it?"

"You're about as funny as a hangover," he said. "Call me."

Break.

So I crossed the plaza, following what seemed marked out as the route of the procession. I thought I might meet some trouble at the House of the Unicorn and need a spell to get in, but no one barred my way.

I entered. It was big and all decked out for the ceremony, with a great variety of pennons on the walls and flowers all over the place. The only other inhabitant was a muffled woman up near the front who appeared to be praying. I moved off to the left into a somewhat darker section.

"Luke," I addressed his Trump. "All clear. Do you read me?"

I felt his presence before I caught the image. "Okay," he said. "Bring me through," and we clasped hands, and he was there.

He clapped me on the shoulders.

"Well, now, let me look at you," he said. "Wonder whatever became of my letter sweater?"

"I think you gave it to Gail."

"I think you may be right."

"Brought you a present," I said, tossing back my cloak and fumbling at the side of my sword belt. "Here. I turned up your father's sword."

"You're kidding."

He took it into his hands, examined the sheath, turned it over many times. Then he drew it partway, and it hissed again and sparks danced along its tracery and a bit of smoke drifted upward from it.

"It really is!" he said. "Werewindle, the Daysword—brother to the Nightblade, Grayswandir!"

"What's that?" I said. "I didn't know there was any connection."

"I'd have to think hard to remember the full story, but they go back a long way. Thank you."

He turned and took several paces, slapping the weapon against his thigh as he walked. Abruptly he returned.

"I've been had," he said. "That woman has done it again, and I am peeved to the extreme. I don't know how to handle this."

"What? What are you talking about?"

"My mother," he explained. "She's done it again. Just when I thought I'd taken the reins and was riding my own course, she's come along and messed up my life."

"How'd she do that?"

"She hired Dalt and his boys to take over here."

"Yeah, we sort of figured that out. By the way, what happened to Arkans?"

"Oh, he's okay. I've got him under arrest, of course. But he's in good quarters and he can have anything he wants. I wouldn't hurt him. I always kind of liked the guy."

"So what's the problem? You win. You've got your own kingdom now."

"Hell," he said, then glanced furtively toward the sanctum. "I think I was conned, but I'm not exactly sure. See, I never wanted this job. Dalt told me we were taking over for Mom. I was coming in with him to establish order, claim the place for the family again, then welcome her back with a lot of pomp and crap. I figured once she had her throne back, she'd be off my case for good. I'd hit it out of here for more congenial turf, and she'd have a whole kingdom to occupy her attention. Nothing was said about me getting stuck with this lousy job."

I shook my head.

"I don't understand at all," I said. "You got it for her. Why not just turn it over to her and do as you planned?"

He gave a humorless laugh.

"Arkans they liked," he said. "Me they like. Mom they're not so fond of. Nobody seems that enthusiastic about having her back. In fact, there were strong indications that if she tried it, there would indeed be a coup-coup."

"I suppose you could still step aside and give it to Arkans."

Luke punched the stone wall.

"I don't know whether she'd be madder at me or at herself for having paid Dalt as much as she did to throw Arkans out. But she'd tell me it's my duty to do it, and I don't know—maybe it is. What do you think?"

"That's a hard one to answer, Luke. Who do you think would do a better job, you or Arkans?"

"I honestly don't know. He's had a lot of experience in government, but I did grow up here, and I do know how the place is run and how to get things done. The only thing I'm sure of is that either of us would be better at it than Mom."

I folded my arms, and I thought hard.

"I can't make this decision for you," I said. "But tell me, what would you most like to do?"

He chuckled.

"You know I've always been a salesman. If I were going to stick around and do something for Kashfa, I'd rather represent her industries abroad, which would be sort of undignified for a monarch. Probably what I'd be best at, though. I don't know."

"It's a problem and a half, Luke. I don't want the responsibility of telling you which way to go."

"If I'd known it was going to come to this, I'd have smeared Dalt back in Arden."

"You really think you could take him?"

"Believe it," he said.

"Well, that doesn't solve your present problem."

"True. I've a strong feeling I may have to go through with this."

The woman up front glanced our way several times. I guess we were talking kind of loud for the surroundings.

"Too bad there are no other good candidates," I said, lowering my voice.

"This must seem like pretty small beer to someone from Amber."

"Hell, it's your home. You've got a right to take it seriously. I'm just sorry it's doing such a job on you."

"Yeah, most problems seem to start at home, don't they? Sometimes I just feel like taking a walk and not coming back."

"What would happen if you did?"

"Either Mom would restore herself to the throne with Dalt's gang to back her up, which would require a mess of executions of people I can think of who'd be against it, or she'd say the game isn't worth the candle and settle for the Keep. If she decided to enjoy her retirement, then the coalition which backed him in the first place would probably spring Arkans and continue things from where they'd had to leave off."

"Which course of action seems most likely to you?" I said.

"She'd go for it and there'd be a civil war. Win or lose, it would mess up the country and doubtless keep us out of the Golden Circle this time around, too. Speaking of which—"

"I don't know," I said quickly. "I'm not empowered to talk Golden Circle Treaty with you."

"I'd kind of guessed that," Luke said, "and that wasn't what I wanted to ask. I was just curious whether anyone back in Amber might have said, 'They just blew it,' or 'Maybe we'll give them another crack at it a little farther down the road,' or 'We'll still deal, but they can forget the Eregnor guarantees.' "

He gave me an artificial grin, and I returned it.

"You can forget Eregnor," I said.

"Figured that," he said. "What about the rest?"

"I get the impression it's 'Let's wait and see what happens.' "

"Guessed that much, too. Give me a good report, even if they don't ask, okay? By the way, I don't suppose your presence here is technically official?"

"Personal," I said, "from a diplomatic standpoint."

The lady up front rose to her feet. Luke sighed.

"Wish I could find my way back to Alice's restaurant. Maybe the Hatter would see something we're missing," he said. Then: "Hey! Where'd he come from? Looks just like you but—"

He was staring past me, and I could already feel the disturbance. I didn't even bother to summon the Logrus, though, because I felt ready for anything.

I turned, smiling.

"Are you ready to die, brother?" Jurt asked. He had either managed to regrow his eye or was wearing an artificial one, and he now had sufficient hair that I could no longer tell about the ear. His little finger was partly regrown also.

"No, but I'm ready to kill," I said. "I'm glad you happened by."

He bowed, mockingly. There was a faint glow about him. I could feel the power that flowed through and around his person.

"Have you been back to the Keep for your final treatment?" I inquired.

"I don't believe that will be necessary," he said. "I am more than adequate for any task I've set myself, now I've control of these forces."

"This is Jurt?" Luke asked.

"Yes," I replied. "This is Jurt."

Jurt cast a quick glance Luke's way. I could feel him focusing on the blade.

"Is that a power object you bear?" he inquired. "Let me see it!"

He extended his hand, and the weapon jerked within Luke's grip but did not come loose.

"No, thanks," Luke said, and Jurt vanished. A moment later he appeared behind Luke, and his arm went around Luke's neck in a choke. Luke gripped it with one hand, bowed, and turned and threw him over his shoulder.

Jurt landed on his back before him, and Luke made no move to follow up on his action.

"Draw that blade," Jurt said, "and let me see it." Then he shook himself like a dog and rose to his feet. "Well?" he said.

"I see no need for a weapon in dealing with the likes of you," Luke told him.

Jurt raised both hands above his head and formed them into

fists. They met, remained in contact for a moment. Then he drew them apart, his right hand somehow drawing a long blade out of his left.

"You ought to take that show on the road," Luke said, "now."

"Draw it!" Jurt said.

"I don't like the idea of fighting in a church," Luke told him.

"You want to step outside?"

"Very funny," Jurt replied. "I know you've got an army out there. No thanks. I'll even take a certain pleasure in bloodying a Unicorn shrine."

"You ought to talk to Dalt," Luke said. "He gets his kicks in weird ways, too. Can I get you a horse—or a chicken? Maybe some white mice and aluminum foil?"

Jurt lunged. Luke stepped backward and drew his father's blade. It hissed and crackled and smoked as he parried lightly and drove it forward. There was a sudden fear on Jurt's face as he threw himself backward, batting at it, stumbling. As he fell, Luke kicked him in the stomach and Jurt's blade went flying.

"That's Werewindle!" Jurt gasped. "How did you come by the sword of Brand?"

"Brand was my father," Luke said.

A momentary look of respect passed over Jurt's face.

"I didn't know . . ." he muttered, and then he vanished.

I waited. I extended magical feelers all over the place. But there was just Luke, myself and the lady, who had halted some distance from us, watching, as if afraid to come any nearer on her way out.

Then Luke collapsed. Jurt was standing behind him, having just struck him on the back of the neck with his elbow. He reached then for Luke's wrist, as if to seize it and wrench the blade from his hand.

"It must be mine!" he said as I reached through the ring and struck him with a bolt of pure energy which I thought would rupture most of his organs and leave him a bleeding mass of jelly. Only for an instant had I considered using anything less than lethal force. I could see that sooner or later one of us was going to kill the other, and I'd decided to get it over with before he got lucky.

But he was already lucky. His bath in the Fount must have toughened him even more than I'd thought. He spun around three times, as if he'd been clipped by a truck, and was slammed up against the wall. He sagged. He slipped to the floor. Blood came out of his mouth. He looked as if he were about to pass out. Then his eyes focused and his hands extended.

A force similar to the one I'd just thrown at him struck at me. I was surprised by his ability to regroup and retaliate at that level with that speed. Not so surprised that I wasn't able to parry it, though. I took a step forward then and tried to set him afire with a beautiful spell the ring suggested. Rising, he was able to shield against it within moments of his clothes' beginning to smolder. I kept coming, and he created a vacuum around me. I pierced it and kept breathing. Then I tried a battering ram spell which the ring showed me, even more forceful than the first working with which I'd hit him.

He vanished before it hit, and a crack ran up three feet of the stone wall which had been behind him. I sent sense-tendrils all over and spotted him seconds later, crouched on a cornice high overhead. He launched himself at me just as I looked up.

I didn't know whether it would break my hand or not, but I felt it would be worth it, even so, as I levitated. I contrived to pass him at about the midway point, and I hit him with a left, which I hoped broke his neck as well as his jaw. Unfortunately it also broke my levitation spell, and I tumbled to the floor along with him.

I heard the lady cry out as we fell, and she came rushing toward us. We lay stunned for several heartbeats. Then he rolled over onto his stomach, reached, hunched and fell, reached again.

His hand fell upon the haft of Werewindle. He must have felt my gaze as his fingers tightened about it, for he glanced at me and smiled. I heard Luke mutter a curse and stir. I threw a deep freeze spell at Jurt, but he trumped out before the cold front hit.

Then the lady screamed again, and even before I turned, I knew that the voice had been Coral's.

Reappearing, Jurt half collapsed against her from the rear, finding her throat with the edge of that bright, smoldering blade.

"Nobody," he gasped, "move . . . or I'll carve her . . . an extra smile."

I sought after a quick spell that would finish him without endangering her.

"Don't try it, Merle," he said. "I'll feel it . . . coming. Just leave me . . . alone . . . for half a minute . . . and you'll get to live . . . a little longer. I don't know where you picked up . . . those extra tricks . . . but they won't save you—"

He was panting and covered with sweat. The blood still dripped from his mouth.

"Let go of my wife," Luke said, rising, "or there'll never be anyplace you'll be able to hide."

"I don't want you for an enemy, son of Brand," Jurt said.

"Then do as I say, fella. I've taken out better men than you."

And then Jurt screamed as if his soul were on fire. Werewindle moved away from Coral's throat, and Jurt backed off and began jerking, like a puppet whose joints have seized up but whose strings are still being yanked. Coral turned toward him, her back to Luke and me. Her right hand rose to her face. After a time Jurt fell to the floor and curled into a fetal position. A red light seemed to be playing upon him. He was shaking steadily, and I could even hear his teeth chattering.

Abruptly, then, he was gone, trailing rainbows, leaving blood and spittle, bearing Werewindle with him. I sent a parting bolt after, but I knew that it did not reach him. I'd felt Julia's presence at the other end of the spectrum, and despite everything else, I was pleased to know that I had not slain her yet. But Jurt—Jurt was very dangerous now, I realized. For this was the first time we'd fought that he hadn't left a piece of himself behind, had even taken something away with him. Something deadly. He was learning, and that did not bode well.

When I turned my head, I caught sight of the red glow before Coral lowered her eyepatch, and I realized what had become of the Jewel of Judgment, though not, of course, why.

"Wife?" I said.

"Well, sort of . . . Yes," she replied.

"Just one of those things," Luke said. "Do you two know each other?"

PRINCE
OF
CHAOS

To Jane Lindskold—

Gramercy, lady, for your help.
This one was yours from the start.

1

See one coronation and you've seen them all. Sounds cynical and probably is, especially when the principal is your best friend and his queen's your inadvertent lover. But there's generally a procession, with a lot of slow music, and uncomfortable, colorful garb, incense, speeches, prayers, the ringing of bells. They are tedious, generally hot, and requiring of one an insincere attention, as at weddings, commencements, and secret initiations.

And so Luke and Coral became the sovereigns of Kashfa, in the same church where we'd fought almost—but, unfortunately, not quite—to the death with my mad brother Jurt but a few hours before. As Amber's only representative at the event—albeit of, technically, unofficial status—I was accorded a ringside standing-place, and eyes were often drifting my way. So I had to keep alert and mouth appropriate responses. While Random would not permit formal status to my presence at the ceremony, I knew he'd be irritated if he heard that my behavior was less than diplomatically sound.

So I wound up with hurting feet, a stiff neck, and colorful garments soaked with sweat. That's show biz. Still, I wouldn't have had it any other way. Luke and I go back through some of the damnedest times, and I couldn't help but think of them—from sword's point to track meets, from art galleries and into Shadow—as I stood there sweltering and wondering what would become of him now he wore a crown. Such an occurrence had changed my uncle Random from a happy-go-lucky musician, footloose and degenerate, into a sage and responsible monarch—though I've only my relatives' reports when it comes to knowing about the first. I found myself hoping it wouldn't mellow Luke out all that much. Still—again—Luke was a very different person than Random, not to mention ages younger. Amazing what years can do, though—or is it just the nature of events? I realized myself to be a lot different than I had been not so very long ago, from all that had happened to me recently. A lot different than I'd been yesterday, come to think of it.

During the recessional Coral managed to pass me a note, saying that she had to see me, giving a time and a place, even including a small map. It proved an apartment to the rear of the palace. We met there that evening and wound up spending the night. She and Luke had been married as kids, by proxy, I learned then, part of the diplomatic arrangement between Jasra and the Begmans. It didn't work out, though—the diplomatic part, that is—and the rest kind of fell by the wayside. The principals had sort of forgotten about the marriage, too, till recent events served as a reminder. Neither had seen the other in years. Still, the record showed that the prince had been married. While it was an annullable thing, she could also be crowned with him. If there were anything in it for Kashfa.

And there was: Eregnor. A Begman queen on the Kashfan throne might help smooth over that particular real estate grab. At least, that had been Jasra's thinking, Coral told me. And Luke had been swayed by this, particularly in the absence of the guarantees from Amber and the now-defunct Golden Circle Treaty had held.

I held her. She was not well, despite what seemed an amazing postoperative recovery. She wore a black patch over her right eye and was more than a little reactive should my hand stray near it— or even if I looked at it for too long. What might have led Dworkin to replace the damaged eye with the Jewel of Judgment, I could not even guess. Unless he somehow considered her proof against the forces of the Pattern and the Logrus in their attempts to recover it. My expertise in this area, though, was nonexistent. Having finally met the diminutive mage, I had become convinced of his sanity—though this feeling in no way served to penetrate those enigmatic qualities that ancient wise men tend to possess.

"How does it feel?" I asked her.

"Very strange," she replied. "Not pain—exactly. More like the way a Trump contact feels. Only it's with me all the time, and I'm not going anywhere or talking to anyone. It's as if I'm standing in some sort of gateway. Forces are moving about me, through me."

In an instant I was at the center that was the gray ring with its wheel of many-spoked reddish metal. From the inside, here, it was like a great web. A bright strand pulsed for my attention. Yes, it was a line to a very potent force in distant Shadow, one that might be used for probing. Carefully, I extended it toward the covered jewel she wore in her eye socket.

There was no immediate resistance. In fact, I felt nothing as I extended the line of power. An image came to me of a curtain of flame, however. Pushing through the fiery veil, I felt my extension of inquiry slowing, slowing, halted. And there I hovered, as it were, at the edge of a void. This was not the way of attunement, as I understood it, and I was loath to invoke the Pattern, which I understood to be a part of it, when employing other forces. I pushed forward and felt a terrible coldness, draining the energies I had called upon.

Still, it was not draining the energy directly from me, only from one of the forces I commanded. I pushed it farther, and I beheld a faint patch of light like some distant nebula. It hung against a background the deep red of port wine. Closer still, and it resolved itself into a form—a complex, three dimensional construct, half-familiar—which must be the pathway one takes in attuning oneself to the Jewel, from my father's description. All right, I was inside the Jewel. Should I essay the initiation?

"Go no further," came an unfamiliar voice, though I realized it to be Coral who was making the sounds. She seemed to have slipped into a trance state. "You are denied the higher initiation."

I drew back on my probe, not eager for any demonstrations that might come my way along it. My Logrus sight, which had remained with me constantly since recent events in Amber, gave me a vision of Coral now fully enfolded and penetrated by the higher version of the Pattern.

"Why?" I asked it.

But I was not vouchsafed a reply. Coral gave a little jerk, shook herself, and stared at me.

"What happened?" she asked.

"You dozed off," I replied. "No wonder. Whatever Dworkin did, plus the day's stress . . ."

She yawned and collapsed back on the bed.

"Yes," she breathed, and then she was really asleep.

I pulled off my boots and discarded my heavier garments. I stretched out beside her and drew a quilt over us. I was tired, too, and I just wanted someone to hold.

How long I slept I do not know. I was troubled by dark,

swirling dreams. Faces—human, animal, demonic, moved about me, none of them bearing particularly cheerful expressions. Forests fell and burst into flame, the ground shook and split, the waters of the sea rose in gigantic waves and assailed the land, the moon dripped blood and there came up a great wailing. Something called my name. . . .

A great wind rattled the shutters till they burst inward, flapping and banging. In my dream, a creature entered then and came to crouch at the foot of the bed, calling softly to me, over and over. The room seemed to be shaking, and my mind went back to California. It seemed that an earthquake was in progress. The wind rose from a shriek to a roar, and I heard crashing sounds from without, as of trees falling, towers toppling. . . .

"Merlin, Prince of the House of Sawall, Prince of Chaos, rise up," it seemed to say. Then it gnashed its fangs and began again.

At the fourth or fifth repetition it struck me that I might not be dreaming. There were screams from somewhere outside, and steady pulses of lightning came and went against almost musical rolls of thunder.

I raised a protective shell before I moved, before I opened my eyes. The sounds were real, as was the broken shutter. So was the creature at the foot of the bed.

"Merlin, Merlin. Rise up, Merlin," it said to me—it being a long-snouted, pointed-eared individual, well-fanged and clawed, of a greenish-silver cast of complexion, eyes large and shining, damp leathery wings folded against its lean sides. From its expression, I couldn't tell whether it was smiling or in pain. "Awaken, Lord of Chaos."

"Gryll," I said, naming an old family servant from the Courts.

"Aye, Lord," it replied. "The same as taught you the bonedance game."

"I'll be damned."

"Business before pleasure, Lord. I've followed the black thread a long and horrid way to come calling."

"The threads didn't reach this far," I said, "without an awful lot of push. Maybe even not then. Do they now?"

"It's easier now," he replied.

"How so?"

"His Majesty Swayvill, King of Chaos, sleeps this night with the ancestors of darkness. I was sent to fetch you back for the ceremonies."

"Now?"

"Now."

"Yeah. Well, okay. Sure. Just let me get my stuff together. How'd it happen, anyhow?"

I pulled on my boots, donned the rest of my garments, buckled on my blade.

"I am not privy to any details. Of course, it is common knowledge that his health was poor."

"I want to leave a note," I said.

He nodded.

"A brief one, I trust."

"Yes."

I scrawled on a piece of parchment from the writing table, *Coral, Called away on family business. I'll be in touch,* and I laid it beside her hand.

"All right," I said. "How do we do this?"

"I will bear you upon my back, Prince Merlin, as I did long ago."

I nodded as a flood of childhood memories returned to me. Gryll was immensely strong, as are most demons. But I recalled our games, at Pit's-edge and out over the darkness, in burial chambers, caves, still-smoking battlefields, ruined temples, chambers of dead sorcerers, private hells. I always seemed to have more fun playing with demons than with my mother's relatives by blood or marriage. I even based my main Chaos form upon one of their kind.

He absorbed a chair from the room's corner for extra mass, changing shape to accommodate my adult size. As I climbed upon his elongated torso, catching a firm hold, he exclaimed, "Ah, Merlin! What magics do you bear these days?"

"I've their control, but not full knowledge of their essence," I answered. "They're a very recent acquisition. What is it that you feel?"

"Heat, cold, strange music," he replied. "From all directions. You have changed."

"Everyone changes," I said as he moved toward the window. "That's life."

A dark thread lay upon the wide sill. He reached out and touched it as he launched himself.

There came a great rushing of wind as we fell downward, moved forward, rose. Towers flashed past, wavering. The stars were bright, a quarter moon just risen, illuminating the bellies of a low line of clouds. We soared, the castle and the town dwindling in an eyeblink. The stars danced, became streaks of light. A band of sheer, rippling blackness spread about us, widening. The Black Road, I suddenly thought. It is like a temporary version of the Black Road, in the sky. I glanced back.

It was not there. It was as if it were somehow reeling in as we rode. Or was it reeling us in?

The countryside passed beneath us like a film played at triple speed. Forest, hill, and mountain peak fled by. Our black way was a great ribbon heaving before us, patches of light and dark like daytime cloud shadows sliding past. And then the tempo increased, staccato. I noted of a sudden that there was no longer any wind. Abruptly, the moon was high overhead, and a crooked mountain range snaked beneath us. The stillness had a dreamlike quality to it, and in an instant the moon had fallen lower. A line of light cracked the world to my right and stars began to go out. There was no feeling of exertion in Gryll's body as we plunged along that black way; and the moon vanished and light grew buttery yellow along a line of clouds, acquiring a pink cast even as I watched.

"The power of Chaos rises," I remarked.

"The energy of disorder," he replied.

"There is more to this than you've told me," I said.

"I am but a servant," Gryll responded, "and not privy to the councils of the mighty."

The world continued to brighten, and for as far ahead as I could see our black ribbon rippled. We were passing high over mountainous terrain. And clouds blew apart and new ones formed at a rapid rate. We had obviously begun our passage through Shadow. After a time, the mountains wore down and rolling plains slid by. Suddenly the sun was in the middle of the sky. We seemed to be passing just above our black way, Gryll's toes barely grazing it as we moved. At times his wings hardly fluttered before me, at other times they thrummed like those of a hummingbird, into invisibility.

The sun grew cherry-red far to my left. A pink desert spread beneath us. . . .

Then it was dark again and the stars turned like a great wheel.

Then we were low, barely passing above the tops of the trees. . . .

We burst into the air over a busy downtown street, lights on poles and the fronts of vehicles, neon in windows. The warm, stuffy, dusty, gassy smell of city rose up about us. A few pedestrians glanced upward, barely seeming to note our passage.

Even as we flashed across a river, cresting the housetops of suburbia, the prospect wavered and we passed over a primordial landscape of rock, lava, avalanche, and shuddering ground, two active volcanoes—one near, one far—spewing smoke against a blue-green sky.

"This, I take it, is a shortcut?" I said.

"It is the shortest cut," Gryll replied.

We entered a long night, and at some point it seemed that our way took us beneath deep waters, bright sea creatures hovering and darting both near at hand and in the middle distance. Dry and uncrushed, the black way protected us.

"It is as major an upheaval as the death of Oberon," Gryll volunteered. "Its effects are rippling across Shadow."

"But Oberon's death coincided with the re-creation of the Pattern," I said. "There was more to it than the death of a monarch of one of the extremes."

"True," Gryll replied, "but now is a time of imbalance among the forces. This adds to it. It will be even more severe."

We plunged into an opening in a dark mass of stone. Lines of light streaked past us. Irregularities were limned in a pale blue. Later—how long, I do not know—we were in a purple sky, with no transition that I can recall from the dark sea bottom. A single star gleamed far ahead. We sped toward it.

"Why?" I asked.

"Because the Pattern has grown stronger than the Logrus," he replied.

"How did that happen?"

"Prince Corwin drew a second Pattern at the time of the confrontation between the Courts and Amber."

"Yes, he told me about it. I've even seen it. He feared Oberon might not be able to repair the original."

"But he did, and so now there are two."

"Yes?"

"Your father's Pattern is also an artifact of order. It served to tip the ancient balance in the favor of Amber."

"How is it you are aware of this, Gryll, when no one back in Amber seems to know it or saw fit to tell me?"

"Your brother Prince Mandor and the Princess Fiona suspected this and sought evidence. They presented their findings to your uncle, Lord Suhuy. He made several journeys into Shadow and became persuaded that this is the case. He was preparing his findings for presentation to the king when Swayvill suffered his final illness. I know these things because it was Suhuy who sent me for you, and he charged me to tell them to you."

"I just assumed it was my mother who'd sent for me."

"Suhuy was certain she would—which is why he wanted to reach you first. What I have told you concerning your father's Pattern is not yet common knowledge."

"What am I supposed to do about it?"

"He did not entrust me with that information."

The star grew brighter. The sky was filled with splashes of orange and pink. Shortly, lines of green light joined them, and they swirled like streamers about us.

We raced on, and the configurations came to dominate the sky fully, like a psychedelic parasol rotating slowly. The landscape became a total blur. I felt as if a part of me dozed, though I am certain I did not lose consciousness. Time seemed to be playing games with my metabolism. I grew enormously hungry and my eyes ached.

The star brightened. Gryll's wings took on a prismatic shimmer. We seemed to be moving at an incredible pace now.

Our strand curved upward at its outer edges. The process continued as we advanced until it seemed we were moving in a trough. Then they met overhead, and it was as if we sped down a gun barrel, aimed at the blue-white star.

"Anything else you're supposed to tell me?"

"Not so far as I know."

I rubbed my left wrist, feeling as if something should have been pulsing there. Oh, yes. Frakir. Where was Frakir, anyway? Then I recalled leaving her behind in Brand's apartment. Why had I done that? I—my mind felt cloudy, the memory dreamlike.

This was the first time since the event that I had examined that memory. Had I looked earlier I would have known sooner what it meant. It was the clouding effect of glamor. I had walked into a spell back in Brand's apartment. I'd no way of knowing whether it had been specific to me or merely something I'd activated in poking about. It could, I supposed, even have been something more general, enlivened by the disaster—possibly even an unintentional side effect of something that had been disturbed. Somehow I doubted the latter, however.

For that matter, I doubted any generality about the business. It was just too *right* to have been a booby-trap Brand had left lying about. It had confounded a trained sorcerer, me. Perhaps it was only my present distancing from the vicinity of its occurrence that had helped to clear my mind. As I reviewed my actions from the time of exposure I could see that I had been moving in something of a haze since then. And the more I reviewed the more I felt the spell to have been specifically tailored to enfold me. Not understanding it, I could not consider myself free of it with this knowledge either.

Whatever it was, it had caused me to abandon Frakir without thinking twice about it, and it had caused me to feel—well—strange. I could not tell exactly how it might have influenced, might still be influencing, my thoughts and my feelings, the usual problem when one is caught up inside a spell. But I didn't see how it could possibly have been the late Brand himself who had set the thing up against such an unpredictable occurrence as my having rooms next to his old ones years after his death, from which I would be prompted to enter his quarters in the disastrous aftermath of an improbable confrontation between the Logrus and the Pattern in an upper hall of Amber Castle. No, it seemed that someone else had to be behind it. Jurt? Julia? It didn't seem too likely that they'd be able to operate undetected in the heart of Amber Castle. Who then? And could it have had anything to do with that episode in the Hall of Mirrors? I drew blanks. Were I back there now I might be able to come up with a spell of my own to ferret out the one responsible. But I wasn't, and any investigation at that end of things would have to wait.

The light ahead flashed more brightly now, winking from heavenly blue to baleful red.

"Gryll," I said. "Do you detect a spell upon me?"

"Aye, m'lord," he replied.

"Why didn't you mention it?"

"I thought it one of your own—for defense, perhaps."

"Can you lift it? I'm at a disadvantage, here on the inside."

"'Tis too tangled in your person. I wouldn't know where to begin."

"Can you tell me anything about it?"

"Only that it's there, m'lord. Does seem rather heavy about the head, though."

"Could be coloring my thoughts a certain way, then?"

"Aye, a pale blue."

"I wasn't referring to your manner of perceiving it. Only to the possibility that it could be influencing my thinking."

His wings flashed blue, then red. Our tunnel expanded suddenly and the sky grew bright with the crazy colors of Chaos. The star we followed now took on the proportions of a small light—magically enhanced, of course—within a high tower of a sepulchral castle, all gray and olive, atop a mountain the bottom and middle of which had been removed. The island of stone floated above a petrified forest. The trees burned with opal fires—orange, purple, green.

"I'd imagine it could be disentangled," Gryll observed. "But its unraveling be a bafflement to this poor demon."

I grunted. I watched the streaking scenery for a few moments. Then, "Speaking of demons . . ." I said.

"Yes?"

"What can you tell me about the sort known as a *ty'iga?*" I asked.

"They dwell far out beyond the Rim," he replied, "and may be the closest of all creatures to the primal Chaos. I do not believe they even possess true bodies of the material sort. They have little to do with other demons, let alone anyone else."

"Ever know any of them—uh—personally?"

"I have encountered a few—now and then," he replied.

We rose higher. The castle had been doing the same. A fall of meteors burned its way, brightly, silently, behind it.

"They can inhabit a human body, take it over."

"That doesn't surprise me."

"I know of one who has done this thing, several times. But an unusual problem has come up. It apparently took control of one on the human's deathbed. The passing of the human seemed to lock the *ty'iga* in place. It cannot vacate the body now. Do you know of any way it might escape?"

Gryll chuckled.

"Jump off a cliff, I suppose. Or fall on a sword."

"But what if it's tied to its host so closely now that this doesn't free it?"

He chuckled again.

"That's the breaks of the game, in the body-stealing business."

"I owe this one something," I said. "I'd like to help her—it."

He was silent for a time, then replied, "An older, wiser *ty'iga*

might know something about these matters. And you know where
they are."

"Yeah."

"Sorry I can't be more help. They're an old breed, *ty'iga*."

And now we bore down upon that tower. Our roadway under
the shifting kaleidoscope that was the sky dwindled before us to
but the tiniest of streaks. Gryll beat his way toward the light in the
window and I peered past him.

I glanced downward. The prospect was dizzying. From some
distant place a growling sound came up, as if portions of the earth
itself were moving slowly against each other—a common enough
occurrence in this vicinity. The winds beat at my garments. A
strand of tangerine clouds beaded the sky to my left. I could make
out detail work in the castle walls. I caught sight of a figure within
the room of the light.

Then we were very near, and then through the window and inside. A large, stooped, gray and red demonic form, horned and
half-scaled, regarded me with elliptically pupiled yellow eyes. Its
fangs were bared in a smile.

"Uncle!" I cried as I dismounted. "Greetings!"

Gryll stretched and shook himself as Suhuy rushed forward
and embraced me—carefully.

"Merlin," he said at last, "welcome home. I regret the occasion
but rejoice in your presence. Gryll has told you . . . ?"

"Of the passing of His Highness? Yes. I'm sorry."

He released me and stepped back a pace.

"It is not as if it were unanticipated," he said. "Just the opposite. Too much so, in fact. Yet there is no proper time for such an
event."

"True," I replied, massaging a certain stiffness out of my left
shoulder and groping in my hip pocket after a comb.

"And he had been ailing for so long that I had grown used to it,"
I said. "It was almost as if he'd come to terms with the weakness."

Suhuy nodded. Then, "Are you going to transform?" he asked.

"It's been a rough day," I told him. "I'd as soon save my energy, unless there's some demand of protocol."

"None at all, just now," he replied. "Have you eaten?"

"Not recently."

"Come then," he said. "Let's find you some nourishment."

He turned and walked toward the far wall. I followed him.
There were no doors in the room, and he had to know all the local

Shadow stress points, the Courts being opposite to Amber in this regard. While it's awfully hard to pass through Shadow in Amber, the shadows are like frayed curtains in the Courts—often, you can look right through into another reality without even trying. And, sometimes, something in the other reality may be looking at you. Care must be taken, too, not to step through into a place where you will find yourself in the middle of the air, underwater, or in the path of a raging torrent. The Courts were never big on tourism.

Fortunately, the stuff of Shadow is so docile at this end of reality that it can be easily manipulated by a shadowmaster—who can stitch together their fabrics to create a way. Shadowmasters are technicians of locally potent skill, whose ability derives from the Logrus, though they need not be initiates. Very few are, although all initiates are automatically members of the Shadowmaster Guild. They're like plumbers or electricians about the Courts, and their skills vary as much as their counterparts on the Shadow Earth—a combination of aptitude and experience. While I'm a guild member I'd much rather follow someone who knows the ways than feel them out for myself. I suppose I should say more about this matter. Maybe I will sometime.

When we reached the wall, of course, it wasn't there. It just sort of grew misty and faded away; and we passed through the space where it had been—or, rather, a different analogous space— and we were passing down a green stairway. Well, it wasn't exactly a stairway. It was a series of unconnected green discs, descending in spiral fashion, proper riser and tread distance apart, sort of floating there in the night air. They passed about the exterior of the castle, finally stopping before a blank wall. Before we reached that wall we passed through several moments of bright daylight, a brief flurry of blue snow, and the apse of something like a cathedral without an altar, skeletons occupying pews at either hand. When we finally came to the wall we passed through it, emerging in a large kitchen. Suhuy led me to the larder and indicated I should help myself. I found some cold meat and bread and made myself a sandwich, washing it down with tepid beer. He nibbled at a piece of bread himself and sipped at a flagon of the same brew. A bird appeared overhead in full flight, cawing raucously, vanishing again before it had passed the entire length of the room.

"When are the services?" I asked.

"Redsky next, almost a whole turning off," he replied. "So you've a chance to sleep and collect yourself before then—perhaps."

"What do you mean, 'perhaps'?"

"As one of the three, you're under black watch. That's why I summoned you here, to one of my places of solitude." He turned and walked through the wall. I followed him, still bearing my flagon, and we seated ourselves beside a still, green pool beneath a rocky overhang, umber sky above. His castle contained places from all over Chaos and Shadow, stitched together into a crazy-quilt pattern of ways within ways. "And since you wear the spikard you've added resources for safety," he observed.

He reached out and touched the many-spoked wheel of my ring. A faint tingling followed in my finger, hand, and arm.

"Uncle, you were often given to cryptic utterances when you were my teacher," I said. "But I've graduated now, and I guess that gives me the right to say I don't know what the hell you're talking about."

He chuckled and sipped his beer.

"On reflection, it always became clear," he said.

"Reflection . . ." I said, and I looked into the pool.

Images swam amid the black ribbons beneath its surface—Swayvill lying in state, yellow and black robes muffling his shrunken form, my mother, my father, demonic forms, all passing and fading, Jurt, myself, Jasra and Julia, Random and Fiona, Mandor and Dworkin, Bill Roth and many faces I did not know. . . .

I shook my head.

"Reflection does not clarify," I said.

"It is not the function of an instant," he replied.

So I returned my attention to the chaos of faces and forms. Jurt returned and remained for a long time. He was dressing himself, in very good taste, and he appeared to be relatively intact. When he finally faded there returned one of the half-familiar faces I had seen earlier. I knew he was a noble of the Courts, and I searched my memory. Of course. It had been a long while, but now I recognized him. It was Tmer, of the House of Jesby, eldest son of the late Prince Rolovians, and now lord himself of the Ways of Jesby—spade beard, heavy brow, sturdily built, not unhandsome, in a rugged sort of way; by all report a brave and possibly even sensitive fellow.

Then there was Prince Tubble of the Ways of Chanicut, phasing back and forth between human and swirling demonic forms. Placid, heavy, subtle; centuries old and very shrewd; he wore a fringed beard, had wide, innocent, pale eyes, was master of many games.

I waited, and Tmer followed Jurt followed Tubble into vanishment amid the coiling ribbons. I waited longer, and nothing new occurred.

"End of reflection," I announced at last. "But I still don't know what it means."

"What did you see?"

"My brother Jurt," I replied, "and Prince Tmer of Jesby. And Tubble of Chanicut, among other attractions."

"Most appropriate," he responded. "Entirely appropriate."

"And so?"

"Like you, Tmer and Tubble are both under black watch. I understand Tmer is at Jesby, though I believe Jurt has gone to earth somewhere other than Dalgarry."

"Jurt's come back?"

He nodded.

"He could be at my mother's Fortress Gantu," I mused. "Or, Sawall did have a second stead—the Ways of Anch, at the very Rim."

Suhuy shrugged.

"I do not know," he said.

"But why the black watch—for any of us?"

"You went off into Shadow to a fine university," he said, "and you have dwelled in the Court of Amber, which I would deem highly educational. Therefore, I bid you take thought. Surely, a mind so well honed—"

"I realize the black watch means we face some sort of danger. . . ."

"Of course."

". . . But its nature eludes me. Unless . . ."

"Yes."

"It has to do with Swayvill's death. So it must involve some sort of political settlement. But I've been away. I don't know what matters are hot just now."

He showed me row upon row of worn but still nasty fangs.

"Try the matter of the succession," he said.

"Okay. Say the Ways of Sawall are supporting one possible successor, Jesby the other, Chanicut the other. Say we're at each other's throats over the matter. Say I've come back into the middle of a vendetta. So whoever's giving the orders right now has declared us under watch as a matter of keeping things from getting messy. I appreciate it."

"Close," he said, "but it's already gone further than that."

I shook my head.

"I give up," I said.

From somewhere there came up a wailing sound.

"Think about it," he replied, "while I welcome a guest."

He rose and stepped into the pool, vanishing immediately.

I finished my beer.

2

It seemed but moments later that a rock to my left shimmered and emitted a bell-like tone. Without conscious intent my attention gathered itself at my ring, which Suhuy had referred to as a spikard. I realized in that instant that I was preparing to use it to defend myself. Interesting, how familiar I felt with it now, how adapted I seemed to have become to it in so short a time. I was on my feet, facing the stone, left hand extended in its direction when Suhuy stepped through the shining place, a taller, darker figure at his rear. A moment later and that figure followed him, emerging into substantiality and shifting from an octopal ape form to that of my brother Mandor, humanized, wearing black as when last I had seen him, though the garments were fresh and of a slightly different cut, his white hair less tousled. He quickly scanned the area about us and gave me a smile.

"I see that all is well," he stated.

I chuckled as I nodded toward his arm in its sling.

"As well as might be expected," I replied. "What happened in Amber after I left?"

"No fresh disasters," he answered. "I stayed only long enough to see whether there was anything I could do to be of assistance. This amounted to a little magical clearing of the vicinity and the summoning of a few planks to lay over holes. Then I begged leave of Random to depart, he granted it, and I came home."

"A disaster? At Amber?" Suhuy asked.

I nodded.

"There was a confrontation between the Unicorn and the

Serpent in the halls of Amber Palace, resulting in considerable damage."

"What could have occasioned the Serpent's venturing that far into the realm of Order?"

"It involved what Amber refers to as the Jewel of Judgment, which the Serpent considers its missing eye."

"I must hear the entire tale."

I proceeded to tell him of the complicated encounter, leaving out my own later experiences in the Corridor of Mirrors and Brand's apartments. While I spoke, Mandor's gaze drifted to the spikard, to Suhuy, and back. When he saw that I noted this he smiled.

"So Dworkin is himself once more . . . ?" Suhuy said.

"I didn't know him before," I replied. "But he seemed to know what he was about."

". . . And the Queen of Kashfa sees with the Eye of the Serpent."

"I don't know that she sees with it," I said. "She's still recovering from the operation. But that's an interesting thought. If she could see with it, what might she behold?"

"The clear, cold lines of eternity, I daresay. Beneath all Shadow. No mortal could bear it for too long."

"She is of the blood of Amber," I said.

"Really? Oberon's?"

I nodded.

"Your late liege was a very active man," he observed. "Still, it would be quite a burden of seeing, though I speak only from guesswork—and a certain knowledge of principles. I've no idea what may come of this. Only Dworkin could say. Be he sane, there is a reason for it. I acknowledge his mastery, though I've never been able to anticipate him."

"You know him, personally?" I asked.

"I knew him," he said, "long ago, before his troubles. And I do not know whether to rejoice or despair in this. Recovered, he may be working for the greater good. Then again, his interests may be totally partisan."

"Sorry I can't enlighten you," I said. "I find his actions cryptic, too."

"I'm baffled also," Mandor said, "by the disposition of the Eye. But it still sounds pretty much a local matter, involving Amber's relations with Kashfa and Begma. I don't see that there is anything to be gained at this point by speculation. It's better keeping most of our attention for more pressing local matters."

•

I felt myself sigh.

"Such as the succession?" I suggested.

Mandor quirked an eyebrow.

"Oh, Lord Suhuy has briefed you already?"

"No," I replied. "No, but I heard so much from my father of the succession in Amber, with all its cabals, intrigues, and double crosses, that I almost feel an authority on the subject. I imagine it could be that way here, too, among the Houses of Swayvill's descendants, there being many more generations involved."

"You have the right idea," he said, "though I think the picture might be a bit more orderly here than it was there."

"That's something, anyway," I said. "For me, I intend to pay my respects and get the hell out. Send me a postcard telling me how it gets settled."

He laughed. He seldom laughs. I felt my wrist prickle where Frakir usually rides.

"He really doesn't know," he said, glancing at Suhuy.

"He's just arrived," Suhuy answered. "I hadn't the time to tell him anything."

I groped in my pocket, located a coin, withdrew it, and flipped it.

"Heads," I announced, on inspection. "You tell me, Mandor. What's going on?"

"You're not next in line for the throne," he said.

It being my turn to laugh, I did.

"I already knew that," I said. "You told me not that long ago, over dinner, how long the line was before me—if someone of my mixed blood could be considered at all."

"Two," he said. "Two stand before you."

"I don't understand," I said. "What happened to all the others?"

"Dead," he replied.

"Bad year for the flu?"

He gave me a nasty smile.

"There has been an unprecedented number of fatal duels and political assassinations recently."

"Which sort dominated the field?"

"The assassinations."

"Fascinating."

". . . And so you three are under black watch protection of the Crown, and were given into the care of your respective Houses' security."

"You're serious."

"Indeed."

"Was this sudden thinning of the ranks a matter of many people simultaneously seeking advancement? Or was it a smaller number, removing roadblocks?"

"The Crown is uncertain."

"When you say 'the Crown,' who, exactly, are you referring to, right now? Who's making decisions in the interim?"

"Lord Bances of Amblerash," he replied, "a distant relative and longtime friend of our late monarch."

"I sort of recall him. Could he have an eye on the throne himself, and be behind any of the—removals?"

"The man's a priest of the Serpent. Their vows bar them from reigning anywhere."

"There are usually ways around vows."

"True, but the man seems genuinely uninterested in such a thing."

"That needn't preclude his having a favorite, and maybe helping him along a bit. Is anybody near the throne particularly fond of his Order?"

"To my knowledge, no."

"Which doesn't mean someone mightn't have cut a deal."

"No, though Bances isn't the sort of man one would approach easily with a proposition."

"In other words, you believe he's above whatever's going on?"

"In the absence of evidence to the contrary."

"Who is next in line?"

"Tubble of Chanicut."

"Who's second?"

"Tmer of Jesby."

"Top of the line, your pool," I said to Suhuy.

He showed me his teeth again. They seemed to rotate.

"Are we at vendetta with either Chanicut or Jesby?" I asked.

"Not really."

"We're all just taking care then, huh?"

"Yes."

"How did it all come to this? I mean, there were a lot of people involved, as I recall. Was it a night of the long knives, or what?"

"No, the deaths have been occurring steadily for some time. There wasn't a sudden bloodbath when Swayvill took his turn for the worse—though a few did occur just recently."

"Well, there must have been some investigation. Do we have any of the perps in custody?"

"No, they either escaped or were killed."

"What of those who were killed? Their identities might indicate their political affiliations."

"Not really. Several were professionals. A couple of others were general malcontents, arguably among the mentally ill."

"You're saying there are no clues as to who might be behind it all?"

"That's right."

"What about suspicions then?"

"Tubble himself is of course suspect, though it is not a good idea to say it aloud. He stood to benefit the most, and now he's in a position to do so. Also, there is much in his career of political connivance, double-dealing, assassination. But that was long ago. Everyone has a few skeletons in the cellar. He has been a quiet and conservative man for many years."

"Tmer, then—He's close enough to generate suspicion. Is there anything to connect him with the bloody business?"

"Not really. His affairs are hardly open. He's a very private man. But he was never associated with such extremes in the past. I do not know him all that well, but he has always struck me as a simpler, more direct person than Tubble. He seems the sort who'd simply attempt a coup if he wanted the throne badly enough, rather than spend a lot of time intriguing."

"There could, of course, be a number of people involved, each acting in his own interest—"

"And now that the matter is imminent they'll have to surface soon?"

"It would seem so, wouldn't it?"

A smile. A shrug.

"No reason for a coronation to end it all," he said. "A crown does not automatically make a person dagger-proof."

"But the successor would come to power with a lot of bad baggage."

"It wouldn't be the first time in history. And if you stop to think about it, some very good monarchs have come to power under such a cloud. By the way, has it occurred to you that the others might be speculating along these lines about you?"

"Yes, and it makes me uncomfortable. My father wanted the throne of Amber for a long time, and it really messed up his life. He was only happy when he said the hell with it. If I learned anything from his story, that's it. I have no such ambition."

But for a moment, I wondered. What would it feel like to control a massive state? Every time I complained about politics, here, in Amber, back in the States on the Shadow Earth, there was the automatic corollary of considering the way I'd manage situations if I were in charge.

"I wonder?" Mandor repeated.

I glanced downward.

"Perhaps the others are looking into their own scrying pools just now," I said, "hoping for clues."

"Doubtless," he responded. "What if Tubble and Tmer did meet untimely ends? What would you do?"

"Don't even think about it," I said. "It won't happen."

"Suppose."

"I don't know."

"You really should make some sort of decision, just to have it out of the way. You're never at a loss for words when you know your own mind."

"Thanks. I'll remember that."

"Tell me more of your story, since last we met."

And so I did, Pattern ghosts and all.

Somewhere near the end the wailing sound began again. Suhuy moved toward the rock.

"Excuse me," he said, and the rock parted and he passed within.

Immediately, I felt Mandor's gaze heavy upon me.

"We probably only have a moment," he said. "Not enough time, really, to go into everything I wanted to cover with you."

"Very private, huh?"

"Yes. So you must arrange to dine with me before the funeral. Say, a quarter-turning hence, bluesky."

"All right. Your place, or the Ways of Sawall?"

"Come to me at Mandorways."

The rock phased again as I nodded, and a lithe demonic figure entered, shimmering bluely within a veil of cloud. I was on my feet in an instant, then bowing to kiss the hand she extended.

"Mother," I said. "I hadn't anticipated the pleasure—this soon."

She smiled, and then it went away in a swirl. The scales faded, the contours of her face and form flowed. The blue went away into a normal though pale flesh color. Her hips and shoulders widened as she lost something of height, though still remained tall. Her brown eyes grew more attractive as the heavy brow ridges receded. A few freckles became visible across her now-human, slightly upturned nose. Her brown hair was longer than when last I had seen her in this form. And she was still smiling. Her red tunic became her, simply belted; a rapier hung at her left hip.

"My dear Merlin," she said, taking my head between her hands and kissing me upon the lips. "I am pleased to see you looking so well. It has been quite a while since last you visited."

"I've had a very active existence of late."

"To be sure," she said. "I've heard some report of your various misadventures."

"I'd imagine you would have. It's not everyone has a *ty'iga* following him about, periodically seducing him in various forms, and making life, in general, very complicated with unwanted efforts at protection."

"It shows that I care, dear."

"It also shows that you have no respect for my privacy nor trust in my judgment."

Mandor cleared his throat.

"Hello, Dara," he said then.

"I suppose it must seem that way to you," she stated. Then, "Hello, Mandor," she went on. "What happened to your arm?"

"A misunderstanding involving some architecture," he replied. "You've been out of sight, though hardly out of mind, for some time."

"Thank you, if that's a compliment," she said. "Yes, I go a bit reclusive every now and then, when the weight of society becomes troublesome. Though you're hardly the one to talk, sir, vanishing for long stretches as you do in the labyrinths of Mandorways—if that be indeed where you take yourself."

He bowed.

"As you say, lady, we appear to be creatures of a kind."

Her eyes narrowed, though her voice was unchanged, as she said, "I wonder. Yes, I can sometimes see us as kindred spirits, perhaps even more than in our simplest cycles of activity. We've both been out and about a lot of late, though, haven't we?"

"But I've been careless," said Mandor, indicating his injured arm. "You, obviously, have not."

"I never argue with architecture," she said.

"Or other imponderables?" he asked.

"I try to work with what is in place," she told him.

"Generally, I do, too."

"And if you cannot?" she asked.

He shrugged.

"Sometimes there are collisions."

"You've survived many in your time, haven't you?"

"I can't deny it, but then it has been a long while. You seem made of very survivable stuff yourself."

"So far," she responded. "We really must compare notes on imponderables and collisions one day. Wouldn't it be strange if we were similar in all respects?"

"I should be very much surprised," he answered.

I was fascinated and slightly frightened by the exchange, though I could go only by feeling and had no notion of specifics. They were somehow similar, and I'd never heard generalities delivered with quite that precision and emphasis outside of Amber, where they often make a game of talking that way.

"Forgive me," Mandor said then, to the company in general, "but I must absent myself to recuperation. Thank you for your hospitality, sir." He bowed to Suhuy. "And for the pleasure of crossing—paths with you"—this to Dara.

"You've barely arrived," Suhuy said, "and you've taken no refreshment. You make me a poor host."

"Rest assured, old friend, there is none could perform such a transformation," he stated. He looked at me as he backed toward the opening way. "Till later," he said, and I nodded.

He passed into the way, and the rock solidified with his vanishment.

"One wonders at his deliveries," my mother said, "without apparent rehearsal."

"Grace," Suhuy commented. "He was born with an abundance."

"I wonder who will die today?" she said.

"I am not certain the implication is warranted," Suhuy replied.

She laughed.

"And if it is," she said, "they will certainly expire in good taste."

"Do you speak in condemnation or envy?" he asked.

"Neither," she said. "For I, too, am an admirer of grace—and a good jest."

"Mother," I said, "just what's going on?"

"Whatever do you mean, Merlin?" she replied.

"I left this place a long time ago. You sent a demon to find me and take care of me. Presumably, it could detect someone of the blood of Amber. So there was some confusion between myself and Luke. So it settled by taking care of both of us—until Luke began his periodic attempts to kill me. Then it protected me from

Luke and tried to determine which of us was the proper party. It even lived with Luke for a time, and later pursued me. I should have guessed at something of this because it was so eager to learn my mother's name. Apparently, Luke was just as closemouthed about his parentage."

She laughed.

"It makes a beautiful picture," she began. "Little Jasra and the Prince of Darkness—"

"Don't try to change the subject. Think how embarrassing that is for a grown man—his mother sending demons to look after him."

"The singular. It was just one demon, dear."

"Who cares? The principle's the same. Where do you get off with this protective business? I resent—"

"The *ty'iga* probably saved your life on more than one occasion, Merlin."

"Well, yes. But—"

"You'd rather be dead than protected? Just because it was coming from me?"

"That's not the point!"

"Then what is the point?"

"It seems you just assumed I couldn't take care of myself, and—"

"Well, you couldn't."

"But you had no way of knowing that. I resented your starting with the assumption that I needed chaperoning in Shadow, that I was naive, gullible, careless—"

"I suppose it would hurt your feelings if I said that you were, going to a place as different from the Courts as that Shadow is."

"Yes, I can take care of myself!"

"You weren't doing that great a job of it. But you are making a number of unwarranted assumptions yourself. What makes you think that the reasons you gave are the only possible ones for my taking such an action?"

"Okay. Tell me that you knew that Luke was going to try to kill me every April thirtieth. And if the answer is yes, why didn't you just tell me?"

"I did not know that Luke was going to try to kill you every April thirtieth."

I turned away. I clenched my fists and relaxed them.

"So you just did it for the hell of it?"

"Merlin, why do you find it so difficult to admit that other people might sometimes know things you don't?"

"Start with their unwillingness to tell me these things."

She was silent a long moment. Then, "I'm afraid there is something to what you say," she replied. "But there were strong reasons for not talking of such matters."

"Then start with the inability to tell me. Tell me now why you didn't trust me then."

"It wasn't a matter of trust."

"Is it okay to tell me now what it was?"

Another, longer silence followed.

"No," she finally said. "Not yet."

I turned toward her, keeping my features composed and my voice level.

"Then nothing has changed," I said, "nor ever shall. You still do not trust me."

"That is not true," she answered, glancing at Suhuy. "It is just that this is not the proper time or the proper place to go into these matters."

"Might I fetch you a drink or something to eat, Dara?" Suhuy said immediately.

"Thank you no," she replied. "I cannot stay much longer."

"Mother, tell me, then, something about the *ty'iga*."

"What do you wish to know?"

"You conjured it from someplace beyond the Rim."

"That is correct."

"Such beings are bodiless themselves, but capable of taking over a living host for their own purposes."

"Yes."

"Supposing such a being took over the body of a person at or near the moment of death, making it the sole animating spirit and controlling intelligence?"

"Interesting. Is this a hypothetical question?"

"No. It's really happened with the one you sent after me. It doesn't seem able to quit that body now. Why not?"

"I am not really certain," she said.

"It is trapped now," Suhuy offered. "It can only come and go by reacting with a resident intelligence."

"The body, with the *ty'iga* in control, recovered from the illness that killed its consciousness," I said. "You mean it's stuck there now for life?"

"Yes. So far as I know."

"Then tell me this: Will it be released when that body dies, or will it die with it?"

"It could go either way," he replied. "But the longer it remains in the body, the more likely it is that it will perish along with it."

I looked back at my mother.

"There you have the end of its story," I stated.

She shrugged.

"I've done with this one and released it," she said, "and one can always conjure another should the need arise."

"Don't do it," I told her.

"I shan't," she said. "There is no need to, now."

"But if you thought there were, you would?"

"A mother tends to value her son's safety, whether the son likes it or not."

I raised my left hand, extending the forefinger in an angry gesture, when I noticed that I was wearing a bright bracelet—it seemed an almost-hologramatic representation of a woven cord. I lowered my hand, bit back my first response, and said, "You know my feelings now."

"I knew them a long time ago," she said. "Let us dine at the Ways of Sawall, half a turning hence, purplesky. Agreed?"

"Agreed," I said.

"Till then. Good turning, Suhuy."

"Good turning, Dara."

She took three paces and was gone, as etiquette prescribed, out the same way by which she had entered.

I turned and strode to the pool's edge, stared into its depths, felt the muscles in my shoulders slowly unknot. Jasra and Julia were down there now, back in the citadel of the Keep, doing something arcane in the lab. And then the strands were flowing over them, some cruel truth beyond all order and beauty, beginning to form themselves into a mask of fascinating, frightening proportion.

I felt a hand on my shoulder.

"Family," Suhuy said, "intrigues and maddens. You are feeling the tyranny of affection at the moment, are you not?"

I nodded.

"Something Mark Twain said about being able to choose your friends but not your relatives," I answered.

"I do not know what they are up to, though I have my suspicions," he said. "There is nothing to do now but rest and wait. I would like to hear more of your story."

"Thanks, Uncle. Yeah," I said. "Why not?"

So I gave him all the rest of my tale. Partway through it, we adjourned to the kitchen for further sustenance, then took another way to a floating balcony above a lime-colored ocean breaking upon pink rocks and beaches under a twilit or otherwise indigo sky without stars. There, I finished my telling.

"This is more than a little interesting," he said, at last.

"Oh? Do you see something in it all that I don't?" I asked.

"You've given me too much to consider for me to give you a hasty judgment," he said. "Let us leave it at that for now."

"Very well."

I leaned on the rail, looked down at the waters.

"You need rest," he said after a time.

"I guess I do."

"Come, I'll show you to your room."

He extended a hand and I took hold of it. Together, we sank through the floor.

And so I slept, surrounded by tapestries and heavy drapes, in a doorless chamber in the Ways of Suhuy. It might have been in a tower, as I could hear the winds passing beyond the walls. Sleeping, I dreamt. . . .

I was back in the castle Amber, walking the sparkling length of the Corridor of Mirrors. Tapers flickered in tall holders. My footsteps made no sound. The mirrors came in all manner of shapes. They covered the walls at either hand, big ones, little ones. I passed myself within their depths, reflected, distorted, sometimes re-reflected. . . .

I was halted before a tall, cracked mirror to my left, framed in tin. Even as I turned toward it I knew that it would not be me whom I regarded this time.

Nor was I mistaken. Coral was looking at me from out of the mirror. She had on a peach-colored blouse and was not wearing her eyepatch. The crack in the mirror divided her face down the middle. Her left eye was the green I remembered, her right was the Jewel of Judgment. Both seemed to be focused upon me.

"Merlin," she said. "Help me. This is too strange. Give me back my eye."

"I don't know how," I said. "I don't understand what was done."

"My eye," she went on, as if she had not heard. "The world is all swarming forces in the Eye of Judgment, cold—so cold!—and not a friendly place. Help me!"

"I'll find a way," I said.

"My eye . . ." she continued.

I hurried by.

From a rectangular mirror in a wooden frame carved at its base in the form of a phoenix, Luke regarded me.

"Hey, old buddy," he said, looking slightly forlorn, "I'd sure like to have my dad's sword back. You haven't come across it again, have you?"

" 'Fraid not," I muttered.

"It's a shame to get to hold your present for such a short period of time. Watch for it, will you? I've a feeling it might come in handy."

"I'll do that," I said.

"After all, you're kind of responsible for what happened," he continued.

"Right," I agreed.

". . . And I'd sure like to have it back."

"Yeah," I said, moving away.

A nasty chuckle emerged from a maroon-framed ellipse to my right. Turning, I beheld the face of Victor Melman, the shadow Earth sorcerer I had confronted back when my troubles were beginning.

"Son of perdition!" he hissed. " 'Tis good to see you wander lost in Limbo. May my blood lie burning on your hands."

"Your blood is on your own hands," I said. "I count you as a suicide."

"Not so!" he snapped back. "You slew me most unfairly."

"Bullshit," I answered. "I may be guilty of a lot of things, but your death is not one of them."

I began to walk away, and his hand emerged from the mirror and clutched at my shoulder.

"Murderer!" he cried.

I brushed his hand away.

"Bugger off!" I said, and I kept going.

Then, from a wide, green-framed mirror with a greenish haze to the glass, Random hailed me from my left, shaking his head.

"Merlin! Merlin! What are you up to, anyway?" he asked. "I've known for some time that you haven't been keeping me abreast of everything that's afoot."

"Well," I replied, regarding him in an orange T-shirt and Levi's, "that's true, sir. Some things I just haven't had time to go into."

"Things that involve the safety of the realm—and you haven't had time?"

"Well, I guess there's something of a judgmental factor involved."

"If it involves our safety, I am the one to do the judging."

"Yes, sir. I realize that—"

"We have to have a talk, Merlin. Is it that your personal life is mixed with this in some way?"

"I guess that's true—"

"It doesn't matter. The kingdom is more important. We must talk."

"Yes, sir. We will as soon as—"

" 'As soon as,' hell! Now! Stop screwing around at whatever you're up to and get your ass back here! We have to talk!"

"I will, as soon as—"

"Don't give me that! It verges on the traitorous if you're withholding important information! I need to see you now! Come home!"

"I will," I said, and I hurried away, his voice joining a continuing chorus of the others, repeating their demands, their pleas, their accusations.

Out of the next one—circular, with a blue braided frame— Julia regarded me.

"And there you go," she said, almost wistfully. "You knew I loved you."

"I loved you, too," I admitted. "It took me a long time to realize it. I guess I messed up, though."

"You didn't love me enough," she said. "Not enough to trust me. And so you lost my trust."

I looked away.

"I'm sorry," I said.

"Not good enough," she responded. "Thus, we are become enemies."

"It doesn't have to be that way."

"Too late," she said. "Too late."

"I'm sorry," I repeated, and I hurried away.

Thus, I came to Jasra, in a red, diamond frame. Her bright-nailed hand reached out and caressed my cheek.

"Going somewhere, dear boy?" she asked.

"I hope so," I said.

She smiled crookedly and pursed her lips.

"I've decided you were a bad influence on my son," she said. "He lost his edge when he became friends with you."

"Sorry about that," I said.

". . . Which may make him unfit to rule."

"Unfit or unwilling?" I asked.

"Whichever, it will be your fault."

"He's a big boy now, Jasra. He makes his own decisions."

"I fear you've taught him to make the wrong ones."

"He's his own man, lady. Don't blame me if he does things you don't like."

"And if Kashfa crumbles because you've softened him?"

"I decline the nomination," I said, taking a step forward. It was good that I was moving, for her hand shot out, nails raking at my face, barely missing. She threw expletives after me as I walked away. Fortunately, they were drowned amid the cries of the others.

"Merlin?"

Turning to my right again I beheld the face of Nayda within a silver mirror, its surface and curled frame of a single piece.

"Nayda! What are *you* down on me for?"

"Nothing," the *ty'iga* lady replied. "I'm just passing through, and I need directions."

"You don't hate me? How refreshing!"

"Hate you? Don't be silly. I could never do that."

"Everyone else in this gallery seems irritated with me."

"It's only a dream, Merlin. You're real, I'm real, and I don't know about the others."

"I'm sorry my mother put you under that spell to protect me— all those years ago. Are you really free of it now? If you're not, perhaps I can—"

"I'm free of it."

"I'm sorry you had so much trouble fulfilling its terms—not knowing whether it was Luke or me you were supposed to be guarding. Who'd have known there'd be two Amberites in the same neighborhood in Berkeley?"

"I'm not sorry."

"What do you mean?"

"I came for directions. I want to know how I can find Luke."

"Why, in Kashfa. He was just crowned king the other day. What do you need him for?"

"Hadn't you guessed?"

"No."

"I'm in love with him. Always was. Now that I'm free of the *geas* and have a body of my own, I want him to know that I was Gail—and how I feel. Thanks, Merlin. Good-bye."

"Wait!"

"Yes?"

"I never said thanks for your protecting me all those years— even if it was only a compulsion for you, even if it got to be a big bother for me. Thanks, and good luck."

She smiled and faded away. I reached out and touched the mirror.

"Luck," I thought I heard her say.

Strange. It was a dream. Still—I couldn't awaken, and it felt real. I—

"You made it back to the Courts in time for all the scheming, I see"—this from a mirror three paces ahead, black-bound and narrow.

I moved to it. My brother Jurt glared out at me.

"What do you want?" I asked.

His face was an angry parody of my own.

"I want you never to have been," he said. "Failing that, I'd like to see you dead."

"What's your third choice?" I asked.

"Your confinement to a private hell, I guess."

"Why?"

"You stand between me and everything I want."

"I'll be glad to step aside. Tell me how."

"There's no way you can or will, on your own."

"So you hate me?"

"Yes."

"I thought your bath in the Fountain destroyed your emotions."

"I didn't get the full treatment, and it only made them stronger."

"Any way we can forget the whole thing and start over again, be friends?"

"Never."

"Didn't think so."

"She always cared more about you than me, and now you're going to have the throne."

"Don't be ridiculous. I don't want it."

"Your desires have nothing to do with the matter."

"I won't have it."

"Yes, you will—unless I kill you first."

"Don't be stupid. It's not worth this."

"One day soon, when you least expect it, you will turn and see me. It will be too late."

The mirror grew entirely black.

"Jurt!"

Nothing. Aggravating, having to put up with him in dream as well as waking.

I turned my head toward a fire-framed mirror several paces ahead and to my left, knowing—somehow—it was next on my route. I moved toward it.

She was smiling.

"And there you have it," she said.

"Aunty, what's going on?"

"It seems to be the sort of conflict generally referred to as 'irreducible,' " Fiona replied.

"That's not the sort of answer I need."

"Too much is afoot to give you a better one."

"And you're a part of it?"

"A very small one. Not one who can do you much good just now."

"What am I to do?"

"Learn your options and choose the best one."

"Best for whom? Best for what?"

"Only you can say."

"Can you give me a hint?"

"Could you have walked Corwin's Pattern that day I took you to it?"

"Yes."

"I thought so. It was drawn under unusual circumstances. It can never be duplicated. Our Pattern would never have permitted its construction had it not been damaged itself and too weak to prevent its coming into being."

"So?"

"Our Pattern is trying to absorb it, incorporate it. If it succeeds, it will be as disastrous as it would have been were the Pattern of Amber destroyed at the time of the war. The balance with Chaos will be totally upset."

"Isn't Chaos strong enough to prevent this? I'd thought they were equally potent."

"They were until you repaired the Shadow Pattern and Amber's was able to absorb it. This increased its strength beyond that of Chaos. Now it is able to reach for your father's against the power of the Logrus."

"I don't understand what is to be done."

"Neither do I, yet. But I charge you to remember what I have said. When the time comes you must make a decision. I've no idea what it will involve, but it will be very important."

"She's right," came a voice from behind my back.

Turning, I saw my father within a shining black frame, a silver rose set at its top.

"Corwin!" I heard Fiona say. "Where are you?"

"In a place where there is no light," he said.

"I thought you somehow in Amber, Father, with Deirdre," I said.

"The ghosts play at being ghosts," he answered. "I have not much time, for my strength is low. I can tell you only this: Trust not the Pattern, nor the Logrus either, nor any of their spawn, till this matter be settled."

He began to fade.

"How can I help you?" I asked.

The words ". . . in the Courts" came to me before he vanished. I turned again.

"Fi, what did he mean by that?" I asked her.

She was frowning.

"I get the impression that the answer lies somewhere in the Courts," she replied slowly.

"Where? Where should I look?"

She shook her head and began to turn away.

"Who would know best?" she said.

Then she, too, was gone.

Voices were still calling to me, from behind, from ahead. There was weeping and laughter, and my name being repeated. I rushed ahead.

"Whatever happens," Bill Roth said, "if you need a good lawyer, I'll handle it—even in Chaos."

And then there was Dworkin, squinting at me from out of a tiny mirror with a twisted frame.

"Nothing to be alarmed about," he remarked, "but all sorts of imponderables are hovering about you."

"What am I to do?" I cried.

"You must become something greater than yourself."

"I don't understand."

"Escape the cage that is your life."

"What cage?"

He was gone.

I ran, and their words rang around me.

Near the end of the hall was a mirror like a piece of yellow silk stretched upon a frame. The Cheshire Cat grinned at me from within.

"It's not worth it. The hell with them all," he said. "Come to the cabaret, old chum. We'll tip a few brews and watch the man paint."

"No!" I cried. "No!"

And then there was only a grin. This time I faded, too. Merciful, black oblivion and the sound of the wind, somewhere, passing.

3

How long I slept, I do not know. I was awakened by Suhuy's repeating my name.

"Merlin, Merlin," he said. "The sky is white."

"And I've a busy day," I answered. "I know. I'd a busy night, too."

"It reached you, then."

"What?"

"A small spell I sent, to open your mind to some enlightenment. I hoped to lead you to answers from within, rather than burden you with my guesswork and suspicions."

"I was back in the Corridor of Mirrors."

"I knew not what form it might take."

"Was it real?"

"As such things go, it should have been."

"Well, thanks—I guess. It reminds me that Gryll said something about your wanting to see me before my mother did."

"I wanted to see how much you knew before you faced her. I wanted to protect your freedom of choice."

"What are you saying?"

"I'm sure she wants to see you on the throne."

I sat up and rubbed my eyes.

"I suppose that's possible," I said.

"I don't know how far she's willing to go to effect this. I wanted to give you a chance to know your own mind before you're exposed to her plans. Would you care for a cup of tea?"

"Yes, thanks."

I accepted a mug he proffered and raised it to my lips.

"What are you saying about her beyond a guess at her wishes?" I asked.

He shook his head.

"I don't know how active her program might be," he said, "if that is what you mean. And whether she was connected with it or another, the spell you came wearing has faded now."

"Your doing?"

He nodded.

I took another swallow.

"I never realized how close I'd gotten to the head of the line," I added. "Jurt *is* number four or five in the succession, isn't he?"

He nodded.

"I've a feeling it's going to be a very busy day," I said.

"Finish your tea," he told me, "and follow me when you would."

He walked away through a dragon tapestry on the far wall.

As I raised the mug again, the bright bracelet on my left wrist came free and drifted before me, losing its braided outline, becoming a circle of pure light. It hovered above the steaming brew, as if enjoying its cinnamony aroma.

"Hi, Ghost," I said. "Why'd you weave yourself about my wrist that way?"

"To look like that piece of rope you usually wear," came the reply. "I thought you must be fond of the effect."

"I mean, what were you up to the whole time?"

"Just listening, Dad. Seeing how I might be of help. These people are all your relatives, too?"

"The ones we've met so far, yes."

"Is it necessary to go back to Amber to speak ill of them?"

"No, it works here in the Courts, too." I took another sip of tea. "Any special ill you have in mind? Or was that a general question?"

"I don't trust your mother or your brother Mandor, even if they are my grandmother and uncle. I think they're setting you up for something."

"Mandor's always been good to me."

". . . And your uncle Suhuy—he seems eminently stable, but he reminds me a lot of Dworkin. Might he be sitting on all sorts of internal turmoils and ready to flip out anytime?"

"I hope not," I said. "He never has."

"Oh-oh, it's been building, and this is a time of stress."

"Where are you getting all this pop psychology, anyway?"

"I've been studying the great psychologists of the Shadow Earth. It's part of my ongoing attempt to understand the human condition. I realized it was time I learned more about the irrational parts."

"What brought all this on?"

"The higher order edition of the Pattern I encountered in the Jewel, actually. There were aspects of it I simply could not understand. This led to considerations of chaos theory, then to Menninger and all the others for its manifestations in consciousness."

"Any conclusions?"

"I am wiser therefor."

"I mean, concerning the Pattern."

"Yes. Either it possesses an element of irrationality itself, like living things, or it is an intelligence of such an order that some of its processes only seem irrational to lesser beings. Either explanation amounts to the same thing from a practical standpoint."

"I never had the opportunity to apply some of the tests I'd designed, but can you say from self-knowledge whether you fall into such a category yourself?"

"Me? Irrational? The notion never occurred to me. I can't see how it could be."

I finished my tea and swung my legs over the side of the bed.

"Too bad," I said. "I think some measure of it is what makes us truly human—that, and recognizing it in ourselves, of course."

"Really?"

I rose and began dressing myself.

"Yes, and controlling it within oneself may have something to do with intelligence and creativity."

"I'm going to have to study this very closely."

"Do that," I said, pulling on my boots, "and let me know your findings."

As I continued dressing, he asked, "When the sky turns blue you will breakfast with your brother Mandor?"

"Yes," I said.

"And later you will take lunch with your mother?"

"That's right."

"Later still, you will attend the late monarch's funeral?"

"I will."

"Will you need me to protect you?"

"I'll be safe with my relatives, Ghost. Even if you don't trust them."

"The last funeral you attended got bombed."

"That's true. But it was Luke, and he's sworn off. I'll be okay. You want to sightsee, go ahead."

"All right," he said. "I do."

I rose and crossed the chamber, to stand before the dragon.

"Can you tell me the way to the Logrus?" Ghost asked.

"Are you joking?"

"No," he stated. "I've seen the Pattern, but I've never seen the place of the Logrus. Where do they keep it?"

"I thought I gave you better memory functions than that. In your last encounter with the thing, you pissed it off in the max."

"I suppose I did. Do you think it would hold a grudge?"

"Offhand, yes. Upon consideration, yes. Stay away from it."

"You just advised me to study the chaos factor, the irrational."

"I didn't advise you to commit suicide. I put a lot of work into you."

"I value myself, too. And you know I have a survival imperative, the same as organic beings."

"It's your judgment I wonder about."

"You know a lot about my abilities."

"It's true you're good at getting the hell out of places."

"And you owe me a decent education."

"Let me think about it."

"That's just stalling. I suppose I can find it myself."

"Fine. Go ahead."

"It's that hard to locate?"

"You gave up on omniscience, remember?"

"Dad, I think I need to see it."

"I haven't the time to take you there."

"Just show me the way. I'm good at concealing myself."

"I'll give you that. All right. Suhuy is Keeper of the Logrus. It lies in a cavern—somewhere. The only way I know to it begins in this place."

"Where?"

"There are something like nine turnings involved. I'll lay a seeing upon you, to lead you."

"I don't know whether your spells would work on something like me—"

I reached out through the ring—pardon me, spikard— superimposed a series of black asterisks upon a map of the ways he must follow, hung it in the space of my Logrus vision before him, and I said, "I designed you, and I designed this spell."

"Uh, yes," Ghost replied. "I feel as if I suddenly possess data that I can't access."

"It will be presented to you at the appropriate times. Form yourself into the likeness of a ring upon my left index finger. We will quit this room in a moment and pass through others. When we are near the proper way I will indicate it by pointing. Proceed in that direction and you will pass through something along your route which will conduct you into another place. Somewhere in that vicinity you will find a black star indicating the next direction you must take—to another place and another star and so on. Eventually, you will emerge in a cavern that houses the Logrus. Conceal yourself as completely as you can and make your observations. When you wish to retreat, reverse the process."

He shrank himself and flew to my finger.

"Look me up later and let me know your experiences."

"I was planning to," came his tiny voice. "I would not wish to add to your probable present paranoia."

"Keep it up," I said.

I crossed the room and entered the dragon.

I emerged in a small sitting room, one window looking out over mountains; the other, a desert. There was no one about, and I stepped out into a long hallway. Yes, just as I recalled.

I moved along it, passing a number of other rooms, till I came to a door on my left, which I opened to discover a collection of mops, brooms, buckets, brushes, a heap of cleaning cloths, a basin. Yes, as I remembered. I pointed to the shelves on my right.

"Find the black star," I said.

"You're serious?" came the small voice.

"Go and see."

A streak of light proceeded from my index finger, grew distorted as it neared the shelves, folded itself into a line so thin it was no longer present.

"Good luck," I breathed, and then I turned away.

I closed the door, wondering whether I had done the right thing, consoling myself with the thought that he would have gone looking and doubtless located the Logrus eventually, anyway. Whatever was to be on this front, would be. And I was curious as to what he might learn.

I turned and took myself back up the hallway to the little sitting room. It might be my last opportunity at being alone for a time, and I was determined to take advantage of it. I seated myself on a pile of cushions and withdrew my Trumps. A quick run through the deck turned up the one I had hastily sketched of Coral on that recent hectic day back in Amber. I studied her features till the card grew cold.

The image became three-dimensional, and then she slipped away and I saw myself, walking the streets of Amber on a bright afternoon, holding her hand as I led her around a knot of merchants. Then we were descending the face of Kolvir, sea bright before us, gulls passing. Then back in the cafe, table flying against the wall. . . .

I covered the card with my hand. She was asleep, dreaming. Odd, to enter another's dreams that way. Odder, to find myself there—unless, of course, the touch of my mind had prompted unconscious reminiscence. . . . One of life's smaller puzzles. No need to awaken the poor lady, just to ask her how she was feeling. I supposed I could call Luke and ask him how she was doing. I began searching for his card, then hesitated. He must be pretty busy, his first few days on the job as monarch. And I already knew she was resting. As I toyed with Luke's card, though, finally pushing it aside, the one beneath it was revealed.

Gray and silver and black. . . . His face was an older, somewhat harder version of my own. Corwin, my father, looked back at me. How many times had I sweated over that card, trying to reach him, till my mind tied itself into aching knots, with no result? The others had told me that it could mean he was dead, or that he was blocking the contact. And then a funny feeling came over me. I recalled his own story, in particular when he'd spoken of the times they had tried to reach Brand through his Trump, being at first unable to because he had been imprisoned in such a distant shadow. Then I remembered his own attempts to reach through to the Courts, and the difficulty imposed by the great distance. Supposing that, rather than being dead or blocking me, he was greatly removed from the places I had been when I had made the efforts?

But then, who was it had come to my aid that night in Shadow, bearing me to that peculiar place between shadows and the bizarre adventures that befell me there? And though I was totally uncertain as to the nature of his appearance to me in the Corridor of Mirrors, I had later encountered indications of his presence in Amber Castle itself. If he'd been in any of those places, it would seem he hadn't really been too far off. And that would mean he'd simply been blocking me, and another attempt to reach him would probably prove equally fruitless. Still, what if there were some other explanation for all these occurrences and . . .

The card seemed to grow cold beneath my touch. Was it just my imagination, or was the strength of my regard beginning to activate it? I moved forward in my mind, focusing. It seemed to grow even colder as I did so.

"Dad?" I said. "Corwin?"

Colder still, and a tingling feeling in my fingertips that touched it. It seemed the beginning of a Trump contact. It could be that he was much nearer to the Courts than to Amber, within a more reachable range now. . . .

"Corwin," I repeated. "It's me, Merlin. Hello."

His image shifted, seemed to move. And then the card went totally black.

Yet, it remained cold, and a sensation like a silent version of contact was present, like a telephone connection during a long pause.

"Dad? Are you there?"

The blackness of the card took on the aspect of depth. And deep within it, something seemed to be stirring.

"Merlin?" The word was faint, yet I was certain it was his voice, speaking my name. "Merlin?"

The movement within the depth was real. Something was rushing toward me.

It erupted from the card into my face, with a beating of black wings, cawing, crow or raven, black, black.

"Forbidden!" it cried. "Forbidden! Go back! Withdraw!"

It flapped about my head as the cards spilled from my hand.

"Stay away!" it screeched, circling the room. "Forbidden place!"

It passed out the doorway and I pursued it. It seemed to have vanished, though, in the moments it was lost to my sight.

"Bird!" I cried. "Come back!"

But there was no reply, no further sounds of beating wings. I peered into the other rooms and there was no sign of the creature in any of them.

"Bird . . . ?"

"Merlin! What's the matter?"—this from high overhead.

I looked up to behold Suhuy, descending a crystal stair behind a quivering veil of light, a sky full of stars at his back.

"Just looking for a bird," I replied.

"Oh," he said, reaching the landing and stepping through the veil which then shook itself out of existence, taking the stair along with it. "Any particular bird?"

"A big black one," I said. "Of the talking sort."

He shook his head.

"I can send for one," he said.

"This was a special bird," I said.

"Sorry you lost it."

We walked out into the hallway and I turned left and headed back to the sitting room.

"Trumps all over the place," my uncle remarked.

"I was attempting to use one and it went black and the bird flew out of it, shouting, 'Forbidden'! I dropped them at that point."

"Sounds as if your correspondent is a practical joker," he said, "or under a spell."

We knelt and he helped me to gather them.

"The latter seems more likely," I said. "It was my father's card. I've been trying to locate him for a long while now, and this was the closest I've come. I actually heard his voice, within the blackout, before the bird interrupted and cut us off."

"Sounds as if he is confined to a dark place, perhaps magically guarded as well."

"Of course!" I said, squaring up the edges of my deck and re-casing it.

One cannot shift the stuff of Shadow in a place of absolute darkness. It is as effective as blindness in stopping one of our blood from escaping confinement. It added an element of rationality to my recent experience. Someone wanting Corwin out of commission *would* have to keep him in a very dark place.

"Did you ever meet my father?" I asked.

"No," Suhuy replied. "I understand that he did visit the Courts briefly, at the end of the war. But I never had the pleasure."

"Did you hear anything of his doings here?"

"I believe he attended a meeting with Swayvill and his counselors, along with Random and the other Amberites, preliminary to the peace treaty. After that, I understand he went his own ways, and I never heard where they might have led him."

"I'd heard as much in Amber," I said. "I wonder. . . . He'd killed a noble—a Lord Borel—near the end of the final battle. Any chance Borel's relatives might have gone after him?"

He clicked his fangs twice, then pursed his lips.

"The House of Hendrake . . ." he mused. "I think not. Your grandmother was Hendrake. . . ."

"I know," I said. "But I didn't have much to do with them. Some disagreement with Helgram. . . ."

"Hendrake Ways is very much of the military sort," he went on. "Glory of battle. Martial honor, you know. I can't see them as holding a peacetime grudge for a wartime happening."

Recalling my father's story, I said, "Even if they considered the killing less than honorable?"

"I don't know," he said to that. "It's hard to guess attitudes on specific questions."

"Who is head of the House of Hendrake now?"

"The Duchess Belissa Minobee."

"The duke, her husband—Larsus. . . . What happened to him?"

"He died at Patternfall. I believe Prince Julian of Amber slew him."

"And Borel was their son?"

"Yes."

"Ouch. Two of them. I didn't realize."

"Borel had two brothers, a half brother and a half sister, many uncles, aunts, cousins. Yes, it's a big House. And the women of Hendrake are as doughty as the men."

"Yes, of course. There are songs, such as 'Never Wed a Hendrake Lass.' Any way of finding out whether Corwin had any doings with Hendrake while he was here?"

"One could ask about a bit, though it's been a long while. Memories fade, trails grow cold. Not easy."

He shook his head.

"How long till bluesky?" I asked him.

"Fairly soon," he said.

"I'd better be heading for Mandorways then. I promised my brother I'd breakfast with him."

"I'll see you later," he said. "At the funeral, if not before."

"Yes," I said. "I guess I'd better clean up and change clothes."

I headed back through the way to my room, where I summoned a basin of water, soap, toothbrush, razor; also, gray trousers, black boots and belt, purple shirt and gloves, charcoal cloak, fresh blade and scabbard. When I had made myself presentable, I took a way through a forested glade to the receiving room. From there, I exited onto a thruway. A quarter mile of mountain trail later, ending abruptly at a chasm, I summoned a filmy and crossed upon it. Then I bore right to Mandorways, traveling a blue beach beneath a double sun for perhaps a hundred yards. I turned right, passing through a remembered archway of stone, moving briefly past a bubbling lava field and through a black obsidian wall, which took me to a pleasant cavern, over a small bridge, through a corner of a graveyard, a few steps along the Rim and into the receiving area of his Ways.

The entire wall to my left was composed of slow flame; that to my right, a non-returnable way, save for light, giving sight of some sea-bottom trench where bright things moved about and ate one another. Mandor was seated humanformed before a bookcase directly ahead, wearing black and white, feet propped on a black ottoman, a copy of Robert Hass's *Praise,* which I had given him, in his hand.

He smiled as he looked up.

" 'Death's hounds feared me,' " he said. "Nice line, that. How are you this cycle?"

"Rested, finally," I said. "Yourself?"

He placed the book upon a small, legless table that floated near just then, and rose to his feet. The fact that he had obviously been reading it because I was coming in no way detracted from the compliment. He had always been that way.

"Quite well, thank you," he replied. "Come, let me feed you."

He took my arm and steered me toward the wall of fire. It fell away as we drew near and our footsteps sounded in a place of momentary darkness, succeeded almost immediately by a small lane, sunlight filtered through arching branches overhead, violets blooming at either hand. The lane took us to a flagged patio, a green and white gazebo at its farther end. We mounted a few stairs to a well-set table within, frosted pitchers of juice and baskets of warm rolls near at hand. He gestured and I seated myself. At his gesture a carafe of coffee appeared beside my setting.

"I see you recall my morning predeliction," I said, "from the Shadow Earth. Thank you."

He smiled faintly as he nodded, seating himself across from me. Bird-songs I could not identify sounded from the trees. A gentle breeze caused leaves to rustle.

"What are you up to these days?" I asked him as I poured a cup of coffee and broke a roll.

"Observing the scene, mainly," he replied.

"Political scene?"

"As always. Though my recent experience in Amber has led me to regard it as part of an even larger picture."

I nodded.

"And your investigations with Fiona?"

"Those, too," he answered. "These are shaping up into very unusual times."

"I've noticed."

"It seems almost as if the Pattern-Logrus conflict were making itself manifest in mundane affairs, as well as on the cosmic scale."

"I feel that way, too. But then I'm prejudiced. I got caught up in the cosmic part early, and without a scorecard. I've been run all over the place and manipulated every which way recently—to the point where all of my affairs seemed part of their bigger picture. I don't like it a bit, and if I had some way to make them back off I'd use it."

"Hm," he said. "And what if your whole life were a study in manipulation?"

"I wouldn't feel good about it," I said. "I guess I'd feel just the way I do now, only perhaps more intensely."

He gestured and an amazing omelet appeared before me, followed, moments later, by a side dish of fried potatoes, mixed with what appeared to be green chilies and onions.

"All of this is hypothetical," I said as I began eating, "isn't it?"

There followed a long pause as he took his first mouthful, then, "I think not," he said.

"I think the Powers have been moving madly for a long while now," he went on, "and we're finally nearing endgame."

"What makes you privy to these matters?"

"It began with a careful consideration of events," he said. "Then followed the formulation and testing of hypotheses."

"Spare me a lecture on the use of the scientific method in theology and human politics," I said.

"You asked."

"True. Go ahead."

"Do you not feel it somewhat odd that Swayvill expired just when he did, when so many things are coming to fruition simultaneously, after having hung on for so long?"

"He had to go sometime," I said, "and all the recent stresses probably proved too much."

"Timing," Mandor said. "Strategic placement. Timing."

"For what?"

"To place you on the throne of Chaos, of course," he replied.

4

Sometimes you hear an unlikely thing and that's all it is. Other times, you hear something improbable and it strikes an echo. There is an immediate feeling of having known it, or known something very like it, all along, and just not having bothered to pick it up and examine it. By rights, I should have choked at Mandor's pronouncement, then snorted something such as "Preposterous!" Yet, I'd a peculiar feeling about this business—whether his conclusion was right or wrong—as if there were something more than conjecture involved, as if there just might be some overall plan moving me toward the circle of power in the Courts.

I took a long, slow drink of coffee. Then, "Really?" I said.

I felt myself smiling as he sought my eyes, studied my face.

"Are you consciously party to the effort?"

I raised my coffee cup again. I had been about to say, "No, of course not. This is the first I've heard of the notion." Then I recalled my father's telling me how he had duped Aunt Flora into giving him vital information his amnesia had washed away. It was not the cleverness with which he had done it that had impressed me so much as the fact that his mistrust of relatives transcended consciousness, existed as a pure existential reflex. Not having been through all the family rivalries Corwin had, I lacked responses of such intensity. And Mandor and I had always gotten along particularly well, even though he was a few centuries older and had very different tastes in some areas. But, suddenly, discussing such a high-stakes matter as we were, that small voice Corwin referred to as his worse-if-wiser self suggested, "Why not? You could use the practice, kid," and as I lowered the cup again I decided to try it out, just to see how it felt, for a few minutes.

"I don't know whether we both have the same thing in mind," I said. "Why don't you tell me about the middle game—or perhaps even the opening—for what you see rushing to conclusion now."

"Both the Pattern and the Logrus are sentient," he said. "We've both seen evidence of that. Whether they are manifestations of the Unicorn and the Serpent or the other way around makes no real difference. Either way, we are talking about a pair of greater-than-human intelligences with vast powers at their disposal. Whichever came first is also one of those useless theological points. We need only concern ourselves with the present situation, as it affects us."

I nodded.

"A fair assessment," I agreed.

"The forces they represent have been opposed but fairly evenly matched for ages," he went on, "and thus a kind of balance has been maintained. They have constantly sought small victories over each other, each attempting to add to its own domain at the expense of the other. It appears to be a zero-sum game. Both Oberon and Swayvill were their agents for a long while, with Dworkin and Suhuy as their intermediaries with the powers themselves."

"So?" I said as he took a sip of juice.

"I believe that Dworkin had touched the Pattern too closely," he continued, "and so became subject to manipulation. He was sufficiently sophisticated, however, that he realized this and resisted. This resulted in his madness, with a reciprocal damaging effect on the Pattern itself because of their close connection. This, in turn, caused the Pattern to leave him alone, rather than risk further trauma. The damage was done, though, and the Logrus gained a small edge. This allowed it to act in the realm of order when Prince Brand began his experiments to increase his personal abilities. I believe he laid himself open to control and became an unwitting agent of the Logrus."

"That's a lot of supposition," I said.

"Consider," he responded, "that his aims seemingly became those of a madman. They make much more sense when seen as the goal of something wanting to destroy all order, to restore the universe to chaos."

"Continue," I said.

"At some point, the Pattern discovered—or perhaps possessed all along—the ability to create 'ghosts,' short-lived simulacra of those who had negotiated it. Fascinating concept, that. I was very interested to learn of it. It provided a major mechanism, supporting my thesis of the Pattern's and possibly the Logrus's, direct action in the promotion of physical events. Might they have figured in the setting up of your father as the Pattern's champion against Brand? I wonder."

"I don't follow," I said. "Setting him up, you say?"

"I've a feeling he was really the Pattern's choice as the next King of Amber, easy to promote, too, as it seemed to coincide with his own wishes. I've wondered about his sudden recovery in that Shadow Earth clinic, and particularly about the circumstances surrounding the accident that put him there, when even with differing time streams it seemed possible that Brand might have had to be in two places at the same time—imprisoned and looking down the sights of a rifle. Of course, Brand is no longer available to clarify the matter."

"More supposition," I said, finishing my omelet. "But not uninteresting. Please continue."

"Your father had second thoughts about the throne, however. Still, he *was* Amber's champion. Amber *did* win the war. The Pattern *was* repaired. The balance *was* restored. Random was the second choice as monarch—a good maintainer of the status quo—and that choice *was* made by the Unicorn, not by the Amberites following any of their versions of the Rules of Succession."

"I never looked at it all that way," I said.

"And your father—inadvertently, I believe—provided a bonus. Afraid that the Pattern had not been repaired, he drew another. Only, it *had* been repaired. Thus, there were two artifacts of order, rather than one. Though, as a separate entity, it probably did not add to the Pattern's strength, it added to order, as such, diminishing the effects of the Logrus. So your father set the balance right, then proceeded to tip it again—in the other direction."

"This is your conclusion from the investigations you and Fiona made of the new Pattern?"

He nodded slowly, took a sip of juice.

"Hence, more Shadow storms than usual, as a mundane effect," he said, "bringing us up to present times."

"Yes, present times," I said, pouring more coffee. "We've noted they've grown interesting."

"Indeed. Your story of the girl Coral, asking the Pattern to send her to an appropriate place, is a case in point. What did it immediately do? It sent her to a Shadow Pattern and turned out the lights. Then it sent you to rescue her, repairing that edition of itself in the process. Once it was repaired it was no longer a Shadow Pattern, but another version of itself that it was then able to absorb. It probably absorbed that entire shadow as well, adding considerably to its own energies. Its edge over the Logrus increased even more. The Logrus would need a big gain to restore the balance after that. So it risked an incursion into the Pattern's domain, in a desperate effort to obtain the Eye of Chaos. That ended in a stalemate, though, because of the intervention of that bizarre entity you call Ghostwheel. So the balance remains tipped in the Pattern's favor, an unhealthy state of affairs."

"For the Logrus."

"For everybody, I'd say. The Powers will be at odds, the shadows in turmoil and disorder in both realms till things have been righted."

"So something should be done to benefit the Logrus?"

"You already know that."

"I suppose I do."

"It communicated with you directly, didn't it?"

I recalled my night in the chapel in the place between shadows, where I had been faced with a choice between the Serpent and the Unicorn, the Logrus and the Pattern. Resenting the bullying in such a forced format, I had refused to choose either.

"Yes, it did," I answered.

"It wanted you for its champion, didn't it?"

"I suppose it did," I said.

"And . . . ?"

". . . And here we are," I replied.

"Did it indicate anything that might support my thesis?"

I thought about that trek through the Undershadow, mixing menace with ghosts—Pattern, Logrus, or both.

"I suppose it did," I repeated.

But, ultimately, it had been the Pattern I had served at the end of that journey, albeit unwittingly.

"You are prepared to execute its design for the good of the Courts?"

"I'm prepared to seek resolution of this matter, for everybody's peace of mind."

He smiled.

"Is that a qualification or an agreement?"

"It's a statement of intent," I said.

"If the Logrus has chosen you, it has its reasons."

"I daresay."

"It almost goes without saying that having you on the throne would strengthen the House of Sawall immensely."

"The thought had occurred to me, now you mention it."

"For one with your background, of course, it would become necessary to determine where your ultimate loyalty lies—with Amber or with the Courts."

"Do you foresee another war?"

"No, of course not. But anything you do to strengthen the Logrus will arouse the Pattern and provoke some response from Amber. Hardly to the point of war, but possibly to that of retaliation."

"Could you be more specific as to what you have in mind?"

"I'm only dealing in generalities at the moment, to give you opportunity to assess your reactions."

I nodded.

"Since we're talking generalities I'll just repeat my statement: I'm prepared to seek a resolution—"

"All right," he said. "We understand each other to this extent. In the event you make it to the throne, you want the same thing we do—"

" 'We'?" I interrupted.

"The House of Sawall, of course.—But you don't want anyone dictating specifics to you."

"That says it nicely," I replied.

"But of course we're speaking hypothetically, there being a couple of others about with stronger claims."

"So why argue contingencies?"

"If the House were able to see you crowned, however, do you acknowledge you would owe consideration for this?"

"Brother," I said, "you *are* the House, for all major purposes. If you're asking for a commitment before taking out Tmer and Tubble, forget it, I'm not all that eager to sit on a throne."

"Your wishes are not paramount in this," he said. "There is no reason for squeamishness when you consider that we've long been at odds with Jesby, and Chanicut's always been a troublemaker."

"Squeamishness has nothing to do with it," I said. "I never said I wanted the throne. And, frankly, I think either Tmer or Tubble would probably do a better job."

"They are not designates of the Logrus."

"And if I am, I should make it without any help."

"Brother, there is a big gap between its world of principles and ours of flesh, stone, and steel."

"And supposing I have my own agenda and it does not include your plan?"

"What is it, then?"

"We're speaking hypothetically, remember?"

"Merlin, you're being obstinate. You've a duty in this, to the House as well as to the Courts and the Logrus."

"I can assess my own duties, Mandor, and I have—so far."

"If you've a plan to set things right, and it's a good one, we'll help you to effectuate it. What have you in mind?"

"I do not require help at this point," I said, "but I'll remember that."

"What do you require right now?"

"Information," I said.

"Ask me. I have a lot."

"All right. What can you tell me about my mother's maternal side, the House of Hendrake?"

He pursed his lips.

"They're into soldiering, professionally," he said. "You know they're always off fighting in Shadow wars. They love it. Belissa Minobee's been in charge since General Larsus's death. Hm." He paused. Then, "Do you ask because of their rather odd fixation involving Amber?"

"Amber?" I said. "What do you mean?"

"I recall a social visit to the Ways of Hendrake one time," he said, "when I wandered into a small, chapellike room. In a niche in one wall there hung a portrait of General Benedict, in full battle regalia. There was an altarlike shelf below it bearing several weapons, and upon which a number of candles were burning. Your mother's picture was there, too."

"Really?" I said. "I wonder whether Benedict knows? Dara once told my father she was descended from Benedict. Later, he figured this an out-and-out lie. . . . Do you think people like that would hold a grudge against my father?"

"For what?"

"Corwin slew Borel of Hendrake at the time of the Patternfall War."

"They tend to take such things philosophically."

"Still, I gather it was a somewhat less than kosher engagement from the way he described it—though I don't believe there were any witnesses."

"So let sleeping wyverns lie."

"I've no intention of rousing them. But what I was wondering was that if they had somehow heard details they might have been out to clear some debt of honor on his behalf. Do you think they could have been behind his disappearance?"

"I just don't know," he replied, "how that would fit in with their code. I suppose you could ask them."

"Just come out and say, 'Hey, are you responsible for whatever happened to my dad?' "

"There are more subtle ways of learning a person's attitudes," he responded. "As I recall, you had a few lessons in them in your youth."

"But I don't even know these people. I mean, I might have met one of the sisters at a party, now I think of it—and I recall having seen Larsus and his wife in the distance a few times—but that's it."

"Hendrake will have a representative at the funeral," he said. "If I were to introduce you, perhaps you could apply a little glamour to obtain an informal audience."

"You know, that may be the way to go," I told him. "Probably the only way. Yes, do that, please."

"Very well."

He cleared the table with a gesture, filled it with another. This time, paper-thin crepes with a variety of fillings and toppings appeared before us; and fresh rolls, variously spiced. We ate for a time in silence, appreciating the balminess and the birds, the breezes.

"I wish I could have seen something of Amber," he said at length, "under less restricted circumstances."

"I'm sure that can be arranged," I replied. "I'd like to show you around. I know a great restaurant in Death Alley."

"That wouldn't be Bloody Eddie's, would it?"

"It would, though the name gets changed periodically."

"I've heard of it, and long been curious."

"We'll do that one day."

"Excellent."

He clapped his hands and bowls of fruit appeared. I freshened my coffee and swirled a Kadota fig in a bowl of whipped cream.

"I'll be dining with my mother later," I remarked.

"Yes. I overheard."

"Have you seen much of her recently? How's she been?"

"As she said, rather reclusive," he replied.

"Do you think she's up to something?"

"Probably," he said. "I can't recall a time when she hasn't been."

"Any idea what?"

"Why should I guess when she'll probably tell you outright?"

"You really think she will?"

"You have an advantage over everyone else, in being her son."

"Also a drawback, for the same reason."

"Still, she's more likely to tell you things than she would anyone else."

"Except, perhaps, Jurt."

"Why do you say that?"

"She always liked him better."

"Funny, I've heard him say the same thing about you."

"You see him often?"

"Often? No."

"When was the last time?"

"About two cycles ago."

"Where is he?"

"Here, in the Courts."

"At Sawall?" I had visions of him joining us for lunch. I wouldn't put something like that past Dara either.

"One of its byways, I think. He's rather reticent concerning his comings and goings—and stayings."

There being something like eight byway residences to Sawall that I knew of, it would be difficult to run him down through byways that could lead well into Shadow. Not that I'd any desire to, at the moment.

"What brings him home?" I asked.

"The same thing as yourself, the funeral," he said, "and all that goes with it."

All that goes with it, indeed! If there were a genuine plot to put me on the throne, I could never forget that—willing or unwilling, successful or unsuccessful—Jurt would be a step or two behind me all the way.

"I may have to kill him," I said. "I don't want to. But he's not giving me a whole lot of choice. Sooner or later, he's going to force us into a position where it has to be one or the other."

"Why do you tell me this?"

"So you'll know how I feel about it, and so that you might use whatever influence you may still have to persuade him to find a different hobby."

He shook his head.

"Jurt moved beyond my influence a long time ago," he said. "Dara's about the only one he'll listen to—though I suspect he's still afraid of Suhuy. You might speak to her concerning this matter, soon."

"It's the one thing neither of us can discuss with her—the other."

"Why not?"

"It's just the way it is. She always misunderstands."

"I'm certain she's not going to want her sons killing each other."

"Of course not, but I don't know how to put the matter to her."

"I suggest you make an effort to find a way. In the meantime, I would contrive not to be alone with Jurt, should your paths cross. And if it were me, in the presence of witnesses, I would make certain that the first blow was not mine."

"Well taken, Mandor," I said.

We sat for a time in silence. Then, "You will think about my proposal," he said.

"As I understand it," I replied.

He frowned.

"If you have any questions. . . ."

"No. I'll be thinking."

He rose. I got to my feet, also. With a gesture, he cleared the table. Then he turned away and I followed him out of the gazebo and across its yard to the trail.

We emerged after a stroll in his external study cum receiving room. He squeezed my shoulder as we headed for the exit.

"I'll see you at the funeral then," he remarked.

"Yes," I said. "Thanks for the breakfast."

"By the way, how well do you like that lady, Coral?" he asked.

"Oh, pretty well," I said. "She's quite—nice. Why?"

He shrugged.

"Just curious. I was concerned about her, having been present at the time of her misadventure, and I wondered how much she meant to you."

"Enough that it bothers me a lot," I said.

"I see. Well, give her my good wishes if you should talk to her."

"Thanks, I will."

"We'll talk again later."

"Yes."

I strode into the way, making no haste. I still had considerable time before I was due by the Ways of Sawall.

I paused when I came to a gibbet-shaped tree. A moment's reflection and I turned left, following an ascending trail among dark rocks. Near its top, I walked directly into a mossy boulder, emerging from a sandbank into a light rain. I ran across the field before me, till I came to the fairy circle beneath the ancient tree. I stepped to its middle, made up a couplet with my name for the rhyme, and sank into the ground. When I was halted and the moment's darkness went away, I found myself beside a damp stone wall, looking downhill across a prospect of headstones and monuments. The sky was fully overcast and a cool breeze wandered by. It felt to be one of the ends of a day, but whether morning or twilight lay near, I could not tell. The place looked exactly as I remembered it—cracked mausoleums hung with ivy, falling stone fences, wandering paths beneath high, dark trees. I moved down familiar trails.

As a child, this had been a favored playground of mine, for a time. I met here almost daily, for dozens of cycles, with a little shadow girl named Rhanda. Kicking through boneheaps, brushing by damp shrubbery, I came at length to the damaged mausoleum where we had played house. Pushing aside the sagging gate, I entered.

Nothing had changed, and I found myself chuckling. The cracked cups and saucers, tarnished utensils, were still stacked in the corner, heavy with dust, stained with seepage. I brushed off the catafalque we'd used as a table, seated myself upon it. One day Rhanda had simply stopped coming, and after a time I had, too. I'd often wondered what sort of woman she had become. I'd left her a note in our hiding place, beneath a loose floor stone, I recalled. I wondered whether she'd ever found it.

I raised the stone. My filthy envelope still lay there, unsealed. I took it out, shook it off, slid out my folded sheet.

I unfolded it, read my faded childish scrawl: *What happened Rhanda? I waited and you didn't come.* Beneath it, in a far neater hand, was written: *I can't come anymore because my folks say you are a demon or a vampire. I'm sorry because you are the nicest demon or vampire I know.* I'd never thought of that possibility. Amazing, the ways one can be misunderstood.

I sat there for a time, remembering growing up. I'd taught Rhanda the bonedance game in here. I snapped my fingers then, and our old ensorcelled heap of them across the way made a sound like stirring leaves. My juvenile spell was still in place; the bones rolled forward, arranged themselves into a pair of manikins, began their small, awkward dance. They circled each other, barely holding their shapes, pieces flaking away, cobwebs trailing; loose ones—spares—began to bounce about them. They made tiny clicking sounds as they touched. I moved them faster.

A shadow crossed the doorway, and I heard a chuckle.

"I'll be damned! All you need's a tin roof. So this is how they spend their time in Chaos."

"Luke!" I exclaimed as he stepped inside, my manikins collapsing as my attention left them, into little gray, sticklike heaps. "What are you doing here?"

"Could say I was selling cemetery lots," he observed. "You interested in one?"

He had on a red shirt and brown khakis tucked into his brown suede boots. A tan cloak hung about his shoulders. He was grinning.

"Why aren't you off ruling?"

His smile went away, to be replaced by a moment of puzzlement, returned almost instantly.

"Oh, felt I needed a break. What about you? There's a funeral soon, isn't there?"

I nodded.

"Later on," I said. "I'm just taking a break myself. How'd you get here, anyway?"

"Followed my nose," he said. "Needed some intelligent conversation."

"Be serious. Nobody knew I was coming here. I didn't even know it till the last minute. I—"

I groped about in my pockets.

"You didn't plant another of those blue stones on me, did you?"

"No, nothing that simple," he replied. "I seem to have some sort of message for you."

I got to my feet, approached him, studying his face.

"Are you okay, Luke?"

"Sure. As okay as I ever am, that is."

"It's no mean stunt, finding your way this near to the Courts. Especially if you've never been here before. How'd you manage it?"

"Well, the Courts and I go back a long ways, old buddy. You might say it's in my—blood."

He moved aside from the doorway and I stepped outside. Almost automatically, we began walking.

"I don't understand what you're saying," I told him.

"Well, my dad spent some time here, back in his plotting days," he said. "It's where he met my mother."

"I didn't know that."

"It never came up. We never talked family, remember?"

"Yeah," I said, "and no one I asked seemed to know where Jasra came from. Still, the Courts. . . . She's a long way from home."

"Actually, she was recruited from a nearby shadow," he explained, "like this one."

"Recruited?"

"Yes, she worked as a servant for a number of years—I think she was fairly young when she started—at the Ways of Helgram."

"Helgram? That's my mother's House!"

"Right. She was a maid-companion to the lady Dara. That's where she learned the Arts."

"Jasra got her instruction in sorcery from my mother? And she met Brand at Helgram? That would make it seem Helgram had something to do with Brand's plot, the Black Road, the war—"

"—and the Lady Dara going looking for your father? I guess so."

"Because she wanted to be a Pattern initiate as well as one of the Logrus?"

"Maybe," he said. "I wasn't present."

We moved down a gravelly trail, turned at a huge cluster of dark shrubbery, passing through a forest of stone and over a bridge that crossed a slow black stream that reflected high branches and sky, monochrome. A few leaves rustled in a stray breeze.

"How come you never mentioned any of this later?" I asked.

"I intended to, but it never seemed urgent," he said, "whereas a lot of other things did."

"True," I said. "The pace did seem to keep picking up each time our trails crossed. But now—Are you saying it's urgent now, that I suddenly need to know this?"

"Oh, not exactly." He halted. He reached out and leaned upon a headstone. His hand began to grip it, growing white about the knuckles, across the back. The stone at his fingertips was ground to powder, fell snowlike to the earth. "Not exactly," he repeated.

"That part was my idea, just because I wanted you to know. Maybe it'll do you some good, maybe it won't. Information is like that. You never know." With a crunching, cracking sound, the top of the headstone suddenly gave way. Luke hardly seemed to notice this, and his hand kept on squeezing. Small pieces fell from the larger one he now held.

"So you came all this way to tell me that?"

"No," he answered, as we turned and began walking back the way we had come. "I was sent to tell you something else, and it's been pretty hard holding off. But I figured if I talked about this first, it couldn't let me go, would keep feeding me till I got around to the message."

There came a huge crunch, and the stone he held turned to gravel, falling to mix with that on the trail.

"Let me see your hand."

He brushed it off and held it out. A tiny flame flickered near the base of his index finger. He ran his thumb over it and it went out. I increased my pace, and he matched it.

"Luke, you know what you are?"

"Something in me seems to, but *I* don't, man. I just feel—I'm not right. I'd probably better tell you what I feel I should pretty quick now."

"No. Hold off," I said, hurrying even more.

Something dark passed overhead, too quick for me to make out its shape, vanishing among the trees. We were buffeted by a sudden gust of wind.

"You know what's going on, Merle?" he asked.

"I think so," I said, "and I want you to do exactly what I tell you, no matter how weird it might seem. Okay?"

"Sure thing. If I can't trust a Lord of Chaos, who can I trust, eh?"

We hurried past the clump of shrubs. My mausoleum was just up ahead.

"You know, there really is something I feel obliged to tell you right now, though," he said.

"Hold it. Please."

"It *is* important, though."

I ran on ahead of him. He began running, too, to keep up.

"It's about your being here at the Courts, just now."

I extended my hands, used them to brake myself when I came up against the wall of the stone building. I swung myself through the doorway and inside. Three big steps, and I was kneeling in the corner, snatching up an old cup, using the corner of my cloak to wipe it out.

"Merle, what the hell are you doing?" Luke asked, entering behind me.

"Just a minute and I'll show you," I told him, drawing my dagger.

Placing the cup upon the stone where I had been seated earlier, I held my hand above it and used the dagger to cut my wrist.

Instead of blood, flame came forth from the incision.

"No! Damn it!" I cried.

And I reached into the spikard, located the proper line, and found the flowing channel of a cooling spell that I laid upon the wound. Immediately, the flames died and it was blood that flowed from me. However, as it fell into the cup it began to smoke. Cursing, I extended the spell to control its liquidity there, also.

"Yeah, it's weird, Merle. I'll give you that," Luke observed.

I laid the dagger aside and used my right hand to squeeze my arm above the wound. The blood flowed faster. The spikard throbbed. I glanced at Luke. There was a look of strain upon his face. I pumped my fist. The cup was more than half-full.

"You said you trust me," I stated.

"Afraid so," he answered.

Three-quarters. . . .

"You've got to drink this, Luke," I said. "I mean it."

"Somehow, I suspected you were leading up to this," he said, "and, really, it doesn't sound like such a bad idea. I've a feeling I need a lot of help just now."

He reached out and took the cup, raised it to his lips. I pressed the palm of my hand against the wound. Outside, the winds were gusting regularly.

"When you've finished, put it back," I said. "You're going to need more."

I could hear the sounds of his swallowing.

"Better than a slug of Jameson," he said then. "Don't know why." He replaced the cup on the stone. "A little salty, though," he added.

I removed my hand from the incision, held the wrist above it again, pumped my fist.

"Hey, man. You're losing a lot of blood there. I feel okay now. Was just a little dizzy, that's all. I don't need any more."

"Yes, you do," I said. "Believe me. I gave a lot more than this in a blood drive once and ran in a meet the next day. It's okay."

The wind rose to a gale, moaning past us now.

"Mind telling me what's going on?" he asked.

"Luke, you're a Pattern ghost," I told him.

"What do you mean?"

"The Pattern can duplicate anybody who ever walked it. You've got all the signs. I know them."

"Hey, I feel real. I didn't even do the Pattern in Amber. I did it in Tir-na Nog'th."

"Apparently, it controls the two images as well, since they're true copies. Do you remember your coronation in Kashfa?"

"Coronation? Hell no! You mean I made it to the throne?"

"Yep. Rinaldo the First."

"God damn! Bet Mom's happy."

"I'm sure."

"This is kind of awkward then, there being two of me. You seem familiar with the phenomenon. How does the Pattern handle it?"

"You guys tend not to last very long. It seems the closer you are to the Pattern itself the stronger you are, too. It must have taken a lot of juice to project you this far. Here, drink this."

"Sure."

He tossed off a half cupful and handed the cup back.

"So what's with the precious bodily fluids?" he asked.

"The blood of Amber seems to have a sustaining effect on Pattern ghosts."

"You mean I'm some kind of vampire?"

"I suppose you could put it that way, in a sort of technical sense."

"I'm not sure I like that—especially such a specialized one."

"It does seem to have certain drawbacks. But one thing at a time. Let's get you stabilized before we start looking for angles."

"All right. You've got a captive audience."

There came a rattle, as of a rolled stone, from outside, followed by a small clanking noise.

Luke turned his head.

"I don't think that's just the wind," he stated.

"Take the last sip," I said, moving away from the cup and groping after my handkerchief. "It'll have to hold you."

He tossed it off as I wrapped my wrist. He knotted it in place for me.

"Let's get out of here," I said. "The vibes are getting bad."

"Fine with me," he replied as a figure appeared at the doorway. It was backlighted, its features lost in shadow.

"You're not going anywhere, Pattern ghost," came an almost-familiar voice.

I willed the spikard to about 150 watts illumination.

It was Borel, showing his teeth in an unfriendly fashion.

"You are about to become a very large candle, Patterner," he said to Luke.

"You're wrong, Borel," I said, raising the spikard.

Suddenly, the Sign of the Logrus swam between us.

"Borel? The master swordsman?" Luke inquired.

"The same," I answered.

"Oh, shit!" Luke said.

5

As I probed forward with two of the more lethal energies of the spikard the Logrus image intercepted them and turned them off.

"I didn't save him for you to take him out this easily," I said, and just then something like the image of the Pattern but not really the same flashed into existence nearby.

The Sign of the Logrus slid to my left. The new thing—whatever it was—kept pace with it, both of them passing silently through the wall. Almost immediately, there followed a thunderclap that shook the building. Even Borel, who was reaching for his blade, paused in mid-gesture, then moved his hand to catch hold of the doorway. As he did this, another figure appeared at his back and a familiar voice addressed him: "Please excuse me. You're blocking my way."

"Corwin!" I cried. "Dad!"

Borel turned his head.

"Corwin, Prince of Amber?" he said.

"Indeed," came the reply, "though I'm afraid I haven't had the pleasure."

"I am Borel, Duke of Hendrake, Master of Arms of the Ways of Hendrake."

"You speak with a lot of capitals, sir, and I'm pleased to make your acquaintance," Corwin said. "Now, if you don't mind, I'd like to get through here to see my son."

Borel's hand moved to the hilt of his blade as he turned. I was already moving forward by then, and so was Luke. But there was a movement beyond Borel—a kick, it seemed, low—causing him to expel a lot of air and double forward. Then a fist descended upon the back of his neck and he fell.

"Come on," Corwin called, gesturing. "I think we'd better get out of here."

Luke and I emerged, stepping over the fallen Master of Arms of the Ways of Hendrake. The ground off to the left was blackened, as if from a recent brushfire, and a light rain had begun to fall. There were other human figures in the distance now, moving toward us.

"I don't know whether the force that brought me here can get me out again," Corwin said, looking about. "It may be otherwise occupied." Several moments passed, then, "I guess it is," he said. "Okay, it's up to you. How do we flee?"

"This way," I told him, turning and breaking into a run.

They followed me up the trails that had brought me to this place. I looked back and saw that six dark figures pursued us.

I headed uphill, past the markers and monuments, coming at last to the place beside the old stone wall. By then, there were shouts from behind us. Ignoring them, I drew my companions to me and came up with an impromptu couplet that described the situation and my desire in somewhat less than perfect meter. Still, the charm held, and a hurled cobble only missed me because we were already sinking into the earth.

We emerged from the fairy ring, coming up like mushrooms, and I led my companions across the field, jogging, to the sandbank. As we entered there I heard another shout. We exited the boulder and descended the rocky trail to the gibbet tree. Turning left on the trail, I began to run.

"Hold up!" Corwin called. "I feel it around here somewhere. There!"

He left the trail to the right and began running toward the base of a small hill. Luke and I followed. From behind us came the sounds of our pursuers' emergence from the way at the boulder.

Ahead, I saw something flickering between two trees. We seemed to be heading toward it. As we drew nearer, its outline became clearer, and I realized that it possessed the contours of that Pattern-like image I had beheld back in the mausoleum.

Dad did not break stride as he approached, but charged right into the thing. And vanished. Another cry rose up behind us. Luke was next through the shimmering screen, and I was close on his heels.

We were running through a straight, glowing, pearly tunnel now, and when I glanced back I saw that it seemed to be closing in behind me.

"They can't follow," Corwin shouted. "That end's already closed."

"Then why are we running?" I asked.

"We're still not safe," he replied. "We're cutting through the Logrus's domain. If we're spotted there could still be trouble."

We raced on through that strange tunnel, and, "We're running through Shadow?" I asked.

"Yes."

"Then it would seem that the farther we go, the better—"

The whole thing shook, and I had to put out a hand to keep from being thrown down.

"Oh-oh," Luke said.

"Yes," I agreed as the tunnel began to come apart. Big chunks seemed to be torn out of the walls, the floor. There was only murk behind these rents. We kept going, leaping the openings. Then something struck again, soundlessly, completely shattering the entire passage—around us, behind us, before us.

We fell.

Well, we didn't exactly fall. We sort of drifted in a twilit fog. There didn't seem to be anything underfoot, or in any other direction either. It was a free-fall sensation, with nothing to measure possible movement against.

"Damn!" I heard Corwin say.

We hovered, fell, drifted—whatever—for a time, and, "So close," I heard him mutter.

"Something that way," Luke suddenly announced, gesturing to his right.

A big shape loomed grayly. I moved my mind into the spikard and probed in that direction. Whatever it was, it was inanimate, and I commanded the spike that had touched it to guide us to it.

I did not feel myself moving, but the thing loomed larger, took on familiar outlines, began to show a reddish complexion. When the fins became apparent, I knew for certain.

"Looks like that Polly Jackson you have," Luke remarked. "Even has the snow on it."

Yes, it was my red and white '57 Chevy that we were approaching, there in Limbo.

"It's a construct. It's been pulled from my mind before," I told him. "Probably because it's vivid, I've studied it so often. Also, it seems very appropriate just now."

I reached, toward the door handle. We were coming up on the driver's side. I caught hold and pushed the button. It was, of course, unlocked. The others touched the vehicle in various places and drew themselves along to the other side. I opened the door, slid in behind the wheel, closed the door. Luke and Corwin were entering by then. The keys were in the ignition, as I'd expected.

When everyone was aboard I tried starting it. The engine caught immediately. I stared out across the bright hood into nothingness. I switched on the headlights and that didn't help.

"What now?" Luke asked.

I shifted into first, released the emergency brake, and let out the clutch. As I gave it the gas, it seemed the wheels were turning. After a few moments I shifted into second. A bit later I put it into third.

Was there the tiniest feeling of traction, or was it only the power of suggestion?

I fed it more gas. The foggy prospect seemed to brighten slightly, far ahead, though I supposed this could simply be some effect of my staring in that direction. There was no particular feedback from the steering wheel. I pushed harder on the accelerator.

Luke reached out suddenly and turned on the radio.

"—hazardous driving conditions," came an announcer's voice. "So keep your speed to a minimum." There immediately followed Wynton Marsalis playing "Caravan."

Taking it as a personal message, I eased up on the gas. This produced a definite feeling of light traction, as if, perhaps, we were gliding on ice.

A sensation of forward movement followed, and there did seem a brightening in the distance. Also, it seemed as if I had acquired some weight, was settling more deeply into the seat. Moments later the sensation of a real surface beneath the car became more pronounced. I wondered what would happen if I turned the wheel. I decided not to try it.

The sound from beneath the tires became more gritty. Dim outlines occurred at either hand, increasing the feeling of movement and direction as we passed them. Far ahead, the world was indeed brighter now.

I slowed even more because it began feeling as if I were negotiating a real road, with very poor visibility. Shortly thereafter, the headlights did seem to be operating with some effect, as they struck a few of the passing shapes, giving them the momentary appearance of trees and embankments, shrub clusters, rocks. The rearview mirror continued to reflect nothingness, however.

"Just like old times," Luke said. "Goin' out for pizza on a bad evening."

"Yeah," I agreed.

"I hope the other me has someone open a pizza parlor in Kashfa. Could use one there, you know?"

"I'll come by and try it, if he does."

"Where do you think this whole business is going to leave me, anyway?"

"I don't know, Luke."

"I mean, I can't keep drinking your blood. And what about the other me?"

"I think I can offer you a job that will take care of the problem," Corwin said to him. "For a while, anyway."

The trees were definitely trees now, the fog real fog—moving about a bit. Beads of moisture began to form on the windshield.

"What do you mean?" Luke asked.

"In a minute."

There were breaks in the fog now, real landscape visible through them. Abruptly, I became aware that it was not a real road surface on which I was driving, but rather a fairly level piece of ground. I slowed even more to accommodate this.

A big section of haze dissolved or blew away then, revealing the presence of an enormous tree. Also, a section of the ground seemed to be glowing. There was a familiar feeling to this partial tableau. . . .

"This is the place of *your* Pattern, isn't it?" I asked, as our way grew even clearer. "Fiona brought me here once."

"Yes," came the reply.

"And its image—That's the thing I saw confronting the Sign of the Logrus back in the graveyard—the same thing that led us into the tunnel."

"Yes."

"Then—It's sentient, too. Like Amber's, like the Logrus—"

"True. Park it over there, in that clear area by the tree."

I turned the wheel and headed toward the level spot he had indicated. Fog still hung about the place, but nowhere near as heavy and all-encompassing as on the trail we had taken. It might have been twilight, from the shading of the mist, but the glow from that eccentric Pattern brightened our cup-shaped world beyond a day's end dimness.

As we climbed out Corwin said to Luke, "Pattern ghosts tend not to last long."

"So I understand," Luke replied. "You know any tricks for someone in this position?"

"I know them all, sir. It takes one to know, as they say."

"Oh?"

"Dad . . . ?" I said. "You mean . . ."

"Yes," he replied. "I do not know where the first version of myself might be."

"You are the one I encountered a while back? The one who might have been present in Amber recently, also?"

"Yes."

"I—see. Yet, you don't seem exactly like others I've encountered."

He reached out and clasped my shoulder.

"I'm not," he said, and he glanced toward the Pattern. "I drew that thing," he went on, a little later, "and I'm the only person ever to have walked it. Consequently, I'm the only ghost it can summon. Also, it seems to regard me with something other than utilitarian attention. We can communicate, in a way, and it seems to have been willing to devote the energy needed to keep me stable—for a long while now. We have our own plans, and our relationship seems almost symbiotic. I gather that those of Amber's Pattern and those of the Logrus are more in the nature of ephemera."

"That's been my experience," I said.

"—except for one, to whom you ministered, for which I am grateful. She is under my protection now, for so long as it shall last."

He released my shoulder.

"I haven't been properly introduced to your friend yet," he said then.

"Excuse me. A bit of extenuation there," I said. "Luke, I'd like you to meet my father, Corwin of Amber. Sir, Luke is properly known as Rinaldo, son of your brother Brand."

Corwin's eyes widened for an instant, then narrowed as he extended his hand, studying Luke's face.

"Good to meet a friend of my son's, as well as a relative," he said.

"Glad to know you, too, sir."

"I'd wondered what it was that seemed so familiar about you."

"It kind of slows down with appearances, if that's what you're getting at. Maybe even stops there."

Dad laughed.

"Where'd you two meet?"

"In school," Luke replied. "Berkeley."

"Where else might a pair of us come together? Not in Amber, of course," he said, turning away then to face his Pattern fully. "I'll get your story yet. But come with me now. I want to do an introduction myself."

He headed off toward the shining design and we followed him, a few wisps of fog drifting past us. Save for our short footfalls, the place was silent.

When we came up to the edge of his Pattern we halted and stared out across it. It was a graceful design, too big to take in at a glance; and a feeling of power seemed to pulse outward from it.

"Hi," he said. "I want you to meet my son and my nephew, Merlin and Rinaldo—though I believe you met Merlin once before. Rinaldo has a problem." There followed a long silence. Then he said, "Yes, that's right," and after a time, "You really think so?" and, "Okay. Sure, I'll tell them."

He stretched and sighed and took a few paces away from the Pattern's edge. Then he extended his arms and put them around both our shoulders.

"Men," he said then, "I've got an answer of sorts. But it means we're all going to have to walk this Pattern, for different reasons."

"I'm game," Luke said. "But what's the reason?"

"It's going to adopt you," Corwin said, "and sustain you as it does me. There's a price, though. The time's getting nearer when it will want to be guarded full-time. We can spell each other."

"Sounds fine," Luke said. "This place is kind of peaceful. And I didn't really want to go back to Kashfa and try to depose myself."

"Okay. I'll lead, and you hold on to my shoulder in case there are any funny vibes to deal with. Merlin, you come last and maintain contact with Luke, for the same reason. All right?"

"Sure," I said. "Let's go."

He released us and moved to the place where the line of the design began. We followed, and Luke's hand was on his shoulder as he took the first step. Soon we were all of us on the Pattern, struggling the familiar struggle. Even when the sparks began to rise, though, this one seemed a little easier than I recalled from

Pattern walks in the past, possibly because someone else was leading the way.

Images of avenues lined with ancient chestnut trees filled my mind as we trudged along and fought our way through the First Veil. By then, the sparks came higher about us and I felt the forces of the Pattern beating about me, penetrating me, body and mind. I recalled my days in school, remembered my greatest efforts on the athletic field. The resistance continued to rise, and we leaned into it. Moving my feet became a great effort, and I realized that—somehow—the effort was more important than the movement. I felt my hair beginning to rise as a current passed entirely through my body. Still, this had not to it the maddening quality of the Logrus the time I had negotiated it, nor the adversarial feeling I had felt upon Amber's Pattern. It was almost as if I traversed the interior of a mind, one not unkindly disposed toward me. There was a feeling—of encouragement, almost—as I struggled along a curve, executed a turn. The resistance was as strong, the sparks came as high as on the other at about this point, yet I somehow knew that this Pattern held me in a different fashion. We pushed our way along the lines. We turned, we burned. . . . Penetrating the Second Veil was a slow-motion exercise in stamina and will. Our way eased for a time after that, and images from all over my life came to frighten and console me.

Walking. One, two. . . . Three. I felt that if I were able to take ten more steps I would have a chance to win through. Four. . . . I was drenched with perspiration. Five. The resistance was awful. It took all the effort of running a hundred meters just to inch my foot ahead. My lungs were working like a bellows. Six. The sparks reached my face, passed my eyes, enveloped me completely. I felt as if I had been transformed into an immortal blue flame and that I must, somehow, burn my way through a block of marble. I burned and I burned and the stone remained unchanged. I could spend all of eternity this way. Perhaps I already had. Seven. And the images were gone. All of memory had fled. Even my identity was on vacation. I was stripped to a thing of pure will. I was an act, an act of striving against resistance. Eight. . . . I no longer felt my body. Time was an alien concept. The striving was no longer striving, but a form of elemental movement now, beside which glaciers rushed. Nine. Now I was only movement—infinitesimal, constant. . . .

Ten.

There came an easing. It would become difficult again at the center end, but I knew that the rest of the walk was anticlimax. Something like a slow, low music buoyed me as I trudged ahead, turned, trudged. It was with me through the Final Veil, and as I passed the mid-point of that final stride, it became something like "Caravan."

We stood there at the center, silent for a long while, breathing deeply. Exactly what I had achieved, I was uncertain. I did feel, though, that, in some way, I knew my father better as a result. Strands of mist still drifted, across the Pattern, across the valley.

"I feel—stronger," Luke announced later. "Yes, I'll help guard this place. It seems a good way to spend some time."

"By the way, Luke, what *was* your message for me?" I asked.

"Oh, to tell you to clear out of the Courts," he replied, "that things were getting dangerous."

"I already knew the danger part," I said. "But there are still things I must do."

He shrugged. "Well, that's the message," he said. "No place really seems safe just now."

"There won't be any problems here yet," Corwin said. "Neither Power knows exactly how to approach this place or what to do with it. It's too strong for Amber's Pattern to absorb, and the Logrus doesn't know how to destroy it."

"Sounds pretty easy, then."

"There will probably come a time later, though, when they will try to move against it."

"Until then, we wait and watch. Okay. If some things do come, what might they be?"

"Probably ghosts—like ourselves—seeking to learn more about it, to test. You any good with that blade?"

"In all modesty, yes. If that's not good enough, I've studied the Arts, as well."

"They'll fall to steel, though it's fire they'll bleed—not blood. You can have the Pattern transport you outside now, if you wish. I'll join you in a few moments to show you where the weapons are cached, and the other supplies. I'd like to take a little trip and leave you in charge for a while."

"Sure thing," Luke said. "What about you, Merle?"

"I've got to get back to the Courts. I've a luncheon engagement with my mother, and then Swayvill's funeral to attend."

"It may not be able to send you all the way to the Courts," Corwin said. "That's getting awfully near the Logrus. But you'll work something out with it, or vice versa. How *is* Dara?"

"It's been a long time since I've seen her for more than a few moments," I answered. "She is still peremptory, arrogant, and over-solicitous when it comes to me. I get the impression, too, that she may be involved in local political scheming as well as aspects of the larger relationship between the Courts and Amber."

Luke closed his eyes for a moment and vanished. Shortly afterward, I saw him beside the Polly Jackson car. He opened the door, slid onto the passenger seat, leaned and fiddled with something inside. A little later I could hear the radio playing music across the distance.

"It's likely," Corwin said. "I never understood her, you know. She came to me out of nowhere at a strange time in my life, she lied to me, we became lovers, she walked the Pattern in Amber, and she vanished. It was like a bizarre dream. It was obvious that she used me. For years I thought that it was only to get knowledge of the Pattern and access to it. But I've had a lot of time for reflection recently, and I'm no longer certain that that was the case."

"Oh?" I said. "What, then?"

"You," he replied. "More and more I'm coming to think, what she really wanted was to bear a son or daughter of Amber."

I felt myself grow cold. Could the reason for my own existence have been such a calculated thing? Had there been no affection there at all? Had I been intentionally conceived to serve some special purpose? I did not at all like the notion. It made me feel the way Ghostwheel must, carefully structured product of my imagination and intellect, built to test design ideas only an Amberite could have come up with. Yet he called me "Dad." He actually seemed to care about me. Oddly, I had begun feeling an irrational affection for him myself. Was it partly because we were even more alike than I had consciously realized?

"Why?" I asked. "Why would it have been so important to her that I be born?"

"I can only remember her final words when she had completed the Pattern, turning into a demon in the process. 'Amber,' she said, 'will be destroyed.' Then she was gone."

I was shaking now. The implications were so unsettling that I wanted to cry, sleep, or get drunk. Anything, for a moment's respite.

"You think that my existence might be part of a long-term plan for the destruction of Amber?" I asked.

" 'Might,' " he said. "I could be wrong, kid. I could be very wrong, and if that's the case I apologize for troubling you this much. On the other hand, it would also be wrong of me not to let you know what the possibility is."

I massaged my temples, my brow, my eyes.

"What should I do?" I said then. "I don't want to help destroy Amber."

He clasped me to his breast for a moment and said, "No matter what you are and no matter what's been done to you, there will have to be some element of choice for you, sooner or later. You are greater than the sum of your parts, Merlin. No matter what went into your birth and your life up to now, you've got eyes and a brain and a set of values. Don't let anybody bullshit you, not even me. And when the time comes, if it comes, make damn sure the choice is your own. Nothing that's gone before will matter then."

His words, general as they had to be, drew me back from the place in my spirit where I had retreated.

"Thanks," I said.

He nodded. Then, "While your first impulse may be to force a confrontation on this matter," he said, "I would advise against it. It would achieve nothing other than making her aware of your suspicions. It would be prudent to play a more careful game and see what you can learn."

I sighed.

"You're right, of course," I said. "You came after me as much to tell me this as to help me escape, didn't you?"

He smiled.

"Only worry about important things," he said. "We'll meet again." And then he was gone.

I saw him, suddenly, over near the car, talking to Luke. I watched as he showed him where the caches were located. I wondered what time it was back in the Courts. After a while, they both waved to me. Then Corwin shook hands with Luke and turned and walked off into the fog. I could hear the radio playing "Lili Marlene."

I focused my mind on the Pattern's transporting me to the Ways of Sawall. There was a momentary swirling of blackness. When it cleared I was still standing at the center of the Pattern. I tried again, this time for Suhuy's castle. Again, it refused to punch my ticket.

"How close can you send me?" I finally asked.

There was another swirling, but this one was bright. It delivered me to a high promontory of white stone beneath a black sky, beside a black sea. Two semicircles of pale flame parenthesized my position. Okay, I could live with that. I was at Fire Gate, a way-exchange in Shadow near to the Courts. I faced the sea and counted. When I'd located the fourteenth flickering tower on my left, I walked toward it.

I emerged before a fallen tower beneath a pink sky. Walking toward it, I was transported to a glassy cavern through which a green river flowed. I paced beside the river till I found the stepping-stones that took me to a trail through an autumn wood. I followed this for almost a mile till I felt the presence of a way near the base of an evergreen. This took me to the side of a mountain, whence three more ways and two filmies had me on the trail to lunch with my mother. According to the sky, I had no time to change clothes.

I halted near a crossroads to dust myself off, straighten my apparel, comb my hair. I wondered, as I was about the business, who might receive my calling were I to try to reach Luke via his Trump—Luke himself, his ghost, both? Could the ghosts receive Trump calls? I found myself wondering what was going on back in Amber, too. And I thought of Coral, and Nayda. . . .

Hell.

I wanted to be somewhere else. I wanted to be far away. The Pattern's warning, via Luke, was well taken. Corwin had given me too much to think about, and I hadn't had time to sort it through properly. I did not want to be involved in whatever was going on here in the Courts. I did not like all of the implications involving my mother. I did not feel like attending a funeral. I felt somehow, also, uninformed. You'd think that if somebody wanted something from me—something very important—they'd at least take the time to explain the situation and ask for my cooperation. If it were a relative, there was a strong possibility I'd go along with it. Getting my cooperation would seem a lot less dicey than any trickery intended to control my actions. I wanted to be away from those who would control me, as well as the games they were playing.

I could turn and head back into Shadow, probably lose myself there. I could head back to Amber, tell Random everything I knew, everything I suspected, and he would protect me against the Courts. I could go back to the Shadow Earth, come up with a new identity, get back into computer design. . . .

Then, of course, I would never know what was going on and what had gone before. As for my father's real whereabouts—I'd

been able to reach him from the Courts, never from anywhere
else. In this sense, he was nearby. And there was no one else
around here likely to help him.

I walked ahead and turned right. I made my way toward a pur-
pling sky. I would be on time.

And so I came, again, into the Ways of Sawall. I had emerged
from the red and yellow starburst design painted high upon the
gateside wall of the front courtyard, descended the Invisible Stair,
and peered for long moments down into the great central pit, with
its view of black turbulence beyond the Rim. A falling star burned
its way down the purple sky as I turned away, headed for the
copper-chased door and the low Maze of Art beyond it.

Within, I recalled the many times I had been lost in that maze
as a child. The House of Sawall had been a serious collector of art
for ages, and the collection was so vast that there were several
ways into which one was cast within the maze itself, leading one
through tunnels, a huge spiral, and what seemed an old train station before being shunted back to miss the next turn. I had been
lost in it for days on one occasion, and was finally found crying
before an assemblage of blue shoes nailed to a board. I walked it
now, slowly, looking at old monstrosities, and some newer ones.
There were also strikingly lovely pieces mixed in, such as the
huge vase that looked as if it had been carved from a single fire
opal, and a set of odd enameled tablets from a distant shadow
whose meaning and function no one in the family could be found
to recall. I had to stop and see both again, rather than shortcutting
the gallery, the tablets being a particular favorite of mine.

I was humming an old tune Gryll had taught me as I came up
to the fiery vase and regarded it. I seemed to hear a small chafing
noise, but glances up and down the corridor revealed no one else
in the vicinity. The almost sensual curves of the vase begged to be
touched. I could remember all of the times I had been forbidden to
do so as a child. I put my left hand forward slowly, rested it upon
it. It was warmer than I'd thought it might be. I slid my hand along
its side. It was like a frozen flame.

"Hello," I muttered, remembering an adventure we'd shared.
"It's been a long time. . . ."

"Merlin?" came a small voice.

I withdrew my hand immediately. It was as if the vase had
spoken.

"Yes," I said then. "Yes."

Again, the chafing sound, and a bit of shadow stirred within the creamy opening, above the fire.

"Ss," said the shadow, rising.

"Glait?" I asked.

"Yess."

"It can't be. You've been dead for years."

"Not dead. Ssleeping."

"I haven't seen you since I was a kid. You were injured. You disappeared. I thought you'd died."

"I ssleep. I ssleep to heal. I ssleep to forget. I ssleep to renew mysself."

I extended my arm. The shaggy snake head rose higher, extended itself, fell upon my forearm, climbed, wrapped itself.

"You certainly chose elegant sleeping quarters."

"I knew the jug to be a favorite of yourss. If I waited long enough I knew you would come by again, sstop to admire it. And I would know and rise up in my ssplendor to greet you. My, you have grown!"

"You look pretty much the same. A little thin, perhaps. . . ."

I stroked her head gently.

"It is good to know you are with us still, like some honored family spirit. You and Gryll and Kergma made my childhood a better thing than it might have been."

She raised her head high, stroked my cheek with her nose.

"It warmss my cold blood to ssee you again, dear boy. You've traveled far?"

"I have. Very."

"One night we shall eat mice and lie besside a fire. You will warm me a ssaucer of milk and tell me of your adventuress ssince you left the Wayss of Ssawall. We will find ssome marrow boness for Gryll, if he be sstill about—"

"He seems to serve my uncle Suhuy these days. What of Kergma?"

"I do not know. It hass been sso long."

I held her close to warm her.

"Thank you for waiting here for me in your great drowse, to greet me—"

"Iss more than friendliess, helloss."

"More? What then, Glait? What is it?"

"A thing to show. Walk that way."

She gestured with her head. I moved in the direction she indicated—the way I had been heading anyhow, to where the cor-

ridors widened. I could feel her vibrating against my arm with the
barely audible purring sound she sometimes made.

Suddenly, she stiffened and her head rose, swaying slightly.

"What is it?" I asked.

"Mi-ice," she said. "Mi-ice nearby. I musst go hunting—after
I show you—the thing. Breakfasst. . . ."

"If you would dine first, I will wait."

"No, Merlin. You musst not be late for whatever—brought you
here. There is importance in the air. Later—feasst—vermin. . . ."

We came into a wide, high, skylighted section of the gallery.
Four large pieces of metal statuary—bronze and copper, mostly—
stood in an asymmetrical arrangement about us.

"Onward," Glait said. "Not here."

I turned right at the next corner and plunged ahead. Shortly,
we came to another display—this one resembling a metal forest.

"Sslow now. Sslow, dear demon child."

I halted and studied the trees, bright, dark, shiny, dull. Iron,
aluminum, brass, it was most impressive. It was also a display that
had not been present the last time I had passed this way, years before. Nothing odd about that, of course. There had also been
changes in other areas I had passed through.

"Now. Here. Turn in. Go back."

I moved on into the forest.

"Bear right. The tall one."

I halted when I came to the curved trunk of the tallest tree to
my right.

"This one?"

"Yess. Negotiate it—upward—pleasse."

"You mean climb it?"

"Yess."

"Right."

One nice thing about a stylized tree—or, at least, *this* stylized
tree—was that it spiraled, swelled, and twisted in such a fashion
as to provide better handholds and footholds than at first seemed
apparent. I caught hold, drew myself up, found a place for my
foot, pulled again, pushed.

Higher. Higher, still. When I was perhaps ten feet above the
floor I halted.

"Uh, what do I do now that I'm here?" I asked.

"Climb higher."

"Why?"

"Ssoon. Ssoon. You'll know."

I drew myself about a foot higher, and then I felt it. It is not so much a tingling as it is a kind of pressure. I only feel a tingling, too, sometimes, if they lead someplace risky.

"There's a way up there," I said.

"Yess. I wass coiled about a branch of the blue tree when a shadow-masster opened it. They sslew him afterwardss."

"It must lead to something very important."

"I ssuppose. I am not a good judge—of people thingss."

"You have been through?"

"Yess."

"Then it *is* safe?"

"Yess."

"All right."

I climbed higher, resisting the force of the way until I'd brought both feet to the same level. Then I relaxed into the tugging and let it take me through.

I extended both hands, too, in case the surface was uneven. But it wasn't. The floor was beautifully tiled in black, silver, gray, and white. To the right was a geometric design, to the left a representation of the Pit of Chaos.

My eyes were directed downward for only a few moments, though.

"Good Lord!" I said.

"Wass I right? It iss important?" Glait said.

"It is important," I replied.

6

There were candles all about the chapel, many of them as tall as I am, and nearly as big around. Some were silver, some were gray; a few were white, a few black. They stood at various heights, in artful disposition, on banks, ledges, pattern points on the floor. They did not provide the main illumination, however. This obtained from overhead, and I first assumed it to proceed from a skylight. When I glanced upward to gauge the height of the vault, though, I saw that the light emanated from a large blue-white globe confined behind a dark metal grate.

I took a step forward. The nearest candle flame flickered.

I faced a stone altar that filled a niche across the way. Black candles burned at either hand before it, smaller silver ones upon it. For a moment, I simply regarded it.

"Lookss like you," Glait remarked.

"I thought your eyes didn't register two-dimensional representations."

"I've lived a long time in a musseum. Why hide your picture up a ssecret way?"

I moved forward, my gaze on the painting.

"It's not me," I said. "It's my father, Corwin of Amber."

A silver rose stood within a bud vase before the portrait. Whether it was a real rose or the product of art or magic, I could not tell.

And Grayswandir lay there before it, drawn a few inches from the scabbard. I'd a feeling this was the real thing, that the version worn by the Pattern ghost of my father was itself a reconstruction.

I reached forward, raised it, drew it.

There was a feeling of power as I held it, swung it, struck an *en garde*, lunged, advanced. The spikard came alive, center of a web of forces. I looked down, suddenly self-conscious.

". . . And this is my father's blade," I said, returning to the altar, where I sheathed it. Reluctantly, I left it there.

As I backed away, Glait asked, "Thiss iss important?"

"Very," I said as the way caught hold of me and sent me back to the treetop.

"What now, Masster Merlin?"

"I must get on to lunch with my mother."

"In that case, you'd besst drop me here."

"I could return you to the vase."

"No. I haven't lurked in a tree for a time. Thiss will be fine."

I extended my arm. She unwound herself and flowed away across gleaming branches.

"Good luck, Merlin. Vissit me."

And I was down the tree, snagging my trousers only once, and off up the corridor at a quick pace.

Two turns later I came to a way to the main hall and decided I'd better take it. I popped through beside the massive fireplace—high flames braiding themselves within it—and turned slowly to survey the huge chamber, trying to seem as if I had been there a long while, waiting.

I seemed the only person present. Which, on reflection, struck me as a bit odd, with the fire roaring that way. I adjusted my shirtfront, brushed myself off, ran my comb through my hair. I was inspecting my fingernails when I became aware of a flash of movement at the head of the great staircase to my left.

She was a blizzard within a ten-foot tower. Lightnings danced at its center, crackling; particles of ice clicked and rattled upon the stair; the banister grew frosted where she passed. My mother. She seemed to see me at about the same time I saw her, for she halted. Then she made the turn onto the stair and began her descent.

As she descended, she shifted smoothly, her appearance changing almost from step to step. As soon as I realized what was occurring I relaxed my own efforts and reversed their small effects. I had commenced changing the moment I had seen her, and presumably she had done the same on viewing me. I hadn't thought she'd go to that extent to humor me, a second time, here on her own turf.

The shift was completed just as she reached the bottommost stair, becoming a lovely woman in black trousers and red shirt with flared sleeves. She looked at me again and smiled, moved toward me, embraced me.

It would have been gauche to say that I'd intended shifting but had forgotten. Or any other remark on the matter.

She pushed me out to arm's distance, lowered her gaze and raised it, shook her head.

"Do you sleep in your clothes before or after violent exercise?" she asked me.

"That's unkind," I said. "I stopped to sightsee on the way over and ran into a few problems."

"That is why you are late?"

"No. I'm late because I stopped in our gallery and took longer than I'd intended. And I'm not very late."

She took hold of my arm and turned me.

"I will forgive you," she said, steering me toward the rose and green and gold-flecked pillar of ways, set in the mirrored alcove across the room to the right.

I didn't feel that called for a response, so I didn't make one. I watched with interest as we entered the alcove, to see whether she would conduct me in a clockwise direction or its opposite about the pillar.

The opposite, it turned out. Interesting.

We were reflected and re-reflected from the three sides. So was the room we had quitted. And with each circuit we made of the pillar it became a different room. I watched it change, kaleidoscopically, until she halted me before the crystal grotto beside the underground sea.

"It's been a long time since I thought of this place," I said, stepping forth upon the pure white sand into the crystal-cast light, variously reminiscent of bonfires, solar reflections, candelabra, and LED displays, functions of size and distancing perhaps, laying occasional pieces of rainbow upon the shore, the walls, the black water.

She took my hand and led me toward a raised and railed platform some small distance off to the right. A table stood full set upon it. A collection of covered trays occupied a larger serving table inland of it. We mounted a small stair, and I seated her and moved to check out the goodies next door.

"Do sit down, Merlin," she said. "I'll serve you."

"That's all right," I answered, raising a lid. "I'm already here. I'll do the first round."

She was on her feet.

"Buffet style then," she said.

"Sure."

We filled our plates and moved to the table. Seconds after we had seated ourselves a brilliant flash of light came to us across the water, illuminating the arching dome of the cavern vault like the ribbed interior of some massive beast that was digesting us.

"You needn't look so apprehensive. You know they can't come in this far."

"Waiting for a thunderclap puts my appetite on hold," I said.

She laughed just as a distant roll of thunder reached us.

"And that makes everything all right?" she asked.

"Yes," I replied, raising my fork.

"Strange, the relatives life gives us," she said.

I looked at her, tried to read her expression, couldn't. So, "Yes," I said.

She studied me for a moment, but I wasn't giving anything away either. So, "When you were a child you went monosyllabic as a sign of petulance," she said.

"Yes," I said.

We began eating. There were more flashes out over the still, dark sea. By light of the last one I thought I caught sight of a distant ship, black sails full-rigged and bellied.

"You kept your engagement with Mandor earlier?"

"Yes."

"How is he?"

"Fine."

"Something bothering you, Merlin?"

"Many things."

"Tell Mother?"

"What if she's a part of it?"

"I would be disappointed if I were not. Still, how long will you hold the business of the *ty'iga* against me? I did what I thought was right. I still think it was."

I nodded and continued chewing. After a time, "You made that clear last cycle," I said.

The waters gave a small sloshing sound. A spectrum drifted across our table, her face.

"Is there something else?" she asked.

"Why don't *you* tell *me*?" I said.

I felt her gaze. I met it.

"I don't know what you mean," she answered.

"Are you aware that the Logrus is sentient? And the Pattern?"
I said.

"Did Mandor tell you that?" she asked.

"Yes. But I already knew it before he did."

"How?"

"We've been in touch."

"You and the Pattern? You and the Logrus?"

"Both."

"To what end?"

"Manipulation, I'd say. They're engaged in a power struggle.
They were asking me to choose sides."

"Which did you choose?"

"Neither. Why?"

"You should have told me."

"Why?"

"For counsel. Possibly for assistance."

"Against the Powers of the universe? How well connected are
you, Mother?"

She smiled.

"It is possible that one such as myself may possess special
knowledge of their workings."

"One such as yourself . . . ?"

"A sorceress of my skills."

"Just how good are you, Mother?"

"I don't think they come much better, Merlin."

"Family is always the last to know, I guess. So why didn't you
train me yourself, instead of sending me off to Suhuy?"

"I'm not a good teacher. I dislike training people."

"You trained Jasra."

She tilted her head to the right and narrowed her eyes.

"Did Mandor tell you that, also?" she asked.

"No."

"Who, then?"

"What difference does it make?"

"Considerable," she replied. "Because I don't believe you
knew it the last time we met."

I recalled suddenly that she had said something about Jasra
back at Suhuy's, something implying her familiarity with her,
something to which I would ordinarily have risen save that I was
driving a load of animus in a different direction at the time and
heading downhill in a thunderstorm with the brakes making funny
noises. I was about to ask her why it mattered *when* I learned it,

when I realized that she was really asking from whom I'd learned it, because she was concerned with whom I might have been speaking on such matters since last we'd met. Mentioning Luke's Pattern ghost did not seem politic, so, "Okay, Mandor let it slip," I said, "and then asked me to forget it."

"In other words," she said, "he expected it to get back to me. Why did he do it just that way? I wonder. The man is damnably subtle."

"Maybe he did just let it slip."

"Mandor lets nothing slip. Never make him an enemy, son."

"Are we talking about the same person?"

She snapped her fingers.

"Of course," she said. "It was only as a child that you knew him. You went away after that. You have seen him but a few times since. Yes, he is subtle, insidious, dangerous."

"We've always gotten along well."

"Of course. He never antagonizes without a good reason."

I shrugged and went on eating.

After a time she said, "I daresay he has made similar comments about me."

"I am unable to recall any," I answered.

"Has he been giving you lessons in circumspection, too?"

"No, though I've felt a need to teach myself, of late."

"Surely, you obtained a few in Amber."

"If I did, they were so subtle I didn't notice."

"Well, well. Can it be I need despair of you no more?"

"I doubt it."

"So, what might the Pattern or the Logrus want of you?"

"I already told you—a choice of sides."

"It is that difficult to decide which you prefer?"

"It is that difficult to decide which I dislike less."

"Because they are, as you say, manipulative of people in their struggle for power?"

"Just so."

She laughed. Then, "While it shows the gods as no better than the rest of us," she said, "at least, it shows them as no worse. See here the sources of human morality. It is still better than none at all. If these grounds be insufficient for the choosing of sides, then let other considerations rule. You are, after all, a son of Chaos."

"And Amber," I said.

"You grew up in the Courts."

"And I have dwelled in Amber. My relatives are as numerous there as they are here."

"It is really that close, then?"

"If it were not, it might have simplified matters."

"In that case," she said, "you must turn it around."

"What do you mean?"

"Ask not which appeals the most to you, but which can do the most for you."

I sipped a fine green tea as the storm rolled nearer. Something splashed within the waters of our inlet.

"All right," I said, "I'm asking."

She leaned forward and smiled and her eyes darkened. She has always had perfect control of her face and form, shifting them to suit her moods. She is obviously the same person, but at times she may choose to appear as little more than a girl, at other times becoming a mature and handsome woman. Generally, she seems somewhere in between. But now, a certain timeless quality came into her features—not age so much as the essence of Time—and I realized suddenly that I had never known her true age. I watched as something like a veil of ancient power came across it.

"The Logrus," she said, "will lead you to greatness."

I continued to stare.

"What sort of greatness?" I asked.

"What sort do you desire?"

"I don't know that I ever wanted greatness, on its own. It seems rather like wanting to be an engineer, rather than wanting to design something—or wanting to be a writer, rather than wanting to write. It should be a by-product, not a thing in itself. Otherwise, it's just an ego trip."

"But if you earn it—if you deserve it—shouldn't you have it?"

"I suppose. But so far I've done nothing"—my eyes fell to a bright circle of light beneath the dark waters, moving as if running before a storm—"except perhaps for an odd piece of equipment, which might fall into that category."

"You are young, of course," she said, "and the times for which you were meant to be uniquely qualified have come sooner than I'd anticipated."

If I were to use magic to summon a cup of coffee, would she resent that? Yes, I believed. She would. So I decided on a glass of wine. As I poured it and took a sip, I said, "I'm afraid I don't understand what you're talking about."

She nodded.

"It is hardly something you could learn from introspection," she said slowly, "and no one would be so rash as to mention the possibility to you."

"What are you talking about, Mother?"

"The throne. To reign in the Courts of Chaos."

"Mandor had sort of suggested I think about it," I said.

"All right. No one, excepting Mandor, would be so rash as to mention it."

"I gather mothers get a certain kick out of seeing their sons do well, but unfortunately you've named a job for which I lack not only skill, aptitude, and training but also any desire."

She steepled her fingers and regarded me from just above them.

"You are better qualified than you think, and your desires have nothing to do with the matter."

"As an interested party, I must beg to differ with you."

"Even if it were the only way to protect friends and relatives both here and in Amber?"

I took another sip of wine.

"Protect them? Against what?"

"The Pattern is about to try redefining the middle regions of Shadow in its own image. It is probably strong enough to do it now."

"You were talking of Amber and the Courts, not of Shadow."

"The Logrus will have to resist this incursion. Since it would probably lose in a direct confrontation with its opposite, it will be forced to employ agents strategically, in a strike against Amber. The most effective agents would, of course, be champions of the Courts—"

"This is mad!" I said. "There must be a better way!"

"Possibly," she replied. "Accept the throne and you'll be giving the orders."

"I don't know enough."

"You will be briefed, of course."

"What about the proper order of succession?"

"That's not your problem."

"I rather think I'd have an interest in how it's achieved—say, whether I'd owe you or Mandor for the majority of deaths."

"In that we're both Sawall, the question becomes academic."

"You mean you're cooperating on this?"

"We have our differences," she said, "and I draw the line at any discussion of methods."

I sighed and took another drink. The storm had grown worse

over the dark waters. If that strange light effect beneath their surface were indeed Ghostwheel, I wondered what he was up to. The
lightnings were becoming a steady backdrop, the thunder a continuing soundtrack.

"What did you mean," I said, "when you spoke of the times for
which I was meant to be uniquely qualified?"

"The present and the immediate future," she said, "with the
conflict that will come."

"No," I responded. "I was referring to the business about my
being 'meant to be uniquely qualified.' How so?"

It must have been the lightning, for I had never seen her blush
before.

"You combine two great bloodlines," she said. "Technically,
your father was King of Amber—briefly—between the reign of
Oberon and that of Eric."

"Since Oberon was still alive at the time and had not abdi-
cated, neither reign should be considered valid," I responded.
"Random is Oberon's proper successor."

"A case can be made for an implied abdication," she said.

"You prefer that reading, don't you?"

"Of course."

I watched the storm. I swallowed some wine.

"That is why you wished to bear Corwin's child?" I asked.

"The Logrus assured me that such a child would be uniquely
qualified to reign here."

"But Dad never really meant that much to you, did he?"

She looked away, out to where the circle of light was now racing toward us, lightnings falling behind it.

"You have no right to ask that question," she said.

"I know that. But it's true, isn't it?"

"You are mistaken. He meant a great deal to me."

"But not in any conventional sense."

"I am not a conventional person."

"I was the result of a breeding experiment. The Logrus selected the mate who would give you—what?"

The circle of light swam nearer. The storm followed it, coming
closer in to the shore than I'd ever seen one reach here before.

"An ideal Lord of Chaos," she said, "fit to rule."

"Somehow I feel there's more to it than that," I said.

Dodging lightning bolts, the bright circle came up out of the
water and flashed across the sand toward us. If she responded to

my last remark, I couldn't hear it. The ensuing thunders were deafening.

The light came onto the decking, paused near to my foot.

"Dad, can you protect me?" Ghost asked in a lull between thunderclaps.

"Rise to my left wrist," I bade.

Dara stared as he found his place, taking on the appearance of Frakir. In the meantime, the final flash of lightning did not depart, but stood for a time like a sizzling stalk at the water's edge. Then it collapsed into a ball that hovered in the middle air for several moments before drifting in our direction. As it came on, its structure began to change.

When it drifted to a position beside our table it had become a bright, pulsing Sign of the Logrus.

"Princess Dara, Prince Merlin," came that awful voice I had last heard on the day of the confrontation at Amber Castle, "I did not wish to disturb your repast, but that thing you harbor makes it necessary." A jagged branch of the image was flipped in the direction of my left wrist.

"It's blocking my ability to shift away," Ghost said.

"Give it to me!"

"Why?" I asked.

"That thing has traversed the Logrus," came the words, differing at seeming random in pitch, volume, accent.

It occurred to me that I might defy it now if I were really as valuable to the Logrus as Dara had indicated. So, "It's theoretically open to all comers," I responded.

"I am my own law, Merlin, and your Ghostwheel has crossed me before. I'll have it now."

"No," I said, moving my awareness into the spikard, seeking and locating a means of instant transport to an area where the Pattern ruled. "I'll not surrender my creation so readily."

The brightness of the Sign increased.

At this, Dara was on her feet, moving to interpose herself between it and myself.

"Stay," she said. "We've more important matters to deal with than vengeance upon a toy. I have dispatched my cousins Hendrake for the bride of Chaos. If you wish this plan to succeed, I suggest you assist them."

"I recall your plan for Prince Brand, setting the lady Jasra to snare him. It could not fail, you told me."

"It brought you closer than you ever came, old Serpent, to the power you desire."

"That is true," it acknowledged.

"And the bearer of the Eye is a simpler being than Jasra."

The Sign slid past her, a tiny sun turning itself into a succession of ideograms.

"Merlin, you will take the throne and serve me when the time comes?"

"I will do what is necessary to redress the balance of power," I replied.

"That is not what I asked! Will you take the throne under the terms I set?"

"If that is what is needed to set things right," I answered.

"This pleases me," it said. "Keep your toy."

Dara moved aside, and it passed near to her before fading.

"Ask him of Luke and Corwin and the new Pattern," it said, and then it was gone.

She turned toward me and stared.

"Pour me a glass of wine," she said.

I did this. She raised it and took a swallow.

"So tell me of Luke and Corwin and the new Pattern," she said.

"Tell me of Jasra and Brand," I countered.

"No. You will go first in this," she said.

"Very well," I said. "It neglected to mention that they were Pattern ghosts. Luke's appeared to me on the way over here, sent by the Pattern to persuade me to depart this realm. The Logrus sent Lord Borel's to dispose of Luke."

"Luke being Rinaldo, the son of Jasra and Brand, husband of Coral and King of Kashfa?"

"Very good. Now tell me of all that business at the end. You set Jasra to snare Brand, to guide him down the path he took?"

"He would have taken it anyhow. He came to the Courts seeking power to further his ends. She merely made things a little easier for him."

"That's not how it sounded to me. But does that mean my father's curse was not really a factor?"

"No, it helped—in a metaphysical way—making it easier to extend the Black Road to Amber. Why is it you are still here, when King Rinaldo bade you depart? Is it loyalty to the Courts?"

"I had a date with you for lunch, and it's been a while. Hated to miss it."

She smiled, very slightly, and took a small sip of wine.
"You change the subject well," she stated. "Let us return to it now. The ghost of Borel dispatched that of Rinaldo, I take it?"
"Not exactly."
"What do you mean?"
"My father's ghost showed up about then and dealt with Borel, permitting us to depart."
"Again? Corwin bested Borel again?"
I nodded.
"Neither remembered their first encounter, of course. Their memories only go back to the time of their recording, and—"
"I understand the principle. Then what happened?"
"We fled," I answered, "and I subsequently came here."
"What did the Logrus mean in referring to the new Pattern?"
"My father's ghost was apparently generated there, rather than by the old one."
She sat upright, eyes suddenly wide.
"How do you know this?" she demanded.
"He told me," I answered.
She stared past me then at the now-silent sea. "So the third power is actually taking a part in things," she mused. "This is fascinating, as well as disconcerting. Damn the man for having drawn it!"
"You really hate him, don't you?" I said.
Her eyes focused again upon my own.
"Let that subject be!" she ordered. "Save for this," she amended a moment later. "Did he give you any indication as to the new Pattern's allegiance—or its plans? The fact that it sent him to protect Luke might be seen as a seconding of the old Pattern's action. On the other hand—either because it was created by your father, or because it has its own uses for you—I can see it simply as an effort at your protection. What did he say?"
"That he wanted to get me away from where I was."
She nodded.
"Which he obviously did," she said. "Did he say anything else? Did anything else happen that might be important?"
"He asked after you."
"Really? And that was all?"
"He had no special message, if that's what you mean."
"I see."
She looked away, was silent for a time. Then, "Those ghosts don't last very long, do they?" she said.

"No," I replied.

"It's infuriating," she said at last, "to think that, despite everything, he is still able to play a hand in this."

"He's alive, isn't he, Mother?" I said. "And you know where he is."

"I'm not his keeper, Merlin."

"I think you are."

"It is impertinent to contradict me this way."

"Yet I must," I responded. "I saw him off on his way to the Courts. Certainly, he wanted to be here with the others for the peace settlement. Even more, though, he must have wanted to see you. There were so many unanswered questions in his mind—where you came from, why you came to him, why you parted as you did—"

"Enough!" she cried. "Let it be!"

I ignored her.

"And I know he was here in the Courts. He was seen here. He must have looked you up. What happened then? What sort of answers did you give him?"

She rose to her feet, glaring at me now.

"That will be all, Merlin," she said. "It seems impossible to conduct a civilized conversation with you."

"Is he your prisoner, Mother? Do you have him locked away somewhere, someplace where he can't bother you, can't interfere with your plans?"

She stepped quickly away from the table, almost stumbling.

"Wretched child!" she said. "You're just like him! Why did you have to resemble him so?"

"You're afraid of him, aren't you?" I said, suddenly realizing this could well be the case. "You're afraid to kill a Prince of Amber, even with the Logrus on your side. You've got him locked away somewhere, and you're afraid he'll come loose and blow your latest plans. You've been scared for a long time now because of what you've had to do to keep him out of action."

"Preposterous!" she said, backing away as I rounded the table. There was a look of genuine fear on her face now. "You're just guessing!" she went on. "He's dead, Merlin! Give up! Leave me alone! Never mention his name in my presence again! Yes, I hate him! He would have destroyed us all! He still would, if he could!"

"He is not dead," I stated.

"How can you say that?"

I bit down on the desire to tell her I'd spoken with him, held it back.

"Only the guilty protest so strongly," I said. "He's alive. Where is he?"

She raised her hands, palms inward, and crossed them upon her breast, elbows low. The fear was gone, the anger was gone. When she spoke again, something like mockery seemed her main humor: "Then seek him, Merlin. By all means, seek him."

"Where?" I demanded.

"Look for him in the Pit of Chaos."

A flame appeared near her left foot and began orbiting her body in a counterclockwise direction, spiraling upward, leaving a line of fire to blaze redly behind it. By the time it reached the crown of her head she was entirely concealed. It went out with a faint whooshing sound then, taking her along with it.

I moved forward and knelt, feeling the area on which she'd stood. It was a little warm, that's all. Nice spell. Nobody'd ever taught me that one. Thinking back on it then, I realized that Mom had always had a flair when it came to entrances and exits.

"Ghost?"

He danced away from my wrist to hover in the air before me. "Yes?"

"Are you still barred from transporting yourself through Shadow?"

"No," he replied. "That was lifted when the Sign of the Logrus departed. I can travel—in or out of Shadow. I can provide transportation for you. Would you like me to?"

"Yes. Take me into the gallery upstairs."

"Gallery? I plunged directly from the place of the Logrus into the dark sea, Dad. I'm not quite sure as to the lay of the land here."

"Never mind," I said. "I'll manage it myself."

I activated the spikard. Energies spiraled from six of its tines, encaging Ghost and myself, swirling us upward to the place of my desire in the Maze of Art. I tried for a flash of fire as we went, but had no way of knowing whether I'd achieved it. Makes you wonder how the really good ones get their practice.

7

I delivered us into that eerie hall that had always been old Sawall's chief delight in the maze. It was a sculpture garden, with no outside light sources and small base lighting only about the huge pieces, making it several times darker than my favorite lounge. The floor was uneven—concave, convex, stepped, ridged—with concavity being the dominant curve. It was difficult to guess at its dimensions, for it seemed of different size and contour depending upon where one stood. Gramble, Lord Sawall, had caused it to be constructed without any plane surfaces—and I believe the job involved some unique shadowmastery.

I stood beside what appeared to be a complicated rigging in the absence of its ship—that, or an elaborate musical instrument fit to be strummed by Titans—and the light turned the lines to silver, running like life from darkness to darkness within some half-seen frame. Other pieces jutted from walls and hung like stalactites. As I strolled, what had seemed walls became floor to me. The pieces that had seemed floored now jutted or depended. The room changed shape as I went, and a breeze blew through it, causing sighs, hums, buzzes, chimes. Gramble, my stepfather, had taken a certain delight in this hall, whereas for me it had long represented an exercise in intrepidity to venture beyond its threshold. As I grew older, however, I, too, came to enjoy it, partly for the occasional *frisson* it provided my adolescence. Now, though—Now I just wanted to wander it a few moments, for old times' sake, as I sorted through my thoughts. There were so damned many of them. Things that had tantalized me for much of my adult life seemed near to explanation now. I was not happy with all of the possibilities that tumbled through my mind. Still, no matter which ones came out on top, it would beat ignorance.

"Dad?"

"Yes?"

"What is this place, anyway?" Ghost asked.

"It's a part of the big art collection here at the Ways of Sawall," I explained. "People come from all over the Courts and nearby Shadow to see it. It was a passion with my stepfather. I spent a lot of time wandering these halls when I was a kid. There are many hidden ways in this place."

"And this particular room? There's something wrong with it."

"Yes and no," I said. "I guess it depends on what you mean by 'wrong.'"

"My perceptions are strangely affected just now."

"That is because the space itself is folded in here, like some odd origami figure. The hall is much larger than it seems. You can wander through many times and witness a different array of displays on each occasion. There may even be some internal movement involved. I was never sure. Only Sawall knew for certain."

"I was right. Something's wrong with it."

"I rather like it this way."

I seated myself on a silver stump beside a sprawled silver tree.

"I want to see how it folds," he said at last.

"Go ahead."

As he drifted off, I thought of my recent interview with my mother. I was reminded of everything Mandor had said or implied, of the conflict between the Pattern and the Logrus, of my father as the champion of the Pattern and intended king in Amber. Had she known this, known it as fact rather than speculation? I imagined she could have, for she seemed to enjoy a special relationship with the Logrus, and it would surely have been aware of its adversary's more prominent decisions. She'd admitted that she did not love the man. It seemed as if she had sought him for whatever genetic material had so impressed the Pattern. Had she really been trying to breed a champion for the Logrus?

I chuckled as I considered the result. She had seen me trained well in arms, but I was nowhere near Dad's league. I'd preferred sorcery, but sorcerers were a dime a dozen in the Courts. Finally, she'd shipped me off to college on that Shadow Earth the Amberites favor. But a degree in Computer Science from Berkeley didn't much qualify me to uphold the banner of Chaos against the forces of Order either. I must have been a disappointment to her.

I thought back to my childhood, to some of the strange adventures for which this place had served as a point of departure. Gryll and I would come here, Glait slithering at our feet, coiled about a limb or riding somewhere amid my garments. I would give that odd ululant cry I had learned in a dream, and sometimes Kergma would join us, come skittering down the folds of darkness, out some frayed area of twisted space. I was never sure exactly what Kergma was, or even of what gender, for Kergma was a shapeshifter and flew, crawled, hopped, or ran in a succession of interesting forms.

On an impulse, I voiced that ancient call. Nothing, of course, happened, and I saw it moments later for what it was: a cry after a vanished childhood, when I had at least felt wanted. Now, now I was nothing—neither Amberite nor Chaosite, and certainly a disappointment to my relatives on both sides. I was a failed experiment. I'd never been wanted for myself, but as something that might come to pass. Suddenly my eyes were moist, and I held back a sob. And I'll never know what sort of mood I might have worked myself into because I was distracted then.

There came a flare of red light from a point high on the wall to my left. It was in the form of a small circle about the feet of a human figure.

"Merlin!" called a voice from that direction, and the flames leapt higher. By their light, I saw that familiar face, reminding me a bit of my own, and I was pleased with the meaning it had just given to my life, even if that meaning was death.

I raised my left hand above my head and willed a flash of blue light from the spikard.

"Over here, Jurt!" I called, rising to my feet. I began forming the ball of light that was to be his distraction while I readied the strike that would electrocute him. On reflection, it had seemed the surest way of taking him out. I'd lost count of the number of attempts he'd made on my life, and I'd resolved to take the initiative the next time he came calling. Frying his nervous system seemed the surest way to ice him, despite what the Fountain had done for him. "Over here, Jurt!"

"Merlin! I want to talk!"

"I don't. I've tried it too often, and I've nothing left to say. Come on over and let's get this done—weapons, hands, magic. I don't care."

He raised both hands, palms outward.

"Truce!" he cried. "It wouldn't be right to do it here in Sawall."

"Don't give me that scruples shit, brother!" I cried, but even as I said it I realized there might be something to it. I could remember how much the old man's approval had meant to him, and I realized that he'd hate to do anything to antagonize Dara here on the premises. "What do you want, anyway?"

"To talk. I mean it," he said. "What do I have to do?"

"Meet me over there," I said, casting my ball of light to shine above a familiar object that looked like a giant house of cards made of glass and aluminum, bouncing light from hundreds of planes.

"All right," came the reply.

I began walking in that direction. I saw him approaching from his, and I angled my course so that our paths would not intersect. Also, I increased my pace so as to arrive ahead of him.

"No tricks," he called out. "And if we do decide we can only take it to the end, let's go outside."

"Okay."

I entered the structure at a point around the corner from his approach. Immediately, I encountered six images of myself.

"Why here?" came his voice from somewhere near at hand.

"I don't suppose you ever saw a movie called *Lady from Shanghai*?"

"No."

"It occurred to me that we could wander around in here and talk, and the place would do a lot to keep us from hurting each other."

I turned a corner. There were more of me in different places. A few moments later, I heard a sharp intake of breath from somewhere near at hand. It was followed almost immediately by a chuckle.

"I begin to understand," I heard him say.

Three steps and another turn. I halted. There were two of him and two of me. He was not looking at me, though. I reached out slowly toward one of the images. He turned, he saw me. His mouth opened as he stepped back and vanished.

"What did you want to talk about?" I asked, halting.

"It's hard to know where to begin."

"That's life."

"You upset Dara quite a bit. . . ."

"That was quick. I only left her ten, fifteen minutes ago. You're staying here at Sawall?"

"Yes. And I knew she was having lunch with you. I just saw her briefly a little while ago."

"Well, she didn't make me feel too good either."

I turned another corner and passed through a doorway in time to see him smile faintly.

"She's that way sometimes. I know," he said. "She tells me the Logrus came by for dessert."

"Yes."

"She said it seems to have chosen you for the throne."

I hoped he saw my shrug.

"It seemed that way. I don't want it, though."

"But you said you'd do it."

"Only if there's no other way to restore a certain balance of forces. It's a last resort sort of thing. It won't come to that, I'm sure."

"But it chose you."

Another shrug.

"Tmer and Tubble precede me."

"That doesn't matter. I'd wanted it, you know."

"I know. Seems a pretty dumb career choice."

Suddenly, he surrounded me.

"It does now," he admitted. "It was getting that way for some time, though, before you got designated. I thought I had the edge each time we met, and each time you came a little closer to killing me."

"It did keep getting messier."

"That last time—in the church—in Kashfa, I was certain I could finally take you out. Instead, you damn near did me in."

"Say that Dara or Mandor removed Tmer and Tubble. You knew you'd have to take care of me yourself, but what about Despil?"

"He'd step aside for me."

"You asked him?"

"No. But I'm sure."

I moved on.

"You always assumed too much, Jurt."

"Maybe you're right," he said, appearing and vanishing again. "Either way, it doesn't matter."

"Why not?"

"I quit. I'm out of the running. The hell with it."

"How come?"

"Even if the Logrus hadn't made its intenti
ginning to feel nervous. It was not just that I wa
me either. I got to thinking about myself, an
What if I made it to the throne? I'm not so sure a
I'm competent to hold it." I turned again, caught a
licking his lips, brows knotted. "I could mess up ι.
verely," he went on, "unless I had good advice. And yo.
that, ultimately, it would come from Mandor or Dara. I'd winu ⹁
a puppet, wouldn't I?"

"Probably. But you've gotten me very curious. When did you
start thinking this way? Might it coincide with your treatment in
the Fountain? What if my interruption made yours closer to the
correct course there?"

"It's possible there's something to that," he said. "I'm glad
now I didn't go the full route. I suspect it might have driven me
mad, as it did Brand. But it may not have been that at all. Or—I
don't know."

There was silence as I sidled along a passageway, my puzzled
images keeping pace in the mirrors at either hand.

"She didn't want me to kill you," he finally blurted from
somewhere off to my right.

"Julia?"

"Yes."

"How is she?"

"Recovering. Pretty rapidly, actually."

"Is she here at Sawall?"

"Yes."

"Look, I'd like to see her. But if she doesn't want to, I understand. I didn't know it was her when I stabbed Mask, and I'm
sorry."

"She never really wanted to hurt you. Her quarrel was with
Jasra. With you, it was an elaborate game. She wanted to prove she
was as good as—maybe better than—you. She wanted to show
you what you'd thrown away."

"Sorry," I muttered.

"Tell me one thing, please," he said. "Did you love her? Did
you ever really love her?"

I didn't answer him immediately. After all, I'd asked myself
that question many times, and I'd had to wait for the answer, too.

"Yes," I finally said. "I didn't realize it till it was too late,
though. Bad timing on my part."

A little later I asked, "What about you?"

ii not going to make the same mistake you did," he replied.
ɜ what got me to thinking about all these things. . . ."

I understand. If she won't see me, tell her that I said I'm
ɪry—about everything."

There was no reply. I stood still for a time, hoping he'd catch
up with me, but he didn't.

Then, "Okay," I called out. "Our duel's ended, so far as I'm
concerned."

I began moving again. After a time, I came to an exit and I
stepped through it.

He was standing outside, looking up at a massive porcelain
face.

"Good," he said.

I drew near.

"There's more," he said, still not looking at me.

"Oh?"

"I think they're stacking the deck," he stated.

"Who? How? What for?"

"Mom and the Logrus," he told me. "To put you on the throne.
Who's the bride of the Jewel?"

"I guess that would be Coral. It seems I did hear Dara use that
term at some point. Why?"

"I overheard her giving orders last cycle, to some of her Hendrake kin. She's sending a special team to kidnap this woman and
bring her here. I got the impression she's intended as your queen."

"That's ridiculous," I said. "She's married to my friend Luke.
She's Queen of Kashfa—"

He shrugged.

"Just telling you what I heard," he said. "It had to do with this
balancing of forces thing."

Indeed. I hadn't thought of that possibility, but it made perfect
sense. With Coral, the Courts would automatically obtain the
Jewel of Judgment, or the Eye of the Serpent as it was known hereabout, and that balance would certainly be affected. A loss for Amber, a gain for the Courts. It could be sufficient to achieve what I
wanted, the harmony that might postpone catastrophe indefinitely.

Too bad I couldn't let it occur. The poor girl had been jerked
around too much, because she happened to be in Amber at the
wrong time, because she happened to take a liking to me. I can recall once feeling philosophical in the abstract and deciding, yes, it
would be okay to sacrifice one innocent for the good of the many.
That was back in college, and had something to do with princi-

ples. But Coral was my friend, my cousin, and technically my lover—though under a set of circumstances that should hardly count; and a quick check of my feelings, so as not to be caught up short again, indicated that I could fall in love with her. All of which meant that philosophy had lost yet another round in the real world.

"How long ago did she send these people off, Jurt?"

"I don't know when they left—or even *if* they've left yet," he replied. "And with the time differential, they could be gone and back already for that matter."

"True," I said, and, "Shit!"

He turned and looked at me.

"It's important in all sorts of other ways, too, I suppose?" he said.

"It is to her, and she is to me," I answered.

His expression changed to one of puzzlement.

"In that case," he said, "why don't you just let them bring her to you? If you have to take the throne, it will sweeten things. If you don't, you'll have her with you, anyhow."

"Feelings are hard enough to keep secret, even around non-sorcerers," I said. "She could be used as a hostage against my behavior."

"Oh. I hate to say this pleases me. What I mean is . . . I'm pleased you care about someone else."

I lowered my head. I wanted to reach out and touch him, but I didn't.

Jurt made a little humming noise, as he sometimes had when pondering things as a kid. Then, "We've got to get her before they do, and move her to someplace safe," he said. "Or take her away from them if they've already got her."

" 'We'?"

He smiled, a rare event.

"You know what I've become. I'm tough."

"I hope so," I said. "But you know what'll happen if there are any witnesses to say it was a couple of the Sawall brothers behind this? Most likely a vendetta with Hendrake."

"Even if Dara talked them into it?"

"It'll look like she set them up."

"Okay," he said. "No witnesses."

I could have said that averting vendetta would save a lot of other lives, but that would have sounded hypocritical even if I didn't mean it that way. Instead, "That power you gained in the

Fountain," I said, "gives you something I've heard referred to as a 'living Trump' effect. Seems to me you were able to transport Julia as well as yourself with it."

He nodded.

"Can it get us from here to Kashfa in a hurry?"

The distant sound of an enormous gong filled the air.

"I can do anything the cards can do," he said, "and I can take someone along with me. The only problem is that the Trumps themselves don't have that range. I'd have to take us there in a series of jumps."

The gong sounded again.

"What's going on?" I asked.

"The noise?" he said. "That's notice that the funeral is about to begin. It can be heard throughout the Courts."

"Bad timing."

"Maybe, maybe not. It's giving me an idea."

"Tell me about it."

"It's our alibi if we have to take out some Hendrakes."

"How so?"

"The time differential. We go to the funeral and get seen. We slip out, run our errand, come back, and attend the rest of the service."

"You think the flow will allow that?"

"I think there's a good chance, yes. I've done a lot of jumping around. I'm starting to get a real feel for flows."

"Then we'll give it a try. The more confusion the better."

Again, the gong.

Red, the color of the fire of life that fills us, is the color of mourning garments in the Courts. I used the spikard rather than the Sign of the Logrus to summon suitable clothing for myself. I'd a desire to avoid any commerce, even the most mundane, with that Power, for now.

Jurt then trumped us to his quarters, where he had suitable garments of his own from the last funeral he'd attended. I'd a small desire to see my old room, too. Sometime, perhaps, when I wasn't rushed. . . .

We washed up, combed, trimmed, dressed quickly. I took on a changed form then, as did Jurt, and we went through the ritual again at this level, before garbing ourselves for the occasion. Shirt, breeches, jacket, cloak, anklets, bracelets, scarf, and bandanna—we looked incendiary. Weapons had to be left behind. We planned to return for them on the way out.

"Ready?" Jurt asked me.

"Yes."

He caught hold of my arm and we were transported, arriving at the inward edge of the Plaza at the End of the World, where a blue sky darkened above a conflagration of mourners milling along the route the procession would take. We passed among them, in hope of being seen by as many as possible. I was greeted by a few old acquaintances. Unfortunately, most wanted to stop and talk, not having seen me for some time. Jurt had similar problems. Most also wondered why we were here, rather than back at the Thelbane, the massive, glassy needle of Chaos far to our rear. Periodically, the air would vibrate as the gong continued its slow sounding. I felt it in the ground, also, as we were very near to its home. We made our way slowly across the Plaza, toward the massive pile of black stone at the very edge of the Pit, its gate an archway of frozen flame, as was its downward stair, each tread and riser time-barred fire, each railing the same. The rough amphitheater below us was also fire-furnished, self-illumed, facing the black block at the end of everything, no wall behind it, but the open emptiness of the Pit and its singularity whence all things came.

No one was entering it yet, and we stood near the gates of fire and looked back along the route the procession would follow. We nodded to friendly demonic faces, quivered to the note of the gong, watched the sky darken a little further. Suddenly, my head was filled with a powerful presence.

"Merlin!"

I immediately had an image of Mandor in a changed form, looking down his red-clothed arm, hand invisible, presumably regarding me through my Trump, wearing the closest thing I'd seen in a long while to an irritated expression.

"Yes?" I said.

His gaze moved past me. His expression suddenly changed, eyebrows rising, lips parting.

"That's Jurt you're with?" he asked.

"That's right."

"I'd thought you not on the best of terms," he said slowly, "as of our last conversation."

"We agreed to put aside our differences for the funeral."

"While it seems very civilized, I'm not certain how wise it is," he said.

I smiled.

"I know what I'm doing," I told him.

"Really?" he said. "Then why are you at the cathedral rather than here at Thelbane?"

"Nobody told me I was supposed to be at Thelbane."

"Odd," he responded. "Your mother was supposed to have informed both you and Jurt that you were to be part of the procession."

I shook my head and turned away.

"Jurt, did you know we were to be in the procession?" I asked.

"No," he said. "On the one hand, it makes sense. On the other, there's the black watch, which might recommend we maintain a low profile. Who's telling you this?"

"Mandor. He says Dara was supposed to let us know."

"She didn't tell me."

"You catch that?" I said to Mandor.

"Yes. It doesn't matter now. Come on through, both of you."

He extended his other hand.

"He wants us now," I said to Jurt.

"Damn!" Jurt mouthed, and came forward.

I reached out and clasped Mandor's hand just as Jurt came up and caught hold of my shoulder. We both moved forward then—

—into the slick and gleaming interior of Thelbane's main hall at ground level, a study in black, gray, mossy green, deep red, chandeliers like stalactites, fire sculptures about the walls, scaly hides hung behind them, drifting globes of water in the middle air, creatures swimming within them. The place was filled with nobles, relatives, courtiers, stirring like a field of flame about the catafalque at the hall's center. The gong sounded again just as Mandor said something to us.

He waited till the vibrations subsided, then spoke again: "I said Dara hasn't arrived yet. Go pay your respects, and let Bances assign you places in the procession."

Glancing toward the catafalque, I caught sight of both Tmer and Tubble in the vicinity. Tmer was talking to Bances, Tubble to someone who had his back turned this way. A horrible thought suddenly struck me.

"What," I asked, "is the security situation for the procession?" Mandor smiled.

"There are quite a few guardsmen mixed in with the group here," he said, "and more spotted along the way. Someone will be watching you every second."

I glanced at Jurt to see whether he'd heard that. He nodded.

"Thanks."

Keeping my litany of obscenities subvocal, I moved toward the casket, Jurt at my back. The only way I could think to produce a double would be to talk the Pattern into sending in a ghost of myself to take my place. But the Logrus would detect the ringer's projected energies in no time. And if I just left, not only would my absence be noticed, but I'd probably be tracked—possibly by the Logrus itself once Dara called a conference. Then it would be learned that I'd gone off to thwart the Logrus's attempt to rebalance order, and the headwaters of Shit Creek are a cruel and treacherous expanse. I would not make the mistake of fancying myself indispensable.

"How are we going to do this, Merlin?" Jurt said softly as we found our way to the end of the slow-moving line.

The gong sounded again, causing the chandeliers to vibrate.

"I don't see how we can," I answered. "I think the best I can hope for is to try getting a message through as I walk along."

"It can't be done by Trump from here," he answered. "Well, maybe under perfect conditions," he amended, "but not with all these distractions."

I tried to think of some spell, some sending, some agent to serve me in this. Ghost would have been ideal. Of course, he'd drifted off to explore the spatial asymmetries of the Sculpture Hall. That could keep him occupied for a long while.

"I could get there pretty quickly," Jurt volunteered, "and with the time differential I might make it back before anyone noticed."

"And you know exactly two people in Kashfa you might tell," I said. "Luke and Coral. They both met you in church, when we were trying to kill each other—and you stole Luke's father's sword. Offhand, I'd say he'd try to kill you on sight and she'd scream for help."

The line advanced somewhat.

"So I don't ask for help," he said.

"Un-uh," I told him. "I know you're tough, but Hendrakes are pros. Also, you'd be faced with a very uncooperative rescuee in Coral."

"You're a sorcerer," Jurt said. "If we find out who the guards are, couldn't you lay a spell on them so that they *think* they see us for this whole affair? Then we disappear and no one's the wiser."

"I've a hunch either Mom or our big brother has laid protective spells on the guards. At such an ideal time for an assassination, I would. I wouldn't want anyone able to mess with my people's heads if I were running security here."

We shuffled a little farther along. By leaning to one side and stretching my neck I was able to get a few glimpses of the wasted demonic form of old Swayvill, resplendently garbed, serpent of red-gold laid upon his breast, there in the flame-formed coffin, Oberon's ancient nemesis, going to join him at last.

As I moved nearer, it occurred to me that there was more than one approach to the problem. Perhaps I'd dwelled too long among the magically naive. I'd gotten out of the habit of thinking of magic against magic, of multiple mixed spells. So what if the guards were protected from any fiddling with their perceptions? Let it be. Find a way to work around it.

The gong sounded again. When the echoes died, Jurt leaned near.

"There's more to it than everything I said," he whispered.

"What do you mean?" I asked.

"Another reason I came to you back at Sawall was because I was scared," he replied.

"Of what?"

"At least one of them—Mandor or Dara—wants more than a balance, wants a total victory for the Logrus, for Chaos. I really believe that. It's not just that I don't want to be party to it. I don't want it to happen. Now that I can visit Shadow I don't want to see it destroyed. I don't want a victory for either side. Total control by the Pattern would probably be just as bad."

"How can you be sure one of them really wants this?"

"They tried it before with Brand, didn't they? He was out to destroy all order."

"No," I said. "He planned to destroy the old order, then replace it with his own. He was a revolutionary, not an anarchist. He was going to create a new Pattern within the Chaos he brought forth—his own, but still the real thing."

"He was duped. He couldn't have managed a thing like that."

"No way of knowing till he tried, and he didn't get the chance."

"Either way, I'm afraid someone's going to pull the plug on reality. If this kidnapping takes place, it'll be a big step in that direction. If you can't manage something to cover our absence, I think we should just go anyway and take our chances."

"Not yet," I said. "Hang on. I'm working something out. How's this sound? I don't locate the guards and hallucinate them. Instead, I do a transformation. I cause a couple of other people to look like us. You trump us out as soon as I do. That won't be a hallucination for anyone. Everyone will see them as us; we can go about our business—and check back if we have to."

"You do it and I'll get us out of here."

"Okay, I'll do it to the two guys in front of us. As soon as I've finished I'll gesture like this," I said, lowering my left hand from shoulder-height to waist-level, "and we both stoop as if one of us had dropped something. Then you take us away."

"I'll be ready."

The spikard made it easier than working out a transform spell. It was like a spell processor. I fed it the two end products, and it ran thousands of variations in a trice and handed me the finished products—a pair of spells it would have taken me a long while to work out along classical lines. I raised my hand as I hung them and accessed one of the many power sources the thing commanded off in Shadow. I fed juice into the constructs, watched the change commence, dropped my hand, and leaned forward.

There followed a moment's vertigo, and when I straightened we were back in Jurt's apartment. I laughed and he slapped my shoulder.

Immediately then, we were changing back into our human forms and garments. As soon as that was done, he caught hold of my arm again and trumped us to Fire Gate. A moment later, and he'd jumped us again, this time to a mountaintop overlooking a blue valley beneath a green sky. Then again, to the middle of a high bridge above a deep gorge, the sky putting away stars or taking them on.

"Okay, now," he said, and we stood atop a gray stone wall damp with dew, possibly even the remains of a storm. Clouds were taking fire in the east. There was a light breeze out of the south.

This was the wall that surrounded the innermost zone of Jidrash, Luke's capital in Kashfa. There were four huge buildings below us—including the palace and the Temple of the Unicorn directly across the Plaza from it—as well as a number of smaller buildings. Diagonally across the way from where we stood was the wing of the palace from which Gryll had fetched me (how long ago?) from my rendezvous with the queen. I could even make out the broken shutter of our window amid an expanse of ivy.

"Over there," I said, gesturing. "That's where I last saw her."

An eyeblink later we stood within the chamber, its only inhabitants. The place had been straightened, the bed made up. I withdrew my Trumps and shuffled out Coral's. Staring then till it grew cold, I felt her presence and reached for it.

She was there yet she wasn't. It was the disjointed sense of presence one encounters in dream or stupor. I passed my hand over the card and ended our tenuous contact.

"What happened?" Jurt asked.

"I think she's drugged," I replied.

"Then it would seem they've already got her," he said. "Any way you can trace her in that state?"

"She could also be in the next building, on medication," I said. "She wasn't well when I left."

"What now?"

"Either way, we've got to talk to Luke," I said, searching for his card.

I reached him in an instant on uncovering it.

"Merlin! Where the hell are you?" he asked.

"If you're in the palace, I'm next door," I said.

He rose to his feet from what I now realized to be the edge of a bedstead, and he picked up a long-sleeved green shirt and drew it on, covering his collection of scars. I thought that I glimpsed someone in the bed behind him. He muttered something in that direction, but I could not overhear it.

"We've got to talk," he said, running his hand through his rusty hair. "Bring me through."

"Okay," I said. "But first, you'd better know that my brother Jurt is here."

"Has he got my dad's sword?"

"Uh—No."

"Guess I won't kill him right now," he said, tucking his shirt into his waistband.

Abruptly, he extended his hand. I clasped it. He stepped forward and joined us.

8

Luke grinned at me, scowled at Jurt.

"Where've you been, anyway?" he asked.

"The Courts of Chaos," I replied. "I was summoned from here at the death of Swayvill. The funeral's in progress right now. We sneaked away when I learned that Coral was in danger."

"I know that—now," Luke said. "She's gone. Kidnapped, I think."

"When did it happen?"

"Night before last, I'd judge. What do you know of it?"

I glanced at Jurt. "Time differential," he said.

"She represented a chance to pick up a few points," I explained, "in the ongoing game between the Pattern and the Logrus. So agents of Chaos were sent for her. They wanted her intact, though. She should be okay."

"What do they want her for?"

"Seems they feel she's specially suited to be queen in Thelbane, what with the Jewel of Judgment as a piece of her anatomy and all."

"Who's going to be the new king?"

My face felt warm of a sudden.

"Well, the people who came for her had me in mind for the job," I replied.

"Hey, congratulations!" he said. "Now I don't have to be the only one having all this fun."

"What do you mean?"

"This king business ain't worth shit, man. I wish I'd never gotten sucked into the deal in the first place. Everybody's got a piece of your time, and when they don't someone still has to know where you are."

"Hell, you were just crowned. Give it a chance to shake down."

" 'Just'? It's been over a month!"

"Time differential," Jurt repeated.

"Come on. I'll buy you a cup of coffee," Luke said.

"You've got coffee here?"

"I require it, man. This way." He led us out the door, turned left, headed down a stair.

"I had a funny thought," he said, "while you were talking back there—about you reigning, and Coral a desirable queen. I could get the marriage annulled pretty damn quick, since I'm in charge here. Now, you want her for your queen and I want that Golden Circle Treaty with Amber. I think I see a way to make everybody happy."

"It's a lot more complicated than that, Luke. I don't want the job, and it would be very bad for us if my kinsmen back in the Courts got custody of Coral. I've learned a lot of things recently."

"Such as?" Luke said, opening a postern that let upon a walkway to the rear of the palace.

I glanced back at Jurt.

"He's scared, too," I said. "That's why we're a little more cordial these days."

Jurt nodded.

"It's possible Brand could have been partly victim of a plan originated in the Courts," he said, "part of an idea that's still alive there."

"We'd better go for the whole breakfast," Luke said. "Let's swing around back and take it in the kitchen."

We followed him down a garden path.

And so we ate and talked as the day brightened about us. Luke insisted I try Coral's Trump again, which I did with the same result. Then he cursed, nodded, and said, "Your timing's actually pretty good. The guys who grabbed her were reported to have taken off along a black trail into the west."

"It figures," I said.

"I've reason to believe they didn't make it back to the Courts with her."

"Oh?"

"I understand these black thoroughfares you guys use are dangerous to outsiders," he observed. "But I can show you what's left of this one—it's a black pathway now, actually. I'd like to follow it, but I don't know that I can get away for long. Also, is there a way to protect me from the trail itself?"

"Just being in our company would keep you from harm as we traveled it," Jurt said.

I stood. The cook and two dishwashers glanced in our direction.

"There is somebody you have to meet, Luke," I told him. "Right now."

"Why not?" he said, rising. "Where is he?"

"Let's take a walk," I said.

"Sure."

We got to our feet, headed back to the servants' door.

"So, whether she was a willing accomplice or a magical time bomb, Mom might have conned Dad into his efforts to take over in Amber—and, ultimately, to change the world," Luke said.

"Well, I gather he didn't exactly come to her with clean hands," I said.

"True, but I wonder how elaborate his plans really were, to begin with," Luke mused. "This is the most cheerful thing I've heard all month."

We exited into the little covered walkway that ran along the side of the palace. Luke halted and looked around.

"Where is he?" he asked.

"Not here," I said. "I just needed a point of departure with no witnesses to say I'd kidnapped the king."

"Where *are* we going, Merlin?" Jurt asked, as I swirled a spiral from the center of the spikard, drawing upon sixteen different power sources.

"Good idea. Kidnap away," Luke was saying as he was caught up along with Jurt.

I used it as I had when I'd transported myself from Amber to Kashfa, forming the target from memory rather than discovered vision. Only this time there were three of us and a long, long way to go.

"Have I got a deal for you," I said.

It was like stepping into a kaleidoscope, and passing through about 120 degrees of cubist fragmentation and reassembly, before emerging on the other side beneath a towering tree, its top lost in the fog, in the vicinity of a red and white '57 Chevy, its radio playing Renbourn's "Nine Maidens."

Luke's ghost emerged from the front seat and stared at the original. Luke stared back.

"Hi," I said. "Meet each other. You hardly need an introduction, though. You have so much in common."

Jurt stared at the Pattern.

"That's my dad's edition," I said.

"I could have guessed that," Jurt told me. "But what are we doing here?"

"An idea I had. But I thought Corwin would be here, and I might discuss it with him."

"He came back, and he left again," said the resident Luke, overhearing me.

"Did he leave a forwarding address, or say when he might return?"

"Nope."

"Damn! Look, something that got said just a little while ago gave me the idea that you Lukes might want to change places for a time—if this Pattern could be persuaded to approve some leave."

Luke, whom I decided to continue calling Luke when his ghost was around, brightened suddenly. I resolved to think of his double as Rinaldo, to keep things sorted.

"It's an experience no man should do without," he said.

"Then why are you so anxious to get away from it?" Rinaldo replied.

"To help Merle find Coral," Luke said. "She's been kidnapped."

"Really? By whom?"

"Agents of Chaos."

"Hm." Rinaldo began to pace. "Okay, you know more about it than I do," he finally said. "If Corwin gets back soon and the Pattern excuses me, I'll help you any way I can."

"The trail will be getting colder while we wait," Luke observed.

"You don't understand," Rinaldo said. "I've got a job to do here, and I can't just take off—even if it's to go and be a king somewhere. What I do is more important."

Luke glanced at me.

"He's right," I said. "He's a guardian of the Pattern. On the other hand, nobody's about to hurt Coral. Why don't Jurt and I pop on back to the Courts for a few minutes, to check on the progress of the funeral? Corwin might show up while we're about it. I'm sure you two will find something to talk about."

"Go ahead," Luke told me.

"Yeah," said Rinaldo. "I'd like to know what we've been doing."

I looked at Jurt, who nodded. I went and stood beside him.

"Your turn to drive," I said.

"Back soon," I remarked as we faded into the first jump.

. . . And so again to the Ways of Sawall, and back into our ruddy garb over demonform. I also changed our facial appearance to the nondescript before Jurt returned us to the funeral party, not wanting a matching set marching along.

The Thelbane proved deserted. A quick check outside, however, showed us the procession, perhaps a quarter way across the Plaza, halted and in a state of confusion.

"Uh-oh," Jurt remarked. "What should I do?"

"Take us down there," I told him.

Moments later, we were at the outer edge of the crowd. Swayvill's blazing casket had been lowered to the ground, a guard posted about it. My attention was immediately attracted to a knot of figures perhaps twenty feet off to the right of it. There was some shouting going on, something lay upon the ground, and two demonic forms were being held tightly by several others. My stomach tightened as I saw that the two were the pair I had ensorcelled to resemble Jurt and myself. Both were protesting something.

As I pushed my way forward, I withdrew my spells, causing the two to revert to their own appearance. There were more shouts as this occurred, including an "I told you!" from the nearest. The response to this was a "Yes, they are!" from someone I suddenly realized to be Mandor. He stood between them and the thing on the ground.

"It was a trick!" Mandor said. "A distraction! Release them!"

I decided the moment was propitious for dropping the spells that masked Jurt and myself. Glorious confusion!

Moments later, Mandor saw me and signaled for me to approach. Jurt, I saw, off to my right, had stopped to talk to someone he knew.

"Merlin!" he said as soon as I was near. "What do you know of this?"

"Nothing," I said. "I was way to the rear, with Jurt. I don't even know what happened."

"Someone gave two of the security guards your appearance and Jurt's. This was obviously intended to create confusion when the assassin struck. They rushed forward insisting they were guards. Obviously, they weren't. Clever—especially with you and Jurt on their black watch list."

"I see," I agreed, wondering whether I had helped an assassin to escape. "Who got hit?"

"Tmer, with a very professional dagger stroke," he explained, left eyelid twitching. A faint wink? Meaning? "And he was gone in an instant."

Four mourners, having made a stretcher of cloaks, raised the fallen body. After they'd moved only a few paces with it, I saw another knot of people beyond them.

Seeing my puzzled expression, Mandor glanced back.

"More security," he said. "They're surrounding Tubble. I think I'll order him out of here for now. You and Jurt, too. You can come to the temple later. I'll see that security's even heavier there."

"Okay," I said. "Is Dara here?"

He glanced about.

"I haven't seen her. Don't now, either. You'd better go."

I nodded. As I turned away, I saw a half-familiar face off to my right. She was tall and dark-eyed, shifting from a swirl of multicolored jewels to a swaying flowerlike form, and she had been staring at me. I had been trying to recall her name earlier, and had failed. Seeing her brought it back, though. I approached her.

"I have to leave for a time," I said. "But I wanted to say hello, Gilva."

"You do remember. I was wondering."

"Of course."

"How are you, Merlin?"

I sighed. She smiled her way into furry, half-human solidity.

"Me, too," she said. "I'll be so glad when this is all settled."

"Yes. Listen, I want to see you—for several reasons. When would be a good time?"

"Why, anytime after the funeral, I guess. What about?"

"No time now. Mandor's giving me angry looks. See you later."

"Yes. Later, Merlin."

I hurried back to Jurt and caught him by the elbow.

"We're ordered to leave," I said. "Security reasons."

"All right." He turned to the man he'd been talking with. "Thanks. I'll see you later," he told him.

The world slipped away. A new one dawned: Jurt's apartment, our clothes strewn about it.

"Good timing for us. Bad for Tmer," he remarked.

"True."

"How's it feel to be number two?" he asked as we changed again—both clothing and form.

"It advances your case, too," I said.

"I've a feeling he died on your account, brother, not mine."

"I hope not," I said.

He laughed.

"It's between Tubble and you."

"If it were, I'd be dead already," I said. "If you're right, it's really between Sawall and Chanicut."

"Wouldn't it be funny, Merlin, if I were sticking with you because it's the safest place to be just now?" he asked. "I'm sure our guards and assassins are better than Chanicut's. Supposing I'm just waiting, saving my final effort till Tubble's out of the way? Then, trusting me and all, you turn your back—Coronation!"

I looked at him. He was smiling, but he also seemed to be studying me.

I was about to say, "You can have it, without the trouble," in a joking way. But I wondered just then: Even in jest, if it were a choice between the two of us . . . It occurred to me that if we were the only options, this was a circumstance under which I'd agree to take the throne. I'd resolved to give him the benefit of the doubt, to meet him more than halfway. But I couldn't help it. For all his conciliatory talk and apparent cooperation, a lifelong habit is a hard thing to break. I couldn't bring myself to trust him anymore than I had to.

"Tell it to the Logrus," I said.

A look of fear—the widening of the eyes, the shifting of the gaze downward, a small forward tightening of the shoulders—then, "You really do have an understanding with it, don't you?" he asked.

"There seems to be an understanding, but it only works one way," I said.

"What do you mean?"

"I'm not about to help either side wreck our world."

"Sounds like you're prepared to double-cross the Logrus."

I raised a finger to my lips.

"It must be your Amber blood," he said then. "I've been told they're all a little crazy."

"Maybe so," I said.

"Sounds like something your father would do."

"What do you know of him?"

"You know, everybody has a favorite Amber story."

"Nobody around here ever told any to me."

"Of course not—considering."

"Me being a half-breed and all?" I said.

He shrugged. Then, "Well, yes."

I pulled on my boots.

"Whatever you're doing with that new Pattern," he said, "it probably won't make the old one too happy."

"Doubtless you're right," I agreed.

"So you won't be able to run to it for protection if the Logrus is after you."

"I guess not."

". . . And if they're both after you, the new one won't be able to stand against them."

"You think they'd really get together on anything?"

"Hard to say. You're playing a wild game. I hope you know what you're doing."

"Me, too," I said, rising. "My turn."

I unwound the spikard at a level I'd never attempted before, and I got us there in a single jump.

Luke and Rinaldo were still talking. I could tell them apart by their garments. Corwin was nowhere in sight.

Both waved as we made our appearance.

"How's everything in the Courts?" Luke asked.

"Chaotic," Jurt replied. "How long have we been away?"

"Six hours, I'd guess," Rinaldo replied.

"No sign of Corwin?" I asked.

"No," Luke said. "But in the meantime, we've worked out a deal with each other—and Rinaldo's been in touch with the Pattern here. It will release him and continue his maintenance as soon as Corwin returns."

"Regarding that . . ." Jurt said.

"Yes?" Rinaldo asked.

"I'll stay here and cover for Rinaldo while you go find the lady with the glass eye."

"Why?" Rinaldo asked.

"Because you'll do a better job together and I'll feel a lot safer here than I would most other places."

"I'd have to see whether that's acceptable," Rinaldo said.

"Do it," said Jurt.

He moved off toward the Pattern. I searched the fog in all directions, hoping to see my father returning. Jurt studied the car, its radio now playing a Bruce Dunlap number from "Los Animales."

"If your father comes back and relieves me," Jurt said, "I'll return to the funeral and make excuses for you if you're not there. If you get back and I'm not there, you do the same. All right?"

"Yes," I said, wisps of mist rising like smoke between us. "And whichever of us is free first and has something worth saying . . ."

"Yes," he agreed. "I'll come looking if you don't get to me."

"Didn't happen to pick up my sword while you were back in the Courts, did you?" Luke asked.

"Didn't have time," Jurt replied.

"Next time you're back, I wish you'd make time."

"I will, I will," Jurt said.

Rinaldo moved away from the Pattern, returned to us.

"You're hired," he said to Jurt. "Come with me. There's a spring I want to show you, and a store of food, some weapons."

Luke turned and watched them move off to our left.

"I'm sorry," he said softly, "but I still don't trust him."

"Don't be sorry. I don't either. I've known him too long. But we have better reasons for trusting each other now than we've had for a long time."

"I'm wondering whether it was wise to let him know where this Pattern is, and now to leave him alone with it."

"I'm pretty sure the Pattern knows what it's doing, and that it can take care of itself."

He raised a pair of crossed fingers.

"I'd've argued against it," he said, "save that I need my double."

When they returned, a deejay's baritone suddenly rolled forth, saying, "It all goes to show, timing is everything. Road conditions are fine. It is a good day for travel." Immediately, there followed a drum solo I'd have sworn was something I once heard Random play.

"You're on duty as of now," Rinaldo said to Jurt. To us, he nodded. "Anytime."

I caught us up with the spikard and spun us back to Kashfa, bringing us into Jidrash near twilight, to the same walltop vantage I had enjoyed earlier with my brother.

"And so at last," Rinaldo said, looking out over the town.

"Yes," Luke replied. "It's all yours—for a time." Then, "Merle, how's about jumping us to my apartment?"

I turned to the west where clouds had gone orange, glanced upward to where several hung purple.

"Before we do that, Luke," I said, "I'd like to use what daylight's left for a look at that black trail."

He nodded.

"Good idea. Okay, take us over there."

His gesture indicated a hilly area to the southwest. I caught us up and spikarded us to it, creating a verb for which I felt a need in the same act. Such is the power of Chaos.

Arriving on a small hilltop, we followed Luke down its far side.

"Over this way," he said.

Long shadows lay all about us, but there is a difference between their dimness and the blackness of a travel-thread from the Courts.

"It was right here," Luke finally said when we came to a place between a pair of boulders.

I moved forward into the area but I felt nothing special.

"You sure this is the place?" I asked.

"Yes."

I advanced another ten paces, twenty.

"If this is really where it was, it's gone now," I told him. "Of course . . . I wonder how long we've been away?"

Luke snapped his fingers.

"Timing," he observed. "Take us back to my apartments."

We kissed the day good-bye as I sent forth a lead and opened our way through the wall of dark. We stepped through into the room I had occupied earlier with Coral.

"Close enough?" I asked. "I'm not sure where your rooms are."

"Come on," he said, taking us out, to the left and down the stair. "Time to consult the resident expert. Merle, do something about this guy's appearance. Too much of a good thing might cause comment."

It was easy, and the first time I'd made anyone look like the big portrait of Oberon back home.

Luke knocked on a door before entering. Somewhere beyond it, a familiar voice spoke his name.

"I have some friends with me," he said.

"Bring them in," came her reply.

He opened the door and did so.

"Both of you know Nayda," Luke announced. "Nayda, this is my double. Let's call him Rinaldo and me Luke while we're together. He's going to run things for me here while Merle and I are off looking for your sister."

I changed Rinaldo back then, in response to her puzzled look.

She had on black trousers and an emerald blouse, her hair bound back by a matching green scarf. She smiled as she greeted us, and when she regarded me she touched her lips lightly, almost casually, with a fingertip. I nodded immediately.

"I trust you are recovered from any misadventures in Amber," I said. "You were, of course, there at a bad time."

"Of course," she responded. "Fully recovered, thank you. Kind of you to ask. Thanks, too, for the recent directions. It was you, I take it, who spirited Luke away these two days past?"

"It's really been that long?" I said.

"It has, sir."

"Sorry about that, my dear," Luke said, squeezing her hand and looking long into her eyes.

"That explains why the trail's faded," I said.

Rinaldo seized her hand and kissed it, while executing an elaborate bow.

"Amazing how much you've changed from the girl I knew," he stated.

"Oh?"

"I share Luke's memories as well as his appearance," he explained.

"I could tell there was something not quite human about you," she remarked. "I see you as a man whose very blood is fire."

"And how might you see that?" he inquired.

"She has her means," Luke said, "though I thought it only a psychic bond with her sister. Apparently it goes somewhat further."

She nodded.

"Speaking of which, I hope you can use it to help us track her," he continued. "With the trail gone and a drug or a spell barring a Trump call, we'll be needing assistance."

"Yes," she answered, "though she is in no danger at the moment."

"Good," he said. "In that case, I'll order us all food and set to briefing this good-looking fellow on what's going on in Kashfa these days."

"Luke," I said. "It sounds like an ideal time for me to head back to the Courts for the rest of the funeral."

"How long would you be gone, Merle?"

"I don't know," I replied.

"Back by morning, I trust?"

"Me, too. What if I'm not, though?"

"I've a feeling I should go looking without you."

"Try reaching me first, though."

"Sure. See you later."

I drew my cloak of space about me, shrugging Kashfa away. When I opened it again I was back in Jurt's quarters at Sawall.

I stretched, I yawned. I did a quick turn about the room, making certain I was alone. I unfastened my cloak and tossed it upon the bed. I paced as I unbuttoned my shirt.

Halt. What was it? Also, where?

I retraced a few paces. I had never spent a great deal of time in my younger brother's rooms, but I would have recalled what I was feeling.

There was a chair and table in the corner formed by the wall and an armoire of dark, almost black wood. Kneeling on the chair and reaching over the table, I could feel it—the presence of a way, not quite strong enough for transport, though. Ergo. . . .

I moved off to my right, opened the armoire. It had to be inside, of course. I wondered how recently he had installed it. I also felt slightly funny about poking about in his quarters this way. Still, he owed me for a lot of misery and inconvenience. A few confidences and a little cooperation hardly cleaned the slate. I hadn't learned to trust him yet, and it was possible he was setting me up for something. Good manners, I decided, would have to be sacrificed to prudence.

I pushed garments aside, making a way clear to the back of the thing. I could feel it strongly. A final shove at the garments, a quick shuffle to the rear, and I was at the focus. I let it take me away.

Once there was a forward yielding, the pressure of the garments at my back gave me a small push. That, plus the fact that someone (Jurt, himself?) had done a sloppy shadowmastering job resulting in mismatched floor levels, sent me sprawling as I achieved destination.

At least, I didn't land in a pit full of sharpened stakes or acid. Or the lair of some half-starved beast. No, it was a green-tiled floor, and I caught myself as I fell. And from the flickering light all about me I guessed there was a mess of candles burning.

Even before I looked up I was sure they'd all be green.

Nor was I incorrect. About that or anything else.

The setup was similar to that of my father's, with a groined vault containing a light source superior to the candles. Only there was no painting above this altar. This one featured a stained-glass window, lots of green in it, and a little red.

Its principal was Brand.

I rose and crossed to it. Lying upon it, drawn a few inches from its sheath, was Werewindle.

I reached out and took hold of it, my first impulse being to bear it away with me for eventual restoration to Luke. Then I hesitated. It wasn't something I could wear to a funeral. If I took it now I'd have to hide it somewhere, and it was already well-hidden right here. I let my hand rest upon it, though, as I thought. It contained a similar feeling of power to that which Grayswandir bore, only somehow brighter, less tragedy-touched and brooding. Ironic. It seemed an ideal blade for a hero.

I looked about. There was a book on a reading stand off to my left, a pentagram upon the floor behind me, worked in different shades of green, a smell—as of a recent wood fire—hung in the air. Idly, I wondered what I might find if I were to knock a hole in the wall. Was this chapel located upon a mountaintop? Beneath a lake? Underground? Was it drifting somewhere in the heavens?

What did it represent? It looked to be religious in nature. And Benedict, Corwin, and Brand were the three I knew about. Were they admired, respected—venerated—by certain of my countrymen and relatives? Or were these hidden chapels somehow more sinister?

I removed my hand from Werewindle, stepped to the vicinity of the pentagram.

My Logrus vision revealed nothing untoward, but an intense scan with the spikard detected the residue of a long-removed magical operation. The traces were too faint to tell me anything of its nature, however. While it seemed possible I might probe further after this and come up with a clearer picture, I also realized I hadn't the time such an operation would require.

Reluctantly, I retreated to the vicinity of the way. Could these places have been used to try to influence the individuals involved?

I shook my head. This was something I would have to save for another day. I located the way and gave myself to it.

I stumbled on my return, also.

Catching hold of the frame with one hand, I seized a garment with another, kept myself upright, straightened, and stepped out. Then I shifted the clothing back into place and shut the doors.

I stripped quickly, altering my form as I was about it, and I donned my mourning garb once again. I felt some activity in the vicinity of the spikard, and for the first time I caught it drawing upon one of the many sources it commanded to alter its shape, accommodating the changing size of my finger. It had obviously done this several times before, though this was the first time I had noted the process. This was interesting, in that it showed the device capable of acting independent of my will.

I didn't really know what the thing was, what its origin might have been. I kept it because it represented a considerable source of power, an acceptable substitute for the use of the Logrus, which I now feared. But as I watched it change shape to remain snug upon my changing finger, I wondered. What if it were somehow booby-trapped to turn upon me at exactly the wrong moment?

I turned it a couple of times upon my finger. I moved into it with my mind, knowing this to be an exercise in futility. It would take ages for me to run down each line to its source, to check out hidden spells along the way. It was like taking a trip through a Swiss watch—custom-made. I was impressed both with the beauty of its design, and with the enormous amount of work that had gone into its creation. It could easily possess hidden imperatives that would only respond to special sets of circumstances. Yet—

It had done nothing untoward, yet. And the alternative was the Logrus. It struck me as a genuine instance of the preferability of the devil one didn't know.

Growling, I adjusted my apparel, focused my attention on the Temple of the Serpent, and bade the spikard deliver me near its entrance. It performed as smoothly and gently as if I had never doubted it, as if I had not discovered in it yet another cause for paranoia.

And for a time, I simply stood outside the doors of frozen flame, there at the great Cathedral of the Serpent at the outer edge of the Plaza at the End of the World, situated exactly at the Rim, opened to the Pit itself—where, on a good day, one can view the creation of the universe, or its ending—and I watched the stars swarm through space that folded and unfolded like the petals of flowers; and as if my life were about to change, my thoughts returned to California and school, of sailing the *Sunburst* with Luke and Gail and Julia, of sitting with my father near the end of the war, of riding with Vinta Bayle through the wine country to the east of Amber, of a long, brisk afternoon spent showing Coral about the town, of the strange encounters of that day; and I turned and raised my scaly hand, stared past it at the spire of Thelbane, and "they cease not fighting, east and west, on the marches of my breast," I thought. How long, how long . . . ?—irony, as usual, a three-to-one favorite whenever sentimentality makes its move.

Turning again, I went in to see the last of the King of Chaos.

9

Down, down into the pile, into the great slag heap, window onto the ends of time and space, where nothing is to be seen at the end, I went, between walls forever afire, never burnt down, walking in one of my bodies toward the sound of a voice reading from the Book of the Serpent Hung upon the Tree of Matter, and at length came into the grotto that backed upon blackness, widening semi-circles of red-clad mourners facing the reader and the grand catafalque beside which he stood, Swayvill clearly in view within it, half-covered with red flowers dropped by mourners, red tapers flickering against the Pit, but a few paces behind them; across the rear of the chamber then, listening to Bances of Amblerash, High Priest of the Serpent, his words sounding as if spoken beside me, for the acoustics of Chaos are good; finding a seat in an otherwise empty arc, where anyone looking back would be certain to notice me; seeking familiar faces, finding Dara, Tubble, and Mandor seated in frontal positions that indicated they were to assist Bances in sliding the casket past the edge into forever when the time came; and in my divided heart I recalled the last funeral I had attended before this: Caine's, back in Amber, beside the sea, and I thought again of Bloom and the way the mind wanders on these occasions.

I sought about me. Jurt was nowhere in sight. Gilva of Hendrake was only a couple of rows below me. I shifted my gaze to the deep blackness beyond the Rim. It was almost as if I were looking down, rather than out—if such terms had any real meaning in that place. Occasionally, I would perceive darting points of light or rolling masses. It served me as a kind of Rorschach for a time, and I half-dozed before the prospect of dark butterflies, clouds, pairs of faces—

I sat upright with a small start, wondering what had broken my reverie.

The silence, it was. Bances had stopped reading.

I was about to lean forward and whisper something to Gilva when Bances began the Consignment. I was startled to discover that I recalled all of the appropriate responses.

As the chanting swelled and focused, I saw Mandor get to his feet, and Dara, and Tubble. They moved forward, joining Bances about the casket—Dara and Mandor at its foot, Tubble and Bances at its head. Service assistants rose from their section and began snuffing candles, until only the large one, at the Rim, behind Bances, still flickered. At this point we all stood.

The ever-eerie light of flame mosaics, worked into the walls at either hand, granted additional illumination to the extent that I could detect the movement below when the chanting ceased.

The four figures stooped slightly, presumably taking hold of the casket's handles. They straightened then and moved toward the Rim. An assistant advanced and stood beside the candle just as they passed it, ready to snuff the final flame as Swayvill's remains were consigned to Chaos.

A half-dozen paces remained. . . . Three. Two. . . .

Bances and Tubble knelt at the verge, positioning the casket within a groove in the stone floor, Bances intoning a final bit of ritual the while, Dara and Mandor remaining standing.

The prayer finished, I heard a curse. Mandor seemed jerked forward. Dara stumbled away to the side. I heard a *clunk* as the casket hit the floor. The assistant's hand had already been moving, and the candle went out at that moment. There followed a skidding sound as the casket moved forward, more curses, a shadowy figure retreating from the Rim. . . .

Then came a wail. A bulky outline fell and was gone. The wail diminished, diminished, diminished. . . .

I raised my left fist, caused the spikard to create a globe of white light as a bubble pipe does a bubble. It was about three feet in diameter when I released it to drift overhead. Suddenly, the place was filled with babbling. Others of sorcerous background having exercised their favorite illumination spells at about the same time I had, the temple was now over-illuminated from dozens of point-sources.

Squinting, I saw Bances, Mandor, and Dara in converse near

the Rim. Tubble and the remains of Swayvill were no longer with us.

My fellow mourners were already moving. I did, too, realizing that my time here was now extremely limited.

I stepped down over the empty row, moved to the right, touched Gilva's still humanized shoulder.

"Merlin!" she said, turning quickly. "Tubble—went over—didn't he?"

"Sure looked that way," I said.

"What will happen now?"

"I've got to leave," I said, "fast!"

"Why?"

"Somebody's going to start thinking about the succession in a few moments, and I'm going to be smothered with protection," I told her. "I can't have that, not just now."

"Why not?"

"No time to go into that. But I'd wanted to talk to you. May I borrow you now?"

There were milling bodies all about us.

"Of course—sir," she said, apparently having just thought about the succession.

"Cut that out," I said, spikard spiraling the energies that caught us and took us away.

I brought us to the forest of metal trees, and Gilva kept hold of my arm and looked about her.

"Lord, what is this place?" she asked.

"I'd rather not say," I replied, "for reasons that will become apparent in a moment. I only had one question for you the last time I spoke with you. But now I have two, and this place figures in one of them, in a way, besides being fairly deserted most of the time."

"Ask," she said, moving to face me. "I'll try to help. If it's important, though, I may not be the best person—"

"Yes, it's important. But I haven't time to make an appointment with Belissa. It concerns my father, Corwin."

"Yes?"

"It was he who slew Borel of Hendrake in the war at Patternfall."

"So I understand," she said.

"After the war, he joined the royal party that came here to the Courts to work out the Treaty."

"Yes," she said. "I know that."

"He disappeared shortly thereafter, and no one seemed to know where he'd gotten off to. For a time, I thought he might be dead. Later, however, I received indications that he was not, but rather was imprisoned somewhere. Can you tell me anything about this?"

She turned away suddenly.

"I am offended," she said, "by what I believe you imply."

"I'm sorry," I said, "but I had to ask."

"Ours is an honorable House," she said. "We accept the fortunes of war. When the fighting is ended, we put it all behind us."

"I apologize," I said. "We're even related, you know, on my mother's side."

"Yes, I know," she said, turning away. "Will that be all, Prince Merlin?"

"Yes," I answered. "Where shall I send you?"

She was silent for a moment, then, "You said there were two questions," she stated.

"Forget it. I changed my mind about the second one."

She turned back.

"Why? Why should I forget it? Because I maintain my family's honor?"

"No, because I believe you."

"And?"

"I'll trouble someone else for an opinion."

"Do you mean it's dangerous, and you've decided against asking me?"

"I don't understand it, so it could be dangerous."

"Do you want to offend me again?"

"Heaven forbid!"

"Ask me your question."

"I'll have to show you."

"Do it."

"Even if it means climbing a tree?"

"Whatever it means."

"Follow me."

So I led her to the tree and climbed it, an enormously simple feat in my present form. She was right behind me.

"There's a way up here," I said. "I'm about to let it take me. Give me a few seconds to move aside."

I moved a little farther upward and was transported. Stepping aside, I surveyed the chapel quickly. Nothing seemed changed.

Then Gilva was at my side. I heard a sharp intake of breath.

"Oh, my!" she said.

"I know what I'm looking at," I said, "but I don't know what I'm seeing, if you follow me."

"It is a shrine," she said, "dedicated to the spirit of a member of the royal house of Amber."

"Yes, it's my father Corwin," I agreed. "That's what I'm looking at. But what am I seeing? Why should there be such a thing here in the Courts, anyway?"

She moved forward slowly, studying Dad's altar.

"I might as well tell you," I added, "that this is not the only such shrine I've seen since my return."

She reached out and touched the hilt of Grayswandir. Searching beneath the altar, she found a supply of candles. Removing a silver one and screwing it into the socket of one of a number of holders, she lit it from one of the others and placed it near Grayswandir. She muttered something while she was about it, but I did not make out the words.

When she turned back to me again she was smiling.

"We both grew up here," I said. "How is it that you seem to know all about this when I don't?"

"The answer is fairly simple, Lord," she told me. "You departed right after the war, to seek an education in other lands. This is a sign of something that came to pass in your absence."

She reached out, took hold of my arm, led me to a bench.

"Nobody thought we would actually lose that war," she said, "though it had long been argued that Amber would be a formidable adversary." We seated ourselves. "Afterward, there was considerable unrest," she continued, "Over the policies that had led to it and the treaty that followed it. No single house or grouping could hope for a deposition against the royal coalition, though. You know the conservatism of the Rim Lords. It would take much, much more to unite a majority against the Crown. Instead, their discontent took another form. There grew up a brisk trade in Amber memorabilia from the war. People became fascinated by our conquerors. Biographical studies of Amber's royal family sold very well. Something like a cult began to take shape. Private chapels such as this began to appear, dedicated to a particular Amberite whose virtues appealed to someone."

She paused, studying my face.

"It smacked too much of a religion," she went on then, "and for time out of mind the Way of the Serpent had been the only significant religion in the Courts. So Swayvill outlawed the Amber cult as heretical, for obvious political reasons. That proved a mistake. Had he done nothing it might have passed quickly. I don't really know, of course. But outlawing it drove it underground, made people take it more seriously as a rebellious thing. I've no idea how many cult chapels there are among the Houses, but that's obviously what this is."

"Fascinating sociological phenomenon," I said, "and your cult figure is Benedict."

She laughed.

"That wouldn't have been hard to guess," she said.

"Actually, I had the chapel described to me by my brother Mandor. He claimed to have wandered into it at a party at Hendrake, not knowing what it was."

She chuckled.

"He must have been testing you," she said. "The practice has been common knowledge for a long while. And I happen to know he's a cultist himself."

"Really? How do you know this?"

"He made no secret of it in the old days, before the general proscription."

"And who might his personal patron be?" I said.

"The Princess Fiona," she replied.

Curiouser and curiouser. . . .

"You've actually seen his chapel to her?" I asked.

"Yes. Before the ban it was not uncommon to have your friends over for a service whenever you were feeling particularly disgruntled with royal policy."

"And after the ban?"

"Everyone claimed publicly that their shrines had been destroyed. Many were simply relocated, I think, up hidden ways."

"And the business of having friends over for services?"

"I'd guess it would depend on how good a friend you're talking about. I don't really know how organized the Amber cult is." She gestured widely. "A place like this is illegal, though. Good thing I don't know where we are."

"I guess so," I said. "What about the relationship between the cult figure and the real thing? I'd say that Mandor really does have a thing about Fiona. He's met her, you know, and I've been present and seen it. Someone else I know stole something belonging to his—patron?—and keeps it in his shrine. And that"—I rose, crossed the altar, and picked up Corwin's sword—"is the real thing. I'd seen Grayswandir close-up, touched it, held it. This is it.

But what I'm getting at is that my father is missing, and the last time I saw him he was wearing that blade. Would it be in keeping with the tenets of this cult to keep your patron prisoner?"

"I never heard of such a thing," she said. "But I don't see why not. It is really the spirit of the person that is being venerated. There is no reason the person could not be imprisoned."

"Or dead?"

"Or dead," she agreed.

"Then fascinating as all this is," I said, turning away from the altar, "it doesn't really help me to find my father."

I moved back to her, across what must have been a representation of Amber, stylized as the pattern on a Caucasian rug, there in the dark and light tile, the Chaotic one far off to my right.

"You would have to ask the person responsible for his blade's being there," she said, rising.

"I already asked the person I believed responsible. The response was not satisfactory."

I took her arm to steer her back toward the way to the tree, and she was suddenly standing very close.

"I would like to serve our next king any way I might," she said. "Though I may not normally speak for our House, I am certain Hendrake would agree to help you bring pressure upon the person responsible."

"Thanks," I said as we embraced. Her scales were cool. Her fangs would have shredded my human ear, but it was only a nibble in demonform. "I will talk to you again if I need help along those lines."

"Talk to me again, anyway."

It was good to hold and be held for a time, and that is what we did, till I saw a shadow move in the vicinity of the way.

"Masster Merlin."

"Glait!"

"Yess. I ssaw you come thiss way. Manform, demonform, grown or ssmall, I know you."

"Merlin, what is it?" Gilva asked.

"An old friend," I told her. "Glait, meet Gilva. And vice versa."

"Pleassed. I came to warn you that ssomeone approachess."

"Who?"

"Princess Dara."

"Oh, dear!" Gilva remarked.

"You suspect where we are," I said to her. "Keep it to yourself."

"I value my head, Lord. What do we do now?"

"Glait, to me," I said, kneeling and extending an arm.

She flowed up it and made herself comfortable. I rose and caught hold of Gilva with the other. I sent my will into the spikard.

Then I hesitated.

I didn't know where the hell we were—really, physically, in terms of geography. A way can deliver you next door, or somewhere thousands of miles distant from its point of origin, or somewhere off in Shadow. It would take a while to have the spikard figure where we were and then work out the way back, if we were going to bypass the way. Too long, I was certain.

I could simply use it to render us invisible. But I feared my mother's sorcerous sensitivity would be sufficient to detect our presence at levels beyond the visual.

I faced the nearest wall and extended my senses past it on a line of the spikard's force. We were not underwater or drifting on a sea of lava or quicksand. We seemed to be in a wooded spot.

So I walked toward the wall and passed us through it when we got there.

Several paces later, in the midst of a shaded glade, I looked back and beheld a grassy hillside, with no singing coming from beneath it. We stood under a blue sky, orange sun nearing its top. There were bird and insect sounds about us.

"Marrow!" Glait exclaimed, unwound herself from my arm and vanished into the grasses.

"Don't stay away long!" I hissed, trying to keep my voice low; and I led Gilva away from the hill.

"Merlin," she said, "I'm frightened at what I've learned."

"I won't tell anyone if you won't," I said. "If you'd like, I can even remove these memories before I send you back to the funeral."

"No, let me keep them. I can even wish there were more."

"I'll figure our location and get you back before you're missed."

"I'll wait with you while your friend hunts."

I half expected her to continue, ". . . in case I never see you again," what with the near skateboarding of Tmer and Tubble off this ever-mortal helix. But no, she was a demure and well-bred battle-maid—with over thirty notches on the haft of her broadsword, I later learned—and she was above stating the distasteful obvious in the presence of her possible future liege.

When Glait returned after an appropriate time, I said,

"Thanks, Gilva. I'm going to send you back to the funeral now. If anyone saw us together and wants to know where I am, tell them I said I was going into hiding."

"If you do need a place to hide . . ."

"Talk to you sometime later perhaps," I said, and I sent her back to the temple at the edge of everything.

"Good vermin," Glait remarked, as I commenced my shift humanward. (It's always easier that way for me than the demon-shift.)

"I'd like to send you back to Sawall's sculpture garden," I said.

"Why there, Masster Merlin?"

"To wait for a time, to see whether you behold a sentient circle of light. And if you do, to address it as Ghostwheel and tell it to come to me."

"Where shall I tell it to sseek you?"

"That I do not know, but it is good at that sort of thing."

"Then ssend me. And if you are not eaten by ssomething bigger, come tell me your sstory one night."

"I shall."

It was the work of but a moment to hang the serpent back in her tree. I've never been sure when she's joking, reptilian humor being more than a little strange.

I summoned fresh garments and garbed myself in gray and purple. Fetched me blades long and short then, also.

I wondered what my mother might have been up to in her chapel, but decided against trying to spy on her. I raised the spikard and regarded it for a moment, then lowered it. It seemed possibly counterproductive to transport myself to Kashfa when I was uncertain how much time had passed and whether Luke was actually still there. I took out my Trumps, which I had had along in my mourning garb, uncased them.

I located Luke's, focused upon it. Before too long it went cold and I felt Luke's presence.

"Yes?" he said. "That you, Merle?" at about the same time as his image swam and altered, causing me to see him mounted and riding through a part-blasted, part-normal countryside.

"Yeah," I answered. "I gather you're no longer in Kashfa."

"Right," he said. "Where're you?"

"Somewhere in Shadow. How's about yourself?"

"Damned if I know for sure," he responded. "We've been following this black path for days—and I can only say 'somewhere in Shadow,' too."

"Oh, you located it?"

"Nayda did. I didn't see anything, but she just led me on. Eventually, the trail got clear to me. Hell of a tracker, that gal."

"She's with you now?"

"That's right. She says we're gaining on them, too."

"Better bring me through then."

"Come ahead."

He extended a hand. I reached forward, clasped it, took a step, released his hand, began walking beside him, a pack horse to the rear.

"Hi, Nayda!" I called, to where she rode at his other side. A grim figure was mounted upon a black horse ahead and to her right.

She smiled.

"Merlin," she said. "Hello."

"How about Merle?" I said.

"If you wish."

The figure on the dark horse turned and regarded me. I halted a death strike that ran from reflex to the spikard so fast that it scared me. The air between us was smudged and filled with a screeching note, as of a car grabbing pavement to avert collision.

He was a big, blond-haired son of a bitch, and he had on a yellow shirt and black trousers, black boots, lots of cutlery. The medallion of the Lion rending the Unicorn bounced upon his broad chest. Every time I'd seen or heard of the man, he'd been about something nasty, damn near killing Luke on one occasion. He was a mercenary, a Robin Hood figure out of Eregnor, and a sworn enemy of Amber—illegitimate son of her late liege Oberon. I believed there was a price on his head within the Golden Circle. On the other hand, he and Luke had been buddies for years, and Luke swore he wasn't all that bad. He was my uncle Dalt, and I'd a feeling that if he moved too quickly the flexing of his muscles would shred his shirt.

". . . And you remember my military adviser, Dalt," Luke said.

"I remember," I stated.

Dalt stared at the black lines in the air that faded, smokelike, between us. He actually smiled then, a little.

"Merlin," he said, "son of Amber, Prince of Chaos, the man who dug my grave."

"What's this?" Luke asked.

"A little conversational gambit," I replied. "You've a good memory, Dalt—for faces."

He chuckled.

"Hard to forget something like a grave opening itself," he said. "But I've no quarrel with you, Merlin."

"Nor I you—now," I said.

He grunted then and I grunted back and considered us introduced. I turned back toward Luke.

"Is the path itself giving you any trouble?" I asked.

"No," he replied. "It's nothing at all like those stories I'd heard about the Black Road. It looks a little bleak at times, but nothing's really threatened us." He glanced downward and chuckled. "Of course it's only a few yards wide," he added, "and this is the broadest it's been, so far."

"Still," I said, opening my senses and studying its emanations with my Logrus sight, "I'd think something might have threatened."

"I guess we've been lucky," he said.

Again, Nayda laughed, and I felt foolish. The presence of a *ty'iga* would count as surely as my own in offsetting the dire effects of a Chaos roadway in the realm of Order.

"Guess you had a little luck coming," I said.

"You're going to need a horse, Merle," he said then.

"I suppose you're right," I agreed.

I was afraid to use Logrus magic and call attention to my location. Still, I had already learned that the spikard could be used in a similar fashion, and I entered it with my will, extended, extended, made contact, summoned. . . .

"It'll be along any minute," I said. "Did you say something about our gaining on them?"

"That's what Nayda tells me," he explained. "She has an amazing rapport with her sister—not to mention a high sensitivity to this pathway itself.

"Knows a lot about demons, too," he added.

"Oh, are we likely to encounter any?" I asked her.

"It was demonformed warriors from the Courts who abducted Coral," she said. "They seem headed toward a tower up ahead."

"How far ahead?" I asked.

"Hard to say, since we're cutting through Shadow," she answered.

The trail, which consisted of blackened grasses and which produced the same effect on any tree or shrub that so much as overhung it, wound its way through a hilly area now; and as I stepped onto and off of it I noted that it seemed brighter and warmer each time I departed. It had reached this point now after having been virtually undetectable in the vicinity of Kashfa—an index of how far we were into the realm of the Logrus.

A little past the next bending of the trail, I heard a whinny from off to the right.

"Excuse me," I said. "Delivery time," and I departed the trail and entered a grove of oval-leafed trees.

Snorting and stamping sounds reached me from ahead, and I followed them down shaded ways.

"Wait up!" Luke called. "We shouldn't separate."

But the wood was fairly dense, not at all easy going for someone on horseback, so I hollered back, "Don't worry!" and plunged ahead.

. . . And that, of course, was why he was there.

Fully saddled and bridled, his reins tangled in the dense foliage, he was cursing in horse-talk, shaking his head from side to side, pawing at the earth. I halted, stared.

I may have given the impression that I would rather pull on a pair of Adidas and jog through Shadow than plunge through on the back of a beast driven half-mad by the changes going on about it. Or ride a bicycle. Or hop through on a pogo stick.

Nor would this impression be incorrect. It is not that I don't know how to drive the things. It is just that I'd never been particularly fond of them. Admitted, I never had the use of one of those wonder horses, such as Julian's Morgenstern, Dad's Star, or Benedict's Glemdenning, which stood to mortal horses in terms of life span, strength, and endurance as did Amberites to the inhabitants of most shadows.

I looked all about, but could detect no injured rider. . . .

"Merlin!" I heard Luke call, but my attention was nearer at hand. I advanced slowly, not wanting to upset him further. "Are you all right?"

I had simply put in an order for a horse. Any old hay burner would have served, for purposes of keeping up with my companions.

I found myself looking at an absolutely lovely animal—black and orange-striped like a tiger. In this, he resembled Glemdenning with his red and black striping. In that I didn't know where Benedict's mount came from either, I was glad to let it be the place of magic.

I advanced slowly.

"Merle! Anything wrong?"

I didn't want to shout back a reply and frighten the poor beast. I placed my hand gently upon his neck.

"It's okay," I said. "I like you. I'll undo it and we'll be friends, all right?"

I took my time untangling the reins, using my other hand to massage his neck and shoulders. When he was free he did not pull away, but seemed to study me.

"Come on," I said, taking up the reins, "this way."

I led him back the way I had come, talking the while. I realized by the time we emerged that I actually liked him. I met Luke about then, a blade in his hand.

"My God!" he said. "No wonder it took you so long! You stopped to paint it!"

"You like, huh?"

"You ever want to get rid of that one, I'll make you a good offer."

"I don't think I'll be getting rid of him," I said.

"What's his name?"

"Tiger," I said without premeditation, and then I mounted.

We headed back to the trail, where even Dalt eyed my mount with something like pleasure. Nayda reached out and stroked the black and orange mane.

"Now we may be able to make it in time," she said, "if we hurry."

I mounted, and I guided Tiger over onto the trail. I anticipated all manner of reactions to the trail, as I recalled from my father's story the possibly intimidating effects of the thing upon animals. It didn't seem to bother him, though, and I released the breath I hadn't realized I was holding.

"In time for what?" I asked as we found a formation—Luke in the lead, Dalt behind him and to the right, Nayda to the left of the trail, rear, me to her right and somewhat back.

"I cannot tell for certain," she said, "because she is still sedated. However, I do know that she is no longer being moved; and I have the impression that her abductors have taken refuge in the tower, where the trail is much wider."

"Hm," I said. "You wouldn't have happened to notice the rate of change in width per unit of distance traveled on this trail, would you?"

"I was in liberal arts," she said, smiling. "Remember?"

She turned suddenly then, glancing in Luke's direction. He

was still an entire horse's length ahead, eyes front—though he had looked back moments before.

"Damn you!" she said softly. "Being with you both this way gets me to thinking about school. Then I start talking that way—"

"In English," I said.

"Did I say that in English?"

"Yes."

"Shit! Help me if you catch me at it, will you?"

"Of course," I said. "It seems to show you'd enjoyed it somewhat, despite its being a job Dara'd laid on you. And you're probably the only *ty'iga* with a degree from Berkeley."

"Yes, I enjoyed it—confused as I was over which of you was which. Those were the happiest days in my life, with you and Luke, back in school. For years I tried to learn your mothers' names so I'd know who I was supposed to be protecting. You were both so cagey, though."

"It's in the genes, I guess," I observed. "I enjoyed your company as Vinta Bayle—appreciated your protection as others, too."

"I suffered," she said, "when Luke began his yearly attempts on your life. If he were the son of Dara I was supposed to protect, it shouldn't have mattered. But it did. I was already very fond of both of you. All I could tell was that you were both of the blood of Amber. I didn't want either of you harmed. The hardest thing was when you went away, and I was sure Luke had lured you into the mountains of New Mexico to kill you. By then, I suspected very strongly that you were the one, but I was not certain. I was in love with Luke, I had taken over the body of Dan Martinez, and I was carrying a pistol. I followed you everywhere I could, knowing that if he tried to harm you the *geas* I was under would force me to shoot the man I loved."

"You shot first, though. We were just standing talking, by the side of the road. He shot back in self-defense."

"I know. But everything seemed to indicate that you were in peril. He'd taken you to a perfect spot for an execution, at an ideal time—"

"No," I said. "Your shot went wide, and you left yourself open for what followed."

"I don't understand what you're saying."

"You solved the problem of possibly having to shoot Luke by setting up a situation where he shot you."

"I couldn't do that, under a *geas*."

"Maybe not consciously," I said. "So something stronger than the *geas* found a way."

"You really believe that?"

"Yes, and it's all right for you to admit it now. You're released foom the *geas*. My mother told me. You told me—I think."

She nodded. "I don't know exactly when it came undone, or how," she said. "But it's gone—though I'd still try to protect you if something threatened. It's good that you and Luke are really friends, and—"

"So why the secret?" I interrupted. "Why not just tell him you were Gail? Surprise the hell out of him—pleasantly."

"You don't understand," she said. "He broke up with me, remember? Now I've another chance. It's like it was, all over again. He—likes me a lot. I'm afraid to say, 'I'm really the girl you once broke up with.' It might get him to thinking of all the reasons why, and make him decide he was right the first time."

"That's silly," I said. "I don't know what reasons he gave. He never told me about it. Just said there'd been an argument. But I'm sure they were specious. I know he liked you. I'm sure he really broke up with you because he was a son of Amber about to come home on some very nasty business, and there was no room for what he thought was a normal shadow girl in the picture. You'd played your part too well."

"Is that why you broke up with Julia?" she asked.

"No," I said.

"Sorry."

I noticed the black trail had widened about a foot since we'd begun talking. I was in the market for a mathematical problem just then.

10

And so we rode—six paces along a city street, amid the blare of horns, our black way edged by skid marks; a quarter mile along a black sand beach, beside a soft green sea, stirring palms to our left; across a tarnished snowfield; beneath a bridge of stone, our way a dead and blackened streambed; then to prairie; back to wooded way—and Tiger never flinched, even when Dalt put a booted foot through a windshield and broke off an antenna.

The way continued to widen, to perhaps twice its width when I had first come upon it. Stark trees were more common within it now, standing like photographic negatives of their bright mates but a few feet off the trail. While the leaves and branches of these latter were regularly stirred, we felt no wind at all. The sounds—of our voices, of our mounts' hooves—came somehow muted now, also. Our entire course had a constant, wavery twilight atmosphere to it, no matter that a few paces away—which brief excursion we essayed many times—it might be high noon or midnight. Dead-looking birds were perched within the blackened trees, though they seemed on occasion to move, and the raspy, croaking sounds that sometimes came to us may well have been theirs.

At one time, a fire raged to our right; at another, we seemed to be passing near the foot of a glacier on the left. Our trail continued to widen—nothing like the great Black Road Corwin had described to me from the days of the war, but big enough now for us all to ride abreast.

"Luke," I said, after a time.

"Yeah?" he answered, from my left. Nayda rode to my right now, and Dalt to her right. "What's up?"

"I don't want to be king."

"Me neither," he said. "How hard they pushing you?"

"I'm afraid they're going to grab me and crown me if I go back. Everybody in my way died suddenly. They really plan to stick me on the throne, to marry me to Coral—"

"Uh-huh," he said, "and I've two questions about it. First, will it work?"

"The Logrus seems to think it will, at least for a time—which is all politics is about, anyhow."

"Second," he said, "if you feel about the place the way I feel about Kashfa, you're not going to let it go to hell if you can help it—even if it means some personal misery. You don't want to take the throne, though, so you must have worked out some alternative remedy. What is it?"

I nodded as the trail turned sharply to the left and headed up-hill. Something small and dark scuttled across our path.

"I've a notion—not even a full idea," I said, "which I want to discuss with my father."

"Tall order," he said. "You know for sure that he's even alive?"

"I talked to him not all that long ago—very briefly. He's a prisoner, somewhere. All I know for sure is that it's somewhere in the vicinity of the Courts—because I can reach him by Trump from there, but nowhere else."

"Tell me about this communication," he said.

And so I did, black bird and all.

"Sounds like busting him out's going to be tricky," he said. "And you think your mom's behind it?"

"Yep."

"I thought I was the only one with these maternal problems. But it figures, seeing as yours trained mine."

"How come we turned out so normal?" I said.

He just stared at me for several seconds. Then he started to laugh.

"Well, I *feel* normal," I said.

"Of course," he said quickly then, "and that's what counts. Tell me, if it came to an out-and-out crossing of powers, do you think you could beat Dara?"

"Hard to say," I told him. "I'm stronger now than I ever was before, because of the spikard. But I'm beginning to believe she's very good."

"What the hell's a spikard?"

So I told him that story, too.

"That's why you were so flashy back in the church when you were fighting with Jurt?" he said.

"That's right."

"Let's see it."

I tried to pull it off, but it wouldn't pass the knuckle. So I simply extended my hand. Luke reached for it. His fingers halted a couple of inches above it.

"It's holding me off, Merle. Protective little devil."

"Hell," I said, "I'm not a shapeshifter for nothing." I took hold of it then, slimmed my finger suddenly, and slid it off. "Here."

He held it in the palm of his left hand as we bounced along, regarding it through narrowed eyes. Suddenly, I felt dizzy. Withdrawal symptoms from the thing? I forced myself upright, reversed my breathing, refused to let it show.

"Heavy," Luke said at last. "I can feel the power there. Other things, too. It won't let me in, though."

I reached for it and he drew his hand away.

"I can feel it in the air all around us," he said. "Merle, this thing lays a spell on anybody who wears it."

I shrugged.

"Yes," I said. "A benign one, though. It's done nothing to harm me, and it's helped me a number of times."

"But can you trust anything that came to you in such an odd way—almost by trickery, caused you to abandon Frakir when she tried to warn you about it, and for all you knew has been influencing your behavior ever since you put it on?"

"I admit to a kind of disorientation at first," I said, "but I think that was just in the way of accommodation to the levels of voltage it draws. I've been back to normal for some time now."

"How can you tell for sure? Maybe it's brainwashed you."

"Do I seem brainwashed to you?"

"No. I was just trying to say that I wouldn't completely trust anything with such questionable credentials."

"Well taken," I agreed, holding forth my hand. "But so far the benefits have outweighed any hypothetical dangers. Consider me warned, and I'll take my chances."

He handed it back.

"If I think it's making you act weird I'm going to hit you over the head and pull it off, though."

"Fair enough," I said, slipping it back on. Immediately, I felt a rush of energy throughout my system as the lines of control were reestablished.

"If you're not sure you can force the information out of your mother," he said, "how do you propose finding Corwin and freeing him?"

"Several things suggest themselves," I said. "The simplest way may be a foot in the door technique. That is, I'd open all of the channels on the spikard and go for another Trump contact. As soon as there's any sort of opening I'd just push ahead with full force, jamming any spells that try to stop me and burning them out."

"Sounds as if it could be dangerous."

"I can't think of any way to go about this that wouldn't be."

"Then why haven't you tried it?"

"It only occurred to me recently, and I haven't had the time since then."

"However you go about it, you're going to need some help," he said. "So count me in."

"Thanks, Luke. I—"

"Now, about the king business," he said. "What happens if you simply refuse to take the throne? Who's next in line?"

"It's a bit tangled when you come to Sawall," I said. "By rights, Mandor should be first in line of succession from our House. He'd removed himself from the line years ago, though."

"Why?"

"I believe he claimed he was unfit to rule."

"No offense, Merle. But he seems like the only one of you who *is* fit for the job."

"Oh, without a doubt," I responded. "Most of the Houses have someone like him, though. There's usually a nominal head and a de facto one, someone for show and someone for scheming. Mandor likes the climate behind the scenes."

"Sounds as if your House has two," he said.

"I'm not really clear on it," I said. "I don't know Dara's status right now in her father's House—Helgram—or her mother's—Hendrake. But it might be worth a power struggle within Sawall if that's where the next king is coming from. Still, the more I learn of Mandor the more intimidating such a struggle would seem. I'd guess they're cooperating."

"I take it you're next in line, and then Jurt?"

"Actually, our brother Despil is next after me. Jurt said that

Despil would probably step aside for him, but I think that was wishful thinking. I'm not at all sure he would. Anyhow, Jurt says now that he isn't interested."

"Ha! I think he's just taking a different approach. You whipped him too many times, and he's trying to get in good with you. Hope that spikard can protect your back."

"I don't know," I said. "I'd like to believe him. He spent a lot of time making sure that it wouldn't be easy, though."

"Supposing you all decline. Who's next?"

"I'm not certain," I said, "but I think it would go to Hendrake then."

"Damn," Luke said. "It's as twisted a place as Amber, isn't it?"

"Neither one's twisted, exactly. Just a little complicated, till you've learned the ropes."

"What say I just listen, and you fill me in on everything that you haven't so far?"

"Good idea."

So I talked for a long while, breaking to summon food and water. We halted twice during that time, causing me to realize just how tired I had become. And briefing Luke reminded me yet again that I should be telling all of this to Random. But if I got in touch and tried it I was certain he would order me back to Amber. And I couldn't disobey a direct order from the king, even if I was almost his opposite number.

"We're getting nearer," Nayda announced somewhat later, and I noted that our roadway had widened even more, almost to the point she'd described. I drew a jolt of energy into my system, digested it, and kept going.

Shortly thereafter, she remarked, "Much nearer."

"Like just around the corner?" Luke asked.

"Could be," she answered. "I can't be more precise, the condition she's in."

But a little later, we heard distant shouts.

Luke drew rein.

"Something about a tower," he said.

She nodded.

"Were they heading for it, holing up in it, or defending themselves there?"

"All of the above," she said. "I understand now. Her captors were pursued, headed for a place of refuge, reached it, are there now."

"How come you're suddenly that precise?"

She gave me a quick look that I took as a request for an explanation other than *ty'iga* powers.

"I was using the spikard," I offered, "trying to see whether I could give her a clearer vision."

"Good," Luke said. "Can you boost it even more, so we can see what we're up against?"

"I can try," I said, narrowing my eyes at her in inquiry. She responded with a very slight nod.

I wasn't certain how to go about it, so I just fed her energy in the way of that jolt I'd given myself a while back.

"Yes," she said after a few moments, "Coral and her captors—six of them, I believe—have taken refuge in a tower near here. They are under attack."

"How large is the party of attackers?" Luke asked.

"Small," she said. "Quite small. I can't give you a number."

"Let's go and see," Luke said, and he led the way, Dalt behind him.

"Three or four," Nayda whispered to me, "but they're Pattern ghosts. That's probably all it can maintain this far from home, on a Black Road."

"Ouch," I said. "This makes it tricky."

"How so?"

"It means I have relatives on both sides."

"It also looks as if Amber's ghosts and the Court's demons are only agents, and that it's really a confrontation between the Logrus and the Pattern."

"Damn! Of course!" I said. "It could easily escalate into another of those. I'm going to have to warn Luke what we're riding into."

"You can't! Not without telling him what I am!"

"I'll tell him I learned it myself—that I had a sudden insight into a new spell."

"But what then? Which side are you on? What do we do?"

"Neither," I said. "We're on our own, and against both of them."

"You're crazy! There's no place you can hide, Merle! The Powers divide the universe between them!"

"Luke!" I cried. "I just probed ahead, learned the attackers are Pattern ghosts!"

"You don't say?" he called back. "Think we should be taking

their side? It's probably better for the Pattern to take her back than for the Courts to get her, wouldn't you think?"

"She shouldn't be used that way," I said. "Let's take her away from both of them."

"I agree with your feelings," he stated. "But what if we succeed? I don't really care to be struck by a meteor or transported to the bottom of the nearest ocean."

"As near as I can tell, the spikard doesn't draw its power from the Pattern or the Logrus. Its sources are scattered through Shadow."

"So? I'm sure it's not a match for either one, let alone both."

"No, but I can use it to start an evasion course. They'll be getting in each other's way if they decide to pursue us."

"But eventually they'd find us, wouldn't they?"

"Maybe, maybe not," I said. "I have some ideas, but we're running out of time."

"Dalt, did you hear all that?" Luke asked.

"I did," Dalt replied.

"If you want out, now's your chance."

"And miss an opportunity to twist the Unicorn's tail?" he said. "Keep riding!"

We did, and the shouts grew louder as we raced ahead. There was a certain timeless feeling to it, though—with the muffled sounds and the dimness—as if we had always been riding here and always would be. . . .

Then we rounded a bend and I saw the top of the tower in the distance, heard more shouts. We slowed as we came to the next turn, advancing more cautiously, working our way through a small stand of black saplings.

Finally, we halted, dismounted, worked our way forward on foot. We pushed aside the final screening branches and looked down a slight slope to a blackened, sandy plain beside a three-story gray tower with slit windows and a narrow entranceway. It took a while to sort out the tableau at its base.

There were two demonformed individuals standing to either side of the tower's entrance. They were armed and their attention seemed focused upon the contest taking place on the sands before them. Familiar figures stood at the far end of this impromptu arena and at either side: Benedict stroked his chin, expressionless; Eric hunkered and smiled; Caine juggled, flipped, palmed, and passed a dagger, reflexively, through some private routine, an expression of amused fascination on his face. From the tower's top, I suddenly noted, two horned demons leaned forward, their gazes as intent as those of Amber's Pattern ghosts.

At the circle's center Gérard faced a demonformed son of Hendrake, of his own height and greater girth. It looked to be Chinaway himself, who was said to have a collection of over two hundred skulls of those he'd dispatched. I preferred Gérard's collection of a thousand or so mugs, steins, and drinking horns, but your ghost will walk, you lover of trees, in an English lane, if you know what I mean.

Both were stripped to the waist, and from the scuffed-up condition of the sands about them I guessed they had been at it for some time. Chinaway tried to trip Gérard just then, who caught his arm and head as he stepped behind him, and sent him cartwheeling away. The demon lord came up on his feet, however, and immediately advanced once again, arms extended, hands weaving a sinuous pattern before him. Gérard simply waited in a ready position. Chinaway stabbed taloned fingers toward Gérard's eyes and hooked a blow against his rib cage. Gérard caught hold of his shoulder, however, as Chinaway dropped and caught him about the thigh.

"Let's wait," Dalt said softly. "I want to watch."

Luke and I both nodded as Gérard's locked Chinaway's head and Chinaway wrapped his other arm about Gérard's waist. Then they simply stood there, muscles bulging beneath two hides, one pale and smooth, the other red and scaly. Their lungs worked like bellows.

"I assume the thing's been dragging out," Luke whispered, "and they decided to settle it champion against champion."

"Looks that way," I said.

"Coral must be inside then, wouldn't you think?"

"Wait a minute."

I ran a quick probe into the structure, locating two people within. I nodded then.

"Her and a single guard, I'd say."

Gérard and Chinaway still stood like statues.

"Now might be the best time to grab Coral," Luke said, "while everybody's watching the fight."

"You're probably right," I told him. "Let me see whether I can make myself invisible. That might simplify matters."

"Okay," he said about a quarter minute later. "Whatever you did just then worked. You're gone."

"Indeed I am," I said. "Back in a bit."

"How will you get her out?"

"I'll decide after I've reached her. Just be ready."

I moved slowly, careful not to scuff the sand. I skirted the circle, passing behind Caine. I approached the door to the tower, soundless, checking about me constantly. Gérard and Chinaway still stood exactly as they had been, locked, and applying enormous pressures to each other.

I passed between the guards, entering the dim interior of the tower. It consisted of a single round room with a bare earth floor, stone pedestals beneath each slit window. A ladder led up to the second floor through a hole in the ceiling. Coral lay upon a blanket to my left; the individual who was ostensibly guarding her stood upon a pedestal, watching the fight through the nearest window.

I moved nearer, knelt, caught up her left wrist and felt her pulse. It was strong and steady. I decided against trying to awaken her, though. Instead, I wrapped the blanket around her, raised her in my arms, and stood.

I was about to try extending the invisibility spell to include her when the watcher at the window turned. I must have made some noise in moving her.

For a moment, the guard stared at the sight of his prisoner drifting below him. Then he opened his mouth, as if to give alarm—leaving me with small choice but to shock his nervous system into insensibility with a charge from my ring.

Unfortunately, there was a rattle of arms as he fell from his pedestal to the floor. Almost immediately, I heard a cry from overhead, followed by sounds of rapid movement.

Turning, I hurried to the door. I had to slow and turn because of its narrowness. I wasn't certain what the guards outside would think when a comatose Coral drifted by, but I didn't want to be trapped inside. Peering ahead, I saw that Gérard and Chinaway seemed in the same position as before. Seconds later, however, as I turned my body and took my first sidling step, there came a sudden, sharp twisting movement from Gérard, followed immediately by a sound like that of a snapping stick.

Gérard let his arms fall and stood erect. The body of Chinaway hit the ground at his side, neck at an unnatural angle. Eric and Caine applauded. The two guards beside the door moved forward. Behind me, within, the ladder rattled at the other side of the room. I heard a cry from that direction.

Two more steps and I turned, headed left. The outside guards were rushing toward their fallen champion. A half-dozen paces, and there were more cries at my back, as my pursuers exited the tower; and there were human cries as well, from the killing circle.

I knew that I couldn't outrun any of them, carrying my burden; and all that motor activity interfered with my concentration to the point where I was incapable of performing magical operations.

So I dropped to my knees, lowering Coral to the ground before me, turned without even rising, and extended my left fist, plunging my mind deep within the ring, calling for extreme measures to halt the pair of Hendrake commandos who were only a few paces away now, edged weapons ready to pierce and to slash.

. . . And then they were caught up in the midst of flames. I think they screamed, but there was a lot of noise just then. Two paces more, perhaps, and they fell, blackened and twitching, before me. My hand was shaking, from its proximity to the powers that caused this; and I hadn't time, even, to think or to feel as I swung toward the sandy place of the recent contest and whatever might be coming at me from that direction.

One of the two guards who had rushed forward lay smoldering on the ground at Eric's feet. Another—who had apparently attacked Caine—clutched at the knife in his gullet, fires spreading outward, downward, upward, from his throat, as he sank slowly, then toppled to the rear.

Immediately, Caine, Eric, and Benedict turned to stare at me. Gérard, having just drawn on a blue shirt, was buckling his sword-belt in place. He turned, too, just as Caine said, "And who, sir, are you?"

"Merlin," I replied, "son of Corwin."

Caine actually looked startled.

"Does Corwin have a son?" he asked the others.

Eric shrugged and Gérard said, "I don't know." But Benedict studied me.

"There is a resemblance," he said.

"True," Caine agreed. "All right, boy. Even if you are Corwin's son, that woman you're making off with belongs to us. We just won her fair and square off these well-done Chaosites."

With that, he began walking toward me. A moment later, Eric joined him. Then Gérard fell into step behind them. I didn't want to harm them, even if they were only ghosts, so I gestured and a line was drawn in the sand before them. Immediately, it caught fire.

They halted.

Suddenly, a huge figure appeared at my left. It was Dalt, a naked blade in his hand. A moment later, Luke was there. Then Nayda. The four of us faced the four of them, across the fire.

"She's ours now," Dalt said, and he took a single step forward.

"You are mistaken," came the reply, and Eric crossed the line, drawing his weapon.

Dalt was a couple of inches taller than Eric, and he had a longer reach. He moved forward immediately. I expected some kind of cut from that big blade he carried, but he went in for a point-attack. Eric, using a lighter weapon, sidestepped and came in under his arm. Dalt dropped the point of his blade, moved to his left, and parried it. The two weapons were suited for very different styles—Eric's being at the heaviest end of the rapier class, Dalt's at the lighter end of broadsword. Dalt's could be a single-handed weapon for a big-enough, strong-enough guy. I'd have had to use it two-handed myself. Dalt tried an upward cut just then, of the sort a Japanese swordsman would refer to as *kiriage*. Eric simply stepped back and tried for a wrist cut as it passed him. Dalt suddenly moved his left hand to the haft and executed a blinding two-handed cut of the sort known as *naname giri*. Eric continued to circle, trying for the wrist yet again.

Suddenly, Dalt opened his right hand and let it drift back, as his right foot performed a huge semicircular step to his rear and his left arm moved forward, leaving him in a left-handed European *en garde* position, from which that massive arm and matching blade immediately extended, performing an inside beat upon Eric's blade followed by a lunge. Eric parried as his right foot crossed behind his left and he sprang backward. Even so, I saw a spark as his guard was creased. He feinted in *sixte,* however, dropped his point beneath the parry that followed, extended his arm in *quatre,* raised himself and his blade into something resembling a stop-thrust targeting the left shoulder as the parry crossed, turned his wrist, and slashed Dalt across the left forearm.

Caine applauded, but Dalt simply brought his hands together and separated them again, executing a little hop-step as he did so, leaving him in a right *en garde* position. Eric drew circles in the air with the point of his weapon and smiled.

"Cute little dance routine you have there," he said.

Then Eric lunged, was parried, retreated, sidestepped, threw a front kick at Dalt's kneecap, missed, then moved with perfect timing as Dalt attempted a head cut. Switching to the Japanese himself, he spun in to the larger man's right, a maneuver I'd seen in a *kumatchi* exercise, his own blade rising and falling as Dalt's cut swept past. Dalt's right forearm went suddenly wet, a thing I did not really notice until after Eric had rotated his weapon, blade pointing outward and upward, and, the guard covering his knuckles, had driven his fist against the right side of Dalt's jaw. He kicked him then behind the knee and struck him with his left shoulder. Dalt stumbled and fell. Eric immediately kicked him, kidney, elbow, thigh—the latter only because he missed the knee—set his boot upon Dalt's weapon and swung his own about to bring its point in line with the man's heart.

I had been hoping all along, I suddenly realized, that Dalt would kick Eric's ass—not just because he was on my side and Eric wasn't, but because of the rough time Eric had given my dad. On the other hand, I doubted there were too many people of such ass-kicking prowess about. Unfortunately, two of them stood on the other side of the line I had drawn. Gérard could have out-wrestled him. Benedict, Master of Arms at Amber, could have beaten him with any weapon. I just didn't see us as having much of a chance against them all, with Caine thrown in for good measure—not even with a *ty'iga* on our side. And if I were suddenly to tell Eric that Dalt was his half brother, it wouldn't slow his thrust by an instant, even if he believed me.

So I made the only decision I could make. They were, after all, only Pattern ghosts. The real Benedict and Gérard were somewhere else at this moment and would in no way be harmed by anything I did to their doubles here. Eric and Caine were, of course, long dead, Caine being the fratricidal hero of the Pattern-fall war and subject of a recent statue on the Grand Concourse, on the occasion of Luke's assassinating him for killing his father. And Eric, of course, had found a hero's death on the slopes of Kolvir, saving him, I suppose, from dying at the hands of my father. The bloody history of my family swam through my head as I raised the spikard to add a footnote to it, calling again for the wave of incineration that had taken out two of my Hendrake kin.

My arm felt as if someone had struck it with a baseball bat. A wisp of smoke rose from the spikard. For a moment, my four upright uncles stood unmoving. And my fifth remained supine.

Then, slowly, Eric raised his weapon. And he continued to raise it, as Benedict, Caine, and Gérard drew theirs. He straightened as he held it before his face. The others did the same. It looked strangely like a salute; and Eric's eyes met mine.

"I know you," he said.

Then they all completed the gesture, and faded, faded, turned to smoke, and blew away.

Dalt bled, my arm ached, and I figured out what was going on just moments before Luke gasped and said, "Over there."

My line of fire had gone out some time ago, but beyond the mark it had left, where my faded kinsmen had just been standing, the air began to shimmer.

"That will be the Pattern," I said to Luke, "come calling."

A moment later the Sign of the Pattern hovered before us.

"Merlin," it said, "you certainly move around a lot."

"My life has become very busy of late," I said.

"You took my advice and left the Courts."

"Yes, that seemed prudent."

"But I do not understand your purposes here."

"What's to understand?"

"You took the lady Coral away from the agents of the Logrus."

"That's right."

"But then you attempted to keep her from my agents as well."

"That, too, is correct."

"You must realize by now that she bears something that contributes to our balance of power."

"Yes."

"So one of us must have her. Yet you would deny us both."

"Yes."

"Why?"

"It's her whom I care about. She has rights and feelings. You're treating her like a game piece."

"True. I recognize her personhood, but unfortunately she is become both."

"Then I would deny her to both of you. Nothing would be changed, in that neither of you has her now, anyway. But I would take her out of the game."

"Merlin, you are a more important piece than she is, but you are still only a piece and you may not dictate to me. Do you understand?"

"I understand my value to you," I said.

"I think not," it responded.

I was wondering just then how strong it really was in this place. It seemed obvious that in terms of energy expenditure, it had been necessary for it to release its four ghosts to be able to manifest itself here. Dared I oppose it with every channel on the spikard opened? I had never tried accessing every Shadow source it controlled simultaneously. If I did this, and if I were to move very quickly, could I get us all out of here before the Pattern reacted? If I couldn't, could I punch through whatever it raised up to stop us? And if I succeeded—either way—to what place should we flee?

Finally, how might this affect the Pattern's attitude toward me?

(. . . if you are not eaten by something bigger, come tell me your story one night.)

What the hell, I decided. It is a good day to be listed à la carte.

I opened all the channels.

It felt as if I had been jogging along at a good clip and a brick wall had suddenly appeared six inches before me.

I felt the smash and I went away.

I lay upon a smooth, cool stone surface. There was a terrible rushing of energies in my mind and body. I reached into their source and took control of them, dampening them to something that didn't threaten to take the top of my head off. Then I opened one eye, slightly.

The sky was very blue. I saw a pair of boots, standing a few feet off, faced away from me. I recognized them as Nayda's, and turning my head slightly, I saw that she wore them. I also saw then that Dalt lay sprawled several yards off to my left.

Nayda was breathing heavily, and my Logrus vision showed a pale red light about her vibrating hands, menacing.

Propping myself upon my left elbow and peering about her, I saw that she stood between me and the Sign of the Pattern that hovered in the air perhaps ten feet away.

When it spoke again it was the first time I'd heard it express anything like amusement: "You would protect him, against me?"

"Yes," she replied.

"Why?"

"I did it for so long that it would be a shame to fail him when he really needs it."

"Creature of the Pit, do you know where you stand?" it asked.

"No," she said.

I looked beyond them both at a perfectly clear blue sky. The surface upon which I lay was a level area of rock, perhaps oval in shape, opening onto nothing. A quick turning of my head showed that it seemed bitten out of a mountainside, however, several dark recesses to the rear indicating the possibility of caves. I saw, too, that Coral lay behind me. Our stony shelf was several hundred meters wide. And there was movement beyond Nayda and the Sign of the Pattern. Luke had just hauled himself up into a kneeling position.

I could have answered the question put to Nayda, but there was no percentage in my doing so. Not when she was doing such a fine job of holding our captor's attention and providing a crucial respite.

To my left, I saw gold-pink swirls within the stone, and though I had never been here I recalled the description from my father's story and knew this to be the place of the primal Pattern, the deeper level of reality that underlay Amber itself.

I rolled onto all fours then, and crawled a few steps, seaward, Patternward.

"You are at the other end of the universe, *ty'iga,* in the place of my greatest power."

Dalt groaned and rolled over, sat up, massaged his eyes with the palms of his hands.

I could feel something like a vibration just at the edge of hearing coming from Nayda now, and her entire form had taken on that reddish glow. I knew that she would die if she attacked the Sign, and I realized that I would attack it myself if it killed her.

I heard a moan from Coral.

"You will not hurt my friends," Nayda said.

I wondered then at its slapping me down before I could use the spikard, and transporting us immediately to its stronghold. Did this mean I might actually have had a chance against it, out there in Logrus territory where it was weakened?

"Creature of the Pit," it told her, "such a doomed, pathetic gesture as yours verges on the heroic. I feel a certain fondness for you. Would that I had such a friend. No, I will not harm your companions. But I must detain Coral and Merlin here as power counters, and the rest of you for political reasons, until this dispute with my adversary is settled."

"Detain?" she said. "Here?"

"There are comfortable quarters within the rock," it said.

I rose carefully to my feet, fumbling at my belt for my dagger.

Luke got up and walked over to Coral, knelt beside her.

"Are you awake?" he asked.

"Sort of," she answered.

"Can you stand?"

"Maybe."

"Let me help you."

Dalt rose while Luke was assisting her. I continued to sidle toward the design. Where was Dworkin when I really needed him?

"You may enter the caves behind you and inspect your quarters," the Sign said. "But first you must remove that ring, Merlin."

"No, now's hardly a time to be unpacking and getting comfortable," I answered, slashing my left palm with the dagger and taking a final step. "We won't be staying long."

A sound like a small thunderclap emerged from the Sign of the Pattern, but there was no lightning, nor did I think there would be. Not when it realized what I was holding in my hand, and where I was holding it.

"A thing I learned from Luke's father," I explained. "Let's talk."

"Yes," said the Sign of the Pattern, "like the reasonable beings that we are. Would you care for some cushions?"

Immediately, three such objects appeared nearby.

"Thanks," I said, drawing up a green one. "I could sure use an iced tea."

"Do you take sugar?"

11

Seated upon a cushion, dagger at my side, I held my left hand out over the Pattern, cupped palm filled with my blood. The Sign of the Pattern hovered in the air before me, seeming, of a sudden, to have forgotten Coral, Nayda, Dalt, and Luke. I sipped from the frosted glass in my right hand, a sprig of fresh mint visible amid the ice.

"Prince Merlin," inquired the Sign, "tell me what it is that you desire and let us resolve this matter quickly. Are you sure I mightn't fetch you a napkin to place at the danger point? It would not minimize your bargaining ability, if you stop to think of it. But it would serve to prevent accidents."

"No, that's okay," I said, half-gesturing with the blood-filled hand, so that its contents were stirred, a small line of red trickling up my wrist. "Thanks, anyhow."

The Sign of the Pattern vibrated, grew still.

"Prince Merlin, you have made your point," it said. "But I do not think you realize the full implications of your threat. A few drops of your blood upon my physical design could disturb the functioning of the universe."

I nodded.

"I know," I said.

"Very well," it answered. "State your demands."

"Our freedom," I said. "Let us go, and you remain intact."

"You give me small choice, but the same applies to your friends."

"What do you mean?"

"You may send Dalt whenever you wish," it said. "As for the

demon lady, I relinquish her with regret, as I feel she would have provided good company—"

Luke regarded Nayda.

"What is this 'creature of the Pit,' 'demon lady' business, anyway?" he asked.

"Well, there are a few things you don't know about me . . ." she responded.

"Is it a long story?" he asked.

"Yes."

"Am I an assignment? Or do you really like me?"

"You're not an assignment, and I really like you."

"Then we'll hear the story later," he said.

"As I said, send her," it went on. "And Dalt. And Luke. I will be happy to send the three of them wherever you wish. But does it occur to you that you and Coral are probably safer here than anywhere else?"

"Maybe. Maybe not," I answered. "Coral, how do you feel about it?"

"Get me out of here," she said.

"So much for that notion," I told it. "Now—"

"Wait. You want to be fair to your friends, don't you?"

"Sure I do."

"Then let me point some things out to them which they may not have considered."

"Go ahead."

"Lady," it said, "they want your eye in the Courts of Chaos. Your feelings on the matter are immaterial. If this can only be achieved by making you a prisoner, then it will be done."

Coral laughed softly.

"The alternative being to remain your prisoner?" she asked.

"Think of yourself as a guest. I will provide for your every comfort. Of course, there is a positive gain for me in this state of affairs—apart from denying the adversary your presence. I acknowledge this. But you must choose one of us, else the other will grab you off."

I looked at Coral, who shook her head slightly.

"So what'll it be?" I asked.

Coral came over and placed her hand upon my shoulder.

"Get me out of here," she said.

"You heard 'em," I told it. "Everybody goes."

"I crave your indulgence a moment more," it said.

"For what?" I asked.

"Consider. Choosing between the Logrus and myself is not a mere matter of politics—of selecting this person or that to do a particular job. My adversary and I represent two fundamental principles by means of which the universe is organized. You may tag us with nouns and adjectives from most languages and dozens of disciplines, but we represent, basically, Order and Chaos— Apollonian and Dionysiac, if you like; reason and feeling, if you prefer; madness and sanity; light and dark; signal and noise. As much as this may seem to indicate it, however, neither of us seeks the other's extinction. Heat death or fireball, classicism or anarchy, each of us proceeds along a single track, and without the other it would lead to a dead end. Both of us know this, and the game we have played since the beginning is a far more subtle thing—ultimately, perhaps, to be judged only esthetically.

"Now, I have gained a significant edge over my ancient adversary, for the first time in ages. I am in a position now to produce a historian's dream throughout Shadow—an age of high civilization and culture such as shall never be forgotten. If the balance were tipped the other way we would be contemplating a period of upheaval at least on par with that of an ice age. When I spoke of you as game pieces it was not to minimize your roles in this. For this is a time of great fluidity, when the Jewel and the man who would be king will make a difference. Stay with me, and I will guarantee the Golden Age of which I spoke, and you a part in it. Leave, and you will be snatched away by the other. Darkness and disorder will follow. Which would you have?"

Luke smiled.

"I know a good sales pitch when I hear it," he said. "Narrow it down to a simple choice. Make them think it's their own."

Coral squeezed my shoulder.

"We're going," I said.

"Very well," said the Sign. "Tell me where you want to go, and I'll send you all there."

"Not all," Luke said suddenly. "Just them."

"I do not understand. What about you?"

He drew a dagger and slashed his palm. He advanced and stood beside me, extending his hand out over the Pattern, also.

"If we go, only three of us may arrive," he said, "if that. I'll stay here and keep you company while you deliver my friends."

"How will you know I've done it in a satisfactory fashion?"

"Good question," he said. "Merle, you got a set of Trumps on you?"

"Yes."

I removed them and showed them to him.

"Still got one of me in there?"

"Last time I looked I did."

"Then get it out and have it ready. Figure your next move before you take off. Stay in touch with me till you make it."

"What about yourself, Luke? You can't sit there forever as a bloody threat to Order. It's only a temporary stalemate. You have to surrender your position sooner or later, and when you do—"

"Do you still have some odd cards in that deck?"

"What do you mean?"

"The ones you once referred to as the Trumps of Doom."

I riffled through. They were mostly near the bottom.

"Yes," I said. "Beautifully executed. I wouldn't have tossed them."

"You really think so?"

"Yeah. Get together a bunch of stuff this good, and I'll get you an exhibit back in Amber."

"You serious? You're not just saying that because—"

The Sign of the Pattern emitted a growling sound.

"Everybody's a critic," Luke observed. "Okay. Pull all the Trumps of Doom."

I did this.

"Mix 'em up a little. Keep 'em face down, please."

"All right."

"Fan 'em."

He leaned forward, took a card.

"Okay," he said. "I'm in business. Whenever you're ready, tell it where to take you. Stay in touch. Hey, Pattern, I want an iced tea of my own."

A frosty glass appeared near his right foot. He stooped and took it up, sipped from it.

"Thanks."

"Luke," Nayda said, "I don't understand what's going on. What will happen to you?"

"Nothing much," he replied. "Don't cry for me, demon lady. I'll see you later."

He looked at me and quirked an eyebrow.

"Send us to Jidrash," I said, "in Kashfa—to the open area between the palace and the church."

I held Luke's Trump in my moist left hand, near to a humming spikard. I felt the card grow cold just as Luke said, "You heard him."

And the world swirled and unswirled, and it was a brisk, windy morning in Jidrash. I regarded Luke through his Trump. I opened channel after channel of the ring.

"Dalt, I might as well leave you here," I said. "You, too, Nayda."

"No," the big man said, just as Nayda said, "Hold on a minute."

"You're both out of the picture now," I explained. "Neither side wants you for anything. But I've got to get Coral someplace safe. Me, too."

"You're a focus of the action," Nayda said, "and I can help Luke by helping you. Take me along."

"I feel the same way about it," Dalt said. "I still owe Luke a big one."

"Okay," I said. "Hey, Luke! You hear all that?"

"Yeah," he said. "Better be about your business then. Shit! I spilled it—"

His Trump went black.

I didn't wait for avenging angels, tongues of fire, lightning bolts, or an opening of the earth. I got us out of jurisdiction real quick.

I sprawled on the green grass beneath the big tree. Wisps of fog drifted by. Dad's Pattern sparkled below me. Jurt was seated cross-legged on the hood of the car, blade across his knees. He hit the ground when we made our appearance. Corwin was nowhere in sight.

"What's going on?" Jurt asked me.

"I am beat, bushed, and whacked-out. I am going to lie here and stare at the fog till my mind goes away," I said. "Meet Coral, Nayda, and Dalt. Hear their story and tell them yours, Jurt. Don't wake me for the end of the world unless it has very good special effects."

I proceeded to do as I had promised, to the tune of a fading guitar and the distant voice of Sara K. The grass was wondrous soft. The fog swirled through my brain. Fade to black.

And then, and then. . . . And then, sir. . . .

Walking. I was walking, almost drifting, through a California shopping mall I used to frequent. Knots of kids, couples with infants, women with parcels, passed, words smothered by sounds from a music store speaker. Potted oases sheltered, deli smells drifted, sale signs promised.

Walking. Past the drugstore. Past the shoe store. Past the candy store. . . .

Narrow corridor to the left. I'd never noticed it. Must turn. . . .

Odd there should be a carpet—and candles in high holders, and sconces, and candelabra atop narrow chests. The walls glittered with their re—

I turned back.

There was no back. The mall was gone. The corridor ended in that direction at a wall. A small tapestry hung upon it, depicting nine figures who looked back at me. I shrugged and turned again.

"Still something left to your spell, Uncle," I remarked. "Let's be about it then."

Walking. In silence now. Ahead. To the place where the mirrors glittered. I had seen this place long ago, I recalled, though its disposition—I suddenly realized—was not peculiar to Amber Castle. It was right there, on the tip of memory—my younger self passing this way, not unaccompanied—but the price of that recollection would be loss of control here, I knew. Reluctantly, I released the image and turned my attention to the small oval mirror to my left.

I smiled. So did my image. I stuck out my tongue and was so saluted in return.

I moved on. Only after several paces did I realize that the image had been my demonformed self, while my person had not.

A soft throat-clearing sound occurred to my right. Turning in that direction, I beheld my brother Mandor within a black-framed lozenge.

"Dear boy," he stated, "the king is dead. Long live your august personage as soon as you have assumed the throne. You had best make haste to return for a crowning at the End of the World, with or without the bride of the Jewel."

"We ran into a few small problems," I said.

"Nothing worth resolving just now. Your presence in the Courts is far more important."

"No, my friends are," I said.

A momentary smile touched his lips.

"You will be in an ideal position to protect your friends," he said, "and to do as you would with your enemies."

"I will be back," I said, "soon. But not to be crowned."

"As you would, Merlin. It is your presence that is desired."

"I promise nothing," I said.

He chuckled, and the mirror was emptied.

I turned away. I walked on.

More laughter. From the left. My mother's.

From within a red frame of carved flowers, she stared at me, a look of vast amusement upon her features.

"Seek him in the Pit!" she said. "Seek him in the Pit!"

I passed, and her laughter continued at my back for a time.

"Hsst!"

To my right, a long, narrow mirror bordered in green.

"Masster Merlin," she said. "I have ssought, but the ghosst-light hass not passsed my way."

"Thanks, Glait. Keep looking, please."

"Yess. We musst ssit together in a warm place by night once again and drink milk and talk of the old dayss."

"That would be nice. Yes, we must. If we are not eaten by something bigger."

"S-s-s-s-s!"

Could that be laughter?

"Good hunting, Glait."

"Yess. S-s-s!"

. . . And on. Walking.

"Son of Amber. Wearer of the spikard"—this from within a shadowy niche to my left.

I halted and stared. The frame was white, the glass was gray. Within was a man I had never met. His shirt was black and opened at the neck. He wore a brown leather vest, his hair dark blond, eyes perhaps green.

"Yes?"

"A spikard was hidden in Amber," he stated, "for you to find. It conveys great powers. It also bears a series of spells that will cause its wearer to act in certain ways under certain circumstances."

"I suspected this," I said. "What is it set to do?"

"Formerly worn by Swayvill, King of Chaos, it will force the chosen successor to take the throne, behave in a certain fashion, and be amenable to the suggestions of certain persons."

"These being?"

"The woman who laughed and cried, 'Seek him in the Pit.' The man in black, who desires your return."

"Dara and Mandor. They laid these spells upon it?"

"Just so. And the man left it for you to find."

"I hate to surrender the thing just now," I said, "when it's proving so useful. Is there a way to lift these spells?"

"Of course. But it should not matter to you."

"Why not?"

"The ring you wear is not the one of which I speak."

"I do not understand."

"But you will. Never fear."

"Who are you, sir?"

"My name is Delwin, and we may never actually meet—unless certain ancient powers come loose."

He raised his hand, and I saw that he, too, wore a spikard. He moved it toward me.

"Touch your ring to mine," he commanded. "Then it can be ordered to bring you to me."

I raised mine and moved it toward the glass. At the moment they seemed to touch, there was a flash of light and Delwin was gone.

I let my arm fall. I walked on. On an impulse, I stopped before a chest and opened its drawer.

I stared. There was no way to one-up this place, it seemed. The drawer contained a miniature, scaled-down representation of my father's chapel—tiny colored tiles, diminutive burning tapers, even a doll-sized Grayswandir upon the altar.

"The answer lies before you, dear friend," came a throaty voice I knew yet did not know.

I raised my gaze to a lavender-bordered mirror I had not realized hung above the chest. The lady within had long, coal-black hair and eyes so dark I could not tell where the pupils left off and the irises began. Her complexion was very pale, emphasized perhaps by her pink eye shadow and lip coloring. Those eyes. . . .

"Rhanda!" I said.

"You remember! You do remember me!"

". . . And the days of our bonedance games," I said. "Grown and lovely. I thought of you but recently."

"And I felt the touch of your regard as I slept, my Merlin. I am sorry we parted so, but my parents—"

"I understand," I said. "They thought me demon or vampire."

"Yes." She extended her pale hand through the mirror, took hold of my own, drew it toward her. Within the looking glass, she pressed it to her lips. They were cold. "They would rather I cultivated the acquaintance of the sons and daughters of men and women, than of our own kind."

When she smiled, I beheld her fangs. They had not been apparent in her childhood.

"Gods! You look human!" she said. "Come visit me in Wildwood one day!"

Impulsively, I leaned forward. Our lips met within the mirror. Whatever she was, we had been friends.

"The answer," she repeated, "lies before you. Come see me!"

The mirror turned red and she was gone. The chapel stood unchanged within the drawer. I closed it and turned away.

Walking. Mirrors to the left. Mirrors to the right. Only myself within them.

Then—

"Well, well, nephew. Confused?"

"As usual."

"Can't say as I blame you."

His eyes were mocking and wise, his hair red as his sister Fiona's or his late brother Brand's. Or Luke's, for that matter.

"Bleys," I said, "what the hell is going on?"

"I've the rest of Delwin's message," he said, reaching into his pocket and extending his hand. "Here."

I reached into the mirror and accepted it. It was yet another spikard, like the one I wore.

"It is the one of which Delwin spoke," he said. "You must never wear it."

I studied it for several moments.

"What am I to do with it?" I asked.

"Put it in your pocket. A use may suggest itself at some point."

"How did you come by it?"

"I switched it after Mandor left it, for the one you wear now."

"How many are there, anyway?"

"Nine," he replied.

"I suppose you know all about them."

"More than most."

"That wouldn't be hard. I don't suppose you know where my father is?"

"No. But you do. Your lady friend with the sanguinary tastes told you."

"Riddles," I said.

"Always preferable to no answer at all," he responded.

Then he was gone and I walked again. After a while, this was gone, too.

Drifting. Black. Good. So good. . . .

* * *

A bit of light found its way through my eyelashes. I shut it out again. But the thunder rolled, and after a time the light leaked in once again.

Dark lines in brown, great horny ridges, ferny forests. . . .

A little later the faculty that evaluates perceptions awoke and pointed out that I was lying on my side staring at the cracked earth between a pair of roots from the tree, clumps of grass dotted here and there across the prospect.

. . . And I continued to stare, and there was a sudden brightness as of a lightning flash followed almost immediately by a crack of thunder. The earth seemed to shudder with it. I heard the pattering of drops upon the leaves of a tree, the hood of a car. I continued to stare at the largest crack that traversed the valley of my regard.

. . . And I realized that I knew.

It was the numb knowledge of awakening. The sources of emotion still dozed. In the distance, I could hear familiar voices in soft converse. I could also hear the sounds of cutlery against china. My stomach would awaken in a bit, I knew, and I would join them. For now, it was so very pleasant to lie here wrapped in my cloak, hearing the gentle rain and knowing. . . .

I returned to my micro-world and its dark canyon. . . .

The ground shook again, this time without benefit of lightning or thunder. And it kept on shaking. This irritated me, for it disturbed my friends and relatives, causing them to raise their voices in something like alarm. Also, it stirred a dormant California reflex at a time when I just wanted to loll and savor my fresh-acquired knowledge.

"Merlin, are you awake?"

"Yes," I said, sitting up suddenly, giving my eyes a quick rub, and running my hands through my hair.

It was the ghost of my father that knelt beside me, having just shaken my shoulder. "We seem to have a problem," he said, "with rather extreme ramifications."

Jurt, standing behind him, nodded several times. The ground shook once again, twigs and leaves fell about us, pebbles bounced, dust rose, the fogs were agitated. I heard a dish break in the vicinity of the heavy red and white cloth about which Luke, Dalt, Coral, and Nayda sat eating.

I untangled my cloak and rose to my feet, realizing then that someone had removed my boots while I slept. I drew them back on. There came another tremor, and I leaned against the tree for support.

"This is the problem?" I said. "Or is something bigger about to eat it?"

He gave me a puzzled look. Then, "Back when I drew the Pattern," he said, "I'd no way of knowing that this area was faulted, or that something like this would one day occur. If these shocks should crack the Pattern, we've had it—in more ways than one. As I understand it, that spikard you wear can draw upon enormous sources of energy. Is there some way you could use it to defuse this thing?"

"I don't know," I told him. "I never tried anything like it."

"Find out fast, okay?" he said.

But I was already spinning my mind about the circle of tines, touching each one to life. Then I seized upon the one possessed of the most juice, drew hard upon it, filled myself, body and mind, with its energy. Ignition completed and engine idling, with me in the driver's seat, I shifted into gear then, extending a line of force from the spikard down into the ground.

I reached for a long while, seeking a conversion metaphor to the subjective for anything I might discover.

. . . Wading out from the beach into the ocean—waves tickling my stomach, my chest—feeling with my toes the rocks, the strands of seaweed. . . . Sometimes a rock would turn, slip, bump against another, slide. . . . I couldn't see to the bottom with my eyes. But I saw the rocks, the wrack, in their disposition and movement, just the same, beheld them as clearly as if the bottom were fully illuminated.

Feeling, feeling my way now, down through the strata, single toe soft as a flashlight's beam running along rocky surfaces, testing the pressures of one upon another, isostatic kisses of mountains beneath the earth, orogenic erogenies of slow movement, flesh caressing mineral in the darkest of secret places—

Slip! The rock slides off. My body follows. . . .

I dive for it, following the sliding passage. I race ahead, pouring forth heat, cracking rock, splintering new pathways, outward, outward. . . . It was coming this way. I broke through a wall of stone, another. Another. I was not certain this was the way to divert it, but it was the only one I knew to try. Go that way! Damn it! That way! I accessed two more channels, a third, a fourth—

There was a slight vibration within the ground. I opened another channel. Within my metaphor the rocks grew stable beneath the waters. Shortly thereafter, the ground ceased its vibration.

I returned to the place where I had first felt the slide begin, stable now, yet still stressed. Feel it, feel it carefully. Describe a vector. Follow. Follow it to the point of original pressure. But no. This point is but a confluence of vectors. Trace them.

Yet again. More junctions. Trace them. Access more channels. The entire pressure structure, intricate as a nervous system, must be described. I must hold its tree within my mind.

Another layer. It may not be possible. I may be courting infinity in my topographic branchings. Freeze frame. Simplify the problem. Ignore everything beyond the tertiary. Trace to the next junction. There are some loops. Good. And a plate is now involved. Better.

Try another jump. No good. Too big a picture to contain. Discard tertiaries.

Yes.

Thus general lines sketched. Vectors of transmission simply drawn—back to plate, almost. Pressure exerted less than full pressure extended. Why? Additional point of input along second vector, redirecting shear forces this valley.

"Merlin? Are you all right?"

"Let me be," I hear my voice respond.

Extend then, input source, into, feeling, transmission signature. . . .

Is this a Logrus that I see before me?

I opened three more channels, focused on the area, began heating it.

Soon rocks were cracking, but a little later they melted. My newly created magma flowed down fault lines. A hollowed-out area occurred at the point whence the precipitating force had originated.

Back.

I withdrew my probes, shut down the spikard.

"What did you do?" he asked me.

"I found the place where the Logrus was messing with underground stresses," I said, "and I removed the place. There's a small grotto there now. If it collapses it may ease the pressure even more."

"So you've stabilized it?"

"At least for now. I don't know the limits of the Logrus, but it's going to have to figure a new route to reach this place. Then it's going to have to test it out. And if it's doing a lot of Pattern watching just now, that may slow it."

"So you've bought some time," he said. "Of course, the Pattern may move against us next."

"It could," I said. "I've brought everyone here because I thought they'd be safe from both Powers."

"Apparently you made the payoff worth the risk."

"Okay," I said. "I guess it's time to give them some other things to worry about."

"Such as?"

I looked at him, Pattern ghost of my father, guardian of this place.

"I know where your flesh-and-blood counterpart is," I said, "and I'm about to set him free."

There came a flash of lightning. A sudden gust of wind lofted the fallen leaves, stirred the fogs.

"I must accompany you," he said.

"Why?"

"I've a personal interest in him, of course."

"All right."

Thunder crashed about us, and the fogs were torn apart by a fresh onslaught of wind.

Jurt came up to us then.

"I think it's begun," he said.

"What?" I asked.

"The duel of Powers," he said. "For a long time the Pattern had an edge. But when Luke damaged it and you snatched away the bride of the Jewel, it must have weakened it more, relative to the Logrus, than it's been in ages. So the Logrus decided to attack, pausing only for a quick attempt to damage this Pattern."

"Unless the Logrus was just testing us," I said, "and this is simply a storm."

A light rain had begun while he was speaking.

"I came here because I thought it was the one place neither of them would touch in the event of a contest," he went on. "I'd assumed neither would care to divert energy from its own attack or defense for a swipe in this direction."

"That reasoning may still hold," I said.

"Just for once I'd like to be on the winning side," he stated. "I'm not sure I care about right or wrong. They're very arguable quantities. I'd just like to be in with the guys who win for a change. What do you think, Merle? What are you going to do?"

"Corwin here and I are going to head for the Courts, and we're going to free my father," I said. "Then we're going to resolve whatever needs resolving and live happily ever after. You know how it goes."

He shook his head.

"I can never decide whether you're a fool or whether your confidence is warranted. Every time I decided you were a fool, though, it cost me." He looked up at the dark sky, wiped rain from his brow. "I'm really torn," he said, "but you could still be King of Chaos."

"No," I said.

". . . And you enjoy some special relationship with the Powers."

"If I do, I don't understand it myself."

"No matter," he said. "I'm still with you."

I crossed to the others, hugged Coral.

"I must return to the Courts," I said. "Guard the Pattern. We'll be back."

The sky was illuminated by three brilliant flashes. The wind shook the tree.

I turned away and created a door in the middle of the air. Corwin's ghost and I stepped through it.

12

Thus did I return to the Courts of Chaos, coming through into Sawall's space-warped sculpture garden.

"Where are we?" my ghost-father asked.

"A museum of sorts," I replied, "in the house of my stepfather. I chose it because the lighting is tricky and there are many places to hide."

He studied some of the pieces, as well as their disposition upon the walls and ceiling.

"This would be a hell of a place to fight a skirmish," he observed.

"I suppose it would."

"You grew up hereabout, huh?"

"Yes."

"What was it like?"

"Oh, I don't know. I don't have anything to compare it to. I had some good times, alone, and with friends—and a few bad times. All a part of being a kid."

"This place . . . ?"

"The Ways of Sawall. I wish I had time to show you the whole thing, take you through all of the ways."

"One day, perhaps."

"Yes."

I began walking, hoping for the Ghostwheel or Kergma to appear. Neither did, however.

We finally passed into a corridor that took us to a hall of tapestries, whence there was a way to a room that I desired—for the room let upon the hallway that passed the gallery of metal trees.

Before we could depart, however, I heard voices from that hall-way. So we waited in the room—which contained the skeleton of a Jabberwock painted in orange, blue, and yellow, Early Psychedelic—as the speakers approached. One of them I recog-nized immediately as my brother Mandor; the other I could not identify by voice alone, but managing a glimpse as they passed, I saw it to be Lord Bances of Amblerash, High Priest of the Serpent Which Manifests the Logrus (to cite a full title just once). In a badly plotted story they'd have paused outside the doorway, and I'd have overheard a conversation telling me everything I needed to know about anything.

They slowed as they passed.

"That's the way it will be then?" Bances said.

"Yes," Mandor replied. "Soon."

And they were by, and I couldn't make out another word. I lis-tened to their receding footsteps till they were gone. Then I waited a little longer. I would have sworn I heard a small voice saying, "Follow. Follow."

"Hear anything just then?" I whispered.

"Nope."

So we stepped out into the hallway and turned right, moving in the opposite direction from that which Mandor and Bances had taken. As we did, I felt a sensation of heat at a point somewhat be-low my left hip.

"You think he is somewhere near here?" the Corwin ghost asked. "Prisoner to Dara?"

"Yes and no," I said. "Ow!"

It felt like a hot coal pressed against my upper leg. I jammed my hand into my pocket as I slid into the nearest display niche, which I shared with a mummified lady in an amber casket.

Even as my hand closed about it, I knew what it was, raising all manner of philosophical speculations I had neither time nor desire to address at the moment and so treated in the time-honored fashion of dealing with such things: I shelved them.

It was a spikard that I withdrew, that lay warmly upon my palm. Almost immediately a small spark leapt between it and the one that I wore upon my finger.

There followed a wordless communication, a sequence of im-ages, ideas, feelings, urging me to find Mandor and place myself in his hands for the preparations for my crowning as the next King of the Courts. I could see why Bleys had told me not to put the thing on. Unmediated by my own spikard, its injunctions would probably have been overpowering. I used mine to shut it off, to build a tiny insulating wall about it.

"You have *two* of the damned things!" Corwin's ghost observed.

I nodded.

"Know anything about them that I don't?" I asked. "That would include almost anything."

He shook his head.

"Only that they were said to be very early power objects, from the days when the universe was still a murky place and the Shadow realms less clearly defined. When the time came, their wielders slept or dissolved or whatever such figures do, and the spikards were withdrawn or stashed or transformed, or whatever becomes of such things when the story's over. There are many versions, of course. There always are. But bringing two of them to the Courts could conceivably draw a lot of attention to yourself, not to mention adding to the general power of Chaos just by virtue of their presence at this pole of existence."

"Oh, my," I said. "I'll order the one I'm wearing to conceal itself, also."

"I don't think that'll work," he said, "though I'm not certain. I'd think they must maintain a constant flux-pin with each source of power, and that would give some indication of the thing's presence because of its broadcast nature."

"I'll tell it to tune itself as low as it can then."

He nodded.

"It can't hurt to make it specific," he said, "though I'd guess it probably does that anyhow, automatically."

I placed the other ring back in my pocket, departed the niche, and hurried on up the hallway.

I slowed when we neared what I thought to be the area. But I seemed mistaken. The metal forest was not there. We passed that section. Shortly, we came to a familiar display—the one that had preceded the metal forest, on approaching it from that direction.

Even as I turned back, I knew. I knew what had happened. When we reached what had been the area, I stopped and studied it.

"What is it?" my ghostly father asked.

"It seems a display of every conceivable variety of edged weapon and tool that Chaos has ever spewed forth," I said, "all of them exhibited point up, you'll note."

"So?" he asked.

"This is the place," I answered, "the place where we were going to climb a metal tree."

"Merle," he said, "maybe this place does something to my thought processes, or yours. I just don't understand."

"It's up near the ceiling," I explained, gesturing. "I know the approximate area—I think. Looks a little different now. . . ."

"What's there, son?"

"A way—a transport area, like the one we passed through to the place of the Jabberwock skeleton. Only this one would take us to your chapel."

"And that's where we're headed?"

"Right."

He rubbed his chin.

"Well, there were some fairly tall items in some of the displays we passed," he observed, "and not all of them were metal or stone. We could wrestle over that totem pole or whatever the hell it is, from back up the hall, clear away some of the sharp displays below that place, set the thing up—"

"No," I said. "Dara obviously caught on to the fact that someone had visited it—probably this last time around, when she almost surprised me. The display was changed because of this. There are only two obvious ways to get up there—transport something unwieldy, as you suggest, and clear away a lot of cutlery before we climb. Or rev up the spikard and levitate ourselves to the spot. The first would take too long and probably get us discovered. The second would employ so much power that it would doubtless set off any magical wards she's installed about the area."

He took hold of my arm and drew me on past the display.

"We've got to talk," he said, leading me into an alcove containing a small bench.

He seated himself and folded his arms.

"I've got to know what the hell's going on," he said. "I can't help properly unless I'm briefed. What's the connection between the man and the chapel?"

"I figured out something I think my mother really meant when she told me, 'Seek him in the Pit,'" I explained. "The floor of the chapel bears stylized representations of the Courts and of Amber worked out in tiles. At the extreme of the Courts' end is a representation of the Pit. I never set foot in that area when I visited the chapel. I'm willing to bet there's a way located there, and at the other end is the place of his imprisonment."

He'd begun nodding as I spoke, then, "So you were going to pass through and free him?" he asked.

"Right."

"Tell me, do these ways have to work both ways?" he said.

"Well, no. . . . Oh, I see what you're getting at."

"Give me a more complete description of the chapel," he said.

I proceeded to do so.

"That magic circle on the floor intrigues me," he said. "It might be a means of communicating with him without risking the dangers of presence. Some sort of image-exchange, perhaps."

"I might have to fool with it a long while to figure it out," I said, "unless I got lucky. What I propose doing is to levitate, enter, use the way at the Pit to reach him, free him, and get the hell out. No subtlety. No finesse. If anything fails to do what we expect, we force our way through it with the spikard. We'll have to move fast because they'll be after us once we start."

He stared past me for a long while, as if thinking hard.

At length, he asked, "Is there any way her wards might be set off accidentally?"

"Hm. The passage of a stray magical current from the real Pit, I suppose. It sometimes spews them forth."

"What would characterize its passage?"

"A magical deposit or transformation," I said.

"Could you fake such a phenomenon?"

"I suppose. But what would be the point? They'd still investigate, and with Corwin gone they'd realize it was just a trick. The effort would be wasted."

He chuckled.

"But he won't be missing," he said. "I'm going to take his place."

"I can't let you do that!"

"My choice," he said. "But he's going to need the time if he's going to help stop Dara and Mandor from advancing the conflict between the Powers beyond anything at Patternfall."

I sighed.

"It's the only way," he said.

"I guess you're right."

He unfolded his arms, stretched, and rose to his feet.

"Let's go do it," he said.

I had to work out a spell, a thing I hadn't done recently—well, half of a spell, the effects half, as I had the spikard to juice it. Then I lay it in a swathe across the display, turning portions of blades into flowers, joined at the molecular level. As I did, I felt a tingling I was certain was the psychic alarm taking note of the enterprise and reporting it to central.

Then I summoned a lot of juice and lofted us. I felt the tug of the way as we neared it. I had been almost dead-on. I let it take us through.

He whistled softly on regarding the chapel.

"Enjoy," I said. "It's the treatment a god gets."

"Yeah. Prisoner in his own church."

He stalked across the room, unbuckling his belt as he went. He substituted it for the one upon the altar.

"Good copy," he said, "but not even the Pattern can duplicate Grayswandir."

"I thought a section of the Pattern was reproduced on the blade."

"Maybe it's the other way around," he said.

"What do you mean?"

"Ask the other Corwin sometime," he said. "It has to do with something we were talking about recently."

He approached and passed the lethal package to me—weapon, sheath, belt.

"Be nice if you take it to him," he said.

I buckled it and hung it over my head and shoulder.

"Okay," I told him. "We'd better move."

I headed toward the far corner of the chapel. As I neared the area where the Pit was represented I felt the unmistakable tug of a way.

"Eureka!" I said, activating channels on the spikard. "Follow me."

I stepped forward and it took me away.

We arrived in a chamber of perhaps fifteen feet square. There was a wooden post at its center and the floor was of stone with some straw strewn upon it. Several of the big candles, as from the chapel, were spotted about. The walls were of stone on two sides, wood on the others. The wooden walls contained unlatched wooden doors. One of the stone walls contained a windowless metal door, a keyhole at its left side. A key, which looked about the right size, hung from a nail in the post.

I took down the key and checked quickly beyond the wooden door to my right, discovering a large barrel of water, a dipper, and a variety of dishes, cups, utensils. Behind the other door were a few blankets and stacks of what were probably toilet tissues.

I crossed to the metal door then and knocked upon it with the key. There was no response. I inserted the key in the lock and felt my companion take hold of my arm.

"Better let me do that," he said. "I think like him, and I think I'll be safer."

I had to agree with the wisdom of this, and I stepped aside.

"Corwin!" he called out. "We're springing you! It's your son Merlin and me, your double. Don't jump me when I open the door, okay? We'll stand still and you can take a look."

"Open it," came a voice from within.

So he did, and we stood there.

"What do you know?" came the voice I remembered, finally. "You guys look for real."

"We are," said his ghost, "and as usual, at times such as this, you'd better hurry."

"Yeah." There came a slow tread from within, and when he emerged he was shielding his eyes with his left hand. "Either of you got a pair of shades? The light hurts."

"Damn!" I said, wishing I'd thought of it. "No, and if I send for them the Logrus might spot me."

"Later, later. I'll squint and stumble. Let's get the hell out."

His ghost entered the cell.

"Now make me bearded, thin, and grimy. Lengthen the hair and tatter the clothes," he said. "Then lock me in."

"What's going on?" my father asked.

"Your ghost will be impersonating you in your cell for a while."

"It's your plan," Corwin stated. "Do what the ghost says." And so I did. He turned and extended his hand back into the cell then. "Thanks, buddy."

"My pleasure," the other replied, clasping his hand and shaking it. "Good luck."

"So long."

I closed and locked the cell door. I hung the key on its nail and steered him to the way. It took us through.

He lowered his hand as we came into the chapel. The dimness must have been sufficient for him to handle now. He drew away from me and crossed to the altar.

"We'd better go, Dad."

He chuckled as he reached across the altar, raised a burning taper, and used it to light one of the others that had apparently gone out in some draft.

"I've pissed on my own grave," he announced. "Can't pass up the pleasure of lighting a candle to myself in my own church."

He extended his left hand in my direction without looking at me.

"Give me Grayswandir," he said.

I slipped it off and passed it to him. He unfastened it and buckled it about his waist, loosened it in its sheath.

"All right. What now?" he asked.

I thought fast. If Dara was aware that I had exited through the wall last time—a distinct possibility, considering—then the walls might well be booby-trapped in some fashion. On the other hand, if we went out the way I had come in we might encounter someone rushing this way in answer to the alarm.

Hell.

"Come on," I said, activating the spikard, ready to whisk us away at the glimpse of an intruder. "It's going to be tricky because it involves levitation on the way out."

I caught hold of him again and we approached the way. I wrapped us in energies as it took us, and I lofted us above the field of blades and flowers as we departed.

There were footfalls from up the corridor. I swirled us away to another place.

I took us to Jurt's apartment, which didn't seem a place anyone was likely to come looking for a man who was still in his cell; and I knew that Jurt had no need of it just then.

Corwin sprawled on the bed and squinted at me.

"By the way," he said, "thanks."

"Anytime," I told him.

"You know your way around this place pretty well?" he said.

"It doesn't seem to have changed that much," I told him.

"Then how's about raiding an icebox for me while I borrow your brother's scissors and razor for a quick shave and haircut."

"What would you like?"

"Meat, bread, cheese, wine, maybe a piece of pie," he said. "Just so it's fresh and there's lots of it. Then you're going to have a lot of story to tell me."

"I guess I am," I said.

And so I made my way to the kitchen, down familiar halls and ways I had traversed as a boy. The place was lit by just a few tapers, the fires banked. No one was about.

I proceeded to raid the larder, heaping a tray with the various viands requested, adding a few pieces of fruit I came across. I almost dropped the wine bottle when I heard a sharp intake of breath near the doorway I had entered.

It was Julia, in a blue silk wrap.

"Merlin!"

I crossed to her.

"I owe you several apologies," I said. "I'm ready to make them."

"I'd heard you were back. I heard you were to be king."

"Funny, I heard that, too."

"Then it would be unpatriotic of me to stay mad, wouldn't it?"

"I never meant to hurt you," I said. "Physically, or any other way."

Suddenly, we were holding each other. It lasted a long time before she told me, "Jurt says you're friends now."

"I guess we sort of are."

I kissed her.

"If we got back together again," she said, "he'd probably try to kill you again."

"I know. This time the consequences could really be cataclysmic, too."

"Where are you going right now?"

"I'm on an errand, and it's going to take me several hours."

"Why don't you stop by when you're finished? We've got a lot to talk about. I'm staying in a place called the Wisteria Room for now. Know where that is?"

"Yes," I said. "This is crazy."

"See you later?"

"Maybe."

The next day I traveled to the Rim, for I'd heard report that the Pitdivers—those who seek after artifacts of creation beyond the Rim—had suspended operations for the first time in a generation. When I questioned them they told me of dangerous activities in the depths—whirlwinds, wings of fire, blasts of new-minted matter.

Sitting in a secluded place and looking down, I used the spikard I wore to question the one I didn't. When I removed the shield in which I'd encased it, it commenced a steady litany, "Go to Mandor. Get crowned. See your brother. See your mother. Begin preparations." I wrapped it again and put it away. If I didn't do something soon he was going to suspect that I was beyond its control. Did I care?

I could just absent myself, perhaps going away with my father, helping him at whatever showdown might finally develop over his Pattern. I could even ditch both spikards there, enhancing the forces in that place. I could still rely on my own magic in a pinch. But—

My problem was right here. I had been bred and conditioned to be a perfect royal flunky, under the control of my mother, and possibly my brother Mandor. I loved Amber, but I loved the Courts as well. Fleeing to Amber, while assuring my safety, would no more solve my personal problem than running off with my dad—or returning to the Shadow Earth I also cared for, with or without Coral. No. The problem was here—and inside me.

I summoned a filmy to bear me to an elevated way to take me back to Sawall. As I traveled, I thought of what I must do, and I realized that I was afraid. If things got pushed as far as they well might, there was a strong possibility that I would die. Alternatively, I might have to kill someone I didn't really want to.

Either way, though, there had to be some resolution or I'd never know peace at this pole of my existence.

I walked beside a purple stream beneath a green sun atop a pearly sky. I summoned a purple and gray bird, which came and sat upon my wrist. I had thought to dispatch it to Amber with a message for Random. Try as I might, however, I could phrase no simple note. Too many things depended on other things. Laughing, I released it and leapt from the bank, where I struck another way above the water.

Returned to Sawall, I made my way to the sculpture hall. By then, I knew what I must try to do and how I must go about it. I stood where I had stood—how long ago?—regarding massive structures, simple figures, intricate ones.

"Ghost?" I said. "You in the neighborhood?"

There was no response.

"Ghost!" I repeated more loudly. "Can you hear me?"

Nothing.

I dug out my Trumps, located the one I had done for Ghostwheel, bright circle.

I regarded it with some intensity, but it was slow to grow cool.

This was understandable, considering some of the odd areas of space to which this hall gave access. Also, it was irritating.

I raised the spikard. Using it here at the level I intended would be like setting off a burglar alarm. Amen.

I touched the Tarot with a line of subtle force, attempting to enhance the instrument's sensitivity. I maintained my concentration.

Again, nothing.

I backed it with more force. There followed a perceptible cooling. But there was no contact.

"Ghost," I said through clenched teeth. "This is important. Come to me."

No reply. So I sent power into the thing. The card began to glow and frost crystals formed upon it. Small crackling sounds occurred in its vicinity.

"Ghost," I repeated.

A weak sense of his presence occurred then, and I poured more juice into the card. It shattered in my hand, and I caught it in a web of forces and held all of the pieces together, looking like a small stained-glass window. I continued to reach through it.

"Dad! I'm in trouble!" came to me then.

"Where are you? What's the matter?" I asked.

"I followed this entity I met. Pursued her—it. Almost a mathematical abstraction. Called Kergma. Got caught here at an odd-even dimensional interface, where I'm spiraling. Was having a good time up until then—"

"I know Kergma well. Kergma is a trickster. I can feel your spatial situation. I am about to send bursts of energy to counter the rotation. Let me know if there are problems. As soon as you're able to Trump through, tell me and come ahead."

I pulsed it through the spikard and the braking effect began. Moments later, he informed me, "I think I can escape now."

"Come on, then."

Suddenly, Ghost was there, spinning about me like a magic circle.

"Thanks, Dad. I really appreciate this. Let me know if there's ever anything—"

"There is," I said.

"What?"

"Shrink yourself down and hide somewhere about my person."

"Wrist okay again?"

"Sure."

He did that thing. Then, "Why?" he asked.

"I may need a sudden ally," I replied.

"Against what?"

"Anything," I said. "It's showdown time."

"I don't like the sound of that."

"Then leave me now. I won't hold it against you."

"I couldn't do that."

"Listen, Ghost. This thing has escalated, and a line must be drawn now. I—"

The air began to shimmer, off to my right. I knew what it meant.

"Later," I said. "Be still."

. . . And there was a doorway, and it opened to admit a tower of green light: eyes, ears, nose, mouth, limbs cycling about its sea-like range—one of the more inspired demonic forms I'd beheld of late. And, of course, I knew the features.

"Merlin," he said. "I felt you ply the spikard here."

"I thought you might," I replied, "and I am at your service, Mandor."

"Really?"

"In all respects, brother."

"Including a certain matter of succession?"

"That in particular."

"Excellent! And what business were you about here?"

"I was but seeking something I had lost."

"That can wait upon another day, Merlin. We have much to do just now."

"Yes, that is true."

"So assume a more pleasing form and come with me. We must discuss the measures you are to take upon assuming the throne—which Houses are to be suppressed, who outlawed—"

"I must speak with Dara immediately."

"I would rather lay some groundwork first. Come! Shift, and let us be away!"

"Would you know where she is just now?"

"Gantu, I believe. But we will confer with her later."

"You wouldn't happen to have her Trump handy, would you?"

"I fear not. I thought you carried a deck of your own?"

"I do. But hers was inadvertently destroyed one night when I was drinking."

"No matter," he said. "We will see her later, as I explained."

I had been opening channels on the spikard as we spoke. I caught him at the center of a whirlwind of forces. I could see the transformation procedure within him, and it was a simple matter to reverse it, collapsing the green and spinning tower into the form of a white-haired man clad in black and white and looking very irritated.

"Merlin!" he cried. "Why have you changed me?"

"This thing fascinates me," I said, waving the spikard. "I just wanted to see whether I could do it."

"Now you've seen it," he said. "Kindly release me to turn back, and find a more fitting form for yourself."

"A moment," I said, as he attempted to melt and flow. "I require you just as you are."

I held him against his effort, and I drew a fiery rectangle in the air. A series of quick movements filled it with a rough likeness of my mother.

"Merlin! What are you doing?" he cried.

I suppressed his effort to extricate himself by means of a transport spell.

"Conference time," I announced. "Bear with me."

I didn't just meditate upon the impromptu Trump I had hung in the air before me, but practically attacked it with a charge of the energies I was cycling through my body and the space about me.

Suddenly, Dara stood within the frame I had created—tall, coal-black, eyes of green flame.

"Merlin! What's happening?" she cried.

I'd never heard of it being done quite this way before, but I held the contact, willed her presence, and blew away the frame. She stood before me then, perhaps seven feet tall, pulsing with indignation.

"What is the meaning of this?" she asked.

I caught her as I had Mandor and collapsed her down to human scale.

"Democracy," I said. "Let's all look alike for a minute."

"This is not amusing," she responded, and she began to change back.

I canceled her effort.

"No, it isn't," I answered. "But I called this meeting, and it will be run on my terms."

"Very well," she said, shrugging. "What has become so terribly urgent?"

"The succession."

"The matter is settled. The throne is yours."

"And whose creature am I to be?" I raised my left hand, hoping they had no way of telling one spikard from another. "This thing confers great powers. It also charges for their use. It bore a spell for control of its wearer."

"It was Swayvill's," Mandor said. "I got it to you when I did to accustom you to the force of its presence. And yes, there is a price. Its wearer must come to terms with it."

"I have wrestled with it," I lied, "and I am its master. But the main problems were not cosmic. They were compulsions of your own installation."

"I do not deny it," he said. "But there was a very good reason for their presence. You were reluctant to take the throne. I felt it necessary to add an element of compulsion."

I shook my head.

"Not good enough," I said. "There was more to it than that. It was a thing designed to make me subservient to you."

"Necessary," he responded. "You've been away. You lack intimate knowledge of the local political scene. We could not simply let you take the reins and go off in your own direction—not in times such as these, when blunders could be very costly. The House needed some means to control you. But this was only to be until your education was complete."

"Permit me to doubt you, brother," I said.

He glanced at Dara, who nodded slightly.

"He is right," she said, "and I see nothing wrong with such temporary control until you learn the business. Too much is at stake to permit otherwise."

"It was a slave-spell," I said. "It would force me to take the throne, to follow orders."

Mandor licked his lips. It was the first time I'd ever seen him betray a sign of nervousness. It instantly made me wary—though I realized moments later that it may have been a calculated distraction. It caused me to guard against him immediately; and, of course, the attack came from Dara.

A wave of heat swept over me. I shifted my attention at once, attempting to raise a barrier. It was not an attack against my person. It was something soothing, coercive. I bared my teeth as I fought to hold it off.

"Mother—" I growled.

"We must restore the imperatives," she said flatly, more to Mandor than to me.

"Why?" I asked. "You're getting what you want."

"The throne is not enough," she answered. "I do not trust you in this, and reliance will be necessary."

"You never trusted me," I said, pushing away the remains of her spell.

"That is not true," she told me, "and this is a technical matter, not a personal one."

"Whatever the matter," I said, "I'm not buying."

Mandor tossed a paralysis spell at me, and I pushed it away, ready for anything now. As I was doing this, Dara hit me with an elaborate working I recognized as a Confusion Storm. I was not about to try matching them both, spell for spell. A good sorcerer may have a half dozen major spells hung. Their judicious employment is generally enough for dealing with most situations. In a sorcerous duel the strategy involved in their employment is a major part of the game. If both parties are still standing when the spells have been exhausted, then they are reduced to fighting with raw energies. Whoever controls a greater quantity usually has the edge then.

I raised an umbrella against the Confusion Storm, parried Mandor's Astral Club, held myself together through Mom's Spirit Split, maintained my senses through Mandor's Well of Blackness. My major spells had all gone stale, and I had hung no new ones since I'd begun relying on the spikard. I was already reduced to reliance on raw power. Fortunately, the spikard gave me control of more of it than I'd ever held before. All I had to do was force them to use up their spells, then all trickiness would be removed from the situation. I would wear them down, drain them.

Mandor sneaked one partway through, hurting me in a brush with an Electric Porcupine. I battered him with a wall of force, however, slamming him into a system of revolving discs that flashed off in all directions. Dara turned into a liquid flame, coiling, waving, flowing through circles and figure-eights, as she advanced and retreated, tossing bubbles of euphoria and pain to orbit me. I tried to blow them away, hurricane-wise, shattering the great porcelain face, uprooting towers, family groups with holes in them, glowing geometries. Mandor turned to sand, which filtered downward through the structure upon which he sprawled, became a yellow carpet, crept toward me.

I ignored the effects and continued to beat at them with energies. I hurled the carpet through the flame and dumped a floating fountain upon them. Brushing out small fires in my clothing and hair, I forced my consciousness through numbed areas in my left shoulder and leg. I fell apart and drew myself back together again as I mastered Dara's spell of Unweaving. I shattered Mandor's Diamond Bubble and digested the Chains of Deliverance. On three occasions, I dropped my human form for things more suitable, but always I returned to it. I hadn't had a workout like this since my final exams with Suhuy.

But the ultimate advantage was obviously mine. Their only real chance had lain in surprise, and that was gone now. I opened all channels on the spikard, a thing which might have intimidated even the Pattern—though, now I thought on it, it had gotten me knocked senseless. I caught Mandor in a cone of force that stripped him down to a skeleton and built him back up again in an instant. Dara was harder to nail, but when I blasted her with all of the channels, she hit me with a Dazzlement spell she'd been holding in reserve, the only thing that saved her from turning into a statue as I'd intended. Instead, it left her in mortal form and restricted to slow motion.

I shook my head and rubbed my eyes. Lights danced before me.

"Congratulations," she said, over a span of perhaps ten seconds. "You're better than I'd thought."

"And I'm not even finished," I replied, breathing deeply. "It's time to do unto you as you'd have done unto me."

I began to craft the working which would place them under my control. It was then that I noticed her small slow smile.

"I'd thought—we might—deal with—you—ourselves," she said as the air began to shimmer before her. "I was—wrong."

The Sign of the Logrus took form before her. Immediately, her features grew more animated.

Then I felt its terrible regard. When it addressed me, that pastiche-voice tore at my nervous system.

"I have been summoned," it said, "to deal with your recalcitrance, oh man who would be king."

There came a crash from downhill as the house of mirrors collapsed. I looked in that direction. So did Dara. Mandor, just now struggling to his feet, did also.

The reflective panels rose into the air and drifted toward us. They were quickly deployed all about us, reflecting and re-reflecting our confrontation from countless angles. The prospect was bewildering, for space itself seemed somehow bent, twisted now in our vicinity. And in each image we were surrounded by a circle of light, though I could not detect its absolute source.

"I stand with Merlin," Ghost said, from somewhere.

"Construct!" the Logrus Sign stated. "You thwarted me in Amber!"

"And a short thwart for the Pattern, too," Ghost observed. "It sort of balances out."

"What are your wishes now?"

"Hands off Merlin," Ghost said. "He'll rule here as well as reign. No strings on him."

Ghost's lights began cycling.

I pulsed the spikard, open on all channels, hoping to locate Ghost, give him access to its energies. I couldn't seem to make contact, though.

"I don't need that, Dad," Ghost stated. "I access sources in Shadow myself."

"What is it that you want for yourself, construct?" the Sign inquired.

"To protect one who cares for me."

"I can offer you cosmic greatness."

"You already did. I turned you down then, too. Remember?"

"I remember. And I will remember." A jagged tentacle of the constantly shifting figure moved toward one of the circles of light. There was a blinding rush of flame when they met. When my vision cleared, however, nothing had changed. "Very well," the Sign acknowledged. "You came prepared. It is not yet time to weaken myself in your destruction. Not when another waits for me to falter.

"Lady of Chaos," it stated, "you must honor Merlin's wishes. If his reign be a foolish thing, he will destroy himself by his own actions. If it be prudent, you will have gained what you sought without interference."

The expression on her face was one of disbelief.

"You would back down before a son of Amber and his toy?" she asked.

"We must give him what he wants," it acknowledged, "for now. For now . . ."

The air squealed about its vanishment. Mandor smiled the smallest of smiles, reflected to infinity.

"I can't believe this," she said, becoming a flower-faced cat and then a tree of green flame.

"Believe as you would," Mandor told her. "He's won."

The tree flared through its autumn and was gone.

Mandor nodded to me.

"I just hope you know what you're doing," he said.

"I know what I'm doing."

"Take it however you would," he said, "but if you need advice I'll try to help you."

"Thanks."

"Care to discuss it over lunch?"

"Not just now."

He shrugged and became a blue whirlwind.

"Till later then," came the voice out of the whirlwind, before it blew away.

"Thanks, Ghost," I said. "Your timing's gotten a lot better."

"Chaos has a weak left," he replied.

I located fresh garments of silver, black, gray, and white. I took them back to Jurt's apartments with me. I had a long story to tell.

We walked little-used ways, passing through Shadow, coming at length to the final battlefield of the Patternfall War. The place had healed itself over the years, leaving no indication of all that had transpired there. Corwin regarded it for a long while in silence.

Then he turned to me and said, "It'll take some doing to sort everything out, to achieve a more permanent balance, to assure its stability."

"Yes."

"You think you can keep things peaceful on this end for a while?"

"That's the idea," I said. "I'll give it my best shot."

"That's all any of us can do," he said. "Okay, Random has to know what's happened, of course. I'm not sure how he's going to take having you as an opposite number, but that's the breaks."

"Give him my regards, and Bill Roth, too."

He nodded.

"And good luck," I said.

"There are still mysteries within mysteries," he told me. "I'll let you know what I find out, as soon as I have something."

He moved forward and embraced me.

Then, "Rev up that ring and send me back to Amber."

"It's already revved," I said. "Good-bye."

". . . And hello," he answered, from the tail end of a rainbow.

I turned away then, for the long walk back to Chaos.

If you enjoyed this book…
Come visit our Web site at

www.sfbc.com

and find hundreds more:
- science fiction • fantasy
  - the newest books
  - the greatest classics

THE SCIENCE FICTION BOOK CLUB

has been bringing the best of science fiction and fantasy
to the doors of discriminating readers for over 50 years.
For a look at currently available books and details on how to join,
just visit us at the address above.